KT-498-957

THE COLLECTED STORIES OF

STEFAN ZWEIG

Translated from the German by
Anthea Bell

PUSHKIN PRESS
LONDON

Pushkin Press
71–75 Shelton Street
London WC2H 9JQ

Original texts © Williams Verlag AG Zurich
English translations © Anthea Bell

Published by Pushkin Press in 2013
003

ISBN 978 1 782270 03 4

All rights reserved. No part of this publication may be reproduced, stored in a retrieval system or transmitted in any form or by any means, electronic, mechanical, photocopying, recording or otherwise, without prior permission in writing from Pushkin Press

Set in 10 on 13 Monotype Baskerville
by Tetragon, London

Proudly printed and bound in Great Britain by
TJ International, Padstow, Cornwall
on Munken Premium Cream 80gsm

www.pushkinpress.com

CONTENTS

FORGOTTEN DREAMS

THE VILLA LAY CLOSE TO THE SEA.

The quiet avenues, lined with pine trees, breathed out the rich strength of salty sea air, and a slight breeze constantly played around the orange trees, now and then removing a colourful bloom from flowering shrubs as if with careful fingers. The sunlit distance, where attractive houses built on hillsides gleamed like white pearls, a lighthouse miles away rose steeply and straight as a candle—the whole scene shone, its contours sharp and clearly outlined, and was set in the deep azure of the sky like a bright mosaic. The waves of the sea, marked by only the few white specks that were the distant sails of isolated ships, lapped against the tiered terrace on which the villa stood; the ground then rose on and on to the green of a broad, shady garden and merged with the rest of the park, a scene drowsy and still, as if under some fairy-tale enchantment.

Outside the sleeping house on which the morning heat lay heavily, a narrow gravel path ran like a white line to the cool viewing point. The waves tossed wildly beneath it, and here and there shimmering spray rose, sparkling in rainbow colours as brightly as diamonds in the strong sunlight. There the shining rays of the sun broke on the small groups of Vistulian pines standing close together, as if in intimate conversation, they also fell on a Japanese parasol with amusing pictures on it in bright, glaring colours, now open wide.

A woman was leaning back in a soft basket chair in the shade of this parasol, her beautiful form comfortably lounging in the yielding weave of the wicker. One slender hand, wearing no rings, dangled down as if forgotten, petting the gleaming, silky coat of a dog with gentle, pleasing movements, while the other hand held a book on which her dark eyes, with their black lashes and the suggestion of a smile in them, were concentrating. They were large and restless eyes, their beauty enhanced by a dark, veiled glow. Altogether the strong, attractive effect of the oval, sharply outlined face did not give the natural impression of simple beauty, but expressed the refinement of certain details tended with careful, delicate coquetry. The apparently unruly confusion of her fragrant, shining curls was the careful construction of an artist, and in the same way the slight smile that hovered around her lips as she read, revealing her white teeth, was the result of many years of practice in front of the mirror, but had already become a firmly established part of the whole design and could not be laid aside now.

There was a slight crunch on the sand.

She looks without changing her position, like a cat lying basking in the dazzling torrent of warm sunlight and merely blinking apathetically at the newcomer with phosphorescent eyes.

The steps quickly come closer, and a servant in livery stands in front of her to hand her a small visiting card, then stands back a little way to wait.

She reads the name with that expression of surprise on her features that appears when you are greeted in the street with great familiarity by someone you do not know. For a moment, small lines appear above her sharply traced black eyebrows, showing how hard she is thinking, and then a happy light plays over her whole face all of a sudden, her eyes sparkle with high spirits as she thinks of the long-ago days of her youth, almost forgotten now. The name has aroused pleasant images in her again. Figures and dreams take on distinct shape once more, and become as clear as reality.

"Ah, yes," she said as she remembered, suddenly turning to the servant, "yes, of course show the gentleman up here."

The servant left, with a soft and obsequious tread. For a moment there was silence except for the never-tiring wind singing softly in the treetops, now full of the heavy golden midday light.

Then vigorous, energetic footsteps were heard on the gravel path, a long shadow fell at her feet, and a tall man stood before her. She had risen from her chair with a lively movement.

Their eyes met first. With a quick glance he took in the elegance of her figure, while a slight ironic smile came into her eyes. "It's really good of you to have thought of me," she began, offering him her slender and well-tended hand, which he touched respectfully with his lips.

"Dear lady, I will be honest with you, since this is our first meeting for years, and also, I fear, the last for many years to come. It is something of a coincidence that I am here; the name of the owner of the castle about which I was enquiring because of its magnificent position recalled you to my mind. So I am really here under false pretences."

"But nonetheless welcome for that, and in fact I myself could not remember your existence at first, although it was once of some significance to me."

Now they both smiled. The sweet, light fragrance of a first youthful, half-unspoken love, with all its intoxicating tenderness, had awoken in them like a dream on which you reflect ironically when you wake, although you really wish for nothing more than to dream it again, to live in the dream. The beautiful dream of young love that ventures only on half-measures, that desires and dares not ask, promises and does not give.

They went on talking. But there was already a warmth in their voices, an affectionate familiarity, that only a rosy if already half-faded secret like theirs can allow. In quiet words, broken by a peal of happy laughter now and then, they talked about the past, or forgotten poems, faded flowers, lost ribbons—little love tokens that they had exchanged in the little town where they spent their youth. The old stories that, like half-remembered legends, rang bells in their hearts that had long ago fallen silent, stifled by dust, were slowly, very slowly invested with a melancholy solemnity; the final notes of their youthful love, now dead, brought profound and almost sad gravity to their conversation.

His darkly melodious voice shook slightly as he said, "All that way across the ocean in America, I heard the news that you were engaged—I heard it at a time when the marriage itself had probably taken place."

She did not reply to that. Her thoughts were ten years back in the past. For several long minutes, a sultry silence hung in the air between them.

Then she asked, almost under her breath, "What did you think of me at the time?"

He looked up in surprise. "I can tell you frankly, since I am going back to my new country tomorrow. I didn't feel angry with you, I had no moments of confused, hostile indecision, since life had cooled the bright blaze of love to a dying glow of friendship by that time. I didn't understand you—I just felt sorry for you."

A faint tinge of red flew to her cheeks, and there was a bright glint in her eyes as she cried, in agitation, "Sorry for me! I can't imagine why."

"Because I was thinking of your future husband, that indolent financier with his mind always bent on making money—don't interrupt me, I really don't mean to insult your husband, whom I always respected in his way—and because I was thinking of you, the girl I had left behind. Because I couldn't see you, the independent idealist who had only ironic contempt for humdrum everyday life, as the conventional wife of an ordinary person."

"Then why would I have married him if it was as you say?"

"I didn't know exactly. Perhaps he had hidden qualities that escaped a superficial glance and came to light only in the intimacy of your life together. And I saw that as the easy solution to the riddle, because one thing I could not and would not believe."

"And that was?"

"That you had accepted him for his aristocratic title of Count and his millions. That was the one thing I considered impossible."

It was as if she had failed to hear those last words, for she was looking through her fingers, which glowed deep rose like a murex shell, staring far into the distance, all the way to the veils of mist on the horizon where the sky dipped its pale-blue garment into the dark magnificence of the waves.

He too was lost in thought, and had almost forgotten that last remark of his when, suddenly and almost inaudibly, she turned away from him and said, "And yet that is what happened."

He looked at her in surprise, almost alarm. She had settled back into her chair with slow and obviously artificial composure, and she went on in a soft melancholy undertone, barely moving her lips.

"None of you understood me when I was still a girl, shy and easily intimidated, not even you who were so close to me. Perhaps not even I myself. I think of it often now, and I don't understand myself at that time, because what do women still know about their girlish hearts that believed in miracles, whose dreams are like delicate little white flowers that will be blown away at the first breath of reality? And I was not like all the other girls who dreamt of virile, strong young heroes who would turn their yearnings into radiant happiness, their quiet guesses into delightful knowledge, and bring them release from the uncertain, ill-defined suffering that they cannot grasp, but that casts its shadow on their girlhood, becoming more menacing as it lies in wait for them. I never felt such things, my soul steered other dreams towards the hidden grove of the future that lay behind the enveloping mists of the coming days. My dreams were my own. I always dreamt of myself as a royal child out of one of the old books of fairy tales, playing with sparkling, radiant jewels, wearing sweeping dresses of great value—I dreamt of luxury and magnificence, because I loved them both. Ah, the pleasure of letting my hands pass over trembling, softly rustling silk, or laying my fingers down in the soft, darkly dreaming pile of a heavy velvet fabric, as if they were asleep! I was happy when I could wear jewels on my slender fingers as they trembled with happiness, when pale gemstones looked out of the thick torrent of my hair, like pearls of foam; my highest aim was to rest in the soft upholstery of an elegant vehicle. At the time I was caught up in a frenzied love of artistic beauty that made me despise my real, everyday life. I hated myself in my ordinary clothes, looking simple and modest as a nun, and I often stayed at home for days on end because I was ashamed of my humdrum appearance, I hid myself in my cramped, ugly room, and my dearest dream was to live alone beside the sea, on a property both magnificent and artistic, in shady, green garden walks that were never touched by the dirty hands of the common workaday world, where rich peace reigned—much like this place, in fact. My husband made my dreams come true, and because he could do that I married him."

She has fallen silent now, and her face is suffused with Bacchanalian beauty. The glow in her eyes has become deep and menacing, and the red in her cheeks burns more and more warmly.

There is a profound silence, broken only by the monotonous rhythmical song of the glittering waves breaking on the tiers of the terrace below, as if casting itself on a beloved breast.

Then he says softly, as if to himself, "But what about love?"

She heard that. A slight smile comes to her lips.

"Do you still have all the ideals, *all* the ideals that you took to that distant world with you? Are they all still intact, or have some of them died or withered away? Haven't they been torn out of you by force and flung in the dirt, where thousands of wheels carrying vehicles to their owners' destination in life crushed them? Or have you lost none of them?"

He nods sadly, and says no more.

Suddenly he carries her hand to his lips and kisses it in silence. Then he says, in a warm voice, "Goodbye, and I wish you well."

She returns his farewell firmly and honestly. She feels no shame at having unveiled her deepest secret and shown her soul to a man who has been a stranger to her for years. Smiling, she watches him go, thinks of the words he said about love, and the past comes up with quiet, inaudible steps to intervene between her and the present. And suddenly she thinks that *he* could have given her life its direction, and her ideas paint that strange notion in bright colours.

And slowly, slowly, imperceptibly, the smile on her dreaming lips dies away.

IN THE SNOW

A SMALL MEDIEVAL German town close to the Polish border, with the sturdy solidity of fourteenth-century building: the colourful, lively picture that it usually presents has faded to a single impression of dazzling, shimmering white. Snow is piled high on the broad walls and weighs down on the tops of the towers, around which night has already cast veils of opaque grey mist.

Darkness is falling fast. The hurry and bustle of the streets, the activity of a crowd of busy people, is dying down to a continuous murmur of sound that seems to come from far away, broken only by the rhythmic, monotonous chime of evening bells. The day's business is over for the weary workers who are longing for sleep, lights become few and far between, and finally they all go out. The town lies there like a single mighty creature fast asleep.

Every sound has died away, even the trembling voice of the wind over the moors is only a gentle lullaby now, and you can hear the soft whisper of snowflakes dusting down on the surfaces where their wandering ends...

But suddenly a faint sound is heard.

It is like the distant, hasty beat of hoofs coming closer. The startled man in the guardhouse at the gate, drowsy with sleep, goes to the window in surprise to listen. And sure enough, a horseman is approaching at full gallop, making straight for the gate, and a minute later a brusque voice, hoarse from the cold, demands entrance. The gate is opened. A man steps through it, leading in a steaming horse which he immediately hands to the gatekeeper. He swiftly allays the man's doubts with a few words and a sizeable sum of money, and then, his confident and rapid strides showing that he knows the place, he crosses the deserted white market place, and goes down quiet streets and along alleys deep in snow, making for the far end of the little town.

Several small houses stand there, crowding close together as if they needed each other's support. They are all plain, unassuming, smoky and crooked, and they stand in eternal silence in these secluded streets. They might never have known cheerful festivities bubbling over with merriment, no cries of delight might ever have shaken those blank, hidden windows, no bright sunshine might ever have been reflected in their panes. Alone, like shy children intimidated by others, the houses press together in the narrow confines of the Jewish quarter.

The stranger stops outside one of these houses, the largest and relatively speaking the finest. It belongs to the richest man in the little community, and also serves as a synagogue.

Bright light filters through the crack between the drawn curtains, and voices are raised in religious song inside the lighted room. This is the peaceful celebration of Chanukah, a festival of rejoicing in memory of the victory of the Maccabaeans, a day that reminds these exiled people, reduced to servitude by Fate, of their former great power. It is one of the few happy days that life and the law will allow them. But the song sounds melancholy, yearning, and the bright metal of the voices singing it has rusted with all the thousands of tears that have been shed. Out in the lonely street, the singing echoes like a hopeless lament, and is blown away on the wind.

The stranger stands outside the house for some time, inactive, lost in thought and dreams, and tears rise in his throat as he instinctively joins in the ancient, sacred melodies that flow from deep within his heart. His soul is full of profound devotion.

Then he pulls himself together. His steps faltering now, he goes to the closed doorway and brings the knocker down heavily, with a dull thud that shakes the door.

The vibration is felt through the entire building as the sound echoes on.

At once the singing in the room above stops dead, as if at an agreed signal. The people inside have turned pale and are looking at one another in alarm. Their festive mood has instantly evaporated. Dreams of the victorious power of such men as Judas Maccabaeus, by whose side they were all standing in spirit a moment ago, have fled; the bright vision of Israel that they saw before their eyes has gone, they are poor, trembling, helpless Jews again. Reality has asserted itself.

There is a terrible silence. The trembling hand of the prayer leader has sunk to his prayer book, the pale lips of his congregation will not obey them. A dreadful sense of foreboding has fallen on the room, seizing all throats in an iron grip.

They well know why.

Some while ago they heard an ominous word, a new and terrible word, but they were aware of its murderous meaning for their own people. The Flagellants were abroad in Germany, wild, fanatically religious men who flailed their own bodies with scourges in Bacchanalian orgies of lust and delight, deranged and drunken hordes who had already slaughtered and tortured thousands of Jews, intending to deprive them of what they held most holy, their age-old belief in the Father. That was their worst fear. With blind, stoical patience they had accepted exile, beatings, robbery, enslavement; they had all known late-night raids with burning and looting, and they shuddered to think of living in such times.

Then, only a few days earlier, rumours had begun spreading that one company of Flagellants was on its way to their own part of the country, which so far had known them only by hearsay, and it was said to be not far off. Perhaps the Flagellants have already arrived?

Terrible fear has seized on them all, making their hearts falter. They already see those forces, greedy for blood, men with faces flushed by wine, brandishing blazing torches and breaking violently into their homes. Already the stifled cries of their women ring in their ears, crying out for help as they pay the price of the murderers' wild lust; they already feel the flashing weapons strike. It is like a clear and vivid dream.

The stranger listens for sounds in the room above, and when no one lets him in he knocks again. Once more the dull echo of his knock resounds through the silence and distress inside the building.

By now the master of the house, the prayer leader, whose flowing white beard and great age give him the look of a patriarch, has been the first to recover some composure. He quietly murmurs, "God's will be done," and then bends down to his granddaughter. She is a pretty girl and, in her fear resembles a deer turning its great, pleading eyes on the huntsman. "Look out and see who's there, Lea."

All eyes are on the girl's face as she goes timidly to the window, and draws back the curtain with pale, trembling fingers. Then comes a cry from the depths of her heart. "Thank God, it's only one man."

"Praise the Lord." It is a sound like a sigh of relief on all sides. Now movement returns to the still figures who had been oppressed by the dreadful nightmare. Separate groups form, some standing in silent prayer, others talking in frightened, uncertain voices, discussing the unexpected arrival of the stranger, who is now being let in through the front gate.

The whole room is full of the hot, stuffy aroma of logs burning and a large crowd of people, all of them gathered around the richly laid festive table on which the sign and symbol of this holy evening stands, the seven-branched candlestick. The candles shine with a dull light in the smouldering vapours. The women wear dresses adorned with jewellery, the men voluminous robes with white prayer bands. There is a sense of deep solemnity in the crowded room, a solemnity such as only genuine piety can bring.

Now the stranger's quick footsteps are coming up the steps, and he enters the room.

At the same time a sharp gust of biting wind blows into the warm room through the open door. Icy cold streams in with the snow-scented air, chilling everyone. The draught puts out the flickering candles on the candlestick; only one of them still wavers unsteadily as it dies down. Suddenly the room is full of a heavy, oppressive twilight, as if cold night might suddenly fall within these walls. All at once the peace and comfort are gone. Everyone feels that the extinguishing of the sacred candles is a bad omen, and superstition makes them shiver again. But no one dares to say a word.

A tall, black-bearded man, who can hardly be more than thirty years old, stands at the door. He quickly divests himself of the scarves and coats in which he had been muffled up against the cold, and as soon as his face is revealed in the faint light of that last little flickering candle flame, Lea runs to him and embraces him.

This is Josua, her fiancé from the neighbouring town.

The others also crowd eagerly around him, greeting him happily, only to fall silent next moment, for he frees himself from his fiancée's arms with a grave, sad expression, and the weight of his terrible knowledge has dug deep furrows on his brow. All eyes are anxiously turned on him, and he cannot defend himself and what he has to say from the raging torrent of his own emotions. He takes the girl's hands as she stands beside him, and quietly forces himself to utter the fateful news.

"The Flagellants are here."

The eyes that had been turned questioningly to him stare, fixed on his face, and he feels the pulse of the hands he is holding falter suddenly. The prayer leader clutches the edge of the heavy table, his fingers trembling, so that the crystal glasses begin to sing softly, sending quavering notes through the air. Fear digs its claws into desperate hearts again, draining the last drops of blood from the frightened, devastated faces staring at the bearer of the news.

The last candle flickers once more and goes out.

Only the lamp hanging from the ceiling now casts a faint light on the dismayed, distraught people; the news has struck them like a thunderbolt.

One voice softly murmurs the resigned phrase with which Fate has made them familiar. "It is God's will."

But the others still cannot grasp it.

However, the newcomer is continuing, his words brusque and disconnected, as if he could hardly bear to hear them himself.

"They're coming—many of them—hundreds. And crowds of people with them—blood on their hands—they've murdered thousands—all our people in the East. They've been in my town already…"

He is interrupted by a woman's dreadful scream. Her floods of tears cannot soften its force. Still young, only recently married, she falls to the floor in front of him.

"They're there? Oh, my parents, my brothers and sisters! Has any harm come to them?"

He bends down to her, and there is grief in his voice as he tells her quietly, making it sound like a consolation, "They can feel no human harm any more."

And once again all is still, perfectly still. The awesome spectre of the fear of death is in the room with them, making them tremble. There is no one present here who did not have a loved one in that town, someone who is now dead.

At this the prayer leader, tears running into his silver beard and unable to control his shaking voice, begins to chant, disjointedly, the ancient, solemn prayer for the dead. They all join in. They are not even aware that they are singing, their minds are not on the words and melody that they utter mechanically; each is thinking only of his dear ones. And the chant grows ever stronger, they breathe more and more deeply, it is increasingly difficult for them to suppress their rising feelings. The words become confused until at last they are all sobbing in wild, uncomprehending sorrow. Infinite pain, a pain beyond words, has brought them all together like brothers.

Deep silence descends. But now and then a great sob can no longer be suppressed. And then comes the heavy, numbing voice of the messenger telling his tale again.

"They are all at rest with the Lord. Not one of them escaped, only I, through the providence of God…"

"Praise be to his name," murmurs the whole circle with instinctive piety. In the mouths of these broken, trembling people, the words sound like a worn-out formula.

"I came home late from a journey, and the Jewish quarter was already full of looters. I wasn't recognized, I could have run for it—but I had to go in, I couldn't help going to my place, my own people, I was among them as they fell under flailing fists. Suddenly a man came riding my way, struck out at me—but he missed, swaying in the saddle. Then all at once the will to live took hold of me, that strange chain that binds us to our misery—passion gave me strength and courage. I pulled him off his horse, mounted it, and rode away on it myself through the dark night, here to you. I've been riding for a day and a night."

He stops for a moment. Then he says, in a firmer voice, "But enough of all that now! First of all, what shall we do?"

The answer comes from all sides.

"Escape!"—"We must get away!"—"Over the border to Poland!"

It is the one way they all know to help themselves, age-old and shameful, yet the only way for the weaker to oppose the strong. No one dreams of physical resistance. Can a Jew defend himself or fight back? As they see it, the idea is ridiculous, unimaginable; they are not living in the time of the Maccabaeans now, they are enslaved again. The Egyptians are back, stamping the mark of eternal weakness and servitude on the people. Even the torrent of the passing years over many centuries cannot wash it away.

Flight, then.

One man did suggest, timidly, that they might appeal to the other citizens of the town for protection, but a scornful smile was all the answer he got. Again and again, their fate has always brought the oppressed back to the necessity of relying on themselves and on their God. No third party could be trusted.

They discussed the practical details. Men who had regarded making money as their sole aim in life, who saw wealth as the peak of human happiness and power, now agreed that they must not shrink from any sacrifice if it could speed their flight. All possessions must be converted into cash, however unfavourable the rate of exchange. There were carts and teams of horses to be bought, the most essential protection from the cold to be found. All at once the fear of death had obliterated what was supposed to be the salient quality of their race, just as their individual characters had been forged together into a single will. In all the pale, weary faces, their thoughts were working towards one aim.

And when morning lit its blazing torches, it had all been discussed and decided. With the flexibility of their people, used to wandering through the world, they adjusted to their sad situation, and their final decisions and arrangements ended in another prayer.

Then each of them went to do his part of the work.

And many sighs died away in the soft singing of the snowflakes, which had already built high walls towering up in the shimmering whiteness of the streets.

The great gates of the town closed with a hollow clang behind the last of the fugitives' carts.

The moon shone only faintly in the sky, but it turned the myriad flakes whirling in their lively dance to silver as they clung to clothes, fluttered around the nostrils of the snorting horses, and crunched under wheels making their way with difficulty through the dense snowdrifts.

Quiet voices whispered in the carts. Women exchanged reminiscences of their home town, which still seemed so close in its security and self-confidence. They spoke in soft, musical and melancholy tones. Children had a thousand things to ask in their clear voices, although their questions grew quieter and less frequent, and finally gave way to regular breathing. The men's voices struck a deeper note as they anxiously discussed the future and murmured quiet prayers. They all pressed close to one another, out of their awareness that they belonged together and instinctive fear of the cold. It blew through all the gaps and cracks in the carts with its icy breath, freezing the drivers' fingers.

The leading cart came to a halt.

Immediately the whole line of carts following behind it stopped too. Pale faces peered out from the tarpaulin covers of these moving tents, wondering what had caused the delay. The patriarch had climbed out of the first cart, and all the others followed his example, understanding the reason for this halt.

They were not far from the town yet; through the falling white flakes you could still, if indistinctly, make out the tower rising from the broad plain as if were a menacing hand, with a light shining from its spire like a jewel on its ringed finger.

Everything here was smooth and white, like the still surface of a lake, broken only by a few small, regular mounds surmounted by fenced-in trees here and there. They knew that this was where their dear ones lay in quiet, everlasting beds, rejected, alone and far from home, like all their kind.

Now the deep silence is broken by quiet sobbing, and although they are so used to suffering hot tears run down their rigid faces, freezing into droplets of bright ice on the snow.

As they contemplate this deep and silent peace, their mortal fears are gone, forgotten. Suddenly, eyes heavy with tears, they all feel an infinite, wild longing for this eternal, quiet peace in the 'good place' with their loved ones. So much of their childhood sleeps under this white blanket, so many good memories, so much happiness that they will never know again. Everyone senses it; everyone longs to be in the 'good place'.

But time is short, and they must go on.

They climb back into the carts, huddling close to each other, for although they did not feel the biting cold while they were out in the open, the icy frost now steals over their shaking, shivering bodies again, making them grit their teeth. And in the darkness of the carts their eyes express unspeakable fear and endless sorrow.

Their thoughts, however, keep going back the way they have come, along the path of broad furrows left by the horse-drawn carts in the snow, back to the 'good place', the place of their desires.

It is past midnight now, and the carts have travelled a long way from the town. They are in the middle of the great plain which lies flooded by bright moonlight, while white, drifting veils seem to hover over it, the shimmering reflections of the snow. The strong horses trudge laboriously through the thick snow, which clings tenaciously, and the carts jolt slowly, almost imperceptibly on, as if they might stop at any moment.

The cold is terrible, like icy knives cutting into limbs that have already lost much of their mobility. And gradually a strong wind rises as well, singing wild songs and howling around the carts. As if with greedy hands reaching out for prey, it tears at the covers of the carts which are constantly shaking loose, and frozen fingers find it hard to fasten them back in place more firmly.

The storm sings louder and louder, and in its song the quiet voices of the men murmuring prayers die away. It is an effort for their frozen lips to form the words. In the shrill whistling of the wind the hopeless sobs of the women, fearful for the future, also fall silent, and so does the persistent crying of children woken from their weariness by the cold.

Creaking, the wheels roll through the snow.

In the cart that brings up the rear, Lea presses close to her fiancé, who is telling her of the terrible things he has seen in a sad, toneless voice. He puts his strong arm firmly around her slender, girlish waist as if to protect her from the assault of the cold and from all pain. She looks at him gratefully, and a few tender, longing words are exchanged through the sounds of wailing and the storm, making them both forget death and danger.

Suddenly an abrupt jolt makes them all sway.

Then the cart stops.

Indistinctly, through the roaring of the storm, they hear loud shouts from the teams of horse-drawn carts in front, the crack of whips, the murmuring of agitated voices. The sounds will not die down. They leave the cart and hurry forward through the biting cold to the place where one horse in a team has fallen, carrying the other down with it. Around the two horses stand men who want to help but can do nothing; the wind blows them about like puppets with no will of their own, the snowflakes blind their eyes, and their hands are frozen, with no strength left in them. Their fingers lie side by side like stiff pieces of wood. And there is no help anywhere in sight, only the plain that runs on and on, a smooth expanse, proudly aware of its vast extent as it loses itself in the dim light from the snow and in the unheeding storm that swallows up their cries.

Once again the full, sad awareness of their situation comes home to them. Death reaches out for them once more in a new and terrible form as they stand together, helpless and defenceless against the irresistible, invincible forces of nature, facing the pitiless weapon of the frost.

Again and again the storm trumpets their doom in their ears. You must die here—you must die here.

And their fear of death turns to hopeless resignation.

No one has spoken the thought out loud, but it came to them all at the same time. Clumsily, stiff-limbed, they climb back into the carts and huddle close together again, waiting to die.

They no longer hope for any help.

They press close, all with their own loved ones, to be with one another in death. Outside, their constant companion the storm sings a song of death, and the flakes build a huge, shining coffin around the carts.

Death comes slowly. The icy, biting cold penetrates every corner of the carts and all their pores, like poison seizing on limb after limb, gently, but never doubting that it will prevail.

The minutes slowly run away, as if giving death time to complete its great work of release. Long and heavy hours pass, carrying these desperate souls away into eternity.

The storm wind sings cheerfully, laughing in wild derision at this everyday drama, and the heedless moon sheds its silver light over life and death.

There is deep silence in the last cart of all. Several of those in it are dead already, others are under the spell of hallucinations brought on by the bitter cold to make death seem kinder. But they are all still and lifeless, only their thoughts still darting in confusion, like sudden hot flashes of lightning.

Josua holds his fiancée with cold hands. She is dead already, although he does not know it.

He dreams.

He is sitting with her in that room with its warm fragrance, the seven candles in the golden candlestick are burning, they are all sitting together as they once used to. The glowing light of the happy festival rests on smiling faces speaking friendly words and prayers. And others, long dead, come in through the doorway, among them his dead parents, but that no longer surprises him. They kiss tenderly, they exchange familiar words. More and more approach, Jews in the bleached garments of their forefathers' time, and now come the heroes, Judas Maccabaeus and all the others; they all sit down together to talk and make merry. More come, and still more. The room is full of figures, his eyes are tiring with the sight of so many, changing more and more quickly, giving way to one another, his ear echoes to the confusion of sounds. There is a hammering and droning in his pulse, hotter and hotter—

And suddenly it is over. All is quiet now.

By this time the sun has risen, and the snowflakes, still falling, shine like diamonds. The sun makes the broad mounds that have risen overnight, covered over and over with snow, gleam as if they were jewels.

It is a strong, joyful sun that has suddenly begun to shine, almost a springtime sun. And sure enough, spring is not far away. Soon it will be bringing buds and green leaves back again, and will lift the white shrouds from the grave of the poor, lost, frozen Jews who have never known true spring in their lives.

THE MIRACLES OF LIFE

To my dear friend Hans Müller

GREY MIST LAY LOW over Antwerp, enveloping the city entirely in its dense and heavy swathes. The shapes of houses were blurred in the fine, smoky vapour, and you could not see to the end of the street, but overhead there was ringing in the air, a deep sound like the word of God coming out of the clouds, for the muted voices of the bells in the church towers, calling their congregations to prayer, had also merged in the great, wild sea of mist filling the city and the countryside around, and encompassing the restless, softly roaring waters of the sea far away in the harbour. Here and there a faint gleam struggled against the damp grey mist, trying to light up a gaudy shop sign, but only muffled noise and throaty laughter told you where to find the taverns in which freezing customers gathered, complaining of the weather. The alleys seemed empty, and any passers-by were seen only as fleeting impressions that soon dissolved into the mist. It was a dismal, depressing Sunday morning.

Only the bells called and pealed as if desperately, while the mist stifled their cries. For the devout were few and far between; foreign heresy had found a foothold in this land, and even those who had not abandoned their old faith were less assiduous and zealous in the service of the Lord. Heavy morning mists were enough to keep many away from their devotions. Wrinkled old women busily telling their beads, poor folk in their plain Sunday best stood looking lost in the long, dark aisles of the churches, where the shining gold of altars and chapels and the priests' bright chasubles shone like a mild and gentle flame. But the mist seemed to have seeped through the high walls, for here, too, the chilly and sad mood of the deserted streets prevailed. The morning sermon itself was cold and austere, without a ray of sunlight to brighten it. It was preached against the Protestants, and the driving force behind it was furious rage, hatred along with a strong sense of power, for the time for moderation was over, and good news from Spain had reached the clerics—the new king served the work of the Church with admirable fervour. In his sermon, the preacher united graphic descriptions of the Last Judgement with dark words of admonition for the immediate future. If there had been a large congregation, his words might have been passed on by the faithful murmuring in their pews to a great crowd of hearers, but as it was they dropped into the dark void with a dull echo, as if frozen in the moist, chilly air.

During the storm two men had quickly entered the main porch of the cathedral, their faces obscured at first by wind-blown hair and voluminous coats with collars turned up high. The taller man shed his damp coat to reveal the honest but not especially striking features of a portly man in the rich clothing suitable for a merchant. The other was a stranger figure, although not because of anything unusual in his clothing; his gentle, unhurried movements and his rather big-boned, rustic but kindly face, surrounded by abundant waving white hair, lent him the mild aspect of an evangelist. They both said a short prayer, and then the merchant signed to his older companion to follow him. They went slowly, with measured steps, into the side aisle, which was almost entirely in darkness because dank air made the candles gutter, and heavy clouds that refused to lift still obscured the bright face of the sun. The merchant stopped at one of the small side chapels, most of which contained devotional items promised to the Church as donations by the old families of the city, and pointing to one of the little altars he said, "Here it is."

The other man came closer and shaded his eyes with his hand to see it better in the dim light. One wing of the altarpiece was occupied by a painting in clear colours made even softer by the twilight, and it immediately caught the old painter's eye. It showed the Virgin Mary, her heart transfixed by a sword, and despite the pain and sorrow of the subject it was a gentle work with an aura of reconciliation about it. Mary had a strangely sweet face, not so much that of the Mother of God as of a dreaming girl in the bloom of youth, but with the idea of pain tingeing the smiling beauty of a playful, carefree nature. Thick black hair tumbling down softly surrounded a small, pale but radiant face with very red lips, glowing like a crimson wound. The features were wonderfully delicate, and many of the brushstrokes, for instance in the assured, slender curve of the eyebrows, gave an almost yearning expression to the beauty of the tender face. The Virgin's dark eyes were deep in thought, as if dreaming of another brighter and sweeter world from which her pain was stealing her away. The hands were folded in gentle devotion, and her breast still seemed to be quivering with slight fear at the cold touch of the sword piercing her. Blood from her wound ran along it. All this was bathed in a wonderful radiance surrounding her head with golden flame, and even her heart glowed like the mystical light of the chalice in the stained glass of the church windows when sunlight fell through them. And the twilight around it took the last touch of worldliness from this picture, so that the halo around the sweet girlish face shone with the true radiance of transfiguration.

Almost abruptly, the painter tore himself away from his lengthy admiration of the picture. "None of our countrymen painted this," he said.

The merchant nodded in agreement.

"No, it is by an Italian. A young painter at the time. But there's quite a long story behind it. I will tell it all to you from the beginning, and then, as you know, I want you to complete the altarpiece by putting the keystone in place. Look, the sermon is over. We should find a better place to tell stories than this church, well as it may suit our joint efforts. Let's go."

The painter lingered for a moment longer before turning his eyes away from the picture. It seemed even more radiant as the smoky darkness outside the windows lifted, and the mist took on a golden hue. He almost felt that if he stayed here, rapt in devout contemplation of the gentle pain on those childish lips, they would smile and reveal new loveliness. But his companion had gone ahead of him already, and he had to quicken his pace to catch up with the merchant in the porch. They left the cathedral together, as they had come.

The heavy cloak of mist thrown over the city by the early spring morning had given way to a dull, silvery light caught like a cobweb among the gabled roofs. The close-set cobblestones had a steely, damp gleam, and the first of the flickering sunlight was beginning to cast its gold on them. The two men made their way down narrow, winding alleys to the clear air of the harbour, where the merchant lived. And as they slowly walked towards it at their leisure, deep in thought and lost in memory, the merchant's story gathered pace.

"As I have told you already," he began, "I spent some time in Venice in my youth. And to cut a long story short, my conduct there was not very Christian. Instead of managing my father's business in the city, I sat in taverns with young men who spent all day carousing and making merry, drinking, gambling, often bawling out some bawdy song or uttering bitter curses, and I was just as bad as the others. I had no intention of going home. I took life easy and ignored my father's letters when he wrote to me more and more urgently and sternly, warning me that people in Venice who knew me had told him that my licentious life would be the end of me. I only laughed, sometimes with annoyance, and a quick draught of sweet, dark wine washed all my bitterness away, or if not that then the kiss of a wanton girl. I tore up my father's letters, I had abandoned myself entirely to a life of intoxicated frenzy, and I did not intend to give it up. But one evening I was suddenly free of it all. It was very strange, and sometimes I still feel as if a miracle had cleared my path. I was sitting in my usual tavern; I can still see it today, with its smoke and vapours and my drinking companions. There were girls of easy virtue there as well, one of them very beautiful, and we seldom made merrier than that night, a stormy and very strange one. Suddenly, just as a lewd story aroused roars of laughter, my servant came in with a letter for me brought by the courier from

Flanders. I was displeased. I did not like receiving my father's letters, which were always admonishing me to do my duty and be a good Christian, two notions that I had long ago drowned in wine. But I was about to take it from the servant when up jumped one of my drinking companions, a handsome, clever fellow, a master of all the arts of chivalry. 'Never mind the croaking old toad. What's it to you?' he cried, throwing the letter up in the air, swiftly drawing his sword, neatly spearing the letter as it fluttered down and pinning it to the wall. The supple blue blade quivered as it stuck there. He carefully withdrew the sword, and the letter, still unopened, stayed where it was. 'There clings the black bat!' he laughed. The others applauded, the girls clustered happily around him, they drank his health. I laughed myself, drank with them, and forgetting the letter and my father, God and myself, I forced myself into wild merriment. I gave the letter not a thought, and we went on to another tavern, where our merriment turned to outright folly. I was drunk as never before, and one of those girls was as beautiful as sin."

The merchant instinctively stopped and passed his hand several times over his brow, as if to banish an unwelcome image from his mind. The painter was quick to realise that this was a painful memory, and did not look at him, but let his eyes rest with apparent interest on a galleon under full sail, swiftly approaching the harbour that the two men had reached, and where they now stood amidst all its colourful hurry and bustle. The merchant's silence did not last long, and he soon continued his tale.

"You can guess how it was. I was young and bewildered, she was beautiful and bold. We came together, and I was full of urgent desire. But a strange thing happened. As I lay in her amorous embrace, with her mouth pressed to mine, I did not feel the kiss as a wild gesture of affection willingly returned. Instead, I was miraculously reminded of the gentle evening kisses we exchanged in my parental home. All at once, strange to say, even as I lay in the whore's arms I thought of my father's crumpled, mistreated, unread letter, and it was as if I felt my drinking companion's sword-thrust in my own bleeding breast. I sat up, so suddenly and looking so pale that the girl asked in alarm what the matter was. However, I was ashamed of my foolish fears, ashamed in front of this woman, a stranger, in whose bed I lay and whose beauty I had been enjoying. I did not want to tell her the foolish thoughts of that moment. Yet my life changed there and then, and today I still feel, as I felt at the time, that only the grace of God can bring such a change. I threw the girl some money, which she took reluctantly because she was afraid I despised her, and she called me a German fool. But I listened to no more from her, and instead stormed away on that cold, rainy night, calling like a desperate man over the dark canals for a gondola. At last one came along, and the price the gondolier asked was high, but my heart was beating with such sudden, merciless, incomprehensible fear that I could think of nothing but the letter, miraculously reminded of it as I suddenly was. By the time I reached the tavern my desire to read it was like a devouring fever; I raced into the place like a madman, ignoring the cheerful, surprised cries of my companions, jumped up on a table, making the glasses on it clink, tore the letter down from the wall and ran out again, taking no notice of the derision and angry curses behind me. At the first corner I unfolded the letter with trembling hands. Rain was pouring down from the overcast sky, and the wind tore at the sheet of paper in my hands. However, I did not stop reading until, with overflowing eyes, I had deciphered the whole of the letter. Not that the words in it were many—they told me that my mother was sick and likely to die, and asked me to come home. Not a word of the usual blame or reproach. But how my heart burnt with shame when I saw that the sword blade had pierced my mother's name…"

"A miracle indeed, an obvious miracle, one to be understood not by everyone but certainly by the man affected," murmured the painter as the merchant, deeply moved, lapsed into silence. For a while they walked along side by side without a word. The merchant's fine house was already visible in the distance, and when he looked up and saw it he quickly went on with his tale.

"I will be brief. I will not tell you what pain and remorseful madness I felt that night. I will say only that next morning found me kneeling on the steps of St Mark's in ardent prayer, vowing to donate an altar to the Mother of God if she would grant me the grace to see my mother again alive and receive her forgiveness. I set off that same day, travelling for many days and hours in despair and fear to Antwerp, where I hurried in wild desperation to my parental home. At the gate stood my mother herself, looking pale and older, but restored to good health. On seeing me she opened her arms to me, rejoicing, and in her embrace I wept tears of sorrow pent up over many days and many shamefully wasted nights. My life was different after that, and I may almost say it was a life well lived. I have buried that letter, the dearest thing I had, under the foundation stone of this house, built by the fruits of my own labour, and I did my best to keep my vow. Soon after my return here I had the altar that you have seen erected, and adorned as well as I could. However, as I knew nothing of those mysteries by which you painters judge your art, and wanted to dedicate a worthy picture to the Mother of God, who had worked a miracle for me, I wrote to a good friend in Venice asking him to send me the best of the painters he knew, to paint me the work that my heart desired.

"Months passed by. One day a young man came to my door, told me what his calling was, and brought me greetings and a letter from my friend. This Italian painter, whose remarkable and strangely sad face I well remember to this day, was not at all like the boastful, noisy drinking companions of my days in Venice. You might have thought him a monk rather than a painter, for he wore a long, black robe, his hair was cut in a plain style, and his face showed the spiritual pallor of asceticism and night watches. The letter merely confirmed my favourable impression, and dispelled any doubts aroused in me by the youthfulness of this Italian master. The older painters of Italy, wrote my friend, were prouder than princes, and even the most tempting offer could not lure them away from their native land, where they were surrounded by great lords and ladies as well as the common people. He had chosen this young master because, for some reason he did not know, the young man's wish to leave Italy weighed more with him than any offer of money, but the young painter's talent was valued highly and honoured in his own country.

"The man my friend had sent was quiet and reserved. I never learnt anything about his life beyond hints that a beautiful woman had played a painful part in his story, and it was because of her that he had left his native Italy. And although I have no proof of it, and such an idea seems heretical and unchristian, I think that the picture you have seen, which he painted within a few weeks without a model, working with careful preparation from memory, bears the features of the woman he had loved. Whenever I came to see him at work I found him painting another version of that same sweet face again, or lost in dreamy contemplation of it. Once the painting was finished, I felt secretly afraid of the godlessness of painting a woman who might be a courtesan as the Mother of God, and asked him to choose a different model for the companion piece that I also wanted. He did not reply, and when I went to see him next day he had left without a word of goodbye. I had some scruples about adorning the altar with that picture, but the priest whom I consulted felt no such doubt in accepting it."

"And he was right," interrupted the painter, almost vehemently. "For how can we imagine the beauty of Our Lady if not from looking at the woman we see in the picture? Are we not made in God's image? If so, such a portrayal, if only a faint copy of the unseen original, must be the closest to perfection that we can offer to human eyes. Now, listen—you want me to paint that second picture. I am one of those poor souls who cannot paint without a living model. I do not have the gift of painting only from within myself, I work from nature in trying to show what is true in it. I would not choose a woman whom I myself loved to model for a portrait worthy of the Mother of God—it would be sinful to see the immaculate Virgin through her face—but I would look for a lovely model and paint the woman whose features seem to me to show the face of the Mother of God as I have seen it in devout dreams. And believe me, although those may be the features of a sinful human woman, if the work is done in pious devotion none of the dross of desire and sin will be left. The magic of such purity, like a miraculous sign, can often be expressed in a woman's face. I think I have often seen that miracle myself."

"Well, however that may be, I trust you. You are a mature man, you have endured and experienced much, and if you see no sin in it..."

"Far from it! I consider it laudable. Only Protestants and other sectarians denounce the adornment of God's house."

"You are right. But I would like you to begin the picture soon, because my vow, still only half-fulfilled, still burns in me like a sin. For twenty years I forgot about the second picture in the altarpiece. Then, quite recently, when I saw my wife's sorrowful face as she wept by our child's sickbed, I thought of the debt I owed and renewed my vow. And as you are aware, once again the Mother of God worked a miracle of healing, when all the doctors had given up in despair. I beg you not to leave it too long before you start work."

"I will do what I can, but to be honest with you, never in my long career as an artist has anything struck me as so difficult. If my picture is not to look a poor daub, carelessly constructed, beside the painting of that young master—and I long to know more about his work—then I shall need to have the hand of God with me."

"God never fails those who are loyal to him. Goodbye, then, and go cheerfully to work. I hope you will soon bring good news to my house."

The merchant shook hands cordially with the painter once again outside the door of his house, looking confidently into the artist's clear eyes, set in his honest German, angular face like the waters of a bright mountain lake surrounded by weathered peaks and rough rocks. The painter had another parting remark on his lips, but left it unspoken and firmly clasped the hand offered to him. The two parted in perfect accord with each other.

The painter walked slowly along beside the harbour, as he always liked to do when his art did not keep him to his studio. He loved the busy, colourful scene presented by the place, with the hurry and bustle of work at the waterside, and sometimes he sat down on a bollard to sketch the curious physical posture of a labourer, or practice the difficult knack of foreshortening a path only a foot wide. He was not at all disturbed by the loud cries of the seamen, the rattling of carts and the monotonous sound of the sea breaking on shore. He had been granted those insights that do not reflect images seen only in the mind's eye, but can recognise in every living thing, however humble or indifferent, the ray of light to illuminate a work of art. For that reason he always liked places where life was at its most colourful, offering a confusing abundance of different delights. He walked among the sailors slowly, with a questing eye, and no one dared to laugh at him, for among all the noisy, useless folk who gather in a harbour, just as the beach is covered with empty shells and pebbles, he stood out with his calm bearing and the dignity of his appearance.

This time, however, he soon gave up his search and got to his feet. The merchant's story had moved him deeply. It touched lightly upon an incident in his own life, and even his usual devotion to the magic of art failed him today. The mild radiance of that picture of the Virgin painted by the young Italian master seemed to illuminate the faces of all the women he saw today, even if they were only stout fishwives. Dreaming and thoughtful, he wandered indecisively for a while past the crowd in its Sunday best, but then he stopped trying to resist his longing to go back to the cathedral and look at the strange portrayal of that beautiful woman again.

A few weeks had passed since the conversation in which the painter agreed to his friend's request for a second picture to complete the altarpiece for the Mother of God, and still the blank canvas in his studio looked reproachfully at the old master. He almost began to fear it, and spent a good deal of time out and about in the streets of the city to keep himself from brooding on its stern admonition and his own despondency. In a life full of busy work—perhaps he had in fact worked *too* hard, failing to keep an enquiring eye on his true self—a change had come over the painter since he first set eyes on the young Italian's picture. Future and past had been wrenched abruptly apart, and looked at him like an empty mirror reflecting only darkness and shadows. And nothing is more terrible than to feel that your life's final peak of achievement already lies just ahead if only you stride on boldly, and then be assailed by a brooding fear that you have taken the wrong path, you have lost your power, you cannot take the last, least step forward. All at once the artist, who had painted hundreds of sacred pictures in the course of his life, seemed to have lost his ability to portray a human face well enough for him to think it worthy of a divine subject. He had looked at women who sold their faces as artist's models to be copied by the hour, at others who sold their bodies, at citizens' wives and gentle girls with the light of inner purity shining in their faces, but whenever they were close to him, and he was on the point of painting the first brushstroke on the canvas, he was aware of their humanity. He saw the blonde, greedy plump figure of one, he saw another's wild addiction to the game of love; he sensed the smooth emptiness behind the brief gleam of a girlish brow, and was disconcerted by the bold gait of whores and the immodest way they swung their hips. Suddenly a world full of such people seemed a bleak place. He felt that the breath of the divine had been extinguished, quenched by the exuberant flesh of these desirable women who knew nothing about mystical virginity, or the tremor of awe in immaculate devotion to dreams of another world. He was ashamed to open the portfolios containing his own work, for it seemed to him as if he had, so to speak, made himself unworthy to live on this earth, had committed a sin in painting pictures where sturdy country folk modelled for the Saviour's disciples and stout countrywomen as the women who served him. His mood became more and more sombre and oppressive. He remembered himself as a young man following his father's plough, long before he took to art instead, he saw his hard peasant hands thrusting the harrow through the black earth, and wondered if he would not have done better to sow yellow seed corn and work to support a family, instead of touching secrets and miraculous signs, mysteries not meant for him, with his clumsy fingers. His whole life seemed to be turned upside down, he had run aground on the fleeting vision of an hour when he saw an image that came back to him in his dreams, and was both torment and blessing in his waking moments. For he could no longer see the Mother of God in his prayers except as she was in the picture that presented so lovely a portrayal of her. It was so different from the beauty of all the earthly women he met, transfigured in the light of feminine humility touched with a presentiment of the divine. In the deceptive twilight of memory, the images of all the women he had ever loved came together in that wonderful figure. And when he tried, for the first time, to ignore reality and create a Mother of God out of the figure of Mary with her child that hovered before his mind's eye, smiling gently in happy, unclouded bliss, then his fingers, wielding the brush, sank powerless as if numbed by cramp. The current was drying up, the skill of his fingers in interpreting the words spoken by the eye seemed helpless in the face of his bright dream, although he saw as clearly in his imagination as if it were painted on a solid wall. His inability to give shape to the fairest and truest of his dreams and bring it into reality was pain that burnt like fire now that reality itself, in all its abundance, did not help him to build a bridge. And he asked himself a terrible question—could he still call himself an artist if such a thing could happen to him, had he been only a hardworking craftsman all his life, fitting colours together as a labourer constructs a building out of stones?

Such self-tormenting reflections gave him not a day's rest, and drove him with compelling power out of his studio, where the empty canvas and carefully prepared tools of his trade reproached him like mocking voices. Several times he thought of confessing his dilemma to the merchant, but he was afraid that the latter, while a pious and well-disposed man, would never understand him, and would think it more of a clumsy excuse than real inability to begin such a work. After all, he had already painted many sacred pictures, to the general acclaim of laymen and master painters alike. So he made it his habit to wander the streets, restless and at his wits' end, secretly alarmed when chance or a hidden magic made him wake from his wandering dreams again and again, finding himself outside the cathedral with the altarpiece in its chapel, as if there were an invisible link between him and the picture, or a divine power ruled his soul even in dreams. Sometimes he went in, half-hoping to find some flaw in the picture and thus break free of its spell, but in front of it he entirely forgot to assess the young artist's creation enviously, judging its art and skill. Instead, he felt the rushing of wings around him, bearing him up into spheres of calm, transfigured contemplation. It was not until he left the cathedral and began thinking of himself and his own efforts that he felt the old pain again, redoubled.

One afternoon he had been wandering through the colourful streets once more, and this time he felt that his tormenting doubt was eased. The first breath of spring wind had begun to blow from the south, bringing with it the brightness, if not the warmth, of many fine spring days to come. For the first time the dull grey gloom that his own cares had cast over the world seemed to leave the painter, and a sense of the grace of God poured into his heart, as it always did when fleeting signs of spring announced the great miracle of resurrection. A clear March sun washed all the rooftops and streets clean, brightly coloured pennants fluttered down in the harbour, the water shone blue between the ships rocking gently there, and the never-ending noise of the city was like jubilant song. A troop of Spanish cavalry trotted over the main square. No hostile glances were cast at them today; the townsfolk enjoyed the sight of the sun reflected from their armour and shining helmets. Women's white headdresses, tugged wilfully back by the wind, revealed fresh, highly coloured complexions. Wooden clogs clattered on the cobblestones as children danced in a ring, holding hands and singing.

And in the usually dark alleys of the harbour district, to which the artist now turned feeling ever lighter at heart, something shimmering flickered like a falling rain of light. The sun could not quite show its bright face between the gabled roofs here as they leant towards each other, densely crowded together, black and crumpled like the hoods of a couple of little old women standing there chattering, one each side of the street. But the light was reflected from window to window, as if sparkling hands were waving in the air, passing back and forth in a high-spirited game. In many places the light remained soft and muted, like a dreaming eye in the first evening twilight. Down below in the street lay darkness where it had lain for years, hidden only occasionally in winter by a cloak of snow. Those who lived there had the sad gloom of constant dusk in their eyes, but the children who longed for light and brightness trusted the enticement of these first rays of spring, playing in their thin clothing on the dirty, potholed streets. The narrow strip of blue sky showing between the rooftops, the golden dance of the sunlight above made them deeply, instinctively happy.

The painter walked on and on, never tiring. He felt as if he, too, were granted secret reasons to rejoice, as if every spark of sunlight was the fleeting reflection of the radiance of God's grace going to his heart. All the bitterness had left his face. It now shone with such a mild and kindly light that the children playing their games were amazed, and greeted him with awe, thinking that he must be a priest. He walked on and on, with never a thought for where he was going. The new force of springtime was in his limbs, just as flower buds tap hopefully at the bast holding old, weather-beaten trees together, willing it to let their young strength shoot out into the light. His step was as spry and light as a young man's, and he seemed to be feeling fresher and livelier even though he had been walking for hours, putting stretches of the road behind him at a faster and more flexible pace.

Suddenly the painter stopped as if turned to stone and shaded his eyes with his hand to protect them, like a man dazzled by a flashing light or some awesome, incredible event. Looking up at a window, he had felt the full beam of sunlight reflected back from it strike his eyes painfully, but through the crimson and gold mist forming in front of them a strange apparition, a wonderful illusion had appeared—there was the Madonna painted by that young Italian master, leaning back dreamily and with a touch of sorrow as she did in the picture. A shudder ran through him as the terrible fear of disappointment united with the trembling ecstasy of a man granted grace, one who had seen a vision of the Mother of God not in the darkness of a dream but in bright daylight. That was a miracle of the kind to which many had borne witness, but few had really seen it! He dared not look up yet, his trembling shoulders did not feel strong enough to bear the shattering effect of finding that he was wrong, and he was afraid that this one moment could crush his life even more cruelly than the merciless self-torment of his despairing heart. Only when his pulse was beating more steadily and slowly, and he no longer felt it like a hammer blow in his throat, did he pull himself together and look up slowly from the shelter of his hand at the window where he had seen that seductive image framed.

He had been mistaken. It was not the girl from the young master's Madonna. Yet all the same, his raised hand did not sink despondently. What he saw also appeared to him a miracle, if a sweeter, milder, more human one than a divine apparition seen in the radiant light of a blessed hour. This girl, looking thoughtfully out of the sunlit window frame, bore only a distant resemblance to the altarpiece in the chapel—her face too was framed by black hair, she too had a delicate complexion of mysterious, fantastic pallor, but her features were harder, sharper, almost angry, and around the mouth there was a tearful defiance that was not moderated even by the lost expression of her dreaming eyes, which held an old, deep grief. There was a childlike wilfulness and a legacy of hidden sorrow in their bright restlessness, which she seemed to control only with difficulty. He felt that her silent composure could dissolve into abrupt and angry movement at any time, and her mood of gentle reverie did not hide it. The painter felt a certain tension in her features, suggesting that this child would grow to be one of those women who live in their dreams and are at one with their longings, whose souls cling to what they love with every fibre of their being, and who die if they are forced away from it. But he marvelled not so much at all this strangeness in her face as at the miraculous play of nature that made the sunny glow behind her head, reflected in the window, look like a saint's halo lying around her hair until it shone like black steel. And he thought he clearly felt here the divine hand showing him how to complete his work in a manner worthy of the subject and pleasing to God.

A carter roughly jostled the painter as he stood in the middle of the street, lost in thought. "God's wrath, can't you watch out, old man, or are you so taken with the lovely Jew girl that you stand there gaping like an idiot and blocking my way?"

The painter started with surprise, but took no offence at the man's rough tone, and indeed he had scarcely noticed it in the light of the information provided by this gruff and heavily clad fellow. "Is she Jewish?" he asked in great surprise.

"So it's said, but I don't know. Anyway, she's not the child of the folk here, they found her or came by her somehow. What's it to me? I've never felt curious about it, and I won't neither. Ask the master of the house himself if you like. He'll know better than me, for sure, how she comes to be here."

The 'master' to whom he referred was an innkeeper, landlord of one of those dark, smoky taverns where the liveliness and noise never quite died down, because it was frequented by so many gamblers and seamen, soldiers and idlers that the place was seldom left entirely empty. Broad-built, with a fleshy but kindly face, he stood in the narrow doorway like an inn sign inviting custom. On impulse the painter approached him. They went into the tavern, and the painter sat down in a corner at a smeared wooden table. He still felt rather agitated, and when the landlord put the glass he had ordered in front of him, he asked him to sit at the table with him for a few moments. Quietly, so as not to attract the attention of a couple of slightly tipsy sailors bawling out songs at the next table, he asked his question. He told the man briefly but with deep feeling of the miraculous sign that had appeared to him—the landlord listened in surprise as his slow understanding, somewhat clouded by wine, tried to follow the painter—and finally asked if he would allow him to paint his daughter as the model for a picture of the Virgin Mary. He did not forget to mention that by giving permission her father too would be taking part in a devout work, and pointed out several times that he would be ready to pay the girl good money for her services.

The innkeeper did not answer at once, but kept rubbing his broad nostrils with a fat finger. At last he began.

"Well, sir, you mustn't take me for a bad Christian, by God no, but it's not as easy as you think. If I was her father and I could say to my daughter, off you go and do as I say, well, sir, the bargain would soon be struck. But with that child, it's different… Good God, what's the matter?"

He had jumped up angrily, for he did not like to be disturbed as he talked. At another table a man was hammering his empty tankard on the bench and demanding another. Roughly, the landlord snatched the tankard from his hand and refilled it, suppressing a curse. At the same time he picked up a glass and bottle, went back to join his new guest, sat down and filled glasses for them both. His own was soon gulped down, and as if well refreshed he wiped his bristling moustache and began his tale.

"I'll tell you how I came by that Jewish girl, sir. I was a soldier, fighting first in Italy, then in Germany. A bad trade, I can tell you, never worse than today, and it was bad enough even back then. I'd had enough of it, I was on my way home through Germany to take up some honest calling, because I didn't have much left to call my own. The money you get as loot in warfare runs through your fingers like water, and I was never a skinflint. So I was in some German town or other, I'd only just arrived, when I heard a great to-do that evening. What set it off I don't know, but the townsfolk had ganged up together to attack the local Jews and I went along with them, partly hoping to pick something up, partly out of curiosity to see what happened. The townsfolk went to work with a will, there was storming of houses, killing, robbing, raping, and the men of the town were roaring with greed and lust. I'd soon had enough of that kind of thing, and I left them to it. I wasn't going to sully my honourable sword with women's blood, or wrestle with whores for what loot I could find. Well then, as I'm about to go back down a side alley, I see an old Jew with his long beard a-quiver, his face distorted, holding in his arms a small child just woken from sleep. He runs to me and stammers out a torrent of words I can't make out. All I understood of his Yiddish German was that he'd give me a good sum of money in return for saving the pair of them. I felt sorry for the child, looking at me all alarmed with her big eyes. And it didn't seem a bad bargain, so I threw my cloak over the old man and took them to my lodgings. There were a few people standing in the alleys, looking like they were inclined to go for the old man, but I'd drawn my sword, and they let all three of us pass. I took them to the inn where I was staying, and when the old man went on his knees to plead with me we left the town that same evening, while the fire-raising and murder went on into the night. We could still see the firelight when we were far away, and the old man stared at it in despair, but the child, she just slept on calmly. The three of us weren't together for long. After a few days the old man fell mortally sick, and he died on the way. But first he gave me all the money he'd brought away with him, and a piece of paper written in strange letters—I was to give a broker in Antwerp, he said, and he told me the man's name. He commended his granddaughter to my care as he died. Well, I came here to Antwerp and showed that piece of paper, and a strange effect it had too—the broker gave me a handsome sum of money, more than I'd have expected. I was glad of it, for now I could be free of the wandering life, so I bought this house and the tavern with the money and soon forgot the war. I kept the child. I was sorry for her, and then I hoped that as she grew up she'd do the work about the place for me, old bachelor that I am. But it didn't turn out like that.

"You saw her just now, and that's the way she is all day. She looks out of the window at empty air, she speaks to no one, she gives timid answers as if she was ducking down expecting someone to hit her. She never speaks to men. At first I thought she'd be an asset here in the tavern, bringing in the guests, like the landlord's young daughter over the road, she'll joke with his customers and encourage them to drink glass after glass. But our girl here's not bold, and if anyone so much as touches her she screams and runs out of the door like a whirlwind. And then if I go looking for her she's sure to be sitting huddled in a corner somewhere, crying fit to break your heart, you'd think God know what harm had come to her. Strange folk, the Jews!"

"Tell me," said the painter, interrupting the storyteller, who was getting more and more thoughtful as he went on, "tell me, is she still of the Jewish religion, or has she converted to the true faith?"

The landlord scratched his head in embarrassment. "Well, sir," he said, "I was a soldier. I couldn't say too much about my own Christianity. I seldom went to church and I don't often go now, though I'm sorry, and as for converting the child, I never felt clever enough for that. I didn't really try, seemed to me it would be a waste of time with that truculent little thing. Folk set the priest on me once, and he read me a right lecture, but I was putting it off until the child reached the age of reason. Still, I reckon we'll be waiting a long time yet for that, although she's past fifteen years old now, but she's so strange and wilful. Odd folk, these Jews, who knows much about them? Her old grandfather seemed to me a good man, and she's not a bad girl, hard as it is to get close to her. And as for your idea, sir, I like it well enough, I think an honest Christian can never do too much for the salvation of his soul, and everything we do will be judged one day… but I'll tell you straight, I have no real power over the child. When she looks at you with those big black eyes you don't have the heart to do anything that might hurt her. But see for yourself. I'll call her down."

He stood up, poured himself another glass, drained it standing there with his legs apart, and then marched across the tavern to some sailors who had just come in and were puffing at their short-stemmed white clay pipes, filling the place with thick smoke. He shook hands with them in friendly fashion, filled their glasses and joked with them. Then he remembered what he was on his way to do, and the painter heard him make his way up the stairs with a heavy tread.

He felt strangely disturbed. The wonderful confidence he had drawn from that happy moment of emotion on seeing the girl began to cloud over in the murky light of this tavern. The dust of the street and the dark smoke were imposed on the shining image he remembered. And back came his sombre fear that it was a sin to take the solid, animal humanity that could not be separated from earthly women, mingling it with sublime ideas and elevating it to the throne of his pious dreams. He shuddered, wondering from what hands he was to receive the gift to which miraculous signs, both secret and revealed, had pointed his way.

The landlord came back into the tavern, and in his heavy, broad black shadow the painter saw the figure of the girl, standing in the doorway indecisively, seeming to be alarmed by the noise and the smoke, holding the doorpost with her slender hands as if seeking for help. An impatient word from the landlord telling her to hurry up alarmed her, and sent her shrinking further back into the darkness of the stairway, but the painter had already risen to approach her. He took her hands in his—old and rough as they were, they were also very gentle—and asked quietly and kindly, looking into her eyes, "Won't you sit down with me for a moment?"

The girl looked at him, astonished by the kindness and affection in the deep, bell-like sound of his voice on hearing it for the first time there in the dark, smoky tavern. She felt how gentle his hands were, and saw the tender goodness in his eyes with the sweet diffidence of a girl who has been hungering for affection for weeks and years, and is amazed to receive it. When she saw his snow-white head and kindly features, the image of her dead grandfather's face rose suddenly before her mind's eye, and forgotten notes sounded in her heart, chiming with loud jubilation through her veins and up into her throat, so that she could not say a word in reply, but blushed and nodded vigorously—almost as if she were angry, so harshly abrupt was the sudden movement. Timidly, she followed him to his table and perched on the edge of the bench beside him.

The painter looked affectionately down at her without saying a word. Before the old man's clear gaze, the tragic loneliness and proud sense of difference that had been present in this child from an early age flared up suddenly in her eyes. He would have liked to draw her close and press a reassuring kiss of benediction on her brow, but he was afraid of alarming her, and he feared the eyes of the other guests, who were pointing the strange couple out to each other and laughing. Before even hearing a word from this child he understood her very well, and warm sympathy rose in him, flowing freely, for he understood the painful defiance, harsh and brusque and defensive, of someone who wants to give an infinite wealth of love, yet who feels rejected. He gently asked, "What is your name, child?"

She looked up at him with trust, but in confusion. All this was still too strange and alien to her. Her voice shook shyly as she replied quietly, half turning away, "Esther."

The old man sensed that she trusted him but dared not show it yet. He began, in a quiet voice, "I am a painter, Esther, and I would like to paint a picture of you. Nothing bad will happen to you, you will see a great many beautiful things in my studio, and perhaps we will sometimes talk to each other like good friends. It will only be for one or two hours a day, as long as you please and no more. Will you come to my studio and let me paint you, Esther?"

The girl blushed even more rosily and did not know what to say. Dark riddles suddenly opened up before her, and she could not find her way to them. Finally she looked at the landlord, who was standing curiously by, with an uneasy, questioning glance.

"Your father will allow it and likes the idea," the painter made haste to say. "The decision is yours alone, for I cannot and do not want to force you into it. So will you let me paint you, Esther?"

He held out his large, brown, rustic hand invitingly. She hesitated for a moment, and then, bashfully and without a word, placed her own small white hand in the painter's to show her consent. His hand enclosed hers for a moment, as if it were prey he had caught. Then he let it go with a kindly look. The landlord, amazed to see the bargain so quickly concluded, called over some of the sailors from the other tables to point out this extraordinary event. But the girl, ashamed to be at the centre of attention, quickly jumped up and ran out of the door like lightning. The whole company watched her go in surprise.

"Good heavens above," said the astonished landlord, "that was a masterstroke, sir. I'd never have expected that shy little thing to agree."

And as if to confirm this statement he poured another glassful down his throat. The painter, who was beginning to feel ill at ease in the company here as it slowly lost its awe of him, threw some money on the table, discussed further details with the landlord, and warmly shook his hand. However, he made haste to leave the tavern; he did not care for its musty air and all the noise, and the drunk, bawling customers repelled him.

When he came out into the street the sun had just set, and only a dull pink twilight lingered in the sky. The evening was mild and pure. Walking slowly, the old man went home musing on events that seemed to him as strange and yet as pleasing as a dream. There was reverence in his heart, and it trembled as happily as when the first bell rang from the church tower calling the congregation to prayers, to be answered by the bells of all the other towers nearby, their voices deep and high, muffled and joyful, chiming and murmuring, like human beings calling out in joy and sorrow and pain. It seemed to him extraordinary that after following a sober and straightforward path all his life, his heart should be inflamed at this late hour by the soft radiance of divine miracles, but he dared not doubt it, and he carried the grace of that radiance for which he had longed home through the dark streets, blessedly awake and yet in a wonderful dream.

Days had passed by, and still the blank canvas stood on the painter's easel. Now, however, it was not despondency paralysing his hands, but a sure inner confidence that no longer counted the days, was in no hurry, and instead waited in serene silence while he held his powers in restraint. Esther had been timid and shy when she first visited the studio, but she soon became more forthcoming, gentler and less timid, basking in his fatherly warmth as he bestowed it on the simple, frightened girl. They spent these days merely talking to each other, like friends meeting after long years apart who have to get acquainted again before putting ardent feeling into heartfelt words and reviving their old intimacy. And soon there was a secret bond between these two people, so dissimilar and yet so like each other in a certain simplicity—one of them a man who had learnt that clarity and silence are at the heart of life, an experienced man schooled in simplicity by long days and years; the other a girl who had never yet truly felt alive, but had dreamt her days away as if surrounded by darkness, and who now felt the first ray from a world of light reach her heart, reflecting it back in a glow of radiance. The difference between the sexes meant nothing to the two of them; such thoughts were now extinguished in him and merely cast the evening light of memory into his life, and as for the girl, her dim sense of her own femininity had not fully awoken and was expressed only as vague, restless longing that had no aim as yet. A barrier still stood between them, but might soon give way—their different races and religions, the discipline of blood that has learnt to see itself as strange and hostile, nurturing distrust that only a moment of great love will overcome. Without that unconscious idea in her mind the girl, whose heart was full of pent-up affection, would long ago have thrown herself in tears on the old man's breast, confessing her secret terrors and growing longings, the pains and joys of her lonely existence. As it was, however, she showed her feelings only in glances and silences, restless gestures and hints. Whenever she felt everything in her trying to flow towards the light and express itself in clear, fluent words of ardent emotion, a secret power took hold of her like a dark, invisible hand and stifled them. And the old man did not forget that all his life he had regarded Jews if not with hatred, at least with a sense that they were alien. He hesitated to begin his picture because he hoped that the girl had been placed in his path only to be converted to the true faith. The miracle was not to be worked for him; he was to work it for her. He wanted to see in her eyes the same deep longing for the Saviour that the Mother of God must herself have felt when she trembled in blessed expectation of his coming. He would like to fill her with faith before painting a Madonna who still felt the awe of the Annunciation, but had already united it with the sweet confidence of coming fulfilment. And around his Madonna he imagined a mild landscape, a day just before the coming of spring, with white clouds moving through the air like swans drawing the warm weather along on invisible threads, with the first tender green showing as the moment of resurrection approached, flowers opening their buds to announce the coming of blessed spring as if in high, childlike voices. But the girl's eyes still seemed to him too timid and humble. He could not yet kindle the mystic flame of the Virgin's Annunciation and her devotion to a sombre promise in those restless glances; the deep, veiled suffering of her race still showed there, and sometimes he sensed the defiance of the Chosen People at odds with their God. They did not yet know humility and gentle, unearthly love.

With care and caution he tried to find ways to bring the Christian faith closer to her heart, knowing that if he showed it to her glowing in all its brightness, like a monstrance with the sun sparkling in it to show a thousand colours, she would not sink down before it in awe but turn brusquely away, seeing it as a hostile sign. There were many pictures taken from the Scriptures in his portfolios, works painted when he was an apprentice and sometimes copied again later when he was overcome by emotion. He took them out now and looked at the pictures side by side, and soon he felt the deep impression that many of them made on his mind in the trembling of his hands, and the warmth of his breath on his cheeks as it came faster. A bright world of beauty suddenly lay before the eyes of the lonely girl, who for years had seen only the swollen figures of guests at the tavern, the wrinkled faces of old, black-clad women, the grubby children shouting and tussling with each other in the street. But here were gentlewomen of enchanting beauty wearing wonderful dresses, ladies proud and sad, dreamy and desirable, knights in armour with long and gorgeous robes laughing or talking to the ladies, kings with flowing white locks on which golden crowns shone, handsome young men who had suffered martyrdom, sinking to the ground pierced by arrows or bleeding to death under torture. And a strange land that she did not know, although it touched her heart sweetly like an unconscious memory of home, opened up before her—a land of green palms and tall cypress trees, with a bright blue sky, always the same deep hue, above deserts and mountains, cities and distant prospects. Its radiant glow seemed much lighter and happier than this northern sky of eternal grey cloud.

Gradually he began telling her little stories about the pictures, explaining the simple, poetic legends of the Bible, speaking of the signs and wonders of that holy time with such enthusiasm that he forgot his own intentions, and he described, in ecstatic terms, the confidence in his faith that had brought him grace so recently. And the old man's deeply felt faith touched the girl's heart; she felt as if a wonderful country were suddenly revealed to her, opening its gates in the dark. She was less and less certain of herself as her life woke from the depths of the dark to see crimson light. She herself was feeling so strange that nothing seemed to her incredible—not the story of the silver star followed by three kings from distant lands, with their horses and camels bearing bright burdens of precious things—nor the idea that a dead man, touched by a hand in blessing, might wake to life again. After all, she felt the same wonderful power at work in herself. Soon the pictures were forgotten. The old man told her about his own life, connecting the old legends with many signs from God. He was bringing to light much that he had thought and dreamt of in his old age, and he himself was surprised by his own eloquence, as if it were something strange taken from another's hand to be tested. He was like a preacher who begins with a text from the word of God, meaning to explain and interpret it, and who then suddenly forgets his hearers and his intentions and gives himself up to the pleasure of letting all the springs of his heart flow into a deep torrent of words, as if into a goblet containing all the sweetness and sanctity of life. And then the preacher's words rise higher and higher above the heads of the humble members of his congregation, who cannot reach up to the world he now inhabits, but murmur and stare at him as he approaches the heavens in his bold dream, forgetting the force of gravity that will weigh down his wings again…

The painter suddenly looked around him as if still surrounded by the rosy mists of his inspired words. Reality showed him its cold and ordered structure once more. But what he saw was itself as beautiful as a dream.

Esther was sitting at his feet looking up at him. Gently leaning on his arm, gazing into the still, blue, clear eyes that suddenly seemed so full of light, she had gradually sunk down beside him, and in his devout emotion he had never noticed. She was crouching at his knees, her eyes turned up to him. Old words from her own childhood were suddenly present in her confused mind, words that her father, wearing his solemn black robe and frayed white bands, had often read from an old and venerable book. Those words too had been so full of resonant ceremony and ardent piety. A world that she had lost, a world of which she now knew little came back to life in muted colours, filling her with poignant longing and bringing the gleam of tears to her eyes. When the old man bent down to those sad eyes and kissed her forehead, he felt a sob shaking her tender, childlike frame in a wild fever. And he misunderstood her. He thought the miracle had happened, and God, in a wonderful moment, had given his usually plain and simple manner of speech the glowing, fiery tongue of eloquence as he once gave it to the prophets when they went out to his people. He thought this awe was the shy, still timorous happiness of one who was on her way home to the true faith, in which all bliss was to be found, and she was trembling and swaying like a flame suddenly lit, still feeling its way up into the air before settling into a clear, steady glow. His heart rejoiced at his mistake; he thought that he was suddenly close to his aim. He spoke to her solemnly.

"I have told you about miracles, Esther. Many say that miracles only happened long ago, but I feel and I tell you now that they still happen today. However, they are quiet miracles, and are only to be found in the souls of those who are ready for them. What has happened here is a miracle—my words and your tears, rising from our blind hearts, have become a miracle of enlightenment worked by an invisible hand. Now that you have understood me you are one of us; at the moment when God gave you those tears you became a Christian…"

He stopped in surprise. When he uttered that word Esther had risen from where she knelt at his feet, putting out her hands to ward off the mere idea. There was horror in her eyes, and the angry, wild truculence that her foster father had mentioned. At that moment, when the severity of her features turned to anger, the lines around her mouth were as sharp as the cut of a knife, and she stood in a defensive attitude like a cat about to pounce. All the ardour in her broke out in that moment of wild self-defence.

Then she calmed down. But the barrier between them was high and dark again, no longer irradiated by supernatural light. Her eyes were cold, restless and ashamed, no longer angry, but no longer full of mystic awe; only reality was in them. Her hands hung limp like wings broken in soaring too high. Life was still a mystery of strange beauty to her, but she dared not love the dream from which she had been so shatteringly woken.

The old painter too felt that his hasty confidence had deceived him, but it was not the first disappointment in his long and questing life of faith and trust. So he felt no pain, only surprise, and then again almost joy to see how quickly *she* felt ashamed. He gently took her two childish hands, still feverishly burning as they were. "Esther, your sudden outburst almost alarmed me. But I do not hold it against you… is that what you are thinking?"

Ashamed, she shook her head, only to raise it again next moment. Again her words were almost defiant.

"But I don't want to be a Christian. I don't want to. I—" She choked on the words for some time before saying, in a muted voice. "I… I hate Christians. I don't know them but I hate them. What you told me about love embracing everything is more beautiful than anything I have ever heard in my life. But the people in the tavern say that they are Christians too, although they are rough and violent. And… I don't even remember it clearly, it's all so long ago… but when they talked about Christians at home, there was fear and hatred in their voices. Everyone hated the Christians. I hate them too… when I was little and went out with my father they shouted at us, and once they threw stones at us. One of the stones hit me and made me bleed and cry, but my father made me go on, he was afraid, and when I shouted for help… I don't remember any more about all that. Or yes, I do. Our alleys were dark and narrow, like the one where I live here. And only Jews lived there. But higher up, the town was beautiful. I once looked down at it from the top of a house… there was a river flowing through it, so blue and clear, and a broad bridge over the river with people crossing it in brightly coloured clothes like the ones you showed me in the pictures. And the houses were decorated with statues and with gilding and gable ends. Among them there were tall, tall towers, where bells rang, and the sun shone all the way down into the streets there. It was all so lovely. But when I told my father he ought to go and see the lovely town with me he looked very serious and said, 'No, Esther, the Christians would kill us.' That frightened me… and ever since then I have hated the Christians."

She stopped in the middle of her dreams, for all around her seemed bright again. What she had forgotten long ago, leaving it to lie dusty and veiled in her soul, was sparkling once again. She was back there walking down the dark alleys of the ghetto to the house she was visiting. And suddenly everything connected and was clear, and she realised that what she sometimes thought was a dream had been reality in her past life. Her words came tumbling out in pursuit of the images hurrying through her mind.

"And then there was that evening… I was suddenly snatched up out of my bed… I saw my grandfather, he was holding me in his arms, his face was pale and trembling… the whole house was in uproar, shaking, there was shouting and noise. Oh, now it's coming back to me. I hear what they were shouting again—it's the others, they were saying, it's the Christians. My father was shouting it, or my mother, or… I don't remember. My grandfather carried me down into the darkness, through black streets and alleys… and there was always that noise and the same shouting—the others, the Christians! How could I have forgotten? And then we went away with a man… when I woke up we were far out in the country, my grandfather and the man I live with now… I never saw that town again, but the sky was very red back where we had come from… and we travelled on…"

Again she stopped. The pictures seemed to be disappearing, getting slowly darker.

"I had three sisters. They were very beautiful, and every evening they came to my bedside to kiss me goodnight… and my father was tall, I couldn't reach up to him, so he often carried me in his arms. And my mother… I never saw her again. I don't know what happened to them, because my grandfather looked away and wouldn't tell me when I asked him. And when he died there was no one I dared to ask."

She stopped once more, and a painful, violent sob burst from her throat. Very quietly, she added, "But now I know it all. How could it all be so dark to me? I feel as if my father were standing beside me saying the words he used to say at that time, it is all so clear in my ears. I won't ask anyone again…"

Her words turned to sobs, to silent, miserable weeping that died away in deep, sad silence. Only a few minutes ago life had shown her an enticing image; now it lay dark and sombre before her again. And the old man had long ago forgotten his intention of converting her as he watched her pain. He stood there in silence, feeling as sad himself as if he must sit down and weep with her, for there were some things that he could not put into words, and with his great love of humanity he felt guilty for unknowingly arousing such pain in her. Shuddering, he felt the fullness of blessing and the weight of a burden to be borne, both coming at the same hour; it was as if heavy waves were rising and falling, and he did not know whether they would raise his life or drag it down into the menacing deeps. But wearily, he felt neither fear nor hope, only pity for this young life with so many different paths opening up before it. He tried to find words; but they were all as heavy as lead and had the ring of false coin. What was all they could express, in the face of such a painful memory?

Sadly, he stroked the hair on her trembling head. She looked up, confused and distracted; then mechanically tidied her hair and rose, her eyes wandering this way and that as if getting used to reality again. Her features became wearier, less tense, and there was only darkness now in her eyes. Abruptly, she pulled herself together, and quickly said, to hide the sobs still rising inside her, "I must go now. It's late. And my father is expecting me."

With a brusque gesture of farewell she shook her head, picked up her skirts and turned to leave. But the old man, who had been watching her with his steady, understanding gaze, called after her. She turned back reluctantly, for there were still tears in her eyes. And again the old man took both her hands in his forceful manner and looked at her. "Esther, I know that you want to go now and not come back again. You do not and will not believe me, because a secret fear deceives you."

He felt her hands relax in his gently, softer now. He went on more confidently, "Come back another day, Esther! We will forget all of this, the happy and the sad part of it alike. Tomorrow we will begin on my picture, and I feel as if it will succeed. And don't be sad any more, let the past rest, don't brood on it. Tomorrow we will begin a new work with new hope—won't we, Esther?"

In tears, she nodded. And she went home again, still timid and uncertain, but with a new and deeper awareness of many things.

The old man stayed there, lost in thought. His belief in miracles had not deserted him, but they had seemed more solemn before; were they only a case of a divine hand playing with life? He abandoned the idea of seeing faith in a mystical promise light up a face when perhaps its owner's soul was too desperate to believe. He would no longer presume to bring God and his own ideas to anyone, he would only be a simple servant of the Lord painting a picture as well as he could, and laying it humbly on God's altar as another man might bring a gift. He felt that it was a mistake to look for signs and portents instead of waiting until they were revealed to him in their own good time.

Humbled, his heart sank to new depths. Why had he wanted to work a miracle on this child when no one had asked him to? Wasn't it enough that when his life was taking bleak and meaningless root, like the trunk of an old tree with only its branches aspiring to reach the sky, another life, a young life full of fear, had come to cling trustfully to him? One of life's miracles, he felt, had happened to him; he had been granted the grace to give and teach the love that still burnt in him in his old age, to sow it like a seed that may yet come to wonderful flower. Hadn't life given him enough with that? And hadn't God shown him the way to serve him? He had wanted a female figure in his picture, and the model for it had come to meet him, wasn't it God's will for him to paint her likeness, and not try converting her to a faith that she might never be able to understand? Lower and lower sank his heart.

Evening and darkness came into his room. The old man stood up, feeling a restlessness unusual to him in his late days, for they were usually as mild as cool rays of autumn sunlight. He slowly kindled a light. Then he went to the cupboard and looked for an old book. His heart was weary of restlessness. He took the Bible, kissed it ardently, and then opened it and read until late into the night.

He began work on the picture. Esther sat leaning thoughtfully back in a soft, comfortable armchair, sometimes listening to the old man as he told her all kinds of stories from his own life and the lives of others, trying to while away the monotonous hours of sitting still for her. Sometimes she just sat calmly dreaming in the large room where the tapestries, pictures and drawings adorning the walls attracted her gaze. The painter's progress was slow. He felt that the studies he was doing of Esther were only first attempts, and had not yet caught the final conviction that he wanted. There was still something lacking in the idea behind his sketches; he could not put it into words, but he felt it deep within him so clearly that feverish haste often drove him on from sketch to sketch, and then, comparing them with each other, he was still not content, faithful as his likenesses of Esther were. He did not mention it to the girl, but he felt as if the harsh set of her lips, a look that never entirely left them even when she was gently dreaming, would detract from the serene expectation that was to transfigure his Madonna. There was too much childish defiance in her for her mood to turn to sweet contemplation of motherhood. He did not think any words would really dispel that darkness in her; it could change only from within. But the soft, feminine emotion he wanted would not come to her face, even when the first spring days cast red-gold sunlight into the room through every window and the whole world stirred as it revived, when all colours seemed to be even softer and deeper, like the warm air wafting through the streets. Finally the painter grew weary. He was an experienced old man, he knew the limits of his art, and he knew he could not overcome them by force. Obeying the insistent voice of sudden intuition, he soon gave up his original plan for the painting. And after weighing up the possibilities, he decided not to paint Esther as the Madonna absorbed in thoughts of the Annunciation, since her face showed no signs of devoutly awakening femininity, but as the most straightforward but deeply felt symbol of his faith, the Madonna with her child. And he wanted to begin it at once, because hesitation was making inroads on his soul, again now that the radiance of the miracle he had dreamt of was fading, and had almost disappeared entirely into darkness. Without telling Esther, he removed the canvas, which bore a few fleeting traces of over-hasty sketches, and replaced it with a fresh one as he tried to give free rein to his new idea.

When Esther sat down in her usual way next day and waited, leaning gently back, for him to begin his work—not an unwelcome prospect to her, since it brought inspiring words and happy moments into the bleakness of her lonely day—she was surprised to hear the painter's voice in the next room, in friendly conversation with a woman whose rough, rustic voice she did not recognise. Curious, she pricked up her ears, but she could not hear what they were saying distinctly. Soon the woman's voice died away, a door latched, and the old man came in and went over to her carrying something pale in his arms. She did not realise at once what it was. He carefully placed a small, naked, sturdy child a few months old on her lap.

At first the baby wriggled, then he lay still. Esther stared wide-eyed at the old man—she had not expected him to play such a strange trick on her. But he only smiled and said nothing. When he saw that her anxious, questioning eyes were still fixed on him, he calmly explained, in a tone that asked her approval, his intention of painting her with the child on her lap. All the warm kindliness of his eyes went into that request. The deep fatherly love that he had come to feel for this strange girl, and his confidence in her restless heart, shone through his words and even his eloquent silence.

Esther's face had flushed rosy red. A great sense of shame tormented her. She hardly dared to look timidly sideways at the healthy little creature whom she reluctantly held on her trembling knees. She had been brought up among people who had a stern abhorrence of the naked human body, and it made her look at this healthy, happy and now peacefully sleeping baby with revulsion and secret fear; she instinctively hid her own nakedness even from herself, and shrank from touching the little boy's soft, pink flesh as if it were a sin. She was afraid, and didn't know why. All her instincts told her to say no, but she did not want to respond so brusquely to the old man's kindly words, for she increasingly loved and revered him. She felt that she could not deny him anything. And his silence and the question in his waiting glance weighed so heavily on her that she could have cried out with a loud, wordless animal scream. She felt unreasonable dislike of the peacefully slumbering child; he had intruded into her one quiet, untroubled hour and destroyed her dreamy melancholy. But she felt weak and defenceless in the face of the calm old man's kindly wisdom. He was like a pale and lonely star above the dark depths of her life. Once again, as she did in answer to all his requests, she bowed her head in humble confusion.

He said no more, but set about beginning the picture. First he only sketched the outline, for Esther was still far too uneasy and bewildered to embody the meaning of his work. Her dreamy expression had entirely disappeared. There was something tense and desperate in her eyes as she avoided looking at the sleeping, naked infant on her lap, and fixed them instead in endless scrutiny on the walls full of pictures and ornaments to which she really felt indifferent. Her stiff hand showed that she was afraid she might have to bring herself to touch the little body. In addition, the weight on her knees was heavy, but she dared not move. However, the tension in her face showed more and more strongly what a painful effort she was making. In the end the painter himself began to have some inkling of her discomfort, although he ascribed it not to her inherited abhorrence of nakedness but to maidenly modesty, and he ended the sitting. The baby himself went on sleeping like a replete little animal, and did not notice when the painter carefully took him off the girl's lap and put him down on the bed in the next room, where he stayed until his mother, a sturdy Dutch seaman's wife brought to Antwerp for a while by chance, came to fetch him. But although Esther was free of the physical burden she felt greatly oppressed by the idea that she would now have to suffer the same alarm every day.

For the next few days she both came to the studio and left it again uneasily. Secretly, she hoped that the painter would give up this plan as well, and her decision to ask him to do so with a few calm words became compelling and overwhelming. Yet she could never quite bring herself do it; personal pride or a secret sense of shame kept the words back even as they came to her lips like birds ready to take flight. However, as she came back day after day, even though she was so restless, her shame gradually became an unconscious lie, for she had already come to terms with it, as you might come to terms with an unwelcome fact about yourself. She simply did not understand what had happened. Meanwhile the picture was making little progress, although the painter described it cautiously to her. In reality the frame of his canvas contained only the empty and unimportant lines of the figures, and a few fleeting attempts at choosing shades of colour. The old man was waiting for Esther to reconcile herself to his idea, and as his hope that she would verged on certainty he did not try to hurry matters along. For the time being, he made her sittings shorter, and talked a great deal of unimportant matters, deliberately ignoring the presence of the baby and Esther's uneasiness. He seemed more confident and cheerful than ever.

And this time his confidence was well-founded. One morning it was bright and warm, the rectangle of the window framed a light, translucent landscape—towers that were far away, yet the golden gleam on them made them look close; rooftops from which smoke rose in a leisurely fashion, curling up into the deep damask blue of the sky and losing itself there; white clouds very close, as if they were about to descend like downy fluttering birds into the darkly flowing sea of roofs. And the sun cast great handfuls of gold on everything, rays and dancing sparks, circles of light like little clinking coins, narrow strips of it like gleaming daggers, fluttering shapes without any real form that leapt nimbly over the floorboards as if they were bright little animals. This dappled, sparkling play of light had woken the baby from sleep as it tapped at his closed eyelids, until his eyes opened and he blinked and stared. He began moving restlessly on Esther's lap as she reluctantly held him. However, he was not trying to get away from her, only grabbing awkwardly with his clumsy little hands at the sparkling light dancing and playing around them, although he could not seize them, and his failure only made him try harder. His fat little fingers tried to move faster and faster. The sunny light showed the warm flow of blood shining rosily through them, and this simple game made the child's clumsy little body such a charming sight that it cast a spell even on Esther. Smiling with her superior knowledge at the baby's vain attempts to catch and hold the light, she watched his endless game without tiring, quite forgetting her reluctance to hold the innocent, helpless infant. For the first time she felt that there was true human life in the smooth little body—all she had felt before was his naked flesh and the dull satisfaction of his senses—and with childish curiosity of her own she followed all his movements. The old man watched in silence. If he spoke he feared he might revive her truculence and the shame she had forgotten, but his kindly lips wore the satisfied smile of a man who knows the world and its creatures. He saw nothing startling in this change, he had expected and counted on it, confident of the deep laws of nature that never fail. Once again he felt very close to one of those miracles of life that are always renewing themselves, a miracle that can suddenly use children to call forth the devoted kindness of women, and they then give it back to the children, so the miracle passes from being to being and never loses its own childhood but lives a double life, in itself and in those it encounters. And was this not the divine miracle of Mary herself, a child who would never become a woman, but would live on in her child? Was that miracle not reflected in reality, and did not every moment of burgeoning life have about it an ineffable radiance and the sound of what can never be understood?

The old man felt again, deeply, that proximity to the miraculous the idea of which, whether divine or earthly, had obsessed him for weeks. But he knew that he stood outside a dark, closed gate, from which he must humbly turn away again, merely leaving a reverent kiss on the forbidden threshold. He picked up a brush to work, and so chase away ideas that were already lost in clouded gloom. However, when he looked to see how close his copy came to reality, he was spellbound for a moment. He felt as if all his searching so far had been in a world hung about with veils, although he did not know it, and only now that they were removed did its power and extravagance burn before him. The picture he had wanted was coming to life. With shining eyes and clutching hands, the healthy, happy child turned to the light that poured its soft radiance over his naked body. And above that playful face was a second, tenderly bent over the child, and itself full of the radiance cast by that bright little body. Esther held her slender, childish hands on both sides of the baby to protect and avert all misfortune from him. And above her head was a fleeting light caught in her hair and seeming to shine out of it from within. Gentle movement united with moving light, unconsciousness joined dreaming memory, they all came together in a brief and beautiful image, airy and made of translucent colours, an image that could be shattered by a moment's abrupt movement.

The old man looked at the couple as if at a vision. The swift play of light seemed to have brought them together, and as if in distant dreams he thought of the Italian master's almost forgotten picture and its divine serenity. Once again he felt as if he heard the call of God. But this time he did not lose himself in dreams, he put all his strength into the moment. With vigorous strokes, he set down the play of the girl's childish hands, the gentle inclination of her bent head, her attitude no longer harsh. It was as if, although the moment was transitory, he wanted to preserve it for ever. He felt creative power in him like hot young blood. His whole life was in flux and flow, light and colour flowed into that moment, forming and holding his painting hand. And as he came closer to the secret of divine power and the unlimited abundance of life than ever before, he did not think about its signs and miracles, he lived them out by creating them himself.

The game did not last long. The child at last got tired of constantly snatching at the light, and Esther was surprised to see the old man suddenly working with feverish haste, his cheeks flushed. His face showed the same visionary light as in the days when he had talked to her about God and his many miracles, and she felt fervent awe in the presence of a mind that could lose itself so entirely in worlds of creation. And in that overwhelming feeling she lost the slight sense of shame she had felt, thinking that the painter had taken her by surprise at the moment when she was entirely fulfilled by the sight of the child. She saw only the abundance of life, and its sublime variety allowed her to feel again the awe that she had first known when the painter showed her pictures of distant, unknown people, cities as lovely as a dream, lush landscapes. The deprivations of her own life, the monotony of her intellectual experience took on colour from the sound of what was strange and the magnificence of what was distant. And a creative longing of her own burnt deep in her soul, like a hidden light burning in darkness.

That day was a turning point in the history of Esther and the picture. The shadows had fallen away from her. Now she walked fast, stepping lightly, to those hours in the studio that seemed to pass so quickly; they strung together a whole series of little incidents each of which was significant to her, for she did not know the true value of life and thought herself rich with the little copper coins of unimportant events. Imperceptibly, the figure of the old man retreated into the background of her mind by comparison with the baby's helpless little pink body. Her hatred had turned to a wild and almost greedy affection, such as girls often feel for small children and little animals. Her whole being was poured into watching and caressing him; unconsciously and in a passionate game, she was living out a woman's most sublime dream, the dream of motherhood. The purpose of her visits to the studio eluded her. She came, sat down in the big armchair with the healthy little baby, who soon recognised her and would laugh back at her, and began her ardent flirtation with him, quite forgetting that she was here for the sake of the picture, and that she had once felt this naked child was nothing but a nuisance. That time seemed as far away as one of the countless deceptive dreams that she used to spin in her long hours in the dark, dismal alley; their fabric dissolved at the first cautious breath of a wind of reality. Only in those hours at the studio did she now seem to live, not in the time she spent at home or the night into which she plunged to sleep. When her fingers held the baby's plump little hands, she felt that this was not an empty dream. And the smile for her in his big blue eyes was not a lie. It was life, and she drank it in with an avidity for abundance that was a rich, unconscious part of her heritage, and also a need to give of herself, a feminine longing before she was a woman yet. This game already had in it the seed of deeper longing and deeper joy. But it was still only a flirtatious dance of affection and admiration, playful charm and foolish dream. She cradled the baby like a child cuddling her doll, but she dreamt as women and mothers dream—sweetly, lovingly, as if in some boundless distant space.

The old man felt the change with all the fullness of his wise heart. He sensed that he was further from her now, but not stranger, and that he was not at the centre of her wishes but left to one side, like a pleasant memory. And he was glad of this change, much as he also loved Esther, for he saw young, strong, kind instincts in her which, he hoped, would do more than his own efforts to break through the defiance and reserve of the nature she had inherited. He knew that her love for him, an old man at the end of his days, was wasteful, although it could bring blessing and promise to her young life.

He owed wonderful hours to the love for the child that had awakened in Esther. Images of great beauty formed before him, all expressing a single idea and yet all different. Soon it was an affectionate game—his sketches showed Esther playing with the child, still a child herself in her unbounded delight, they showed flexible movements without harshness or passion, mild colours blending gently, the tender merging of tender forms. And then again there were moments of silence when the child had fallen asleep on her soft lap, and Esther's little hands watched over him like two hovering angels, when the tender joy of possession lit in her eyes, and a silent longing to wake the sleeping face with loving play. Then again there were seconds when the two pairs of eyes, hers and the baby's, were drawn to each other unconsciously, unintentionally, each seeking the other in loving devotion. Again, there were moments of charming confusion when the child's clumsy hands felt for the girl's breast, expecting to find his mother's milk there. Esther's cheeks would flush bashfully at that, but she felt no fear now, no reluctance, only a shy surge of emotion that turned to a happy smile.

These days were the creative hours that went into the picture. The painter made it out of a thousand touches of tenderness, a thousand loving, blissful, fearful, happy, ardent maternal glances. A great work full of serenity was coming into being. It was plain and simple—just a child playing and a girl's head gently bending down.

But the colours were milder and clearer than he had ever painted colours before, and the forms stood out as sharply and distinctly as dark trees against the glow of an evening sky. It was as if there must be some inner light hidden in the picture, shedding that secret brightness, as if air blew in it more softly, caressingly and clearly than in any other earthly work. There was nothing supernatural about it, and yet it showed the mystical mind of the man who had created it. For the first time the old man felt that in his long and busy creative life he had always been painting, brushstroke after brushstroke, some being of which he really knew nothing. It was like the old folk tale of the magical imps who do their work in hiding, yet so industriously that people marvel in the morning to see all they did overnight. That was how the painter felt when, after moments of creative inspiration, he stepped back from the picture and looked critically at it. Once again the idea of a miracle knocked on the door of his heart, and this time he hardly hesitated to let it in. For this work seemed to him not only the flower of his entire achievement, but something more distant and sublime of which his humble work was not worthy, although it was also the crown of his artistic career. Then his cheerful creativity would die away and turn to a strange mood when he felt fear of his own work, no longer daring to see himself in it.

So he distanced himself from Esther, who now seemed to him only the means of expressing the earthly miracle that he had worked. He showed her all his old kindness, but once again his mind was full of the pious dreams that he had thought far away. The simple power of life suddenly seemed to him so wonderful. Who could give him answers? The Bible was old and sacred, but his heart was earthly and still bound to this life. Where could he ask whether the wings of God descended to this world? Were there signs of God still abroad today, or only the ordinary miracles of life?

The old man did not venture to wish for the answer, although he had seen strange things during his life. But he was no longer as sure of himself as in the old days when he believed in life and in

God, and did not stop to wonder which of them was really true. Every evening he carefully covered up the picture, because once recently, on coming home to see silver moonlight resting on it like a blessing, he felt as if the Mother of God herself had shown him her face, and he could almost have thrown himself down in prayer before the work of his own hands.

Something else, however, happened at this time in Esther's life, nothing in itself strange or unlikely, but it affected the depths of her being like a rising storm and left her trembling in pain that she did not understand. She was experiencing the mystery of maturity, turning from a child into a woman. She was bewildered, since no one had taught her anything about it in advance; she had gone her own strange way alone between deep darkness and mystical light. Now longing awoke in her and did not know where to turn. The defiance that used to make her avoid playing with other children or speaking an unnecessary word burnt like a dark curse at this time. She did not feel the secret sweetness of the change in her, the promise of a seed not yet ready to come to life, only a dull, mysterious pain that she had to bear alone. In her ignorance, she saw the legends and miracles of which the old painter had spoken like lights leading her astray, while her dreams followed them through the most unlikely of possibilities. The story of the mild woman whose picture she had seen, the girl who became a mother after a wonderful Annunciation, suddenly struck her with almost joyful fear. She dared not believe it, because she had heard many other things that she did not understand. However, she thought that some miracle must be taking place inside her because she felt so different in every way, the world and everyone in it also suddenly seemed so different, deeper, stranger, full of secret urges. It all appeared to come together into an inner life trying to get out, then retreating again. There was some common factor at work; she did not know where it lay, but it seemed to hold everything that had once been separate together. She herself felt a force that was trying to take her out into life, to other human beings, but it did not know where to turn, and left behind only that urgent, pressing, tormenting pain of unspent longing and unused power.

In these hours when she was overwhelmed by desperation and needed some kind of support to cling to, Esther tried something that she had thought impossible before. She spoke to her foster father. Until now she had instinctively avoided him, because she felt the distance between them. But now she was driven over that threshold. She told him all about it, and talked about the picture, she looked deep into herself to find something gleaned from those hours that could be useful to her. And the landlord, visibly pleased to hear of the change in her, patted her cheeks with rough kindness and listened. Sometimes he put in a word, but it was as casual and impersonal as the way he spat out tobacco. Then he told her, in his own clumsy fashion, what had just happened to her. Esther listened, but it was no use. He didn't know what else to say to her and didn't even try. Nothing seemed to touch him except outwardly, there was no real sympathy between them, and his words suggested an indifference that repelled her. She knew now what she had only guessed before—people like him could never understand her. They might live side by side, but they did not know each other; it was like living in a desert. And in fact she thought her foster father was the best of all those who went in and out of this dismal tavern, because he had a certain rough plainness about him that could turn to kindness.

However, this disappointment could not daunt the power of her longings, and they all streamed back towards the two living beings she knew who spanned the morning and evening of human life. She desperately counted the lonely night hours still separating her from morning, and then she counted the morning hours separating her from her visit to the painter. Her ardent longings showed in her face. And once out in the street she abandoned herself entirely to her passion like a swimmer plunging into a foaming torrent, and raced through the hurrying crowd, stopping only when, with flushed face and untidy hair, she reached the door of the house she longed to see. In this time of the change in her, she was overcome by an instinctive urge to make free, passionate gestures, and it gave her a wild and desirable beauty.

That greedy, almost desperate need for affection made her prefer the baby to the old man, in whose friendly kindness there was a serenity that rejected stormy passion. He knew nothing about the feminine change in Esther, but he guessed it from her demeanour, and her sudden ecstatic transports made him uneasy. Sensing the nature of the elemental urge driving her on, he did not try to rein it in. Nor did he lose his fatherly love for this lonely child, although his mind had gone back to contemplation of the abstract interplay of the secret forces of life. He was glad to see her, and tried to keep her with him. The picture was in fact finished, but he did not tell Esther so, not wishing to part her from the baby on whom she lavished such affection. Now and then he added a few brushstrokes, but they were minor details—the design of a fold, a slight shading in the background, a fleeting nuance added to the play of light. He dared not touch the real idea behind the picture any more, for the magic of reality had slowly retreated, and he thought the dual aspect of the painting conveyed the spiritual nature of the wonderful creativity that now, as the memory of his execution of it faded, seemed to him less and less like the work of earthly powers. Any further attempt at improvement, he thought, would be not only folly but a sin. And he made up his mind that after this work, in which his hand had clearly been guided, he would do no more paintings, for they could only be lesser works, but spend his days in prayer and in searching for a way to reach those heights whose golden evening glow had rested on him in these late hours of his life.

With the fine instinct that the orphaned and rejected harbour in their hearts, like a secret network of sensitive fibres encompassing everything said and unsaid, Esther sensed the slight distance that the old man who was so dear to her had placed between them, and his mild tenderness, which was still the same, almost distressed her. She felt that at this moment she needed his whole attention and the free abundance of his love so that she could tell him all that was in her heart, all that now troubled it, and ask for answers to the riddles around her. She waited for the right moment to let out the words to express her mental turmoil, but the waiting was endless and tired her out. So all her affection was bent on the child. Her love concentrated on that helpless little body; she would catch the baby up and smother him with warm kisses so impetuously, forgetting his vulnerability, that she hurt him and he began to cry. Then she was less fiercely loving, more protective and reassuring, but even her anxieties were a kind of ecstasy, just as her feelings were not truly maternal, but more of a surge of longing erotic instincts dimly sensed. A force was trying to emerge in her, and her ignorance led her to turn it on the child. She was living out a dream, in a painful dazed state; she clung convulsively to the baby because he had a warm, beating heart, like hers, because she could lavish all the tenderness in her on his silent lips, because with him, unconsciously longing for a human touch, she could clasp another living creature without fearing the shame that came over her if she said a single word to a stranger. She spent hours and hours like that, never tiring, and never realising how she was giving herself away.

For her, all the life for which she longed so wildly was now contained in the child. These were dark times, growing even darker, but she never noticed. The citizens of Antwerp gathered in the evenings and talked of the old liberties and good King Charles, who had loved his land of Flanders so much, with regret and secret anger. There was unrest in the city. The Protestants were secretly uniting. Rabble who feared the daylight assembled, as ominous news arrived from Spain. Minor skirmishes and clashes with the soldiers became more frequent, and in this uneasy, hostile atmosphere the first flames of war and rebellion flared up. Prudent people began to look abroad, others consoled and reassured themselves as well as they could, but the whole country was in a state of fearful expectation, and it was reflected in all faces. At the tavern, the men sat together in corners talking in muted voices, while the landlord spoke of the horrors of war, and joked in his rough way, but no one felt like laughing. The carefree cheerfulness of easy-going folk was extinguished by fear and restless waiting.

Esther felt nothing of this world, neither its muted alarms nor its secret fevers. The child was contented as always, and laughed back at her in his own way—and so she noticed no change in her surroundings. Confused as she was, her life followed a single course. The darkness around her made her fantastic dreams seem real, and it was a reality so distant and strange that she was incapable of any sober, thoughtful understanding of the world. Her femininity, once awakened, cried out for a child, but she did not know the dark mystery involved. She only dreamt a thousand dreams of having a child herself, thinking of the simple marvels of biblical legends and the magical possibility conjured up by her lonely imagination. If anyone had explained this everyday miracle to her in simple words, she might perhaps have looked at the men passing her by with the bashful but considering gaze that was to be seen in the eyes of girls at that time. As it was, however, she never thought of men, only of the children playing in the street, and dreamt of the miracle that might, perhaps, give her a rosy, playful baby some day, a baby all her own who would be her whole happiness. So wild was her wish for one that she might even have given herself to the first comer, throwing aside all shame and fear, just for the sake of the happiness she longed for, but she knew nothing about the creative union of man and woman, and her instincts led her blindly astray. So she returned, again and again, to the other woman's baby. By now she loved him so deeply that he seemed like her own.

One day she came to visit the painter, who had noticed with secret uneasiness her extreme, almost unhealthily passionate love of the child. She arrived with a radiant face and eagerness sparkling in her eyes. The baby was not there as usual. That made her anxious, but she would not admit it, so she went up to the old man and asked him about the progress of his picture. As she put this question the blood rose to her face, for all at once she felt the silent reproach of the many hours when she had paid neither him nor his work any attention. Her neglect of this kindly man weighed on her conscience. But he did not seem to notice.

"It is finished, Esther," he said with a quiet smile. "It was finished long ago. I shall be delivering it tomorrow."

She turned pale, and felt a terrible presentiment that she dared not consider more closely. Very quietly and slowly she asked, "Then I can't come and see you any more?"

He put out both hands to her in the old, warm, compelling gesture that always captivated her. "As often as you like, my child. And the more often that is the happier I shall be. As you see, I am lonely here in this old room of mine, and when you are here it is bright and cheerful all day. Come to see me often, Esther, very often."

All her old love for the old man came welling up, as if to break down all barriers and pour itself out in words. How good and kind he was! Was he not real, and the baby only her own dream? At that moment she felt confident again, but other ideas still hung over that budding confidence like a storm cloud. And the thought of the child tormented her. She wanted to suppress her pain, she kept swallowing the words, but they came out at last in a wild, desperate cry. "What about the baby?"

The old man said nothing, but there was a harsh, almost unsparing expression on his face. Her neglect of him at this moment, when he had hoped to make her soul entirely his own, was like an angry arm warding him off. His voice was cold and indifferent as he said, "The baby has gone away."

He felt her glance hanging on his lips in wild desperation. But a dark force in him made him cruel. He added nothing to what he had said. At that moment he even hated the girl who could so ungratefully forget all the love he had given her, and for a second this kind and gentle man felt a desire to hurt her. But it was only a brief moment of weakness and denial, like a single ripple running away into the endless sea of his gentle kindness. Full of pity for what he saw in her eyes, he turned away.

She could not bear this silence. With a wild gesture, she flung herself on his breast and clung to him, sobbing and moaning. Torment had never burnt more fiercely in her than in the desperate words she cried out between her tears. "I want the baby back, my baby. I can't live without him, they've stolen my one small happiness from me. Why do you want to take the baby away from me? I know I've been unkind to you… Oh, please forgive me and let me have the baby back! Where is he? Tell me! Tell me! I want the baby back…"

The words died away into silent sobbing. Deeply shaken, the old man bent down to her as she clung to him, her convulsive weeping slowly dying down, and she sank lower and lower like a dying flower. Her long, dark hair had come loose, and he gently stroked it. "Be sensible, Esther, and don't cry. The baby has gone away, but—"

"It's not true, oh no, it can't be true!" she cried.

"It *is* true, Esther. His mother has left the country. Times are bad for foreigners and heretics here—and for the faithful and God-fearing as well. They have gone to France, or perhaps England. But why so despairing? Be sensible, Esther, wait a few days and you'll see, you will feel better again."

"I can't, I won't," she cried through more tears. "Why have they taken the baby away from me? He was all I had… I must have him back, I must, I must. He loved me, he was the only creature in the world who was mine, all mine… how am I to live now? Tell me where he is, oh, tell me…"

Her mingled sobs and lamentations became confused, desperate murmuring growing softer and more meaningless, and finally turning to hopeless weeping. Ideas shot like lightning through her tormented mind, she was unable to think clearly and calm down. All she thought and felt circled crazily, restlessly and with pitiless force around the one painful thought obsessing her. The endless silent sea of her questing love surged with loud, despairing pain, and her words flowed on, hot and confused, like blood running from a wound that would not close. The old man had tried to calm her distress with gentle words, but now, in despair, he could say nothing. The elemental force and dark fire of her passion seemed to him stronger than any way he knew of pacifying her. He waited and waited. Sometimes her torrent of feeling seemed to hesitate briefly and grow a little calmer, but again and again a sob set off words that were half a scream, half weeping. Her young soul, rich with love to give, was bleeding to death in her pain.

At last he was able to speak to Esther, but she wouldn't listen. Her eyes were fixed on a single image, and a single thought filled her heart. She stammered it all out, as if she were seeing hallucinations. "He had such a sweet laugh... he was mine, all mine for all those lovely days, I was his mother... and now I can't have him any more. If only I could see him again, just once... if I could only see him just once." And again her voice died away in helpless sobs. She had slowly slipped down from her resting place against the old man's breast, and was clinging to his knees with weary, shaking hands, crouching there surrounded by the flowing locks of her dark hair. As she stooped down, moving convulsively, her face hidden by her hair, she seemed to be crushed by pain and anger. Monotonously, her desperate mind tiring now, she babbled those words again and again. "Just to see him again... only once... if I could see him again just once!"

The old man bent over her.

"Esther?"

She did not move. Her lips went on babbling the same words, without meaning or intonation. He tried to raise her. When he took her arm it was powerless and limp like a broken branch, and fell straight back again. Only her lips kept stammering, "Just to see him again... see him again, oh, see him again just once..."

At that a strange idea came into his baffled mind as he tried to comfort her. He leant down close to her ear. "Esther? You *shall* see him again, not just once but as often as you like."

She started up as if woken from a dream. The words seemed to flow through all her limbs, for suddenly her body moved and straightened up. Her mind seemed to be slowly clearing. Her thoughts were not quite lucid yet, for instinctively she did not believe in so much happiness revealing itself after such pain. Uncertainly she looked up at the old man as if her senses were reeling. She did not entirely understand him, and waited for him to say more, because everything was so indistinct to her. However, he said nothing, but looked at her with a kindly promise in his eyes and nodded. Gently, he put his arm around her, as if afraid of hurting her. So it was not a dream or a lie spoken on impulse. Her heart beat fast in expectation. Willing as a child, she leant against him as he moved away, not knowing where he was going. But he led her only a few steps across the room to his easel. With a swift movement, he removed the cloth covering the picture.

At first Esther was motionless. Her heart stood still. But then, her glance avid, she ran up to the picture as if to snatch the dear, rosy, smiling baby out of his frame and bring him back to life, cradle him in her arms, caress him, feel the tenderness of his clumsy limbs and bring a smile to his comical little mouth. She did not stop to think that this was only a picture, a piece of painted canvas, only a dream of real life; in fact she did not think at all, she only felt, and her eyelids fluttered in blissful ecstasy. She stood close to the painting, never moving. Her fingers trembled and tingled, longing to feel the child's sweet softness again, her lips burnt to cover the little body with loving kisses again. A fever, but a blessed one, ran through her own body. Then warm tears came to her eyes, no longer angry and despairing, but happy as well as melancholy, the overflowing expression of many strange feelings that suddenly filled her heart and must come out. The convulsions that had shaken her died down, and an uncertain but mild mood of reconciliation enveloped her and gently, sweetly lulled her into a wonderful waking dream far from all reality.

The old man again felt a questioning awe in the midst of his delight. How miraculous was this work that could mysteriously inspire even the man who had created it himself, how unearthly was the sublimity that radiated from it! Was this not like the signs and images of the saints whom he honoured, and who could suddenly make the poor and oppressed forget their troubles and go home liberated and inspired by a miracle? And did not a sacred fire now burn in the eyes of the girl looking at her own portrait without curiosity or shame, in pure devotion to God? He felt that these strange paths must have some destination, there must be a will at work that was not blind like his own, but clear-sighted and master of all its wishes. These ideas rejoiced in his heart like a peal of bells, and he felt he had been touched by the grace of Heaven.

Carefully, he took Esther's hand and led her away from the picture. He did not speak, for he too felt warm tears coming to his eyes and did not want to show them. A warm radiance seemed to rest on her head as it did in the picture of the Madonna. It was as if something great beyond all words was in the room with them, rushing by on invisible wings. He looked into Esther's eyes. They were no longer tearfully defiant, but shadowed only by a gentle reflective bloom. Everything around them seemed to him brighter, milder, transfigured. God's sanctity, miraculously close, was revealing itself to him in all things.

They stood together like that for a long time. Then they began to talk as they used to do, but calmly and sensibly, like two human beings who now understood each other entirely and had no more to search for. Esther was quiet. The sight of the picture had moved her strangely, and made her happy because it restored the happiness of her dearest memory to her, because she had her baby back, but her feelings were far more solemn, deeper and more maternal than they had ever been in reality. For now the child was not just the outward appearance of her dream but part of her own soul. No one could take him away from her. He was all hers when she looked at the picture, and she could see it at any time. The old man, shaken by mystical portents, had willingly answered her desperate request. And now she could feel the same blessed abundance of life every day, her longings need no longer be timid and fearful, and the little childlike figure who to others was the Saviour of the world also, unwittingly, embodied a God of love and life to the lonely Jewish girl.

She visited the studio several more days running. But the painter was aware of his commission, which he had almost forgotten. The merchant came to look at the picture and he too, although he knew nothing about the secret miracles of its creation, was overwhelmed by the gentle figure of the Mother of God and the simple expression of an eternal symbol in its execution. He warmly shook hands with his friend, who, however, turned away his lavish praise with a modest, pious gesture, as if he were not standing in front of his own work. The two of them decided not to keep the altar deprived of this adornment any longer.

Next day the picture occupied the other wing of the altarpiece, and the first was no longer alone. And the pair of Madonnas, strangers but with a slight similarity, were a curious sight. They seemed like two sisters, one of them still confidently abandoning herself to the sweetness of life, while the other had already tasted the dark fruit of pain and knew a terror of times yet to come. But the same radiance hung over both their heads, as if stars of love shone above them, and they would take their path through life with its joy and pain under those stars.

Esther herself followed the picture to church, as if she found her own child there. Gradually the memory that the child was a stranger to her was dying away, and true maternal feelings were aroused in her, making her dream into reality. For hours on end she would lie prostrated before the painting, like a Christian before the image of the Saviour. But hers was another faith, and the deep voices of the bells called the congregation to devotions that she did not know. Priests whose words she could not understand sang, loud choral chanting swept like dark waves through the church, rising into the mystic twilight above the pews like a fragrant cloud. And men and women whose faith she hated surrounded her, their murmured prayers drowning out the quiet, loving words she spoke to her baby. However, she was unaware of any of that. Her heart was too bewildered to look around and take any notice of other people; she merely gave herself up to her one wish, to see her child every day, and thought of nothing else in the world. The stormy weather of her budding youth had died down, all her longings had gone away or had flowed into the one idea that drew her back to the picture again and again, as if it were a magical magnet that no other power could withstand. She had never been so happy as she was in those long hours in the church, sensing its solemnity and its secret pleasures without understanding them. She was hurt only when some stranger now and then knelt in front of the picture, looking adoringly up at the child who was hers, all hers. Then she was defiantly jealous, with anger in her heart that made her want to hit out and shed tears. At such moments her mind was increasingly troubled, and she could not distinguish between the real world and the world of her dreams. Only when she lay in front of the picture again did stillness return to her heart.

Spring passed on, the mild, warm weather in which the picture had been finished still held, and it seemed that after all her stormy suffering, summer too would give her the same great and solemn gift of quiet maternal love. The nights were warm and bright, but her fever had died away, and gentle, loving dreams came over Esther's mind. She seemed to be at peace, rocking to a rhythm of calm passion as the regular hours went by, and all that had been lost in the darkness now pointed her ahead along a bright path into the future.

At last the summer approached its climax, the Feast of St Mary, the greatest day in Flanders. Long processions decked out with pennants blowing in the breeze and billowing banners went through the golden harvest fields that were usually full of busy workers.

The monstrance held above the seed corn in the priest's hands as he blessed it shone like the sun, and voices raised in prayer made a gentle sound, so that the sheaves in the fields shook and humbly bowed down. But high in the air clear bells rang in the distance, to be answered joyfully from church towers far away. It was a mighty sound, as if the earth itself were singing together with the woods and the roaring sea.

The glory of the day flowed back from the fertile land into the city and washed over its menacing walls. The noise of craftsmen at work died down, the day labourers' hoarse voices fell silent, only musicians playing fife and bagpipes went from street to street, and the clear silvery voices of dancing children joined the music-making. Silken robes trimmed with yellowing lace, kept waiting in wardrobes all the last year, saw the light of day again, men and women in their best clothes, talking cheerfully, set out for church. And in the cathedral, with its doors open to invite in the pious with clouds of blue incense and fragrant coolness, a springtime of scattered flowers bloomed, pictures and altars were adorned with lavish garlands made by careful hands. Thousands of candles cast magical light into the sweet-scented darkness where the organ roared, and singing, mysterious radiance and mystical twilight reached the heights and depths of the great building.

And then, suddenly a pious and God-fearing mood seemed to flow out into the streets. A procession of the devout formed; up by the main altar the priests raised the famous portrait of St Mary, which seemed to be surrounded by whispered rumours of many miracles, it was borne aloft on the shoulders of the pious, and a solemn procession began. The picture being carried along brought silence to the noisy street, for the crowd fell quiet as people bowed down, and a broad furrow of prayer followed the portrait until it was returned to the cool depths of the cathedral that received it like a fragrant grave.

That year, however, the pious festival was under a dark cloud. For weeks the country had been bearing a heavy burden. Gloomy and as yet unconfirmed news said that the old privileges were to be declared null and void. The freedom fighters known as the Beggars who opposed Spanish rule were making common cause with the Protestants. Dreadful rumours came from the countryside of Protestant divines preaching to crowds of thousands in open places outside the towns and cities, and giving Communion to the armed citizens. Spanish soldiers had been attacked, and churches were said to have been stormed to the sound of the singing of the Geneva Psalms. There was still no definite word of any of this, but the secret flickering of a coming conflagration was felt, and the armed resistance planned by the more thoughtful at secret meetings in their homes degenerated into wild violence and defiance among the many who had nothing to lose.

The festival day had brought the first wave of rioting to Antwerp in the shape of a rabble united in nothing but an instinct to join sudden uprisings. Sinister figures whom no one knew suddenly appeared in the taverns, cursing and uttering wild threats against Spaniards and clerics. Strange people of defiant and angry appearance who avoided the light of day emerged from nooks and crannies and disreputable alleys. There was more and more trouble. Now and then there were minor skirmishes. They did not spill over into a general movement, but were extinguished like sparks hissing out in isolation. The Prince of Orange still maintained strict discipline, and controlled the greedy, quarrelsome and ill-intentioned mob who were joining the Protestants only for the sake of profit.

The magnificence of the great procession merely provoked repressed instincts. For the first time coarse jokes mingled with the singing of the faithful, wild threats were uttered and scornful laughter. Some sang the text of the Beggars' song to a pious melody, a young fellow imitated the croaking voice of the preacher, to the delight of his companions, others greeted the portrait of the Virgin by sweeping off their hats with ostentatious gallantry as if to their lady love. The soldiers and the few faithful Catholics who had ventured to take part in the procession were powerless, and had to grit their teeth and watch this mockery as it became ever wilder. And now that the common people had tasted defiant power, they were becoming less and less amenable. Almost all of them were already armed. The dark impulse that had so far broken out only in curses and threats called for action. This menacing unrest lay over the city like a storm cloud on the feast day of St Mary and the days that followed.

Women and the more sober of the men had kept to their houses since the angry scenes had endangered the procession. The streets now belonged to the mob and the Protestants. Esther, too, had stayed at home for the last few days. But she knew nothing of all these dark events. She vaguely noticed that there were more and more people crowding into the tavern, that the shrill sound of whores' voices mingled with the agitated talk of quarrelling, cursing men, she saw distraught women, she saw figures secretly whispering together, but she felt such indifference to all these things that she did not even ask her foster father about them. She thought of nothing but the baby, the baby who, in her dreams, had long ago become her own. All memory paled beside this one image. The world was no longer so strange to her, but it had no value because it had nothing to give her; her loving devotion and youthful need of God were lost in her thoughts of the child. Only the single hour a day when she stole out to see the picture—it was both her God and her child—breathed real life into her. Otherwise she was like a woman lost in dreams, passing everything else by like a sleepwalker. Day after day, and even once on a long summer night heavy with warm fragrance, when she had fled the tavern and made sure she was shut up in the cathedral, she prostrated herself before the picture on her knees. Her ignorant soul had made a God of it.

And these days were difficult for her, because they kept her from her child. While festive crowds thronged the tall aisles on the Feast of St Mary, and surging organ music filled the nave, she had to turn back and leave the cathedral with the rest of the people crowding it, feeling humbled like a beggar woman because worshippers kept standing in front of the two pictures of St Mary in the chapel that day, and she feared she might be recognised. Sad and almost despairing, she went back, never noticing the sunlight of the day because she had been denied a sight of her child. Envy and anger came over her when she saw the crowds making pilgrimage to the altarpiece, piously coming through the tall porch of the cathedral into that fragrant blue darkness.

She was even sadder next day, when she was not allowed to go out into the streets, now so full of menacing figures. Her room, to which the noise of the tavern rose like a thick, ugly smoke, became intolerable to her. To her confused heart, a day when she could not see the baby in the picture was like a dark and gloomy sleepless night, a night of torment. She was not strong enough yet to bear deprivation. Late in the evening, when her foster father was sitting in the tavern with his guests, she very quietly went down the stairs. She tried the door, and breathed a sigh of relief; it was not locked. Softly, already feeling the mild fresh air that she had missed for a long time, she slipped through the door and hurried to the cathedral.

The streets through which she swiftly walked were dark and full of muffled noise. Single groups had come together from all sides, and news of the departure of the Prince of Orange had let violence loose. Threatening remarks, heard only occasionally and uttered at random in daytime, now sounded like shouts of command. Here and there drunks were bawling, and enthusiasts were singing rebel songs so loud that the windows echoed. Weapons were no longer hidden; hatchets and hooks, swords and stakes glinted in the flickering torchlight. Like a greedy torrent, hesitating only briefly before its foaming waves sweep away all barriers, these dark troops whom no one dared to resist gathered together.

Esther had taken no notice of this unruly crowd, although she once had to push aside a rough arm reaching for her as she slipped by when its owner tried to grab her headscarf. She never wondered why such madness had suddenly come into the rabble; she did not understand their shouting and cries. She simply overcame her fear and disgust, and quickened her pace until at last, breathless, she reached the tall cathedral deep in the shadow of the houses, white moonlit cloud hovering in the air above it.

Reassured, shivering only slightly, she came into the cathedral through a side door. It was dark in the tall, unlit aisles, with only a mysterious silvery light trembling around the dull glass of the windows. The pews were empty. No shadow moved through the wide, breathless expanses of the building, and the statues of the saints stood black and still before the altars. And like the gentle flickering of a glow-worm there came, from what seemed endless depths, the swaying light of the eternal flame above the chapels. All was quiet and sacred here, and the silent majesty of the place so impressed Esther that she muted her tapping footsteps. Carefully, she groped her way towards the chapel in the side aisle and then, trembling, knelt down in front of the picture in boundless quiet rejoicing. In the flowing darkness, it seemed to look down from dense, fragrant clouds, endlessly far away yet very close. And now she did not think any more. As always, the confused longings of her maturing girlish heart relaxed in fantastic dreams. Ardour seemed to stream from every fibre of her being and gather around her brow like an intoxicating cloud. These long hours of unconscious devotion, united with the longing for love, were like a sweet, gently numbing drug; they were a dark wellspring, the blessed fruit of the Hesperides containing and nourishing all divine life. For all bliss was present in her sweet, vague dreams, through which tremors of longing passed. Her agitated heart beat alone in the great silence of the empty church. A soft, bright radiance like misty silver came from the picture, as if shed by a light within, carrying her up from the cold stone of the steps to the mild warm region of light that she knew in dreams. It was a long time since she had thought of the baby as a stranger to her. She dreamt of the God in him and the God in every woman, the essence of her own body, warm with her blood. Vague yearning for the divine, questing ecstasy and the rise of maternal feelings in her spun the deceptive network of her life's dream between them. For her, there was brightness in the wide, oppressive darkness of the church, gentle music played in the awed silence that knew nothing of human language and the passing of the hours. Above her prostrated body, time went its inexorable way.

Something suddenly thudded against the door, shaking it. Then came a second and a third thud, so that she leapt up in alarm, staring into the dreadful darkness. Further thunderous crashing sounds shook the whole tall, proud building, and the isolated lamps rolled like fiery eyes in the dark. Someone was filing through the bolt of the door, now knocked half off its hinges, with a shrill sound like helpless screams in the empty space. The walls flung back the terrifying sounds in violent confusion. Men possessed by greedy rage were hammering at the door, and a roar of excited voices boomed through the hollow shell of the church as if the sea had broken its bounds to come roaring in, and its waves were now beating against the groaning walls of the house of God.

Esther listened, distraught, as if woken suddenly from sleep. But at last the door fell in with a crash. A dark torrent of humanity poured in, filling the mighty building with wild bawling and raging. More came, and more. Thousands of others seemed to be standing outside egging them on. Torches suddenly flared drunkenly up like clutching, greedy hands, and their mad, blood-red light fell on wild faces distorted by blind excitement, their swollen eyes popping as if with sinful desires. Only now did Esther vaguely sense the intentions of the dark rabble that she had already met on her way. The first axe-blows were already falling on the wood of the pulpit, pictures crashed to the floor, statues tipped over, curses and derisive cries swirled up out of this dark flood, above which the torches danced unsteadily as if alarmed by such crazy behaviour. In confusion, the torrent poured onto the high altar, looting and destroying, defiling and desecrating. Wafers of the Host fluttered to the floor like white flower petals, a lamp with the eternal flame in it, flung by a violent hand, rushed like a meteor through the dark. And more and more figures crowded in, with more and more torches burning. A picture caught fire, and the flame licked high like a coiling snake. Someone had laid hands on the organ, smashing its pipes, and their mad notes screamed shrilly for help in the dark. More figures appeared as if out of a wild, deranged dream. A fellow with a bloodstained face smeared his boots with holy oil, to the raucous jubilation of the others, ragged villains strutted about in richly embroidered episcopal vestments, a squealing whore had perched the golden circlet from a statue in her tousled, dirty hair. Thieves drank toasts in wine from the sacred vessels, and up by the high altar two men were fighting with bright knives for possession of a monstrance set with jewels. Prostitutes performed lascivious, drunken dances in front of the shrines, drunks spewed in the fonts of holy water. Angry men armed with flashing axes smashed anything within reach, whatever it was. The sounds rose to a chaotic thunder of noise and screaming voices; like a dense and repellent cloud of plague vapours, the crowd's raging reached to the black heights of the cathedral that looked darkly down on the leaping flames of torches, and seemed immovable, out of reach of this desperate derision.

Esther had hidden in the shadow of the altar in the side chapel, half fainting. It was as if all this must be a dream, and would suddenly disappear like a deceptive illusion. But already the first torches were storming into the side aisles. Figures shaking with fanatical passion as if intoxicated leapt over gratings or smashed them down, overturned the statues and pulled pictures off the shrines. Daggers flashed like fiery snakes in the flickering torchlight, angrily tearing into cupboards and pictures, which fell to the ground with their frames smashed. Closer and closer came the crowd with its smoking, unsteady lights. Esther, breathless, stayed where she was, retreating further into the dark. Her heart missed a beat with alarm and dreadful anticipation. She still did not know quite what was happening, and felt only fear, wild, uncontrollable fear. A few footsteps were coming closer, and then a sturdy, furious fellow broke down the grating with a blow.

She thought she had been seen. But next moment she saw the intruders' purpose, when a statue of the Madonna on the next altar crashed to the floor in pieces. A terrible new fear came to her—they would want to destroy her picture too, her child—and the fear became certainty when picture after picture was pulled down in the flickering torchlight to the sound of jubilant derision, to be torn and trampled underfoot. A terrible idea flashed through her head—they were going to murder the picture, and in her mind it had long ago become her own living child. In a second everything in her flared up as if bathed in dazzling light. One thought, multiplied a thousand times over, inflamed her heart in that single second. She must save the baby, *her* baby. Then dream and reality came together in her mind with desperate fervour. The destructive zealots were already making for the altar. An axe was raised in the air—and at that moment she lost all conscious power of thought and leapt in front of the picture, arms outstretched to protect it…

It was like a magic spell. The axe crashed to the floor from the now powerless hand holding it. The torch fell from the man's other hand and went out as it fell. The sight struck these noisy, frenzied people like lightning. They all fell silent, except for one in whose throat the gasping cry of "The Madonna! The Madonna!" died away.

The mob stood there white as chalk, trembling. A few dropped to their knees in prayer. They were all deeply shaken. The strange illusion was compelling. For them, there was no doubt that a miracle had happened, one of the kind often authenticated, told and retold—the Madonna, whose features were obviously those of the young mother in the picture, was protecting her own likeness. Pangs of conscience were aroused in them when they saw the girl's face, which seemed to them nothing short of the picture come to life. They had never been more devout that in that fleeting moment.

But others were already storming up. Torches illuminated the group standing there rigid and the girl pressing close to the altar, hardly moving herself. Noise flooded into the silence. At the back a woman's shrill voice cried, "Go on, go on, it's only the Jew girl from the tavern." And suddenly the spell was broken. In shame and rage, the humiliated rioters stormed on. A rough fist pushed Esther aside. She swayed. But she kept on her feet, she was fighting for the picture as if it really were her own warm life. Swinging a heavy silver candlestick, she hit out furiously at the iconoclasts with her old defiance; one of them fell, cursing, but another took his place. A dagger glinted like a short red lightning flash, and Esther stumbled and fell. Already the pieces of the splintered altar were raining down on her, but she felt no more pain. The picture of the Madonna and Child, and the picture of the Madonna of the Wounded Heart both fell under a single furious blow from an axe.

And the raving crowd stormed on; from church to church went the looters, filling the streets with terrible noise. A dreadful night fell over Antwerp. Terror and trembling made its way into houses with the news, and hearts beat in fear behind barred gates. But the flame of rebellion was waving like a banner over the whole country.

The old painter, too, shuddered with fear when he heard the news that the iconoclasts were abroad. His knees trembled, and he held a crucifix in his imploring hands to pray for the safety of his picture, the picture given him by the revelation of God's grace. For a whole wild, dark night dreadful ideas tormented him. And at first light of dawn he could not stay at home any longer.

Outside the cathedral, his last hope faded and fell like one of the overturned statues. The doors had been broken down, and rags and splinters showed where the iconoclasts had been like a bloody trail left behind them. He groped his laborious way through the dark to his picture. His hands went out to the shrine, but they met empty air, and sank wearily to his sides again. The faith in his breast that had sung its pious song in praise of God's grace for so many years suddenly flew away like a frightened swallow.

At last he pulled himself together and struck a light, which flared briefly from his tinder, illuminating a scene that made him stagger back. On the ground, among ruins, lay the Italian master's sweetly sad Madonna, the Madonna of the Wounded Heart, transfixed by a dagger thrust. But it was not the picture, it was the figure of the Madonna herself. Cold sweat stood out on his brow as the flame went out again. He thought this must be a bad dream. When he struck his tinder again, however, he recognised Esther lying there dead of her wound. And by a strange miracle she, who in life had been the embodiment of his own picture of the Virgin, revealed in death the features of the Italian master's Madonna and her bleeding, mortal injury.

Yes, it was a miracle, an obvious miracle. But the old man would not believe in any more miracles. At that hour, when he saw the girl who had brought mild light into the late days of his life lying there dead beside his smashed picture, a string broke in his soul that had so often played the music of faith. He denied the God he had revered for seventy years in a single minute. Could this be the work of God's wise, kind hand, giving so much blessed creativity and bringing splendour into being, only to snatch them back into darkness for no good purpose? This could not be a benign will, only a heartless game. It was a miracle of life and not of God, a coincidence like thousands of others that happen at random every day, coming together and then moving apart again. No more! Could good, pure souls mean so little to God that he threw them away in his casual game? For the first time he stood in a church and doubted God, because he had thought him good and kind, and now he could not understand the ways of his creator.

For a long time he looked down at the dead girl who had shed such gentle evening light over his old age. And when he saw the smile of bliss on her broken lips, he felt less savage and did God more justice. Humility came back into his kindly heart. Could he really ask who had performed this strange miracle, making the lonely Jewish girl honour the Madonna in her death? Could he judge whether it was the work of God or the work of life? Could he clothe love in words that he did not know, could he reject God because he did not understand his nature?

The old man shuddered. He felt poor and needy in that lonely hour. He felt that he had wandered alone between God and earthly life all these long years, trying to understand them as twofold when they were one and yet defied understanding. Had it not been like the work of some miraculous star watching over the tentative path of this young girl's soul—had not God and Love been at one in her and in all things?

Above the windows the first light of dawn was showing. But it did not bring light to him, for he did not want to see new days dawning in the life he had lived for so many years, touched by its miracles yet never really transfigured by them. And now, without fear, he felt close to the last miracle, the miracle that ceases to be dream and illusion, and is only the dark eternal truth.

THE STAR ABOVE THE FOREST

A STRANGE THING HAPPENED one day when the slender, elegantly groomed waiter François was leaning over the beautiful Polish Baroness Ostrovska's shoulder to serve her. It lasted for only a second, it was not marked by any start or sudden movement of surprise, any restlessness or momentary agitation. Yet it was one of those seconds in which thousands of hours and days of rejoicing and torment are held spellbound, just as all the wild force of a forest of tall, dark, rustling oak trees, with their rocking branches and swaying crowns, is contained in a single tiny acorn dropping through the air. To outward appearance, nothing happened during that second. With a supple movement François, the waiter in the grand hotel on the Riviera, leaned further down to place the serving platter at a more convenient angle for the Baroness's questing knife. For that one moment, however, his face was just above her softly curling, fragrant waves of hair, and when he instinctively opened the eyes that he had respectfully closed, his reeling gaze saw the gentle white radiance of the line of her neck as it disappeared from that dark cascade of hair, to be lost in her dark red, full-skirted dress. He felt as if crimson flames were flaring up in him. And her knife clinked quietly on the platter, which was imperceptibly shaking. But although in that second he foresaw all the fateful consequences of his sudden enchantment, he expertly mastered his emotion and went on serving at the table with the cool, slightly debonair stylishness of a well-trained waiter with impeccable good taste. He handed the platter calmly to the Baroness's usual companion at table, an elderly aristocrat with gracefully assured manners, who was talking of unimportant matters in crystal-clear French with a very faint accent. Then he walked away from the table without a gesture or a backward glance.

Those minutes were the beginning of his abandoning himself to a very strange kind of devotion, such a reeling, intoxicated sensation that the proud and portentous word 'love' is not quite right for it. It was that faithful, dog-like devotion without desire that those in mid-life seldom feel, and is known only to the very young and the very old. A love devoid of any deliberation, not thinking but only dreaming. He entirely forgot the unjust yet ineradicable disdain that even the clever and considerate show to those who wear a waiter's tailcoat, he did not look for opportunities and chance meetings, but nurtured this strange affection in his blood until its secret fervour was beyond all mockery and criticism. His love was not a matter of secret winks and lurking glances, the sudden boldness of audacious gestures, the senseless ardour of salivating lips and trembling hands; it was quiet toil, the performance of those small services that are all the more sacred and sublime in their humility because they are intended to go unnoticed. After the evening meal he smoothed out the crumpled folds of the tablecloth where she had been sitting with tender, caressing fingers, as one would stroke a beloved woman's soft hands at rest; he adjusted everything close to her with devout symmetry, as if he were preparing it for a special occasion. He carefully carried the glasses that her lips had touched up to his own small, musty attic bedroom, and watched them sparkle like precious jewellery by night when the moonlight streamed in. He was always to be found in some corner, secretly attentive to her as she strolled and walked about. He drank in what she said as you might relish a sweet, fragrantly intoxicating wine on the tongue, and responded to every one of her words and orders as eagerly as children run to catch a ball flying through the air. So his intoxicated soul brought an ever-changing, rich glow into his dull, ordinary life. The wise folly of clothing the whole experience in the cold, destructive words of reality was an idea that never entered his mind: the poor waiter François was in love with an exotic Baroness who would be for ever unattainable. For he did not think of her as reality, but as something very distant, very high above him, sufficient in its mere reflection of life. He loved the imperious pride of her orders, the commanding arch of her black eyebrows that almost touched one another, the wilful lines around her small mouth, the confident grace of her bearing. Subservience seemed to him quite natural, and he felt the humiliating intimacy of menial labour as good fortune, because it enabled him to step so often into the magic circle that surrounded her.

So a dream suddenly awakened in the life of a simple man, like a beautiful, carefully raised garden flower blooming by a roadside where the dust of travel obliterates all other seedlings. It was the frenzy of someone plain and ordinary, an enchanting narcotic dream in the midst of a cold and monotonous life. And such people's dreams are like a rudderless boat drifting aimlessly on quiet, shining waters, rocking with delight, until suddenly its keel grounds abruptly on an unknown bank.

However, reality is stronger and more robust than any dreams. One evening the stout hotel porter from Waadland told him in passing, "Baroness Ostrovska is leaving tomorrow night on the eight o'clock train." And he added a couple of other names which meant nothing to François, and which he did not note. For those words had turned to a confused, tumultuous roaring in his head. A couple of times he mechanically ran his fingers over his aching brow, as if to push away an oppressive weight lying there and dimming his understanding. He took a few steps; he was unsteady on his feet. Alarmed and uncertain, he passed a tall, gilt-framed mirror from which a pale strange face looked back at him, white as a sheet. No ideas would come to him; they seemed to be held captive behind a dark and misty wall. Almost unconsciously, he felt his way down by the hand-rail of the broad flight of steps into the twilit garden, where tall pines stood alone like dark thoughts. His restless figure took a few more shaky steps, like the low reeling flight of a large dark nocturnal bird, and then he sank down on a bench with his head pressed to its cool back. It was perfectly quiet. The sea sparkled here and there beyond the round shapes of shrubs. Faint, trembling lights shone out on the water, and the monotonous, murmuring sing-song of distant breakers was lost in the silence.

Suddenly everything was clear to him, perfectly clear. So painfully clear that he could almost summon up a smile. It was all over. Baroness Ostrovska was going home, and François the waiter would stay at his post. Was that so strange? Didn't all the foreign guests who came to the hotel leave again after two, three or four weeks? How foolish not to have thought of it before. It was so clear, it was enough to make you laugh or cry. And ideas kept whirring through his head. Tomorrow evening on the eight o'clock train to Warsaw. To Warsaw—hours and hours of travel through forests and valleys, passing hills and mountains, steppes and rivers and noisy towns. Warsaw! It was so far away! He couldn't even imagine it, but he felt it in the depths of his heart, that proud and threatening, harsh and distant word Warsaw. While he…

For a second a small, dream-like hope fluttered up in his heart. He could follow. He could hire himself out there as a servant, a secretary, could stand in the street as a freezing beggar, anything not to be so dreadfully far away, just to breathe the air of the same city, perhaps see her sometimes driving past, catch a glimpse of her shadow, her dress, her dark hair. Daydreams flashed hastily through his mind. But this was a hard and pitiless hour. Clear and plain, he saw how unattainable his dreams were. He worked it out: at the most he had savings of a hundred or two hundred francs. That would scarcely take him half the way. And then what? As if through a torn veil he suddenly saw his own life, knew how wretched, pitiful, hateful it must be now. Empty, desolate years working as a waiter, tormented by foolish longing—was something so ridiculous to be his future? The idea made him shudder. And suddenly all these trains of thoughts came stormily and inevitably together. There was only one way out…

The treetops swayed quietly in an imperceptible breeze. A dark, black night menacingly faced him. He rose from his bench, confident and composed, and walked over the crunching gravel up to the great building of the hotel where it slumbered in white silence. He stopped outside her windows. They were dark, with no spark of light at which his dreamy longing could have been kindled. Now his blood was flowing calmly, and he walked like a man whom nothing will ever confuse or deceive again. In his room, he flung himself on the bed without any sign of agitation, and slept a dull, dreamless sleep until the alarm summoned him to get up in the morning.

Next day his demeanour was entirely within the bounds of carefully calculated reflection and self-imposed calm. He carried out his duties with cool indifference, and his gestures were so sure and easy that no one could have guessed at the bitter decision behind his deceptive mask. Just before dinner he hurried out with his small savings to the best florist in the resort and bought choice flowers whose colourful glory spoke to him like words: tulips glowing with fiery, passionate gold—shaggy white chrysanthemums resembling light, exotic dreams—slender orchids, the graceful images of longing—and a few proud, intoxicating roses. And then he bought a magnificent vase of sparkling, opalescent glass. He gave the few francs he still had left to a beggar child in passing, with a quick and carefree movement. Then he hurried back. With sad solemnity, he put the vase of flowers down in front of the Baroness's place at table, which he now prepared for the last time with slow, voluptuously meticulous attention.

Then came the dinner. He served it as usual: cool, silent, skilful, without looking up. Only at the end did he embrace her supple, proud figure with an endlessly long look of which she never knew. And she had never seemed to him so beautiful as in that last, perfect look. Then he stepped calmly back from the table, without any gesture of farewell, and left the dining room. Bearing himself like a guest to whom the staff would bow and nod their heads, he walked down the corridors and the handsome flight of steps outside the reception area and out into the street: any observer must surely have been able to tell that, at that moment, he was leaving his past behind. He stood outside the hotel for a moment, undecided, and then turned to the bright villas and wide gardens, following the road past them, walking on, ever on with his thoughtful, dignified stride, with no idea where he was going.

He wandered restlessly like this until evening, in a lost, dreamy state of mind. He was not thinking of anything any more. Not about the past, or the inevitable moment to come. He was no longer playing with ideas of death, not in the way one might well pick up a shining revolver with its deep, menacing mouth in those last moments, weighing it in the hand, and then lower it again. He had passed sentence on himself long ago. Only images came to him now in rapid flight, like swallows soaring. First images of his youthful days, up to a fateful moment at school when a foolish adventure had suddenly closed an alluring future to him and thrust him out into the turmoil of the world. Then his restless wanderings, his efforts to earn a living, all the attempts that kept failing, until the great black wave that we call destiny broke his pride and he ended up in a position unworthy of him. Many colourful memories whirled past. And finally the gentle reflection of these last few days glowed in his waking dreams, suddenly pushing the dark door of reality open again. He had to go through it. He remembered that he intended to die today.

For a while he thought of the many ways leading to death, assessing their comparative bitterness and speed, until suddenly an idea shot through his mind. His clouded senses abruptly showed him a dark symbol: just as she had unknowingly, destructively driven over his fate, so she should also crush his body. She herself would do it. She would finish her own work. And now his ideas came thick and fast with strange certainty. In just under an hour, at eight, the express carrying her away from him left. He would throw himself under its wheels, let himself be trampled down by the same violent force that was tearing the woman of his dreams from him. He would bleed to death beneath her feet. The ideas stormed on after one another as if in jubilation. He knew the right place too: further off, near the wooded slope, where the swaying treetops hid the sight of the last bend in the railway line nearby. He looked at his watch; the seconds and his hammering blood were beating out the same rhythm. It was time to set off. Now a spring returned to his sluggish footsteps, along with the certainty of his destination. He walked at that brisk, hasty pace that does away with dreaming as one goes forward, restlessly striding on in the twilight glory of the Mediterranean evening towards the place where the sky was a streak of purple lying embedded between distant, wooded hills. And he hurried on until he came to the two silver lines of the railway track shining ahead of him, guiding him on his way. The track led him by winding paths on through the deep, fragrant valleys, their veils of mist now silvered by the soft moonlight, it took him into the hilly landscape where the sight of sparkling lights along the beach showed how far away the nocturnal, black expanse of the sea was now. And at last it presented him with the deep, restlessly whispering forest that hid the railway line in its lowering shadows.

It was late when, breathing heavily, he reached the dark wooded slope. The trees stood around him, black and ominous, but high above, in their shimmering crowns, faint, quivering moonlight was caught in the branches that moaned as they embraced the slight nocturnal breeze. Sometimes this hollow silence was broken by the strange cries of night birds. In this alarming isolation, his thoughts froze entirely. He was merely waiting, waiting and straining his eyes to see the red light of the train appearing down by the curve of the first bend. Sometimes he looked nervously at his watch again, counting seconds. Then he listened once more, thinking that he heard the distant whistle of the locomotive. But it was a false alarm. All was perfectly silent again. Time seemed to stand still.

At last, far away, he saw the light. At that moment he felt a pang in his heart, and could not have said if it was fear or jubilation. He flung himself down on the rails with a brusque movement. At first he felt the pleasantly cool sensation of the strips of iron against his temples for a moment. Then he listened. The train was still far off. It might be several minutes yet. There was nothing to be heard but the whispering of the trees in the wind. His thoughts went this way and that in confusion, until suddenly one stopped and pierced his heart painfully, like an arrow: he was dying for her sake, and she would never know. Not a single gentle ripple of his life as it came to its turbulent end had ever touched hers. She would never know that a stranger's life had depended on her own, and had been crushed by it.

Very quietly, the rhythmic chugging of the approaching engine came through the breathless air from afar. But that idea burned on, tormenting the dying man in his last minutes. The train rattled closer and closer. Then he opened his eyes once more. Above him was a silent, blue-black sky, with the tops of a few trees swaying in front of it. And above the forest stood a shining, white star. A single star above the forest… the rails beneath his head were already beginning to vibrate and sing faintly. But the idea burned on like fire in his heart, and in his eyes as they saw all the fire and despair of his love. His whole longing and that last painful question flowed into the white and shining star that looked mildly down on him. Closer and closer thundered the train. And once more, with a last inexpressible look, the dying man took the sparkling star above the forest to his heart. Then he closed his eyes. The rails were trembling and swaying, closer and closer came the rattling of the express train, making the forest echo as if great bells were hammering out a rhythm. The earth seemed to sway. One more deafening, rushing, whirring sound, a whirlwind of noise, then a shrill scream, the terrifyingly animal scream of the steam whistle, and the screech and groan of brakes applied in vain…

*

The beautiful Baroness Ostrovska had a reserved compartment to herself in the express. She had been reading a French magazine since the train left, gently cradled by the rocking movement of the carriage. The air in the enclosed space was sultry, and drenched with the heavy fragrance of many fading flowers. Clusters of white lilac were already hanging heavily, like over-ripe fruit, from the magnificent farewell baskets that she had been given, flowers hung limp on their stems, and the broad, heavy cups of the roses seemed to be withering in the hot cloud of intoxicating perfumes. Even in the haste of the express as it rushed along, a suffocatingly close atmosphere heated the heavy drifts of perfume weighing oppressively down.

Suddenly she lowered her book with limp fingers. She herself did not know why. Some secret feeling was tearing at her. She felt a dull but painful pressure. A sudden sense of constriction that she couldn't explain clutched her heart. She thought she would choke on the heavy, intoxicating aroma of the flowers. And that terrifying pain did not pass, she felt every revolution of the rushing wheels, their blind, pounding, forward movement was an unspeakable torment. Suddenly she longed to be able to halt the swift momentum of the train, to haul it back from the dark pain towards which it was racing. She had never in her life felt such fear of something terrible, invisible and cruel seizing on her heart as she did now, in those seconds of incomprehensible, incredible pain and fear. And that unspeakable feeling grew stronger and stronger, tightening its grasp around her throat. The idea of being able to stop the train was like a prayer moaned out loud in her mind…

Then she hears a sudden shrill whistle, the wild, warning scream of the locomotive, the wailing groan and crunch of the brakes. And the rhythm of the flying wheels slackens, goes slower and slower, until there is a stuttering rattle and a faltering jerk.

With difficulty, she makes her way to the window to fill her lungs with fresh air. The pane rattles down. Dark figures are hurrying around… words fly back and forth, different voices: a suicide… under the wheels… dead… yes, out here in the open…

She starts. Instinctively, her eyes go to the high and silent sky and the dark trees whispering above it. And beyond them, a single star is shining over the forest. She is aware of its gaze on her like a sparkling tear. Looking at it, she abruptly feels such grief as she has never known before. A fiery grief, full of a longing that has not been part of her own life…

Slowly, the train rattles on. She leans back in the corner and feels soft tears running down over her cheeks. That dull fear has gone away, she feels only a deep, strange pain, and seeks in vain to discover its source. A pain such as terrified children feel when they suddenly wake on a dark, impenetrable night, and feel that they are all alone…

A SUMMER NOVELLA

I SPENT THE MONTH OF AUGUST last summer in Cadenabbia, one of those little places on Lake Como that nestle so charmingly between white villas and dark woods. Probably quiet and peaceful even in the livelier days of spring, when travellers from Bellagio and Menaggio gather in crowds on the narrow strip of beach, in these warm summer weeks the little town was fragrant, sunny and isolated. The hotel was almost entirely deserted: a few occasional guests, each an object of curiosity to the others by virtue of having chosen to spend a summer holiday in this remote place, surprised every morning to find anyone else still here. Most surprising of all to me was the continued presence of an elderly gentleman, very distinguished in appearance and very cultivated—he looked something like a cross between a very correct English statesman and a Parisian man of the world—who, instead of amusing himself by enjoying some lakeside sporting activity, spent his days thoughtfully watching the smoke from his cigarettes dispersing in the air, or now and then leafing through a book.

The oppressive isolation of two rainy days, and his frank, open manner, soon gave our acquaintanceship a warmth that almost entirely bridged the gap in years between us. Born in Estonia, brought up in France and later in England, a man who had never practised any profession and for years had not lived in any one place, he was homeless in the noble sense of those who, like the Vikings and pirates of beauty, have collected in their intellectual raids all that is most precious in many great cities. He was close to all the arts in the manner of a dilettante, but stronger than his love for them was his sublime disdain to serve them. He had them to thank for a thousand delightful hours, but had never devoted a single creative impulse to any of them. He lived one of those lives that seem otiose because they are not linked to any community of interest, because all the riches stored in them by a thousand separate valuable experiences will pass when their last breath is drawn, without anyone to inherit them.

I said as much to him one evening when we were sitting outside the hotel after dinner, watching the bright lake slowly darken before our eyes. He smiled. "You may be right. I don't believe in memoirs; what you have experienced is in the past as soon as its moment is over. And as for literature: doesn't that perish as well twenty, fifty, a hundred years later? However, I'll tell you something today that I think would make a pretty novella. Come with me—such things are better told as one walks along."

So we set off on the beautiful path along the beach, overshadowed by the eternal cypresses and tangled chestnut trees, with the lake casting restless reflections through their branches. Over there lay the white cloud of Bellagio, softly tinted by sunset colours, and high, high above the dark hill gleamed the sparkling crown of the walls of the Villa Serbelloni. The atmosphere was still slightly sultry, but not oppressive; like a woman's gentle arm, it leant tenderly on the shadows and filled the night with the fragrance of invisible flowers. Then he began his tale.

"I will introduce the story with a confession. Until now I haven't told you that I have been in Cadenabbia before, last year, at the same season and in the same hotel. That may surprise you, especially as I have mentioned that I always avoid doing anything twice. But listen to my story. Last year this place was, of course, as deserted as it is now. The same gentleman from Milan was here—the one who spends all day catching fish and throws them back into the lake in the evening, only to catch them again next day; there were two old Englishwomen whose quietly vegetative existence one hardly noticed, and in addition a handsome young man with a pretty, pale girl, who I don't believe to this day was his wife, because they seemed far too fond of each other for that. Finally, there was also a German family, the most typical kind of north Germans. A flaxen-haired, raw-boned woman getting on in years, with angular, graceless movements, piercing steely eyes and a sharp, quarrelsome mouth like a cut made with a knife. She had a sister with her, unmistakably her sister because she had the same features, only lined and somehow softened; the two of them were always together, yet never seemed to talk to each other, and were always intent on their embroidery, into which they seemed to weave all their absence of thought, implacable Fates in a restricted world of tedium. And between them a young girl some sixteen years old, the daughter of one of them, I don't know which, for the pronounced immaturity of her features was already mingling with a slight indication of feminine curves. She was not really pretty, too thin, not fully grown yet, but there was something touching in her look of helpless yearning. Her eyes were large, and probably full of dark light, but they always shyly avoided the glance of others, their glow dispersed into fitful glints. She too always had some needlework with her, but her hands often moved slowly, her fingers slackened, and then she would sit still, looking out over the lake.

"I don't know what it was about that sight that so strangely attracted my attention. Was it the banal yet inevitable idea that struck me, on seeing the faded mother beside her daughter coming into the bloom of youth? Was it the shadow behind her figure, the thought that lines wait hidden in every cheek, weariness in all laughter, disappointment in every dream? Or was it that wild, unfocused longing just breaking out, giving away everything about the girl, every wonderful moment in her life when her eyes were fixed on the whole universe in desire, because they had not yet found one desirable object to cling to, then to remain there rotting like algae on a piece of floating wood? I found it infinitely fascinating to watch her, to see her dreamy, dewy-eyed glance, the wildly exuberant caresses she lavished on every dog and cat, the restlessness that made her begin so many projects and then leave them unfinished. And then the ardent haste with which she raced through the few wretched books in the hotel library in the evening, or leafed through the two volumes of poetry, worn with much reading, that she had brought with her, books containing the poetry of Goethe and Baumbach… but why do you smile?

I had to apologize. "It's the juxtaposition of Goethe and Baumbach."

"I see! Yes, of course, it's comical. And then again, it isn't. You may believe me when I say that it is immaterial to young girls of that age whether the poetry they read is good or bad, the real essence of poetry or an imitation. To them, poems are only vessels for quenching their thirst, and they pay no attention to the quality of the wine in those vessels; it is intoxicating even before it is drunk. And this girl was like that, so full to the brim of longing that it glowed in her eyes, made her fingertips tremble on the table, and she moved in a manner somewhere between awkwardness and elation. You could see she was hungry to talk to someone, to give away something of all that filled her mind, but there was no one there, only a void, only the slight sound of the embroidery needles to right and left of her, and the cold, deliberate glances of the two older ladies.

"I felt a great sense of pity for her. And yet I could not approach her, for first, what does a man of my age mean to a girl at this moment in her life, and secondly, my dislike of becoming acquainted with family groups, and in particular ageing middle-class ladies, stood in the way of any opportunity to do so. Then an odd approach occurred to me. I thought: here is a young girl, unfledged, inexperienced, probably visiting Italy for the first time, a country that in Germany, thanks to Shakespeare, the Englishman who never went there, is regarded as the land of romantic love—the land of Romeos, secret adventures, dropped fans, flashing daggers, of masks, duennas and tender letters. She surely dreams of such adventures, I thought, and who knows a girl's dreams? They are white, wafting clouds hovering aimlessly in the blue sky, and like real clouds always more intensely coloured in the evening, glowing pink and then an ardent red. Nothing will strike her as improbable or unlikely here. So I decided to invent a secret lover for her.

"And that same evening I wrote a long letter, humbly and respectfully tender, full of strange hints, and unsigned. A letter demanding nothing, promising nothing, exuberant and restrained at the same time—in short a romantic letter that would not have been out of place in a verse drama. As I knew that she was the first to come down to breakfast every day, driven by her restlessness, I folded it into her napkin. Morning came. Watching from the garden, I saw her incredulous surprise, her sudden alarm, the red flame that shot into her pale cheeks and quickly spread down her throat. I saw her looking around helplessly, fidgeting, I saw the nervous movement with which she hid the letter, and then I saw her sit there, nervous and uneasy, scarcely touching her breakfast and soon running away, out of the dining room, to somewhere in the dark, deserted corridors of the hotel, to find a place where she could decipher her mysterious letter… Did you want to say something?"

I had made an involuntary movement, and now I had to explain it. "Wasn't that a bold step to take? Didn't you stop to think she might want to find out how the letter came to be in her napkin, or simplest of all ask the waiter? Or show it to her mother?"

"Of course I thought of that. But if you had seen the girl, that timid, scared, sweet creature who was always looking around anxiously if for once she had raised her voice, any doubts would have been dispelled. There are girls whose modesty is so great that you can go to considerable lengths with them, because they are so helpless and would rather put up with anything than confide so much as a word about it to others. I smiled as I watched her going, and was pleased with the success of my little game. Then she came back, and I felt the blood rush suddenly to my temples; this was another girl, moving in a different way. She came in, looking restless and confused, a glowing wave of red had suffused her face, and a sweet awkwardness made her clumsy. And it was the same all day. Her glance flew to every window as if to find the answer to the mystery there, circled around every passer-by, and once fell on me. I carefully avoided it, so as not to give myself away by any sign, but in that fleeting second I had felt a fiery questioning that almost alarmed me; and it struck me again, from years of experience, that there is no more dangerous, tempting and corrupt desire than to light that first spark in a girl's eyes. Then I saw her sitting between the two older ladies, her fingers idle, and noticed that she sometimes quickly felt a place in her dress, where I was sure she was hiding the letter.

"Now the game really did tempt me. That very evening I wrote her a second letter, and so on over the next few days; I found it exciting to be playing the part of a young man in love in my letters, exaggerating an imaginary passion. It became a fascinating sport such as I suppose huntsmen feel when they set snares or entice game to within the firing line of their guns. And my own success was so indescribable, almost frightening me, that I was thinking of putting an end to it, but temptation now bound me ardently to the game I had begun. It was so easy. Her bearing became light, wildly confused as if by dancing, her features radiated a hectic beauty all their own; her sleep must have been a matter of watching and waiting for next morning's letter, for her eyes were darkly shadowed early in the day, and the fire in them unsteady. She began looking after herself, wore flowers in her hair, a wonderful tenderness for everything calmed her hands, and there was always a question in her eyes, for she sensed, from a thousand small indications in my letters, that the writer of them must be near her—an Ariel filling the air with music, hovering nearby, listening for the sound of the slightest things she did, yet invisible by his own will. She became so cheerful that even the two dull-witted ladies noticed the change, for sometimes they let their eyes linger with kindly curiosity on her hurrying form and her budding cheeks, and then looked at her with a surreptitious smile. There was a new sound in her voice, louder, brighter, bolder, and her throat often vibrated and swelled as if she were about to burst into a song full of joyous trills, as if… but there you go, smiling again!"

"No, no, please go on. I only mean that you tell a very good story. You have—forgive me for taking the liberty—you have talent, you could tell as good a tale as one of our novelists."

"You say that, I suppose, for the sake of courtesy, suggesting that I tell a story like your German novelists, that's to say with lyrical fancies, broad, sentimental, tedious. Very well, I'll cut it short! The marionette was dancing, and I pulled the strings with care. To divert any suspicion from me—for sometimes I felt her eyes resting on mine with a question in them—I had suggested that the writer was not staying here but in one of the nearby spa resorts, and came over the lake in a boat or on the steamer every day. And now I saw that when the bell of the approaching steamer rang, she would always escape her mother's supervision on some pretext, hurry away, and keep watch, with bated breath, on the passengers disembarking from a corner of the pier.

"And then one day it happened. It was a gloomy afternoon, and I had nothing better to do than to watch her, when something remarkable occurred. One of the passengers was a handsome young man with the showy elegance of young Italians, and as he scanned the place as if in search of something, the desperately enquiring, questioning, intent look in the young girl's face met his eye. And at once, flooding wildly over her gentle smile, a modest blush swiftly rose in her face. The young man stopped in surprise, his attention drawn to her—something easily understood when you are the recipient of so warm a glance, full of a thousand unsaid things—and he smiled and tried to follow her. She fled, came to a halt in the certainty that this was the man she had been looking out for so long—hurried on again, but looked round once more. It was the eternal interplay of wanting and fearing, longing and shame, in which the sweet, weak partner is always really the stronger. Obviously encouraged, if surprised, he hurried after her, and was getting close. I was feeling, apprehensively, that all this must surely collapse into an alarming state of chaos—when the two older ladies came along the path. The girl flew to them like a shy bird, the young man cautiously withdrew, but still their eyes met once more as they turned to look back, feverishly fixed on one another. This incident was a warning to me to bring my game to an end, yet the temptation was still too strong, and I made up my mind to make use of this coincidence as an aid. I wrote her an unusually long letter that evening, one that was bound to confirm her assumption. It intrigued me to be directing two characters in my play.

"Next morning the quivering confusion of her features alarmed me. Her pretty unrest had given way to nervous agitation that I did not understand; her eyes were moist and red-rimmed, as if by tears, and she seemed to feel a piercing pain. It was as if all her silence were trying to emerge in a wild scream. Darkness lay on her brow, and there was a gloomy astringency in her eyes, while this time above all I had expected bright joy. I was frightened. For the first time a strange element had entered the game; the marionette didn't obey me and wouldn't dance as I had planned. I thought of all possible reasons, and couldn't find one. I began to be afraid of the play I myself had staged, and I did not return to the hotel until evening, to avoid the accusation in her eyes.

"When I did get back, I understood it all. The family's table was no longer laid. They had left. She had been obliged to go away without a chance to say a word to him, and she could not let her family see how her heart was still attached to that one day, that single hour—she had been dragged away from a sweet dream and back to some miserable small town. I had forgotten to think of that. And I still feel that last look of hers as an accusation, its terrible force of mingled anger, torment, despair and the most bitter pain—something that I had brought into her life, and who knew how long it would last?"

He fell silent. The night had been walking with us, and the moon, partly covered with clouds, was shedding a fitful light. Sparkling stars seemed to hang between the trees and the pale surface of the lake. We went on without a word. At last my companion broke our silence. "Well, that was my story. Don't you think it would make a novella?"

"I don't know. At any rate, it's a story that I will remember, along with the others for which I already have to thank you. But a novella? A good opening for one that might perhaps tempt me. For these people are only ships passing in the night, they are not entirely in control of themselves, they mark the beginning of human stories, but there is no real story. You would have to think it out to the end."

"I see what you mean. The young girl's life, her return to the small town, the dreadful tragedy of ordinary life..."

"No, that's not quite it. The girl doesn't interest me so much. Young girls are never interesting, remarkable as they may think themselves, because all that they've experienced is negative, and so their stories are all the same. In this case the girl marries some good solid citizen at home when the time for it comes, and this affair remains a flower petal among her memories. I'm not, as I said, interested in the girl."

"That's strange. I don't know what you can find in the young man to interest you. Everyone catches such glances in his youth, a fire kindled between one pair of eyes and another, most don't even notice it, others quickly forget. You have to grow older to know that this is perhaps the noblest and deepest thing you ever receive, the sacred privilege of youth."

"I'm not interested in the young man either..."

"Then?"

"I'd develop the character of the older man, the letter-writer, trace it all the way through the story. I don't think that you write ardent letters with impunity at any age, or meddle with the feelings of someone else's love. I would try to show how the game becomes serious, how he thinks he is in control of it, when the game now controls him. The girl's awakening beauty, beauty that he thinks he sees only as an observer, intrigues him and fascinates him more deeply. And the moment when it all slips away from him makes him feel a wild longing for the game—and his plaything. I would be intrigued by the reversal in love that is bound to make an old man's passion very like a boy's, because neither feels entirely adequate as a lover, I would give him the fears and expectations of that state of mind. I would make him uncertain, I'd have him travelling after her to see her, yet at the last minute not venturing near her, I'd have him coming back to the same place in the hope of seeing her again, imploring coincidence, which is always cruel in such cases. I would plan my novella along those lines, and then it would be…"

"A lie, false, impossible!"

I was startled. His voice interrupted me harshly, hoarse and shaking, almost menacing. I had never seen my companion so agitated before. Instantly I realized what note I had incautiously struck in him. And when he stopped suddenly, I was painfully moved to see his white hair in the moonlight.

I wanted to change the subject quickly, broach another. But then he spoke again, this time warmly and softly in his calm, deep voice, pleasantly tinged with slight melancholy. "Or you may be right. Yes, it's more interesting: *L'amour coûte cher aux vieillards*—I think that was the title of one of Balzac's most moving stories, and many could be written on the subject. But the old people who know most about it are happy to talk only about their successes, not their failures. They are afraid of looking ridiculous in circumstances that only, so to speak, illustrate the pendulum of eternity swinging. Do you really think it was chance that the 'lost' chapters of Casanova's memoirs are those describing him in later life, when the cockerel becomes a cuckold, the betrayer the betrayed? Maybe his hand was too reluctant and his heart too heavy to write about that."

He offered me his own hand. Now his voice was cool, calm and placid again. "Goodnight! I see it's dangerous to tell young people stories on summer nights. It easily leads to foolish thoughts and all kinds of unnecessary dreams. Goodnight to you!"

And he walked back into the dark, his step still with a spring in it, but slower now. It was late, but the weariness that usually came over me early in the warmth of these mild nights had been dispersed today by the agitation that rings in the blood when something strange happens, or for a moment you feel another man's experience as if it were your own. So I went along the quiet, dark path to the Villa Carlotta with its marble stairway leading down to the lake, and sat on the cool steps. It was a wonderful night. The lights of Bellagio that had been sparkling among the trees like fireflies earlier now seemed endlessly far away across the water, and slowly, one by one, they fell back into the deep darkness. The lake lay there silent, shining like a black jewel, yet edged with sparkling fire. And the splashing waves, like white hands on the pale keys of an instrument, moved up and down the marble steps with a slight swell. The pale sky seemed endlessly high above, decked with thousands of sparkling stars. They stood there calmly, in bright silence; only occasionally did one suddenly break free of that diamantine dance and fall into the summer night, into the dark, into valleys, ravines, mountains or distant water, knowing nothing of it, slung like a human life into the steep depths of unknown destinies.

THE GOVERNESS

THE TWO CHILDREN are alone in their room. The light has been put out; they are surrounded by darkness except for the faint white shimmer showing where their beds are. They are both breathing so quietly that you might think they were asleep.

One of them speaks up. "I say…" she begins. It is the twelve-year-old, and her voice is quiet, almost anxious in the dark.

"What is it?" asks her sister from the other bed. She is only a year older.

"Good, you're still awake. I… there's something I want to tell you."

No answer from across the room, only a rustle of bedclothes. The elder sister is sitting up, looking expectant. Her eyes are sparkling.

"Listen… I wanted to ask you… but no, you tell me first, haven't you noticed anything about our Fräulein in the last few days?"

The other girl hesitates, thinking it over. Then she says, "Yes, but I'm not sure what it is. She isn't as strict as usual. I didn't do any school homework for two whole days recently, and she never told me off. And then she's so… oh, I don't know exactly how to put it. I don't think she's bothering about us any more. She sits somewhere all the time, she doesn't play with us the way she used to."

"I think she's feeling sad, she just doesn't want to show it. She doesn't even play the piano any more."

Silence descends again.

"You wanted to tell me something," the elder girl reminds her sister.

"Yes, but you mustn't tell anyone else, really not anyone, not Mama and not your best friend."

"No, no, I won't!" She is impatient now. "Come on, what is it?"

"Well, when we were going to bed just now, I suddenly remembered that I hadn't said goodnight to Fräulein. I'd taken my shoes off, but I went to her room all the same, ever so quietly, to give her a surprise. And I opened the door of her room very carefully too. I thought at first she wasn't there. There was a light on, but I couldn't see her. Then all at once—it gave me a terrible fright—I heard somebody crying, and I suddenly saw her lying on the bed with all her clothes on and her head in the pillows. She was sobbing so hard that it made me jump. But she didn't notice me. And then I closed the door very quietly again. I had to stand there outside it for a little while because I was trembling so much. And then that sobbing sound came through the door again, quite clearly, and I ran back down here."

The girls keep quiet for a while. Then one of them says, very softly, "Oh, poor Fräulein!" The words linger in the air of the room like a lost, low musical phrase, and then die away again.

"I do wish I knew why she was crying," says the younger sister. "She hasn't quarrelled with anyone these last few days. Mama's leaving her in peace at last instead of scolding her all the time, and I'm sure we haven't done anything bad, not to her. So why was she crying like that?"

"I can think of a reason," says the elder girl.

"What is it? Go on, tell me."

Her sister hesitates, but at last she says, "I think she's in love."

"In love?" The younger girl is baffled. "In love? Who with?"

"Haven't you noticed anything?"

"You don't mean in love with Otto!"

"Oh, don't I? And isn't he in love with her? He's been staying with us for three years while he studies at the university, so why do you think he's suddenly taken to going out with us every day these last few months? Did he ever bother with you or me before Fräulein came to be our governess? He's been hanging around us all the time lately. We keep meeting him by accident in the People's Garden or the City Park or the Prater when we go out with Fräulein. Didn't you notice?"

Startled, the younger girl stammers, "Yes... yes, of course I noticed. Only I always thought it was..."

Her voice fails her. She doesn't go on.

"So did I at first," says her elder sister. "You know how people always say girls are silly. Then I realised that he was only using us as an excuse."

Now they are both silent. It sounds as if the conversation is over. Both girls seem to be deep in thought, or already far away in their dreams.

Then the younger sister breaks the silence in the darkness again. Her voice sounds helpless. "But then why was she crying? He likes her, doesn't he? And I always thought being in love must be wonderful."

"I don't know," says her elder sister, dreamily. "I thought it must be wonderful too."

And once again sleepy lips say, softly and sorrowfully, "Oh, poor Fräulein!"

Then all is quiet in the room.

Next morning they do not discuss the subject again, and yet they are both aware that their thoughts are circling around it. They walk past one another, avoid each other, yet their eyes involuntarily meet when they are glancing surreptitiously at their governess. At mealtimes they watch their cousin Otto as if he were a stranger, although he has been living here with them for years. They do not talk to him, but they keep looking at him from under lowered eyelids to see if he is communicating with Fräulein in some way. Both sisters feel uneasy. They do not play today, and instead do useless, unnecessary things in their nervous anxiety to fathom the mystery. That evening, however, one of them asks the other in a cool tone, as if it were of no importance to her, "Did you notice anything else today?" To which her sister says, "No," and turns away. They are both somehow afraid of talking about it. And so it goes on for a few days, both children silently observing as their minds go round in circles, feeling restlessly and unconsciously close to some sparkling secret.

At last, after a few days, one of them, the younger girl, notices the governess discreetly giving Otto a look full of meaning. He nods in answer. The child quietly takes her sister's hand under the table. When her sister turns to her, she flashes her a meaning glance of her own. The elder girl understands at once, and she too is on the alert.

As soon as they rise from table, the governess tells the girls, "Go to your room and occupy yourselves quietly with something. I have a headache, I'd like to rest for half-an-hour." The children look down. Cautiously, they communicate by touching hands. And as soon as the governess has left, the younger girl hurries over to her sister. "You wait and see—Otto will go to her room now."

"Of course! That's why she sent us to ours."

"We must listen outside her door."

"But suppose someone comes along?"

"Who?"

"Well, Mama."

The younger girl takes fright. "Yes, then…"

"I tell you what. I'll listen at the door, you stay further along the corridor and warn me if there's anyone coming. That way we'll be safe."

The smaller girl looks cross. "But then you won't tell me anything!"

"Yes, I will. I'll tell you all about it."

"Really *all* about it?"

"Yes, I promise. You must cough as a signal if you hear someone coming."

They wait in the corridor, trembling with excitement. Their hearts are beating fast. What will happen? They press close to each other.

Footsteps are approaching. The girls retreat into the shadows. Sure enough, it is Otto. He takes hold of the door handle, and the door closes after him. The elder girl shoots up to it like an arrow from the bow, pressing close to the door, holding her breath as she listens. The younger sister looks wistfully at her from a distance.

She is burning with curiosity, and it tears her away from her post. She creeps up, but her sister angrily pushes her away. So she waits at a distance for two or three more minutes that seem to her like an eternity. She is quivering with impatience, stepping from foot to foot as if the floor were burning hot. In her excitement and anger she is near tears—to think that her sister can hear it all and she can't hear anything! Then, in a third room, a door closes. She coughs. And both girls hurry away back to their room. They stand there for a moment breathless, their hearts thudding.

"Come on then, tell me all about it," demands the younger girl avidly.

Her elder sister looks thoughtful. At last she says, dreamily, as if to herself, "I can't make it out!"

"What?"

"It's so strange."

"What? What's so strange?" The younger girl is impatient to know. Her sister tries to collect her thoughts. The smaller girl is pressing very close to her so as not to miss a word.

"It was really funny… not at all what I expected. I think when he came into the room he was going to hug her or kiss her, but then she said, 'Don't do that, I have something serious to discuss with you.' I couldn't see anything, because the key was in the lock on the inside of the door, but I could hear every word. 'Well, what is it?' asked Otto, but I've never heard him speak like that before. You know his usual cheerful, loud way of talking, but he sounded uncertain of himself when he said that, and I felt at once that he was somehow scared. And she must have noticed that he was pretending, too, because she just said very quietly, 'You know what it is.' 'No, I don't, I have no idea,' he said. 'Oh,' she said, so sadly, so terribly sadly, 'then why are you avoiding me all of a sudden? It's a week since you spoke a word to me, you avoid me whenever you can, you don't go out with the children or to the park with us any more. Am I such a stranger all at once? Oh, you know very well why you're keeping away from me.' He said nothing for a bit, then he said, 'I'm about to sit my examinations, I have a great deal of work to do and no time for anything else. It can't be helped.' Then she began crying, and she said to him, through her tears but so kindly, she wasn't angry, 'Otto, why are you lying to me? Tell the truth. I really haven't deserved this from you. I never asked for anything, but now the two of us have to discuss something after all. You know what I am going to say to you, I can see it from your eyes.' And then he said, 'Well, what is it?' But very faintly. And she said…"

Suddenly the girl began trembling, and in her emotion she could get no further. Her younger sister pressed close, saying, "And then what?"

"Then she said, 'What am I going to do about our baby?'"

The smaller girl started with surprise, and cried, "Their baby? What baby? That's not possible!"

"But she said it."

"You can't have heard properly."

"I did, I did. And he repeated it, he sounded just as surprised as you, he cried, 'A baby!' She didn't say anything for quite a time, and then she asked, 'What's to become of me now?' And then…"

"And then?"

"Then you coughed, and I had to run away."

The younger girl stares ahead of her, dismayed. "A baby! But that's impossible. Where *is* the baby?"

"I don't know. That's what I don't understand."

"Maybe at home where… well, where she was living before she came to be our governess. Mama probably wouldn't let her bring the baby with her because of us. And that's why she's so sad."

They both fall silent again, baffled, brooding, unable to come to any conclusions. The thought of the baby is weighing on their minds. Once again it is the smaller girl who speaks first. "A baby, I mean it isn't possible! How can she have a baby? She isn't married, and only married people have babies, I know that!"

"Perhaps she *was* married."

"Don't be so silly. Not to Otto."

"Then how?…"

They stare at each other, at a loss.

"Oh, poor Fräulein," says one of the girls very sadly. They keep repeating the same phrase, and it dies away into a sigh of sympathy. But their curiosity also keeps flaring up.

"I wonder if it's a girl or a boy?"

"How could we find out?"

"Suppose I asked her some time, very, very carefully… What do you think?"

"I think you're crazy!"

"Why? She's so nice to us."

"Oh, do stop and think! No one tells us *that* sort of thing. They hush everything up. When we come into a room they break off their conversation and start talking to us in a silly way as if we were little children. And I'm thirteen already! What's the point of asking? Grown-ups always tell lies."

"But I really, really would like to know."

"Do you think I wouldn't?"

"I tell you what, the bit I understand least is why Otto didn't sound as if he knew about it. You know if you have a baby, the way you know that you have a mother and a father."

"He was only pretending not to know. He's horrid. Otto is always pretending."

"But you wouldn't pretend about something like that. Perhaps he's just trying to fool people…"

However, at this point the governess comes in. They stop talking at once and seem to be doing homework. However, they surreptitiously glance at her. Her eyes look reddened, her voice is rather huskier and more vibrant than usual. The children keep very quiet, suddenly regarding her with awed timidity. She has a baby, they keep thinking, that's why she's so sad. And soon they are feeling sad themselves.

*

At the dining-room table next day they hear unexpected news. Otto is leaving the family apartment. He has told his uncle that with his examinations so close he has to work very hard, and there are too many distractions here. He will rent a room somewhere for the next month or so, he says, until the exams are over.

The children are very interested to hear this. They guess there is a secret connection with yesterday's conversation, and alert as their instincts now are they pick up the scent of cowardice and flight. When Otto comes to say goodbye to them, they sulk and turn their backs. But they watch surreptitiously as he faces their governess. Her lips are trembling, but she offers him her hand calmly, without a word.

The children have changed a great deal over the last few days. They have lost their playfulness and laughter, the old happy, carefree light has left their eyes. They are full of uneasiness and uncertainty, deeply suspicious of everyone around them. They no longer believe what they are told, they think they detect deliberate lies behind every word. They keep their eyes and ears open all day long, watching every movement, picking up any sudden start of surprise or tone of voice. They haunt the place like shadows in search of clues, listening at doors to overhear anything of interest, possessed by a passionate desire to shake the dark net of secrets off their reluctant shoulders, or at least see through some gap in it and get a glimpse of the real world outside. They have lost their childish trustfulness, their blindly carefree merriment. Moreover, they guess that the tense, sultry atmosphere resulting from recent events will discharge itself in some unexpected way, and they don't want to miss it. Ever since discovering that the people around them are liars they have become persistent and watchful; they are sly and deceitful themselves. With their parents, they take refuge in pretended childishness flaring up into hectic activity. They are a prey to nervous restlessness; their eyes, once shining with a soft, gentle glow, now look deeper and are more likely to flash. In all this constant watching and spying, they feel so helpless that their love for each other is stronger. Sometimes they hug stormily, abandoning themselves to a need for affection suddenly welling up in them, sometimes they burst into tears. All at once, and for no apparent reason, life seems to be in a state of crisis.

Among the many emotional injuries that they now realise they have suffered, there is one that they feel particularly deeply. Seeing how sad Fräulein is these days, they have set out silently, without a word, to please her as much as they possibly can. They do their school exercises carefully and industriously, they help each other, they are quiet and uncomplaining, they try to anticipate her every wish. But Fräulein doesn't even notice, and that hurts them badly. She is entirely different these days. Sometimes, when one of the girls speaks to her, she starts as if woken from sleep. And then her gaze, at first searching, returns from some distant horizon. She will often sit for hours looking dreamily into space, and then the girls go about on tiptoe so as not to disturb her. They have a vague, mysterious idea that she is thinking about her baby who is somewhere far away. And out of the depths of their own awakening femininity they love Fräulein more and more. She is so kind and gentle, her once brisk, high-spirited manner is more thoughtful now, her movements more careful, and the children guess at a secret sadness in all this. They have never seen her shed tears, but her eyelids are often red. They realise that Fräulein is trying to keep her pain secret from them, and are in despair to think that they cannot help her.

And once, when Fräulein has turned to the window and is dabbing her eyes with her handkerchief, the younger girl suddenly plucks up her courage, takes the governess's hand gently, and says, "Fräulein, you're so sad these days. It isn't our fault, is it?"

Much moved, the governess looks at her and caresses her soft hair. "No, my dear, no," she says. "It certainly is not your fault." And she gently kisses the girl's forehead.

*

It is at this time, when they are keeping watch, letting nothing that moves within their field of vision pass unnoticed, that one of them picks up a remark when she suddenly enters a room. It is only a few words, because the girls' parents break off their conversation at once, but anything they hear now can make them suspicious. "I thought I'd noticed something of that sort myself," their mother was saying. "Well, I'll question her." The child thinks at first that this means her, and almost anxiously runs to her sister for advice and help. But at mid-day they realise that their parents' eyes are resting enquiringly on the governess's dreamy, abstracted face, and then their mother and father look at each other.

After lunch their mother says casually to Fräulein, "Will you come to my room, please? I want to speak to you." Fräulein bows her head slightly. The girls are trembling violently. They can feel that something is brewing.

As soon as the governess goes into their mother's room they hurry after her. This eavesdropping, rummaging about in nooks and crannies, listening and lying in wait has become second nature to them. They are no longer even aware that their conduct is improperly bold and sly, they have just one idea in their heads—to get possession of all the secrets being kept from them. They listen. But all they hear is whispered words, and a soft but angry tone of voice. Their bodies tremble nervously. They are afraid of failing to catch something important.

Then one of the voices inside the room rises higher. It is their mother's. She sounds angry and cantankerous.

"Did you really think everyone's blind, and no one would notice anything? I can well imagine how you've carried out your duties with such ideas in your head, and with morals like that! And it is to such a woman that I have entrusted the upbringing of my children, my daughters, a task that God knows you have neglected…"

Fräulein seems to be saying something in reply, but too quietly for the children to make out what it is.

"Excuses, excuses! Every promiscuous girl will offer that excuse!

She'll blame the first man who comes to mind and think nothing of it, hoping the good Lord will come to her aid. And a woman like that claims to be a governess and fit to educate girls. It's outrageous. You surely don't imagine that, in your condition, I shall keep you in my household any longer?"

The children listen intently outside the door. Shivers run through them. They don't understand what their mother is saying, but it is terrible to hear her voice raised in such anger—and the only answer is their governess's quiet, uncontrollable sobbing. Tears come to their own eyes. But the sobbing only seems to make their mother angrier.

"So all you can do now is burst into tears! You don't touch my heart like that. I have no sympathy for such females. What becomes of you now is none of my business. You'll know where to turn, I'm sure, I'm not asking you for the details. All I know is that I shall not tolerate the presence of someone who has so shamefully neglected her duty in my house a day longer."

Only sobs answered her, desperate, wild, animal sobs that shake the children outside the door like a fever. They have never heard anyone cry so hard. And they feel, vaguely, that someone crying like that can't be in the wrong. Their mother is silent now, waiting. Then she says suddenly, brusquely, "Very well, that's all I wanted to say to you. Pack your bags today and come to collect your wages first thing tomorrow. Goodbye."

The children scurry away from the door, and take refuge in their room. What was all that about? They feel as if a bolt of lightning has struck them. Standing there pale and shuddering, for the first time they somehow guess the truth. For the first time, too, they dare to feel hostile to their parents.

"It was wrong of Mama to speak to her like that," says the elder girl, biting her lower lip.

Her younger sister still shrinks from such a bold statement. "But we don't know what she did," she stammers plaintively.

"It can't have been anything bad. Fräulein can't have done anything bad. Mama doesn't know what she's really like."

"And the way she cried—it scared me."

"Yes, it was terrible. So was the way Mama shouted at her. It was wrong of Mama, I tell you it was wrong."

She stamps her foot. Her eyes are blurred with tears. Then the governess comes in, looking very tired.

"Children, there are things I have to do this afternoon. You can be left on your own, can't you? I'm sure I can rely on you, and then I'll see you this evening."

She goes out without noticing how upset the children are.

"Did you see her eyes? They were all red with crying. I can't understand how Mama could treat her like that."

"Oh, poor Fräulein!"

That deep, tearful sigh of sympathy again. The children are standing there in distress when their mother comes in to ask if they would like to go for a walk with her. The girls are evasive. They are afraid of their mother. In addition they are indignant; no one has said a word to them about their governess's departure. They would rather be on their own. Like two swallows in a small cage they swoop back and forth, upset by this atmosphere of lies and silence. They wonder whether to go and see Fräulein in her room and ask her questions, talk to her about it all, tell her they want her to stay and Mama is wrong. But they are afraid of hurting her feelings. And they are also ashamed of themselves for having found out all they know on the sly, by dint of eavesdropping. They must pretend to be stupid, as stupid as they were two or three weeks ago. So they spend the long, endless afternoon on their own, brooding over what they have heard and crying, always with those terrible voices ringing in their ears, their mother's vicious, heartless fury and the desperate sobs of their governess.

Fräulein looks in on them fleetingly that evening and says goodnight. The children tremble when they see her going out; they would like to say something to her. But when Fräulein reaches the door she turns back suddenly, as if their silent wish has brought her back once more of her own accord. Something is gleaming in her eyes; they are moist and clouded. She hugs both children, who begin sobbing wildly, kisses them once again, and then quickly goes out.

The children are in tears. They sense that she was saying goodbye.

"We won't see her any more!" wails one of the girls.

"No, when we get back from school at mid-day tomorrow she's sure to have gone."

"Maybe we can go and visit her later. And then I'm sure she'll show us her baby."

"Oh yes, she's so nice."

"Oh, poor Fräulein!" It is a sigh for their own loss again.

"Can you imagine what it will be like now without her?"

"I'll never be able to take to another governess."

"Nor me."

"No one else will be so kind to us. And then..."

She dares not say it. But an unconscious sense of femininity has made them revere Fräulein even more since they found out about her baby. They both keep thinking about it, and no longer with mere childish curiosity, but deeply moved and sympathetic.

"Listen," says one of the girls. "I know what!"

"Yes?"

"I'd like to do something nice for Fräulein before she goes. So that she'll know we love her and we're not like Mama. What about you?"

"How can you ask?"

"What I thought was, she's always liked white roses so much. Suppose we go out to buy her some first thing tomorrow, before we go to school, and then we can put them in her room."

"But when?"

"At mid-day when we come home."

"She'll be gone by then. I tell you what, suppose I run out very early and buy them before anyone notices I'm gone? And then we can take them to her in her room before we go to school."

"Yes, and we'll get up really early."

They fetch their money boxes, shake out the contents and put all their money together. They feel happier now they know that they can still give Fräulein proof of their silent, devoted love.

They get up very early in the morning. They stand outside the governess's door holding the beautiful double white roses—their hands tremble slightly—but when they knock there is no answer. They think Fräulein must be asleep, and cautiously slip into the room. But it is empty, and the bed has not been slept in. Everything lies scattered around in disorder. A couple of letters in white envelopes lie on the dark tabletop.

The two children take fright. What has happened?

"I'm going to see Mama," says the elder girl with determination. And defiantly, her eyes sombre and entirely fearless, she faces her mother head on and asks, "Where is our Fräulein?"

"She'll be in her room," says her mother, surprised.

"Her room's empty and she hasn't slept in her bed. She must have gone away yesterday evening. Why didn't anyone tell us?"

Her mother doesn't even notice the harsh, challenging tone of the girl's voice. She has turned pale, and goes to see her husband, who quickly disappears into the governess's room.

He stays there for a long time. The child watches her mother, who seems to be upset, with a steady angry gaze that the mother's eyes dare not meet.

Then her father comes back. He is very pale in the face, and is carrying a letter. He goes into the sitting room with her mother and talks to her quietly. The children stand outside, not venturing to listen at the door any more. They are afraid of their father's wrath. Just now he looked as they have never seen him before.

Their mother comes out of the sitting room, her eyes red with tears and appearing distressed. Instinctively, as if attracted to her fear, the children go to meet her, wanting to ask questions. But she says brusquely, "Off you go to school. You're late already."

And the children have to go. As if in a dream they sit there for four or five hours among all the other girls, hearing not a word. They rush home when lessons are over.

Home would be the same as usual except that everyone seems to be in the grip of a terrible idea. No one says anything, but they all, even the servants, look so strange. The children's mother comes to meet them. She seems to have prepared something to tell them. She begins, "Girls, your Fräulein will not be coming back, she has..."

But she does not venture to finish what she was going to say. As her children's eyes meet hers, they flash with such dangerous menace that she dares not tell them a lie. She turns and leaves them, taking refuge in her room.

Otto suddenly turns up that afternoon. He has been summoned; one of the letters left was for him. He too is pale and stands around looking upset. No one speaks to him. They all avoid him. Then he sees the two children huddled together in a corner and goes over to say hello.

"Don't you touch me!" says one of the girls, shuddering with disgust. Her sister actually spits on the floor in front of him. He wanders around for a little longer, looking confused and embarrassed. Then he disappears.

No one talks to the children. They themselves do not exchange a word with anyone. They pace around like caged animals, pale-faced, restless and agitated; they keep coming together, meeting one another's tear-stained gaze, but saying nothing. They know all about it now. They know that they have been told lies, all human beings can be bad and despicable. They do not love their parents any more, they don't believe in them. They know that they can never trust anyone, the whole monstrous weight of life will weigh down on their slender shoulders. They have been cast out of the cheerful comfort of their childhood, as if into an abyss. They cannot quite grasp the terrible nature of what has happened, but the thought of it makes them choke and threatens to stifle them. Their cheeks burn feverishly, and they have an angry, agitated look in their eyes. As if freezing in their isolation, they wander up and down. No one, not even their parents, dares speak to them, they look at everyone with such ill will, and their constant pacing back and forth reflects the agitation working inside them. Although the two girls do not talk to each other about it, they have something dreadful in common. Their impenetrable, unquestioning silence and viciously self-contained pain makes them seem strange and dangerous to everyone. No one comes close to them; access to their minds has been cut off, perhaps for many years to come. Everyone around them feels that they are enemies, and determined enemies at that who will not easily forgive again. For yesterday their childhood came to an end.

That afternoon they grow many years older. And only when they are alone in the darkness of their room in the evening do childish fears surface in them, the fear of loneliness, of images of dead people, as well as a presentiment of indistinct terrors. In the general agitation of the house, no one has remembered to heat the rooms. So they get into one bed together, freezing, holding each other tightly in their thin childish arms, pressing their slender bodies, not yet in the full bloom of youth, close to each other as if seeking help in their fear. They still dare not talk freely. But now the younger girl at last bursts into tears, and her elder sister joins her, sobbing wildly. They weep, closely entwined, warm tears rolling down their faces hesitantly at first, then falling faster, hugging one another breast to breast, shaking as they share their sobs. They are united in pain, a single weeping body in the darkness. They are not crying for the governess now, or for the parents who are lost to them; they are shaken by a sudden horror and fear of the unknown world lying ahead of them, after the first terrifying glimpse that they had of it today. They are afraid of the life ahead of them into which they will now pass, dark and menacing like a gloomy forest through which they must go. Their confused fears become dimmer, almost dreamlike, their sobbing is softer and softer. Their breath mingles gently now, as their tears mingled before. And so at last they fall asleep.

TWILIGHT

MADAM DE PRIE, returning from her morning drive on the day when the King dismissed her lover the Duke of Bourbon from his position as prime-minister in charge of the affairs of state, thought, as the two footmen at the door bowed low to her, that she caught them suppressing a smile at the same time, which vexed her. She did not let it show for the moment, and walked past them and up the steps with composure. But when she reached the first landing on the stairs she abruptly turned her head back, and she saw a broad grin on the lips of the garrulous pair, although it rapidly disappeared as they bowed again in alarm.

Now she knew enough. And up in her salon, where an officer of the royal bodyguard with much gold braid about his person was waiting for her with a letter, she appeared to be in as serene and almost exuberant a mood as if this were merely a conventional call on a friend. Although she noticed the royal seal on the letter and the rather awkward manner of the officer who was aware of the embarrassing nature of his message, she showed neither curiosity nor concern. Without opening the letter or even examining it more closely she made light conversation with the aristocratic young soldier, and on recognising him as a Breton by his accent told him the story of a lady who could never stand Bretons, because one of his countrymen had once become her lover against her will. She was in high spirits and made risqué jokes, partly from a deliberate intention of showing how carefree she was, partly from habit, for in general a careless and easy levity made all her dissimulations seem natural, even transforming them into sincerity. She talked until she really forgot the royal letter, which she creased as she held it in her hands. But finally, after all, she broke the seal.

The letter contained the royal order, expressed briefly and with remarkably little civility, for her to leave court at once and retire to her estate of Courbépine in Normandy. She had fallen into disfavour, her enemies had won at last; even before the King's message arrived she had known it from the smiles of her footmen at the door. But she did not give herself away. The officer carefully observed her eyes as they ran along the lines. They did not flicker, and now that she turned to him again a smile sparkled in them. "His Majesty is very anxious about my health, and would like me to leave the heat of the city and retire to my château. Tell his Majesty that I will comply with his wishes immediately." She smiled as she spoke, as if there were some secret meaning in her words. The officer raised his hat to her and left, with a bow.

But the door had hardly closed behind him before the smile fell from her lips like a withered leaf. She angrily crumpled up the letter. How many such missives, each sealing a human fate, had been sent out into the world under the royal name when she herself had dictated their contents! And now, after she had ruled all France for two years, her enemies dared to banish her from court with a sheet of paper like this! She hadn't expected so much courage from them. To be sure, the young King had never liked her and was ill-disposed towards her, but had she made Marie Leszczynska Queen of France only to be exiled now, just because a mob had rioted outside her windows and there was some kind of famine in the country? For a moment she wondered whether to resist the King's command: the Regent of France, the Duke of Orléans, had been her lover, and anyone who now held power and a high position at court owed it all to her. She did not lack for friends. But she was too proud to appear as a beggar where she was known as a mistress; no one in France was ever to see her with anything but a smiling face. Her exile couldn't last more than a few days, until tempers had calmed down, and then her friends would make sure she was recalled. In her mind, she was already looking forward to her revenge, and soothed her anger with that idea.

Madame de Prie went about her departure with the utmost secrecy. She gave no one a chance to feel sorry for her and received no callers, to avoid having to tell them she was going away. She wanted to disappear suddenly, in mysterious and dashing style, leaving a riddle calculated to confuse the whole court permanently linked to her absence, for it was a peculiarity of her character that she always wished to deceive, to veil whatever she was really doing with a lie. The only person she herself visited was the Count of Belle-Isle, her mortal enemy and the man behind her banishment. She sought him out to show him her smile, her unconcern, her self-confidence. She told him how she welcomed the opportunity of a rest from the stress of life at court, she told blatant lies that clearly showed him the depth of her hatred and contempt. The Count only smiled coldly and said he thought that she would find it hard to bear so long a period of solitude, and he gave the word "long" a strange emphasis that alarmed her. But she controlled herself, and civilly invited him to come and hunt on her estate.

In the afternoon she did meet one of her lovers in her little house in the rue Apolline, and told him to keep her well informed about everything that went on at court. She left that evening. She did not want to drive through the city in her open chaise during the day, because the common people had been hostile to her since the riot that cost human lives, and in addition she was determined to keep her disappearance a mystery. She intended to leave by night and return by day. She left her house just as it was, as if she were going away for only a day or so, and at the moment when the carriage began to move off she said out loud—knowing that her words would find their way back to court—that she was taking a short journey for the sake of her health and would soon be back. And she had schooled herself to wear the mask of dissimulation so well that, genuinely reassured by her own lie, she soon fell into an easy sleep in the jolting carriage, and woke only when she was well outside Paris and past the first posting station, surprised to find herself in a carriage at all, bound for something new, not knowing yet whether it would be good or bad. She felt only that the wheels were turning under her and she had no control over them, that she was gliding into the unknown, but she could not feel any serious anxiety, and soon fell asleep again.

The journey to Normandy was long and tedious, but her first day in Courbépine restored her cheerfulness. Her restless, fanciful mind, always lusting after novelty, discovered an unaccustomed charm in giving itself up to the crystalline purity of a summer's day in the country. She lost herself in a thousand follies, amused herself by walking down the avenues of the park, jumping hedges and trying to catch fluttering butterflies, clad in a dress white as blossom with pale ribbons in her hair, like the little girl she had once been and whom she had thought long dead in her. She walked and walked, and for the first time in years felt the pleasure of letting her limbs relax in the rhythm of her pace, just as she delightedly rediscovered everything about the simple life that she had forgotten in her days at court. She lay in the emerald grass and looked up at the clouds. How strange it was: she hadn't looked at a cloud for years, and she wondered whether clouds were as beautifully outlined, as fluffily white, as pure and airy above the buildings of Paris. For the first time she saw the sky as something real, and its blue vault, sprinkled with white, reminded her of the wonderful Chinese vase that a German prince had recently given her as a present, except that the sky was even lovelier, bluer, more rounded, and full of mild, fragrant air that felt as soft as silk. After hurrying from one entertainment to the next in Paris, she delighted in doing nothing, and the silence around her was as delicious as a cool drink. She now realised, for the first time, that she felt nothing for all the people who had flocked around her at Versailles, she neither loved nor hated any of them, she felt no more for them than for the peasants standing there on the outskirts of the wood with their large, flashing scythes, sometimes shading their eyes with a hand to peer curiously at her. She became more and more exuberant; she played with the young trees, jumped in the air until she could catch the hanging branches, let them spring up again, and laughed out loud when a few white blossoms, as if struck by an arrow, fell into the hand she held out to catch them or the hair she was wearing loose for the first time in years. With the wonderful facility of forgetfulness available to women of no great depth throughout their lives, she did not remember that she was in exile and before that had ruled France, playing with the fate of others as casually as she played now with butterflies and glimmering trees. She cast aside five, ten, fifteen years of her life and was Mademoiselle Pleuneuf again, daughter of the Geneva banker, playing in the convent garden, a small, thin, high-spirited girl of fifteen who knew nothing of Paris and the wide world.

In the afternoon she helped the maids with the harvest: she thought it uncommonly amusing to bind up the big sheaves and fling them exuberantly up to the farm cart. And she sat among them—they had been awestruck at first and behaved shyly—on top of the fully loaded wagon, dangling her legs, laughing with the young fellows and then, when the dancing began, whirling around with the best. It all felt to her like a successful masquerade at court, and she looked forward to telling everyone in Paris how charmingly she had spent her time, dancing with wild flowers in her hair and drinking from the same pitcher as the peasants. She noticed the reality of these things as little as she had felt, at Versailles, that the games of shepherds and shepherdesses were only pretence. Her heart was lost to the pleasure of the moment, it lied in telling the truth and was honest even while it intended to deceive, for she only ever knew what she felt. And what she felt now was delight and rapture running through her veins. The idea that she was out of favour was laughable.

But next morning a dark vestige of ill humour seeped in, mingling with the crystalline merriment of her hours. Waking itself was painful; she tumbled from the black night of dreamless sleep into day as if from warm, sultry air into icy water. She didn't know what had woken her. It was not the light, for a dull, rainy day was dawning outside the tear-stained windows. And it was not the noise either, for there were no voices here, only the fixed, piercing eyes of the dead looking down at her from their pictures on the wall. She was awakc and didn't know why or what for; nothing appealed to her here or tempted her.

And she thought how different waking up in Paris had been. She had danced and talked all evening, had spent half the night with her friends, and then came the wonderful sleep of exhaustion, with bright images still flickering on in her excited mind. And in the morning, with her eyes closed and as if still in a dream, she heard muted voices in the anterooms, and no sooner did her *levée* begin than they came streaming in: the royal dukes of France, petitioners, lovers, friends, all vying for her favour and bringing the suitor's gift of solicitous cheerfulness. Everyone had a story to tell, laughed, chattered, all the latest news and gossip came to her bedside, and her moment of waking carried her straight from those bright dreams into the full tide of life. The smile she had worn on her sleeping lips did not vanish but remained at the corners of her mouth, hovering there in high spirits like a bird swinging in its cage.

The day led her on from these images of her friends to those friends themselves, and they stayed with her as she dressed, as she drove out, as she ate, until far into the night again. She felt herself constantly carried on by this murmuring torrent, restless as the waves, dancing in never-ending rhythm and rocking the flowery boat of her life.

Here, however, the torrent cast her moment of awakening upon a rock, where it lay stranded on the beach of the hours, immobile and useless. Nothing tempted her to get up. Yesterday's innocent amusements had lost their charm; her curiosity, used to being indulged, was of the kind that quickly wore off. Her room was empty, as if airless, and she felt empty too in this solitude where no one asked for her: empty, useless, washed out and drained; she had to remind herself slowly why and how she had come to be here. What did she expect of the day that made her stare so hard at the clock, as it paced indefatigably through the silence with its gentle, tremulous gait?

At last she remembered. She had asked the Prince of Alincourt, the only one of her former lovers for whom she felt any real affection, to send her news from court daily by a mounted messenger. All yesterday she had forgotten what a sensation her disappearance must have been in Paris; now she longed to enjoy that triumph. And the messenger soon arrived, but not the message. Alincourt wrote her a few indifferent banalities, news of the King's health, visits from foreign princes, and let the letter peter out in friendly wishes for her well-being. Not a word about herself and her disappearance. She was angry. Hadn't the news been made public? Or had no one really believed her pretence that she was coming to this tedious place for the sake of her health?

The messenger, a simple, bull-necked groom, shrugged his shoulders. He knew nothing. She concealed her annoyance and wrote back to Alincourt—without showing her displeasure—to thank him for his news and urge him to continue writing to her, telling her everything, all the details. She hoped not to stay in the country long, she said, although she liked it here very well. She didn't even notice that she was lying to him.

But then the rest of the day was so long. The hours here, like the people themselves, seemed to go at a more sedate pace, and she knew no means of making them pass any faster. She didn't know what to do with herself: everything in her was mute, all the brilliant music of her heart dead as a musical clock when the key has been lost. She tried all kinds of things, she sent for books, but even the wittiest of them seemed to her mere printed pages. Disquiet came over her, she missed all the people among whom she had lived for years. She sent the servants hither and thither to no good purpose with imperious commands: she wanted to hear footsteps on the stairs, to see people, to create an illusion of the busy hum of messages, to deceive herself, but like all her plans at present, it didn't work.

Eating disgusted her, like the room and the sky and her servants: all she wanted now was night and deep, black, dreamless sleep until morning, when a more satisfactory message would arrive.

At last evening came, but it was dismal here! Nothing but the coming of darkness, the disappearance of everything, the extinction of the light. Evening here was an end, whereas in Paris it had been the beginning of all pleasures. Here it let the night pour in, there it lit gilded candles in the royal halls, made the air sparkle in your eyes, kindled, warmed, intoxicated and inspired the heart. Here it only made you more anxious. She wandered from room to room: silence lurked in all of them, like a savage animal sated with all the years when no one had been here, and she feared it might leap on her. The floorboards groaned, the books creaked in their bindings as soon as you touched them; something in the spinet moaned in fright like a beaten child when she touched the keys and summoned up a tearful sound. Everything joined in the darkness to resist her, the intruder.

Then, shivering, she had lights lit all over the house. She tried to stay in one room, but she was constantly impelled to move on, she fled from room to room as if that would calm her. But everywhere she came up against the invisible wall of the silence that had ruled this place by right for years, and would not be dismissed. Even the lights seemed to feel it; they hissed quietly and wept hot drops of wax.

Seen from outside, however, the château shone brightly with its thirty sparkling windows, as if there were great festivities here. Groups of villagers stood outside, amazed and wondering aloud where so many people had suddenly come from. But the figure that they saw flitting like a shadow past first one window and then another was always the same: Madame de Prie, pacing desperately up and down like a wild beast in the prison of her inner solitude, looking through the window for something that never came.

On the third day she lost control of her impatience and it turned violent. The solitude oppressed her; she needed people, or at least news of people, of the court, the natural home of her whole being with all its ramifications, of her friends, something to excite or merely touch her. She couldn't wait for the messenger, and early in the morning she rode for three hours to meet him. It was raining, and there was a high wind; her hair, heavy with water, pulled her head back, and the wind blew rain in her face so hard that she saw nothing. Her freezing hands could hardly hold the reins. Finally she galloped back, had her wet clothes stripped off, and took refuge in bed again. She waited feverishly, clenching her teeth on the covers. Now she understood the Count of Belle-Isle's menacing smile as he said that she would find so long a period of solitude hard to bear. And it had been only three days!

At last the courier came. She did not pretend any longer, but avidly tore the seal off the letter with her nails, like a starving man tearing the husk off a fruit. There was a great deal about the court in it: her eye ran down the lines in search of her name. Nothing, nothing. But one name did stand out like fire: her position as lady-in-waiting had been given to Madame de Calaincourt.

For a moment she trembled and felt quite weak. So it was not a case of fleeting disfavour but permanent exile: it was her death sentence, and she loved life. She leaped suddenly out of bed, feeling no shame in front of the courier, and half-naked, shaking with the cold, she wrote letter after letter with a wild craving. She abandoned her show of pride. She wrote to the King, although she knew he hated her; she promised in the humblest, most pitifully grovelling of terms never to try meddling in affairs of state again. She wrote to Marie Leszczynska, reminding her that she was Queen of France only through the agency of Madame de Prie; she wrote to the ministers, promising them money; she turned to her friends. She urged Voltaire, whom she had saved from the Bastille, to write an elegy on her departure from court and to read it aloud. She ordered her secretary to commission lampoons on her enemies and have them distributed in pamphlet form. She wrote twenty such letters with her fevered hand, all begging for just one thing:

Paris, the world, salvation from this solitude. They were no longer letters but screams. Then she opened a casket, gave the courier a handful of gold pieces, told him that even if he rode his horse to death he must be in Paris tonight. Only here had she learned what an hour really meant. Startled, he was going to thank her, but she drove him out.

Then she sought shelter in bed again. She was freezing. A harsh cough shook her thin frame. She lay staring ahead, always waiting for the clock on the mantelpiece to reach the hour and strike at last. But the hours were stubborn, they were not to be hounded with curses, with pleas, with gold, they went sleepily around. The servants came, she sent them all out, she would show no one her despair, she did not want food, or words, she wanted nothing from anyone. The rain fell incessantly outside, and she was as chilly as if she were standing out there shivering like the shrubs with their arms helplessly outstretched. One question went up and down in her mind like the swing of a pendulum: why, why, why, why? Why had God done this to her? Had she sinned so much?

She tugged at the bell-pull and told them to fetch the local priest. It soothed her to think that someone lived here to whom she could talk and confide her fears.

The priest did not delay, more particularly as he had been told that madame was ill. She could not help smiling when he came in, thinking of her abbé in Paris with his fine and delicate hands, the bright glance that rested on her almost tenderly, his courtly conversation which made you quite forget that he was taking confession. The abbé of Courbépine was portly and broad-shouldered, and his boots creaked as he trudged through the doorway. Everything about him was red: his plump hands, his face, weathered by the wind, his big ears, but there was something friendly about him as he offered her his great paw in greeting and sat down in an armchair. The horror in the room seemed to fear his weighty presence and cringed in a corner: filled by his loud voice the room appeared warmer, livelier, and it seemed to Madame de Prie that she breathed more easily now that he was here. He did not know exactly why he had been summoned, and made clumsy conversation, spoke of his parish work, and Paris which he knew only by hearsay, he demonstrated his scholarship, spoke of Descartes and the dangerous works of the sieur de Montaigne. She put in a word here and there, abstractedly; her thoughts were buzzing like a swarm of flies, she just wanted to listen, to hear a human voice, to raise it like a dam holding back the sea of loneliness that threatened to drown her. When, afraid he was disturbing her he was about to stop talking, she encouraged him with ardent kindness which was really nothing but fear. She promised to call on the reverend gentleman, invited him to visit her often; the seductive side of her nature, which had cast such a spell in Paris, emerged extravagantly from her dreamy silence. And the abbé stayed until it was dark.

But as soon as he left she felt as if the weight of the silence were descending on her twice as heavily as before, as if she alone had to hold up the high ceiling, she alone must keep back the advancing darkness. She had never known how much a single human being can mean to another, because she had never been lonely before. She had never thought more of other people than of air, and one does not feel the air, but now that solitude was choking her, only now did she realise how much she needed them, recognising how much they meant to her even when they deceived and told lies, how she herself drew everything from their presence, their easy manners, their confidence and cheerfulness. She had been immersed for decades in the tide of society, never knowing that it nourished and bore her up, but now, stranded like a fish on the beach of solitude, she flinched in despair and convulsive pain. She was freezing and feverishly hot at once. She felt her own body, was startled to find how cold it was; all its sensuous warmth seemed to have died away, her blood surged sluggishly through her veins like gelatine, she felt as if she were lying here in the silence inside the coffin of her own corpse. And suddenly a hot sob of despair tore through her. Alarmed at first, she tried to suppress it, but there was no one here,

here she did not have to dissimulate, she was alone with herself for the first time. And she willingly abandoned herself to the sweet pain of feeling hot tears run down her icy cheeks, while she heard her own sobbing in the terrible silence.

She made haste to return the abbé's visit. The house was deserted, no letters came—she herself knew that no one in Paris had much time for petitioners, and she had to do something, anything, even if it was just playing backgammon, or talking, or simply finding out how someone else talked. Somehow she must defy the tedium advancing ever more menacingly and murderously on her heart. She hurried through the village; she felt nauseated by everything that partook in any way of the name of Courbépine and reminded her of her exile. The abbé's little house lay at the end of the village street, surrounded by green countryside. It was not much higher than a barn, but flowers framed the tiny windows and their tangled foliage hung down over the door, so that she had to bend down to avoid being caught in their fragrant toils.

The abbé was not alone. With him at his desk sat a young man whom, in great confusion at the honour of such a visit, he introduced as his nephew. The abbé was preparing him for his studies, although he was not to be a priest—a vocation for which so much must be given up! This was meant as a gallant jest. Madame de Prie smiled, not so much at the rather clumsy compliment as at the amusing embarrassment of the young man, who blushed red and didn't know where to look. He was a tall country fellow with a bony, red-cheeked face, yellow hair and a rather artless expression: he seemed clumsy and brutish with his awkward limbs, but at the moment his extreme respect for her kept his boorishness within bounds and made him look childishly helpless. He scarcely dared to answer her questions, stuttered and stammered, put his hands in his pockets, took them out again, and Madame de Prie, enchanted by his embarrassment, asked him question after question—it did her good to find someone who was confused and small in her presence again, who felt that he was a supplicant, subservient to her. The abbé spoke for him, praised his passion for the noble vocation of scholarship, his other good qualities, and told her it was the boy's great wish to be able to complete his studies at the university in Paris. He himself, to be sure, was poor and could not help his nephew much, the boy also lacked the patronage that alone smoothed the path to high office, and he pressingly recommended him to her favour. He knew that she was all-powerful at court; a single word would suffice to make the young student's boldest dreams come true.

Madame de Prie smiled bitterly into the darkness: so she was supposed to be all-powerful at court, and couldn't even compel anyone to answer a single letter or grant a single request. Yet it was good to feel that no one here knew of her helplessness and her fall from grace. Even the semblance of power warmed her heart now. She controlled herself: yes, she would certainly recommend the young man, who from what so estimable an advocate as the abbé said of him must surely be worthy of every favour. She asked him to come and talk to her tomorrow so that she could assess his qualities. She would recommend him at court, she said, she would give him a letter of introduction to her friend the Queen and the members of the Academy (reminding herself, as she said so, that not one of them had sent a single line in reply to her letters).

The old abbé was quivering with delight, and tears ran down his fat cheeks. He kissed her hands, wandered around the room as if drunk, while the young fellow stood there with a dazed expression, unable to utter a word. When Madame de Prie decided to leave he did not budge, but stayed rooted to the spot, until the abbé surreptitiously indicated, with a vigorous gesture, that he should escort his benefactress back to the château. He walked beside her, stammering out thanks, and tangling his words up whenever she looked at him. It made her feel quite cheerful. For the first time she felt the old relish, mingled with slight contempt, of seeing a human being powerless before her. It revived the desire to toy with others which had become a necessity of life to her during her years of power. He stopped at the gateway of the château, bowed clumsily and strode away with his stiff, rustic gait, hardly giving her time to remind him to come and see her tomorrow.

She watched him go, smiling to herself. He was clumsy and naïve, but all the same he was alive and passionate, not dead like everything else around her. He was fire, and she was freezing. Her body was starved here too, accustomed as it was to caresses and embraces; her eyes, if they were to have any lively brilliance, must reflect the sparkling desires of the young that came her way daily in Paris. She watched for a long time as he walked away: this could be a toy, admittedly made of hard wood, rough-hewn and artless, but still a toy to help her pass the time.

Next morning the young man called. Madame de Prie, who weary as she was with inactivity and discontent did not usually rise until late in the afternoon, decided to receive the caller in her bed. First she had herself carefully adorned by her lady's maid, with a little red colour on her lips, which were getting paler and paler. Then she told the maid to admit her visitor.

The door slowly creaked open. Hesitantly and very awkwardly, the young man made his way in. He had put on his best garments, which nonetheless were the Sunday clothes of a rustic, and smelled rather too strongly of various greasy ointments. His gaze wandered searchingly from the floor to the ceiling of the darkened room, and he seemed relieved to find no one there, until an encouraging greeting came from beneath the pink cloud of the canopy over the bed. He started, for he either did not know or had forgotten that great ladies in Paris received visitors at their *levée*. He made some kind of backwards movement, as if he had stepped into deep water, and his cheeks flushed a deep red, betraying embarrassment which she enjoyed to the full and which charmed her. In honeyed tones, she invited him to come closer. It amused her to treat him with the utmost civility.

He carefully approached, as if walking a narrow plank with great depths of foaming water to right and left of him. And she held out her small, slim hand, which he cautiously took in his sturdy fingers as if he were afraid of breaking it, raising it reverently to his lips. With a friendly gesture, she invited him to sit in a comfortable armchair beside her bed, and he dropped into it as if his knees had suddenly been broken.

He felt a little safer sitting there. Now the whole room couldn't go on circling wildly around him, the floor couldn't rock like waves. However, the unusual sight still confused him, the loose silk of the covers seemed to mould the shape of her naked body, and the pink cloud of the canopy hovered like mist. He dared not look, yet he felt that he couldn't keep his eyes fixed on the floor for ever. His hands, his useless large, red hands, moved up and down the arms of the chair as if he had to hold on tight. Then they took fright at their own restlessness, and lay in his lap, frozen like heavy clods. There was a burning, almost tearful sensation in his eyes, fear tore at all his muscles, and his throat felt powerless to utter a word.

She was delighted by his awkwardness. It pleased her to let the silence drag mercilessly on, to watch, smiling, as he struggled to utter his first word, repeatedly unable to bring out anything but a stammer. She liked to see a young man as strong as an ox trembling and looking helplessly around him. Finally she took pity on him, and began asking him about his intentions, in which she contrived to pretend an uncommon amount of interest, so that he gradually plucked up his courage again. He talked about his studies, the church fathers and philosophers, and she chatted to him without knowing much about it. And when the self-important sobriety with which he put forward his opinions and expanded on them began to bore her, she amused herself by making little movements to discompose him. Sometimes she plucked at the bedspread as if it were about to slide off; at an abrupt gesture from the speaker she suddenly raised a bare arm from the crumpled silk; she wriggled her feet under the covers; and every time she did this he stopped, became confused, stumbled over his words or brought them out tumbling over each other, his face assumed an increasingly tortured and tense expression, and now and then she saw a vein run swift as a snake across his forehead. The game entertained her. She liked his boyish confusion a thousand times better than his well-turned rhetoric. And now she sought to discomfit him verbally too.

"You mustn't keep thinking so much of your studies and your sterling qualities! There are certain skills that matter more in Paris. You must learn to put yourself forward. You're an attractive man; be clever, make good use of your youth, above all, don't neglect women. Women mean everything in Paris, so our weakness must be your strength. Learn to choose your lovers and exploit them well, and you'll become a minister. Have you ever had a lover here?"

The young man started. All of a sudden his face was dark as blood. An overpowering sense of intolerable strain urged him to run to the door, but there was a heaviness in him, as if he were dazed by the fragrance of this woman's perfume, by her breath. All his muscles felt cramped, his chest was tense, he felt himself running crazily wild.

Then there was a crack. His clutching fingers had broken the arm of the chair. He jumped up in alarm, unspeakably humiliated by this mishap, but she, charmed by his elemental passion, just smiled and said, "Oh, you mustn't take fright like that when you're asked a question that you're not used to. You'll find it often happens in Paris. But you must learn a few more courtly manners, and I'll help you. I find it difficult to do without my secretary anyway; I would like it if you'd take his place here."

His eyes shining, he stammered effusive thanks and pressed her hand so hard that it hurt. She smiled, a sad smile—here it was again, the old delusion of imagining herself loved, when the reality was that one man had a position in mind, another his vanity, a third his career. All the same, it was so delightful to keep forgetting that. And here she had no one to delude but herself. Three days later he was her lover.

But the dangerous boredom had only been scared away, not mortally wounded. It dragged itself through the empty rooms again, lying in wait behind their doors. Only unwelcome news came from Paris. The King did not reply to her at all; Marie Leszczynska sent a few frosty lines inquiring after her health and carefully avoiding any hint of friendly feeling. She thought the lampoons were tasteless and offensive, besides showing too clearly who had commissioned them, which was enough to make her position at court even at worse, in so far as anyone there still remembered her. Nor was there a word in the letter she received from her friend Alincourt about any return, not even a glimmer of hope. She felt like a woman who was thought dead but wakes in her coffin underground, screaming and raving and hammering on its sides, while no one hears her up above, men and women walk lightly over the ground, and her voice chokes alone in the solitude. Madame de Prie wrote a few more letters, but with the same feeling that she was buried alive and screaming, well aware that no one would hear her, that she was hammering helplessly against the walls of her isolation. However, writing them passed the time, and here in Courbépine time was her bitterest enemy.

Her game with the young man soon bored her too. She had never shown any constancy in her affections (it was the main reason behind her fall from favour), and this young fellow's few words of love, the awkwardness that he soon forgot once she had given him good clothes, silk stockings and fine buckles for his shoes, could not keep her mind occupied. Her nature was so sated with the company of crowds that she soon wearied of a single man, and as soon as she was alone she seemed to herself repulsive and wretched. Seducing this timid peasant, schooling his clumsy caresses, making the bear dance had been a pretty game; she found possessing him was tedious, indeed positively embarrassing.

And furthermore, he no longer pleased her. She had been charmed by the adoration he had shown her, his devotion, his confusion. But he soon shed those qualities and developed a familiarity that repelled her; his once humble gaze was now full of relish and self-satisfaction. He preened in his fine clothes, and she suspected that he showed off to the village in them. A kind of hatred gradually arose in her, because he had gained all this from her unhappiness and loneliness, because he was healthy and ate with a hearty appetite, while she ate less and less out of rage and her injured feelings, and grew thin and weak. He took her for granted as his lover, oaf that he was, he lolled contentedly in the idle bed of his conquest, instead of showing his first amazement when she gave him the gift of herself, he grew apathetic and lazy, and she, bitterly envious, burning with unhappiness and ignominy, hated his repellent satisfaction, his boorish avarice and base pride. And she hated herself for sinking so low that she must reach out to such crude folk if she was not to founder in the mud of solitude.

She began to provoke and torment him. She had never really been vicious, but she felt a need to avenge herself on someone for everything, for her enemies' triumph, her exile from Paris, her unanswered letters, for Courbépine. And she had no one else to hand. She wanted to rouse him from his lethargic ease, make him feel small again, not so happy, make him cringe. She mercilessly reproached him for his red hands, his lack of sophistication, his bad manners, but he, with a man's healthy instinct, took little notice now of the woman who had once summoned him to her. He was defiant, he laughed, and indignantly shook off her sarcasm. But she did not stop: irritating someone made a nice game to relieve her boredom. She tried to make him jealous, told him on every occasion about her lovers in Paris, counted them on her fingers for him. She showed him presents she had been given, she exaggerated and told lies. But he merely felt flattered to think that, after all those dukes and princes, she had chosen him. He smacked his lips with satisfaction and was not discomposed. That enraged her even more. She told him other, worse things, she lied to him about the grooms and valets she had had. His brow darkened at last. She saw it, laughed, and went on. Suddenly he struck the table with his fist.

"That's enough! Why are you telling me all this?"

Her expression was perfectly innocent. "Because I like to."

"But I don't want to hear it."

"I do, my dear, or I wouldn't do it."

He said nothing, but bit his lip. She had so naturally commanding a tone of voice that he felt like a servant. He clenched his fists. How like an animal he is when he's angry, she thought, feeling both revulsion and fear. She sensed the danger in the atmosphere. But there was too much anger pent up in her, she couldn't stop tormenting him. She began again.

"What strange ideas you have of life, my dear. Do you think Parisians live as you do in your hovels here, where one is slowly bored to death?"

His nostrils flared; he snorted. Then he said, "People don't have to come here if they think it's so boring."

She felt the pang deep within her. So he knew about her exile too. She supposed the valet had spread the news. She felt weaker now that he knew, and smiled to veil her fear.

"My dear, there are reasons that you may not necessarily understand even if you've learned a little Latin. Perhaps you would have found it more useful to study better manners."

He said nothing, but she heard him snorting quietly with rage. That aroused her even more and she felt something like a sensual desire to hurt him.

"And there you stand proud as a cockerel on the dunghill. Why do you snort like that? You're acting like a lout!"

"We can't all be princes or dukes or grooms."

He was red in the face and had clenched his fists. She, however, poisoned by unhappiness, leaped to her feet.

"Be quiet! You forget who I am. I won't be spoken to like that by a rustic oaf!"

He made a gesture.

"Be quiet! Or else…"

"Or else?"

He impudently faced her. And it occurred to her that she had no "or else" left. She couldn't have anyone sent to the Bastille, or reduced to the ranks or dismissed, she couldn't command or forbid anyone to do or not to do something. She was nothing, only a defenceless woman like hundreds of thousands in France, vulnerable to any insult, any injustice.

"Or else," she said, fighting for breath, "I'll have you thrown out by the servants."

He shrugged his shoulders and turned. He was going to leave.

But she wouldn't let him. He was not to be the one to throw her over! Another man rejecting her—least of all must it be this one. All her anger suddenly broke out, the accumulated bitterness of days, and she went for him as if she were drunk.

"Get out! Do you think I need you, you fool of a peasant, just because I felt sorry for you? Go away! Don't soil my floors any more. Go where you like but not to Paris, and not to me. Get out! I hate you, your avarice, your simplicity, your stupid satisfaction—you disgust me. Get out!"

Then the unexpected happened. As she so suddenly flung her hatred at him, he had been holding his fists clenched in front of him like an invisible shield, but now they suddenly came down on her with the impact of falling stones. She screamed and stared at him. But he struck and struck in blind, vengeful rage, intoxicated by the awareness of his strength, he struck her, taking out on her all a peasant's envy of the distinguished and clever aristocrat, all the hatred of a man despised for a woman, he hammered it all into her weak, flinching, convulsed body. She screamed at first, then whimpered quietly and fell silent. The humiliation hurt her more than the blows. She fell silent, felt his rage, and still preserved her silence.

Then he stopped, exhausted, and horrified by what he had done. A shudder ran through her body. He thought she was about to stand up, and he fled, afraid of her glance. But it was only the weeping that she had held back suddenly tearing convulsively through her body.

And so she broke her last toy herself.

The door had closed behind him long ago, and still she did not move. She lay there like an animal hunted to death, breathing quietly but stertorously, and quite without fear, without feelings, without any sense of pain or shame. She was full of an unspeakable weariness, she felt no wish for revenge, no indignation, just weariness, an unspeakable weariness as if all her blood had flowed out of her together with her tears and only her lifeless body lay here, held down by its own weight. She did not try to stand up, she didn't know what to do with herself after such an experience.

The evening slowly entered the room, and she did not feel it. For evening comes quietly. It does not look boldly through the window like mid-day, it seeps from the walls like dark water, raises the ceiling into a void, brings everything gently floating down into its soundless torrent. When she looked up, there was darkness around her and silence, except for the sound of the little clock mincing along into infinity somewhere. The curtains fell in dark folds as if some fearful monster were hiding behind them, the doors seemed to have sunk into the wall in some way, making the room look sealed and black around her, like a nailed-up coffin. There was no way in or out any more, it was all boundless yet barred, everything seemed to weigh down, compressing the air so that she could gasp, not breathe.

At the far end of the room shone a path into the unknown: the tall mirror there gleamed faintly in the dark like the nocturnal surface of a marshy pool, and now, as she rose, something white swirled out of it. She got to her feet, went closer, it surged from the mirror like smoke, a ghostly creature: she herself, coming closer and quickly withdrawing again.

She felt dread. Something in her cried out for light, but she did not want to call anyone. She struck the tinder herself, and then one by one lit the candles in the dully glowing bronze candelabrum standing on its marble console. The flames flickered, quivering as they felt their way into the dark, like someone overheated stepping into a cool bath; they retreated, came forward again, and at last a trembling, circular cloud of light rose above the candelabrum and hovered there, casting more and more circles of light on the ceiling. High above, where delicate *amoretti* with wings of cloud usually rocked in the blue sky, grey, misty shadows now lay, with the soft lightning of the quivering candle-flames flashing fitfully through them. The objects all around seemed to have been roused from sleep; they stood there motionless, with shadows creeping high behind them as if animals had been crouching there, giving them a fearful look.

However, the mirror enticed and allured her. Something was always moving in it when she looked. Otherwise, all around her was silent and hostile, the objects were sleepy, human beings rejected her. She could ask no questions, couldn't complain to anyone, but there was something in the mirror that gave an answer, did not remain indifferent, moved and looked significantly at her. But what should she ask it? She had seldom asked if she was beautiful in Paris. The bright eyes of the men who desired her had been her mirror. She knew she was beautiful from her triumphs, her passionate nights, from the amazement of the common people when she drove to Versailles in her carriage. She had believed them even when they lied, for confidence in her own power was the secret of her strength. But now, what was she now that she had been humbled?

She looked anxiously into the flickering light in the glass, as if her fate stood in the mirror looking back at her. She started in alarm: was that really herself? Her cheeks looked hollow and dull, a bitter set to her mouth mocked her, her eyes lay deep in their sockets and looked out in fear as if searching for help. She shook herself. This was just a nightmare. And she smiled at the mirror. But the smile was returned frostily, scornfully. She felt her body: no, the mirror did not lie, she had grown thin, thin as a child, and the rings hung loose on her fingers. She felt the blood flow more coldly in her veins. She was full of dread. Was everything over, youth as well? A furious desire came over her to mock herself, celebrated as she was, the mistress of France, and as if in a dream she spoke the lines that Voltaire had written when dedicating his play to her, the lines that her flatterers liked to repeat:

Vous qui possedez la beauté
Sans être vaine et coquette
Et l'extrême vivacité
Sans être jamais indiscrète,
Vous à qui donnèrent les Dieux
Tant des lumières naturelles
Un esprit juste, gracieux,
Solide dans le sérieux
*Et charmant dans les bagatelles.**

Every word now seemed to express derision, and she stared and stared into the mirror to see if the woman there was not mocking her too.

She raised the candelabrum to get a better view of herself. And the closer she held it the more she seemed to age. Every minute she spent looking into the mirror seemed to put years on her life, she saw herself grow paler and paler, becoming more wan, sicklier, older all the time, she felt herself aging, her whole life seemed to be passing away. She trembled. She saw her fate horribly revealed in the mirror, the entire story of her decline, and she couldn't take

* Lady, yours is a beauty bright, never flirtatious, never vain; your liveliness will show no spite, and never seeks to inflict pain. Yours, all the bounty of the mind, a spirit gracious, full of love. In graver questions wise you prove, in matters light, charming and kind.

her eyes off it, but stared and stared at the white, distorted mask of the old woman who was herself.

Then, suddenly, the candles all flickered at once as if in alarm, the flames turned blue and tried to fly up from their wicks. A dark figure stood in the mirror, its hand reaching out to her.

She uttered a piercing scream, and in self-defence flung the bronze candelabrum at the mirror. A thousand sparks sprang from the glass. The candles fell to the floor and went out. There was darkness around her and in her as she collapsed unconscious. She had seen her fate.

The courier who had entered the room with news from Paris, and whose sudden appearance in the mirror-frame had so alarmed Madame de Prie, saw only the shimmering of the broken shards of glass, and heard the sound of a fall in the darkness. He ran to fetch the servants. They found Madame de Prie lying motionless on the floor among the sparkling glass splinters and the extinguished candles, her eyes closed. Only her bluish lips trembled slightly, showing a sign of life. They carried her to her bed, and a servant set out to ride to Amfreville and fetch the doctor.

But the sick woman soon came round, and with difficulty brought herself back to reality amidst the frightened faces. She did not know exactly how she had come here, but she controlled her fear and weariness in front of the others, kept her ever-ready smile on her bloodless lips, although her face had now frozen to a mask, and asked in a voice that endeavoured to be carefree, even cheerful, what had happened to her. In alarm, and evasively, the servants told her. She did not reply, but smiled and reached for the letter.

However, it was difficult for her to keep that smile on her face. Her friend wrote to say that he had succeeded in speaking to the King at last. The King was still extremely angry with her, because she had wrecked the country's finances and roused the people against her, but there was some hope of having her recalled to Paris in two or three years' time. The letter shook in her hands. Was she to live away from Paris for two years without people around her, without power? She was not strong enough to bear such solitude. It was her death sentence. She knew that she couldn't breathe without happiness, without power, without youth, without love; after ruling France, she couldn't live here like a peasant woman.

And all of a sudden she understood the figure in the mirror that had reached out for her, and the extinguishing of the flames: she must put an end to it before she grew really old, wholly ugly and wholly unhappy. She refused to see the doctor, who had now arrived; only the King could have helped her. And as he would not, she must help herself. The thought no longer hurt her. She had died long ago, on the day when the officer stood in her room and took everything from her that kept her alive: the air of Paris, the only place where she could breathe; the power that was her plaything; the admiration and triumph to which she owed her strength. The woman who roamed these empty rooms, lonely, bored, and humiliated, was no longer Madame de Prie, was an aging, unhappy, ugly creature whom she must kill so that it would not dishonour the name that had once shone brightly over France.

Now that the exiled woman had decided to put an end to it herself, her sense of frozen heaviness, her urgent disquiet had left her. She had a purpose again, an occupation, something that kept her going, excited her and intrigued her with the various possibilities it offered. For she would not die here like an animal breathing its last in a corner; she wanted an aura of the mysterious and mystical to hover around her death. She would come to a heroic, legendary end like the queens of antiquity. Her life had burned bright, and so must her death; it must arouse the somnolent admiration of the multitude once again. No one in Paris was to guess that she died here in torment, choked by loneliness and disfavour, burnt up by her unsatisfied greed for power; she would deceive them all by staging her death as a drama. Deception, the delight of her life, opened up her heart again. She would end it all in a blazing fire of merriment, as if at random, she wouldn't die squirming like a discarded wax taper coiling on the ground, trodden out in pity. She would go down into the abyss dancing.

Next day a number of notes flew away from her desk: affectionate, appealing, seductive, imperious, promising and softly perfumed lines. She scattered her invitations around Paris and the provinces, she held out the prospect of their favourite occupations to everyone, offered some hunting, others gaming, others again masked balls. She had actors, singers and dancers hired by her agents in Paris, she ordered expensive costumes, announced the founding of a second court in France, with all the refinements and pleasures of Versailles. She enticed and invited strangers and acquaintances, the distinguished and the less distinguished, but she must have people here, a great many people, an audience for the comedy of happiness and satisfaction that she was going to stage before the end came.

And soon a new life began in Courbépine. Parisian society, always craving pleasure, sought out this novelty. In addition, its members all felt a secret, slightly contemptuous curiosity to see how the former mistress of France, now toppled, took her exile. One festivity followed another. Carriages came emblazoned with noble coats of arms, large country coaches arrived crammed with high-spirited passengers, army officers came on horseback—more visitors flooded in every day, and with them an army of hangers-on and servants. Many had brought pastoral costumes with them, as if for a rustic game, others came in great pomp and ceremony. The little village was like a military camp.

And the château awoke, its once unlighted windows shining proudly, for it was enlivened by talking and laughter, games and music. People walked up and down, couples whispered in corners where only grey silence had lurked. Women's dresses glowed in bright hues in the shade of the shrubberies, the cheerfully plangent tunes of risqué songs were plucked on mandolins far into the night. Servants hurried along the corridors, the windows were framed by flowers, coloured lights sparkled among the bushes. They lived out the carefree life of Versailles, the light charm of heedlessness. The absence of the real court did take a little of the bloom off it all, but increased the exuberance that encouraged the guests to dance, free from all constraints of etiquette.

At the centre of this whirlwind of activity, Madame de Prie felt her sluggish blood begin to circulate feverishly again. She was one of those women, and they are not rare, who are shaped entirely by other people's attitudes. She was beautiful when she was desired, witty in clever company, proud when she was flattered, in love when she was loved. The more that was expected of her, the more she gave. But in solitude, where no one saw her, spoke to her, heard her or wanted anything of her, she had become ugly, dull-witted, helpless, unhappy. She could be lively only in the midst of life; in isolation she dwindled to a shadow. And now that the reflected light of her earlier life shone around her, all her merriment and her carefree charm sparkled in the air again, she was witty once more, agreeable, she wove her enchantments, made conversation, caught fire from the glances that lingered on her. She forgot that she meant to deceive these people with her cheerfulness, and was in genuine high spirits, she took every smile as a piece of good fortune, every word as true, plunged feverishly into enjoying the company she had been deprived of so long, as if falling into the arms of a lover.

She made the festivities wilder and wilder, she summoned more and more guests, enticing them to Courbépine. And more and more came. For at the time, after the failure of John Law's financial system, the land was impoverished, but she herself was rich, and she was casting the millions she had extorted during her time of power to the wind. Money was thrown down on the gaming tables, went up in smoke in expensive firework displays, was squandered on exotic fancies, but she threw it away more and more wildly, like a woman desperate. The guests were amazed, surprised by her lavish expenditure and the magnificence of the festivities; no one knew in whose honour they were really given. And in all the wild merriment, she herself almost forgot.

The festivities continued unabated for the whole month of August. September came, the trees wore colourful fruits in their hair, and the evening clouds were shot with gold. The guests were fewer now; time was pressing.

But amidst the pleasures, Madame de Prie had almost forgotten her purpose. Wishing to deceive others with such magnificent frenzies, she deceived herself; her carefree mood matched this imitation of her former life so well that she took it for real, and even believed in her power, her beauty, her *joie de vivre*.

To be sure, one thing was different, and that hurt. People were all kinder to her now that she was of no importance, they were warmer and yet cooler. The women no longer envied her, did not inflict malicious little pinpricks, the men did not flock around her. They all laughed with her, treated her as a good friend, but they told no more lies about love, they did not beg, they did not flatter, they did not make an enemy of her, and that was what made her feel that she was quite powerless. A life without envy, hatred and lies was not a life worth living. She realised, with horror, that in fact she had already been forgotten; the social whirl was as wild as ever, but she was not at its centre now. The men laughed with other women, whose freshness and youth they saw for the first time; the moment had come to remind the world of herself again before she grew old and a stranger to them all.

She put off her decision from day to day. A sensation quivered within her, half fear, half hope that something might yet hold her back, might keep her from that despairing leap into the irrevocable. Among all those pairs of hands reaching for the food on her tables, holding women close in the dance, rolling gold coins over the gaming tables, might there not be one who could hold her back, would want to hold her back, one who loved her so much that she could happily dispense with the bright show of a large company, and exchange the unstable possession of royal power for him? Without knowing it, she was looking for such a thing; she courted the passion of all the men, for she was courting her own life. But they all passed her by.

Then, one day, she met a young captain in the royal guard, a handsome, amusing fellow whom she had noticed before. They met as twilight fell over the park, and she saw him walking up and down among the trees, his eyes wild, his teeth clenched, and sometimes he struck the tree trunks with his fist. She spoke to him. He gave her a distracted answer; she saw that some secret was troubling him, and asked the reason for his desperation. At last he confessed that he had lost a hundred *louis d'or* at the gaming table, money entrusted to him by his regiment. That made him a thief, and now he must carry out sentence on himself. She felt it strangely ominous that here, amidst this happy tumult, someone else had come to the same dark conclusion too. But this man was young, had rosy cheeks, could laugh again; there was still help for him. She summoned him to her room and gave him five hundred *louis d'or*. Trembling with joy, he kissed her hands. She kept him there a long time, but that was all he wanted from her, he asked no more with any glance or gesture. She was shaken; she couldn't even buy love now. That fortified her in her decision.

She sent him away, and stepped quickly out into the hall. Laughter met her as she opened the door, happy voices and lively people filled the room like a cloud. Suddenly she felt that she hated them all, cheerful as they were, dancing and laughing on her grave. Envy took hold of her when she thought that they would all live on, and be happy.

She was burning with a malicious desire to disturb her guests, alarm and confuse them, stop their laughter. And suddenly, when their exuberance died down for a second and silence fell, she said directly, "Don't you notice that there's a death in the house?"

For a moment confusion reigned. Even to a drunk, the word "death" is like a hammer falling on his heart. Baffled, they asked each other who was dead. "I am," Madame de Prie said coldly, without any change of expression, "I shall not see this winter come."

She spoke so gravely, in so sombre a tone, that they all looked at one another in silence. But only for a second. Then a jest flew from somewhere in the room like a coloured ball, someone else threw it back, and as if enlivened by the curious notion of death the wave of exuberance surged foaming and high again, and buried the discomfort of that initial surprise.

Madame de Prie remained very calm. She felt that there was no going back now. But it amused her to stage her prophecy even more dramatically. She went up to one of the round tables where her guests were playing faro, and waited for the next card to be turned over. It was a seven of one of the black suits, clubs or spades. "The seventh of October, then." Without meaning to, she had said it out loud under her breath.

"What's the seventh of October?" one of the onlookers asked casually.

She looked at him calmly. "The day of my death."

They all laughed. The joke was passed on. Madame de Prie was delighted to find that no one believed her. If they didn't trust her in life any more, then at least they should see how she and her comedy had fooled them in death. A wonderful sense of superiority, pleasure and ease ran through her limbs. She felt as if she must rejoice aloud in high spirits and derision.

In the next room music was playing. A dance had just begun. She joined the dancers, and had never danced better.

From that moment on, her life had meaning again. She knew she was preparing to do something that would certainly make her immortal. She imagined the King's amazement, the horror of her guests when her prophecy of her death came true to the very day. And she was staging the comedy most carefully; she invited more and more guests, doubled her expenditure, worked on the multifarious magnificence of these last days as if it were a work of art, something that would make her sudden fall even more keenly felt. She aired the prediction of her death again at every opportunity, but always drew a glittering curtain of merriment over it; she wanted everyone to know that it had been announced, and no one to believe it. Only death would raise her name once again to the ranks of those who could never be forgotten, from which the King had cast her down.

Two days before she was to carry out her irrevocable purpose, she gave the last and most magnificent festivities of all. Since the Persian and other Islamic embassies had set up for the first time in Paris, all things Oriental had been the fashion in France: books were written in Eastern guise, the fairy tales and legends of the Orient were translated, Arab costume was popular, and people imitated the flowery style of Eastern language. At enormous expense, Madame de Prie had turned the whole château into an Oriental palace. Costly rugs lay on the floor, squawking parrots and white-feathered cockatoos rocked on their perches on the window bars, held there by silver chains; servants hurried soundlessly down the corridors in turbans and baggy silk trousers, taking Turkish sweetmeats and other refreshments entirely unknown at the time to the guests, who were dazzled by such daring splendour. Coloured tents were erected in the garden, boys cooled them by waving broad fans, music rang out from the dark shadows of the shrubberies, everything possible was done to make the evening an unforgettable fairy-tale experience, and the silvery half-moon hanging in the starry sky that night encouraged the imagination to conjure up the mysteriously sultry atmosphere of a night by the Bosphorus.

But the real surprise was a particularly spacious tent, containing a stage hung with red velvet curtains. Wishing to appear to her guests in the full radiance of her fame and beauty, Madame de Prie had decided to act a play herself; a final display of all the merriment and levity of her life to an audience was to be her last and finest deception. In the few days she still had left, she had commissioned a young author to write a play to her exact requirements. Time was short and his alexandrines bad, but that was not what mattered to her. The tragedy was set in the Orient, and she herself was to play the part of Zengane, a young queen whose realm is captured by enemies and who goes proudly to her death, although the magnanimous victor offers to share all his royal power with her if she will be his wife. She had insisted on these details: she wanted to give a dress rehearsal of her voluntary death in front of the unsuspecting audience before she put the plan into practice.

And in addition she wanted to experience the past once more, if only in game, she wanted to be queen again, and show that she was born to it and must die once she was deprived of power.

Her aim was to be beautiful and royal in the eyes of others on that last evening; she would adorn her past image with an invisible crown, ensuring that her name aroused that pure shiver of veneration which attends all that is sublime. Cosmetics veiled the pallor of her sunken cheeks, her thin figure was concealed by the flowing Oriental robes she wore, the confusing brightness of the jewels gleaming on her hair, like dew on a dark flower in the morning moisture, outshone her tired eyes. And when she appeared like this in the brightness behind the curtain as it swept back, a brightness further intensified by her passion, when she appeared on stage surrounded by kneeling servants and the awe-stricken populace, a rustle passed through the ranks of her guests. Her heart was thudding: for the first time in these bitter weeks she felt the delightful wave of admiration that had borne her life up for so long surging towards her, and a wonderful feeling arose in her, a sweet sadness mingled with melancholy pleasure, a regret that kept receding, flowing back into a great sense of happiness. Before her, the surf of the wave flickered, she did not see individuals any more, only a great crowd, perhaps her guests, perhaps all France, perhaps generations yet to come, perhaps eternity. And she felt only, and blissfully, one thing: she was standing on a great height again, envied, admired, the cynosure of all those curious and nameless eyes, and at last, after such a long time, she felt aware of living again, of being really alive. Death was not too high a price to pay for this second of life.

She played her part magnificently, although she had never tried acting before. She had shed everything that prevents most people from making a show of emotion to others—fear, timidity, shame, awkwardness—she had shed all that, and was now playing only with objects. She wanted to be queen, and she was queen again for the length of an hour. Only once did her breath fail her, when she spoke the line, "*Je vais mourir, oh ne me plaignez pas!*"*, for she felt that she was expressing her deep wish for life, and was afraid they might not be deceived, might understand her, warn her, hold her back. But in fact the pause after that cry seemed in itself to be acted with such irresistible credibility that a shudder ran through the audience. And when, with a wild gesture, she turned the dagger against her heart, fell, and seemed to die smiling, when the play was over—although only now did it really begin—they stormed to applaud her, paying her tribute with an enthusiasm that she had not known even in the days of her greatest power.

However, she had only a smile for all the uproar, and when she was complimented on her magnificent performance of the death of Zengane, she said calmly, "I suppose that, today, I should know how to die. Death dwells in me already. It will all be over the day after tomorrow."

They laughed again, but it no longer hurt her. There was blessed, painless merriment inside her, and such a childishly exuberant joy at having deceived all these enthusiastic people that she instinctively joined in the peals of laughter. Once she had played only with men and power; now she saw that there was no better toy than death.

Next day, the last full day of her life, the guests went away; she meant to receive death alone. The coaches churned up white dust like clouds in the distance, the horsemen trotted away, the halls were emptied of light and laughter, a restless wind howled down the chimney. She felt as if the blood were slowly flowing out of her

* Now I shall die, oh do not mourn for me!

veins with the departing guests, she felt herself becoming colder and colder, weaker, more defenceless, more fearful. Death had seemed to her so easy yesterday, just a game; now that she was alone again, it suddenly showed her its horror and its power once more.

And everything that she thought she had tamed and trodden underfoot awoke again. The last evening came, and once more the snake-like shadows that, alarmed by the light, had hidden behind objects came crawling out of hiding with flickering tongues. Dread, stifled by laughter and veiled by the bright images of human company, gradually returned all-powerful to the deserted rooms. The silence had only been cowering under the surging sound of voices; now it spread abroad again like mist, filled the rooms, the halls, the stairways, the corridors, and her shuddering heart as well.

She would have liked to make an end of it at once. But she had chosen the seventh of October, and must not destroy the deception, that artificial, glimmering, lying construct of her triumph, just for the sake of a whim. She must wait. It was worse than being dead, though, to wait for the hour of death while the wind outside mocked her, and dark shadows in here reached for her heart. How could she bear this long last night before death, this endless time until dawn? Dark objects, spectre-like, pressed closer and closer, all the shades of her past life rose from their burial vaults—she fled before them from room to room, but they stared at her from the pictures, grinned behind the windows, crouched down behind cupboards. The dead reached out to her, though she was still alive and wanted human company, company just for one night. She longed for a human being as if for a coat in which to wrap her shivering form until day dawned.

Suddenly she rang the bell, which screeched shrilly like a wounded animal. A servant, drowsy with sleep, came upstairs to her. She told him to go at once to the priest's nephew, wake him and bring him here. She had important news for him.

The servant stared as if she were mad. But she did not feel it, she felt nothing at all, every emotion had died in her. She was not ashamed to summon the man who had beaten her, she did not hesitate to summon a man to her bedroom at night in front of the servant. There was only a cold void in her, she felt that her poor shivering body needed warmth if it were not to freeze. Her soul was dead already; she had only to kill her body now.

After a while the door opened. Her former lover came in. His face was chilly and contemptuous, he seemed unspeakably strange to her. And yet the horror shrank back slightly under the objects in the room, just because he opened the door and she was no longer entirely alone with them.

He took pains to seem very decided and not betray his inner astonishment, since this summons was entirely unexpected. For days, while the festivities were in full swing in the château, he had slunk around the barred gateways of the park, his eyes narrowed with rage; he had eaten his heart out with self-reproaches, for he, as her lover, should have been able to stride through the midst of this brilliance. He was consumed with anger for having so humiliated her; those extravagant festivities had suddenly made the power of the wealth that he had failed to exploit very clear to him again. And moreover, his hours with Madame de Prie had made him desire these fine, fragrant, spoilt ladies with their delicate, fragile limbs, their strangely provocative lusts, their rustling silken dresses. He had taken himself back to the priest's poverty-stricken house, where everything suddenly seemed to him crude, dirty and worn. His greed, once roused, made him look avidly at all the ladies who came from Paris, but none of them looked back at him, their coaches scornfully splashed him with the mud their wheels threw up, and the great lords didn't even see him when he humbly raised his hat to them. A hundred times he had felt impelled to go into the château and fling himself at Madame de Prie's feet, and every time fear had held him back.

But now she had summoned him, and that made him arrogant. Inwardly, he straightened his back: it was the proudest moment of his life to think that she needed him again after all.

For a moment they looked at one another, barely able to hide the hatred in their eyes. At that moment, each despised the other because each intended to misuse the other. Madame de Prie controlled herself. Her voice was very cool.

"The Duke of Berlington asked me yesterday if I could recommend him a secretary. If you would like the post, I'll send you to Paris tomorrow with a letter for him."

The young man trembled. He had already assumed a haughty bearing, intending to be condescending and gracious if she was seeking his favours. But all that was gone now. Greed overcame him. Paris gleamed before his eyes.

"If madame were to be so kind—I—I can't think of anything that would make me happier," he stammered. His eyes had the pleading expression of a beaten dog in them.

She nodded. Then she looked at him, commandingly yet milder again. He understood. Everything would be the way it had once been…

And not for a second of that passionate night did she forget that she hated him, despised him, and was deceiving him—for there was no Duke of Berlington —she knew how contemptible she herself was, driven to buy a man's caresses with a lie, yet it was life, real life that she felt in his limbs, drank from his lips, not the darkness and silence already coming to hold her fast. She felt the warmth of his youth driving death away, and knew at every moment that she was trying to deceive death itself, the death that was coming closer and closer, and of whose power she now, for the first time, had some inkling.

The morning of the seventh of October was clear. Sunlight shimmered above the fields, even the shadows were translucent and pure. Madame de Prie dressed carefully, as if for a great feast, put her affairs in order, burned letters. She locked her jewellery, which was very valuable, in an ebony casket, tore up all her promissory notes and contracts. Now that it was day again, everything in her was clear and determined once more, and she wanted clarity above all else.

Her lover came in. She spoke to him kindly and without resentment; it pained her to think that she was so pitilessly deceiving the last man who had meant anything to her, even if he had not meant much. She did not want anyone to speak of her with resentment, only with admiration and gratitude. And she felt an urge to lavish the jewellery from the casket on him, in return for that one last night. It was a fortune.

But he was half-asleep and inattentive. In his boorish greed for gain, he thought of nothing but his position, his future. The memory of their passionate caresses made him yet bolder. Abruptly, he said he must set off for Paris at once, or he might arrive too late, and he demanded rather than requested the letter of recommendation. Something froze inside her. She had hired him, and now he was asking for payment.

She wrote the letter, a letter to a man who did not exist and whom he could never find. But she still hesitated to give it to him. Once more she put off her decision. She asked if he couldn't stay one day longer; she would like that very much, she said. And as she spoke she balanced the casket in her hand. She felt that if he said yes it might yet save her. But all their decisions led the same way. He was in a hurry. He didn't want to stay. If he had not said it in such a surly manner, making her feel so clearly that he had let himself be bought only for one night, she would have given him the jewellery, which was worth hundreds of thousands of livres. But he was brusque, his glance impudent and with no love in it. So she took a single, very small jewel with only a dull glow to it—dull as his eyes—and gave it to him in return for taking the casket, of whose contents he had no idea, to the Ursuline convent in Paris. She added a letter asking the nuns to say Masses for her soul. Then she sent the impatient young man off to find the Duke of Berlington.

He thanked her, not effusively, and left, unaware of the value of the casket that he himself was carrying. And so, after acting out a comedy of her feelings in front of them all, she deceived even the last man to cross her path.

Then she closed the door and quickly took a small flask from a drawer. It was made of fine Chinese porcelain, with strange, monstrous dragons coiling and curling in blue on it. She looked at it with curiosity, toyed with it as carelessly as she had toyed with her fellow men and women, with princes, with France, with love and death. She unscrewed the stopper and poured the clear liquid into a small dish. For a moment she hesitated, really just from a childish fear that it might have a bitter flavour. Cautiously, like a kitten sniffing warm milk, she touched it with her tongue; no, it didn't taste bad. And so she drank the contents of the dish down in a single draught.

The whole thing, at that moment, seemed to her somehow amusing and extremely ludicrous: to think that you had only to take that one tiny sip, and tomorrow you wouldn't see the clouds, the fields, the woods any more, messengers would go riding, the King would be horrified and all of France amazed. So this was the great step that she had feared taking so much. She thought of the astonishment of her guests, of the legends that would be told of the way she had foretold the day of her death, and failed to understand only one thing: that she had given herself to death because she missed the company of humans, those same gullible humans who could be deceived with such a little comedy. Dying seemed to her altogether easy, you could even smile as you died—yes, you could indeed, she tried it—you could perfectly well smile, and it wasn't difficult to preserve a beautiful and tranquil face in death, a face radiant with unearthly bliss. It was true, even after death you could act happiness. She hadn't known that. She found everything, human beings, the world, death and life, suddenly so very amusing that the smile she had prepared sprang involuntarily to her carefree lips. She straightened up, as if there were a mirror opposite her somewhere, waited for death, and smiled and smiled and smiled.

*

But death was not to be deceived, and broke her laughter. When Madame de Prie was found her face was distorted into a terrible grimace. Those dreadful features showed everything that she had really suffered in the last few weeks: her rage, her torment, her aimless fear, her wild and desperate pain. The deceptive smile for which she had struggled so avidly had been helpless, had drained away. Her feet were twisted together in torment, her hands had clutched a curtain so convulsively that scraps of it were left between her fingers, her mouth was open as if in a shrill scream.

And all that show of apparent merriment, the mystic prophecy of the day of her death had been for nothing too. The news of her suicide arrived in Paris on the evening when an Italian conjuror was displaying his arts at court. He made rabbits disappear into a hat, he brought grown geese out of eggshells. When the message arrived people were slightly interested, were surprised, whispered, the name of Madame de Prie went around for a few minutes, but then the conjuror performed another amazing trick and she was forgotten, just as she herself would have forgotten someone else's fate at such a moment. Interest in her strange end did not last long in France, and her desperate efforts to stage a drama that would never be forgotten were in vain. The fame she longed for, the immortality she thought to seize by force with her death, passed her name by: her story was buried under the dust and ashes of trivial events. For the history of the world will not tolerate intruders; it chooses its own heroes and implacably dismisses those not summoned to that rank, however hard they may try; someone who has fallen off the carriage of fate as it goes along will never catch up with it again. And nothing was left of the strange end of Madame de Prie, her real life and the ingeniously devised deception of her death but a few dry lines in some book of memoirs or other, conveying to their reader as little of the passionate emotions of her life as a pressed flower allows one to guess at the fragrant marvel of its long-forgotten spring.

A STORY TOLD IN TWILIGHT

HAS RAIN BEEN SWEEPING over the city again in the wind? Is that what suddenly makes it so dim in our room? No. The air is silvery clear and still, as it seldom is on these summer days, but it is getting late, and we didn't notice. Only the dormer windows opposite still smile with a faint glow, and the sky above the roof ridge is veiled by golden mist. In an hour's time it will be night. That will be a wonderful hour, for there is no lovelier sight than the slow fading of sunset colour into shadow, to be followed by darkness rising from the ground below, until finally its black tide engulfs the walls, carrying us away into its obscurity. If we sit opposite one another, looking at each other without a word, it will seem, at that hour, as if our familiar faces in the shadows were older and stranger and farther away, as if we had never known them like that, and each of us was now seeing the other across a wide space and over many years. But you say you don't want silence now, because in silence one hears, apprehensively, the clock breaking time into a hundred tiny splinters, and our breathing will sound as loud as the breathing of a sick man. You want me to tell you a story. Willingly. But not about me, for our life in these big cities is short of experience, or so it seems to us, because we do not yet know what is really our own in them. However, I will tell you a story fit for this hour that really loves only silence, and I would wish it to have something about it of the warm, soft, flowing twilight now hovering mistily outside our windows.

I don't remember just how I came to know this story. All I do know is that I was sitting here for a long time early this afternoon, reading a book, then putting it down again, drowsing in my dreams, perhaps sleeping lightly. And suddenly I saw figures stealing past the walls, and I could hear what they were saying and look into their lives. But when I wanted to watch them moving away, I found myself awake again and on my own. The book lay at my feet. When I picked it up to look for those characters in it, I couldn't find the story any more; it was as if it had fallen out of the pages into my hands, or as if it had never been there at all. Perhaps I had dreamt it, or seen it in one of those bright clouds that came to our city today from distant lands, to carry away the rain that has been depressing us for so long. Did I hear it in the artless old song that an organ-grinder was playing with a melancholy creaking sound under my window, or had someone told it to me years ago? I don't know. Such stories often come into my mind, and I let them take their playful course, running through my fingers, which I allow to drop them as you might caress ears of wheat and long-stemmed flowers in passing without picking them. All I do is dream them, beginning with a sudden brightly coloured image and moving towards a gentler end, but I do not hold and keep them. However, you want me to tell you a story today, so I will tell it to you now, when twilight fills us with a longing to see some bright, lively thing before our eyes, starved as they are in this grey light.

How shall I begin? I feel I must pluck a moment out of the darkness, an image and a character, because that is how those strange dreams of mine begin. Yes, now I remember. I see a slender youth walking down a broad flight of steps leading out of a castle. It is night, and a night of dim moonlight, but I see the whole outline of his supple body, and his features stand out clearly. He is remarkably good-looking. His black hair falls smoothly over his high—almost too high—forehead, combed in a childish style, and his hands, reaching out before him in the dark to feel the warmth of the air after a sunlit day, are delicate and finely formed. His footsteps are hesitant. Dreamily, he climbs down to the large garden, where the rounded treetops rustle; the white path of a single broad avenue leads through it.

I don't know when all this is set, whether yesterday or fifty years ago, and I don't know where; but I think it must be in England or Scotland, the only places where I am sure there are such tall, massive stone castles. From a distance they look menacing, like fortresses, and reveal their bright gardens full of flowers only to an eye familiar with them. Yes, now I know for certain: it is to the north, in Scotland. Only there are the summer nights so light that the sky has a milky, opalescent glow, and the fields are never entirely dark, so that everything seems full of a soft radiance, and only the shadows drop, like huge black birds, down to pale expanses of countryside. Yes, it's in Scotland, I remember that now for certain; and if I racked my brain I would also find the names of this baronial castle and the boy, because now the darkness around my dream is beginning to peel away, and I feel it all as distinctly as if it were not memory but experience. The boy has come to spend the summer with his married sister, and in the hospitable way of distinguished British families he finds that he is not alone; in the evening there is a whole party of gentlemen who have come for the field sports of shooting and fishing, and their wives, with a few young girls, tall, handsome people, who in their cheerfulness and youth play laughing, but not noisily, to the sound of the echo from the ancient walls. By day they ride horses, there are dogs about, two or three boats glitter on the river, and liveliness without frantic activity helps the day to pass quickly and pleasantly.

But it is evening now, the company around the dinner table has broken up. The gentlemen are sitting in the great hall, smoking and playing cards; until midnight, white light, quivering at the edges, spills out of the bright windows into the park, sometimes accompanied by a full-throated, jocular roar of laughter. Most of the ladies have already gone to their rooms, although a few of them may still be talking to each other in the entrance hall of the castle. So the boy is on his own in the evening. He is not allowed to join the gentlemen yet, or only briefly, and he feels shy in the presence of ladies because when he opens a door they suddenly lower their voices, and he senses that they are discussing matters he isn't meant to hear. And he doesn't like their company anyway, because they ask him questions as if he were still a child, and only half-listen to his answers; they make use of him to do them all sorts of small favours, and then thank him in the tone they would use with a good little boy. He thought he would go to bed, but his room was too hot, full of still, sultry air. They had forgotten to close the windows during the day, so the sun had made itself at home in here, almost setting light to the table, leaving the bedstead hot to the touch, clinging heavily to the walls, and its warm breath still comes out of the corners and from behind curtains. And moreover it was still so early—and outside, the summer night shone like a white candle, peaceful, with no wind, as motionless as if it longed for nothing. So the boy goes down the tall castle steps again and towards the garden, which is rimmed by the dark sky like a saint's halo. Here the rich fragrance given off by many invisible flowers comes enticingly to meet him. He feels strange. In all the confused sensations of his fifteen years of life, he couldn't have said exactly why, but his lips are quivering as if he has to say something in the night air, or must raise his hands and close his eyes for a long time. He seems to have some mysterious familiarity with this summer night, now at rest, something that calls for words or a gesture of greeting.

Then, all of a sudden, as he goes deeper into the darkness, an extraordinary thing happens. The gravel behind him crunches slightly, and as he turns, startled, all he sees is a tall white form, bright and fluttering, coming towards him, and in astonishment he feels strong and yet caught, without any violence, in a woman's embrace. A soft, warm body presses close to his, a trembling hand quickly caresses his hair and bends his head back; reeling, he feels a stranger's open mouth like a fruit against his own, quivering lips fastening on his. The face is so close to him that he cannot see its features. And he dares not look, because shudders are running through his body like pain, so that he has to close his eyes and give himself up to those burning lips without any will of his own; he is their prey. Hesitantly, uncertainly, as if asking a question, his arms now go round the stranger's body, and, suddenly intoxicated, he holds it close to his own. Avidly, his hands move over its soft outline, fall still and then tremble as they move on again more and more feverishly, carried away. And now the whole weight of her body, pressing ever more urgently against him, bending forward, a delightful burden, rests on his own yielding breast. He feels as if he were sinking and flowing away under her fast-breathing urgency, and is already weak at the knees. He thinks of nothing, he does not wonder how this woman came to him, or what her name is, he merely drinks in the desire of those strange, moist lips with his eyes closed, until he is intoxicated by them, drifting away with no will or mind of his own on a vast tide of passion. He feels as if stars had suddenly fallen to earth, there is such a shimmering before his eyes, everything flickers in the air like sparks, burning whatever he touches. He does not know how long all this lasts, whether he has been held in this soft chain for hours or seconds; in this wild, sensual struggle he feels that everything is blazing up and drifting away, he is staggering in a wonderful kind of vertigo.

Then suddenly, with an abrupt movement, the chain of heat holding them breaks. Brusquely, almost angrily, the woman loosens the embrace that held him so close; she stands erect, and already a shaft of white light is running past the trees, clear and fast, and has gone before he can raise his hands to seize it and stop her.

Who was she? And how long had it lasted? Dazed, with a sense of oppressive uneasiness, he stands up, propping himself against a tree. Slowly, cool thought returns to the space between his fevered temples: his life suddenly seems to him to have moved forward a thousand hours. Could his confused dreams of women and passion suddenly have come true? Or was it only a dream? He feels himself, touches his hair. Yes, it is damp at his hammering temples, damp and cool from the dew on the grass into which they had fallen. Now it all flashes before his mind's eye again, he feels those burning lips once more, breathes in the strange, exciting, sensual perfume clinging to her dress, tries to remember every word she spoke—but none of them come back to him.

And now, with a sudden shock of alarm, he remembers that in fact she said nothing at all, not even his name; that he heard only her sighs spilling over and her convulsively restrained sobs of desire threatening to break out, that he knows the fragrance of her tousled hair, the hot pressure of her breasts, the smooth enamel of her skin, he knows that her figure, her breath, all her quivering feelings were his—and yet he has no idea of the identity of this woman who has overwhelmed him with her love in the dark. He knows that he must now try to find a name to give to his happy astonishment.

And then the extraordinary experience that he has just shared with a woman seems to him a poor thing, very petty compared to the sparkling mystery staring at him out of the dark with alluring eyes. Who was she? He swiftly reviews all the possible candidates, assembling in his mind's eye the images of all the women staying here at the castle; he recalls every strange hour, excavates from his memory every conversation he has had with them, every smile of the only five or six women who could be part of this puzzle. Young Countess E., perhaps, who so often quarrelled violently with her ageing husband, or his uncle's young wife, who had such curiously gentle yet iridescent eyes, or—and he was startled by this idea—one of the three sisters, his cousins, who are so like each other in their proud, haughty, abrupt manner. No—these were all cool, circumspect people. In recent years he had often felt sick, or an outcast, when secret stirrings in him began disturbing and flickering in his dreams. He had envied all who were, or seemed to be, so calm, so well-balanced and lacking in desires, had been afraid of his awakening passion as if it were an infirmity. And now?… But who, which of them all could be so deceptive?

Slowly, that insistent question drives the frenzy out of his blood. It is late now, the lights in the hall where guests were playing cards are out, he is the only guest in the castle still awake, he—and perhaps also that unknown woman. Slowly, weariness comes over him. Why go on thinking about it? A glance, a spark glimpsed between someone's eyelids, the secret pressure of his hand must surely tell him everything tomorrow. Dreamily, he climbs the steps, as dreamily as he climbed down them, but he feels so very different now. His blood is still slightly agitated, but the warm room seems to him clearer and cooler than it was.

When he wakes next morning, the horses down outside the castle are already stamping and scraping their hooves on the ground; he hears voices, laughter, and his name is called now and then. He quickly leaps out of bed—he has missed breakfast—dresses at high speed and runs downstairs, where the rest of the party cheerfully wish him a good morning. "What a late riser you are!" laughs Countess E., and there is laughter in her clear eyes as well. His avid look falls on her face; no, it couldn't be the Countess, her laughter is too carefree. "I hope you had sweet dreams," the young woman teases him, but her delicate build seems to him too slight for his companion last night. With a question in his eyes, he looks from face to face, but sees no smiling reflection answering it on any of them.

They ride out into the country. He assesses each voice, his eyes dwell on every line and undulation of the women's bodies as they move on horseback, he observes the way they bend, the way they raise their arms. At the luncheon table he leans close to them in conversation, to catch the scent of their lips or the sultry warmth of their hair, but nothing, nothing gives him any sign, not a fleeting trail for his heated thoughts to pursue. The day draws out endlessly towards evening. If he tries to read a book, the lines run over the edge of the pages and suddenly lead out into the garden, and it is night again, that strange night, and he feels the unknown woman's arms embracing him once more. Then he drops the book from his trembling hands and decides to go down to the little pool. But suddenly, surprised by himself, he finds that he is standing on that very spot again. He feels feverish at dinner that evening, his hands are distracted, moving restlessly back and forth as if pursued, his eyes retreat shyly under their lids. Not until the others—at last, at last!—push back their chairs is he happy, and soon he is running out of his room and into the park, up and down the white path that seems to shimmer like milky mist beneath his feet, going up and down it, up and down hundreds, thousands of times. Are the lights on in the great hall yet? Yes, they come on at last, and at last there is light in a few of the first-floor windows. The ladies have gone upstairs. Now, if she is going to come, it can be only a matter of minutes; but every minute stretches to breaking point, fuming with impatience. Up and down the path, up and down, he is moving convulsively back and forth as if worked by invisible wires.

And then, suddenly, the white figure comes hurrying down the steps, fast, much too fast for him to recognize her. She seems to be made of glinting moonlight, or a lost, drifting wisp of mist among the trees, chased this way by the wind and now, now in his arms. They close firmly as a claw around that wild body, heated and throbbing from her fast running. It is the same as yesterday, a single moment with this warm wave beating against his breast, and he thinks he will faint with the sweet throbbing of her heart and flow away in a stream of dark desire. But then the frenzy abruptly dies down, and he holds back his fiery feelings. He must not lose himself in that wonderful pleasure, give himself up to those lips fixed on his, before he knows what name to give this body pressed so close that it is as if her heart were beating loudly in his own chest! He bends his head back from her kiss to see her face, but shadows are falling, mingling with her hair; the twilight makes it look dark. The tangled trees grow too close together, and the light of the moon, veiled in cloud, is not strong enough for him to make out her features. He sees only her eyes shining, glowing stones sprinkled deep down somewhere, set in faintly gleaming marble.

Now he wants to hear a word, just one splinter of her voice breaking away. "Who are you?" he demands. "Tell me who you are!" But that soft, moist mouth offers only kisses, no words. He tries to force a word out of her, a cry of pain, he squeezes her arm, digs his nails into its flesh; but he is aware only of his own gasping, heated breath, and of the sultry heat of her obstinately silent lips that only moan a little now and then—whether in pain or pleasure he does not know. And it sends him nearly mad to realize that he has no power over this defiant will, that this woman coming out of the dark takes him without giving herself away to him, that he has unbounded power over her body and its desires, yet cannot command her name. Anger rises in him and he fends off her embrace; but she, feeling his arms slacken and aware of his uneasiness, caresses his hair soothingly, enticingly with her excited hand. And then, as her fingers move, he feels something make a slight ringing sound against his forehead, something metal, a medallion or coin that hangs loose from her bracelet. An idea suddenly occurs to him. As if in the transports of passion, he presses her hand to him, and in so doing embeds the coin deep in his half-bared arm until he feels its surface digging into his skin. He is sure of having a sign to follow now, and with it burning against him he willingly gives himself up to the passion he has held back. Now he presses deep into her body, sucks the desire from her lips, falling into the mysteriously pleasurable ardour of a wordless embrace.

And then, when she suddenly jumps up and takes flight, just as she did yesterday, he does not try to hold her back, for he is already feverish with curiosity to see the sign. He runs to his room, turns up the dim lamplight until it is bright, and bends avidly over the mark left by the coin in his arm.

It is no longer entirely clear, the full outline is indistinct; but one corner is still engraved red and sharp on his flesh, unmistakably precise. There are angular corners; the coin must have eight sides, medium-sized like a penny but with more of a raised surface, because the impression here is still deep, corresponding to the height of the surface. The mark burns like fire as he examines it so greedily; it suddenly hurts him, like a wound, and only now that he dips his hand in cold water does the painful burning go away. So the medallion is octagonal; he feels certain of that now. Triumph sparkles in his eyes. Tomorrow he will know everything.

Next morning he is one of the first down at the breakfast table. The only ladies present are an elderly old maid, his sister and Countess E.

They are all in a cheerful mood, and their lively conversation passes him by. He has all the more opportunity for his observations. His glance swiftly falls on the Countess's slim wrist; she is not wearing a bracelet. He can speak to her without agitation now, but his eyes keep going nervously to the door. Then his cousins, the three sisters, come in together. Uneasiness stirs in him again. He catches a glimpse of the jewellery they wear pushed up under their sleeves, but they sit down too quickly for a good view: Kitty with her chestnut-brown hair opposite him; blonde Margot; and Elisabeth, whose hair is so fair that it shines like silver in the dark and flows golden in the sun. All three, as usual, are cool, quiet and reserved, stiff with the dignity he dislikes so much about them; after all, they are not much older than he is, and were his playmates for years. His uncle's young wife has not come down yet. The boy's heart is more and more restless now that he feels the moment of revelation is so close, and suddenly he decides that he almost likes the mysterious torment of secrecy. However, his eyes are full of curiosity; they move around the edge of the table, where the women's hands lie at rest on the white cloth or wander slowly like ships in a bright bay. He sees only their hands, and they suddenly seem to him like creatures with a life and soul of their own, characters on a stage. Why is the blood throbbing at his temples like that? All three cousins, he sees in alarm, are wearing bracelets, and the idea that it could be one of these three proud and outwardly immaculate young women, whom he has never known, even in childhood, as anything but unapproachable and reserved, confuses him. Which of them could it be? Kitty, whom he knows least because she is the eldest, Margot with her abrupt manner, or little Elisabeth? He dares not wish it to be any of them. Secretly, he wants it to be none of them, or he wants not to know. But now his desire carries him away.

"Could I ask you to pour me another cup of tea, please, Kitty?" His voice sounds as if he has sand in his throat. He passes her his cup; now she must raise her arm and reach over the table to him. Now—he sees a medallion dangling from her bracelet and for a moment his hand stops dead, but no, it is a green stone in a round setting that clinks softly against the porcelain. His glance gratefully rests on Kitty's brown hair.

It takes him a moment to get his breath back.

"May I trouble you for a lump of sugar, Margot?" A slender hand comes to life on the table, stretches, picks up a silver bowl and passes it over. And there—his hand shakes slightly—he sees, where the wrist disappears into her sleeve, an old silver coin dangling from a flexible bracelet. The coin has eight sides, is the size of a penny and is obviously a family heirloom of some kind. But octagonal, with the sharp corners that dug into his flesh yesterday. His hand is no steadier, and he misses his aim with the sugar tongs at first; only then does he drop a lump of sugar into his tea, which he forgets to drink.

Margot! The name is burning on his lips in a cry of the utmost surprise, but he clenches his teeth and bites it back. He hears her speaking now—and her voice sounds to him as strange as if someone were speaking from a stand at a show—cool, composed, slightly humorous, and her breath is so calm that he almost takes fright at the thought of the terrible lie she is living. Is this really the same woman whose unsteady breath he soothed yesterday, from whose moist lips he drank kisses, who falls on him by night like a beast of prey? Again and again he stares at those lips. Yes, the pride, the reserve, could be taking refuge there and nowhere else, but what is there to show the fire within her?

He looks harder at her face, as if seeing it for the first time. And for the first time he really feels, rejoicing, trembling with happiness and almost near tears, how beautiful she is in her pride, how enticing in her secrecy. His gaze traces, with delight, the curving line of her eyebrows suddenly rising to a sharp angle, looks deep into the cool, gemstone hue of her grey-green eyes, kisses the pale, slightly translucent skin of her cheeks, imagines her lips, now sharply tensed, curving more softly for a kiss, wanders around her pale hair, and, quickly moving down again, takes in her whole figure with delight.

He has never known her until this moment. Now he rises from the table and finds that his knees are trembling. He is drunk with looking at her as if on strong wine.

Then his sister calls down below. The horses are ready for the morning ride, prancing nervously, impatiently champing at the bit. One guest after another mounts, and then they ride in a bright cavalcade down the broad avenue through the garden. First at a slow trot, with a sedate harmony that is out of tune with the racing rhythm of the boy's blood. But then, beyond the gate, they give the horses their heads, storming down the road and into the meadows to left and right, where a slight morning mist still lingers. There must have been a heavy fall of dew overnight, for under the veil of mist, trembling dewdrops glitter like sparks, and the air is deliciously cool, as if chilled by a waterfall somewhere near. The close-packed group soon strings out, the chain breaks into colourful separate links and a few riders have already disappeared into the woods among the hills.

Margot is one of the riders in the lead. She loves the wild exhilaration, the passionate tug of the wind at her hair, the indescribable sense of pressing forward at a fast gallop. The boy is storming on behind her; he sees her proud body sitting very erect, tracing a beautiful line in her swift movement. He sometimes sees her slightly flushed face, the light in her eyes, and now that she is living out her own strength with such passion he knows her again. Desperately, he feels his love and longing flare vehemently up. He is overcome by an impetuous wish to take hold of her all of a sudden, sweep her off her horse and into his arms, to drink from those ravenous lips again, to feel the shattering throb of her agitated heart against his breast. He strikes his horse's flank, and it leaps forward with a whinny. Now he is beside her, his knee almost touching hers, their stirrups clink slightly together. He must say it now, he must.

"Margot," he stammers.

She turns her head, her arched brows shoot up. "Yes, what is it, Bob?" Her tone of voice is perfectly cool. And her eyes are cool as well, showing no emotion.

A shiver runs all the way down him to his knees. What had he been going to say? He can't remember. He stammers something about turning back.

"Are you tired?" she says, with what sounds to him like a touch of sarcasm.

"No, but the others are so far behind," he manages to say. Another moment, he feels, and he will be impelled to do something senseless—reach his arms out to her, or begin shedding tears, or strike out at her with the riding crop that is shaking in his hand as if it were electrically charged. Abruptly he pulls his horse back, making it rear for a moment. She races on ahead, erect, proud, unapproachable.

The others soon catch up with him. There is a lively conversation in progress to both sides of him, but the words and laughter pass him by, making no sense, like the hard clatter of the horses' hooves. He is tormenting himself for his failure to summon up the courage to tell her about his love and force her to confess hers, and his desire to tame her grows wilder and wilder, veiling his eyes like a red mist above the land before him. Why didn't he answer scorn with scorn? Unconsciously he urges his horse on, and now the heat of his speed eases his mind. Then the others call out that it is time to turn back. The sun has crept above the hills and is high in the midday sky. A soft, smoky fragrance wafts from the fields, colours are bright now and burn the eyes like molten gold. Sultry, heavy heat billows out over the land, the sweating horses are trotting more drowsily, with warm steam rising from them, breathing hard. Slowly the procession forms again, cheerfulness is more muted than before, conversation more desultory.

Margot too is in sight again. Her horse is foaming at the mouth, white specks of foam cling trembling to her riding habit, and the round bun into which she has pinned up her hair threatens to come undone, held in place only loosely by its clasps. The boy stares as if enchanted at the tangle of blonde hair, and the idea that it might suddenly all come down, flowing in wild tresses, maddens him with excitement. Already the arched garden gate at the end of the avenue is in sight, and beyond it the broad avenue up to the castle. Carefully, he guides his horse past the others, is the first to arrive, jumps down, hands the reins to a groom and waits for the cavalcade. Margot comes last. She trots up very slowly, her body relaxed, leaning back, exhausted as if by pleasure. She must look like that, he senses, when she has blunted the edge of her frenzy, she must have looked like that yesterday and the evening before. The memory makes him impetuous again. He goes over to her and, breathlessly, helps her down from the horse.

As he is holding the stirrup, his hand feverishly clasps her slender ankle. "Margot," he groans, murmuring her name softly. She does not so much as look at him in answer, taking the hand he is holding out casually as she gets down.

"Margot, you're so wonderful," he stammers again.

She gives him a sharp look, her eyebrows rising steeply again. "I think you must be drunk, Bob! What on earth are you talking about?"

But angry with her for pretending, blind with passion, he presses the hand that he is still holding firmly to himself as if to plunge it into his breast. At that, Margot, flushing angrily, gives him such a vigorous push that he sways, and she walks rapidly past him. All this has happened so fast and so abruptly that no one has noticed, and now it seems to him, too, like nothing but an alarming dream.

He is so pale and distracted all the rest of the day that the blonde Countess strokes his hair in passing and asks if he is all right. He is so angry that when his dog jumps up at him, barking, he chases it away with a kick; he is so clumsy in playing games that the girls laugh at him. The idea that now she will not come this evening poisons his blood, makes him bad-tempered and surly. They all sit out in the garden together at teatime, Margot opposite him, but she does not look at him. Magnetically attracted, his eyes keep tentatively glancing at hers, which are cool as grey stone, returning no echo. It embitters him to think that she is playing with him like this. Now, as she turns brusquely away from him, he clenches his fist and feels he could easily knock her down.

"What's the matter, Bob? You look so pale," says a voice suddenly. It is little Elisabeth, Margot's sister. There is a soft, warm light in her eyes, but he does not notice it. He feels rather as if he were caught in some disreputable act, and says angrily, "Leave me alone, will you? You and your damned concern for me!" Then he regrets it, because the colour drains out of Elisabeth's own face, she turns away and says, with a hint of tears in her voice, "How oddly you're behaving today." Everyone is looking at him with disapproval, almost menacingly, and he himself feels that he is in the wrong. But then, before he can apologize, a hard voice, bright and sharp as the blade of a knife, Margot's voice, speaks across the table. "If you ask me, Bob is behaving very badly for his age. We're wrong to treat him as a gentleman or even an adult." This from Margot, Margot who gave him her lips only last night! He feels everything going round in circles, there is a mist before his eyes. Rage seizes him. "You of all people should know!" he says in an unpleasant tone of voice, and gets up from the table. His movement was so abrupt that his chair falls over behind him, but he does not turn back.

And yet, senseless as it seems even to him, that evening he is down in the garden again, praying to God that she may come. Perhaps all that had been nothing but pretence and waywardness—no, he wouldn't ask her any more questions or be angry with her, if only she would come, if only he could feel once again the bitter desire of those soft, moist lips against his mouth, sealing all its questions. The hours seem to have gone to sleep; night, an apathetic, limp animal, lies in front of the castle; time drags out to an insane length. The faintly buzzing grass around him seems to be animated by mocking voices; the twigs and branches gently moving, playing with their shadows and the faint glow of evening light, are like mocking hands. All sounds are confused and strange, they irritate him more painfully than silence. Once a dog begins barking out in the countryside, and once a shooting star crosses the sky and falls somewhere behind the castle. The night seems brighter and brighter, the shadows of the trees above the garden path darker and darker, and those soft sounds are more and more confused. Drifting clouds envelop the sky in sombre, melancholy darkness. This loneliness falls on his burning heart.

The boy walks up and down, more and more vigorously, faster and faster. Sometimes he angrily strikes a tree, or rubs a piece of its bark in his fingers, rubbing so furiously that they bleed. No, she is not going to come, he knew it all along, but he doesn't want to believe it because then she will never come again, never. It is the bitterest moment of his life. And he is still so youthfully passionate that he flings himself down hard in the damp moss, digging his hands into the earth, tears on his cheeks, sobbing softly and bitterly as he never wept as a child, and as he will never be able to weep again.

Then a faint cracking sound in the undergrowth suddenly rouses him from his despair. And as he leaps up, blindly holding out his searching hands, he finds that he is holding—and how wonderful is its sudden, warm impact on his breast—he is holding the body of which he dreamt so wildly in his arms again. A sob breaks from his throat, his whole being is dissolved in a vast convulsion, and he holds her tall, curving body so masterfully to his that a moan comes from those strange, silent lips. As he feels her groan, held in his power, he knows for the first time that he has mastered her and is not, as he was yesterday and the day before, the prey of her moods; a desire overcomes him to torment her for the torment he has felt for what seems like a hundred hours, to chastise her for her defiance, for those scornful words this evening in front of the others, for the mendacious game she is playing. Hatred is so inextricably intertwined with his burning desire that their embrace is more of a battle than a loving encounter. He catches hold of her slim wrists so that her whole breathless body writhes, trembling, and then holds her so stormily against him again that she cannot move, only groan quietly again and again, whether in pleasure or pain he does not know. But he cannot get a word out of her. Now, when he forces his lips on hers, sucking at them to stifle that faint moaning, he feels something warm and wet on them, blood, blood running where her teeth have bitten so hard into his lips. And so he torments her until he suddenly feels his strength flagging, and the hot wave of desire rises in him, and now they are both gasping, breast to breast. Flames have fallen overnight, stars seem to flicker in front of his eyes, everything is crazy, his thoughts circle more wildly, and all of it has only one name: Margot. Muted, but from the depths of his heart, he finally, in a burning torrent, gets out her name in mingled rejoicing and despair, expressing longing, hatred, anger and love at the same time. It comes out in a single cry filled with his three days of torment: Margot, Margot. And to his ears, all the music in the world lies in those two syllables.

A shock passes through his body. All at once the fervour of their embrace dies down, a brief, wild thrust, a sob, weeping comes from her throat, and again there is fire in her movements, but only to tear herself away as if from a touch she hates. Surprised, he tries to hold her, but she struggles with him; as she bends her face close he feels tears of anger running down her cheeks, and her slender body writhes like a snake. Suddenly, with an embittered movement of violence, she throws him off and runs. Her white dress shows among the trees, and is then drowned in darkness.

So there he stands, alone again, shocked and confused as he was the first time, when warmth and passion suddenly fell into his arms. The stars gleam with moisture before his eyes, and his blood thrusts sharp sparks into his brow from within. What has happened? He makes his way through the row of trees, growing less densely here, and farther into the garden, where he knows the little fountain will be playing. He lets its water soothe his hand, white, silvery water that murmurs softly to him and shines beautifully in the reflection of the moon as it slowly emerges from the clouds again. And then, now that he sees more clearly, wild grief comes over him as if the mild wind had blown it down out of the trees. His warm tears rise, and now he feels, more strongly and clearly than in those moments of their convulsive embrace, how much he loves Margot. Everything that went before has fallen away from him, the shuddering frenzy of possession, his anger at her withholding of her secret; love in all its fullness, sweetly melancholy, surrounds him, a love almost without longing; but it is overpowering.

Why did he torment her like that? Hasn't she shown him incredible generosity on these three nights, hasn't his life suddenly emerged from a gloomy twilight into a sparkling, dangerously bright light since she taught him tenderness and the wild ardour of love? And then she left him, in tears of anger! A soft, irresistible wish for reconciliation wells up in him, for a mild, calm word, a wish to hold her quiet in his arms, asking nothing, and tell her how grateful he is to her. Yes, he will go to her in all humility and tell her how purely he loves her, saying he will never mention her name again or force an answer out of her that she does not want to give.

The silvery water flows softly, and he thinks of her tears. Perhaps she is all alone in her room now, he thinks, with only this whispering night to listen to her, a night that listens to all and consoles no one. This night when he is both far from her and near her, without seeing a glimmer of her hair, hearing a word in her voice half lost on the wind, and yet he is caught inextricably, his soul in hers—this night becomes unbearable agony to him. And his longing to be near her, even lying outside her door like a dog or standing as a beggar below her window, is irresistible.

As he hesitantly steals out of the darkness of the trees, he sees that there is still light in her window on the first floor. It is a faint light; its yellow shimmering scarcely even illuminates the leaves of the spreading sycamore tree that is trying to knock on the window with its branches as if they were hands, stretching them out, then withdrawing them again in the gentle breeze, a dark, gigantic eavesdropper outside the small, shining pane. The idea that Margot is awake behind the shining glass, perhaps still shedding tears or thinking about him, upsets the boy so much that he has to lean against the tree to keep himself from swaying.

He stares up as if spellbound. The white curtains waft restlessly out, playing in the light wind, seeming now deep gold in the radiance of the warm lamplight, now silvery when they blow forward into the shaft of moonlight that seeps, flickering, through the leaves. And the window, opening inward, mirrors the play of light and shade as a loosely strung tissue of light reflections. But to the fevered boy now staring up out of the shadows, hot-eyed, dark runes telling a tale seem to be written there on a blank surface. The flowing shadows, the silvery gleam that passes over that black surface like faint smoke—these fleeting perceptions fill his imagination with trembling images. He sees Margot, tall and beautiful, her hair—oh, that wild, blonde hair—flowing loose, his own restlessness in her blood, pacing up and down her room, sees her feverish in her sultry passion, sobbing with rage. As if through glass, he now sees, through the high walls, the smallest of her movements when she raises her hands or sinks into an armchair, and her silent, desperate staring at the starlit sky. He even thinks, when the pane lights up for a moment, that he sees her face anxiously bend to look down into the slumbering garden, looking for him. And then his wild emotion gets the better of him; keeping his voice low, and yet urgent, he calls up her name: Margot! Margot!

Wasn't that something scurrying over the blank surface like a veil, white and fast? He thinks he saw it clearly. He strains his ears, but nothing is moving. The soft breath of the drowsy trees and the silken whispering in the grass swell, carried on the gentle wind, now farther away, now louder again, a warm wave gently dying down. The night is peaceful, the window is silent, a silver frame round a darkened picture. Didn't she hear him? Or doesn't she want to hear him any more? That trembling glow around the window confuses him. His heart beats hard, expressing the longing in his breast, beats against the bark of the tree, and the bark itself seems to tremble at such passion. All he knows is that he must see her now, must speak to her now, even if he were to call her name so loud that people came to see what was going on, and others woke from sleep. He feels that something must happen at this point, the most senseless of ideas seems to him desirable, just as everything is easily achieved in a dream. Now that his glance moves up to the window again, he suddenly sees the tree leaning against it reach out a branch like a signpost, and his hand clings harder to its trunk. Suddenly it is all clear to him: he must climb up there—the trunk is broad, but feels soft and silken—and once up the tree he will call to her just outside her window. Close to her up there, he will talk to her, and he won't come down again until she has forgiven him. He does not stop to think for a second, he sees only the window, enticing him, gleaming faintly, and feels that the tree is on his side, sturdy and broad enough to take his weight. With a couple of quick movements he swings himself up, and already his hands are holding a branch. He energetically hauls his body after them, and now he is high in the tree, almost at the top of the leaf canopy swaying beneath him as it might do in alarm. The rustling sound of the leaves ripples on to the last of them, and the branch bends closer to the window as if to warn the unsuspecting girl. Now the boy, as he climbs, can see the white ceiling of her room, and in the middle of it, sparkling gold, the circle of light cast by the lamp. And he knows, trembling slightly with excitement, that in a moment he will see Margot herself, weeping or still sobbing or in the naked desire of her body. His arms slacken, but he catches himself again. Slowly, he makes his way along the branch turned to her window; his knees are bleeding a little, there is a cut on his hand, but he climbs on, and is now almost within the light from the window. A broad tangle of leaves still conceals the view, the final scene he longs so much to see, and the ray of light is already falling on him as he bends forward, trembling—and his body rocks, he loses his balance and falls tumbling to the ground.

He hits the grass with a soft, hollow impact, like a heavy fruit falling. Up in the castle, a figure leans out of the window, looking around uneasily, but nothing moves in the darkness, which is still as a millpond that has swallowed up a drowning man. Soon the light at the window goes out and the garden is left to itself again, in the uncertain twilight gleam above the silent shadows.

After a few minutes the fallen figure wakes to consciousness. His eyes stare up for a second to where a pale sky with a few wandering stars in it looks coldly down on him. But then he feels a sudden piercing, agonizing pain in his right foot, a pain that almost makes him scream at the first movement he attempts. Suddenly he knows what has happened to him. He also knows that he can't stay lying here under Margot's window, he can't call for help to anyone, must not raise his voice or make much noise as he moves. Blood is running from his forehead; he must have hit a stone or a piece of wood on the turf, but he wipes it away with his hand to keep it from running into his eyes. Then, curled on his left side, he tries slowly working his way forward by ramming his hands into the earth. Every time something touches or merely jars his broken leg, pain flares up, and he is afraid of losing consciousness again. But he drags himself slowly on. It takes him almost half an hour to reach the steps, and his arms already feel weak. Cold sweat mingles on his brow with the sticky blood still oozing out. The last and worst of it is still to come: he must get to the top of the steps, and he works his way very slowly up them, in agony. When he is right at the top, reaching for the balustrade, his breath rattles in his throat. He drags himself a little farther, to the door into the room where the gentlemen play cards, and where he can hear voices and see a light. He hauls himself up by the handle, and suddenly, as if flung in, he falls into the brightly lit room as the door gives way.

He must present a gruesome sight, stumbling in like that, blood all over his face, smeared with garden soil, and then falling to the floor like a clod of earth, because the gentlemen spring up wildly. Chairs fall over backwards with a clatter, they all hurry to help him. He is carefully laid on the sofa. He just manages to babble something about tumbling down the steps on his way to go for a walk in the park, and then it is as if black ribbons fall on his eyes, waver back and forth, and surround him entirely. He falls into a faint, and knows no more.

A horse is saddled, and someone rides to the nearest town to fetch a doctor. The castle, startled into wakefulness, is full of ghostly activity: lights tremble like glow-worms in the corridors, voices whisper, asking what has happened from their bedroom doors, the servants timidly appear, drowsy with sleep, and finally the unconscious boy is carried up to his room.

The doctor ascertains that he has indeed broken his leg, and reassures everyone by telling them that there is no danger. However, the victim of the accident will have to lie motionless with his leg bound up for a long time. When the boy is told, he smiles faintly. It does not trouble him much. If you want to dream of someone you love, it is good to lie alone like this for lengthy periods—no noise, no other people, in a bright, high-ceilinged room with treetops rustling outside. It is sweet to think everything over in peace, dream gentle dreams of your love, undisturbed by any arrangements and duties, alone and at your ease with the tender dream images that approach the bed when you close your eyes for a moment. Love may have no more quietly beautiful moments than these pale, twilight dreams.

He still feels severe pain for the first few days, but it is mingled with a curious kind of pleasure. The idea that he has suffered this pain for the sake of his beloved Margot gives the boy a highly romantic, almost ecstatic sense of self-confidence. He wishes he had a wound, he thinks, a blood-red injury to his face that he could have taken around openly, all the time, like a knight wearing his lady's favours; alternatively, it would have been good never to wake up again at all but stay lying down there, broken to pieces outside her window. His dream is already under way; he imagines her awakened in the morning by the sound of voices under her window, all talking together, sees her bending curiously down and discovering him—him!—shattered there below the window, dead for her sake. He pictures her collapsing with a scream; he hears that shrill cry in his ears, and then sees her grief and despair as she lives on, sad and serious all her life, dressed in black, her lips quivering faintly when she is asked the reason for her sorrow.

He dreams like this for days, at first only in the dark, then with open eyes, getting accustomed to the pleasant memory of her dear image. Not an hour is so bright or full of activity as to keep her picture from coming to him, a slight shadow stealing over the walls, or her voice from reaching his ears through the rippling rustle of the leaves and the crunch of sand outside in the strong sunlight. He converses with Margot for hours like this, or dreams of accompanying her on their travels, on wonderful journeys. Sometimes, however, he wakes from these reveries distraught. Would she really mourn for him if he were dead? Would she even remember him?

To be sure, she sometimes comes in person to visit the invalid. Often, when he is talking to her in his mind and seems to see her lovely image before him, the door opens and she comes in, tall and beautiful, but so different from the being in his dreams. For she is not gentle, nor does she bend down with emotion to kiss his brow, like the Margot of his dreams; she just sits down beside his chaise longue, asks how he is and whether he is in any pain, and then tells him a few interesting stories. He is always so sweetly startled and confused by her presence that he dares not look at her; often he closes his eyes to hear her voice the better, drinking in the sound of her words more deeply, that unique music that will then hover around him for hours. He answers her hesitantly, because he loves the silence when he hears only her breathing, and is most profoundly alone with her in this room, in space itself. And then, when she stands up and turns to the door, he stretches and straightens up with difficulty, despite the pain, so that he can memorize the outline of her figure in movement, see her in her living form before she lapses into the uncertain reality of his dreams.

Margot visits him almost every day. But doesn't Kitty visit him too, and Elisabeth, little Elisabeth who always looks so startled, and asks whether he feels better yet in such kind tones of concern? Doesn't his sister come to see him daily, and the other women, and aren't they all equally kind to him? Don't they stay with him, telling him amusing stories? In fact they even stay too long, because their presence drives away his mood of reverie, rouses it from its meditative peace and forces him to make casual conversation and utter silly phrases. He would rather none of them came except for Margot, and even she only for an hour, only for a few minutes, and then he would be on his own again to dream of her undisturbed, uninterrupted, quietly happy as if buoyed up on soft clouds, entirely absorbed in the consoling images of his love.

So sometimes, when he hears a hand opening the door, he closes his eyes and pretends to be asleep. Then the visitors steal out again on tiptoe, he hears the handle quietly closing, and knows that now he can plunge back into the warm tide of his dreams gently bearing him away to enticingly faraway places.

And one day a strange thing happens: Margot has already been to visit him, only for a moment, but she brought all the scents of the garden in her hair, the sultry perfume of jasmine in flower, and the bright sparkling of the August sun was in her eyes. Now, he knew, he could not expect her again today. It would be a long, bright afternoon, shining with sweet reverie, because no one would disturb him; they had all gone riding. And when the door moves again, hesitantly, he squeezes his eyes shut, imitating sleep. However, the woman coming in—as he can clearly hear in the breathless stillness of the room—does not retreat, but closes the door without a sound so as not to wake him. Now she steals towards him, stepping carefully, her feet barely touching the floor. He hears the soft rustle of a dress, and knows that she is sitting down beside him. And through the crimson mist behind his closed eyelids, he feels that her gaze is on his face.

His heart begins to thud. Is it Margot? It must be. He senses it, but it is sweeter, wilder, more exciting, a secret, intriguing pleasure not to open his eyes yet but merely guess at her presence beside him. What will she do now? The seconds seem to him endless. She is only looking at him, listening to him sleeping, and that idea sends an electric tingling through his pores, the uncomfortable yet intoxicating sense of being vulnerable to her observation, blind and defenceless, to know that if he opened his eyes now they would suddenly, like a cloak, envelop Margot's startled face in tender mood. But he does not move, although his breath comes unsteadily from a chest too constricted for it, and he waits and waits.

Nothing happens. He feels as if she were bending down closer to him, as if he sensed, closer to his face now, her faint perfume, a soft, moist lilac scent that he knows from her lips. And now she has placed her hand on the chaise longue and is gently stroking his arm above the rug spread over him—the blood surges from that hand in a hot wave through his whole body—stroking his arm calmly and carefully. He feels that her touch is magnetic, and his blood flows in response to it. This gentle affection, intoxicating and intriguing him at the same time, is a wonderful feeling.

Slowly, almost rhythmically, her hand is still moving along his arm. He peers up surreptitiously between his eyelids. At first he sees only a crimson mist of restless light, then he can make out the dark, speckled rug, and now, as if it came from far away, the hand caressing him; he sees it very, very dimly, only a narrow glimpse of something white, coming down like a bright cloud and moving away again. The gap between his eyelids is wider and wider now. He sees her fingers clearly, pale and white as porcelain, sees them curving gently to stroke forward and then back again, dallying with him, but full of life. They move on like feelers and then withdraw; and at that moment the hand seems to take on a life of its own, like a cat snuggling close to a dress, a small white cat with its claws retracted, purring affectionately, and he would not be surprised if the cat's eyes suddenly began to shoot sparks. And sure enough, isn't something blinking brightly in that white caress? No, it's only the glint of metal, a golden shimmer. But now, as the hand moves forward again, he sees clearly that it is the medallion dangling from her bracelet, that mysterious, giveaway medallion, octagonal and the size of a penny. It is Margot's hand caressing his arm, and a longing rises in him to snatch up that soft, white hand—it wears no rings—carry it to his lips and kiss it. But then he feels her breath, senses that Margot's face is very close to his, and he cannot keep his eyelids pressed together any longer. Happily, radiantly, he turns his gaze on the face now so close, and sees it retreat in alarm.

And then, as the shadows cast by the face bent down to him disperse and light shows her features, stirred by emotion, he recognizes—it is like an electric shock going through his limbs—he recognizes Elisabeth, Margot's sister, that strange girl young Elisabeth. Was this a dream? No, he is staring into a face now quickly blushing red, she is turning her eyes away in alarm, and yes, it is Elisabeth. All at once he guesses at the terrible mistake he has made; his eyes gaze avidly at her hand, and the medallion really is there on her bracelet.

Mists begin swirling before his eyes. He feels exactly as he did when he fainted after his fall, but he grits his teeth; he doesn't want to lose his ability to think straight. Suddenly it all passes rapidly before his mind's eye, concentrated into a single second: Margot's surprise and haughty attitude, Elisabeth's smile, that strange look of hers touching him like a discreet hand—no, there was no possible mistake about it.

He feels one last moment of hope, and stares at the medallion; perhaps Margot gave it to her, today or yesterday or earlier.

But Elisabeth is speaking to him. His fevered thinking must have distorted his features, for she asks him anxiously, "Are you in pain, Bob?"

How alike their voices are, he thinks. And he replies only, without thinking, "Yes, yes… I mean no… I'm perfectly all right!"

There is silence again. The thought keeps coming back to him in a surge of heat: perhaps Margot has given it to her, and that's all. He knows it can't be true, but he has to ask her.

"What's that medallion?"

"Oh, a coin from some American republic or other, I don't know which. Uncle Robert gave it to us once."

"Us?"

He holds his breath. She must say it now.

"Margot and me. Kitty didn't want one, I don't know why."

He feels something wet flowing into his eyes. Carefully, he turns his head aside so that Elisabeth will not see the tear that must be very close to his eyelids now; it cannot be forced back, it slowly, slowly rolls down his cheek. He wants to say something, but he is afraid that his voice might break under the rising pressure of a sob. They are both silent, watching one another anxiously. Then Elisabeth stands up. "I'll go now, Bob. Get well soon." He shuts his eyes, and the door creaks quietly as it closes.

His thoughts fly up like a startled flock of pigeons. Only now does he understand the enormity of his mistake. Shame and anger at his folly overcome him, and at the same time a fierce pain. He knows now that Margot is lost to him for ever, but he feels that he still loves her, if not yet, perhaps, with a desperate longing for the unattainable. And Elisabeth—as if in anger, he rejects her image, because all her devotion and the now muted fire of her passion cannot mean as much to him as a smile from Margot or the touch of her hand in passing. If Elisabeth had revealed herself to him from the first he would have loved her, for in those early hours he was still childlike in his passion; but now, in his thousand dreams of Margot, he has burnt her name too deeply into his heart for it to be extinguished now.

He feels everything darkening before his eyes as his constantly whirling thoughts are gradually washed away by tears. He tries in vain to conjure up Margot's face in his mind as he has done in all the long, lonely hours and days of his illness; a shadow of Elisabeth always comes in front of it, Elisabeth with her deep, yearning eyes, and then he is in confusion and has to think again, in torment, of how it all happened. He is overcome by shame to think how he stood outside Margot's window calling her name, and again he feels sorry for quiet, fair-haired Elisabeth, for whom he never had a word or a look to spare in all these days, when his gratitude ought to have been bent on her like fire.

Next morning Margot comes to visit him for a moment. He trembles at her closeness, and dares not look her in the eye. What is she saying to him? He hardly hears it; the wild buzzing in his temples is louder than her voice. Only when she leaves him does he gaze again, with longing, at her figure. He feels that he has never loved her more.

Elisabeth visits him in the afternoon. There is a gentle familiarity in her hands, which sometimes brush against his, and her voice is very quiet, slightly sad. She speaks, with a certain anxiety, of indifferent things, as if she were afraid of giving herself away if she talked about the two of them. He does not know quite what he feels for her. Sometimes he feels pity for her, sometimes gratitude for her love, but he cannot tell her so. He hardly dares to look at her for fear of lying to her.

She comes every day now, and stays longer too. It is as if, since the hour when the nature of their shared secret dawned on them, their uncertainty has disappeared as well. Yet they never dare to talk about those hours in the dark of the garden.

One day Elisabeth is sitting beside his chaise longue again. The sun is shining brightly outside, a reflection of the green treetops in the wind trembles on the walls. At such moments her hair is as fiery as burning clouds, her skin pale and translucent, her whole being shines and seems airy. From his cushions, which lie in shadow, he sees her face smiling close to him, and yet it looks far away because it is radiant with light that no longer reaches him. He forgets everything that has happened at this sight. And when she bends down to him, so that her eyes seem to be more profound, moving darkly inward, when she leans forward he puts his arm round her, brings her head close to his and kisses her delicate, moist mouth. She trembles like a leaf but does not resist, only caresses his hair with her hand. And then she says, merely breathing the words, with loving sorrow in her voice, "But Margot is the only one you love." He feels that tone of devotion go straight to his heart, that gentle, unresisting despair, and the name that shakes him with emotion strikes at his very soul. But he dares not lie at that minute. He says nothing in reply.

She kisses him once more, very lightly, an almost sisterly kiss on the lips, and then she goes out without a word. That is the only time they talk about it. A few more days, and then the convalescent is taken down to the garden, where the first faded leaves are already chasing across the path and early evening breathes an autumnal melancholy. Another few days, and he is walking alone with some difficulty, for the last time that year, under the colourful autumn canopy of leaves. The trees speak louder and more angrily now than on those three mild summer nights. The boy, in melancholy mood himself, goes to the place where they were once together. He feels as if an invisible, dark wall were standing here behind which, blurred in twilight already, his childhood lies; and now there is another land before him, strange and dangerous.

He said goodbye to the whole party that evening, looked hard once more at Margot's face, as if he had to drink enough of it in to last for the rest of his life, placed his hand restlessly in Elisabeth's, which clasped it with warm ardour, almost looked past Kitty, their friends and his sister—his heart was so full of the realization that he loved one of the sisters and the other loved him. He was very pale, with a bitter expression on his face that made him seem more than a boy; for the first time, he looked like a man.

And yet, when the horses were brought up and he saw Margot turn indifferently away to go back up the steps, and when Elisabeth's eyes suddenly shone with moisture, and she held the balustrade, the full extent of his new experience overwhelmed him so entirely that he gave himself up to tears of his own like a child.

The castle retreated farther into the distance, and through the dust raised by the carriage the dark garden looked smaller and smaller. Then came the countryside, and finally all that he had experienced was hidden from his eyes—but his memory was all the more vivid. Two hours of driving took him to the nearest railway station, and next morning he was in London.

A few more years and he was no longer a boy. But that first experience had left too strong an impression ever to fade. Margot and Elisabeth had both married, but he did not want to see them again, for the memory of those hours sometimes came back to him so forcefully that his entire later life seemed to him merely a dream and an illusion by comparison with its reality. He became one of those men who cannot find a way of relating to women, because in one second of his life the sensation of both loving and being loved had united in him entirely; and now no longing urged him to look for what had fallen into his trembling, anxiously yielding boyish hands so early. He travelled in many countries, one of those correct, silent Englishmen whom many consider unemotional because they are so reserved, and their eyes look coolly away from the faces and smiles of women. For who thinks that they may bear in them, inextricably mingled with their blood, images on which their gaze is always fixed, with an eternal flame burning around them as it does before icons of the Madonna? And now I remember how I heard this story. A card had been left inside the book that I was reading this afternoon, a postcard sent to me by a friend in Canada. He is a young Englishman whom I met once on a journey. We often talked in the long evenings, and in what he said the memory of two women sometimes suddenly and mysteriously flared up, as if they were distant statues, and always in connection with a moment of his youth. It is a long time, a very long time since I spoke to him, and I had probably forgotten those conversations. But today, on receiving that postcard, the memory was revived, mingling dreamily in my mind with experiences of my own; and I felt as if I had read his story in the book that slipped out of my hands, or as if I had found it in a dream.

But how dark it is now in this room, and how far away you are from me in the deep twilight! I can see only a faint pale light where I think your face is, and I do not know if you are smiling or sad. Are you smiling because I make up strange stories for people whom I knew fleetingly, dream of whole destinies for them, and then calmly let them slip back into their lives and their own world? Or are you sad for that boy who rejected love and found himself all at once cast out of the garden of his sweet dream for ever? There, I didn't mean my story to be dark and melancholy—I only wanted to tell you about a boy suddenly surprised by love, his own and someone else's. But stories told in the evening all tread the gentle path of melancholy. Twilight falls with its veils, the sorrow that rests in the evening is a starless vault above them, darkness seeps into their blood, and all the bright, colourful words in them have as full and heavy a sound as if they came from our inmost hearts.

WONDRAK

IN THE AUTUMN OF 1899, the incredible, improbable news that that ugly creature Ruzena Sedlak, known to everyone far and wide as 'the Death's Head', had had a baby aroused much mirth in the small Southern Bohemian town of Dobitzan. Her alarmingly and indeed distressingly ugly appearance had often enough caused amusement that none the less was more pitying than spiteful, but even the most inventive joker would never have ventured to speculate that such a battered, unattractive pot would ever find its lid. Now, however, a young huntsman had vouched for what was surely a miracle, if a miracle in the worst of taste. He had actually seen the baby in the remote part of the forest where Ruzena Sedlak lived, had seen it suckling happily from her breast, and the maidservants who heard this amazing news made haste to carry it back with their buckets to all the shops, inns and houses of Dobitzan. All that grey October evening, no one talked of anything but the unexpected infant and its presumed father. Forthright souls drinking at the regulars' table dug one another meaningfully in the ribs, spluttering with laughter as they accused each other of that unappetizing claim to fame, and the pharmacist, who had a certain amount of medical knowledge, described the probable course of the amorous scene in such realistic detail that everyone had to put back another schnapps or so in order to recover. For the first time in her twenty-eight years, the unfortunate Ruzena had provided her fellow citizens with piquant and abundant material for jokes.

Of course Nature herself, long ago, had been the first to play a cruel and ineradicable joke on the poor monstrosity, the daughter of a syphilitic brewer's man, by squashing her nose while she was still in the womb, and the derisive nickname that clung so terribly came into the world with her. For as soon as the midwife, who had seen plenty of strange and ugly creatures born in forty years, set eyes on the newborn baby she hastily made the sign of the cross and cried, losing all control of herself, "A death's head!" For where the arch of the nose normally rises clear and distinct in a human face, protecting the eyes and shading the lips, dividing light and shadow on the human countenance, there yawned in this child only a deep-set, empty Nothing: just two breathing holes, black as bullet wounds and shockingly empty in the pink surface of flesh. The sight, which no one could stand for long, reminded people forcibly of a skull, where a similarly monstrous and disturbing void lies between the bony forehead and the white teeth. Then, recovering from her first shock, the midwife examined the baby and found that otherwise the little girl was well proportioned, healthy and shapely. The unfortunate child needed nothing to be the same as other babies but an inch of bone and gristle and a small amount of flesh. But Nature has made us so accustomed to the regularity of her laws that the slightest deviation from their familiar harmony seems repellent and alarming. Every mistake made by the creator arouses our bitter dislike of the failed creation—an injustice for which there is no remedy. Fatally, we feel revulsion not for the negligent designer but for the innocent thing it has designed. Every maimed and malformed being is doomed to suffer horribly not only from its own torment, but from the ill-concealed discomfort of those who are normally formed. And so a squinting eye, a twisted lip, a split palate, all of them just single mistakes of Nature, become the lasting torment of a human being, the inescapable misery of a soul—indeed, such diabolical misery that the sufferer finds it hard to believe in any sense of justice on the circling star we call the Earth.

Even as a child Ruzena Sedlak learned, to her shame, that she was known with good reason as the Death's Head, at the same time as she learned to talk, and every second she was reminded yet again that because of that missing inch of bone she was mercilessly banished from the cheerful company of other human beings. Pregnant women quickly turned away if they met her in the street;

farmer's wives from the local countryside, bringing their eggs to sell at market, crossed themselves on seeing her, for these simple souls could not help thinking that the Devil himself had squashed the child's nose. And even those who were more kindly disposed and talked to her kept their eyes obviously lowered as they talked; she could not remember ever having seen the pupil of an eye clearly and at close quarters, except in the eyes of animals, who sense only kindness and not ugliness in human beings. It was lucky that her mind was dull and lethargic, so that she suffered only vaguely from this injustice of God's when she was with other people. She did not have the strength to hate them, or any wish to love them; she took little notice of the whole town, which remained strange to her, so she was very pleased when kind Father Nossal put in a good word for her and found her a post as housekeeper at a hunting lodge out in the forest. It was eight hours' walk from town, and very remote from any human company. In the middle of his extensive woods, which reached from Dobitzan to the Schwarzenberg Forests, Count R had had a log cabin built in the foreign style for his guests, and apart from those few weeks in autumn when they came visiting, it was always empty. Ruzena Sedlak was installed as caretaker, with a ground-floor room to live in. Her only duties were to look after the hunting lodge, and feed the deer and the small game in hard winters. Otherwise her time was her own to use as she pleased, which she did by rearing goats, rabbits, chickens, and other small livestock, cultivating a vegetable garden, and trading a little in eggs, chickens, and kids. She lived entirely in the woods for eight years, and the animals, which she loved dearly, made her forget human beings. In their own turn human beings forgot her. Only the miraculous fact that some specimen of masculinity, either blind or dead drunk (no one could explain the aberration in any other way), had made the Death's Head pregnant, brought this forgotten creature of God back to the amused attention of the people of Dobitzan after many years.

One man in town, to be sure, did not laugh at the news but growled angrily, and that was the Mayor. For if Nature is unkind to one of her offspring now and then, and God forgets one of his creatures, an official would be no kind of official if he allowed himself to forget any human being, and there must be no omissions from a well-kept register. A child five months old and not yet registered, with no name in the records, grumbled the Mayor (who was a baker by profession) in great indignation. The priest was upset too: a child of five months and not yet baptised! These were heathen ways. After long discussion between the two of them, as representing the earthly and divine powers, the town clerk Wondrak was sent off to the forest to remind Ruzena Sedlak of her duty as a citizen. At first she told him roughly that the child was hers, no business of anyone else, and no concern of God or the Devil either. But when Wondrak, a sturdy figure and sticking to his point, replied that she was wrong there, the Devil would indeed take an interest in an unbaptised child, he'd carry its mother off to Hell if she failed to have the baby christened, the poor simple creature felt terrified of good Father Nossal, and she obediently brought the child to town next Sunday, wrapped in blue cotton. The baptism was celebrated early in the morning, to keep curious mockers away, the sponsors being a half-blind beggar woman and the good clerk Wondrak, who gave his own first name of Karel to the crying boy. The civil formalities proved a little more awkward, for when the Mayor asked as in duty bound for the father's name, a small, unseemly smile escaped both him and the kindly Wondrak. Ruzena did not reply, but bit her lip. So the unknown man's son was registered in her name, and thereafter was known as Karel Sedlak.

It was a fact that Ruzena, the Death's Head, could not have said who Karel's father was. One misty October evening the previous year, she had come back from town very late with her pannier on her back. Three fellows met her deep in the forest, out to steal timber, perhaps, or poachers or gypsies, at any rate not local men. The thick leaves cast far too much shade for her to tell their faces apart, and they could not make out who they had in front of them either (a sight which might have spared her their unwanted attentions). They saw only from her full, bell-shaped skirts that they were looking at a woman, and they attacked her. Ruzena quickly turned to run away, but one of them leaped at her from behind, moving faster than she did, and knocked her to the ground so hard that her back crashed down on her smashed pannier. Now she wanted to scream, but the three men quickly pulled her skirt up over her head, tore her shift in two, knotted the rags of it together and used them to tie her hands as she hit out wildly, punching and scratching. That was when it happened. There were three of them, she couldn't tell one from the other with her skirts up over her face, and none of them said a word. She heard only laughter, deep, rumbling and spiteful, and then satisfied grunts. She smelled tobacco, felt bearded faces, hard hands inflicting pain, weight falling on her, and more pain. When the last man had finished with her she tried to get up and free herself, but one of them hit her on the head with a cudgel so hard that she fell down. They weren't standing for any nonsense.

They must have been a long way off by the time Ruzena Sedlak ventured to get up again, bleeding, angry, abused and beaten. Her knees were trembling with exhaustion and rage. Not that she felt ashamed: her own hated body meant far too little to her, and she had known too much humiliation to feel that this vicious attack was anything out of the ordinary, but her shift was torn, her green skirt and her apron, and in addition the rogues had broken her pannier, which had cost her good money. She thought of going back to town to complain of the vagabonds, but the people there would only mock her; no one would help her. So she angrily dragged herself home, and once among her animals, good, gentle creatures who nuzzled her hands affectionately with their soft noses, she forgot all about the vile attack on her.

Only months later did she realize, in alarm, that she was going to be a mother. She immediately decided to get rid of the unwanted child. She didn't want to bring another monstrosity like herself into the world! No other innocent child should suffer as she had suffered herself. Better to kill it at once, get rid of it, bury it. For the next few weeks she avoided going to town so that no one would notice her condition, and as her pregnancy went on she dug a deep pit beside the compost heap ahead of time. She would bury the child there as soon as it was born, she thought; who would ever know? No one came into these woods.

One May night her pains began, so suddenly and savagely that she lay writhing on the floor, groaning as hot claws tore at her inside, and had no time to find a light. She bit her lips until they bled. Alone, helpless and in agony, she bore her child on the bare floor like an animal. She had just enough strength left afterwards to drag herself to her bed, where she collapsed, exhausted, in a wet and bleeding heap, and slept until it was day. Waking up when it grew light, she remembered what had happened, and the thought of what she must do now immediately came back into her mind. She hoped she wouldn't have to kill the brat, she hoped it was dead already. She listened. And then, very faintly, she heard a thin sound, a squeaking sound on the floor. She dragged herself over to it; the child was still alive. She felt it with a shaking hand: first the forehead, then the tiny ears, the chin, the nose, and she trembled worse than ever. It was a wild yet at the same time pleasant feeling, for an extraordinary thing had happened—the baby was well-formed. She, the monstrosity, had brought a real, pure, healthy child into the world. The curse had run its course. In amazement, she stared at the pink little thing. The child looked fair, she even thought beautiful, he was a little boy, not a death's head but made like other human beings, and a tiny smile was just forming on his tadpole of a mouth. She no longer had the strength to do what she had meant to do; she picked up the faintly breathing little creature and put it to her breast.

Many things altered for the better now. Life no longer went pointlessly by; it came running to her with tiny gasps and little cries, now it touched her with two small, clumsy baby hands. She had never had anything but her own malformed body; now she had something of her own. She had made a creature that would outlast and survive her, a child who needed and made use of her. For those first five months Ruzena Sedlak was perfectly happy. The baby grew for her alone, no one else knew about him, which was all to the good. And he had no father; that was good too. No one on earth knew about him, and once again that was excellent. He belonged entirely to her, and her alone.

That was why she snapped so angrily at poor Wondrak when he came from the offices in town with the message to say she had to take the baby to be baptised and registered. Her dull, rural sense of greed instinctively if vaguely felt that if people knew about her baby, he would be taken away from her. Now he was hers, all hers, but if those people in the offices, if the State and the Mayor wrote his name in one of their stupid books, a part of the baby as a human being would belong to them. They would have got a grip on his ankle, so to speak, they could summon him and order him about. And indeed, this was the one and only time that she took her Karel as a baby to town to see other people. To her own surprise, he grew to be a sturdy, brown, pretty boy with a pert, curious nose and quick straight legs, a lad with an ear for music who could whistle like a thrush, imitate the cry of the jay and the cuckoo, who climbed trees like a cat and ran races with the white dog Horcek. Knowing no one else, he was not afraid of her deformed face, and she laughed and was carefree and happy when she talked to him and his round, chestnut-brown eyes were turned on her. He was soon helping her to milk the goats, gather berries and split wood with his firm little hands. It was at this time that she, who had seldom been to church, began to pray again. She was never entirely free of the fear that he might be taken away from her as suddenly as he had arrived.

But once, when she went to town to sell a kid, Wondrak suddenly barred her way, which he was well able to do, for in these seven years his good Bohemian belly had grown even bigger and broader. It was a good thing he'd happened to meet her, he growled, that would save him another trek into the woods. He had a bone to pick with her. Didn't Ruzena Sedlak know that at the age of seven a boy ought to be at school? And when she said angrily it was none of his business how old her boy was, or where he ought to be, then Wondrak tightened his braces and his broad moon-face assumed a menacing expression of official dignity. Now the town clerk spoke forcefully; he didn't give a damn for her impertinence. Hadn't she ever heard of the law on elementary schooling for all? Why did she think the expensive new schoolhouse had been put up two years ago? She must go the Mayor at once, he'd soon make her understand that a Christian child in the Imperial state couldn't be allowed to grow up like the beasts of the field. And if she didn't like it, he supposed there was still a place in the lockup for her, and the child would be taken away and put in the orphanage.

At this last threat Ruzena turned pale. Of course the thought of school had long ago occurred to her, but she had always hoped they would forget. This was all because of that wretched book in the Mayor's office. Anyone whose name was written in it didn't own himself any more. And they were already beginning to take him away from her. For Karel, sturdy as his legs were, couldn't spend eight hours a day walking to school, and what was she to live on in the town? Finally, yet again, Father Nossal came to the rescue. He would have the boy to live with him during the week, he said, and he could go home to her every Saturday and Sunday and in the school holidays. His housekeeper would look after Karel very well. Ruzena stared angrily at the kindly, plump woman, who assured her in friendly tones that Father Nossal was right. She would have liked to strike the housekeeper—a woman who would now have more of her Karel than she did herself. But she was afraid in front of Father Nossal, so there was nothing she could do but agree. However, her skin was pale as stone, and in her hatred those terrible holes looked so black in her ruined face that the housekeeper hastily crossed herself in the kitchen, as if she had seen the Devil.

After that Ruzena often went to town. She had to walk all night, for eight hours, just to get a glimpse from the corner of her Karel and feel proud of him: neatly dressed, sponge dangling from his slate, walking to school with the other boys. He was strong, lively, and better-looking than most of them, not a fright like her, shunned by everyone. She would walk eight hours there and eight hours back for that sight of him, she brought eggs and butter with her out of the forest, and she worked harder and did more business than ever simply so that she could pay to have new clothes made for him. And now, too, she understood for the first time that Sundays were a God-given gift to man. Karel studied hard and did well, and the priest even spoke of sending him to high school in the big city at his own expense. But she balked frantically at this: no, no, he must stay here, and she found him a job with a woodcutter in the forest where she lived. It was hard work but closer to her, only four hours from her part of the woods, in a place where they were cutting rides through the forest. She was sometimes able to take him his mid-day meal and sit with him for an hour. And even when she didn't see him but just heard the firm, ringing axe strokes in the distance, they echoed cheerfully in her heart. It was her own blood she heard, her own strength.

Only Karel mattered to her. She even neglected the animals. There was no one else in the world. So she hardly noticed that a war began in the year 1914, and when she did notice it seemed to her, oddly enough, rather a good thing. The boys were paid better wages now, because the men were away, and when she took her eggs and chickens to town she didn't feel she must wait humbly for the women to arrive, as she used to, but went further and further down the road to meet them, and soon sold her shining eggs for shining coins, haggling with her customers. She already had a whole hidden drawer full of money and banknotes; another three years like this, and she would be able to move into town with her Karel. That was all she knew about the war, and all she thought of it.

But one day in this period that could hardly be measured in months, when she took her son's meal to the workmen's hut, he said, bending his head and swallowing the words along with his soup, that he couldn't come out to see her this Sunday. She was dumbfounded.

Why not? It was the first time since she had given birth to him that he wouldn't be spending Sunday with her. Well, it was like this, he said, chewing, he had to go off to Budweis with the others for acceptance. Acceptance? She didn't know what he was talking about. Acceptance for military service, he explained, eighteen-year-olds were soon going to be called up, it had been in the newspapers for a long time, and yesterday they'd had official notification.

Ruzena turned pale. All at once the blood drained from her face. She had never thought of that—she had never thought that he too would turn eighteen, her own child, and then they could take him away from her. Now she saw it all: that was why they had written him down in their wretched book in the Mayor's office all that time ago, so that they could drag him off to their accursed war. She sat perfectly still, and when Karel looked at her in surprise, he was frightened of his mother for the first time, because the figure sitting there was no longer a human being. He himself felt the force of the terrible nickname of 'the Death's Head', as he never had before—he had once punched a friend in the face for thoughtlessly uttering it. Out of a face drained of blood and white as bone, her black eyes stared straight into space, and her mouth had fallen open to show an empty cavern under those two dark holes in her flesh. He shuddered. Then she stood up and took his hand.

"Come over here," she said. And her voice was brittle as hard bone too. She led him to the nearby barn where the woodcutters kept their tools. No one was there; she closed the door. "Go over there," she told him sternly, and once again her voice in the dark might have come from the world beyond. Then she unbuttoned her dress. It was some time before her trembling fingers found and took out the silver crucifix that she wore on a thong around her neck. She placed it on the window-sill.

"There," she told him. "Now swear."

"What do you want me to swear?"

"Swear on that cross, by God and all his saints and the crucified Christ, that you will do as I say!"

He would have asked questions, but her bony fingers forced his hand down on the crucifix. Outside the sound of plates clattering could be heard, the laughter and talking of the workmen, and over there the grasshoppers were chirping in the grass, but here in the barn all was silent. Only her death's head shone menacingly out of the shadows. Her dark passion made him shudder. But he swore.

She breathed a sigh of relief, and tucked the crucifix back into place. "You've sworn on the crucified Christ to obey me. You will not go to that damned war. Let them find others in Vienna. Not you!"

"But suppose they come looking for me?"

She laughed again, shrill, malicious laughter. "Those donkeys, they won't get you. If they do come in search of you, you must go out to me in the woods. Now, go back and tell everyone you're going to Budweis on Sunday, hand in your notice and say you'll be off to the war."

Karel obeyed. He had inherited her stubborn cast of mind that could cope with anything. And on Saturday night he stole out to the house in the forest—she had already taken his clothes there little by little—and she showed him a room in the attic. He must stay here during the day, she said. He could come out at night, she said (they wouldn't come then), but he must not go too close to town, and he must always take Horcek the dog with him. The dog would start barking if anyone moved within a mile of them. And he mustn't be afraid of the townsfolk, said Ruzena, no one had ever come out to her house yet except for Wondrak and the huntsman. But now the huntsman was buried somewhere in the rocks of Italy, and she could deal with that fat fool Wondrak, ha, ha.

However, she laughed only to give the lad courage. In reality, fear weighed on her breast by night like a great block of stone. Only the Count and the guests at his hunting parties, it was true, had ever made their way out to this remote and isolated house. But small, dull-minded, ignorant creature that she was, she feared the unknown in the shape of the power with which they had begun this war. What did they really have all those books for in Dobitzan, in Budweis and Vienna? What was in them? Somehow or other, thanks to those accursed books, they must know all about everyone, every single person. They had summoned the tailor Wrba's brother back from America, and someone had come from Holland too, the bastards had reached everyone. Might they perhaps lay hands on Karel after all? Might they not work out that he hadn't gone to Budweis, but was hiding here in the forest? Oh, it was so hard to be alone against everyone, without anyone to talk to! Ought she to tell the priest? Perhaps he might advise her; over the years she had become used to that. And while her son's strong breathing regularly broke the silence, its sound coming through the thin floor above her, she tormented herself: a mother on her own against the monstrosity of the world, how could she deceive all those people in town with their mean-minded books and notes and certificates? She tossed and turned, unable to sleep, and now and then bit her lip so that her child up above, knowing nothing of her fears, would not hear her groans, and then she lay there with her eyes open, a prey to all the cruel torments of dark night and horror until well into the early hours of morning. At last she thought she had an idea, and she immediately leaped out of bed, gathered up her things, and made her way fast to town.

She had eggs with her, a great many eggs, and a few young chickens, and she hurried with those from house to house. One woman wanted to buy all she had, but she would let her have only two chickens, because she wanted to talk to a large number of people—that was her cunning trick. She wanted to talk to everyone in town so that the news would spread rapidly. So everywhere she went, from house to house, she complained bitterly. It was a shame, she said, taking her child off to Budweis, her Karel. They were dragging all the young fellows off to war these days, oh, surely God couldn't suffer them to take a poor woman's breadwinner away from her. Couldn't the Emperor see that it was all over if they needed such children, wouldn't he do better to stop the war? People listened to her, sad and sympathetic, frowning gloomily. Many cautiously turned and put a finger to their lips to warn her to be careful. For long ago the whole Czech people had broken away in their hearts from the Habsburgs, those strange gentlemen in Vienna, they had been surreptitiously keeping banners and candles ready to receive the Russians and set up their own kingdom. In secret and mysterious ways, passing the news from mouth to mouth, they all knew that their leaders Kramarc and Klopitsch were in jail, that Masaryk, who was on their side, was in exile, and the soldiers had brought back from the front vague news of German legions forming in Russia and Siberia. So there had been a secret understanding at work in people's minds all over the country for a long time before any individuals ventured to take action, and by mutual consent they approved of any kind of resistance and indignation. The townsfolk therefore gave Ruzena a sympathetic hearing, and looked regretful, and with secret delight she felt that the whole town believed her lying tale. When she passed, she heard them talking behind her back: they've taken even that poor woman's son away, folk said. And good Father Nossal himself spoke to her and said, with a strange twinkle in his eye, she mustn't worry too much, because he'd heard that this business wouldn't last much longer. The poor silly creature's heart beat high when she heard people talking like that: how stupid they were! Now she had fooled the whole town, all by herself, and they would pass the news that Karel had been called up on to Budweis, and then it would go from Budweis to Vienna. So he would be forgotten, and afterwards, when the war was over, she would take the consequences on herself. And to hammer the lie home, to make other people feel sure of it, she came to town week after week and went on spinning her tale: he had written, she said, saying he had to go to Italy, and telling her how bad the food was in wartime. She sent him butter every week, she said, but God knew if it wasn't stolen on the way. Oh, if he were only back from the war, if only she had him home again!

This went on for several weeks, but one day when she had come to town yet again, and was embarking on the litany of her woes,

Wondrak accosted her in a rather strange way and said, "Come along to my house and let's drink a glass of something." She dared not say no. But she felt cold all the way to her knees when she was alone with Wondrak in his parlour, and realized that he wanted to talk about one particular subject. He began by walking up and down, apparently undecided, and then he carefully closed the windows and sat down facing her.

"Well, and how's your Karel?"

She stammered that he knew Karel had joined the army, his regiment had marched off to Italy yesterday. Oh, if only the war were over, she said, she prayed for her child daily.

Wondrak did not reply, but just whistled quietly to himself. Then he rose and checked that the door was well closed. She concluded from this that he meant her no ill, although he so persistently avoided looking at her.

Well, that's all to the good, he muttered, but he, Wondrak, had just been wondering whether Karel hadn't secretly made off? No business of his, of course, and after all, you could understand a fellow who didn't want to throw his bones into another man's soup—let the Germans manage this stupid war of theirs on their own. But (and here he turned to the door again) three days ago an armed troop had arrived, a contingent of military police from Prague with Carinthian soldiers, and they were searching the houses now for lads who hadn't obeyed the call-up to join the army. There was Jennisch the locksmith, who after all had sprained his forefinger, they'd taken him out of his house and led him over the marketplace in handcuffs. It was a shame, such a good, honest man. And in the neighbouring village they were said to have shot a man who ran away, a shocking thing, it really was! They hadn't finished yet either, said Wondrak. They had brought a whole list from Budweis or Prague or somewhere, a list of the names of all the men who hadn't joined. Well, his lips were sealed on account of his official position, but maybe a number of men shouldn't be on that list at all.

As he spoke, Wondrak did not look at her, but stared with curious interest at the smoke rings rising from his pipe to the ceiling. Then he stood up and growled, unruffled, "But if your Karel really did join up, they'll have had their trouble for nothing, and it will all turn out well."

Ruzena sat there, frozen. It was all over. So her trick had done no good, they had found out, those bastards in Vienna with their books, they'd discovered that her child hadn't joined up. However, she asked no more questions, and merely got to her feet. Wondrak didn't look at her, but elaborately knocked out his pipe; they had understood one another.

"Thank you," she said quietly, and left.

She went to the end of the street with her knees stiff and cold, and then she suddenly began to run. If only she wasn't still on the way when they came—her child wouldn't defend himself, silly boy. She ran faster and faster, she threw her basket away, she tore open the dress clinging damply to her skin, she ran on and on and on, further into the forest, she ran as she had never run before in her life.

Night lay black above the house when she heard, from afar, the dog barking. That good dog Horcek, she thought, he gives us plenty of warning. All was still. Thank God, she had come in time. I'll have a Mass said, she thought, gasping for breath and only now aware of her exhaustion, two Masses, three Masses, and I'll offer candles, she added, lots of candles, all the rest of my life. Then she quietly went in, held her breath and listened. And suddenly the blood flowed strongly back into her trembling body as she heard the regular breath of the sleeping man. He was safe and sound, the child who had grown from her body. She climbed the stairs to the attic, a lighted candle in her shaking hand. Karel was fast asleep, sleeping deeply. His thick, heavy brown hair hung damp over his forehead, his broad, handsome, masculine mouth stood open to show his strong, firm white teeth. Tenderly, uncertainly, the candlelight flickered over the clear planes and shadows of that carefree boyish face. She saw again how handsome he was, and how young. His muscles stood out like white roots on his arms, which were bare, crossed above the blanket, and his shoulders might have been made of smooth marble; they were broad, strong and firm. There was power to last for decades in the flesh that she had formed from her own, there was an unimaginable wealth of life in his body, which had only just grown to manhood. And was she to give it up to Vienna for the sake of a silly piece of paper? Instinctively, she uttered a sharp laugh. Karel started up in alarm and shook himself, blinking foolishly at the light. Then, seeing her, he laughed too, his good, hearty, childlike Bohemian laugh. "What's up?" he asked, yawning and cracking his finger joints. "Is it day?"

But she shook him fully awake. He must get out of bed at once, she told him, he must get out of the house, she'd make him a place to stay for the next few days far in the forest and on no account must he move from it, even if a week passed before she came back for him. Then she tied up a great bundle of hay, put it on her back, and led him along a secret path for about quarter-of-an-hour into the thickest, most inaccessible part of the forest, to a place where a small huntsman's hide had once been erected.

He had to stay here, she told him, he mustn't show himself by day, but he could walk around at night. And she'd bring him food, she assured him of that. As usual, Karel obeyed her. He didn't understand, but he obeyed her. She would bring him food and tobacco in the middle of the day, she said. And then she went away, feeling relieved. Thank God, she had saved him. The house was cleared of his traces, so now let them come.

And come they did, quite a large troop of them. They knew their trade, they had studied it. Wondrak had done well to warn her. At five in the morning, when she had gone to bed and had been there for two hours (they must have been marching all night), the dog began to bark. She lay awake with her heart thudding. They were here. The enemy had come. But she did not stir, even when a harsh voice downstairs shouted, "Open up there!" Slowly, very slowly she dragged herself to the door, muttering in a deliberately loud voice, as if she had just been woken from deep sleep. Slow-witted she might be thought, but deception came naturally to her.

She yawned, a loud yawn. Then she opened the door. A military police officer stood outside in the wan, misty light of early morning with dew on his cap, a stranger. He had four soldiers and a dog with him, and he immediately stuck his foot in the door.

Did her son Karel Sedlak live here, he asked.

"Oh mercy me, he left long ago. He went to Budweis to join the army, all our town knows that," she was quick to answer. A little too quick—noticeably quick. As she spoke, she did not forget that she should look these men in the eye. She had worked that out for herself.

"We'll see," grunted the officer through his red moustache, which was moist from the mist. Then he barked out an order in German. Two men stationed themselves outside the door, two more went round behind the house, unslinging the guns from their shoulders. The dog leaped around sniffing at her own Horcek, who distrustfully avoided him. As soon as the soldiers had taken up their positions, the officer told them something else in German and then, turning to her, addressed her in Czech.

"Let's see the house now."

She followed him, feeling both fear and angry glee. There's nothing in the house, look as long as you like, she thought. You won't find anything.

He stepped briskly into her living-room, pushed open the shutters so that grey light fell on everything inside, and looked around. He opened the chest, looked under the bed, raised the bolster—nothing. "The other rooms," he ordered.

As if to trying to fool him and make him tired of all this, she replied, "I don't have any. The others all belong to His Excellency the Count. And His Excellency just has me here to keep house for him. I had to swear my oath on it."

He ignored this. "Open up."

She showed him the Count's dining-room, the kitchen, the servants' quarters, the bedrooms where the gentry slept. He searched the whole place. He had had practice; he tapped at the walls. Nothing. An expression of annoyance came over his face, and joy leaped up in her, sharp and full of malice.

Then he pointed to the stairs. "The attics," he ordered. Once more she felt that surge of glee. Yes, Karel had indeed been sleeping in the attics. Thank heaven that good man Wondrak had warned her, or they would have caught him there.

The officer climbed the stairs and she followed. There was his empty bed. And only now did it strike her that some of his clothes still lay there; she ought to have cleared them away, she should have stowed them in a chest. The straw was untidy too; she'd forgotten about that.

He noticed it himself. Who, he asked, slept here?

She made herself out simple-minded. "Oh, it's only the servant ever sleeps here—that's the Count's huntsman when there's a hunting party. Sometimes he has a couple of others with him."

"There's no hunting parties these days. Who last slept here?"

No one, she assured him. But the straw, he pointed out, was all churned up. Oh, she replied, the dog often lay down there to sleep in winter.

"Indeed?" said the man sharply. "The dog." And he reached for the table. There lay a pipe, half knocked-out. There were ashes on the floor. "So the dog smokes a pipe too, eh?"

Ruzena did not answer. She was lost for words. He did not wait for her to reply, but opened the chest and took out clothes. Whose, he asked, were these?

"My Karel's. He left them there when he went away to join the army."

The officer stood there, thwarted. She seemed to have an answer for everything. He knocked on the walls here too, searched the floor, but there was nothing there, only the straw. At last he had finished his inspection, and her heart leaped up with relief. He stood up, adjusted his braces, and when he turned to the stairs she thought, now he'll go. Saved! And her blood began flowing again.

However, the officer stopped in the doorway, raised two fingers to his mouth, and gave a shrill whistle.

Ruzena started in alarm. The whistle went right through her ear and penetrated deep inside her. What did it mean? She was overcome by fear of the unknown. And now along came the dog, wagging his tail, carrying himself proudly because his master had called him. His paws danced on the ground, padding on it with fast, light sounds.

He was a kind of German shepherd dog, with intelligent eyes and a bushy tail. He pressed close to the officer's leg and looked up at him, thumping his tail on the floor.

"Here, Hektor," said the officer. He took clothes out of the chest, a pair of shoes, a shirt, and threw them all down. "Here, seek!"

Hektor came up, his pointed muzzle reaching a little way forward to burrow into the clothes, and sniffing a shoe as well. His nose quivered as he sniffed, and he uttered a short, sharp yelp as he took a deep breath, his sides quivering, wagging his tail hard. He was excited, his movements rapid, his flanks were heaving. He had picked up the scent, and now he had a job to do. The officer called something to him, raised his arm to point at the bed, and the dog padded over to it, sniffing. Then he put his head down and ran back and forth.

The devil must be in that dog, she thought. His eyes sparkled. He had picked up a scent on the floor and was now sniffing its trail, which led him to the top of the stairs. The officer followed him. "Seek, seek!" he encouraged the dog. Now Hektor was in the attic doorway, still following the trail, and it led him downstairs. The military police officer was following him.

Once he was down again, he shouted an order to his men. The four soldiers all assembled and followed the dog. Hektor moved swiftly from bush to bush, then back into the house. Finally he followed the scent slowly out of the door again, and at last towards the forest. Ruzena's heart missed a beat. She ran down the stairs herself and instinctively went to the door; she wanted to follow the dog, run ahead of him, scream, warn Karel, stop them… she herself didn't know just what she could do. But the officer in command of the party of military police snapped at her, standing at the door to bar her way, "You stay there! Sit down!" And he pointed to the bench around the stove. She dared not reply, she simply huddled there.

She heard the soldiers' steps, she heard the snapping sound of straps being fastened. And then she was alone with the officer, who sat down at the table as if she were not there at all. He calmly knocked out his own tobacco pipe, refilled it and began to smoke, drawing on it very slowly. He could wait patiently, he was sure of himself. It was very quiet now. Ruzena heard only the way he puffed smoke from his lungs into the air. His calm composure made her tremble. She sat and stared at him, her cold hands hanging down, feeling that her blood had congealed inside her, was frozen there. Yet everything in her was stretched to breaking point. She felt numb. She forced herself to hold her breath to listen for any sounds from the forest, then she heard her own breathing coming louder than the throbbing in her ears, and in her numb brain she wondered whether he might yet escape. Suddenly she raised her hands and felt through her blouse for the place where the crucifix hung. She clutched it and began praying, reciting the Lord's Prayer and all the intercessions she knew. Involuntarily, she uttered one word out loud. The officer half turned, looking at her sharply and, as she thought, with derision. Got you, Death's Head, just you wait, he was thinking. For at that moment she did indeed resemble a skull, with her forehead white as bone below her falling hair, her mouth open to show her white teeth, and then there were the black holes that were her eyes and her nose. He turned away again, instinctively spat on the floor, and then trod out the slimy spittle from his pipe with his foot, slowly, without haste or any agitation.

She felt as if she must scream. She couldn't bear this; time and eternity weighed down on her. She trembled, she wanted to fall down before him, beg him on her knees, plead with him, kiss his feet. He was a human being, after all, but unapproachable in his uniform, in the impregnability of his power, sent out by the enemy. But doing any such thing would surely give her away. After all, they might not find Karel. She strained her ears again, listening as if she were nothing but her sense of hearing. She listened for an eternity. This was more cruel than anything she had borne in all her forty years.

It seemed to her a longer time than the whole nine months when she was carrying her child, but in fact she waited for only half-an-hour. Then there was a clinking outside, and a footstep. More footsteps were heard, and finally a small sharp sound. The officer stood up and glanced at the door. He uttered a brief laugh, and patted the dog, who came leaping up to him. "Good dog, Hektor, good dog." Then, without looking back, he went out. Ruzena was stunned by horror.

She stood perfectly still like that for a moment. Then, with a sudden movement, she banished the leaden feeling from her legs and rushed out. Oh, how terrible, they had him! Karel, her Karel stood between them, his hands cuffed behind his back, stooping, bent, his eyes lowered in shame. They had caught him just as he was going to the stream to wash and had brought him back as he was, barefoot, in his trousers and loose shirt. His mother cried out in shrill tones, and she was already making for the officer. She fell on her knees in front of him and clutched his feet. Let her son go, she cried, he was her child, her only child! Let him go for the Saviour's sake, he was only a child still, her Karel, not yet seventeen. He was sixteen, only sixteen, she pleaded, they had made a mistake. And he was sick too, very sick, she could swear it, everyone knew, he had spent all this time lying sick in bed.

The military police officer, feeling uncomfortable (and his men were looking darkly at him too), tried to free his feet. But she only clung even more firmly, weeping and raving. The Saviour would reward him, she cried, if he spared her innocent child. Why in heaven's name take her child, who was so weak? Have pity, she begged the officer, there were others around here, tall, powerful, strong young fellows, so many of them in the country round about, why take Karel, why him? Let him leave her child to her, she begged the officer, for the Saviour's sake—God would reward him for his good deed, she herself would pray for him every day. Every day. And for his mother. She would kiss his feet—and indeed, in her frenzy she actually did fling herself down to kiss the officer's dirty, muddy shoes.

Shame made him rough. Tearing himself free, he pushed the desperate woman away. What a fuss she was making! Thousands and thousands of men had marched away for the Emperor, and none of them had uttered a squeak of protest. The doctors would soon find out if the lad was sick. She should be glad he wasn't put up against the wall at once as a deserter. A fellow who makes off like that ought by rights to be shot, and if it was up to him, the officer, he said, he knew what he'd do with him, he would…

He got no further. In the middle of this speech she leaped at him. Suddenly, from down on the floor at his feet, she sprang at him and made him stagger, both hands going for his throat like claws. He was a strong man, but he rocked back on his heels. Hitting out, he struck her, punching her flesh, her forehead. Then he seized her in his two hard hands and twisted a joint until she writhed in pain. But although she was defenceless now, she bit, snapping like an animal, bit his arm and hung there with her teeth in it. He yelled. And now his men came up, tore her away, got her down on the ground and kicked her.

The officer was shaking with pain and anger—to be shamed like this in front of his soldiers! "Handcuff her," he ordered. "We'll show you, you bitch." His arm hurt like hell. Her teeth had gone through his coat and the fabric of his shirt; red blood was running out. He felt it trickling down, but he wasn't going to show that. As they put the handcuffs on her, he bound up the place under his shirt with his handkerchief, and then, composed again, ordered the men: "Forward march. Two of you go ahead with the lad, two of you follow with her."

Her hands were fastened behind her back now, and the officer had drawn his revolver. "If either of them moves, shoot them down."

The soldiers took Karel between them. He twisted and turned, but when they told him, "March!" he marched. He walked on with fixed eyes, mechanically, without resisting; the shock had broken his strength. His mother followed without defending herself either; violence would do no good now. She would have gone anywhere with Karel, she'd have gone to the ends of the earth, just so long as she was with him, could stay with him. So long as she could see him: his fine broad back, his curly brown shock of hair above his firm neck, oh, and his hands, tortured now, bound behind his back, the hands she had known when they were tiny, with small pink nails, with sweet little folds on them. She would have walked on without any soldiers, without any orders, just so as to be with him and not leave him. All she wanted was to know that she was still near him. She felt no weariness in spite of walking for so long—eight hours. She did not feel her sore feet, although they had both gone barefoot all this time, she did not feel the pressure of her hands cuffed behind her back, all she felt was that he was close, she had him, she was with him.

They marched through the forest and along the dusty country road. Bells were pealing out over the town, striking twelve noon, all was at rest when the unusual procession made its way along the main street of Dobitzan, Karel first, with the weary soldiers trotting along to right and left of him to guard him, then Ruzena Sedlak, her eyes glazed, still dishevelled and battered from the blows, with her own hands cuffed behind her back, and bringing up the rear the military police officer, a grave, stern figure, obviously making a great effort to bear himself well. He had put his revolver back into its holster.

The buzz of noise in the marketplace died down. People came out of their doors to look darkly at the scene. Drivers on their carts cracked the whip at their horses angrily and spat, as if by chance. Men frowned and murmured, looked away and then back again, it was a shame, they muttered, first the children, the lads of seventeen, now they were dragging women off too. All the ill will and resentment of a people who had long felt that this Austrian war was nothing to do with them, yet dared not show any violent opposition, stood mute but menacing in hundreds of eyes, the eyes of the people of Dobitzan.

No one said a word; they were all silent. The steps of the marching soldiers could be heard in the street.

Somehow or other, Ruzena's animal nature must have sensed the magnetic force of that embitterment, for suddenly, in the middle of the road, the handcuffed woman flung herself down flat among the soldiers, her skirts flying, and began shouting at the top of her voice, "Help me, brothers! For God's sake help me! Don't let them do this."

The soldiers had to seize her, and then she cried out again, to Karel, "Throw yourself down! They'll have to drag us to the slaughter! Let God see this!" And Karel obediently lay down in the middle of the wet road too.

The furious military police officer intervened. "Get them up!" he shouted at his startled men. They tried to haul Ruzena and her son to their feet. But she twisted and turned, flung herself about with her bound hands like a fish landed on the bank, uttering shrill cries. She snapped and bit; it was a terrible sight. "God must see this," she howled, "God must see this." Finally the soldiers had to drag both of them away like beasts going to be butchered. But she went on shouting, her voice cracking horribly, "God must see this, God must see this!"

She was forced away as they waited for reinforcements, and was taken off to a cell under arrest, half-naked now, with her greying hair coming down. It was high time; the townsfolk were gathering together. Their looks were even darker than before. One farmer spat. Several women began talking angrily out loud. There was whistling, you could see men nudging the women and warning them; children stared, wide-eyed and alarmed, at all this tumultuous confusion.

Mother and son were taken off to the cells together, but the hatred in the air for the open display of violence was palpable.

Meanwhile, pacing furiously up and down in his office, his collar, trimmed with gold lace, torn open in his rage, the District Commissioner was bawling out the military police officer. He was a fool, he told the man, he was a godforsaken idiot to bring a deserter in along the road in broad daylight, and a woman in handcuffs with him. This kind of thing would get around the whole region, and then he personally would have trouble with Vienna. Didn't the officer think there had been quite enough of all this chasing people around here in Bohemia? This evening would have been a better time to bring the young man in. And why the devil had he brought the woman along too?

The officer showed his torn coat, pointing out that the mad bitch had attacked and bitten him. He'd had to have her arrested, he said, if only for the sake of the men's morale.

But the Commissioner was not mollified, and went on: "So did you have to drag her through the town in broad daylight? You can't treat women like that. People won't stand for it. What a mess! It gets folk really annoyed when you start in on women. Much better leave them out of it."

Finally the police officer asked, in muted tones, what he ought to do now.

"Oh, get the lad sent off tonight, send him to Budweis with the others. What business is all this of ours? Let those…" (he was about to say "bloody bureaucrats", but thought better of it in time), "let those responsible take care of it, we've done our duty. Keep the Sedlak woman under arrest until he's gone. She'll calm down in the morning. You can release her as soon as he's left. After all, women do calm down when they've had a good cry. And after that they go to church—or to some other man's bed."

The officer protested; he was most unwilling to agree. Had he marched all night for this? To himself, he vowed that this was the last time he'd go to so much trouble.

The District Commissioner had been right, it seemed. The Sedlak woman did indeed calm down in the cells. She did not move, but lay still on her bed. However, she felt no weariness. She was merely straining her ears to listen. She knew that her child was somewhere in another part of this building. Karel was still here, but she couldn't see him, couldn't hear him. She felt his presence, all the same. She knew he was close. Despite her dull nature, she felt a link with him through all these doors. Something could still make it turn out well for them. Perhaps the priest could help; he must have heard them both being dragged off under arrest. Perhaps the war was already over. Somewhere she listened for a sign, for a word. Karel was still there. As long as he was still there, there was hope. That was why everything was so quiet, so breathlessly still. The prison warder went up to see the District Commissioner, who duly noted the fact that the Sedlak woman had calmed down. Just as he'd said she would. Tomorrow they'd send Karel off, and then there would be peace and quiet again.

[*Here ends Zweig's unfinished manuscript*]

COMPULSION

To Pierre J Jouve
in fraternal friendship

THE WOMAN WAS STILL fast asleep, her breath coming full and strong. Her mouth, slightly open, seemed to be on the verge of smiling or speaking, and her curved young breasts rose softly under the covers. The first glimmer of dawn showed at the windows, but the light was poor this winter morning. Somewhere between darkness and day, it hovered uncertainly over sleeping things, veiling their forms.

Ferdinand had risen and dressed quietly, he himself did not know why. It often happened these days that, in the middle of working, he would suddenly pick up his hat and hurry out of the house, into the fields, striding faster and faster until he had walked to the point of exhaustion, and all at once found himself somewhere far away, in a place he did not know, his knees shaking and the pulse throbbing at his temples. Or he would suddenly freeze in the middle of an animated conversation and lose track of the words, failing to hear questions, and he would have to force himself back into awareness. Then again, he might forget what he was doing when he undressed in the evening, and would sit perfectly still on the edge of the bed, holding the shoe he had just taken off, until a word from his wife startled him out of his reverie or the shoe fell to the floor with a bang.

As he now left the slightly close atmosphere of the bedroom and stepped out on to the balcony, he shivered. Instinctively he drew his elbows in, closer to the warmth of his body. The landscape deep below him was still enveloped in mist. Dense, milky vapours hovered over the Lake of Zürich, which from his little house, perched high up here, usually looked as smooth as a mirror, reflecting every white cloud that hurried past in the sky. Wherever his eyes looked, whatever his hands felt, it was all damp, dark, slippery and grey.

Water dripped from the trees, moisture trickled from the rafters of the house. The world rising from the mists was like a man who has just emerged from a river with water streaming off him. The murmur of human voices came through the misty night, but muted and disjointed like the stertorous breathing of a drunk. Sometimes he also heard hammer blows and the distant chime of the bell from the church tower, but its usually clear tone sounded damp and rusty. Dank darkness stood between him and his world.

He shivered. Yet he stayed there, his hands thrust deeper into his pockets, waiting for the view to clear. The mist began slowly rolling up from below, like a sheet of grey paper, and he longed to see the beloved landscape that, he knew, lay down there in its usual orderly fashion, with its clear lines that normally brought clarity and order to his own life, although now it was hidden by these morning mists. He had so often gone to the window here in a mood of inner turmoil to find reassurance in the peaceful view: the houses over on the opposite bank of the lake, turning to each other as if in friendship, a steamer dividing the blue water with delicate precision, gulls flocking cheerfully over the banks, smoke rising in silver coils from red chimneys as the noonday chimes rang out. Peace! Peace! was the message it conveyed for all to see. At such moments, in the face of his own knowledge and despite the madness of the world, he believed in the beautiful signal it gave him, and for hours could forget his own homeland as he looked at this new one that he had chosen. Months ago, in flight from the present times and from other human beings, coming away from a country at war and arriving in Switzerland, he had felt his soul, crumpled, furrowed and ploughed into disorder as it was by horror and dismay, smoothing out here and growing scar tissue as the landscape softly welcomed him in, and its pure lines and colours called on his art to set to work. As a result he always felt alienated from himself, an exile once again, when the sight was obscured, as it was by the mist hiding everything from him at this time of the morning. He felt infinite pity for everyone shut up down in the dark, and for the people in the world of his old home, far away now—infinite pity, and a longing to be linked to them and their fate.

Somewhere out in the mist, the bell in the church tower gave four strokes and then, telling itself the time of day, chimed eight in clearer tones that pealed out into the March morning. He felt as if he were on top of a tower himself, indescribably isolated, with the world before him and his wife behind him in the darkness of her slumbers. His innermost will strained to tear that soft wall of mist apart and to sense, somewhere, the message of awakening, the certainty of life. And as he sent his eyes out into the mist, so to speak, he thought he did see something, either a man or an animal, moving slowly down there in the grey penumbra where the village ended and the winding path climbed up the hill to this house. Small, softly veiled in mist, it was coming towards him. He felt first pleasure to see something awake besides himself, then curiosity too, an avid and unhealthy curiosity. The grey figure of a man was making its way to a crossroads, with tracks leading to the next village in one direction and up here in the other. For a moment the stranger seemed to hesitate and draw breath at the crossroads. Then, slowly, he began climbing the bridle path.

Ferdinand felt uneasy. Who is this man, he wondered, what compulsion drives him out of the warmth of his dark bedroom and into the morning as mine has driven me? Is he coming up to see me, and if so what does he want? Then, through the mist which was thinner at close quarters now, he recognized the postman. He climbed up here every morning on the stroke of eight, and Ferdinand knew and pictured the man's rough-hewn face, his red seaman's beard turning grey at the ends, and his blue-framed glasses. His name was Nussbaum, meaning 'nut tree', and to himself Ferdinand called him Nutcracker because of his stiff movements and the ceremony with which he always swung his big, black leather bag over to the right before delivering the post with an air of self-importance. Ferdinand could not help smiling as he saw him trudging up, step by step, bag at the moment slung over his left shoulder, careful to impart great dignity to his short-legged gait.

But suddenly he felt weak at the knees. His hand, which had been shielding his eyes, dropped as if suddenly numb. His uneasiness today, yesterday, all these last weeks was back. He thought he sensed that the man was coming step by step inexorably towards him, coming to him alone. Without knowing just what he was about, he opened the bedroom door, stole past his sleeping wife, and hurried downstairs to intercept the postman on his way up the fenced path. They met at the garden gate.

"Do you have… do you have…"—he had to try again three times—"do you have any post for me?"

The postman pushed up his wet glasses to look at him. "Let's have a look." He hauled the black bag round to his right, and his fingers—they were like large worms, damp and red with the frosty mist—rummaged among the letters. Ferdinand was shivering. In the end the postman took one letter out. It was in a large brown envelope, with the word '*Official*' stamped in large letters on it, and his name underneath. "To be signed for," said the postman, moistening his indelible pencil and holding out the book to Ferdinand, who signed his name with a flourish. In his agitation the signature was illegible.

Then he took the letter that the sturdy red hand was offering him. But his fingers were so awkward that it slipped out of them, and fell to the ground to lie on the wet soil and damp leaves. And as he bent to pick it up, a bitter smell of decomposition and decay rose to his nostrils.

This, he now knew for certain, was what had been lurking under the surface for weeks, destroying his peace: the thought of this letter, which he had expected and was reluctant to receive, sent to him from far away, from a pointless, formless distance. Its rigid, typewritten words were groping for him, his warm life and his freedom. He had felt it approaching from somewhere or other, like a mounted man on patrol who senses the cold steel tube invisibly aimed at him from green forest undergrowth, and the little piece of lead in it that wants to penetrate the darkness beneath his skin. So resistance had been useless, and so had the little tricks he had practised to occupy his mind for nights on end. They had caught up with him. Barely eight months ago he had been standing naked, shivering with cold and revulsion, in front of an army doctor who felt the muscles in his arms like a horse-dealer. The humiliation of it illustrated the human indignity of the times and the slavery into which Europe had declined. He bore life in the stifling atmosphere of the patriotic phase of the war for two months, but after a while he found the air too difficult to breathe, and when the people around him opened their lips to speak he thought he saw their lies lying yellow on their tongues. The sight of the women, shivering with cold, who sat on the marketplace steps with their empty potato sacks in the first light of dawn broke his heart; he went around with his fists clenched, he felt that he was turning mean-minded and spiteful, he hated himself in his powerless rage. At last, thanks to a good word that someone put in for him, he succeeded in moving to Switzerland with his wife, and when he crossed the border the blood suddenly returned to his cheeks. He was swaying so much that he had to hold on to a post for support, but he felt like a human being again at last, full of life, will, strength, and capable of action. His lungs opened to breathe the air of freedom. All his fatherland meant to him now was prison and compulsion. His home in the world was outside his country, Europe was humanity.

But that light-hearted happiness did not last long. The fear came back. He felt that somehow or other his name had hooked him from behind to haul him back into that bloodstained thicket, that something he didn't know, although it knew him, was not about to let him go. He retreated inside himself, read no newspapers in order to avoid anything about men being called up, moved house to blur his trail, had letters sent to his wife *poste restante*, and avoided company so as to be asked no questions. He never went into town, he sent his wife to buy canvas and paints. He hid away in anonymity in this little village on the Lake of Zürich, where he had rented a small house from a farming family. But still he knew that in a drawer somewhere, among hundreds of thousands of other sheets of paper, there was one with his name on it. And one day, somewhere, some time, they would be bound to open that drawer—he could hear it being pulled out, he imagined the staccato hammer of his name being typed, and he knew that the letter would be sent on its travels until at last it found him.

Now here it was, crackling and cold, physically present in his fingers. Ferdinand made an effort to keep calm. What does this letter matter to me? he asked himself. Why should I take out the sheet of paper inside the envelope and read what it says overleaf? Tomorrow and the day after tomorrow the bushes will bear a thousand, ten thousand, a hundred thousand leaves, and this is no more to me than any of them. What does that word '*Official*' mean? Does that say I *have* to read it? I hold no office anywhere, and no one holds office over me. What's my name there for—is that really me? Who can compel me to say it means me, who can force me to read what's written on the paper? If I just tear it up unread, the scraps will flutter down to the lake, I won't know anything about it and nor will the world; it will be gone as fast as a drop of water falling from a tree to the ground, as fast as every breath that passes my lips! Why should this piece of paper make me uneasy? I won't know anything about it unless I want to. And I don't want to. All I want is my freedom.

His fingers tensed, ready to tear the stout envelope into small scraps. But oddly enough, his muscles would not do it. Something or other had taken over his own hands against his own will, for they did not obey him. And as he wished with all his heart that they would tear up the envelope, they very carefully opened it and, trembling, unfolded the white sheet of paper. It said what he already knew.

'No 34.729F. On the orders of District Headquarters at M, your honour is hereby requested hereby to present yourself in Room Number 8, District Headquarters at M, by 22nd March at the latest for a further medical examination with a view to establishing your fitness for service in the army. You will be issued with the military papers by the Consulate in Zürich, where you are to go for that purpose.'

When he went back indoors an hour later his wife came to meet him, smiling, a bunch of spring flowers loosely held in her hand. She was radiant with carefree delight. "Look," she said, "look what I've found! They're already flowering in the meadow behind the house, even though the snow still lies in the shade among the trees." He took the flowers to please her, bent over them so as not to catch his beloved wife's untroubled gaze, and was quick to take refuge in the little attic room that he had made into a studio.

But his work did not go well. No sooner did he face his blank canvas than the typewritten words of the letter suddenly stood there as if hammered out on it. The colours on his palette seemed to him like mud and blood. He kept thinking of pus and wounds. His self-portrait, painted in half-shade, showed him a military collar under his chin. "Madness! Madness!" he said out loud, stamping his foot to dispel these deranged images. But his hands trembled and the floor shook beneath his feet. He had to sit down, and he went on sitting there on his small stool, overwhelmed by his thoughts, until his wife called him to luncheon.

Every morsel choked him. Something bitter was stuck high up in his throat, it had to be swallowed with every mouthful, and it always came up again. Hunched there in silence, he realized that his wife was watching him. Suddenly he felt her hand softly placed on his own.

"What's the matter, Ferdinand?" He did not reply. "Have you had bad news?"

He just nodded, and gulped.

"From the army?"

He nodded again. She said no more, and nor did he. The looming, oppressive idea of it was suddenly there in the room, pushing everything else aside. It weighed down, broad and sticky, on the food they had begun to eat. It crawled, a damp slug, over the backs of their necks and made them shudder. They dared not look at each other, but just sat there in silence with their shoulders bent, and the intolerable burden of that thought pressing down on them.

There was a faltering note in her voice when at last she asked, "Have they told you to go to the Consulate?"

"Yes."

"And will you go?"

He was trembling. "I don't know. But I have to."

"Why do you have to? They can't order you about here in Switzerland. You're a free man here."

"Free!" he said savagely, through gritted teeth. "Who's still free today?"

"Anyone who wants to be. You most of all. What *is* this?" Contemptuously, she snatched away the sheet of paper that he had placed in front of him. "What power does this scrap of paper have over you, scribbled by some wretched clerk in an office—what power does it have over you? You're a free, living man! What can it do to you?"

"In itself it can't do anything, but the people who sent it can."

"So who sent it? What human being does it come from? It's from no one but a machine, a vast, murderous machine. But it can't touch you."

"It's touched millions, so why not me?"

"Because you don't want to go?"

"Nor did all the others."

"But they weren't free. They were caught between the guns, that's why they went. Not of their own free will, not one of them. No one would willingly have left Switzerland to go back to that hell."

But when she saw how he was tormenting himself, she checked her wildness. Pity welled up in her, as if for a child. "Ferdinand," she said, leaning against him, "try to think perfectly clearly now. You're afraid, and I understand how distressing it is to have this evil beast suddenly pouncing on you. But remember, we were expecting this letter. We've discussed what to do in this event hundreds of times, and I was proud of you because I knew you'd just tear it to pieces, you wouldn't give yourself up to go and murder people. Don't you remember?"

"I know, Paula, I know, but…"

"Don't say any more now," she urged him. "Somehow or other, this thing has got its teeth into you. But think of our conversations, of the statement you drew up—it's there in the left-hand drawer of the desk—saying that you would never carry arms. You had firmly decided…"

He reacted to that. "No, I hadn't firmly decided! I was never sure! All that was lies. I was hiding from my own fear. I intoxicated myself with those words. But it was all true only as long as I was free, and I always knew that if I was summoned I'd be weak. Do you think I trembled before them? They're nothing as long as their ideas aren't really in my heart, otherwise they're just air, words, nothing. But I trembled before myself, because I always knew that as soon as they called me up I'd go."

"Ferdinand, do you *want* to go?"

"No, no, no," he cried, stamping his foot, "I don't want to, I don't, nothing in me wants to. But I *shall* go, against my own will. That's the terrible part of these people's power, you serve them against your will, against your own convictions. If you still had a will of your own—but the moment you have a letter like that in your hands, your free will is gone. You obey. You're a schoolboy, the teacher's calling to you, you stand up and tremble."

"But Ferdinand, who's calling you? The Fatherland? Some clerk in an office! Some bored bureaucrat! And what's more, even the state has no right to force a man to commit murder, no right…"

"I know, I know. Why not quote Tolstoy too? I know all the arguments: don't you understand, I myself don't believe they have any right to call me up, I don't believe it's my duty to obey them. I acknowledge only one kind of duty: to act as a human being and to work. I have no Fatherland beyond mankind in general, no ambition to kill other people, I know all that, Paula, I see it as clearly as you do—except that they've caught me already, they're summoning me and I know, in spite of everything, I shall go."

"But why? Why? I ask you, why?"

He groaned. "I don't know why. Perhaps because madness is stronger than reason in the world these days. Perhaps it's just because I'm no hero and I daren't run away… there's no explaining it. It's a kind of compulsion; I can't break the chain that is throttling twenty million people. I can't do it."

He hid his face in his hands. The clock above them ticked on and on, a guard on duty outside the sentry-box of time. She was trembling slightly. "It's calling to you, yes, I can understand that, although… well, I don't *really* understand it. But can't you hear anything here calling to you as well? Is there nothing to keep you here?"

He flared up. "My pictures? My work? No! I can't paint any more. I realized that today. I'm already living over there, not here any more. It's a crime to work for your own pleasure now while the world falls into ruin. You can't feel and live for yourself alone!"

She stood up and turned away. "I never thought you lived for yourself alone. I thought… I thought I was part of your world too." She couldn't go on; her tears were forcing their way out along with her words. He tried to soothe her. But there was anger behind her tears, and he shrank from that. "Go, then," she said, "you'd better go! What do I mean to you? Less than a scrap of paper. So go if you want to."

"I don't want to!" He struck the table with his fists in helpless rage. "I don't want to. But they want me to. They are strong and I'm weak. They've forged their iron will over thousands of years, they're well-organized and subtle, they've made preparations and now it breaks over us like a thunderstorm. Their will is strong and my nerves are weak. It's an unequal battle. You can't fight back against a machine. You could resist men, yes, but this is a machine, a slaughtering machine, a soulless tool without a heart or mind. There's nothing you can do to oppose it."

"Yes, you can if you must." She was shouting like a madwoman now. "I can do it if you can't. If you're weak I'm not, I don't knuckle under to a piece of paper, I don't give up any living creature for a word. You won't go as long as I have any power over you. You're sick, I can swear it. You're highly strung. If a plate so much as clinks you jump nervously. Any doctor must see that. Get yourself examined here, I'll go with you, I'll tell the doctor everything. He's sure to say you're unfit. You just have to defend yourself, take the bit between your teeth—the bit of your own will. Remember your friend Jeannot in Paris, who had himself put under observation in the psychiatric hospital for three months—and how they tormented him with their investigations, but he held out until they discharged him. You just have to show that you're not going along with them. You can't give up. This means everything; don't forget, they want your life, your liberty, everything. You have to fight back."

"Fight back! How can I fight back? They're stronger than anyone, they're stronger than anything in the whole world."

"That's not true! They're only strong as long as the world allows it. The individual is always stronger than any idea, he just has to be true to himself and his own will. He just has to know that he's a human being and wants to stay human, and then those words they use to anaesthetize people these days—the Fatherland, duty, heroism—then they're simply phrases stinking of blood, warm, living human blood. Be honest, is your Fatherland as important to you as your life? Is a province that will switch overnight from one Serene Highness to another as dear to you as the hand you paint with? Do you believe in some kind of justice beyond the invisible knowledge of what's just and right that we build into ourselves with our thoughts, our blood? No, I know you don't, no! You're lying to yourself if you say you want to go…"

"I don't want to."

"But you don't feel that strongly enough! You don't want to stay any more. You're letting yourself want to do this thing, that's your crime. You're giving yourself up to something you hate and staking your life on it. Why not on something you really believe in? Shedding blood for your own ideas is one thing, but why do it for someone else's? Ferdinand, don't forget, if you really want strongly enough to stay free, what are those people over the border but wicked fools? If you *don't* want it enough, and they get hold of you, then you're the fool. You always said…"

"Yes, I said, I said it all, I talked and talked just to give myself courage. I was boasting, the way children sing in a dark wood because they're afraid of their own fears. It was all a lie, that's cruelly clear to me now. Because I always knew that if they sent for me I'd go…"

"You're really going? Oh, Ferdinand, Ferdinand!"

"Not me! Not me! It's something else in me that's going—has gone already. Something or other stands up in me like the schoolboy obediently standing up for the teacher, I told you so. It trembles and obeys! Yet at the same time I hear all you say, and I know it's right and true and human and necessary—it's the one thing I ought to do, I must do—I know that, I know it, that's why it's so despicable of me to go. But I *am* going, something compels me. Despise me! I despise myself. But there's nothing else I can do, nothing!"

He hammered on the table with both fists. There was a dull, animal, captive expression in his eyes. She couldn't bear to look at him. In her love, she was afraid that she might indeed despise him. The table was still laid, the meat standing on it was cold now and looked like carrion, the bread was black and crumbling; it might have been slag. The heavy smell of food filled the room. Nausea rose to her throat in her disgust at all this. She pushed the window open to let in some fresh air. Her shoulders were shaking slightly, and above them rose the blue March sky, with its white clouds caressing her hair.

"Look," she said more quietly, "look out there! Just once, I beg you. Perhaps all I'm saying isn't entirely true. Words always miss the mark. But what I can see is true all the same. That doesn't lie. There's a farmer down there following the plough. He's young and strong. Why doesn't *he* go off to be murdered? Because his country isn't at war, because his fields lie a little way beyond the border, so the law doesn't apply to him. And now that you're in this country it doesn't apply to you either. Can an invisible law that's in force only as far as a few milestones and then not beyond them be true? Don't you feel how senseless it is when you look at the peace here? Look, Ferdinand, look, see how clear the sky is above the lake, see how the colours wait for us to enjoy them, come here to the window and then tell me just once more that you want to go…"

"I don't want to go! I don't want to! You know I don't! Why should I look out at this scene? I know all about it, everything, everything! You're just tormenting me! Every word you say hurts. And nothing, nothing, nothing can help me!"

She felt weak in the face of his pain. Pity broke her strength. She quietly turned around.

"So when… oh, Ferdinand… when do you have to go to the Consulate?"

"Tomorrow. Well, it ought to have been yesterday, but the letter didn't reach me in time. They didn't track me down until today. So I'll have to go tomorrow."

"But suppose you don't go tomorrow? Keep them waiting. They can't do anything to you here. And there's no hurry. Let them wait a week. I'll write and tell them you were ill, you were in bed. My brother did that and gained two weeks' grace. At the worst they won't believe you and they'll send the doctor from the Consulate up here. Perhaps we could talk to him. People are still human beings if they don't wear a uniform. Maybe he'll look at your pictures and see that someone like you is right out of place at the front. And even if that doesn't work we'll have gained a week."

He said nothing, and she felt that his silence was opposing her.

"Ferdinand, promise me not to go tomorrow! Let them wait. You need to be well prepared in your mind. At the moment you're upset, and they're doing what they like with you. They'd be stronger than you tomorrow, but in a week's time you'll be stronger than them. Think of the happy days we'll enjoy then. Oh, Ferdinand, Ferdinand, are you listening to me?"

She shook him. He looked at her, empty-eyed. That apathetic, lost gaze showed no response to her words, only horror and fear from a depth that she could not plumb. He pulled himself together only slowly.

"You're right," he said at last. "You're right, there's no hurry. What can they do to me? Has the letter necessarily reached me? Couldn't I have gone away for a little while? Or I could have been ill. No—I signed a receipt for the postman. But that makes no difference. We have to think things over. You're right, you're right."

He had risen to his feet and began pacing up and down the room. "You're right, you're right," he mechanically repeated, but there was no conviction in his voice. "You're right, you're right"—it sounded abstracted, he was repeating the words vacantly. She felt that his thoughts were somewhere else, far away, still with the people over the border, still heading for disaster. She couldn't bear to hear his constant "You're right, you're right" any more. Quietly, she went out of the room, and then heard him walking up and down it for hours on end, like a prisoner in his dungeon.

He did not touch dinner that evening either. There was something far away and frozen in him. It was only that night that she felt her living husband's fear as he lay beside her, clasping her soft, warm body as if taking refuge in it, embracing her passionately, convulsively. But this, she knew, was not love but escape. It was a spasmodic reaction, and under his kisses she sensed bitter, salty tears. Then he lay in silence again. Sometimes she heard him groan. Then she held her hand out to him, and he took it as if he could cling to it. They did not talk. Only once, when she heard him sob, did she try to comfort him. "You still have a week. Don't think about it." But then she was ashamed of herself for advising him to think of something else, for she felt from the chill of his hand, the pulsing of his heart, that this one idea possessed and commanded him. And there was no miracle to release him from it.

Never before had silence and the dark weighed so heavily in this house. The horror of the whole world stood there within its walls, cold and chilly. Only the clock, undeterred, ticked on, an iron sentry marching up, marching down, and she knew that with every marching step of that clock the living man at her side, the man she loved, was moving further away from her. She couldn't bear it any more; she jumped out of bed and stopped the pendulum. Now there was no time any more, only terror and silence. And they both lay mute and wakeful, side by side, until the new day dawned, with the idea of what was to come marching up and down in their hearts.

It was still wintry twilight. Hoarfrost was hovering over the lake in heavy drifts of mist when he got up, quickly threw on his clothes, hurried hesitantly and uncertainly from room to room and back again, until he suddenly took his hat and coat and quietly opened the front door. Later, he often remembered how his hand had trembled when it touched the bolt, which was cold with frost, and he turned furtively to see if anyone was watching him. Sure enough, the dog rushed at him as if he were a thief stealing in, but on recognizing him got down, responded affectionately to his patting, and then raced around wagging his tail, eager to go for a walk with him. However, he shooed the dog away with his hand—he dared not speak. Then, not sure himself why he was in such haste, he suddenly hurried down the bridle path. Sometimes he stopped and looked back at his house as it slowly disappeared from sight in the mist, but then the urge to go on came over him once more and he ran downhill to the station, stumbling over stones as if someone were after him. Only when he arrived did he stop, warm vapour rising from his moist clothes, sweat on his forehead.

A few farmers and other folk who knew him were standing there. They wished him good morning, and one or two seemed inclined to strike up a conversation with him, but he turned away from them. He felt a bashful fear of having to talk to other people at this moment, and yet waiting idly beside the wet rails was painful. Without attending to what he was doing he stood on the scales, put a coin in the slot, stared into his pale, sweating face in the little mirror above the dial that showed his weight, and only when he got off and his coin clinked down inside the machine did he notice that he had failed to register what the pointers said. "I'm going out of my mind, right out of my mind," he murmured quietly, and felt a chill of horror at himself. He sat down on a bench and tried to force himself to think everything over clearly. But then the signal bell rang, very close to him, a harsh, jangling sound, and he jumped, startled. The locomotive was already whistling in the distance. The train raced in, and he sat down in a compartment. A dirty newspaper lay on the floor. He picked the newspaper up and stared at it without taking in what he was reading, seeing only his own hands holding it and shaking more and more all the time.

The train stopped. Zürich. He staggered out. He knew where he was going, and sensed his own reluctance to go there, but it was growing weaker all the time. Now and then he set himself small trials of strength. He stopped in front of a poster and, to prove that he was in command of himself, forced himself to read it from top to bottom. "There's no hurry," he told himself in an undertone, but even as his lips murmured the words he was overcome by haste again. His frantic, thrusting impatience was like an engine driving him on. Helplessly, he looked around for a cab. His legs were trembling. A taxi drove by and he hailed it, flinging himself into it like a suicide plunging into the river. He gave a name; the street where the Consulate stood.

The car engine hummed. He leaned back with his eyes closed. He felt as if he were racing into an abyss, and even took some slight pleasure in the speed of the cab carrying him to his doom. It felt good to observe himself passively. But the car was already stopping. He got out, paid the driver, and entered the lift of the building where the Consulate had its offices. In an odd way he again felt a sense of pleasure at being mechanically raised up and carried onwards. As if it were not himself doing all this, but the unknown, unimaginable power of his compulsion forcing him to go on his way.

The door of the Consulate was locked. He rang the bell. No answer. A thought flashed urgently through his mind: go back, get away from here quickly, go down the stairs and out! But he rang the bell again. Steps came slowly dragging along inside. A servant in his shirt-sleeves, duster in hand, made a great business of opening the door. Obviously he was tidying the offices. "Yes, what do you want?" he growled.

"I—I was told to come to the Consulate,' he managed to say, retreating, and ashamed of stammering in front of this servant.

The man turned, sounding peevish and annoyed. "Can't you read what it says on the plate? Office hours ten to twelve. There's nobody here yet." And without waiting for any answer he closed the door.

Ferdinand stood there, flinching, as a sense of boundless shame struck him to the heart. He looked at his watch. It was ten-past seven. "This is mad! I'm out of my mind!" he stammered, and went down the steps trembling like an old man.

Two-and-a-half hours—this dead, empty time was terrible to him, for he felt that with every minute of waiting some of his strength slipped away. Just now he had been braced and prepared, he had worked out what he would say in advance, every word was ready, the whole scene was constructed in his mind, and now this iron curtain of two hours had fallen between him and the strength he had screwed to the sticking-point. Afraid, he sensed all the warmth in him dissipating, obliterating word after word from his memory as they tumbled over one another and nervously took to flight.

He had worked it out like this: he would go to the Consulate and have himself announced there at once to the military attaché, whom he knew slightly. They had once met and made casual conversation at the house of mutual friends. So he would at least know the man he faced: an aristocrat, elegant, worldly, proud of his joviality, a man who liked to appear generous-minded and did not want to be thought a mere bureaucrat. They all had that ambition, they wanted to figure as diplomats, men of importance, and he planned to work on that: he would have himself announced, speak of general things at first in a civil, sociable tone, ask after the health of the attaché's wife. The attaché would be sure to ask him to sit down, offer him a cigarette, and finally, as silence fell, would say politely, "Well, how can I help you?" The other man must ask him first, that was very important, that was not to be forgotten. In answer he would say, very cool and casual, "I've had a letter asking me to go to M for a medical examination. There must be some mistake; I've already been expressly declared unfit for military service." He must say that very calmly, it must be immediately obvious that he regarded the whole thing as a mere trifle.

At this point the attaché—he remembered the man's casual manner—would take the piece of paper and explain that this was to be a new examination; surely, he would say, he must have seen in the newspapers, some time ago, that even those previously exempted must now report again.

To this, still very coolly, he would say, "Ah, I see! The fact is I don't read the papers, I just don't have time for it. I have work to do." He wanted the other man to see at once how indifferent he was to the whole war, how much he felt himself a free agent.

Of course the attaché would then explain that Ferdinand must comply with this call-up order, he himself was sorry, but the military authorities… and so on and so forth. That would be his moment to speak more forcefully. "Yes, I understand that," he must say, "but the fact is, it's quite impossible for me to interrupt my work just now. I've agreed to have an exhibition of my paintings held, and I can't let the curator down. I've given my word." And then he would suggest to the attaché that he should either be given a longer deadline, or have himself re-examined here by the Consulate doctor.

So far he was sure he knew how it would go. Only after this point were there a number of possibilities. The attaché might agree at once, and then at least he would have gained time. But if the attaché said politely—with cold, evasive civility, suddenly sounding official—that such decisions were inadmissible and outside his jurisdiction, then he had to be resolute. First he must stand up, go over to the desk and say firmly, very, very firmly, his manner conveying an inner sense of inflexible determination, "I understand that, but I would like to put it on record that my economic obligations prevent me from complying with this call-up immediately. I will take it upon myself to postpone matters for three weeks, until I have satisfied my moral liabilities. Naturally I have no intention of failing in my duty to the Fatherland." He was particularly proud of these remarks, which he had planned with care. "I would like to put it on record", "economic obligations"—it all sounded so objective and official. If the attaché then pointed out that there might be legal consequences, that would be the time to make his tone a little sharper and reply coldly, "I know the law, I am well aware of the consequences. But once I have given my word, I regard keeping it the highest law of all, and I must accept any difficulty in order to do so." Then he must be quick to bow, thus cutting the conversation short, and go to the door. He'd show them that he was no workman or apprentice to wait for dismissal, but a man who decided for himself when a conversation was over.

He acted out this scene in his mind three times, pacing up and down. He liked the whole structure, the entire tone of it, he was waiting impatiently for the moment to come like an actor waiting for his cue. There was just one passage that still didn't seem quite right to him. "I have no intention of failing in my duty to the Fatherland." There absolutely had to be some kind of sop to patriotic values in the conversation, it was necessary to show that he was not being purposely obstructive, but he wasn't ready to go either. He would acknowledge the necessity of showing patriotism, for their ears only, of course, not for himself. However, that "duty to the Fatherland"—the phrase was too literary, it came too pat. He thought it over again. Perhaps: "I know that the Fatherland needs me." No, that was even more ridiculous. Or better: "I have no intention of shirking my responsibility to answer the call of the Fatherland." Yes, that was an improvement. But he still didn't like this part of the scene; it was too servile. He was bowing just a little too low. He thought yet again. He had better keep it perfectly simple. "I know my duty"—yes, that was it, you could turn the phrase this way and that, understand or misunderstand it. And it sounded clear and brief. You could say it in a masterful tone—"I know my duty"—almost like a threat. Now it was all perfect. Yet he glanced nervously at his watch again. Time refused to go forward. It was only eight o'clock.

People jostled him in the street, he didn't know which way to turn. He went into a café and tried to read the papers. But he felt the words disturbing him; they were all about duty and the Fatherland here too, and the phrases left him confused. He drank a cognac and then another, to get rid of the bitter taste in his throat. Frantically, he wondered how he could get the better of time, and kept reassembling the pieces of his imaginary conversation in his head. Suddenly he put a hand to his cheek—"Unshaved! I haven't shaved!" He hurried to a barber's, where he also had his hair cut and washed. That disposed of half-an-hour of waiting. And then, it occurred to him, he ought to look elegant. That was important in such offices. They took an arrogant tone only with the riffraff, they'd snap at people like that, but if you appeared looking elegant, a man of the world, at ease, they'd soon change their tune. The idea went to his head. He had his coat brushed and went to buy a pair of gloves, taking a long time over his choice. Yellow gloves somehow seemed too striking, something a gigolo might wear; a discreet pearl-grey pair would be better. Then he went up and down the street again, looked at himself in a tailor's mirror, adjusted his tie. His hand felt too empty—a walking-stick, it occurred to him, a walking-stick would impart a sense of occasion, a touch of worldliness to his visit. He quickly went into the shop and bought one. When he came out again the clock in the tower was striking quarter-to-ten. He recited his lines to himself once more. The new version, with the words, "I know my duty," was now the strongest part of it. Very sure of himself, very firmly he strode out and ran up the stairs to the Consulate, as light on his feet as a boy.

A minute later, as soon as the servant opened the door, a sudden presentiment that his calculations might be all wrong descended on him. And indeed, nothing went as he had expected. When he asked to see the attaché he was told that His Honour the Secretary was with a visitor, and he must wait. A not particularly civil gesture showed him to a chair in the middle of a row where three men of downcast appearance were already sitting. Reluctantly, he sat down, feeling with annoyance that his was just an ordinary affair here, he was a case, something to be dealt with. The men beside him were exchanging their own little stories; one of them was saying, in plaintive and depressed tones, that he had been interned in France for two years and now the people here wouldn't give him the money for his fare home; another complained that no one would help him to find a job, even though he had three children. Privately, Ferdinand was quivering with fury; they had left him on a bench with common petitioners, yet he noticed that somehow he was also irritated by the petty, fault-finding tone of these ordinary people. He wanted to rehearse his conversation once more, but their fatuous remarks put him off his stroke. He felt like shouting at them, "Be quiet, you fools!" or bringing money out of his pocket and sending them home, but his will was crippled and he just sat there with them, hat in hand like his companions. The constant coming and going of people opening and closing doors also confused him; all the time he was afraid that someone he knew might see him here with the petitioners, and yet whenever a door opened he was ready to leap up, only to sit back again disappointed. Once he pulled himself together and told the servant, who was standing beside them like a sentry on duty, "I can always come back tomorrow, you know." But the man reassured him—"His Honour the Secretary will be able to see you soon"—and his knees gave way again. He was trapped here; there was nothing he could do about it.

At last a lady came out, skirts rustling, smiling and preening, passed the waiting petitioners with an air of superiority, and the servant called, "His Honour the Secretary can see you now."

Ferdinand stood up. Only when it was too late did he realize that he had left his walking-stick and gloves on the window-sill, but he couldn't go back for them now, the door was already open. Half looking back, confused by these random thoughts, he went in. The attaché sat at his desk reading. Now he looked up, nodded to Ferdinand, and gave him a courteous but cold smile, without asking him to sit down. "Ah, our *magister artium*. Just a minute." He rose and called to someone in the next room. "The Ferdinand R file, please, you remember, the one that came the day before yesterday, his call-up papers were sent on here." Sitting down again, he said, "So you're another one who's leaving us again! Well, I hope you've enjoyed your stay here in Switzerland. You're looking very well," and then he was leafing through the file that a clerk brought him. "Report to M… yes… yes, that's right… all in order. I've had the papers made out… I don't suppose you want to claim travel expenses, do you?"

Ferdinand stood up and heard his own voice stammering, "No… no."

The attaché signed the call-up order and handed it to him. "You're really supposed to leave tomorrow, but I don't suppose it's all that urgent. Let the paint dry on your latest masterpiece. If you need another day or so to put your affairs in order, I'll take the responsibility for that. A couple of days won't matter to the Fatherland."

Ferdinand sensed that this was a joke, and he ought to smile. To his private horror, he actually did feel his lips stretching in a polite grimace. Say something, he told himself, I must say something now, not just stand around like a dolt. And at last he managed to get out, "Is the call-up letter enough… I don't need anything else… some kind of special pass?"

"No, no," smiled the attaché. "They won't make any trouble for you at the border. They'll be expecting you anyway. Well, *bon voyage*." And he offered his hand.

Ferdinand felt that he had been dismissed. Everything went dark before his eyes as he quickly made his way to the door. Nausea rose in his throat.

"The door on the right, please, the one on the right," said the voice behind him. He had tried the wrong door, and now—with a slight smile, as he thought he saw in the dim light of his bewildered senses—the attaché was holding the correct door open for him.

"Thank you, thank you, please don't trouble yourself," he stammered, furious with himself for this unnecessary civility. And no sooner was he out of the room, with the servant handing him his stick and gloves, than he remembered all he had planned to say. "Economic obligations… put it on the record." He felt more ashamed than ever before in his life, and he had even thanked the man, thanked him politely! But his emotional capacity would no longer suffice even for rage. Pale-faced, he went down the stairs, feeling only that this man walking along couldn't be himself, and that he had been defeated by force, a strange and pitiless force treading a whole world underfoot.

It was not until late in the afternoon that he arrived home. The soles of his feet were sore; he had been walking aimlessly around for hours, and had turned back from his own door three times. Finally he tried stealing up to it from the back, along hidden paths through the vineyards. However, the faithful dog had detected him. Barking wildly, he jumped up at him, tail wagging passionately. His wife stood at the door, and he saw at first glance that she knew everything. He followed her without a word, shame weighing heavily on the back of his neck.

But she was not harsh. She did not look at him, she was visibly avoiding anything that would upset him. She placed some cold meat on the table, and when he obediently sat down she went to his side. "Ferdinand," she said, and her voice was shaking badly, "you're not well. This is not the time for me to talk to you. I won't blame you, you're not acting of your own free will, and I feel how much you're suffering. But promise me one thing: don't do anything else in this business without discussing it first with me."

He said nothing. Her voice became more agitated.

"I've never interfered in your personal affairs, I always aimed to leave you the freedom to make your own decisions absolutely. But now you're playing not just with your life, you're playing with mine too. It took us years to find our happiness, and I'm not giving it up as easily as you. Not to the state, not to murder, not to your vanity and weakness. Not to anyone, do you hear? Not to anyone! If you are weak when you face them, I'm not. I know what this is all about, and I'm not giving up."

He still remained silent, and his servile, guilty silence began to make her bitter. "I'm not letting this scrap of paper take something away from me, I don't acknowledge any law that ends in murder. I'm not bowing to any bureaucracy. You men are all ruined by ideologies now, you think in terms of politics and ethics, we women still have straightforward feelings. I know what the word Fatherland means too, but I know what our Fatherland means today: murder and enslavement. You can feel a sense of belonging to your own nation, but that doesn't mean that when the nations have run mad you have to join them. You may be just a number to them, a tool, cannon-fodder, but to me you're still a living man and I won't let them have you. I'm not giving you up. I've never ventured to decide anything for you, but now it's my duty to protect you. You've always been a clear-minded, responsible human being who knew what he wanted; now you're a broken, disturbed, dutiful mechanism without any will of your own—it's dead, like those millions of victims out there. They've worked on you through your nerves, but they forgot me. I was never stronger than I am now."

He still remained silent, lost in gloomy thought. There was no ability in him to resist either his adversary or her.

She stood up very straight, like someone arming for battle. Her voice was hard, tense, braced.

"What did they say to you at the Consulate? I want to know." It was an order. Wearily, he took out the paper and handed it to her. She read it, frowning. Then she tossed it scornfully on to the table.

"What a hurry those good gentlemen are in! Tomorrow! And I expect you even thanked them, clicked your heels, obedient already. 'Ordered to make yourself available at once.' Available! They should have said make yourself a slave. We haven't fallen so low yet, that point hasn't come, not by a long way!"

Ferdinand stood up. He was pale, and his hand clutched the chair convulsively. "Paula, let's not deceive ourselves. That point *has* come. We can't escape it. I tried to defend myself, and it was no use. I'm—I *am* this piece of paper. Even if I tear it up, I still am. Don't make it difficult for me. There'd be no freedom here. Every hour I'd feel something out there calling, groping for me, pulling and tugging at me. It will be easier for me there. There's freedom to be found in the dungeon itself. It's only while I still feel I'm a fugitive, evading them, that I'm not free. And anyway, why jump to the worst conclusions? They rejected me once, why not this time too? Or perhaps they won't give me a weapon, in fact I feel sure they won't, I'll be employed on some lighter kind of service. Why think the worst now? It may not be so dangerous, perhaps I'll be lucky."

She did not relent. "That's not the point any more, Ferdinand. It makes no difference whether they give you light or heavy work to do. It's a case of whether you have to go into service under what you hate, whether you're willing to lend yourself to the greatest crime in the world against your own convictions. Because everyone who isn't against them is with them. And you *can* reject them, you can do it, so you must."

"I can do it? I can't do anything! Not any more. Everything that once made me strong—my abhorrence of this absurdity, my hatred for it, my indignation—all that is such a burden on me now. Don't torment me, please, don't torment me, don't tell me that."

"I'm not. You have to tell yourself: they have no rights over a living man."

"Rights! Rights! Where are there any rights in the world? We've murdered rights. Every individual person has his rights, but they have power, and nothing else matters any more."

"And why do they have power? Because the rest of you hand it to them. And they'll have it only while you're still cowards. What humanity now calls monstrous consists of ten men with strong wills in the countries concerned, and ten men can destroy the monstrosity again. A man, a single living man can destroy their power by saying no to them. But while you and those like you cower, thinking perhaps you'll muddle through, while you dodge and duck and hope to slip through their fingers instead of striking them to the heart, you'll be their servants and you'll deserve no better. A man ought not to crawl away, he ought to say no, that's the only duty there is today, there's no duty to go and get yourself killed."

"But Paula… what do you think… what should I…"

"You should say no if something says no inside you. You know I love life, I love your freedom, I love your work. And if you tell me today: I have to go there, I have to lay down the law with a gun, and if I know you truly believe you must, then I'll say: Go! But if you go for the sake of a lie that you don't believe yourself, out of weakness and lack of nerve and just hoping you can muddle through, then I despise you, yes, I despise you! If you want to go as a man standing for humanity, for what you believe in, then I won't try to stop you. But if you go to be a beast among beasts, a slave among slaves, I shall stand up to you. It's all right for people to sacrifice themselves for their own ideas, not for the madness of others. Let those who believe in the Fatherland die for it."

"Paula!" Instinctively, he rose to his feet.

"Oh, am I speaking too freely for you? Do you feel the corporal's stick behind you already? Never fear! We're still in Switzerland. You'd like me to keep quiet, or tell you you'll be all right, nothing will happen to you. But this is no time for sentimentality. Everything is at stake now. You and I are at stake."

"Paula!" he said, trying to interrupt again.

"No, I have no more sympathy with you. I chose you and lived with you as a free human being. And I despise weaklings and those who lie to themselves. Why should I sympathize with you? What do I mean to you? A sergeant hands you a few words on a piece of paper, and you cast me aside and run after him. But I'm not to be cast aside and then picked up again: you must decide now. Decide between them and me! Despise them or despise me. I know there are hard times ahead for us if you stay; I'll never see my parents and family again, we shall never be allowed to go back, but I can face that if you are with me. If you tear us apart now, though, then it's for ever."

He merely groaned, but she was blazing with angry strength.

"Choose them or me! There's no third choice. Ferdinand, think better of it while there's still time. I've often felt sorry we have no child. Now, for the first time, I'm glad of it. I don't want a weakling's child, and I don't want to bring up a war orphan. I've never stood by you more than I do now that I'm making it hard for you. But I tell you: this is not a trial separation, this is goodbye for ever. If you leave me to join the army and follow those uniformed murderers, there's no coming back. I don't share my life with criminals, I don't share a man with that vampire the state. It or me—you must choose now."

He still stood there shivering as she went to the door and slammed it behind her. The loud slam brought him to his knees. He had to sit down, and collapsed there, sombre, at a loss. And at last he broke down and cried like a small child.

She did not come back into the room all afternoon, but he felt that her strong will stood outside it, hostile and armed. And at the same time he knew about that other will, with a steel driving-wheel set cold under its breast, forcing him on. Sometimes he tried to think about this or that, but his thoughts slipped away, and as he sat there still, apparently thoughtful, the last of his peace flowed away into a state of burning nervous agitation. He felt the two ends of his life taken and tugged both ways by superhuman powers, and wished only that it would split like a rope in the middle.

To occupy himself he went through the desk drawers, tore up some letters, stared at others without taking in a word, stumbled round the room, sat down again, forced up by restlessness and down again by exhaustion. And suddenly he saw his hands putting together necessities for the journey, bringing out his rucksack from under the sofa. He stared at his own hands doing all this deliberately and against his own will. When the rucksack was packed he began to tremble, and suddenly there it was on the table. His shoulders felt weighed down, as if it were already resting on them, and with it the whole weight of these times.

The door opened, and his wife came in with a paraffin lamp. When she placed it on the table, the circle of light it cast fell on the packed rucksack. His secret ignominy, thus brightly lit, emerged starkly from the darkness. He stammered, "It's only in case… I still have time… I…" But a glance, fixed, stony, mask-like, met his words and crushed them. She stared at him for several minutes, her lips tightly pressed over her teeth. She stood motionless at first, then swayed slightly as if she might faint, while her eyes bored into him.

The tension of her lips relaxed, but she turned, a shudder ran over her shoulders, and she left him without looking back.

A few minutes later the maid came in, bringing supper for him alone. The usual place at his side was empty, and when, full of incoherent emotion, he looked at it, he saw the cruel symbol of the rucksack placed there. He felt as if he had left already, was already dead to this house; its walls were dark, the circle of light from the lamp did not reach all the way to them, and outside, beyond the lights in other houses, night and the *föhn* wind pressed down. All was still in the distance, and the height of the sky, its vast expanse spanning the depths below, only increased his sense of isolation. He felt everything around him gradually dying, dropping away from him: the house, the landscape, his work, his wife, as the broad sea of his life suddenly dried up, compressing his beating heart. A great need for love overcame him, for warm and kindly words. He felt ready to agree to anything, if he could only somehow get back to the past. Melancholy prevailed over his nervous restlessness, and the strong emotions of his imminent farewell were lost in childish longing for a little tenderness.

He went to the bedroom door and softly tried the handle. It did not move; it was locked. He knocked, hesitantly. No answer. He knocked again. His heart beat in time with his knocking. Still silence. Now he knew it was all over and he had lost; the chilly knowledge came home to him. He put out the lamp, lay down on the sofa in his clothes and wrapped himself in a rug. Everything in him now longed to fall into sleep and oblivion. Once more he listened, and thought he had heard something close. He strained his ears, looking at the door, but it was solid wood. Nothing. His head fell back again.

Then something low down touched him. He started up in alarm, but it soon changed to emotion. The dog, who had slipped in with the maid and hidden under the sofa, came up to him and licked his hand with a warm tongue. And the animal's instinctive love touched him deeply because it came from the world now dead to him, and was all of his past life that still was his. He bent down and hugged the dog like a human being. Something on this earth still loves me and does not despise me, he felt, to him I am not a machine yet, not just a tool of murder, not a willing weakling, only a creature linked to him by love. Again and again, his hand tenderly stroked the soft coat. The dog moved closer to him, as if he knew his master was lonely, and both of them, breathing softly, began to fall asleep.

When he woke up he felt fresher, and the morning was bright and clear outside the shining window. The *föhn* wind had blown away the darkness, and the white silhouette of the distant mountain chain gleamed above the lake. Ferdinand got up, still a little unsteady from the hours he had slept away, and when he was fully awake his eyes fell on the fastened rucksack. Suddenly he remembered it all, but now, in bright daylight, it did not weigh so heavily on his mind.

Why did I pack it? he asked himself. Why? I have no intention of going away. The spring is just beginning. I want to paint. There's no great hurry. He told me himself I could take a couple of days. Even animals don't run to the slaughter. My wife is right: it's a crime against her, against myself, against everyone. Nothing can happen to me, after all. A few weeks under arrest, maybe, if I report for duty late, but isn't military service a prison in itself? I have no ambition to cut a fine figure in society, in fact I'd feel it an honour to have disobeyed at this time of slavery. I've no idea of setting out now. I'll stay here. I want to paint the landscape first, so that some day I'll remember where I was happy. And I won't go until the picture is in its frame. They can't herd me like a cow. I'm in no hurry.

He took the rucksack, swung it up in the air and tossed it into a corner. He enjoyed trying his own strength as he did so. And his new mood made him feel a need for a quick test of his will power. He took the call-up order from his wallet to tear it into pieces, and unfolded it.

But strangely, the military jargon cast its spell over him again. He began to read. "You are under orders to…". The words struck him to the heart. This was an order that would not be denied. Somehow he felt himself wavering; that unknown sensation was back. His hands began to shake. His strength faded. Cold came from somewhere, like a draught of wind blowing around him, uneasiness returned, inside him the steel clockwork of the alien will began to stir, tensing all his nerves and making its way to his joints. Instinctively he looked at his watch. "Plenty of time," he murmured, but he no longer knew what he himself meant: time to catch the morning train to the border, or did he mean the extended deadline he had granted himself? And now it came back, that mysterious internal compulsion, the ebb tide carrying him away, stronger than ever because it faced both his last resistance and his fear, his surely hopeless fear of succumbing. He knew that if no one held fast to him now he would be lost.

He made his way to the door of his wife's room and listened intently. Nothing moved. Hesitantly, he knocked with his knuckles. Silence. He knocked again. Still silence. He cautiously tried the handle. The door was not locked, and opened, but the room was empty, the bed empty too and unmade. He felt alarmed. Softly, he called her name, and when there was no reply repeated, more uneasily, "Paula!" Then, like a man under attack, he shouted at the top of his voice, "Paula! Paula! Paula!" Nothing moved. He tried the kitchen, which was empty. The terrible sense of abandonment asserted its rights over him, and he trembled. He groped his way up to the studio, not knowing what he wanted to do: say goodbye or be prevented from leaving. But here again there was no one. There wasn't even any trace of the faithful dog. Everything was deserting him, loneliness washed around him and broke the last of his strength.

He went back through the empty house and picked up the rucksack. In giving way to the compulsion he somehow felt relieved of the burden of himself. It's her fault, he told himself, her fault. Why has she gone? She ought to have kept me here, it was her duty.

She could have saved me from myself, but she didn't want to. She despises me. She doesn't love me any more. She's let me down, so I'll let myself down too. My blood will be on her conscience! It's her fault, not mine, all her fault.

Outside the house, he turned once more. Would no call come from somewhere, no word of love? Would nothing raise its fists against that steely mechanism of obedience inside him and smash it? But nothing spoke. Nothing called. Nothing showed itself. Everything was deserting him, and already he felt himself falling into an abyss. And the thought came to him: might it not be better to take another ten steps towards the lake, let himself fall from the bridge and find peace?

The clock in the church tower struck, a ponderous, heavy sound. Its severe call out of the clear sky he had once loved so much goaded him on like a whiplash. Ten more minutes: then the train would come in, then it would all be over, finally, hopelessly over. Ten more minutes: but he no longer felt they were minutes of freedom. Like a hunted man he raced forward, staggered, hesitated, ran on, gasped in frantic fear of being late, went faster and faster until suddenly, just before reaching the platform, he almost collided with someone standing at the barrier.

He started in alarm. The rucksack fell from his trembling hand. It was his wife standing there, pale, as if she hadn't slept, her grave, sad eyes turned on him again.

"I knew you'd come. For the last three days I've known you would do it. But I'm not leaving you. I've been waiting here since early in the morning, since the first trains came in, and I'll wait until the last have left. As long as I breathe they won't lay hands on you, Ferdinand, remember that. You said yourself there was plenty of time. Why are you in such a hurry?"

He looked at her uncertainly.

"It's just that… my name's been sent in… they're expecting me…"

"Who are expecting you? Slavery and death, maybe, no one else! Wake up, Ferdinand, realize that you're free, entirely free, no one has power over you, no one can give you orders—listen, you're free, free, free! I'll tell you so a thousand times, ten thousand times, every hour, every minute, until you feel it yourself! You're free. Free! Free!"

"Please," he said quietly, as two farmers turned curiously to glance at them in passing. "Please, not so loud. People are looking..."

"People! People!" she cried in a rage. "What do I care about people? How will they help me when you're shot dead, or limping home, a broken man? What do I care for people, their pity, their love, their gratitude? I want you as a human being, a free, living human being. I want you free, free, as a man should be, not cannon-fodder."

"Paula!" He tried to calm her fury. She pushed him away.

"Let me alone, you and your stupid, cowardly fear! I'm in a free country here, I can say what I like, I'm not a servant and I won't give you up to servitude! Ferdinand, if you go I'll throw myself in front of the locomotive."

"Paula!" He took hold of her again, but her face was suddenly bitter.

"But no," she said, "I won't lie. I may be too cowardly to do it. Millions of women have been too cowardly when their husbands and children were dragged away—not one of them did what she ought to have done. Your cowardice poisons us. What will I do if you go away? Weep and wail, go to church and ask God to let you off with some light kind of service. And then perhaps I'll mock men who didn't go. Anything's possible these days."

"Paula." He held her hands. "Why are you making it so hard for me, when you know it must be done?"

"Am I to make it easy for you? It ought to be hard for you, very, very hard, as hard as I can make it. Here I am, you'll have to push me away by force, use your fists, you'll have to kick me when I'm down. I'm not giving you up."

The signals clattered. He straightened up, pale and agitated, and reached for his rucksack. But she had already snatched it and was standing foursquare in front of him.

"Give me that!" he groaned.

"Never! Never!" she gasped, wrestling with him. The farmers gathered around, laughing out loud. There was shouting as the bystanders egged them on, encouraging one or the other, children ran from their games to look. But the pair were struggling for possession of the rucksack with the strength of bitter despair, as if fighting for their lives.

At that moment the locomotive was heard as the train steamed in. Suddenly he let go of the rucksack and ran, without turning back. He hurried on, stumbling over the rails to reach a carriage and fling himself into it. Loud laughter broke out as the farmers roared with glee, pursuing him with shouts of, "You'll have to jump out again, mister, the missus has got it!" Their raucous laughter lashed at his shame. And now the train was moving out.

She stood there holding the rucksack, with the laughter of the crowd all around her, and stared at the train vanishing faster and faster into the distance. He did not wave from the window, he gave her no sign. Sudden tears veiled her eyes, and she saw no more.

He sat hunched in the corner of the carriage, and did not venture to look out of the window as the train gathered speed. Outside, torn to a thousand pieces by the speed of the train, everything he owned passed by: the little house on the hill with his pictures, his table and chair and bed, his wife, the dog, many days of happiness. And the wide landscape at which he had often gazed, his eyes shining, was gone as if hurled away, like his freedom and his whole life. He seemed to feel his life's blood streaming out of all his veins; he was nothing now but the white call-up order crackling in his pocket, and he was driven on with it by the ill will of Fate.

In dull bewilderment, he merely registered events as they happened. The conductor asked for his ticket; he had none, but in the voice of a sleepwalker named the town on the border as his destination, and passively changed to another train. The mechanism inside him did everything, and it had stopped hurting. At the Swiss customs office they asked to see his papers. He showed them what he had: only that one sheet of paper. Now and then some lost remnant of himself made a slight effort to think, murmuring as if in a dream, "Turn back! You're still free! You don't have to go." But the mechanism in his blood that did not speak, and yet made his nerves and limbs move by force, thrust him implacably on with its invisible command, "You must."

He was standing on the platform of the transit station where he had to change trains again for his native land. Over there, clearly visible in the dull light, a bridge crossed the river which was the border. His weary mind tried to understand the meaning of the word; on this side of the border you could still live, breathe, and speak freely, act as you liked, do work that mattered. Eight hundred paces further on, once over that bridge, your will would be removed from your body like an animal's entrails being gutted, you would have to obey strangers and stab other strangers to death. And the little bridge there, a structure of just ten dozen wooden posts and two crossbeams meant all those things. That was why two men, each in a different, colourful and pointless uniform, stood one at each end with guns to guard the bridge. A sombre sensation tormented him, he knew he couldn't think clearly any more, but his thoughts rolled on. What exactly were they guarding in the form of that wooden structure? They were preventing anyone passing from one country to the other, making sure no one got out of the country where men's wills were gutted, and went to the country on the other side of the border. And was he himself going to cross the bridge? Yes, but the other way, out of freedom into…

He stood still, musing, hypnotized by the idea of the border. Now that he saw its intrinsic nature, a physical object guarded by two bored citizens in military uniforms, there was something in himself that he could no longer entirely understand. He tried to stand back and think: there was a war going on. But only in the country over there—the war was going on a kilometre away, or rather a kilometre minus two hundred metres away. Or perhaps, it occurred to him, it was ten metres closer than that, say a kilometre minus eight hundred metres minus ten metres away. He felt some kind of odd urge to find out whether there was still a war in progress on those last ten metres or not. The comical aspect of the idea amused him. There ought to be a line drawn somewhere, the dividing line. Suppose when you reached the border you had one foot on the bridge and one on the ground, what were you then—were you still free, or already a soldier? You'd have to be wearing a civilian boot on one foot and a military boot on the other. His confused thoughts became more and more childish. Suppose you were standing on the bridge, you were already over it, and then you ran back, were you a deserter? And the water under the bridge—was it warlike or peaceful? And *was* there a line drawn somewhere in the national colours? What about the fish, were they allowed to swim across into the war zone? What about the animals? He thought of his dog. If the dog had come along too, they'd probably have called him up as well, he'd have had to fire machine guns or go tracking down wounded men under a hail of bullets. Thank God the dog had stayed at home.

Thank God! The thought gave him a shock, and he shook himself. He sensed that since he had seen the border in physical form, a bridge between life and death, something in him that was not the mechanism was beginning to work, understanding and resistance were coming back to life in him. The train that had brought him in still stood on the opposite track, except that the locomotive had been moved and its gigantic glass eyes were now looking the other way, ready to pull the carriages back into Switzerland. It was a reminder that there was still time. He felt painful life return to the numbed nerve of his longing for his lost home, and the man he had once been began to revive. Over there, on the far side of bridge, he saw a soldier strapped into a strange uniform, he saw him marching pointlessly up and down with his gun over his shoulder, and he saw himself reflected in this stranger. Only now was his destiny clear to him, and now that he understood it he saw that it meant death and destruction. And life cried out in his soul.

Then the signals clattered, and the harsh sound shattered his still tentative feelings. Now, he knew, all was lost—if he got into the train just coming in and spent three minutes in it, travelling to the bridge and over it. And he knew that he would. Another quarter-of-an-hour and he would have been saved. He stood there feeling dizzy.

But the train did not come in from the distance into which he looked as he stood there trembling; it rumbled slowly over the bridge from the other side. And suddenly the station concourse was full of movement, people were streaming out of the waiting rooms, women crowded forward, crying out, pushing, Swiss soldiers quickly lined up. And all at once music began to play—he listened, amazed, he couldn't believe it. But there it was, blaring out, unmistakeable: the Marseillaise. The enemy's national anthem, sung on a train coming out of German territory!

The train thundered up, puffing, and stopped. And now everything was fast and frantic: carriage doors were flung open, pale-faced men stumbled out, delight in their glowing eyes—Frenchmen in uniform, wounded Frenchmen, enemies, enemies! In his dreamlike state, it was some seconds before he realized that this was a train with wounded prisoners being exchanged, freed from captivity over there, saved from the madness of the war. And they knew it, they all felt it; how they waved and shouted and laughed, although even laughter still hurt many of them! One man, staggering and hesitant, stumbled out on a wooden leg, clung to a post and shouted, "*La Suisse! La Suisse! Dieu soit béni*!" Sobbing women hurried from window to window until they found the beloved faces they were looking for, voices called out in confusion, sobbing, shouting, but all of them rising high in the golden moment of rejoicing. The music died away, and for some time nothing could be heard but great waves of emotion breaking over these people as they shouted and cried out.

Then they gradually calmed down. Groups formed, happily united in quiet joy and rapid talk. A few women were still wandering around, calling out names. Nurses brought refreshment and presents. The very sick were carried out on their stretchers, pale in white bandages, tenderly surrounded by care and comfort. The whole debris of suffering could be seen concentrated in those forms: maimed men with empty sleeves, the emaciated and half-burnt, the lingering remnants of youth gone to seed and growing old. But all eyes gleamed happily as they looked up at the sky; they all sensed that they were near the end of their pilgrimage.

Ferdinand stood as if paralysed amidst this unexpected throng of new arrivals; his heart was suddenly beating strongly again under the sheet of paper in his breast pocket. Standing alone and apart from the others, with no one expecting him, he saw a stretcher come to a halt. Slowly, with unsteady steps, he went over to the wounded man, who seemed to have been forgotten in the joy of all these strangers. The man's face was white as a sheet, his beard straggled wildly, a limp, injured arm dangled from the stretcher. His eyes were closed, his lips pale. Ferdinand shivered. Gently, he raised the dangling arm and placed it carefully on the sick man's breast. Then the stranger opened his eyes, looked at Ferdinand, and out of distant regions of unknown torment the man formed a grateful smile of greeting.

It came to Ferdinand like a flash as he stood, still trembling: was he to do such things himself? Injure people like this, look his fellow men in the eye with no emotion but hatred, take part in this terrible crime of his own free will? The truth of what he felt revived strongly again, breaking the mechanism inside him. Freedom rose up, great and blessed freedom, destroying obedience. Never, never! something in him cried in a primal, mighty, unknown voice. It struck him down. Sobbing, he collapsed beside the stretcher.

People hurried to him, thinking he must have had an epileptic fit; the doctor came along. But he was already getting slowly to his feet and refused help. His face was calm and cheerful. He found his wallet, took out his last banknote and placed it on the wounded man's stretcher; then he took the call-up order and read it once more, slowly and deliberately. After that he tore it in two and scattered the scraps on the platform. People stared at him as if he were mad. But he was not ashamed any more. I am well again, he felt, and that was all. The music began once more. And his own heart drowned out all the musical notes with its resonant song.

Late that evening, he came home to his house. It was dark and closed, like a coffin. He knocked. Footsteps slowly made their way to the door; his wife opened it. When she saw him, she gave a start of surprise. But he gently took her arm and led her back to the doorway. They said nothing, just stood there, both of them trembling with happiness. He went into the living-room and saw his pictures in it. She had brought them all down from the studio so that she could be close to him through his work. He felt infinite love for her at this sign of her own for him, and realized how much he had just saved. In silence, he pressed her hand. The dog came racing out of the kitchen and jumped up at him; everything had been waiting for him, it seemed as if his real self had never left this place, and yet he felt like a man coming back from the dead.

Still they said nothing. But she took his hand gently and led him to the window. Outside, untouched by the self-inflicted torment of humanity run mad, lay the everlasting world, with endless stars shining for him under an endless sky. He looked up and saw, in a devout and solemn mood, that there was no law on earth for mankind except the law of humanity itself, that nothing unites men more truly than their own union. His wife's breath close to his lips was sweet and blessed, and sometimes their two bodies trembled slightly in the pleasure of holding each other close. But still they said nothing. Their hearts soared freely in the eternal freedom of things, released from the confusion of words and man-made laws.

MOONBEAM ALLEY

The ship, delayed by a storm, could not land at the small French seaport until late in the evening, and I missed the night train to Germany. So I had an unexpected day to spend in this foreign town, and an evening which offered nothing more alluring than the melancholy music of a ladies' ensemble in a suburban nightclub, or a tedious conversation with my chance-met travelling companions. The air in the small hotel dining-room seemed to me intolerable, greasy with oil, stifling with smoke, and I suffered doubly from its murky impurity because I still tasted the pure breath of the sea on my lips, cool and salty. So I went out and walked down the broad, brightly lit street, going nowhere in particular, until I reached a square where an outdoor band was playing. I went on amidst the casually flowing tide of people who were out for a stroll. At first it did me good to be carried passively away by this current of provincially dressed persons who meant nothing to me, but soon I could no longer tolerate the company of strangers surging up close to me with their disconnected laughter, their eyes resting on me in surprise, with odd looks or a grin, the touches that imperceptibly urged me on, the light coming from a thousand small sources, the constant sound of footsteps. The sea voyage had been turbulent, and I still felt a reeling, slightly intoxicated sensation in my blood, a rocking and gliding beneath my feet, the earth seemed to move as if it were breathing and the street to rise to the sky. All this loud confusion suddenly made me dizzy, and to save myself I turned into a side street without looking at its name, and then into a yet smaller street, where the senseless noise gradually ebbed away. I walked aimlessly on through the tangle of alleys branching off each other like veins, and becoming darker and darker the further I went from the main square. The large electrical arc lamps that lit the broad avenues like moons did not shine here, and the stars at last began coming into view again above the few street lamps, in a black and partly overcast sky.

I must have reached the sailors' quarter near the harbour. I could tell from the smell of rotting fish, from the sweetish aroma of seaweed and decay that bladderwrack gives off when the breakers wash it ashore, from the typical fumes of pollution and unaired rooms that linger dankly in these nooks and crannies until a great storm rises, bringing in fresh air. The nebulous darkness and unexpected solitude did me good. I slowed my pace, glancing down alley after alley now, each different from its neighbour, here a quiet alley, there an inviting one, but all dark, with the muted sound of music and voices rising so mysteriously from invisible vaults that one could scarcely guess at its underground sources. For the doors to all the cellars were closed, with only the light of a red or yellow lamp showing.

I liked such alleyways in foreign towns, places that are a disreputable marketplace for all the passions, a secret accumulation of temptations for the sailors who, after many lonely days on strange and dangerous seas, come here for just one night to fulfil all their many sensuous dreams within an hour. These little side-streets have to lurk somewhere in the poorer part of any big city, lying low, because they say so boldly and importunately things that are hidden beneath a hundred disguises in the brightly lit buildings with their shining window panes and distinguished denizens. Enticing music wafts from small rooms here, garish cinematograph posters promise unimaginable splendours, small, square lanterns hang under gateways, winking in very clear invitation, issuing an intimate greeting, and naked flesh glimpsed through a door left ajar shimmers under gilded fripperies. Drunks shout in the bars, gamblers argue in loud voices. The sailors grin when they meet each other here, their dull eyes glinting in anticipation, for they can find everything in such places, women and gaming, drink and a show to watch, adventures both grubby and great. But all this is hidden in modestly muted yet tell-tale fashion behind shutters lowered for the look of the thing, it all goes on behind closed doors, and that apparent seclusion is intriguing, is twice as seductive because it is both hidden and accessible. Such streets are the same in Hamburg and Colombo and Havana, similar in all seaports, just as the wide and luxurious avenues resemble each other, for the upper side and underside of life share the same form. These shady streets are the last fantastic remnants of a sensually unregulated world where instinct still has free rein, brutal and unbridled; they are a dark wood of passions, a thicket full of the animal kingdom, exciting visitors with what they reveal and enticing them with what they hide. One can weave them into dreams.

And the alley where I suddenly felt myself a captive was such a street. I had been idly following a couple of cuirassiers whose swords, dragging along after them, clinked on the uneven road surface. Women called to them from a bar, they laughed and shouted coarse jests back at the girls, one of the soldiers knocked at the window, then a voice somewhere swore at them and they went on. Their laughter faded in the distance, and soon they were out of my hearing. The alley was silent again; a couple of windows shone faintly, mistily reflecting the pale moon. I stood drinking in that silence, which struck me as a strange one because something behind it seemed to be murmuring words of mystery, lust and danger. I clearly felt that the silence was deceptive, and something of the world's decay shimmered in the murky haze. But I went on standing there, listening to the empty air. I was no longer aware of the town and the alley, of their names or my own, I just sensed that I was a stranger here, miraculously detached in the unknown, with no purpose in mind, no message to deliver, no links with anything, and yet I sensed all the dark life around me as fully as I felt the blood flowing beneath my own skin. I had only the impression that nothing here was for me and yet it all was all mine: it was the delightful sensation of an experience made deepest and most genuine because one is not personally involved. That sensation is one of the wellsprings of my inmost being, and in an unknown situation it always comes over me like desire. Then suddenly, as I stood listening in the lonely alley as if waiting for something that was bound to happen, something to urge me on, out of this somnambulistic sensation of listening to the void, I heard, muted by either distance or a wall between us, the very faint sound of a song in German coming from somewhere. It was that simple air from *Der Freischütz*, 'Fairest, greenest bridal wreath'. A woman's voice was singing it, very badly, but it was still a German tune, something German here in a foreign part of the world, and so it affected me in a way all its own. It was being sung some way off, but I felt it like a greeting, the first word I had heard in my native tongue for weeks. Who, I asked myself, speaks my language here, whose memory impels her to lift her voice from the heart in singing this poor little song here in this remote, disreputable alley? I followed the voice, going from house to house. They all stood half asleep, their shutters closed, but light shining behind the shutters gave their nature away, and sometimes a hand waved. Outside there were garish signs, screaming posters, and the words "Ale, Whisky, Beer" promised a hidden bar, but it all appeared sealed and uninviting, yet enticing at the same time. Now and then—and I heard a few footsteps in the distance—now and then the voice came again, singing the refrain more clearly this time, sounding closer and closer. I identified the house. For a moment I hesitated, and then pushed my foot against the inner door, which was heavily draped with white net curtains. However, as I stooped to go in, having made up my mind, something came to life in the shadow of the entrance and gave a start of alarm, a figure that had obviously been waiting there, its face pressed close to the pane. The lantern over the door cast red light on that face, yet it was pale with fright—a man was staring at me, wide-eyed. He muttered something like an apology and disappeared down the dimly lit alley. It was a strange greeting. I looked the way he had gone. Something still seemed to be moving in the vanishing shadows of the alley, but indistinctly. Inside the building the voice was still singing, and seemed to me even clearer now. That lured me on. I turned the door-handle and quickly stepped inside.

The last word of the song stopped short, as if cut off by a knife. And in some alarm I felt a void before me, a sense of silent hostility as if I had broken something. Only slowly did my eyes adjust to the room, which was almost empty: it contained a bar counter and a table, and the whole place was obviously just a means of access to other rooms behind it, whose real purpose was immediately made obvious by their opened doors, muted lamplight, and beds made up and ready. A girl sat at the table, leaning her elbows on it, her tired face made up, and behind her at the bar was the landlady, stout and dingy grey, with another girl who was not bad-looking. My greeting sounded harsh in the space, and a bored response came back with some delay. Finding that I had stepped into such a void, so tense and bleak a silence, I was ill at ease and would rather have left at once, but in my embarrassment I could think of no excuse, so I resigned myself to sitting down at the table in front of the bar. The girl, remembering her duties, asked what I would like to drink, and I recognised her as German at once from the harsh accent of her French. I ordered beer, she went out and came back again with the lethargic bearing that betrayed even more indifference than the empty look in her eyes, which glowed faintly under their lids like lights going out. Automatically, and in accordance with the custom of such places, she put a second glass down next to mine for herself. As she raised her glass she did not turn her blank gaze on me, so I was able to observe her. Her face was in fact still beautiful, with regular features, but inner weariness seemed to make it coarse, like a mask; everything about her drooped, her eyelids were heavy, her hair hung loose, her cheeks, badly made up and smudged, were already beginning to fall in, and broad lines ran down to her mouth. Her dress too was carelessly draped, her voice hoarse, roughened by smoke and beer. All things considered, I felt that this was an exhausted woman who went on living only out of habit and without feelings, so to speak. Self-consciously and with a sense of dread I asked a question. She replied with dull indifference, scarcely moving her lips, and without looking at me. I felt I was unwelcome. At the back of the room the landlady was yawning, and the other girl was sitting in a corner glancing in my direction, as if waiting for me to summon her. I would have liked to leave, but everything about me felt heavy, and I sat in that sated, smouldering air, swaying slightly as the sailors do, kept there by both distaste and curiosity, for this indifference was, in a way, intriguing.

Then I suddenly gave a start, alarmed by raucous laughter near me. At the same time the flame of the light wavered, and the draught told me that someone must have opened the door behind my back. "Oh, so here you are again, are you?" said the voice beside me shrilly, in German. "Slinking round the house again, you skinflint? Well, come along in, I won't hurt you."

I spun round, to look first at her as she uttered this greeting, in tones as piercing as if her body had suddenly caught fire, then at the door. Even before it was fully open I recognised the trembling figure and humble glance of the man who had been almost glued to the outside of the pane just now. Intimidated, he held his hat in his hand like a beggar, trembling at the sound of the raucous greeting and the laughter which suddenly seemed to shake her apathetic figure convulsively, and which was accompanied by the landlady's rapid whispering from the bar counter at the back of the room.

"Sit down there with Françoise, then," the woman beside me ordered the poor man as he came closer with a craven, shuffling step. "You can see I have a gentleman here."

She said this to him in German. The landlady and the other girl laughed out loud, although they couldn't understand her, but they seemed to know the new guest.

"Give him champagne, Françoise, the expensive brand, give him a bottle of it!" she called out, laughing, and turning to him again added with derision, "And if it's too expensive for you then you can stay outside, you miserable miser. I suppose you'd like to stare at me for free—you want everything for free, don't you?"

The tall figure seemed almost to collapse at the sound of this vicious laughter; he hunched his back as if his face were trying to creep away and hide like a dog, and his hand shook as he reached for the bottle and spilled some of the wine in pouring it. He was still trying to look up at her face, but he could not lift his gaze from the floor, where it wandered over the tiles. And only now, in the lamplight, did I clearly see that emaciated face, worn and pale, his hair damp and thin on his bony skull, his joints loose and looking as if they were broken, a pitiful creature without any strength, yet not devoid of malice. Everything about him was crooked, awry, cringing, and now, when he raised his eyes, though he immediately lowered them again in alarm, they had a gleam of ill will in them.

"Don't trouble yourself about him!" the girl told me in French, roughly taking my arm as if to turn me round. "This is old business between the two of us, it's nothing new." And again, baring her teeth as if ready to bite, she called out to him, "Listen to me, you old lynx! You just hear what I say. I said I'd rather jump into the sea than go with you, didn't I?"

Once again the landlady and the other girl laughed, loud and foolish laughter. It seemed to be a familiar joke to them, a daily jest. But I found it unpleasant to see that other girl, Françoise, suddenly press close to him with pretended affection, wheedling him with flattery from which he shrank, though he didn't have the courage to shake her off, and I was alarmed when his wandering gaze, awkward, anxious, abject, rested on me. And I felt dread of the woman beside me, who had suddenly been roused from her apathy and was full of such burning malice that her hands trembled. I threw some money on the table and was going to leave, but she wouldn't take it.

"If he annoys you I'll throw him out, the bastard. He must do as he's told. Come along, drink another glass with me!"

She pressed close to me with a wild, abrupt kind of tenderness which I knew at once was only pretended, to torment the other man. At every movement she quickly looked askance across the table, and it was dreadful to me to see how he began to wince whenever she paid me some little attention, as if he felt hot steel branding his flesh. Without paying any attention to her, I stared only at him, and shuddered to see something in the nature of anger, rage, envy and greed arising in him, yet he cringed again if she so much as turned her head. She now pressed very close to me, her body trembling with her vicious pleasure in this game, and I felt horror at her garishly painted face with its smell of cheap powder, at the fumes emanating from her slack flesh. I reached for a cigar to keep her away from my face, and while my eyes were searching the table for a match she ordered him, "Bring us a light!"

I was more horrified than he was at such an imposition, making him serve me, and quickly set about looking for a light myself. But he snapped to attention at her words as if at the crack of a whip, came over to us, reeling, with unsteady footsteps, and put his own lighter on the table quickly, as if he might burn up if he touched the tabletop. For a second I met his eyes: there was boundless shame in them, and crushing embitterment. That servile glance of his struck a chord in me as another man, a brother. I felt the force of his humiliation at the woman's hands and was ashamed for him.

"Thank you very much," I said in German—she started at that—"but you shouldn't have troubled." Then I offered him my hand. A hesitation, a long one, then I felt damp, bony fingers, and suddenly, convulsively, an abrupt pressure in thanks. For a second his eyes shone as they looked at mine, and then they were hidden again by those slack eyelids. In defiance of the woman, I was going to ask him to sit down with us, and I must already have begun to trace the gesture of invitation, for she quickly ordered him, "You sit down again and don't disturb us here."

All at once I was overcome by disgust at the sound of her caustic voice and this scene of torture. What did I care for this smoky bar, this unpleasant whore and the feeble man, these fumes of beer, smoke and cheap perfume? I craved fresh air. I pushed the money over to her, stood up and moved away with decision as she came flatteringly closer to me. It revolted me to help her humiliate another human being, and the determined manner of my withdrawal clearly showed how little she attracted me sensually. Her blood was up now, a line appeared around her mouth, but whatever word sprang to her lips she took care not to utter it, just turning on him and flouncing with undisguised hatred. But he was expecting the worst, and at this threatening movement he rapidly, with a hunted look, put his hand in his pocket and brought out a purse. It was obvious that he was afraid of being left alone with her now, and in his haste he had trouble untying the purse-strings—it was the kind of knitted purse adorned with glass beads that peasants and the lower classes carry. Anyone could see that he wasn't used to throwing his money about, unlike the sailors who produce the coins clinking in their pockets with a sweeping gesture and fling them down on the table; he was clearly in the habit of counting money carefully and weighing the coins up in his fingers. "How he trembles for his dear, sweet *pfennigs*! Are we going too slowly for you? Wait!" she mocked, and came a step closer. He shrank back, and seeing his alarm she said, shrugging her shoulders and with unspeakable revulsion in her eyes, "Oh, I won't take anything from you, I spit on your money. I know you've counted all your dear, nice little *pfennigs*. No one in the world must have too much money. And then of course," she added, suddenly tapping his chest, "there's the banknotes you've sewn in there so that no one will steal them!"

Sure enough, like a man with a weak heart suddenly clutching at his breast, he reached with a pale and trembling hand for a certain place on his coat, his fingers instinctively felt for the secret hiding-place and came away again, reassured. "Miser!" she spat. But then, suddenly, a flush rose to her victim's face; he threw the purse abruptly at the other girl, who first cried out in alarm, then laughed aloud, and he stormed past her and out of the door as if escaping from a fire.

For a moment she still stood there, eyes flashing with fury. Then her eyelids fell apathetically again, weariness relaxed her body from its tension. She seemed to grow old and tired within a moment. Something uncertain and lost blurred the gaze now resting on me.

She stood there like a drunk waking up, feeling numb and empty with shame. "He'll be weeping and wailing for his money outside. Maybe he'll go to the police and say we stole it. And he'll be back tomorrow, but he won't have me all the same. Anyone else can, but not him!"

She went to the bar, threw coins down on it and swallowed a glass of brandy in a single draught. The vicious light was back in her eyes, but blurred as if by tears of rage and shame. I felt nauseated by her, and that destroyed pity. "Good evening," I said, and left. "*Bonsoir*," replied the landlady. She did not look round but just laughed, shrill and scornful laughter.

When I stepped outside there was nothing in the alley but night and the sky, a sultry darkness with the moonlight veiled and endlessly far away. I greedily took great breaths of the warm yet reviving air, my sense of dread turned to amazement at the diversity of human fate, and I felt again—it is a feeling that can make me happy to the point of tears—how fate is always waiting behind every window, every door opens on new experience, the wide variety of this world is omnipresent, and even its dirtiest corners swarm with predestined events as if with the iridescent gleam of beetles decomposing. Gone was the distasteful part of the encounter, and my tension was pleasantly resolved, turning to a sweet weariness that longed to turn all I had just seen and heard into a more attractive dream. Instinctively I looked around me, trying to work out my way back through this tangle of winding alleys. Then a shadow—he must have come close without making any noise—approached me.

"Forgive me,"—and I immediately recognised that humble tone of voice—"but I don't think you know your way around here. May I—may I show you which way to go? You are staying, sir, at…?"

I told him the name of my hotel.

"I'll go with you… if you'll permit me," he immediately added humbly.

Dread came over me again. This stealthy, spectral step, almost soundless yet close beside me, the darkness of the sailors' alley and the memory of what I had just witnessed all gradually turned to a dreamlike confusion of the emotions, leaving me devoid of judgement and unable to say no. I felt without seeing the subservience in his eyes, and noticed how his lips trembled; I knew that he wanted to talk to me, but in my daze, where the curiosity of my heart mingled uncertainly with physical numbness, I did nothing to encourage or discourage him. He cleared his throat several times, I noticed that he was trying and failing to speak, but some kind of cruelty which had, mysteriously, passed from the woman in the bar to me enjoyed watching him wrestle with shame and mental torment, and I did not help him, but let the silence lie black and heavy between us. And our steps, his quietly shuffling like an old man's, mine deliberately firm and decided, as if to escape this dirty world, sounded odd together. I felt the tension between us more strongly all the time; it was a shrill silence now, full of unheard cries, and it already resembled a violin string stretched too taut by the time he at last—and at first with dreadful hesitation—managed to bring out his words.

"You saw… you saw… sir, you saw a strange scene in there. Forgive me… forgive me if I mention it again… but it must seem strange to you… and I must look very ridiculous. That woman, you see…"

He stopped again. Something was constricting his throat. Then his voice sank very low, and he whispered rapidly, "That woman… she's my wife." I must have given a start of surprise, for he quickly went on as if to apologise. "That's to say, she was my wife… four or five years ago, it was in Geratzheim back in Hesse where I come from… sir, I wouldn't like you to think ill of her… perhaps it's my fault she's like that. She wasn't always… I… I tormented her. I took her although she was very poor, she didn't even have any household linen, nothing, nothing at all… and I'm rich, or that's to say well off… not rich… at least, I was then… and you see, sir, perhaps—she's right there—perhaps I was tight-fisted with money… but then I always was, sir, before this misfortune… and my father and mother before me, we all were… and I worked hard for every *pfennig*… and she was light-minded, she liked pretty things… but she was poor, and I was always reproaching her for it… I shouldn't have done it, I know that now, sir, for she is proud, very proud. You mustn't think she's really the way she makes out… that's a lie, and she does herself violence only… only to hurt me, to torment me… and… and because she's ashamed. Perhaps she's gone to the bad, but I… I don't think so, because, sir, she was very good, very good…"

He wiped his eyes in great agitation and stood still. Instinctively, I looked at him, and he suddenly no longer struck me as ridiculous. I found that I could even ignore his curiously servile manner of speech, the way he kept calling me "sir", as only the lower classes do in Germany. His face was greatly exercised by his internal struggle to put his story into words, and his eyes were fixed as he began walking unsteadily forward again, on the roadway itself, as if there, in the flickering light, he were laboriously reading the tale that so painfully tore its way out of his constricted throat.

"Yes, sir," he uttered now, breathing deeply, and in quite a different voice, a deep voice that seemed to come from a gentler world within him, "yes, she was very good… to me too, she was very grateful to me for saving her from poverty… and I knew that she was grateful, too, but… but I wanted to hear her say so… again and again, again and again… it did me good to hear her thank me… sir, it was so good, so very good, to feel… to feel that you are a better human being, when… when you know all the same that you're not… I'd have given all my money to hear it again and again… and she was very proud, so when she realised that I was insisting she must be grateful, she wanted to say so less and less. That's why… that, sir, is the only reason why I always made her ask… I never gave anything of my own free will… I felt good, making her come to beg for every dress, every ribbon… I tormented her like that for three years, I tormented her more and more… but it was only because I loved her, sir… I liked her pride, yet I still wanted to make her bow to me, madman that I was, and when she wanted something I was angry… but I wasn't really, sir… I was glad of any chance to humiliate her, for… for I didn't know how much I loved her…"

He stopped again. He was staggering as he walked now, and had obviously forgotten me. He spoke mechanically, as if in his sleep, in a louder and louder voice.

"And I didn't know… I didn't know it until that dreadful day when… when I'd refused to give her money for her mother, only a very little money… that is, I had it ready for her, but I wanted her to come and ask me once again… oh, what am I saying?… yes, I knew then, when I came home in the evening and she was gone, leaving just a note on the table… 'Keep your damned money, I want no more to do with you,' it said… nothing more… sir, I was like a lunatic for three days and three nights. I had the river searched and the woods, I gave the police large sums of money, I went to all the neighbours, but they just laughed and mocked me… there was no trace of her, nothing. At last a man came with news from the next village… he said he'd seen her… in the train with a soldier, she'd gone to Berlin. I followed her that very day… I neglected my business, I lost thousands… they stole from me, my servants, my manager, all of them… but I swear to you, sir, it was all the same to me… I stayed in Berlin, I stayed there a week until I found her among all those people… and went to her…" He was breathing heavily.

"Sir, I swear to you… I didn't say a harsh word to her… I wept, I went on my knees… I offered her money, all my fortune, said she should control it, because then I knew… I knew I couldn't live without her. I love every hair on her head… her mouth… her body, everything, everything… and I was the one who thrust her out, I alone… She was pale as death when I suddenly came in… I'd bribed the woman she was staying with… a procuress, a bad, vicious woman… she looked white as chalk standing there by the wall… she heard me out. Sir, I believe she was… yes, I think she was almost glad to see me, but when I mentioned the money… and I did so, I promise you, only to show her that I wasn't thinking of it any more… then she spat… and then… because I still wouldn't go… then she called her lover, and they both laughed at me… But, sir, I went back again day after day. The people of the house told me everything, I knew that the rascal had left her and she was in dire need, so I went once again… once again, sir, but she flew at me and tore up a banknote that I'd secretly left on the table, and when I next came back she was gone… What didn't I do, sir, to find her again? For a year, I swear to you, I didn't live, I just kept looking for her, I paid detective agencies until at last I found out that she was in Argentina… in… in a house of ill repute…" He hesitated a moment. The last words were spoken like a death rattle. And his voice grew deeper yet.

"I was horrified… at first… but then I remembered that it was I, no one else, who had sent her there… and I thought how she must be suffering, the poor creature… for more than anything else she's proud… I went to my lawyer, who wrote to the consul and sent money… not telling her who it came from… just so that she would come back. I received a telegram to say it had all succeeded… I knew what the ship was, and I waited to meet it in Amsterdam… I was there three days early, burning with impatience… at last it came in, I was so happy just to see the smoke of the steamer on the horizon, and I thought I couldn't wait for it to come in and tie up, so slowly, so slowly, and then the passengers came down the gangplank and at last, at last she was there… I didn't know her at first… she was different, her face painted… and as… as you saw her… and when she saw me waiting… she went pale. Two sailors had to hold her up or she'd have fallen off the gangplank. As soon as she was on shore I came up to her… I said nothing, my throat was too dry… She said nothing either, and didn't look at me… The porter carried her bags, we walked and walked… Then, suddenly, she stopped and said… oh, sir, how she said it… 'Do you still want me for your wife, even now?' I took her hand… she was trembling, but she said nothing. Yet I felt that everything was all right again… sir, how happy I was! I danced around her like a child when I had her in the room, I fell at her feet… I must have said foolish things… for she laughed through her tears and caressed me… very hesitantly, of course… but sir… it did me so much good. My heart was overflowing. I ran upstairs, downstairs, ordered a dinner in the hotel… our wedding feast… I helped her to dress… and we went down, we ate and drank and made merry… oh, she was so cheerful, like a child, so warm and good-hearted, and she talked of home… and how we would see to everything again… And then…" His voice suddenly roughened, and he made a movement with his hand as if to knock someone down. "There… there was a waiter… a bad, dishonest man… who thought I was drunk because I was raving and dancing and laughing madly… although it was just that I was happy, oh, so happy. And then, when I paid him, he gave me back my change twenty francs short… I shouted at him and demanded the rest… he was embarrassed, and brought out the money… And then she began laughing aloud again. I stared at her, but her face was different… mocking, hard, hostile all at once. 'How pernickety you still are… even on our wedding day!' she said very coldly, so sharply, with such… such pity. I was horrified, and cursed myself for being so punctilious… I went to great pains to laugh again, but her merriment was gone, had died. She demanded a room of her own… what wouldn't I have given her?… and I lay alone all night, thinking of nothing but what I could buy her next morning… what I could give her… how to show her that I'm not miserly… would never be miserly with her again. And in the morning I went out, I bought a bracelet, very early, and when I went into her room… it… it was empty, just the same as before. And I knew there'd be a note on the table… I went away and prayed to God it wasn't true… but… but it was there… And it said…" Here he hesitated. Instinctively, I had stopped and was looking at him. He bent his head. Then he whispered, hoarsely:

"It said… 'Leave me alone. I find you repulsive.'"

We had reached the harbour, and suddenly the roar of the nearby breakers broke the silence. There lay the ships at anchor, near and far, lights winking like the eyes of large black animals, and from somewhere came the sound of singing. Nothing was distinct, yet there was so much to feel, an immensity of sleep, with the seaport dreaming deeply.

I sensed the man's shadow beside me, a flickering, spectral shape at my feet, now disintegrating, now coming together again as the light of the dim street lamps changed. I could say nothing, I could give no comfort and had no questions, but I felt his silence clinging to me, heavy and oppressive. Then, suddenly, he clutched my arm. He was trembling.

"But I won't leave this place without her… I've found her again, after months… She torments me, but I won't give up… I beg you, sir, talk to her… I must have her, tell her that, she won't listen to me… I can't go on living like this… I can't watch the men going in to her… and wait outside the house until they come down again, drunk and laughing… The whole alley knows me now, they laugh when they see me waiting… it drives me mad… and yet I go back again every evening. Sir, I beg you, speak to her… I don't know you, but do it for God's merciful sake… speak to her…"

Instinctively, and with horror, I tried to free my arm. But as he felt my resistance to his unhappiness, he suddenly fell on his knees in the middle of the road and embraced my feet.

"I beg you, sir… you must speak to her… you must, or… or something terrible will happen. I've spent all I have looking for her, and I won't… I won't leave her here alive. I've bought a knife… I have a knife, sir… I won't leave her here alive, I can't bear it… Speak to her, sir…"

He was rolling about on the ground in front of me like a madman. At that moment two police officers came down the street. I violently wrenched him up and to his feet. He stared at me for a moment, astonished. Then he said in a dry and very different voice, "Turn down that side-street, and you'll see your hotel." Once more he stared at me with eyes whose pupils seemed to have merged into something terribly white and empty. Then he walked away.

I wrapped my coat around me. I was shivering. I felt nothing but exhaustion, I was in a confused daze, black and devoid of any emotion, a darkly moving slumber. I wanted to think all this over, but that black wave of weariness kept rising inside me, carrying me away. I staggered into the hotel, fell into bed, and slept as soundly as a brute beast.

Next morning I didn't know how much of it all had been a dream and how much was real, and something in me didn't want to know. I had woken late, a stranger in a strange town, and I went to look at a church where there were said to be some very famous mosaics dating from the days of classical antiquity. But I stared blankly at them. Last night's encounter rose more and more clearly before my mind's eye, and I felt an irresistible urge to go in search of that alley and that house. But those strange alleys come to life only at night; by day they wear cold, grey disguises, and only those who know them well can recognise them. However hard I looked, I couldn't find the alley. I came back tired and disappointed, pursued by images of something that was either memory or delusion.

The time of my train was nine in the evening. I left the town with regret. A porter fetched my bags and carried them to the station for me. On our way, I suddenly turned at a crossing; I recognised the alley leading to the house, told the porter to wait, and—while he smiled first in surprise, then knowingly—went to look at the scene of my adventure once more.

There it lay in the dark, as dark as yesterday, and in the faint moonlight I saw the glass pane in the house door gleaming. Once again I was going closer when, with a rustling sound, a figure emerged from the darkness. With a shudder, I saw him waiting there in the doorway and beckoning me to approach. Dread took hold of me—I fled quickly, in cowardly fear of getting involved here and missing my train.

But then, just before I turned the corner of the alley, I looked back once again. When my gaze fell on him he pulled himself together and strode to the door. He quickly opened his hand, and I saw the glint of metal in it. From a distance, I couldn't tell whether the moonlight showed money or a knife gleaming there in his fingers…

AMOK

IN MARCH 1912 a strange accident occurred in Naples harbour during the unloading of a large ocean-going liner which was reported at length by the newspapers, although in extremely fanciful terms. Although I was a passenger on the *Oceania*, I did not myself witness this strange incident—nor did any of the others—since it happened while coal was being taken on board and cargo unloaded, and to escape the noise we had all gone ashore to pass the time in coffee-houses or theatres. It is my personal opinion however, that a number of conjectures which I did not voice publicly at the time provide the true explanation of that sensational event, and I think that, at a distance of some years, I may now be permitted to give an account of a conversation I had in confidence immediately before the curious episode.

When I went to the Calcutta shipping agency trying to book a passage on the *Oceania* for my voyage home to Europe, the clerk apologetically shrugged his shoulders. He didn't know if it would be possible for him to get me a cabin, he said; at this time of year, with the rainy season imminent, the ship was likely to be fully booked all the way from Australia, and he would have to wait for a telegram from Singapore. Next day, I was glad to hear, he told me that yes, he could still reserve me a cabin, although not a particularly comfortable one; it would be below deck and amidships. As I was impatient to get home I did not hesitate for long, but took it.

The clerk had not misinformed me. The ship was over-crowded and my cabin a poor one: a cramped little rectangle of a place near the engine room, lit only dimly through a circular porthole.

The thick, curdled air smelled greasy and musty, and I could not for a moment escape the electric ventilator fan that hummed as it circled overhead like a steel bat gone mad. Down below the engines clattered and groaned like a breathless coal-heaver constantly climbing the same flight of stairs, up above I heard the tramp of footsteps pacing the promenade deck the whole time. As soon as I had stowed my luggage away amidst the dingy girders in my stuffy tomb, I then went back on deck to get away from the place, and as I came up from the depths I drank in the soft, sweet wind blowing off the land as if it were ambrosia.

But the atmosphere of the promenade deck was crowded and restless too, full of people chattering incessantly, hurrying up and down with the uneasy nervousness of those forced to be inactive in a confined space. The arch flirtatiousness of the women, the constant pacing up and down on the bottleneck of the deck as flocks of passengers surged past the deckchairs, always meeting the same faces again, were actually painful to me. I had seen a new world, I had taken in turbulent, confused images that raced wildly through my mind. Now I wanted leisure to think, to analyse and organise them, make sense of all that had impressed itself on my eyes, but there wasn't a moment of rest and peace to be had here on the crowded deck. The lines of a book I was trying to read blurred as the fleeting shadows of the chattering passengers moved by. It was impossible to be alone with myself on the unshaded, busy thoroughfare of the deck of this ship.

I tried for three days; resigned to my lot, I watched the passengers and the sea. But the sea was always the same, blue and empty, and only at sunset was it abruptly flooded with every imaginable colour. As for the passengers, after seventy-two hours I knew them all by heart. Every face was tediously familiar, the women's shrill laughter no longer irritated me, even the loud voices of two Dutch officers quarrelling nearby were not such a source of annoyance any more. There was nothing for it but to escape the deck, although my cabin was hot and stuffy, and in the saloon English girls kept playing waltzes badly on the piano, staccato-fashion. Finally I decided to turn the day's normal timetable upside down, and in the afternoon, having anaesthetized myself with a few glasses of beer, I went to my cabin to sleep through the evening with its dinner and dancing.

When I woke it was dark and oppressive in the little coffin of my cabin. I had switched off the ventilator, so the air around my temples felt greasy and humid. My senses were bemused, and it took me some minutes to remember my surroundings and wonder what the time was. It must have been after midnight, anyway, for I could not hear music or those restless footsteps pacing overhead. Only the engine, the breathing heart of the leviathan, throbbed as it thrust the body of the ship on into the unseen.

I made my way up to the deck. It was deserted. And as I looked above the steam from the funnel and the ghostly gleam of the spars, a magical brightness suddenly met my eyes. The sky was radiant, dark behind the white stars wheeling through it and yet radiant, as if a velvet curtain up there veiled a great light, and the twinkling stars were merely gaps and cracks through which that indescribable brightness shone. I had never before seen the sky as I saw it that night, glowing with such radiance, hard and steely blue, and yet light came sparkling, dripping, pouring, gushing down, falling from the moon and stars as if burning in some mysterious inner space. The white-painted outlines of the ship stood out bright against the velvety dark sea in the moonlight, while all the detailed contours of the ropes and the yards dissolved in that flowing brilliance; the lights on the masts seemed to hang in space, with the round eye of the lookout post above them, earthly yellow stars amidst the shining stars of the sky.

And right above my head stood the magical constellation of the Southern Cross, hammered into the invisible void with shining diamond nails and seeming to hover, although only the ship was really moving, quivering slightly as it made its way up and down with heaving breast, up and down, a gigantic swimmer passing through the dark waves. I stood there looking up; I felt as if I were bathed by warm water falling from above, except that it was light washing over my hands, mild, white light pouring around my shoulders, my head, and seeming to permeate me entirely, for all at once everything sombre about me was brightly lit. I breathed freely, purely, and full of sudden delight I felt the air on my lips like a clear drink. It was soft, effervescent air carrying on it the aroma of fruits, the scent of distant islands, and making me feel slightly drunk. Now, for the first time since I had set foot on the ship's planks, I knew the blessed joy of reverie, and the other more sensual pleasure of abandoning my body, woman-like, to the softness surrounding me. I wanted to lie down and look up at the white hieroglyphs in the sky. But the loungers and deckchairs had been cleared away, and there was nowhere for me to rest and dream on the deserted promenade deck.

So I made my way on, gradually approaching the bows of the ship, dazzled by the light that seemed to be shining more and more intensely on everything around me. It almost hurt, that bright, glaring, burning starlight, and I wanted to find a place to lie on a mat in deep shade, feeling the glow not on me but only above me, reflected in the ship's gear around me as one sees a landscape from a darkened room. At last, stumbling over cables and past iron hoists, I reached the ship's side and looked down over the keel to see the bows moving on into the blackness, while molten moonlight sprayed up, foaming, on both sides of their path. The ship kept rising and falling, rising and falling in the flowing dark, cutting through the black water as a plough cuts through soil, and in that sparkling interplay I felt all the torment of the conquered element and all the pleasures of earthly power. As I watched I lost all sense of time. Did I stand there for an hour, or was it only minutes? The vast cradle of the ship moving up and down rocked me away from time, and I felt only a pleasant weariness coming over me, a sensuous feeling. I wanted to sleep, to dream, yet I did not wish to leave this magic and go back down into my coffin. I instinctively felt around with my foot and found a coil of ropes. I sat down on it with my eyes closed yet not fully darkened, for above them, above me, that silver glow streamed on. Below me I felt the water rushing quietly on, above me the white torrent flowed by with inaudible resonance. And gradually the rushing sound passed into my blood; I was no longer conscious of myself, I didn't know if I heard my own breathing or the distant, throbbing heart of the ship, I myself was streaming, pouring away in the never-resting midnight world as it raced past.

A dry, harsh cough quite close to me made me jump. I came out of my half-intoxicated reverie with a start. My eyes, which even through closed lids had been dazzled by the white brightness, now searched around: quite close, and opposite me in the shadow of the ship's side, something glinted like light reflected off a pair of glasses, and now I saw the concentrated and circular glow of a lighted pipe. As I sat down, looking only below at the foaming bows as they cut through the waves or up at the Southern Cross, I had obviously failed to notice my neighbour, who must have been sitting here perfectly still all the time. Instinctively, my reactions still slow, I said in German, "Oh, I do apologise!" "Don't mention it," replied the voice from the darkness, in the same language.

I can't say how strange and eerie it was to be sitting next to someone like that in the dark, very close to a man I couldn't see. I felt as if he were staring at me just as I was staring at him, but the flowing, shimmering white light above us was so intense that neither of us could see more of the other than his outline in the shadows. And I thought I could hear his breathing and the faint hissing sound as he drew on his pipe, but that was all.

The silence was unbearable. I wanted to move away, but that seemed too brusque, too sudden. In my embarrassment I took out a cigarette. The match spluttered, and for a second its light flickered over the narrow space where we were sitting. I saw a stranger's face behind the lenses of his glasses, a face I had never seen on board at any meal or on the promenade deck, and whether the sudden flame hurt the man's eyes, or whether it was just an illusion, his face suddenly seemed dreadfully distorted, dark and goblin-like. But before I could make out any details, darkness swallowed up the fleetingly illuminated features again, and I saw only the outline of a figure darkly imprinted on the darkness, and sometimes the circular, fiery ring of the bowl of his pipe hovering in space. Neither of us spoke, and our silence was as sultry and oppressive as the tropical air itself.

Finally I could stand it no longer. I stood up and said a civil, "Goodnight."

"Goodnight," came the reply from the darkness, in a hoarse, harsh, rusty voice.

I stumbled forward with some difficulty, over hawsers and past some posts. Then I heard footsteps behind me, hasty and uncertain. It was my companion of a moment ago. I instinctively stopped. He did not come right up to me, and through the darkness I sensed something like anxiety and awkwardness in his gait.

"Forgive me," he said quickly "if I ask you a favour. I… I…" he stammered, for a moment too embarrassed to go on at once. "I… I have private… very private reasons for staying out of sight… a bereavement… I prefer to avoid company on board. Oh, I didn't mean you, no, no… I'd just like to ask… well, I would be very much obliged if you wouldn't mention seeing me here to anyone on board. There are… are private reasons, I might call them, to keep me from mingling with people just now… yes, well, it would put me in an awkward position if you mentioned that someone… here at night… that I…" And he stopped again. I put an end to his confusion at once by assuring him that I would do as he wished. We shook hands. Then I went back to my cabin and slept a heavy, curiously disturbed sleep, troubled by strange images.

I kept my promise, and told no one on board of my strange meeting, although the temptation to do so was great. For on a sea voyage every little thing becomes an event: a sail on the horizon, a dolphin leaping, a new flirtation, a joke made in passing. And I was full of curiosity to know more about the vessel's unusual passenger. I searched the ship's list for a name that might be his, I scrutinized other people, wondering if they could be somehow related to him; all day I was a prey to nervous impatience, just waiting for evening and wondering if I would meet him again. Odd psychological states have a positively disquieting power over me; I find tracking down the reasons for them deeply intriguing, and the mere presence of unusual characters can kindle a passionate desire in me to know more about them, a desire not much less strong than a woman's wish to acquire some possession. The day seemed long and crumbled tediously away between my fingers. I went to bed early, knowing that my curiosity would wake me at midnight.

Sure enough, I woke at the same time as the night before. The two hands on the illuminated dial of my clock covered one another in a single bright line. I quickly left my sultry cabin and climbed up into the even sultrier night.

The stars were shining as they had shone yesterday, casting a diffuse light over the quivering ship, and the Southern Cross blazed high overhead. It was all just the same as yesterday, where days and nights in the tropics resemble each other more than in our latitudes, but I myself did not feel yesterday's soft, flowing, dreamy sensation of being gently cradled. Something was drawing me on, confusing me, and I knew where it was taking me: to the black hoist by the ship's side, to see if my mysterious acquaintance was sitting immobile there again. I heard the ship's bell striking above me, and it urged me on. Step by step, reluctantly yet fascinated, I followed my instincts. I had not yet reached the prow of the ship when something like a red eye suddenly hovered in front of me: the pipe. So he was there.

I instinctively stepped back and stopped. Next moment I would have left again, but there was movement over there in the dark, something rose, took a couple of steps, and suddenly I heard his voice very close to me, civil and melancholy.

"Forgive me," he said. "You obviously want to sit there again, and I have a feeling that you hesitated when you saw me. Do please sit down, and I'll go away."

I made haste to say he was very welcome to stay so far as I was concerned. I had stepped back, I said, only for fear of disturbing him.

"Oh, you won't disturb me," he said, with some bitterness. "Far from it, I'm glad to have company for a change. I haven't spoken a word to anyone for ten days… well, not for years, really, and then it seems so difficult, perhaps because forcing it all back inside myself chokes me. I can't sit in my cabin any more, in that… that coffin, I can't bear it, and I can't bear the company of human beings either because they laugh all day… I can't endure that now, I hear it in my cabin and stop my ears against it. Of course, they don't know that I… well, they don't know that… they don't know it, and what business is it of theirs, after all, they're strangers…"

He stopped again, and then very suddenly and hastily said, "But I don't want to bother you… forgive me for speaking so freely."

He made a bow, and was about to leave, but I urged him to stay. "You're not bothering me in the least. I'm glad to have a few quiet words with someone up here myself… may I offer you a cigarette?"

He took one, and I lit it. Once again his face moved away from the ship's black side, flickering in the light of the match, but now he turned it fully to me: his eyes behind his glasses looking inquiringly into my face, avidly and with demented force. A shudder passed through me. I could feel that this man wanted to speak, had to speak. And I knew that I must help him by saying nothing.

We sat down again. He had a second deckchair there, and offered it to me. Our cigarettes glowed, and from the way that the ring of light traced by his in the darkness shook, I could tell that his hand was trembling. But I kept silent, and so did he. Then, suddenly, he asked in a quiet voice, "Are you very tired?"

"No, not at all."

The voice in the dark hesitated again. "I would like to ask you something… that's to say, I'd like to tell you something. Oh, I know,

I know very well how absurd it is to turn to the first man I meet, but… I'm… I'm in a terrible mental condition, I have reached a point where I absolutely must talk to someone, or it will be the end of me… You'll understand that when I… well, if I tell you… I mean, I know you can't help me, but this silence is almost making me ill, and a sick man always looks ridiculous to others…"

Here I interrupted, begging him not to distress himself. He could tell me anything he liked, I said. Naturally I couldn't promise him anything, but to show willingness is a human duty. If you see someone in trouble, I added, of course it is your duty to help…

"Duty… to show willing… a duty to try to… so you too think it is a man's duty… yes, his duty to show himself willing to help."

He repeated it three times. I shuddered at the blunt, grim tone of his repetition. Was the man mad? Was he drunk?

As if I had uttered my suspicions aloud, he suddenly said in quite a different voice, "You may think me mad or drunk. No, I'm not—not yet. Only what you said moved me so… so strangely, because that's exactly what torments me now, wondering if it's a duty… a duty…"

He was beginning to stammer again. He broke off for a moment, pulled himself together, and began again.

"The fact is, I am a doctor of medicine, and in that profession we often come upon such cases, such fateful cases… borderline cases, let's call them, when we don't know whether or not it is our duty… or rather, when there's more than one duty involved, not just to another human being but to ourselves too, to the state, to science… yes, of course, we must help, that's what we are there for… but such maxims are never more than theory. How far should we go with our help? Here are you, a stranger to me, and I'm a stranger to you, and I ask you not to mention seeing me… well, so you don't say anything, you do that duty… and now I ask you to talk to me because my own silence is killing me, and you say you are ready to listen. Good, but that's easy… suppose I were to ask you to take hold of me and throw me overboard, though, your willingness to help would be over. The duty has to end somewhere… it ends where we begin thinking of our own lives, our own responsibilities, it has to end somewhere, it has to end… or perhaps for doctors, of all people, it ought *not* to end? Must a doctor always come to the rescue, be ready to help one and all, just because he has a diploma full of Latin words, must he really throw away his life and water down his own blood if some woman… if someone comes along wanting him to be noble, helpful, good? Yes, duty ends somewhere… it ends where no more can be done, that's where it ends…"

He stopped again, and regained control.

"Forgive me, I know I sound agitated… but I'm not drunk, not yet… although I often am, I freely confess it, in this hellish isolation… bear in mind that for seven years I've lived almost entirely with the local natives and with animals… you forget how to talk calmly. And then if you do open up, everything comes flooding out… but wait… Yes, I know… I was going to ask you, I wanted to tell you about a certain case, wondering whether you think one has a duty to help… just help, with motives as pure as an angel's, or whether… Although I fear it will be a long story. Are you sure you're not tired?"

"No, not in the least."

"Thank you… thank you. Will you have a drink?"

He had been groping in the dark behind him somewhere. There was a clinking sound: two or three, at any rate several bottles stood ranged there. He offered me a glass of whisky, which I sipped briefly, while he drained his glass in a single draught. For a moment there was silence between us. Then the ship's bell struck half-past midnight.

"Well then… I'd like to tell you about a case. Suppose that a doctor in a small town… or right out in the country, a doctor who… a doctor who…" He stopped again, and then suddenly moved his chair closer to mine.

"This is no good. I must tell you everything directly, from the beginning, or you won't understand it… no, I can't put it as a theoretical example, I must tell you the story of my own case. There'll be no shame about it, I will hide nothing… people strip naked in front of me, after all, and show me their scabs, their urine, their excrement… if someone is to help there can be no beating about the bush, no concealment. So I won't describe the case of some fictional doctor, I will strip myself naked and say that I… I forgot all shame in that filthy isolation, that accursed country that eats the soul and sucks the marrow from a man's loins."

I must have made a movement of some kind, for he interrupted himself.

"Ah, you protest… oh, I understand, you are fascinated by India, by its temples and palm trees, all the romance of a two-month visit. Yes, the tropics are magical when you're travelling through them by rail, road or rickshaw: I felt just the same when I first arrived seven years ago. I had so many dreams, I was going to learn the language and read the sacred texts in the original, I was going to study the diseases, do scientific work, explore the native psyche—as we would put it in European jargon—I was on a mission for humanity and civilisation. Everyone who comes here dreams the same dream. But then a man's strength ebbs away in this invisible hothouse, the fever strikes deep into him—and we all get the fever, however much quinine we take—he becomes listless, indolent, flabby as a jellyfish. As a European, he is cut off from his true nature, so to speak, when he leaves the big cities for some wretched swamp-ridden station. Sooner or later we all succumb to our weaknesses, some drink, others smoke opium, others again brawl and act like brutes—some kind of folly comes over us all. We long for Europe, we dream of walking down a street again some day, sitting among white people in a well-lit room in a solidly built house, we dream of it year after year, and if a time does come when we could go on leave we're too listless to take the chance. A man knows he's been forgotten back at home, he's a stranger there, a shell in the sea, anyone can tread on him. So he stays, he degenerates and goes to the bad in these hot, humid jungles. It was a bad day when I sold my services to that filthy place…

Not that I did it entirely of my own free will. I had studied in Germany, I was a qualified doctor, indeed a good doctor with a post at the big hospital in Leipzig; in some long-forgotten issue of a medical journal a great deal was made of a new injection that I was the first to introduce. And then I had trouble over a woman, I met her in the hospital; she had driven her lover so crazy that he shot her with a revolver, and soon I was as crazy as he had been. She had a cold, proud manner that drove me to distraction—bold domineering women had always had a hold over me, but she tightened that hold until my bones were breaking. I did what she wanted, I—well, why not say it? It's eight years ago now—I dipped into the hospital funds for her, and when it came out all hell was let loose. An uncle of mine covered up for me when I was dismissed, but my career was over. It was then that I heard the Dutch government was recruiting doctors for the colonies, offering a lump sum in payment. Well, I understood at once the kind of job it would be if they were offering payment like that. For I knew that the crosses on graves in the fever-zone plantations grow three times as fast as at home, but when you're young you think fever and death affect only others. However, I had little choice; I went to Rotterdam, signed up for ten years, and was given a big bundle of banknotes. I sent half home to my uncle, and as for the other half, a woman in the harbour district got it out of me, just because she was so like the vicious cat I'd loved. I sailed away from Europe without money, without even a watch, without illusions, and I wasn't particularly sorry to leave harbour. And then I sat on deck like you, like everyone, and saw the Southern Cross and the palm trees, and my heart rose. Ah, forests, isolation, silence, I dreamed! Well—I'd soon had enough of isolation. I wasn't stationed in Batavia or Surabaya, in a city with other people and clubs, golf, books and newspapers, instead I went to—well, the name doesn't matter—to one of the district stations, two days' journey from the nearest town. A couple of tedious, desiccated officials and a few half-castes were all the society I had, apart from that, nothing for miles around but jungle, plantations, thickets and swamps.

It was tolerable at first. I pursued all kinds of studies; once, when the vice-resident was on a journey of inspection, had a motor accident and broke a leg, I operated on him without assistants, and there was a lot of talk about it. I collected native poisons and weapons, I turned my attention to a hundred little things to keep my mind alert. But that lasted only as long as the strength of Europe was still active in me, and then I dried up. The few Europeans on the station bored me, I stopped mixing with them, I drank and I dreamed. I had only two more years to go before I'd be free, with a pension, and could go back to Europe and begin life again. I wasn't really doing anything but waiting; I lay low and waited. And that's what I would be doing today if she… if it hadn't happened."

The voice in the darkness stopped. The pipe had stopped glowing too. It was so quiet that all of a sudden I could hear the water foaming as it broke against the keel, and the dull, distant throbbing of the engines. I would have liked to light a cigarette, but I was afraid of the bright flash of the lit match and its reflection in his face. He remained silent for a long time. I didn't know if he had finished what he had to say, or was dozing, or had fallen asleep, so profound was his silence.

Then the ship's bell struck a single powerful note: one o'clock. He started. I heard his glass clink again. His hand was obviously feeling around for the whisky. A shot gurgled quietly into his glass, and then the voice suddenly began again, but now it seemed tenser and more passionate.

"So… wait a moment… so yes, there I was, sitting in my damned cobweb, I'd been crouching motionless as a spider in its web for months. It was just after the rainy season. Rain had poured down on the roof for weeks on end, not a human being had come along, no European, I'd been stuck there in the house day after day with my yellow-skinned women and my good whisky. I was feeling very 'down' at the time, homesick for Europe. If I read a novel describing clean streets and white women my fingers began to tremble. I can't really describe the condition to you, but it's like a tropical disease, a raging, feverish, yet helpless nostalgia that sometimes comes over a man. So there I was, sitting over an atlas, I think, dreaming of journeys. Then there's a hammering at the door. My boy is there and one of the women, eyes wide with amazement. They make dramatic gestures: there's a woman here, they say, a lady, a white woman.

I jump up in surprise. I didn't hear a carriage or a car approaching. A white woman, here in this wilderness?

I am about to go down the steps, but then I pull myself together. A glance in the mirror, and I hastily tidy myself up a little. I am nervous, restless, I have ominous forebodings, for I know no one in the world who would be coming to visit me out of friendship. At last I go down.

The lady is waiting in the hall, and hastily comes to meet me. A thick motoring veil hides her face. I am about to greet her, but she is quick to get her word in first. 'Good day, doctor,' she says in fluent English—slightly too fluent, as if she had learnt her speech by heart in advance. 'Do forgive me for descending on you like this, but we have just been visiting the station, our car is over there'—here a thought flashes through my mind: why didn't she drive up to the house?—'And then I remembered that you live here. I've heard so much about you—you worked miracles for the vice-resident, his leg is perfectly all right now, he can play golf as well as ever. Oh yes, imagine all of us in the city are still talking about it, we'd happily dispense with our own cross-grained surgeon and the other doctors if you would only come to us instead. Now, why do you never go to the city? You live like a yogi here… '

And so she chatters on, faster and faster, without letting me get a word in. Her loquacity is nervous and agitated, and makes me uneasy. Why is she talking so much, I ask myself, why doesn't she introduce herself, why doesn't she put that veil back? Is she feverish? Is she ill? Is she mad? I feel increasingly nervous, aware that I look ridiculous, standing silently in front of her while her flood of chatter sweeps over me. At last she slows down slightly, and I am able to ask her upstairs. She signs to the boy to stay where he is, and goes up the stairs ahead of me.

'You have a nice place here,' she says, looking around my room. 'Ah, such lovely books! I'd like to read them all!' She goes up to the bookcase and looks at the titles. For the first time since I set eyes on her, she falls silent for a minute.

'May I offer you a cup of tea?' I ask.

She doesn't turn, but just looks at the spines of the books. 'No thank you, doctor… we have to be off again in a moment, and I don't have much time… this was just a little detour. Ah, I see you have Flaubert as well, I love him so much… *L'Education sentimentale*, wonderful, really wonderful… So you read French too! A man of many talents! Ah, you Germans, you learn everything at school. How splendid to know so many languages! The vice-resident swears by you, he always says he wouldn't go under the knife with anyone else… our residency surgeon is good for playing bridge but… the fact is,' she said, still with her face turned away, 'it crossed my mind today that I might consult you myself some time… and since we happened to be passing anyway, I thought… oh, but I'm sure you are very busy… I can come back another time.'

Showing your hand at last, I thought. But I didn't show any reaction, I merely assured her that it would be an honour to be of service to her now or whenever she liked.

'It's nothing serious,' she said, half-turning and at the same time leafing through a book she had taken off the shelf. 'Nothing serious… just small things, women's troubles… dizziness, fainting. This morning I suddenly fainted as we were driving round a bend, fainted right away, the boy had to prop me up in the car and fetch water… but perhaps the chauffeur was just driving too fast, do you think, doctor?'

'I can't say, just like that. Do you often have fainting fits?'

'No… that is, yes… recently, in fact very recently. Yes, I have had such fainting fits, and attacks of nausea.' She is standing in front of the bookcase again, puts the book back, takes another out and riffles the pages. Strange, I think, why does she keep leafing through the pages so nervously, why doesn't she look up behind that veil? Deliberately, I say nothing. I enjoy making her wait. At last she starts talking again in her nonchalant, loquacious way.

'There's nothing to worry about, doctor, is there? No tropical disease… nothing dangerous… ?'

'I'd have to see if you are feverish first. May I take your pulse?'

I approach her, but she moves slightly aside.

'No, no, I'm not feverish… certainly not, certainly not, I've been taking my own temperature every day since… since this fainting began. Never any higher, always exactly 36.4°. And my digestion is healthy too.'

I hesitate briefly. All this time a suspicion has been lurking at the back of my mind: I sense that this woman wants something from me. You certainly don't go into the wilderness to talk about Flaubert. I keep her waiting for a minute or two, then I say, straight out, 'Forgive me, but may I ask you a few frank questions?'

'Of course, doctor! You are a medical man, after all,' she replies, but she has her back turned to me again and is playing with the books.

'Do you have children?'

'Yes, a son.'

'And have you… did you previously… I mean with your son, did you experience anything similar?'

'Yes.'

Her voice is quite different now. Very clear, very firm, no longer loquacious or nervous.

'And is it possible… forgive my asking… that you are now in the same situation?'

'Yes.'

She utters the word in a tone as sharp and cutting as a knife. Her averted head does not move at all.

'Perhaps it would be best, ma'am, if I gave you a general examination. May I perhaps ask you to… to go to the trouble of coming into the next room?'

Then she does turn, suddenly. I feel a cold, determined gaze bent straight on me through her veil.

'No, that won't be necessary… I am fully aware of my condition.'"

The voice hesitated for a moment. The glass that he had refilled shone briefly in the darkness again.

"So listen… but first try to think a little about it for a moment. A woman forces herself on someone who is desperate with loneliness, the first white woman in years to set foot in his room… and suddenly I feel that there is something wrong here, a danger. A shiver runs down my spine: I am afraid of the steely determination of this woman, who arrived with her careless chatter and then suddenly came out with her demand like a knife. For I knew what she wanted me to do, I knew at once—it was not the first time women had made me such requests, but they approached me differently, ashamed or pleading, they came to me with tears and entreaties. But here was a steely… yes, a virile determination. I felt from the first second that this woman was stronger than me, that she could force me to do as she wanted. And yet, and yet… there was some evil purpose in me, a man on his guard, some kind of bitterness, for as I said before… from the first second, indeed even before I had seen her, I sensed that this woman was an enemy.

At first I said nothing. I remained doggedly, grimly silent. I felt that she was looking at me under her veil—looking at me straight and challengingly, I felt that she wanted to force me to speak, but evasively, or indeed unconsciously, I emulated her casual, chattering manner. I acted as if I didn't understand her, for—I don't know if you can understand this—I wanted to force her to speak clearly, I didn't want to offer anything, I wanted to be asked, particularly by her, because her manner was so imperious… and because I knew that I am particularly vulnerable to women with that cold, proud manner.

So I remained non-committal, saying there was no cause for concern, such fainting fits occurred in the natural course of events, indeed they almost guaranteed a happy outcome. I quoted cases from the medical press… I talked and talked, smoothly and effortlessly, always suggesting that this was something very banal, and… well, I kept waiting for her to interrupt me. Because I knew she wouldn't stand for that.

Then she did interrupt me sharply, waving aside all my reassuring talk.

'That's not what worries me, doctor. When my son was born I was in a better state of health, but now I'm not all right any more… I have a heart condition… '

'Ah, a heart condition,' I repeated, apparently concerned. 'We must look into that at once.' And I made as if to stand up and fetch my stethoscope.

But she stopped me again. Her voice was very sharp and firm now—like an officer's on a parade ground.

'I *do* have a heart condition, doctor, and I must ask you to believe what I tell you. I don't want to waste a lot of time with examinations—I think you might show a little more confidence in me. For my part, I've shown sufficient confidence in you.'

Now it was battle, an open challenge, and I accepted it.

'Confidence calls for frank disclosure, with nothing held back. Please speak frankly. I am a doctor. And for heaven's sake take that veil off, sit down, never mind the books and the roundaboutation. You don't go to visit a doctor in a veil.'

Proud and erect, she looked at me. For one moment she hesitated. Then she sat down and lifted her veil. I saw the kind of face I had feared to see, an impenetrable face, hard, controlled, a face of ageless beauty, a face with grey English eyes in which all seemed at peace, and yet behind which one could dream that all was passion. That narrow, compressed mouth gave nothing away if it didn't want to. For a moment we looked at each other—she commandingly and at the same time inquiringly, with such cold, steely cruelty that I couldn't hold her gaze, but instinctively looked away.

She tapped the table lightly with her knuckles. So she was nervous too. Then she said, quickly and suddenly, 'Do you know what I want you to do for me, doctor, or don't you?'

'I believe I do. But let's be quite plain about it. You want an end put to your condition… you want me to cure you of your fainting fits and nausea by… by removing their cause. Is that it?'

'Yes.'

The word fell like a guillotine.

'And do you know that such attempts are dangerous… for both parties concerned?'

'Yes.'

'That I am legally forbidden to do such a thing?'

'There are cases when it isn't forbidden but actually recommended.'

'They call for medical indications, however.'

'Then you'll find such indications. You're a doctor.'

Clear, fixed, unflinching, her eyes looked at me as she spoke. It was an order, and weakling that I am, I trembled with admiration for her demonically imperious will. But I was still evasive, I didn't want to show that I was already crushed. Some spark of desire in me said: don't go too fast! Make difficulties. Force her to beg!

'That is not always within a doctor's competence. But I am ready to ask a colleague at the hospital… '

'I don't want your colleague… I came to you.'

'May I ask why?'

She looked coldly at me. 'I have no reservations about telling you. Because you live in seclusion, because you don't know me—because you are a good doctor, and because,' she added, hesitating for the first time, 'you probably won't stay here very much longer, particularly if you… if you can go home with a large sum of money.'

I felt cold. The adamant, commercial clarity of her calculation bemused me. So far her lips had uttered no request—she had already worked it all out, she had been lying in wait for me and then tracked me down. I felt the demonic force of her will enter into me, but embittered as I was—I resisted. Once again I made myself sound objective, indeed almost ironic.

'Oh, and you would… would place this large sum of money at my disposal?'

'For your help, and then your immediate departure.'

'Do you realise that would lose me my pension?'

'I will compensate you.'

'You're very clear in your mind about it… but I would like even more clarity. What sum did you envisage as a fee?'

'Twelve thousand guilders, payable by cheque when you reach Amsterdam.'

I trembled… I trembled with anger and… yes, with admiration again too. She had worked it all out, the sum and the manner of its payment, which would oblige me to leave this part of the world, she had assessed me and bought me before she even met me, had made arrangements for me in anticipation of getting her own way. I would have liked to strike her in the face, but as I stood there shaking—she too had risen to her feet—and I looked her straight in the eye, the sight of her closed mouth that refused to plead, her haughty brow that would not bend, a… a kind of violent desire overcame me. She must have felt something of it, for she raised her eyebrows as one would to dismiss a trouble-maker; the hostility between us was suddenly in the open. I knew she hated me because she needed me, and I hated her because… well, because she would not plead. In that one single second of silence we spoke to each other honestly for the first time. Then an idea suddenly came to me, like the bite of a reptile, and I told her… I told her…

But wait a moment, or you'll misunderstand what I did... what I said. First I must explain how... well, how that deranged idea came into my mind."

Once again the glass clinked softly in the dark, and the voice became more agitated.

"Not that I want to make excuses, justify myself, clear myself of blame... but otherwise you won't understand. I don't know if I have ever been what might be called a good man, but... well, I think I was always helpful. In the wretched life I lived over there, the only pleasure I had was using what knowledge was contained in my brain to keep some living creature breathing... an almost divine pleasure. It's a fact, those were my happiest moments, for instance when one of the natives came along, pale with fright, his swollen foot bitten by a snake, howling not to have his leg cut off, and I managed to save him. I've travelled for hours to see a woman in a fever—and as for the kind of help my visitor wanted, I'd already given that in the hospital in Europe. But then I could at least feel that these people *needed* me, that I was saving someone from death or despair—and the feeling of being needed was my way of helping myself.

But this woman—I don't know if I can describe it to you—she had irritated and intrigued me from the moment when she had arrived, apparently just strolling casually in. Her provocative arrogance made me resist, she caused everything in me that was—how shall I put it?—everything in me that was suppressed, hidden, wicked, to oppose her. Playing the part of a great lady, meddling in matters of life and death with unapproachable aplomb... it drove me mad. And then... well, after all, no woman gets pregnant just from playing golf. I knew, that is to say I reminded myself with terrible clarity—and this is when my idea came to me—that this cool, haughty, cold woman, raising her eyebrows above her steely eyes if

I so much as looked at her askance and parried her demands, had been rolling in bed with a man in the heat of passion two or three months ago, naked as an animal and perhaps groaning with desire, their bodies pressing as close as a pair of lips. That was the idea burning in my mind as she looked at me with such unapproachable coolness, proud as an English army officer… and then everything in me braced itself, I was possessed by the idea of humiliating her. From that moment on, I felt I could see her naked body through her dress… from that moment on I lived for nothing but the idea of taking her, forcing a groan from her hard lips, feeling this cold, arrogant woman a prey to desire like anyone else, as that other man had done, the man I didn't know. That… that's what I wanted to explain to you. Low as I had sunk, I had never before thought of exploiting such a situation as a doctor… and this time it wasn't desire, the rutting instinct, nothing sexual, I swear it wasn't, I can vouch for it… just a wish to break her pride, dominate her as a man. I think I told you that I have always been susceptible to proud and apparently cold women… and add to that the fact that I had lived here for seven years without sleeping with a white woman, and had met with no resistance… for the girls here, twittering, fragile little creatures who tremble with awe if a white man, a 'master' takes them… they efface themselves in humility, they're always available, always at your service with their soft, gurgling laughter, but that submissive, slavish attitude in itself spoils the pleasure. So can you understand the shattering effect on me when a woman full of pride and hostility suddenly came along, reserved in every fibre of her being, glittering with mystery and at the same time carrying the burden of an earlier passion? When such a woman boldly enters the cage of a man like me, a lonely, starved, isolated brute of a man… well, that's what I wanted to tell you, just so that you'll understand the rest, what happened next. So, full of some kind of wicked greed, poisoned by the thought of her stripped naked, sensuous, submitting, I pulled myself together with pretended indifference. I said coolly, 'Twelve thousand guilders? No, I won't do it for that.'

She looked at me, turning a little pale. She probably sensed already that my refusal was not a matter of avarice, but she said, 'Then what do you want?'

I was not putting up with her cool tone any more. 'Let's show our hands, shall we? I am not a tradesman… I'm not the poor apothecary in *Romeo and Juliet* who sells his poison for 'corrupted gold'. Perhaps I'm the opposite of a tradesman… you won't get what you want by those means.'

'So you won't do it?'

'Not for money.'

All was very still between us for a second. So still that for the first time I heard her breathing.

'What else can you want, then?'

Now I could control myself no longer. 'First, I want you to stop… stop speaking to me as if I were a tradesman and address me like a human being. And when you need help, I don't want you to… to come straight out with your shameful offer of money, but to ask me… ask me to help you as one human being to another. I am not just a doctor, I don't spend all my time in consultations… I spend some of it in other ways too, and perhaps you have come at such a time.'

She says nothing for a moment, and then her lip curls very slightly, trembles, and she says quickly, 'Then if I were to ask you… would you do it?'

'You're trying to drive a bargain again—you won't ask me unless I promise first. You must ask me first—then I will give you an answer.'

She tosses her head like a defiant horse, and looks angrily at me.

'No, I will not ask you. I'd rather go to my ruin!'

At that anger seized upon me, red, senseless anger.

'Then if you won't ask, I will make my own demand. I don't think I have to put it crudely—you know what I want from you. And then—then I will help you.'

She stared at me for a moment. Then—oh, I can't, I can't tell you how terrible it was—then her features froze and she… she suddenly *laughed*, she laughed at me with unspeakable contempt in her face, contempt that was scattered all over me… and at the same time intoxicated me. That derisive laughter was like a sudden explosion, breaking out so abruptly and with such monstrous force behind it that I… yes, I could have sunk to the ground and kissed her feet. It lasted only a second… it was like lightning, and it had set my whole body on fire. Then she turned and went quickly to the door. I instinctively moved to follow her… to apologise, to beg her… well, my strength was entirely broken. She turned once more and said… no, *ordered*, 'Don't dare to follow me or try to track me down. You would regret it.'

And the door slammed shut behind her."

Another hesitation. Another silence… again, there was only the faint rushing sound, as if of moonlight pouring down. Then, at last, the voice spoke again.

"The door slammed, but I stood there motionless on the spot, as if hypnotized by her order. I heard her go downstairs, open the front door… I heard it all, and my whole will urged me to follow her… to… oh, I don't know what, to call her back, strike her, strangle her, but to follow her… to follow. Yet I couldn't. My limbs were crippled as if by an electric shock… I had been cut to the quick by the imperious gleam of those eyes. I know there's no explaining it, it can't be described… it may sound ridiculous, but I just stood there, and it was several minutes, perhaps five, perhaps ten, before I could raise a foot from the floor…

But no sooner had I moved that foot than I instantly, swiftly, feverishly hurried down the stairs. She could only have gone along the road back to civilisation… I hurry to the shed for my bicycle, I find I have forgotten the door key, I wrench the lock off, splitting and breaking the bamboo of the shed door… and next moment I am on my bicycle and hurrying after her… I have to reach her, I must, before she gets back to her car. I must speak to her. The road rushes past me… only now do I realise how long I must have stood there motionless. Then, where the road through the forest bends just before reaching the buildings of the district station, I see her hurrying along, stepping firmly, walking straight ahead accompanied by her boy… but she must have seen me too, for now she speaks to the boy, who stays behind while she goes on alone. What is she doing? Why does she want to be on her own? Does she want to speak to me out of his hearing? I pedal fast and furiously… then something suddenly springs into my path. It's the boy… I am only just in time to swerve and fall. I rise, cursing… involuntarily I raise my fist to hit the fool, but he leaps aside. I pick up my bicycle to remount it, but then the scoundrel lunges forward, takes hold of the bicycle, and says in his pitiful English, 'You not go on.'

You haven't lived in the tropics… you don't know how unheard-of it is for a yellow bastard like that to seize the bicycle of a white 'master' and tell him, the master, to stay where he is. Instead of answering I strike him in the face with my fist. He staggers, but keeps hold of the bicycle… his eyes, his narrow, frightened eyes are wide open in slavish fear, but he holds the handlebars infernally tight. 'You not go on,' he stammers again. It's lucky I don't have my revolver with me, or I'd shoot him down. 'Out of the way, scum!' is all I say. He cringes and stares at me, but he does not let go of the handlebars. At this rage comes over me… I see that she is well away, she may have escaped me entirely… and I hit him under the chin with a boxer's punch and send him flying. Now I have my bicycle back, but as I jump on it the mechanism jams. A spoke has bent in our tussle. I try to straighten it with trembling hands. I can't, so I fling the bicycle across the road at the scoundrel, who gets up, bleeding, and flinches aside. And then—no, you won't understand how ridiculous it looks to everyone there for a European… well, anyway, I didn't know what I was doing any more. I had only one thought in my mind: to go after her, to reach her. And so I *ran*, ran like a madman along the road and past the huts, where the yellow riff-raff were gathered in amazement to see a white man, the doctor, *running*.

I reach the station, dripping with sweat. My first question is: where is the car? Just driven away… People stare at me in surprise. I must look to them like a lunatic, arriving wet and muddy, screaming my question ahead of me before coming to a halt… Down in the road, I see the white fumes of the car exhaust. She has succeeded… succeeded, just as all her harsh, cruelly harsh calculations must succeed.

But flight won't help her. There are no secrets among Europeans in the tropics. Everyone knows everyone else, everything is a notable event. And not for nothing did her driver spend an hour in the government bungalow… in a few minutes, I know all about it. I know who she is, I know that she lives in… well, in the capital of the colony, eight hours from here by rail. I know that she is… let's say the wife of a big businessman, enormously rich, distinguished, an Englishwoman. I know that her husband has been in America for five months, and is to arrive here next day to take her back to Europe with him…

And meanwhile—the thought burns in my veins like poison—meanwhile she can't be more than two or three months pregnant…

So far I hope I have made it easy for you to understand… but perhaps only because up to that point I still understood myself, and as a doctor I could diagnose my own condition. From now on, however, something began to work in me like a fever… I lost control. That's to say, I knew exactly how pointless everything I did was, but I had no power over myself any more… I no longer understood myself. I was merely racing forward, obsessed by my purpose… No, wait. Perhaps I can make you understand it after all. Do you know what the expression 'running amok' means?"

"'Running amok?' Yes, I think I do… a kind of intoxication affecting the Malays…"

"It's more than intoxication… it's madness, a sort of human rabies, an attack of murderous, pointless monomania that bears no comparison with ordinary alcohol poisoning. I've studied several cases myself during my time in the East —it's easy to be very wise and objective about other people—but I was never able to uncover the terrible secret of its origin. It may have something to do with the climate, the sultry, oppressive atmosphere that weighs on the nervous system like a storm until it suddenly breaks… well then, this is how it goes: a Malay, an ordinary, good-natured man, sits drinking his brew, impassive, indifferent, apathetic… just as I was sitting in my room… when suddenly he leaps to his feet, snatches his dagger and runs out into the street, going straight ahead of him, always straight ahead, with no idea of any destination. With his *kris* he strikes down anything that crosses his path, man or beast, and this murderous frenzy makes him even more deranged. He froths at the mouth as he runs, he howls like a lunatic… but he still runs and runs and runs, he doesn't look right, he doesn't look left, he just runs on screaming shrilly, brandishing his bloodstained *kris* as he forges straight ahead in that dreadful way. The people of the villages know that no power can halt a man running amok, so they shout warnings ahead when they see him coming —'Amok! Amok!'—and everyone flees… but he runs on without hearing, without seeing, striking down anything he meets… until he is either shot dead like a mad dog or collapses of his own accord, still frothing at the mouth…

I once saw a case from the window of my bungalow. It was a terrible sight, but it's only because I saw it that I can understand myself in those days… because I stormed off like that, just like that, obsessed in the same way, going straight ahead with that dreadful expression, seeing nothing to right or to left, following the woman. I don't remember exactly what I did, it all went at such breakneck speed, with such mindless haste… Ten minutes, no, five—no, two—after I had found out all about the woman, her name, where she lived and her story, I was racing back to my house on a borrowed bicycle, I threw a suit into my case, took some money and drove to the railway station in my carriage. I went without informing the district officer, without finding a locum for myself, I left the house just as it was, unlocked. The servants were standing around, the astonished women were asking questions. I didn't answer, didn't turn, drove to the station and took the next train to the city… only an hour after that woman had entered my room, I had thrown my life away and was running amok, careering into empty space.

I ran straight on, headlong… I arrived in the city at six in the evening, and at ten past six I was at her house asking to see her. It was… well, as you will understand, it was the most pointless, stupid thing I could have done, but a man runs amok with empty eyes, he doesn't see where he is going. The servant came back after a few minutes, cool and polite: his mistress was not well and couldn't see anyone.

I staggered away. I prowled around the house for an hour, possessed by the insane hope that she might perhaps come looking for me. Only then did I book into the hotel on the beach and went to my room with two bottles of whisky which, with a double dose of veronal, helped to calm me. At last I fell asleep… and that dull, troubled sleep was the only momentary respite in my race between life and death."

The ship's bell sounded. Two hard, full strokes that vibrated on, trembling, in the soft pool of near-motionless air and then ebbed away in the quiet, endless rushing of the water washing around the keel, its sound mingling with his passionate tale. The man opposite me in the dark must have started in alarm, for his voice hesitated. Once again I heard his hand move down to find a bottle, and the soft gurgling. Then, as if reassured, he began again in a firmer voice.

"I can scarcely tell you about the hours I passed from that moment on. I think, today, that I was in a fever at the time; at the least I was in a state of over-stimulation bordering on madness—as I told you,

I was running amok. But don't forget, it was Tuesday night when I arrived, and on Saturday—as I had now discovered—her husband was to arrive on the P&O steamer from Yokohama. So there were just three days left, three brief days for the decision to be made and for me to help her. You'll understand that I knew I must help her at once, yet I couldn't speak a word to her. And my need to apologise for my ridiculous, deranged behaviour drove me on. I knew how valuable every moment was, I knew it was a matter of life and death to her, yet I had no opportunity of approaching her with so much as a whisper or a sign, because my tempestuous foolishness in chasing after her had frightened her off. It was… wait, yes… it was like running after someone warning that a murderer is on the way, and that person thinks you are the murderer yourself and so runs on to ruin… She saw me only as a man running amok, pursuing her in order to humiliate her, but I… and this was the terrible absurdity of it… I wasn't thinking of that any more at all. I was destroyed already, I just wanted to help her, do her a service. I would have committed murder, any crime, to help her… but she didn't understand that. When I woke in the morning and went straight back to her house, the boy was standing in the doorway, the servant whose face I had punched, and when he saw me coming—he must have been looking out for me—he hurried in through the door. Perhaps he went in only to announce my arrival discreetly… perhaps… oh, that uncertainty, how it torments me now… perhaps everything was ready to receive me, but then, when I saw him, I remembered my disgrace, and this time I didn't even dare to try calling on her again. I was weak at the knees. Just before reaching the doorway I turned and went away again… went away, while she, perhaps, was waiting for me in a similar state of torment.

I didn't know what to do in this strange city that seemed to burn like fire beneath my feet. Suddenly I thought of something, called for a carriage, went to see the vice-resident on whose leg I had operated back at my own district station, and had myself announced. Something in my appearance must have seemed strange, for he looked at me with slight alarm, and there was an uneasiness about his civility… perhaps he recognised me as a man running amok. I told him, briefly, that I wanted a transfer to the city, I couldn't exist in my present post any longer, I said, I had to move at once. He looked at me… I can't tell you how he looked at me… perhaps as a doctor looks at a sick man. 'A nervous breakdown, my dear doctor?' he said. 'I understand that only too well. I'm sure it can be arranged, but wait… let's say for four weeks, while I find a replacement.'

'I can't wait, I can't wait even a day,' I replied. Again he gave me that strange look. 'You must, doctor,' he said gravely. 'We can't leave the station without a medical man. But I promise you I'll set everything in motion this very day.' I stood there with my teeth gritted; for the first time I felt clearly that I was a man whose services had been bought, I was a slave. I was preparing to defy him when, diplomat that he was, he got his word in first. 'You're unused to mixing with other people, doctor, and in the end that becomes an illness. We've all been surprised that you never came here to the city or went on leave. You need more company, more stimulation. Do at least come to the government reception this evening. You'll find the entire colony, and many of them have long wanted to meet you, they've often asked about you and hoped to see you here.'

That last remark pulled me up short. People had asked about me? Could he mean *her*? I was suddenly a different man: I immediately thanked him courteously for his invitation and assured him that I would be there punctually. And punctual I was, over-punctual. I hardly have to tell you that, driven by my impatience, I was the first in the great hall of the government building, surrounded by the silent, yellow-skinned servants whose bare feet hurried back and forth, and who—so it seemed to me in my confused state of mind—were laughing at me behind my back. For a quarter of an hour I was the only European among all the soundless preparations, so alone with myself that I could hear the ticking of my watch in my waistcoat pocket. Then a few government officials at last appeared with their families, and finally the Governor too entered, and drew me into a long conversation in which I assiduously and I think skilfully played my part, until… until suddenly, attacked by a mysterious attack of nerves, I lost all my diplomatic manner and began stammering. Although my back was to the entrance of the hall, I suddenly felt that she must have entered and was present there. I can't tell you how that sudden certainty confused me, but even as I was talking to the Governor and heard his words echo in my ears, I sensed her presence somewhere behind me. Luckily the Governor soon ended the conversation—or I think I would suddenly and abruptly have turned, so strong was that mysterious tugging of my nerves, so burning and agitated my desire. And sure enough, I had hardly turned before I saw her exactly where my senses had unconsciously guessed she would be. She wore a yellow ball-dress that made her slender, immaculate shoulders glow like dull ivory, and was talking to a group of guests. She was smiling, but I thought there was a tense expression on her face. I came closer—she either could not or would not see me—and looked at the attractive smile civilly hovering on her narrow lips. And that smile intoxicated me again, because… well, because I knew it was a lie born of art or artifice, a masterpiece of deception. Today is Wednesday, I thought, on Saturday the ship with her husband on board will arrive… how can she smile like that, so… so confidently, with such a carefree look, casually playing with the fan she holds instead of crushing it in her fear? I… I, a stranger, had been trembling for two days at the thought of this moment… Strange to her as I was, I experienced her fear and horror intensely… and she herself went to this ball and smiled, smiled, smiled…

Music started to play at the back of the hall. The dancing began. An elderly officer had asked her to dance; she left the chattering circle with a word of excuse and walked on his arm towards the other hall and past me. When she saw me her face suddenly froze—but only for a second, and then, before I could make up my mind whether or not to greet her, she gave me a civil nod of recognition, as she would to a chance acquaintance, said, 'Good evening, doctor,' and was gone. No one could have guessed what that grey-green glance concealed; I didn't know myself. Why did she speak to me… why did she suddenly acknowledge me? Was it rejection, was it a *rapprochement*, was it just the embarrassment of surprise? I can't describe the agitation into which I was cast; everything was in turmoil, explosively concentrated within me, and as I saw her like that—casually waltzing in the officer's arms, with such a cool, carefree look on her brow, while I knew that she… that she, like me, was thinking of only one thing… that we two alone, out of everyone here, had a terrible secret in common… and she was waltzing… well, in those few seconds my fear, my longing and my admiration became more passionate than ever. I don't know if anyone was watching me, but certainly my conduct gave away no more than hers—I just could not look in any other direction, I had to… I absolutely had to look at her from a distance, my eyes fastening on her closed face to see if the mask would not drop for a second. She must have found the force of my gaze uncomfortable. As she moved away on her dancing partner's arm, she glanced my way for a split second with imperious sharpness, as if repelling me; once again that little frown of haughty anger, the one I knew already, disfigured her brow.

But… but, as I told you, I was running amok; I looked neither to right nor to left. I understood her at once—her glance said: don't attract attention! Control yourself! I knew that she… how can I put it?… that she expected me to behave discreetly here in the hall, in public. I realised that if I went home at this point, I could be certain she would see me in the morning… that all she wanted to avoid just now was being exposed to my obvious familiarity with her, I knew she feared—and rightly—that my clumsiness would cause a scene. You see, I knew everything, I understood that imperious grey gaze, but… but my feelings were too strong, I had to speak to her. So I moved unsteadily over to the group where she stood talking, joined its loose-knit circle although I knew only a few of the people in it, merely in the hope of hearing her speak, yet always flinching from her eyes timidly, like a whipped dog, when they coldly rested on me as if I were one of the linen curtains hanging behind me, or the air that lightly moved it. But I stood there thirsty for a word spoken to me, for a sign of our understanding, I stood like a block, gazing at her amidst all the chatter. It cannot have passed unnoticed, for no one addressed a word to me, and she had to suffer my ridiculous presence.

I don't know how long I would have stood there… for ever, perhaps… I *could* not leave that enchantment of my own volition. The very force of my frenzy crippled me. But she could not bear it any more… she suddenly turned to the gentlemen, with the magnificent ease that came naturally to her, and said, 'I am a little tired… I think I'll go to bed early for once. Good night!' And she was walking past me with a distant social nod of her head… I could still see the frown on her face, and then nothing but her back, her white, cool, bare back. It was a second before I realised that she was leaving… that I wouldn't be able to see her or speak to her again this evening, this last evening before I could help her. For a moment I stood there rooted to the spot until I realised it, and then… then…

But wait… wait, or you will not understand how stupid and pointless what I did was. I must describe the whole room to you first. It was the great hall of the government building, entirely illuminated by lights and almost empty… the couples had gone into the other room to dance, gentlemen had gone to play cards… only a few groups were still talking in the corners, so the hall was empty, every movement conspicuous and visible in the bright light. And she walked slowly and lightly through that great hall with her shoulders straight, exchanging greetings now and then with indescribable composure, with the magnificent, frozen, proud calm that so enchanted me. I… I had stayed behind, as I told you, as if paralysed, before I realised that she was leaving… and then, when I did realise, she was already at the far side of the hall and just approaching the doors. Then… and I am still ashamed to think of it now… something suddenly came over me and I *ran*… I ran, do you hear?… I did not walk but *ran* through the hall after her, my shoes clattering on the floor. I heard my own footsteps, I saw all eyes turning to me in surprise… I could have died of shame… even as I ran I understood my own derangement, but I could not… could not go back now. I caught up with her in the doorway. She turned to me… her eyes stabbed like grey steel, her nostrils were quivering with anger… I was just going to stammer something out when… when she suddenly *laughed* aloud… a clear, carefree, whole-hearted laugh, and said, in a voice loud enough for everyone to hear, 'Oh, doctor, have you only just remembered my little boy's prescription? Ah, you learned scientists!' A couple of people standing nearby laughed kindly… I understood, and was shattered by the masterly way she had saved the situation. I put my hand in my wallet and tore a blank leaf off my prescription block, and she took it casually before… again with a cold smile of thanks… before she went. For one second I felt easy in my mind… I saw that her skill in dealing with my blunder had made up for it and put things right—but next moment I also knew that all was over for me now, she hated me for my intemperate folly… hated me worse than death itself. I could come to her door hundreds upon hundreds of times, and she would always have me turned away like a dog.

I staggered through the room… I realised that people were looking at me, and I must have appeared strange. I went to the buffet and drank two, three, four glasses of cognac one after another, which saved me from collapsing. My nerves could bear no more, they were in shreds. Then I slunk out through a side entrance, as secretly as a criminal. Not for any principality in the world could I have walked back through that hall, with her carefree laughter still echoing from its walls. I went… I really can't say now exactly where I went, but into a couple of bars where I got drunk, like a man trying to drink his consciousness away… but I could not numb my senses, the laughter was there in me, high and dreadful… I could not silence that damned laughter. I wandered around the harbour… I had left my revolver in my room, or I would have shot myself. I could think of nothing else, and with that thought I went back to the hotel with one idea in my mind… the left-hand drawer of the chest where my revolver lay… with that single idea in mind.

The fact that I didn't shoot myself after all… I swear it wasn't cowardice, it would have been a release to take off the safety catch and press the cold trigger… how can I explain it? I still felt I had a duty… yes, that damned duty to help. The thought that she might still need me, that she did need me, made me mad… it was Thursday morning before I was back in my room, and on Saturday, as I have told you, on Saturday the ship would come in, and I knew that *this* woman, this proud and haughty woman would not survive being shamed before her husband and the world… Oh, how my thoughts tortured me, thoughts of the precious time I had unthinkingly wasted, the crazy haste that had thwarted any prospect of bringing her help in time… for hours, I swear, for hours on end I paced up and down my room, racking my brains to think of a way to approach her, put matters right, help her… for I was certain that she wouldn't let me into her house now. Her laughter was still there in all my nerves, I still saw her nostrils quivering with anger. For hours I paced up and down the three metres of my cramped room… and day had dawned, morning was here already.

Suddenly an idea sent me to the desk… I snatched up a sheaf of notepaper and began to write to her, write it all down… a whining, servile letter in which I begged her forgiveness, called myself a madman, a criminal, and begged her to entrust herself to me. I swore that the hour after it was done I would disappear from the city, from the colony, from the world if she wanted… only she must forgive me and trust me to help her at the last, the very last minute. I feverishly wrote twenty pages like this… it must have been a mad, indescribable letter, like a missive written in delirium, for when I rose from the desk I was bathed in sweat… the room swayed, and I had to drink a glass of water. Only then did I try reading the letter through again, but the very first words horrified me, so I folded it up, trembling, found an envelope… and suddenly a new thought came to me. All at once I knew the right, the crucial thing to say.

I picked up the pen again, and wrote on the last sheet, 'I will wait here in the beach hotel for a word of forgiveness. If no answer comes by seven this evening, I shall shoot myself.'

Then I took the letter, rang for a boy, and told him to deliver the envelope at once. At last I had said everything—everything!"

Something clinked and fell down beside us. As he moved abruptly he had knocked over the whisky bottle; I heard his hand feeling over the deck for it, and then he picked it up with sudden vigour. He threw the empty bottle high in the air and over the ship's side. The voice fell silent for a few minutes, and then feverishly continued, even faster and more agitated than before.

"I am not a believing Christian any more… I don't believe in heaven or hell, and if hell does exist I am not afraid of it, for it can't be worse than those hours I passed between morning and evening… think of a small room, hot in the sunlight, red-hot at blazing noon… a small room, just a desk and a chair and the bed… and nothing on the desk but a watch and a revolver, and sitting at the desk a man… a man who does nothing but stare at that desk and the second hand of his watch, a man who eats and drinks nothing, doesn't smoke, doesn't move, who only… listen to me… who only stares for three long hours at the white circle of the dial and the hand of the watch ticking as it goes around. That… that was how I spent the day, just waiting, waiting, waiting… but waiting like a man running amok, senselessly, like an animal, with that headlong, direct persistence.

Well, I won't try to describe those hours to you… they are beyond description. I myself don't understand now how one can go through such an experience without going mad. Then, at twenty-two minutes past three… I remember the time exactly, I was staring at my watch… there was a sudden knock at the door. I leap up… leap like a tiger leaping on its prey, in one bound I am across the room and at the door, I fling it open, and there stands a timid little

Chinese boy with a folded note in his hand. As I avidly reach for it, he scurries away and is gone.

I tear the note open to read it… and find that I can't. A red mist blurs my vision… imagine my agony, I have word from her at last, and now everything is quivering and dancing before my eyes. I dip my head in water, and my sight clears… once again I take the note and read it. 'Too late! But wait where you are. I may yet send for you.'

No signature on the crumpled paper torn from some old brochure… the writing of someone whose handwriting is usually steady, now scribbling hastily, untidily, in pencil. I don't know why that note shook me so much. Some kind of horror, some mystery clung to it, it might have been written in flight, by someone standing in a window bay or a moving vehicle. An unspeakably cold aura of fear, haste and terror about that furtive note chilled me to the heart… and yet, and yet I was happy. She had written to me, I need not die yet, I could help her… perhaps I could… oh, I lost myself in the craziest hopes and conjectures. I read the little note a hundred, a thousand times over, I kissed it… I examined it for some word I might have forgotten or overlooked. My reverie grew ever deeper and more confused, I was in a strange condition, sleeping with open eyes, a kind of paralysis, a torpid yet turbulent state between sleep and waking. It lasted perhaps for quarter of an hour or so, perhaps for hours.

Suddenly I gave a start. Wasn't that a knock at the door? I held my breath for a minute, two minutes of perfect silence… and then it came again, like a mouse nibbling, a soft but urgent knock. I leaped to my feet, still dizzy, flung the door open, and there outside it stood her boy, the same boy whom I had once struck in the face with my fist. His brown face was pale as ashes, his confused glance spoke of some misfortune. I immediately felt horror. 'What… what's happened?' I managed to stammer. He said, 'Come quickly!' That was all, no more, but I was immediately racing down the stairs with the boy after me. A *sado*, a kind of small carriage, stood waiting. We got in. 'What's happened?' I asked him. He looked at me, trembling, and remained silent, lips compressed. I asked again… still he was silent. I could have struck him with my fist once more, but his doglike devotion to her touched me, and I asked no more questions. The little carriage trotted through the crowded street so fast that people scattered, cursing. It left the European quarter near the beach in the lower town and went on into the noisy turmoil of the city's Chinatown district. At last we reached a narrow, very remote alley… and the carriage stopped outside a low-built house. The place was dirty, with a kind of hunched look about it and a little shop window where a tallow candle stood… one of those places where you would expect to find opium dens or brothels, a thieves' lair or a receivers' cellar full of stolen goods. The boy quickly knocked… a voice whispered through a crack in the door, which stood ajar, there were questions and more questions. I could stand it no longer. I leaped up, pushed the door right open, and an old Chinese woman shrank back with a little scream. The boy followed me, led me along the passage… opened another door… another door, leading to a dark room with a foul smell of brandy and clotted blood. Something in the room groaned. I groped my way in…"

Once again his voice failed. And what he next uttered was more of a sob than words.

"I… I groped my way in… And there… there on a dirty mat, doubled up with pain… a groaning piece of human flesh… there she lay…

I couldn't see her face in the darkness. My eyes weren't yet used to it… so I only groped about and found… found her hand, hot, burning hot… she had a temperature, a very high one, and I shuddered, for I instantly knew it all… how she had fled here from me, had let some dirty Chinese woman mutilate her, only because she hoped for more silence in that quarter… she had allowed some diabolical witch to murder her rather than trust me… because, deranged as I was, I hadn't spared her pride, I hadn't helped her at once… because she feared me more than she feared death.

I shouted for light. The boy ran off; the appalling Chinese woman, her hands trembling, brought a smoking oil lamp. I had to stop myself taking her by her filthy yellow throat as she put the lamp on the table. Its light fell bright and yellow on the tortured body. And suddenly… suddenly all my emotions were gone, all my apathy, my anger, all the impure filth of my accumulated passion… I was nothing but a doctor now, a human being who could understand and feel and help. I had forgotten myself, I was fighting the horror of it with my senses alert and clear… I felt the naked body I had desired in my dreams only as… how can I put it?… as matter, an organism. I did not see *her* any more, only life defending itself against death, a human being bent double in dreadful agony. Her blood, her hot, holy blood streamed over my hands, but I felt no desire and no horror, I was only a doctor. I saw only her suffering… and I saw…

And I saw at once that barring a miracle, all was lost… the woman's criminally clumsy hand had injured her, and she had bled half to death… and I had nothing to stop the bleeding in that stinking den, not even clean water. Everything I touched was stiff with dirt…

'We must go straight to the hospital,' I said. But no sooner had I spoken than her tortured body reared convulsively.

'No… no… would rather die… no one must know… no one… home… home… '

I understood. She was fighting now only to keep her secret, to preserve her honour… not to save her life. And—and I obeyed. The boy brought a litter, we placed her in it… and so we carried her home, already like a corpse, limp and feverish, through the night, fending off the frightened servants' inquiries. Like thieves, we carried her into her own room and closed the doors. And then… then the battle began, the long battle with death…"

*

Suddenly a hand clutched my arm, and I almost cried out with the shock and pain of it. His face in the dark was suddenly hideously close to mine, I saw his white teeth gleam in his sudden outburst, saw his glasses shine like two huge cat's eyes in the pale reflection of the moonlight. And now he was not talking any more but screaming, shaken by howling rage.

"Do you know, stranger, sitting here so casually in your deckchair, travelling at leisure around the world, do you know what it's like to watch someone dying? Have you even been at a deathbed, have you seen the body contort, blue nails scrabbling at the empty air while breath rattles in the dying throat, every limb fights back, every finger is braced against the terror of it, and the eye stares into horror for which there are no words? Have you ever experienced that, idle tourist that you are, you who call it a duty to help? As a doctor I've often seen it, seen it as… as a clinical case, a fact… I have studied it, so to speak—but I *experienced* it only once, there with her, I died with her that night… that dreadful night when I sat there racking my brains to think of something, some way to staunch the blood that kept on flowing, soothe the fever consuming her before my eyes, ward off death as it came closer and closer, and I couldn't keep it from her bed. Can you guess what it means to be a doctor, to know how to combat every illness—to feel the duty of helping, as you so sagely put it, and yet to sit helpless by a dying woman, knowing what is happening but powerless… just knowing the one terrible truth, that there is nothing you can do, although you would open every vein in your own body for her? Watching a beloved body bleed miserably to death in agonising pain, feeling a pulse that flutters and grows faint… ebbing away under your fingers. To be a doctor yet know of nothing, nothing, nothing you can do… just sitting there stammering out some kind of prayer like a little old lady in church, shaking your fist in the face of a merciful god who you know doesn't exist… can you understand that? Can you understand it? There's just one thing I don't understand myself: how… how a man can manage not to die too at such moments, but wake from sleep the next morning, clean his teeth, put on a tie... go on living, when he has experienced what I felt as her breath failed, as the first human being for whom I was really wrestling, fighting, whom I wanted to keep alive with all the force of my being... as she slipped away from me to somewhere else, faster and faster, minute after minute, and my feverish brain could do nothing to keep that one woman alive...

And then, to add to my torment, there was something else too... as I sat at her bedside—I had given her morphine to relieve the pain—and I saw her lying there with burning cheeks, hot and ashen, as I sat there, I felt two eyes constantly fixed on me from behind, gazing at me with terrible expectation. The boy sat there on the floor, quietly murmuring some kind of prayer, and when my eyes met his I saw... oh, I cannot describe it... I saw something so pleading, so... so grateful in his doglike gaze! And at the same time he raised his hands to me as if urging me to save her... to me, you understand, he raised his hands to *me* as if to a god... to me, the helpless weakling who knew the battle was lost, that I was as useless here as an ant scuttling over the floor. How that gaze tormented me, that fanatical, animal hope of what my art could do... I could have shouted at him, kicked him, it hurt so much... and yet I felt that we were both linked by our love for her... by the secret. A waiting animal, an apathetic tangle of limbs, he sat hunched up just behind me. The moment I asked for anything he leaped to his bare, silent feet and handed it to me, trembling... expectantly, as if that might help, might save her. I know he would have cut his veins to help her... she was that kind of woman, she had such power over people... and I... I didn't even have the power to save her from bleeding... oh, that night, that appalling night, an endless night spent between life and death!

Towards morning she woke again and opened her eyes... they were not cold and proud now... there was a moist gleam of fever in them as they looked around the room, as if it were strange... Then she looked at me. She seemed to be thinking, trying to remember my face… and suddenly, I saw, she did remember, because some kind of shock, rejection… a hostile, horrified expression came over her features. She flailed her arms as if to flee… far, far away from me… I saw she was thinking of *that*… of the time back at my house. But then she thought again and looked at me more calmly, breathing heavily… I felt that she wanted to speak, to say something. Again her hands began to flex… she tried to sit up, but she was too weak. I calmed her, leaned down to her… and she gave me a long and tormented look… her lips moved slightly in a last, failing sound as she said, 'Will no one ever know? No one?'

'No one,' I said, with all the strength of my conviction. 'I promise you.'

But her eyes were still restless. Her fevered lips managed, indistinctly, to get it out.

'Swear to me… that no one will know… swear.'

I raised my hand as if taking an oath. She looked at me with… with an indescribable expression… it was soft, warm, grateful… yes, truly, truly grateful. She tried to say something else, but it was too difficult for her. She lay there for a long time, exhausted by the effort, with her eyes closed. Then the terrible part began… the terrible part… she fought for another entire and difficult hour. Not until morning was it all over…"

He was silent for some time. I did not notice until the bell struck from amidships, once, twice, three times—three o'clock. The moon was not shining so brightly now, but a different, faint yellow glow was already trembling in the air, and the wind blew light as a breeze from time to time. Half-an-hour more, an hour more, and it would be day, the grey around us would be extinguished by clear light. I saw his features more distinctly now that the shadows were not so dense and dark in the corner where we sat—he had taken off his cap, and now that his head was bared his tormented face looked even more terrible. But already the gleaming lenses of his glasses were turned to me again, he pulled himself together, and his voice took on a sharp and derisive tone.

"It was all over for her now—but not for me. I was alone with the body—but I was also alone in a strange house and in a city that would permit no secrets, and I… I had to keep hers. Think about it, think about the circumstances: a woman from the colony's high society, a perfectly healthy woman who had been dancing at the government ball only the evening before, suddenly dead in her bed… and a strange doctor with her, apparently called by her servant… no one in the house saw when he arrived or where he came from… she was carried in by night in a litter, and then the doors were closed… and in the morning she was dead. Only then were the servants called, and suddenly the house echoes with screams… the neighbours will know at once, the whole city will know, and there's only one man who can explain it all… I, the stranger, the doctor from a remote country station. A delightful situation, don't you agree?

I knew what lay ahead of me now. Fortunately the boy was with me, the good fellow who read every thought of mine in my eyes—that yellow-skinned, dull-minded creature knew that there was still a battle to be fought. I had said to him only, 'Your mistress did not want anyone to know what happened.' He returned my glance with his moist, doglike, yet determined gaze. All he said was, 'Yes, sir.' But he washed the blood off the floor, tidied everything—and his very determination restored mine to me.

Never in my life before, I know, was I master of such concentrated energy, and I never shall be again. When you have lost everything, you fight desperately for the last that is left—and the last was her legacy to me, my obligation to keep her secret. I calmly received the servants, told them all the same invented story: how the boy she had sent for the doctor happened to meet me by chance on his way. But while I talked, apparently calmly, I was waiting… waiting all the time for the crucial appearance of the medical officer who would have to make out the death certificate before we could put her in her coffin, and her secret with her. Don't forget, this was Thursday, and her husband would arrive on Saturday…

At last, at nine o'clock, I heard the medical officer announced. I had told the servants to send for him—he was my superior in rank and at the same time my rival, the same doctor of whom she had once spoken with such contempt, and who had obviously already heard about my application for a transfer. I sensed his hostility at once, but that in itself stiffened my backbone.

In the front hall he immediately asked, 'When did Frau… naming her by her surname—when did she die?'

'At six in the morning.'

'When did she send for you?'

'Eleven last night.'

'Did you know that I was her doctor?'

'Yes, but this was an emergency… and then… well, she asked especially for me. She wouldn't let them call any other doctor.'

He stared at me, and a flush of red came into his pale, rather plump face. I could tell that he felt bitter. But that was exactly what I needed—all my energies were concentrating on getting a quick decision, for I could feel that my nerves wouldn't hold out much longer. He was going to return a hostile reply, but then said more mildly, 'You may think that you can dispense with my services, but it is still my official duty to confirm death—and establish the cause of death.'

I did not reply, but let him go into the room ahead of me. Then I stepped back, locked the door and put the key on the table. He raised his eyebrows in surprise.

'What's the meaning of this?'

I faced him calmly. 'We don't have to establish the cause of death, we have to think of a different one. This lady called me to treat her after… after suffering the consequences of an operation that went wrong. It was too late for me to save her, but I promised I would save her reputation, and that is what I'm going to do. And I am asking you to help me.'

His eyes were wide with astonishment. 'You surely aren't saying,' he stammered, 'that you're asking me, as medical officer, to conceal a crime?'

'Yes, I am. I must.'

'So I'm to pay for your crime?'

'I've told you, I didn't touch this lady, or… or I wouldn't be here talking to you, I would have put an end to myself by now. She has paid for her transgression, if that's what you want to call it. There's no need for the world to know about it. And I will not allow this lady's reputation to be tarnished now for no good reason.'

My firm tone made him even angrier. 'You will not allow… oh, so I suppose you're my superior, or at least you think you are! Just try giving me orders… when you were summoned here from your country outpost I thought at once there was something fishy going on… nice practices you get up to, I must say, here's a pretty sample of your skill! But now *I* will examine her, *I* will do it, and you may depend upon it that any account to which my name is signed will be correct. I won't put my name to a lie.'

I kept quite calm. 'This time you must. You won't leave the room until you do.'

I put my hand in my pocket. In fact I did not have my revolver with me, but he jumped in alarm. I came a step closer and looked at him.

'Listen, let me tell you something… and then we need not resort to desperate measures. I have reached a point where I set no store by my life or anyone else's… I am anxious only to keep my promise that the manner of this death will remain secret. And listen to this too: I give you my word of honour that if you will sign the certificate saying that this lady died of… well, died accidentally, I will leave this city and the East Indies too in the course of this week… and if you want, I will take my revolver and shoot myself as soon as the coffin is in the ground and I can be sure that no one… *no one*, you understand—can make any more inquiries. That ought to satisfy you—it *must* satisfy you.'

There must have been something menacing in my voice, something quite dangerous, because as I instinctively came closer he retreated with the obvious horror of… of someone fleeing from a man in frenzy running amok, wielding a *kris*. And suddenly he had changed… he cringed, so to speak, he was bemused, his hard attitude crumbled. He murmured something with a last faint protest. 'It will be the first time in my life that I've signed a false certificate… still, I expect some form of words can be found… Who knows what would happen if… but I can't simply… '

'Of course not,' I said helpfully, to strengthen his will—only move fast, move fast, said the tingling sensation in my temples—'but now that you know you would only be hurting a living man and doing a terrible injury to a dead woman, I am sure you will not hesitate.'

He nodded. We approached the table. A few minutes later the certificate was made out; it was published later in the newspaper, and told a credible story of a heart attack. Then he rose and looked at me.

'And you'll leave this week, then?'

'My word of honour.'

He looked at me again. I realised that he wanted to appear stern and objective. 'I'll see about a coffin at once,' he said, to hide his embarrassment. But whatever it was about me that made me so… so dreadful, so tormented—he suddenly offered me his hand and shook mine with hearty good feeling. 'I hope you will be better soon,' he said—I didn't know what he meant. Was I sick? Was I… was I mad? I accompanied him to the door and unlocked it—and it was with the last of my strength that I closed it again behind him. Then the tingling in my temples returned, everything swayed and went round before my eyes, and I collapsed beside her bed… just as a man running amok falls senseless at the end of his frenzied career, his nerves broken."

*

Once again he paused. I shivered slightly: was it the first shower carried on the morning wind that blew softly over the deck? But the tormented face, now partly visible in the reflected light of dawn, was getting control of itself again.

"I don't know how long I lay on the mat like that. Then someone touched me. I came to myself with a start. It was the boy, timidly standing before me with his look of devotion and gazing uneasily at me.

'Someone wants come in… wants see her… '

'No one may come in.'

'Yes… but… '

There was alarm in his eyes. He wanted to say something, but dared not. The faithful creature was in some kind of torment.

'Who is it?'

He looked at me, trembling as if he feared a blow. And then he said—he named a name—how does such a lowly creature suddenly come by so much knowledge, how is it that at some moments these dull human souls show unspeakable tenderness?—then he said, very, very timidly, 'It is *him*.'

I started again, understood at once, and I was immediately avid, impatient to set eyes on the unknown man. For strangely enough, you see, in the midst of all my agony, my fevered longing, fear and haste, I had entirely forgotten 'him', I had forgotten there was a man involved too… the man whom this woman had loved, to whom she had passionately given what she denied to me. Twelve, twenty-four hours ago I would still have hated him, I would have been ready to tear him to pieces. Now… well, I can't tell you how much I wanted to see him, to… to love him because she had loved him.

I was suddenly at the door. There stood a young, very young fair-haired officer, very awkward, very slender, very pale. He looked like a child, so… so touchingly young, and I was unutterably shaken to see how hard he was trying to be a man and maintain his composure, hide his emotion. I saw at once that his hands were trembling as he raised them to his cap. I could have embraced him… because he was so exactly what I would have wished the man who had possessed her to be, not a seducer, not proud… no, still half a child, a pure, affectionate creature to whom she had given herself.

The young man stood before me awkwardly. My avid glance, my passionate haste as I rushed to let him in confused him yet more. The small moustache on his upper lip trembled treacherously… this young officer, this child, had to force himself not to sob out loud.

'Forgive me,' he said at last. 'I would have liked to see Frau… I would so much have liked to see her again.'

Unconsciously, without any deliberate intention, I put my arm around the young stranger's shoulders and led him in as if he were an invalid. He looked at me in surprise, with an infinitely warm and grateful expression… at that moment, some kind of understanding existed between the two of us of what we had in common. We went over to the dead woman. There she lay, white-faced, in white linen—I felt that my presence troubled him, so I stepped back to leave him alone with her. He went slowly closer with… with such reluctant, hesitant steps. I saw from the set of his shoulders the kind of turmoil that was ranging in him. He walked like… like a man walking into a mighty gale. And suddenly he fell to his knees beside the bed, just as I had done.

I came forward at once, raised him and led him to an armchair. He was not ashamed any more, but sobbed out his grief. I could say nothing—I just instinctively stroked his fair, childishly soft hair. He reached for my hand… very gently, yet anxiously… and suddenly I felt his eyes on me. 'Tell me the truth, doctor,' he stammered. 'Did she lay hands on herself?'

'No,' I said.

'And… I mean… is anyone… is someone to blame for her death?'

'No,' I said again, although a desire was rising in me to cry out, 'I am! I am! I am! And so are you! The pair of us! And her obstinacy, her ill-starred obstinacy.' But I controlled myself. I repeated, 'No… no one is to blame. It was fate!'

'I can't believe it,' he groaned, 'I can't believe it. She was at the ball only the day before yesterday, she waved to me. How is it possible, how could it happen?'

I told a lengthy lie. I did not betray her secret even to him. We talked together like two brothers over the next few days, as if irradiated by the emotion that bound us… we did not confess it to each other, but we both felt that our whole lives had depended on that woman. Sometimes the truth rose to my lips, choking me, but I gritted my teeth, and he never learned that she had been carrying his child, or that I had been asked to kill the child, his offspring, and she had taken it down into the abyss with her. Yet we talked of nothing but her in those days, when I was hiding away with him—for I forgot to tell you that they were looking for me. Her husband had arrived after the coffin was closed, and wouldn't accept the medical findings. There were all kinds of rumours, and he was looking for me… but I couldn't bear to see him when I knew that she had suffered in her marriage to him… I hid away, for four days I didn't go out of the house, we neither of us left her lover's apartment. He had booked me a passage under a false name so that I could get away easily. I went on board by night, like a thief, in case anyone recognised me. I have left everything I own behind… my house, all my work of the last seven years, my possessions, they're all there for anyone who wants them… and the government gentlemen will have struck me off their records for deserting my post without leave. But I couldn't live any longer in that house or in that city… in that world where everything reminded me of her. I fled like a thief in the night, just to escape her, just to forget. But… as I came on board at night, it was midnight, my friend was with me… they… they were just hauling something up by crane, something rectangular and black… her coffin… do you hear that, her coffin? She has followed me here, just as I followed her… and I had to stand by and pretend to be a stranger, because he, her husband, was with it, it's going back to England with him. Perhaps he plans to have an autopsy carried out there… he has snatched her back, she's his again now, not ours, she no longer belongs to the two of us. But I am still here… I will go with her to the end… he will not, must not ever know about it. I will defend her secret against any attempt to… against this ruffian from whom she fled to her death. He will learn nothing, nothing… her secret is mine alone…

So now do you understand… do you realise why I can't endure the company of human beings? I can't bear their laughter, to hear them flirting and mating… for her coffin is stowed away down there in the hold, between bales of tea and Brazil nuts. I can't get at it, the hold is locked, but I'm aware of it with all my senses, I know it is there every second of the day… even if they play waltzes and tangos up here. It's stupid, the sea there washes over millions of dead, a corpse is rotting beneath every plot of ground on which we step… yet I can't bear it, I cannot bear it when they give fancy dress balls and laugh so lasciviously. I feel her dead presence, and I know what she wants. I know it, I still have a duty to do… I'm not finished yet, her secret is not quite safe, she won't let me go yet…"

Slow footsteps and slapping sounds came from amidships; the sailors were beginning to scour the deck. He started as if caught in a guilty act, and his strained face looked anxious. Rising, he murmured, "I'll be off… I'll be off." It was painful to see him: his devastated glance, his swollen eyes, red with drink or tears. He didn't want my pity; I sensed shame in his hunched form, endless shame for giving his story away to me during the night. On impulse, I asked him, "May I visit you in your cabin this afternoon?"

He looked at me—there was a derisive, harsh, sardonic set to his mouth. A touch of malevolence came out with every word, distorting it.

"Ah, your famous duty—the duty to help! I see. You were fortunate enough to make me talk by quoting that maxim. But no thank you, sir. Don't think I feel better now that I have torn my guts out before you, shown you the filth inside me. There's no mending my spoiled life any more… I have served the honourable Dutch government for nothing, I can wave goodbye to my pension—I come back to Europe a poor, penniless cur… a cur whining behind a coffin. You don't run amok for long with impunity, you're bound to be struck down in the end, and I hope it will soon all be over for me. No thank you, sir, I'll turn down your kind offer… I have my own friends in my cabin, a few good bottles of old whisky that sometimes comfort me, and then I have my old friend of the past, although I didn't turn it against myself when I should have done, my faithful Browning. In the end it will help me better than any talk. Please don't try to… the one human right one has left is to die as one wishes, and keep well away from any stranger's help."

Once more he gave me a derisive, indeed challenging look, but I felt that it was really only in shame, endless shame. Then he hunched his shoulders, turned without a word of farewell and crossed the foredeck, which was already in bright sunlight, making for the cabins and holding himself in that curious way, leaning sideways, footsteps dragging. I never saw him again. I looked for him in our usual place that night, and the next night too. He kept out of sight, and I might have thought he was a dream of mine or a fantastic apparition had I not then noticed, among the passengers, a man with a black mourning band around his arm, a Dutch merchant, I was told, whose wife had just died of some tropical disease. I saw him walking up and down, grave and grieving, keeping away from the others, and the idea that I knew about his secret sorrow made me oddly timid. I always turned aside when he passed by, so as not to give away with so much as a glance that I knew more about his sad story than he did himself.

Then, in Naples harbour, there was that remarkable accident, and I believe I can find its cause in the stranger's story. For most of the passengers had gone ashore that evening—I myself went to the opera, and then to one of the brightly lit cafés on the Via Roma. As we were on our way back to the ship in a dinghy, I noticed several boats circling the vessel with torches and acetylene lamps as if in search of something, and up on the dark deck there was much mysterious coming-and-going of *carabinieri* and of other policemen. I asked a sailor what had happened. He avoided giving a direct answer in a way that immediately told me the crew had orders to keep quiet, and next day too, when all was calm on board again and we sailed on to Genoa without a hint of any further incident, there was nothing to be learned on board. Not until I saw the Italian newspapers did I read accounts, written up in flowery terms, of the alleged accident in Naples harbour. On the night in question, they wrote, at a quiet time in order to avoid upsetting the passengers, the coffin of a distinguished lady from the Dutch colonies was to be moved from the ship to a boat, and it had just been let down the ship's side on a rope ladder in her husband's presence when something heavy fell from the deck above, carrying the coffin away into the sea, along with the men handling it and the woman's husband, who was helping them to hoist it down. One newspaper said that a madman had flung himself down the steps and onto the rope ladder; another stated that the ladder had broken of itself under too much weight. In any case, the shipping company had done all it could to cover up what exactly had happened. The handlers of the coffin and the dead woman's husband had been pulled out of the water and into boats, not without some difficulty, but the lead coffin itself sank straight to the bottom, and could not be retrieved. The brief mention in another report of the fact that, at the same time, the body of a man of about forty had been washed ashore in the harbour did not seem to be connected in the public mind with the romantic account of the accident. But as soon as I had read those few lines, I felt as if that white, moonlit face with its gleaming glasses were staring back at me again, in ghostly fashion, from behind the sheet of newsprint.

FANTASTIC NIGHT

A SEALED PACKET *containing the following pages was found in the desk of Baron Friedrich Michael von R… after he fell at the battle of Rawaruska in the autumn of 1914, fighting with a regiment of dragoons as a lieutenant in the Austrian reserve. His family, assuming from the title and a fleeting glance at the contents that this was merely a literary work by their relative, gave it to me to assess and entrusted me with its publication. I myself do not by any means regard these papers as fiction; instead, I believe them to be a record of the dead man's own experience, faithful in every detail, and I therefore publish his psychological self-revelation without any alteration or addition, suppressing only his surname.*

This morning I suddenly conceived the notion of writing, for my own benefit, an account of my experiences on that fantastic night, in order to survey the entire incident in its natural order of occurrence. And ever since that abrupt moment of decision I have felt an inexplicable compulsion to set my adventure down in words, although I doubt whether I can describe its strange nature at all adequately. I have not a trace of what people call artistic talent, nor any literary experience, and apart from a few rather light-hearted squibs for the *Theresianum* I have never tried to write anything. I don't even know, for instance, if there is some special technique to be learnt for arranging the sequence of outward events and their simultaneous inner reflection in order, and I wonder whether I am capable of always finding the right word for a certain meaning and the right meaning for a certain word, so as to achieve the equilibrium which I have always subconsciously felt in reading the work of every true storyteller. But I write these lines solely for my own satisfaction, and they are certainly not intended to make something that I can hardly explain even to myself intelligible to others. They are merely an attempt to confront an incident which constantly occupies my mind, keeping it in a state of painfully active fermentation, and to draw a line under it at last: to set it all down, place it before me, and cover it from every angle.

I have not told any of my friends about the incident, first because I felt that I could not make them understand its essential aspects, and then out of a certain sense of shame at having been so shattered and agitated by something that happened quite by chance. For the whole thing is really just a small episode. But even as I write this, I begin to realise how difficult it is for an amateur to choose words of the right significance when he is writing, and what ambiguity, what possibilities of misunderstanding can attach to the simplest of terms. For if I describe the episode as small, of course I mean it only as relatively small, by comparison with those mighty dramatic events that sweep whole nations and human destinies along with them, and then again I mean it as small in terms of time, since the whole sequence of events occupied no more than a bare six hours. To me, however, that experience—which in the general sense was minor, insignificant, unimportant—meant so extraordinarily much that even today, four months after that fantastic night, I still burn with the memory of it, and must exert all my intellectual powers to keep it to myself. Daily, hourly, I go over all the details again, for in a way it has become the pivot on which my whole existence turns; everything I do and say is unconsciously determined by it, my thoughts are solely concerned with going over and over its sudden intrusion into my life, and thereby confirming that it really did happen to me. And now I suddenly know, too, what I certainly had not yet guessed ten minutes ago when I picked up my pen: that I am recording my experience only in order to have it securely and, so to speak, objectively fixed before me, to enjoy it again in my emotions while at the same time understanding it intellectually. It was quite wrong, quite untrue when I said just now that I wanted to draw a line under it by writing it down; on the contrary, I want to make what I lived through all too quickly even more alive, to have it warm and breathing beside me, so that I can clasp it to me again and again. Oh, I am not afraid of forgetting so much as a second of that sultry afternoon, that fantastic night, I need no markers or milestones to help me trace the path I took in those hours step by step in memory: like a sleepwalker I find myself back under its spell at any time, in the middle of the day or the middle of the night, seeing every detail with that clarity of vision that only the heart and not the feeble memory knows. I could draw the outline of every single leaf in that green spring landscape on this paper, even now in autumn I feel the mild air, the soft and pollen-laden wafts of chestnut blossom. So if I am about to describe those hours again, it is done not for fear of forgetting them but for the joy of bringing them to life again. And if I now describe the changes that took place that night, all exactly as they occurred, then I must control myself for the sake of an orderly account, for whenever I begin to think of the details of my experience ecstasy wells up from my emotions, a kind of intoxication overcomes me, and I have to hold back the images of memory to keep them from tumbling over one another in wild confusion, colourful and frenzied. With passionate ardour, I still relive what I experienced on that day, the 7th of June, 1913, when I took a cab at noon…

But once more I feel I must pause, for yet again, and with some alarm, I become aware of the double-edged ambiguity of a single word. Only now that, for the first time, I am to tell a story in its full context do I understand the difficulty of expressing the ever-changing aspect of all that lives in concentrated form. I have just written "I", and said that I took a cab at noon on the 7th of June, 1913. But the word itself is not really straightforward, for I am by no means still the "I" of that time, that 7th of June, although only four months have passed since that day, although I live in the apartment of that former "I" and write at his desk, with his pen, and with his own hand. I am quite distinct from the man I was then, because of this experience of mine, I see him now from the outside, looking coolly at a stranger, and I can describe him like a playmate, a comrade, a friend whom I know well and whose essential nature I also know, but I am not that man any longer. I could speak of him, blame or condemn him, without any sense that he was once a part of me.

The man I was then differed very little, either outwardly or inwardly, from most of his social class, which we usually describe here in Vienna, without any particular pride but as something to be taken entirely for granted, as 'fashionable society'. I was entering my thirty-sixth year, my parents had died prematurely just before I came of age, leaving me a fortune which proved large enough to make it entirely superfluous for me to think thereafter of earning a living or pursuing a career. I was thus unexpectedly spared a decision which weighed on my mind a great deal at the time. For I had just finished my university studies and was facing the choice of a future profession. Thanks to our family connections and my own early inclination for a contemplative existence proceeding at a tranquil pace, I would probably have opted for the civil service, when this parental fortune came to me as sole heir, suddenly assuring me of an independence sufficient to satisfy extensive and even luxurious wishes without working. Ambition had never troubled me, so I decided to begin by watching life at my leisure for a few years, waiting until I finally felt tempted to find some circle of influence for myself. However, I never got beyond this watching and waiting, for as there was nothing in particular that I wanted, I could have anything within the narrow scope of my wishes: the mellow and sensuous city of Vienna, which excels like no other in bringing leisurely strolls, idle observation and the cultivation of elegance to a peak of positively artistic perfection, a purpose in life of itself, enabled me to forget entirely my intention of taking up some real activity. I had all the satisfactions an elegant, noble, well-to-do, good-looking young man without ambition could desire: the harmless excitement of gambling, hunting, the regular refreshment of travels and excursions, and soon I began cultivating this peaceful way of life more and more elaborately, with expertise and artistic inclination. I collected rare glasses, not so much from a true passion for them as for the pleasure of acquiring solid knowledge in the context of an undemanding hobby, I hung my apartment with a particular kind of Italian Baroque engravings and landscapes in the style of Canaletto—acquiring them from second-hand shops or bidding for them at auction provided the excitement of the chase without any dangers—I followed many other pursuits out of a liking for them and always with good taste, and I was seldom absent from performances of good music or the studios of our painters. I did not lack for success with women, and here too, with the secret collector's urge which in a way indicates a lack of real involvement, I chalked up many memorable and precious hours of varied experience. In this field I gradually moved from being a mere sensualist to the status of a knowledgeable connoisseur. All things considered, I had enjoyed many experiences which occupied my days pleasantly and allowed me to feel that my life was a full one, and increasingly I began to relish the easygoing, pleasant atmosphere of a youthful existence that was lively but never agitated. I formed almost no new wishes, for quite small things could blossom into pleasures in the calm climate of my days. A well-chosen tie could make me almost merry; a good book, an excursion in a motor car or an hour with a woman left me fully satisfied. It particularly pleased me to ensure that this way of life, like a faultlessly correct suit of English tailoring, did not make me conspicuous in any way. I believe I was considered pleasant company, I was popular and welcome in society, and most who knew me called me a happy man.

I cannot now say whether the man of that time, whom I am trying to conjure up here, thought himself as happy as those others did, for now that this experience of mine has made me expect a much fuller and more fulfilled significance in every emotion, I find it almost impossible to assess his happiness in retrospect. But I can say with certainty that I felt myself by no means unhappy at the time, for my wishes almost never went unsatisfied and nothing I required of life was withheld. But the very fact that I had become accustomed to getting all I asked from destiny, and demanded no more, led gradually to a certain absence of excitement, a lifelessness in life itself. Those yearnings that then stirred unconsciously in me at many moments of half-realisation were not really wishes, but only the wish for wishes, a craving for desires that would be stronger, wilder, more ambitious, less easily satisfied, a wish to live more and perhaps to suffer more as well. I had removed all obstacles from my life by a method that was only too reasonable, and my vitality was sapped by that absence of obstacles. I noticed that I wanted fewer things and did not want them so much, that a kind of paralysis had come over my feelings, so that—perhaps this is the best way to express it—so that I was suffering from emotional impotence, an inability to take passionate possession of life. I recognised this defect from small signs at first. I noticed that I was absent more and more often from the theatre and society on certain occasions of great note, that I ordered books which had been praised to me and then left them lying on my desk for weeks with their pages still uncut, that although I automatically continued to pursue my hobbies, buying glasses and antiques, I did not trouble to classify them once they were mine, nor did I feel any particular pleasure in unexpectedly acquiring a rare piece which it had taken me a long time to find.

However, I became really aware of this lessening of my emotional vigour, slight but indicative of change, on a certain occasion which I still remember clearly. I had stayed in Vienna for the summer—again, as a result of that curious lethargy which left me feeling no lively attraction to anything new—when I suddenly received a letter written in a spa resort. It was from a woman with whom I had had an intimate relationship for three years, and I even truly thought I loved her. She wrote fourteen agitated pages to tell me that in her weeks at the spa she had met a man who meant a great deal to her, indeed everything, she was going to marry him in the autumn, and the relationship between us must now come to an end. She said that she thought of our time together without regret, indeed with happiness, the memory of me would accompany her into her marriage as the dearest of her past life, and she hoped I would forgive her for her sudden decision. After this factual information, her agitated missive surpassed itself in truly moving entreaties, begging me not to be angry with her, not to feel too much pain at her sudden termination of our relationship; I mustn't try to get her back by force, or do anything foolish to myself. Her lines ran on, becoming more and more passionate: I must and would find comfort with someone better, I must write to her at once, for she was very anxious about my reception of her message. And as a postscript she had hastily scribbled, in pencil: "*Don't do anything stupid, understand me, forgive me!*" I read this letter, surprised at first by her news, and then, when I had skimmed all through it, I read it a second time, now with a certain shame which, on making itself felt, soon became a sense of inner alarm. For none of the strong yet natural feelings which my lover supposed were to be taken for granted had even suggested themselves to me. I had not suffered on hearing her news, I had not been angry with her, and I had certainly not for a second contemplated any violence against either her or myself, and this coldness of my emotions was too strange not to alarm me. A woman was leaving me, a woman who had been my companion for years, whose warm and supple body had offered itself to me, whose breath had mingled with mine in long nights together, and nothing stirred in me, nothing protested, nothing sought to get her back, I had none of those feelings that this woman's pure instinct assumed were natural in any human being. At that moment I was fully aware for the first time how far advanced the process of paralysis already was in me—it was as if I were moving through flowing, bright water without being halted or taking root anywhere, and I knew very well that this chill was something dead and corpse-like, not yet surrounded by the foul breath of decomposition but already numbed beyond recovery, a grimly cold lack of emotion. It was the moment that precedes real, physical death and outwardly visible decay.

After that episode I began carefully observing myself and this curious paralysis of my feelings, as a sick man observes his sickness. When, shortly afterwards, a friend of mine died and I followed his coffin to the grave, I listened to myself to see if I did not feel grief, if some emotion did not move in me at the knowledge that this man, who had been close to me since our childhood, was now lost to me for ever. But nothing stirred, I felt as if I were made of glass, with the world outside shining straight through me and never lingering within, and hard as I attempted on this and many similar occasions to feel something, however much I tried, through reasonable argument, to make myself feel emotion, no response came from my rigid state of mind. People parted from me, women came and went, and I felt much like a man sitting in a room with rain beating on the window panes; there was a kind of sheet of glass between me and my immediate surroundings, and my will was not strong enough to break it.

Although I felt this clearly, the realisation caused me no real uneasiness, for as I have said, I took even what affected myself with indifference. I no longer had feeling enough to suffer. It was enough for me that this internal flaw was hardly perceptible from the outside, in the same way as a man's physical impotence becomes obvious only at the moment of intimacy, and in company I often put on a certain elaborate show, employing artificially passionate admiration and spontaneous exaggeration to hide the extent to which I knew I was dead and unfeeling inside. Outwardly I continued my old comfortable, unconstrained way of life without any change of direction; weeks, months passed easily by and slowly, gathering darkly into years. One morning when I looked in the glass I saw a streak of grey at my temple, and felt that my youth was slowly departing. But what others call youth had long ago ended in me, so taking leave of it did not hurt very much, since I did not love even my own youth enough for that. My refractory emotions preserved their silence even to me.

This inner rigidity made my days more and more similar, despite all the varied occupations and events that filled them, they ranged themselves side by side without emphasis, they grew and faded like the leaves of a tree. And the single day I am about to describe for my own benefit began in a perfectly ordinary way too, without anything odd to mark it, without any internal premonition. On that day, the 7th of June, 1913, I had got up later than usual because of a subconscious Sunday feeling, something that lingered from my childhood and schooldays. I had taken my bath, read the paper, dipped into some books, and then, lured out by the warm summer day that compassionately made its way into my room, I went for a walk. I crossed the Graben in my usual way, greeted friends and acquaintances and conducted brief conversations with some of them, and then I lunched with friends. I had avoided any engagement for the afternoon, since I particularly liked to have a few uninterrupted hours on Sunday which I could use just as my mood, my pleasure or some spontaneous decision dictated. As I left my friends and crossed the Ringstrasse, I felt the beauty of the sunny city doing me good, and enjoyed its early summer finery. All the people seemed cheerful, as if they were in love with the Sunday atmosphere of the lively street, and many details struck me, in particular the way the broad, bushy trees rose from the middle of the asphalt wearing their new green foliage. Although I went this way almost daily, I suddenly became aware of the Sunday crowd as if it were a miracle, and involuntarily I felt a longing for a great deal of greenery, brightness and colour. I thought with a certain interest of the Prater, where in late spring and early summer the great trees stand to right and left of the main avenue down which the carriages drive, motionless like huge green footmen as they hold up their white candles of blossom to the many well-groomed and elegant passers-by. Used as I was to indulging the most fleeting whim at once, I hailed the first cab I saw, and when the cabby asked where I was going I told him the Prater. "Ah, to the races, Baron, am I right?" he replied obsequiously, as if that was to be taken for granted. Only then did I remember that there was a fashionable race meeting today, a preview of the local Derby, where Viennese high society foregathered. How strange, I thought as I got into the cab, only a few years ago how could I possibly have forgotten or failed to attend such a day? When I thought of my forgetfulness I once again felt all the rigidity of the indifference to which I had fallen victim, just as a sick man feels his injury when he moves.

The main avenue was quite empty when we arrived, and the racing must have begun long ago, for I did not see what was usually a handsome procession of carriages; there were only a few cabs racing along, hooves clattering, as if catching up with some invisible omission. The driver turned on his box and asked whether he should make the horses trot faster, but I told him to let them walk slowly, I didn't mind arriving late. I had seen too many races, and had seen the racegoers too often as well, to mind about arriving on time, and as the vehicle rocked gently along it matched my idle mood better to feel the blue air, with a soft rushing sound in it like the sea when you are on board ship, and at my leisure to view the handsome, broad and bushy chestnut trees which sometimes gave up a few flower petals as playthings to the warm, coaxing wind, which then raised them gently and sent them whirling through the air before letting them fall like white flakes on the avenue. It was pleasant to be rocked like that, to sense the presence of spring with eyes closed, to feel carried away and elated without any effort at all. I was quite sorry when the cab reached the Freudenau and stopped at the entrance. I would have liked to turn round and let the soft, early summer day continue to cradle me. But it was already too late, the cab was drawing up outside the racecourse. A muffled roar came to meet me. It re-echoed with a dull, hollow sound on the far side of the tiers of seats, and although I could not see the excited crowd making that concentrated noise I couldn't help thinking of Ostend, where if you walk up the small side streets from the low-lying town to the beach promenade you feel the keen, salty wind blowing over you, and hear a hollow boom before you ever set eyes on the broad, grey, foaming expanse of the sea with its roaring waves. There must be a race going on at the moment, but between me and the turf on which the horses were probably galloping stood a colourful, noisy, dense mass swaying back and forth as if shaken by some inner turmoil: the crowd of spectators and gamblers. I couldn't see the track, but I followed every stage of the race as their heightened excitement reflected it. The jockeys must have started some time ago, the bunched formation at the beginning of the race had thinned out, and a couple of horses were disputing the lead, for already shouts and excited cries were coming from the people who mysteriously, as it seemed, were watching the progress of a race which was invisible to me. The turn of their heads indicated the bend which the horses and jockeys must just have reached on the long oval of turf, for the whole chaotic crowd was now moving its gaze as if craning a single neck to see something out of my line of vision, and its single taut throat roared and gurgled with thousands of hoarse, individual sounds, like a great breaker foaming as it rises higher and higher. And the wave rose and swelled, it already filled the whole space right up to the blue indifferent sky. I looked at a few of the faces. They were distorted as if by some inner spasm, their eyes were fixed and sparkling, they were biting their lips, chins avidly thrust forwards, nostrils flaring like a horse's. Sober as I was, I found their frenzied intemperance both a comic and a dreadful sight. Beside me a man was standing on a chair. He was elegantly dressed, and had what was probably a good-looking face in the usual way, but now he was raving, possessed by an invisible demon, waving his cane in the air as if lashing something forwards; his whole body—in a manner unspeakably ridiculous to a spectator—passionately mimed the movement of rapid riding. He kept bobbing his heels up and down on the chair, as if standing in the stirrups, his right hand constantly whipped the air like a riding crop, his left hand convulsively clutched a slip of white card. And there were more and more of those white slips fluttering around, like sparkling wine spraying above the grey and stormy tide that swelled so noisily. A few horses must be very close to each other on the bend now, for suddenly the shouting divided into three or four individual names roared out like battle cries again and again by separate groups, and the shouts seemed like an outlet for their delirious state of possession.

I stood amidst this roaring frenzy cold as a rock in the raging sea, and I remember to this day exactly what I felt at that moment. First I thought how ridiculous those grotesque gestures were, I felt ironic contempt for the vulgarity of the outburst, but there was something else too, something that I was unwilling to admit to myself—a kind of quiet envy of such excitement, such heated passion, envy of the life in this display of fervour. What, I thought, would have to happen to excite me so much, rouse me to such fever pitch that my body would burn so ardently, my voice would issue from my mouth against my own will? I could not imagine any sum of money that would so spur me on to possess it, any woman who could excite me so much, there was nothing, nothing that could kindle such fire within me in my emotional apathy! If I faced a pistol suddenly aimed at me, my heart would not thud as wildly in the second before I froze as did the hearts of these people around me, a thousand, ten thousand of them, just for a handful of money. But now one horse must be very near the finishing line, for a certain name rang out above the tumult like a string stretched taut, uttered by a thousand voices and rising higher and higher, only to end all at once on an abrupt, shrill note. The music began to play, the crowd suddenly dispersed. One of the races was over, the contest was decided, their tension was resolved into swirling movement as the excited vibrations died down. The throng, just a moment ago a fervent concentration of passion, broke up into many individuals walking, laughing, talking; calm faces emerged from behind the Maenad mask of frenzy; social groups formed again out of the chaos of the game that for seconds on end had forged these thousands of racegoers into a single ardent whole, those groups came together, they parted, I saw people I knew who hailed me, and strangers who scrutinised and observed each other with cool courtesy. The women assessed one another's new outfits, the men cast avid glances, that fashionable curiosity which is the real occupation of the indifferent began to show, the racegoers looked around, counted others, checked up on their presence and their degree of elegance. Scarcely brought down to earth again from their delirium, none of them knew whether the real object of their meeting in company here was the races themselves or this interlude of walking about the racecourse.

I walked through this relaxed, milling crowd, offering and returning greetings, and breathing in with pleasure—for this was the world in which I lived—the aura of perfume and elegance that wafted around the kaleidoscopic confusion. With even more pleasure I felt the soft breeze that sometimes blew out of the summery warmth of the woods from the direction of the Prater meadows, sometimes rippling like a wave among the racegoers and fingering the women's white muslins as if in amorous play. A couple of acquaintances hailed me; the pretty actress Diane nodded invitingly to me from a box, but I joined no one. I was not interested in talking to any of these fashionable folk today; I found it tedious to see myself reflected in them. All I wanted was to experience the spectacle, the crackling, sensuous excitement that pervaded the heightened emotion of the hour (for the excitement of others is the most delightful of spectacles to a man who himself is in a state of indifference). A couple of pretty women passed by, I boldly but without any inward desire scrutinised the breasts under the thin gauze they wore, moving at every step they took, and smiled to myself to see their half-awkward, half-gratified embarrassment when they felt that I was assessing them sensuously and undressing them with my eyes. In fact none of the women aroused me, it simply gave me a certain satisfaction to pretend to them that they did; it pleased me to play with their idea that I wanted to touch them physically and felt a magnetic attraction of the eye, for like all who are cold at heart I found more intense erotic enjoyment in arousing warmth and restlessness in others than in waxing ardent myself. It was only the downy warmth lent to sensuality by the presence of women that I loved to feel, not any genuine arousal, only stimulation and not real excitement. So I walked through the promenading crowd as usual, caught glances, tossed them back as lightly as a shuttlecock, took my pleasure without reaching out a hand, fondled women without physical contact, warmed only slightly by the mildly amorous game.

But soon I found this tedious too. The same people kept passing; I knew their faces and gestures by heart now. There was a chair nearby, and I took it. A new turbulence began in the groups around me, passers-by moved and pushed more restively in the confusion; obviously another race was about to start. I was not interested in that, but sat at my ease and as if submerged beneath the smoke from my cigarette, which rose in white rings against the sky, turning brighter and brighter and disintegrating like a little cloud in the springtime blue. And at that very second the extraordinary, unique experience that still rules my life today began. I can fix the moment exactly, because it so happens that I had just looked at my watch: the hands were crossing, and I watched with idle curiosity as they overlapped for a second. It was sixteen minutes past three on the afternoon of the 7th of June, 1913. With cigarette in hand, then, I was looking at the white dial of the watch, entirely absorbed in this childish and ridiculous contemplation, when I heard a woman laugh out loud just behind my back with the ringing, excited laughter that I love in women, springing warm and startled out of the hot thickets of the senses. I instinctively leant my head back to see the woman whose sensuality, boldly proclaimed aloud, was forcing its way into my carefree reverie like a sparkling white stone dropped into a dull and muddy pond—and then I controlled myself. A curious fancy for an intellectual game, a fancy of the kind I often felt for a small and harmless psychological experiment, held me back.

I didn't want to see the laughing woman just yet; it intrigued me to let my imagination work on her first in a kind of anticipation of pleasure, to conjure up her appearance, giving that laughter a face, a mouth, a throat, a neck, a breast, making a whole living, breathing woman of her.

At this moment she was obviously standing directly behind me. Her laughter had turned to conversation again. I listened intently. She spoke with a slight Hungarian accent, very fast and expressively, her vowels soaring as if in song. It amused me to speculate on the figure that went with her voice, elaborating my imaginary picture as richly as I could. I gave her dark hair, dark eyes, a wide and sensuously curving mouth with strong, very white teeth, a little nose that was very narrow but had flared, quivering nostrils. I put a beauty spot on her left cheek and a riding crop in her hand; as she laughed she slapped it lightly against her thigh. She talked on and on. And each of her words added some new detail to my rapidly formed image of her: a slender, girlish breast, a dark-green dress with a diamond brooch pinned to it at a slant, a pale hat with a white feather. The picture became clearer and clearer, and I already felt as if this stranger standing invisible behind my back was also on a lit photographic plate in the pupil of my eye. But I didn't want to turn round yet, I preferred to enhance my imaginary game further. A touch of lust mingled with my audacious reverie, and I closed both eyes, certain that when I opened them again and turned to her my imagined picture would coincide exactly with her real appearance.

At that moment she stepped forwards. Instinctively I opened my eyes—and felt disappointment. I had guessed quite wrong. Everything was different from my imaginary idea, and indeed was distressingly at odds with it. She wore not a green but a white dress, she was not slim but voluptuous and broad-hipped, the beauty spot I had dreamt up was nowhere to be seen on her plump cheek, her hair under her helmet-shaped hat was pale red, not black. None of my details fitted her real appearance; however, this woman was beautiful, challengingly beautiful, although with my psychological vanity injured, foolishly overweening as it was, I would not acknowledge her beauty. I looked up at her almost with hostility, but even in my resistance to it I felt the strong sensuous attraction emanating from this woman, the enticing, demanding, animal desirability in her firm yet softly plump opulence. Now she laughed aloud again, showing her strong white teeth, and I had to admit that this warm, sensuous laughter was in harmony with her voluptuous appearance; everything about her was vehement and challenging, the curve of her breasts, the way she thrust her chin out as she laughed, her keen glance, her curved nose, the hand pressing her parasol firmly to the ground. Here was the feminine element incarnate, a primeval power, deliberate, pervasive enticement, a beacon of lust made flesh. Beside her stood an elegant, rather colourless officer talking earnestly to her. She listened to him, smiled, laughed, contradicted him, but all this was only by the way, for at the same time her nostrils were quivering as her glance wandered here and there as if to light on everyone; she attracted attention, smiles, glances from every passing man, and from the whole male part of the crowd standing around her too. Her eyes moved all the time, sometimes searching the tiers of seats and suddenly, with joyful recognition, responding to someone's wave, turning now to right, now to left as she listened to the officer, smiling idly. But they had not yet rested on me, for I was outside her field of vision, hidden from her by her companion. I felt some annoyance and stood up—she did not see me. I came closer—now she looked up at the tiers of seats again. I stepped firmly up to her, raised my hat to her companion, and offered her my chair. She looked at me in surprise, a smiling light flickered in her eyes, and she curved her lips into a cajoling smile. But then she simply thanked me briefly and took the chair without sitting down. She merely leant her voluptuous arm, which was bare to the elbow, lightly on the back of the chair, employing this slight bending movement to show off her figure more visibly.

My vexation over my psychological failure was long forgotten; now I was intrigued by the game I was playing with this woman. I retreated slightly, moving to the side of the stand, where I could look at her freely but unobtrusively, leaning on my cane and trying to meet her eyes. She noticed, turned slightly towards my observation post, but in such a way that the movement seemed to be made quite by chance, did not avoid my glance and now and then answered it, but non-committally. Her eyes kept moving, touching on everything, never resting anywhere—was it I alone whose gaze she met with a dark smile, or did she give that smile to everyone? There was no telling, and that very uncertainty piqued me. At the moments when her own gaze fell on me like a flashing light it seemed full of promise, although she responded indiscriminately and with the same steely gleam of her pupils to every other glance that came her way, out of sheer flirtatious pleasure in the game, but without letting her apparent interest in her companion's conversation lapse for an instant. There was something dazzlingly audacious about that passionate display, which was either virtuoso dalliance or an outburst of overflowing sensuality. Involuntarily, I came a step closer: her cold audacity had transferred itself to me. I no longer gazed into her eyes but looked her up and down like a connoisseur, undressed her in my mind and felt her naked. She followed my glance without appearing insulted in any way, smiled at the loquacious officer with the corners of her mouth, but I noticed that her knowing smile was acknowledging my intentions. And now, when I looked at her small, delicate foot just peeping out from under the hem of her white dress, she checked it and smoothed her skirt down with a casual air. Next moment, as if by chance, she raised the same foot and placed it on the first rung of the chair I had offered her, so that through the open-work fabric of her dress I could see her stockings up to the knee. At the same time, the smile she gave her companion seemed to take on a touch of irony or malice. She was obviously playing with me as impersonally as I with her, and I was obliged, with some animosity, to admire the subtle technique of her bold conduct, for while she was offering me the sensuousness of her body in pretended secrecy, she appeared to be flattered by and immersing herself in her companion's whispered remarks at the same time, giving and taking in the game she was playing with both of us. In fact I felt vexed, for in other women I disliked this kind of cold, viciously calculating sensuality, feeling that it was incestuously related to the absence of feeling of which I was conscious in myself. Yet I was aroused, perhaps more in dislike than in desire. I boldly came closer and made a brutal assault on her with my eyes. My gestures clearly said, "I want you, you beautiful animal", and I must involuntarily have moved my lips, for she smiled with faint contempt, turning her head away from me, and draped her skirt over the foot she had just revealed. Next moment, however, those flashing black eyes were wandering here and there again. It was quite obvious that she was as cold as I myself and was a match for me, that we were both playing coolly with a strange arousal that itself was only a pretence of ardour, though it was a pretty sight and amusing to play with on a dull day.

Suddenly the intent look left her face, her sparkling eyes clouded over, and a small line of annoyance appeared around her still smiling mouth. I followed the direction of her gaze; a small, stout gentleman, his garments rumpled, was steering a rapid course towards her, his face and brow, which he was nervously drying with his handkerchief, damp with agitation. His hat, which he had perched askew on his head in his hurry, revealed a large bald patch on one side (I could not help thinking that when he took the hat off there were sure to be large beads of sweat gathering on it, and I found him repulsive). His ringed hand held a whole bundle of betting slips. He was puffing and blowing excitedly, and paying no attention to his wife, addressed the officer at once in loud Hungarian. I immediately recognised him as an aficionado of the turf, some horse-dealer of the better kind for whom the sport was the only form of ecstasy he knew, a surrogate for sublimity. His wife must obviously have admonished him in some way (she was evidently irked, and disturbed in her elemental confidence by his presence), for he straightened his hat, apparently at her behest, then laughed jovially and clapped her on the shoulder with good-natured affection. She angrily raised her eyebrows, repelled by this marital familiarity, which embarrassed her in the officer's presence and perhaps even more in mine. He seemed to be apologising, said a few more words in Hungarian to the officer, who replied with an agreeable smile, and then took her arm, tenderly and a little deferentially. I felt that she was ashamed of his intimacy in front of us, and with mingled feelings of derision and disgust I relished her humiliation. But she was soon in control of herself again, and as she pressed softly against his arm she gave me an ironic sideways glance, as if to say, "There, you see, he has me and you don't." I felt both anger and distaste. I really wanted to turn my back on her and walk away, showing her that I was no longer interested in the wife of such a vulgar, fat fellow. But the attraction was too strong. I stayed.

At that moment the shrill starting signal was heard, and all of a sudden it was as if the whole chattering, dull, sluggish crowd had been shaken into life. Once again, and from all directions, it surged forwards to the barrier in wild turmoil. It cost me some effort not to be carried along with it, for I wanted to stay near her in all this confusion; there might be an opportunity for a meaningful glance, for a touch, a chance for me to take some spontaneous liberty, though just what I didn't yet know, so I doggedly made my way towards her through the hurrying people. At that very moment the stout husband was forging his own path through the crowd, obviously to get a good place in the stand, and so it was that the pair of us, each impelled by a different passion, collided with each other so violently that his hat flew to the ground, and the betting slips loosely tucked into the hatband were scattered wide, drifting like red, blue, yellow and white butterflies. He stared at me for a moment. I was about to offer an automatic apology, but some kind of perverse ill will sealed my lips, and instead I looked coolly at him with a slight but bold, offensive touch of provocation. As red-hot anger rose in him but then timidly gave way, his glance flickered uncertainly for a moment and then cravenly sank before mine. With unforgettable, almost touching anxiety he looked me in the eye for just a second, then turned away, suddenly seemed to remember his betting slips, and bent to pick them and his hat up from the ground. His wife, who had let go of his arm, flashed me a glance of unconcealed fury, her face flushed with agitation, and I saw with a kind of erotic pleasure that she would have liked to strike me. But I stood there very cool and nonchalant, watched the fat husband, smiling and offering no help as he bent, puffing and panting, and crawled around at my feet picking up his betting slips. When he bent over his collar stood away from him like the ruffled feathers of a chicken, a broad roll of fat was visible at the nape of his red neck and he gasped asthmatically at every movement he made. Seeing him panting like that, I involuntarily entertained an improper and distasteful idea: I imagined him alone with his wife engaged in conjugal relations, and this thought put me in such high spirits that I smiled in her face at the sight of the anger she could barely rein in. There she stood, impatient and pale again now, scarcely able to control herself—at last I had wrested a real, genuine feeling from her: hatred, unbridled rage! I would have liked to prolong this distressing scene to infinity; I watched with cold relish as he struggled to gather his betting slips together one by one. Some kind of devil of amusement was in my throat, chuckling continuously and trying to burst into laughter; I would have liked to laugh heartily at that soft, scrabbling mass of flesh, or to tickle him up a little with my cane. I really couldn't remember ever before being so possessed by an evil demon as I was in that delightful moment of triumph at his bold wife's humiliation. Now the unfortunate man finally seemed to have picked up all his slips except one, a blue betting slip which had fallen a little further away and was lying on the ground just in front of me. He turned, puffing and panting, looked round with his short-sighted eyes—his pince-nez had slipped to the end of his damp, sweating nose—and my sense of mischief used that second to prolong his ridiculous search. Obeying the boyish high spirits that had seized on me without my own volition, I quickly moved my foot forwards and placed the sole of my shoe on the slip, so that for all his efforts he couldn't find it as long as it pleased me to let him go on looking. And he did go on looking for it, on and on, now and then counting the coloured slips of card again and again, panting as he did so; it was obvious that he knew one of them—mine!—was still missing, and he was about to start searching again in the middle of the noisy crowd when his wife, deliberately avoiding my scornful gaze and with a grim expression on her face, could no longer restrain her angry impatience. "Lajos!" she suddenly and imperiously called, and he started like a horse hearing the sound of the trumpet, cast one last searching glance at the ground—I felt as if the slip hidden under the sole of my shoe were tickling me, and could hardly conceal an urge to laugh—and then turned obediently to his wife, who led him away from me with a certain ostentatious haste and into the tumultuous crowd, where excitement was rising higher and higher.

I stayed behind, feeling no wish to follow the two of them. The episode was over as far as I was concerned, the sense of erotic tension had resolved into mirth, doing me good. I was no longer aroused, nothing was left but a sense of sound satisfaction after following my sudden mischievous impulse, a jaunty, almost boisterous complacency at the thought of the trick I had played. Ahead of me the crowd was thronging close together, waves of excitement were beginning to rise, surging up to the barrier in a single black, murky mass, but I did not watch, it bored me now. I thought of walking over to the Krieau or going home. But as soon as I instinctively raised my foot to step forwards I noticed the blue betting slip lying forgotten on the ground. I picked it up and held it idly between my fingers, not sure what to do with the thing. I vaguely thought of returning it to 'Lajos', which might serve as an excellent excuse to be introduced to his wife, but I realised that she no longer interested me, that the fleeting ardour this adventure had made me feel had long since cooled into my old apathy. I wanted no more of Lajos's wife than that single combative, challenging exchange of glances—I found the fat man too unappetising to wish to share anything physical with him. I had experienced a tingling of the nerves, but now felt only mild curiosity and a pleasant sense of relaxation.

There was the chair, abandoned and alone. I made myself comfortable on it and lit a cigarette. Ahead of me the breakers of excitement were rising again, but I did not even listen; repetition held no charms for me. I watched the pale smoke rising and thought of the Merano golf course promenade where I had sat two months ago, looking down at the spray of the waterfall. It was just like this: at Merano too you heard a strongly swelling roar that was neither hot nor cold, meaningless sound rising in the silent blue landscape. But now impassioned enthusiasm for the race had reached its climax again; once more parasols, hats, handkerchiefs and loud cries were flying like sea-spray above the black breakers of the throng, once again the voices were swirling together, once again a shout—but of a different kind—issued from the crowd's gigantic mouth. I heard a name called out a thousand, ten thousand times, exultantly, piercing, ecstatically, frantically. "*Cressy! Cressy! Cressy!*" And once again the sound was suddenly cut short, as if it were a taut string breaking (ah, how repetition makes even passion monotonous!). The music began to play, the crowd dispersed. Boards were raised aloft showing the numbers of the winning horses. I looked at them, without conscious intent. The first number was a distinct *SEVEN*. Automatically, I glanced at the blue slip I was still holding and had forgotten. It said *SEVEN* too. I couldn't help laughing. The slip had won; friend Lajos had placed a lucky bet. So my mischief had actually tricked the fat husband out of money: all of a sudden my exuberant mood had returned, and I felt interested to know how much my jealous intervention had cost him. I looked at the piece of blue card more closely for the first time: it was a twenty-crown bet, and Lajos had put it on the horse to win. That could amount to a considerable sum. Without thinking more about it, merely obeying my itch of curiosity, I let myself be carried along with the hurrying crowd to the tote windows. I was pushed into some kind of queue, put down the betting slip, and next moment two busy, bony hands—I couldn't see the face that went with them behind the window—were counting out nine twenty-crown notes on the marble slab in front of me.

At that moment, when the money, real money in blue banknotes was paid out to me, the laughter died in my throat. I immediately felt an unpleasant sensation. Involuntarily, I withdrew my hands so as not to touch the money which was not mine. I would have liked to leave the blue notes lying on the marble slab, but people were pushing forwards behind me, impatient to cash their winnings. So there was nothing I could do but, feeling very awkward, take the notes with reluctant fingers: the banknotes burned like blue fire, and I unconsciously held my spread fingers well away from me, as if the hand that had taken them was not my own any more than the money was. I immediately saw all the difficulty of the situation. Without my own volition, the joke had turned to something that a decent man, a gentleman, an officer in the reserve ought not to have done, and I hesitated to call it by its true name even to myself. For this was not money that had been withheld; it had been obtained by cunning. It was stolen money.

Voices hummed and buzzed around me, people came thronging up on their way to and from the tote windows. I still stood there motionless, my spread hand held away from me. What was I to do? I thought first of the most natural solution: to find the real winner, apologise, and give him back the money. But that wouldn't do, least of all in front of that officer. After all, I was a lieutenant in the reserve, and such a confession would have cost me my commission at once, for even if I had found the betting slip by chance, cashing it in was a dishonest act. I also thought of obeying the instinct of my twitching fingers, crumpling up the notes and throwing them away, although that would also be too easily visible in the middle of such a crowd of people, and would look suspicious. However, I didn't want to keep the money that was not mine on me for a moment, let alone put it in my wallet and give it to someone later: the sense of cleanliness instilled into me from childhood, like the habit of wearing clean underclothes, was revolted by any contact, however fleeting, with those banknotes. I must get rid of the money, I thought feverishly, I must get rid of it somewhere, anywhere! I instinctively looked around me, at a loss, wondering if I could see a hiding place anywhere, a chance of concealing it unobserved; I noticed that people were beginning to flock to the tote windows again, but this time with banknotes in their hands. The idea was my salvation. I would throw the money back to the malicious chance that had given it to me, back into the all-consuming maw that was now greedily swallowing up new bets in notes and silver—yes, that was the thing to do, that was the way to free myself of it.

I impetuously hurried, indeed ran as I pushed my way in among the crowd. But by the time I realised that I didn't know the name of any horse on which to bet there were only two men in front of me, and the first was already at the tote window. I listened avidly to the conversation around me. "Are you backing Ravachol?" one man asked. "Yes, of course, Ravachol," his companion replied. "Don't you think Teddy has a chance?" "Teddy? Not a hope. He failed miserably in his maiden race. All show, no substance."

I drank in these words. So Teddy was a bad horse. Teddy was sure to lose. I immediately decided to bet on him. I pushed the money over, put it on Teddy, the horse I had only just heard of, to win, and a hand gave me the betting slips. All of a sudden I now had nine pieces of card in my fingers instead of just the one, this time red and white. I still felt awkward, but at least the slips didn't burn in so fiery, so humiliating a way as the crumpled banknotes.

I felt light at heart again, almost carefree: the money was gone now, the unpleasant part of the adventure was over, it had begun as a joke and now it was all a joke again. I leant back at ease in my chair, lit a cigarette and blew the smoke into the air at my leisure. But I did not stay there long; I rose, walked around, sat down again. How odd: my sense of pleasant reverie was gone. Some kind of nervousness was tingling in my limbs. At first I thought it was discomfort at the idea that I might meet Lajos and his wife in the crowd of people walking by, but how could they guess that these new betting slips were really theirs? Nor did the restlessness of the crowd disturb me; on the contrary, I watched closely to see when they would begin pressing forwards again, indeed I caught myself getting to my feet again and again to look for the flag that would be hoisted at the beginning of the race. So that was it—impatience, a leaping inward fever of expectation as I wished the race would begin soon and the tiresome affair be over for good.

A boy ran past with a racing paper. I stopped him, bought the programme of today's meeting, and began searching the text and the tips, written in a strange and incomprehensible jargon, until I finally found Teddy, the names of his jockey and the owner of the racing stables, and the information that his colours were red and white. But why was I so interested? Annoyed, I crumpled up the newspaper and tossed it away, stood up, sat down again. I suddenly felt hot, I had to pass my handkerchief over my damp brow, my collar felt tight. And still the race did not begin.

At last the bell rang, people came surging up, and at that moment I felt, to my horror, that the ringing of that bell, like an alarm clock, had woken me from some kind of sleep. I jumped up from the chair so abruptly that it fell over, and eagerly hurried—no, ran forwards into the crowd, betting slips held firmly between my fingers, as if consumed by a frantic fear of arriving too late, of missing something very important. I reached the barrier at the front of the stand by forcibly pushing people aside, and ruthlessly seized a chair on which a lady was about to sit down. Her glance of astonishment showed me just how wild and discourteous my conduct was—she was a lady I knew well, Countess R, and I saw her brows raised in anger—but out of shame and defiance I coldly ignored her and climbed up on the chair to get a good view of the field.

Somewhere in the distance, at the start, several horses were standing close together on the turf, kept in line with difficulty by small jockeys who looked like brightly clad versions of Punchinello. I immediately looked for my horse's colours among them, but my eyes were unpractised, and everything was swimming before them in such a hot, strange blur that I couldn't make out the red-and-white figure among all the other splashes of colour. At that moment the bell rang for the second time, and the horses shot off down the green racetrack like six coloured arrows flying from a bow. It would surely have been a fine sight to watch calmly, purely from an aesthetic point of view, as the slender animals stretched their legs in the gallop, hardly touching the ground as they skimmed the turf, but I felt none of that, I was making desperate attempts to pick out my horse, my jockey, and cursing myself for not bringing a pair of field glasses with me. Lean forwards and crane my neck as I might, I saw nothing but four or five insects tangled together in a blurred, flying knot; however, at last I saw its shape begin to change as the small group reached the bend and strung out into a wedge shape, leaders came to the front while some of the other horses were already falling away at the back. It was a close race: three or four horses galloping full speed stuck together like coloured strips of paper, now one and now another getting its nose ahead. I instinctively stretched and tensed my whole body as if my imitative, springy and impassioned movement could increase their speed and carry them along.

The excitement was rising around me. Some of the more knowledgeable racegoers must have recognised the colours as the horses came round the bend, for names were now flying up like bright rockets from the murky tumult below. A man with his hands raised in a frenzy was standing beside me, and as one horse got its head forwards he stamped his feet and yelled in an ear-splitting tone of triumph, "Ravachol! Ravachol!" I saw that the jockey riding this horse did indeed wear blue, and I felt furious that my horse wasn't winning. I found the piercing cries of "Ravachol! Ravachol!" from the idiot beside me more and more intolerable, I felt cold fury, I would have liked to slam my fist into the wide, black hole of his shouting mouth. I quivered with rage, I was in a fever, and felt I might do something senseless at any moment. But here came another horse, sticking close behind the first. Perhaps it was Teddy, perhaps, perhaps—and that hope spurred my enthusiasm again. I really did think it was a red arm now rising above the saddle and bringing something down on the horse's crupper—it could be red, it must be, it must, it must! But why wasn't the fool of a jockey urging him on? The whip again! Go on, again! Now, now he was quite close to the first horse. Hardly anything between them now. Why should Ravachol win? Ravachol! No, not Ravachol! Not Ravachol! Teddy! Teddy! Come on, Teddy! Teddy!

Suddenly and violently, I caught myself up. What on earth was all this? Who was shouting like that? Who was yelling "Teddy! Teddy!" I was shouting the name! And in the midst of my impassioned outburst I felt afraid of myself. I wanted to stop, control myself, in the middle of my fever I felt a sudden shame. But I couldn't tear my eyes away, for the two horses were sticking very close to each other, and it must really be Teddy hanging on to Ravachol, the wretched horse Ravachol that I fervently hated, for others were now shouting louder around me, many voices in a piercing descant: "Teddy, Teddy!" The yells plunged me back into the frenzy from which I had emerged for one sober second. He should, he must win, and now, now a head did push forwards past the flying horse ridden by the other jockey, just by the span of a hand, and then another, and now—now you could see the neck—and then the shrill bell rang, and there was a great cry of jubilation, despair and fury. For a second the name I longed to hear filled the whole vault of the blue sky above. Then it died away, and somewhere music started playing.

Hot, drenched in sweat, my heart thudding, I got off the chair. I had to sit down for a moment, so confused had my excited enthusiasm left me. Ecstasy such as I had never known before flooded through me, a mindless joy at seeing chance bow to my challenge with such slavish obedience; I tried in vain to pretend to myself it was against my will that the horse had won, I had really wanted to lose the money. But I didn't believe it myself, and I already felt a terrible ache in my limbs urging me, as if magically, to be off somewhere, and I knew where: I wanted to see my triumph, feel it, hold it, money, a great deal of money, I wanted to feel the crisp blue notes in my fingers and sense that tingling of my nerves. A strange and pernicious lust had come over me, and no sense of shame now stood in its way. As soon as I stood up I was hurrying, running to the tote window, I pushed brusquely in among the people waiting in the queue, using my elbows, I impatiently pushed others aside just to see the money, the money itself. "Oaf!" muttered someone whom I had jostled behind me; I heard him, but I had no intention of picking a quarrel. I was shaking with a strange, pathological impatience. At last my turn came, my hands greedily seized a blue bundle of banknotes. I counted them, both trembling and delighted. I had won six hundred and forty crowns.

I clutched them avidly. My first thought was to go on betting, to win more, much more. What had I done with my racing paper? Oh yes, I'd thrown it away in all the excitement. I looked round to see where I could buy another. Then, to my inexpressible dismay, I saw that the people around me were suddenly dispersing, making for the exit, the tote windows were closing, the fluttering flag came down. The meeting was over. That had been the last race. I stood there frozen for a moment. Then anger flared in me as if I had suffered some injustice. I couldn't reconcile myself to the fact that it was all over, not now that all my nerves were tense and quivering, the blood was coursing through my veins, hot as I hadn't felt it for years. But it was no use feeding hope artificially with the deceptive idea that I might have been mistaken, that was just wishful thinking, for the motley crowd was flowing away faster and faster, and the well-trodden turf already showed green among the few people still left. I gradually felt it ridiculous to be lingering here in a state of tension, so I took my hat—I had obviously left my cane at the tote turnstile in my excitement—and went towards the exit. A servant with cap obsequiously raised hurried to meet me, I told him the number of my cab, he shouted it across the open space through his cupped hands, and soon the horses came trotting smartly up. I told the cabby to drive slowly down the main avenue. For now that the excitement was beginning to fade, leaving a pleasurable sensation behind, I felt an almost prurient desire to go over the whole scene again in my thoughts.

At that moment another carriage drove past; I instinctively looked at it, only to look away again very deliberately. It was the woman and her stout husband. They had not noticed me, but I felt a horrible choking sensation, as if I had been caught in the guilty act. I could almost have told the cabby to urge the horses on, just to get away from them quickly.

The cab moved smoothly along on its rubber tyres among all the other carriages, swaying along with their brightly clad cargoes of women like boats full of flowers passing the green banks of the chestnut-lined avenue. The air was mild and sweet, the first cool evening breeze was already wafting faint perfume through the dust. But my pleasant mood of reverie refused to return; the meeting with the man I had swindled had struck me a painful blow. In my overheated and impassioned state it suddenly went through me like a draught of cold air blowing through a crack. I now thought through the whole scene again soberly, and could not understand myself: for no good reason I, a gentleman, a member of fashionable society, an officer in the reserve, highly esteemed in general, had taken money which I did not need, had put it in my wallet, had even done so with a greedy and lustful pleasure that rendered any excuse invalid. An hour ago I had been a man of upright and blameless character; now I had stolen. I was a thief. And as if to frighten myself I spoke my condemnation half-aloud under my breath as the cab gently trotted on, the words unconsciously falling into the rhythm of the horses' hooves: "Thief! Thief! Thief! Thief!"

But strange to say—oh, how am I to describe what happened now? It is so inexplicable, so very odd, and yet I know that I am not deceiving myself in retrospect. I am aware of every second's feelings in those moments, every oscillation of my mind, with a supernatural clarity, more clearly than almost any other experience in my thirty-six years, yet I hardly dare reveal that absurd chain of events, those baffling mood swings, and I really don't know whether any writer or psychologist could describe them logically at all. I can only set them down in order, faithfully reflecting the way they unexpectedly flared up within me. Well, so I was saying to myself, "Thief, thief, thief." Then came a very strange moment, as it were an empty one, a moment when nothing happened, when I was only—oh, how difficult it is to express this!—when I was only listening, listening to my inner voice. I had summoned myself before the court, I had accused myself, and now it was for the plaintiff to answer the judge. So I listened—and nothing happened. The whiplash of that word 'thief', which I had expected to terrify me and then fill me with inexpressible shame and remorse, had no effect. I waited patiently for several minutes, I then bent, as it were, yet closer to myself—for I could feel something moving beneath that defiant silence—and listened with feverish expectation for the echo that did not come, for the cry of disgust, horror, and despair that must follow my self-accusation. And still nothing happened. There was no answer. I said the word "Thief" to myself again, I said it out loud, "Thief", to rouse my numbed conscience at last, hard of hearing as it was. Again there was no answer. And suddenly—in a bright lightning flash of awareness, as if a match had suddenly been struck and held above the twilit depths—I realised that I only wanted to feel shame, I was not really ashamed, that down in those depths I was in some mysterious way proud of my foolish action, even pleased with it.

How was that possible? I resisted this unexpected revelation, for now I really did feel afraid of myself, but it broke over me with too strong and impetuous a force. No, it was not shame seething in my blood with such warmth, not indignation or self-disgust—it was joy, intoxicated joy blazing up in me, sparkling with bright, darting, exuberant flames, for I felt that in those moments I had been truly alive for the first time in many years, that my feelings had only been numb and were not yet dead, that somewhere under the arid surface of my indifference the hot springs of passion still mysteriously flowed, and now, touched by the magic wand of chance, had leapt high, reaching my heart. In me too, in me too, part as I was of the living, breathing universe, there still glowed the mysterious volcanic core of all earthly things, a volcano that sometimes erupts in whirling spasms of desire. I too lived, I was alive, I was a human being with hot, pernicious lusts. The storm of passion had flung wide a door, depths had opened up in me, and I was staring down at the unknown in myself with vertiginous joy. It frightened and at the same time delighted me. And slowly—as the carriage wheeled my dreaming body easily along through the world of bourgeois society—I climbed down, step by step, into the depths of my own humanity, inexpressibly alone in my silent progress, with nothing above me but the bright torch of my suddenly rekindled awareness. And as a thousand people surged around me, laughing and talking, I sought for my lost self in myself, I felt for past years in the magical process of contemplation. Things entirely lost suddenly emerged from the dusty, blank mirrors of my life. I remembered once, as a schoolboy, stealing a penknife from a classmate and then watching, with just the same demonic glee, as he looked for it everywhere, asking everyone if they had seen it, going to great pains to find it; I suddenly understood the mysteriously stormy nature of many sexual encounters, I realised that my passions had been only atrophied, only crushed by social delusions, by the lordly ideal of the perfect gentleman—but that in me too, although deep, deep down in clogged pipes and wellsprings, the hot streams of life flowed as they flowed in everyone else. I had always lived without daring to live to the full, I had restrained myself and hidden from myself, but now a concentrated force had broken out, I was overwhelmed by rich and inexpressibly powerful life. And now I knew that I still valued it; I knew it with the blissful emotion of a woman who feels her child move within her for the first time. I felt—how else can I put it?—real, true, genuine life burgeon within me, I felt—and I am almost ashamed to write this—I felt myself, desiccated as I was, suddenly flowering again, I felt red blood coursing restlessly through my veins, feelings gently unfolded in the warmth, and I matured into an unknown fruit which might be sweet or bitter. The miracle of Tannhäuser had come to me in the bright light of a racecourse, among the buzz of thousands of people enjoying their leisure; I had begun to feel again, the dry staff was putting out green leaves and buds.

A gentleman waved to me from a passing carriage and called my name—obviously I had failed to notice his first greeting. I gave an abrupt start, angry to be disturbed in the sweet flow of the stream pouring forth within me, in the deepest dream I had ever known. But a glance at the man hailing me brought me out of myself; it was my friend Alfons, a dear schoolmate of mine and now a public prosecutor. Suddenly a thought ran through me: now, for the first time, this man who greets you like a brother has power over you; you will be his quarry as soon as he is aware of your crime. If he knew about you and what you have done, he would be bound to snatch you out of this carriage, take you away from your whole comfortable bourgeois life, and thrust you down for three to five years into a dismal world behind barred windows, amidst the dregs of human life, other thieves driven to their dirty cells only by the lash of destitution. But it was only for a moment that cold fear grasped the wrist of my trembling hand, only for a moment did it halt my heartbeat—then this idea too turned to warmth of feeling, to a fantastic, audacious pride that now scrutinised everyone else around me with confidence, almost with contempt. How your sweet, friendly smiles, I thought, how the smiles with which you all greet me as one of yourselves would freeze on your lips if you guessed what I really am! You would wipe away my own greeting with a scornful, angry hand, as if it were a splash of excrement. But before you reject me I have already rejected you; this afternoon I broke out of your chilly, skeletal world, where I was a cogwheel performing its silent function in the great machine that coldly drives its pistons, circling vainly around itself—I have fallen to depths that

I do not know, but I was more alive in that one hour than in all the frozen years I spent among you. I am not one of you any more, no, I am outside you somewhere, on some height or in some depth, but never to tread the flat plain of your bourgeois comfort again. For the first time I have felt all mankind's desire for good and evil, but you will never know where I have been, you will never recognise me: what do any of you know about my secret?

How could I express what I felt in that moment as I, an elegantly clad gentleman, drove past the rows of carriages greeting acquaintances and returning greetings, my face impassive? For while my larva, the outward man of the past, still saw and recognised faces, so delirious a music was playing inside me that I had to control myself to keep from shouting something of that raging tumult aloud. I was so full of emotion that its inner swell hurt me physically, like a man choking I had to press my hand hard to the place on my chest beneath which my heart was painfully seething. But pain, desire, alarm, horror or regret—I felt none of these separately and apart from the others, they were all merged and I felt only that I was alive, that I was breathing and feeling. And this simplest, most primeval of feelings, one I had not known for years, intoxicated me. I have never felt myself as ecstatically alive for even a second of my thirty-six years as I did in the airy lightness of that hour.

With a slight jolt, the cab stopped: the driver had reined in his horses, turned on the box and asked if he should drive me home. I came back to myself, feeling dizzy, looked at the avenue, and was dismayed to see how long I had been dreaming, how far my delirium had spread out over the hours. It was growing dark, a soft wind stirred the tops of the trees, the chestnut blossom was beginning to waft its evening perfume through the cool air. And behind the treetops a veiled glimpse of the moon already shone silver. It was enough, it must be enough. But I would not go home yet, not back to my usual world! I paid the cabby. As I took out my wallet and counted the banknotes, holding them in my fingers, something like a slight electric shock ran from my wrist to my fingertips. So there must be something of my old self left in me, the man who was ashamed. The dying conscience of a gentleman was still twitching, but my hand dipped cheerfully into the stolen money again, and in my joy I was generous with a tip. The driver thanked me so fervently that I had to smile, thinking: if only you knew! The horses began to move, the cab rolled away. I watched it go as you might look back from shipboard at a shore where you have been happy.

For a moment I stood dreamy and undecided in the midst of the murmuring, laughing crowd, with music drifting above it. It was about seven o'clock, and I instinctively turned towards the Sachergarten, where I usually ate with companions after going to the Prater. The cabby had probably set me down here on purpose. But no sooner did I touch the handle of the door in the fence of that superior garden restaurant than I felt a scruple: no, I still did not want to go back to my own world yet, I didn't want to let the wonderful fermentation so mysteriously filling me disperse in the flow of casual conversation, I didn't want to detach myself from the sparkling magic of the adventure in which I had been involved for hours.

The confused music echoed faintly somewhere, and I instinctively went that way, for everything tempted me today. I felt it delightful to give myself up entirely to chance, and there was something extraordinarily intriguing in being aimlessly adrift in this gently moving crowd of people. My blood was seething in this thick, swirling, hot and human mass: I was suddenly on the alert, all my senses stimulated and intensified by that acrid, smoky aroma of human breath, dust, sweat and tobacco. All that even yesterday used to repel me because it seemed vulgar, common, plebeian, all that the elegant gentleman in me had haughtily avoided for a lifetime now magically attracted my new responses as if, for the first time, I felt some relationship in myself with what was animal, instinctive, common. Here among the dregs of the city, mixing with soldiers, servant girls, ruffians, I felt at ease in a way I could not understand at all; I almost greedily drank in the acridity of the air, I found the pushing and shoving of the crowd gathered around me pleasant, and with delighted curiosity I waited to see where this hour would take me, devoid as I was of any will of my own. The cymbals crashed and the brass band blared closer now, the mechanical orchestrions thumped out staccato polkas and boisterous waltzes with insistent monotony, and now and then I heard dull thuds from the sideshows, ripples of laughter, drunken shouting. Now I saw the carousels of my childhood going round and round among the trees, with lights crazily flashing. I stood in the middle of the square, letting all the tumult break over me, filling my eyes and ears: these cascades of sound, the infernal confusion of it all did me good, for there was something in this hurly-burly that stilled my own inner torrent of feeling. I watched the servant girls, skirts flying, getting themselves pushed up in the air on the swings with loud cries of glee that might have issued from their sexual orifices, I saw butchers' boys laughing as they brought heavy hammers down on the try-your-strength machine, barkers with hoarse voices and ape-like gestures cried their wares above the noise of the orchestrions, and all this whirling activity mingled with the thousand sounds and constant movement of the crowd, which was inebriated, as if it had imbibed cheap spirits, on the music of the brass band, the flickering of the light, and their own warm pleasure in company. Now that I myself had been awakened, I suddenly felt other people's lives, I felt the heated arousal of the city as, hot and pent-up, it poured out with its millions in the few leisure hours of a Sunday, as its own fullness spurred it on to sultry, animal, yet somehow healthy and instinctive enjoyment. And gradually, feeling people rub against me, feeling the constant touch of their hot bodies passionately pressing close, I sensed their warm arousal passing into me too: my nerves, stimulated by the sharp aroma, tensed and reached out of me, my senses played deliriously with the roar of the crowd and felt that vague stupor that inevitably mingles with all strong sensual gratification. For the first time in years, perhaps for the first time in my life, I felt the crowd, I felt human beings as a force from which lust passed into my own once separate being; some dam had been burst, and what was in my veins passed out into this world, flowed rhythmically back, and I felt a new desire, to break down that last barrier between me and them, a passionate longing to copulate with this hot, strange press of humanity. With male lust I longed to plunge into the gushing vulva of that hot, giant body; with female lust I was open to every touch, every cry, every allurement, every embrace—and now I knew that love was in me, and a need for love such as I had not felt since my twilight boyhood days. Oh, to plunge in, into the living entity, to be linked somehow to the convulsive, laughing, breathing passion of others, to stream on, to pour my fluids into their veins; to become a small and nameless part of the hurly-burly, something infused into the dirt of the world, a creature quivering with lust, sparkling in the slough with those myriads of beings—oh, to plunge into that fullness, down into the circling ripples, shot like an arrow from the bow of my own tension into the unknown, into some heaven of collective experience.

I know now that I was drunk at the time. Everything was roaring in my blood at once, the ringing bells on the carousel, the high lusty laughter of the women as the men swung them up in the air, the chaotic music, the whirling skirts. Every single sound fell sharply into me and then flickered up again, red and quivering, past my temples, I felt every touch, every glance with fantastically stimulated nerves (it was rather like sea-sickness), yet it came all together in a delirious whole. I cannot possibly explain my complex state in words, it can perhaps best be done by means of a comparison if I say I was brimming over with sound, noise, feeling, overheated like a machine operating with all its wheels racing to escape the monstrous pressure that must surely burst the boiler of my chest any moment. My fingertips twitched, my temples thudded, my heated blood pressed in my throat, surged in my temples—from a state of half-hearted apathy lasting many years I had suddenly plunged into a fever that consumed me. I felt that I must open up, come out of myself with a word, with a glance, unburden myself, flow out of myself, give my inner self away, bring myself down to the common level, be resolved—save myself somehow from the hard barrier of silence dividing me from the warm, flowing, living element. I had not spoken for hours, had pressed no one's hand, felt no one's glance rest on me, questioning and sympathetic, and now, under the pressure of events, this excitement was building up against the dam of silence. Never, never had I so strongly felt a need for communication, for another human being than now, when I was in the middle of a surging throng of thousands and tens of thousands, warmth and words washing around me, yet cut off from the circulating blood of that abundance. I was like a man dying of thirst out at sea. And at the same time, this torment increasing with every glance, I saw strangers meeting at every moment to right and left, touching lightly, coming together and parting in play like little balls of quicksilver. Envy came over me when I saw young men addressing strange girls as they passed by, taking their arms after the first word, seeing people find each other and join forces: a word exchanged beside the carousel, a glance as they brushed past each other was enough, and strangeness melted away in conversation, which might be broken off again after a few minutes, but still it was a link, a union, communication, and all my nerves burned for it now. But practised as I was in social intercourse, a popular purveyor of small talk and confident in all the social forms, I was now afraid, ashamed to address one of these broad-hipped servant girls for fear that she might laugh at me. Indeed, I cast my eyes down when someone looked at me by chance, yet inside I was dying of desire for a word. What I wanted from these people was not clear even to myself, but I could no longer endure to be alone and consumed by my fever. However, they all looked past me, every glance moved away from me, no one wanted to be with me. Once a lad of about twelve in ragged clothes did come near me, his eyes bright in the reflected lights as he stared longingly at the wooden horses going up and down. His narrow mouth was open as if with thirst; he obviously had no money left for a ride, and was simply enjoying the screams and laughter of others. I made my way up to him and asked—though why did my voice tremble and break, ending on a high note?—I asked: "Wouldn't you like a ride?" He looked up, took fright—why? why?—turned bright red and ran away without a word. Not even a barefoot child would let me give him pleasure; I felt there must be something terribly strange about me that meant I could never mingle with anyone, but was separate from the dense mass, floating like a drop of oil on moving water.

However, I did not give in; I could no longer be alone. My feet were burning in my dusty patent leather shoes, my throat was sore from the turbulent air. I looked round me: small islands of green stood to right and left among the flowing human crowds, taverns with red tablecloths and bare wooden benches where ordinary citizens sat with their glasses of beer and Sunday cigarettes. The sight was enticing: strangers could sit together here and fall into conversation, there was a little peace here among the wild frenzy. I went into one such tavern, looked round the tables until I found one where a family was sitting: a stout, sturdy artisan with his wife, two cheerful daughters and a little boy. They were nodding their heads together, joking with each other, and their happy, carefree glances did me good. I greeted them civilly, moved to a chair and asked if I might sit down. Their laughter stopped at once, for a moment they were silent as if each was waiting for another to give consent, and then the woman, in tones almost of dismay, said, "Oh yes, certainly, do." I sat down and then felt that in doing so I had spoilt their carefree mood, for an uncomfortable silence immediately fell around the table. Without daring to take my eyes off the red check tablecloth where salt and pepper had been untidily spilt, I felt that they were all watching me uneasily, and at once—but too late!—it struck me that I was too elegant for this servants' tavern in my race-going suit, my top hat from Paris and the pearl pin in my dove-grey tie, that my elegance, the aura of luxury about me at once enveloped me in an invisible layer of hostility and confusion. The silence of these five people made me sink my head lower and lower to look at the table, grimly, desperately counting the red squares on the cloth again and again, kept where I was by the shame of suddenly standing up again, yet too cowardly to raise my tormented glance. It was a relief when the waiter finally came and put the heavy beer glass down in front of me. Then I could at last move a hand and glance timidly over the rim of the glass as I drank: sure enough, all five were watching me, not as if they disliked me but in silent embarrassment. They recognised an intruder into the musty atmosphere of their world, with the naive instinct of their class they felt that I wanted something here, was looking for something that did not belong in my own environment, that I was brought here not by love or liking, not by the simple pleasure of a waltz, a beer, a wish to sit quietly in a tavern on a Sunday, but by some kind of desire which they did not understand and which they distrusted, just as the boy by the carousel had distrusted my offer, just as the thousands of others out there in the throng avoided my elegance and sophistication with unconscious hostility. Yet I felt that if I could find something careless, easy, heartfelt, truly human to say, the father or mother would respond to me, the daughters would smile back, flattered, I could go to a shooting range with the boy and play childish games with him. Within five, ten minutes I would be released from myself, immersed in the carefree atmosphere of simple conversation, of readily granted, even gratified familiarity—but I could not think of that simple remark, that first step in the conversation. A false, foolish, but overpowering shame stuck in my throat, and I sat with my eyes downcast like a criminal at the table with these simple folk, immersed in the torment of feeling that my grim presence had spoilt the last hour of their Sunday. And as I doggedly sat there, I did penance for all the years of haughty indifference when I had passed thousands and thousands of such tables and millions and millions of my fellow men without a glance, thinking only of ingratiating myself or succeeding in the narrow circles of elegant society, and I felt that the direct way to reach these people and talk to them easily, now that I was cast out and wanted contact in my hour of need, was barred to me on the inside.

So I sat, once a free man, now painfully inward-looking, still counting the red squares on the tablecloth until at last the waiter came by. I called him over, paid, left my almost untouched glass of beer and said a civil good evening. They thanked me in tones of friendly surprise; I knew, without turning round, that as soon as my back was turned they would resume their lively cheerfulness, and the warm circle of their conversation would close in as soon as I, the foreign body, had been thrust out of it.

Once again, but now more greedily, fervently and desperately, I threw myself back into the human whirlpool. The crowd had thinned out under the black trees that merged with the sky, there was not so dense and restless a torrent of people in the circle of light around the carousel, only shadowy forms scurrying around on the outskirts of the square. And the deep roar of the crowd, a noise like breathing in desire, was separating into many little sounds, always ringing out when the music somewhere grew strong and frenzied, as if to snatch back the people who were leaving. Faces of another kind emerged now: the children with their balloons and paper confetti had gone home, and so had families on a leisurely Sunday outing. Now there were loud-mouthed drunks about; shabby characters with a sauntering yet purposeful gait came out of side alleys. During the hour when I had sat transfixed at the strangers' table, this curious world had descended to a lower plane. But in itself this phosphorescent atmosphere of audacity and danger somehow pleased me more than the earlier Sunday respectability. The instinct that had been aroused in me scented a similarly intent desire; I felt myself somehow reflected in the sauntering of these dubious figures, these social outcasts who were also roaming here with restless expectation in search of an adventure, of sudden excitement, and I envied even these ragged fellows the way they roamed so freely and openly, for I was standing beside the wooden post of a carousel and breathing with difficulty, impatient to thrust the pressure of silence and the pain of my isolation away from me and yet incapable of a movement, of a cry, of a word. I just stood there staring at the square that was illuminated by the flickering reflection of the circling lights, looking out from my island of light into the darkness, glancing with foolish hope at any human being who, attracted by the bright light, turned my way for a moment. But all eyes moved coldly away from me. No one wanted me, no one would release me.

I know it would be mad to try to describe or actually explain to anyone how I, a cultured and elegant man, a figure in high society, rich, independent, acquainted with the most distinguished figures of a city with a population of millions, spent a whole hour that night standing by the post of a tunelessly squeaking, constantly rocking carousel in the Prater, hearing the same thumping polka, the same slowly dragging waltz circle past me with the same silly horses' heads of painted wood, twenty, forty, a hundred times, never moving from the spot out of dogged defiance, a magical feeling that I could force fate to do my will. I know I was acting senselessly, but there was a tension of feeling in that senseless persistence, a steely spasm of all the muscles such as people usually feel, perhaps, only at the moment of a fatal fall and just before death. My whole life, a life that had passed so emptily, had suddenly come flooding back and was building up in me like pent-up water behind a dam. And tormented as I was by my pointless delusion, my intention of staying, holding out there until some word or glance from a human being released me, yet I relished it too. In standing at the stake like that I did penance not so much for the theft as for the dull, lethargic vacuity of my earlier life, and I had sworn to myself not to leave until I received a sign that fate had let me go free.

And the more that hour progressed, the more night came on. Lights went out in one after another of the sideshows, and then there was always a kind of rising tide of darkness, swallowing up the light patch of that particular booth on the grass. The bright island where I stood was more and more isolated, and I looked at the time, trembling. Another quarter of an hour and then the dappled wooden horses would stand still, the red and green lights on their foolish foreheads would be switched off, the bloated orchestrion would stop thumping out its music. Then I would be wholly in the dark, all alone here in the faintly rustling night, entirely outcast, entirely desolate. I looked with increasing uneasiness at the now dimly lit square, where a couple on their way home now hurried past or a few drunken fellows staggered about only very occasionally: but over in the shadows hidden life quivered, restless and enticing. Sometimes there was a quiet whistle or a snap of the fingers when a couple of men passed by. And if the men, lured by the sound, moved into the darkness you would hear women's voices whispering in the shadows, and sometimes the wind blew scraps of shrill laughter my way. Gradually that hidden life emerged more boldly from the dark outskirts, coming closer to the circle of light in the illuminated square, only to plunge back into the shadows again as soon as the spiked helmet of a passing policeman shone in the reflected street light. But no sooner had he continued on his beat than the ghostly shadows returned, and now I could see their outlines clearly, so close did they venture to the light. They were the last dregs of that nocturnal world, the mud left behind now that the flowing torrent of humanity had subsided: a couple of whores, the poorest and most despised who have no bedstead of their own, sleep on a mattress by day and by night walk the streets restlessly, giving their worn, abused, thin bodies to any man here in the dark for a small silver coin, with the police after them, driven by hunger or by some ruffian, always roaming the darkness, hunters and hunted alike. They gradually emerged like hungry dogs, sniffing about near the lit square for something male, for a forgotten denizen of the night whose lust they could slake for a crown or so to buy a Glühwein in a café and keep the flickering candle-end of life going; it would soon enough be extinguished in a hospice or a prison. These girls were the refuse, the last liquid muck left after the sensuous tide of the Sunday crowd had ebbed away—it was with boundless horror that I now saw those hungry figures flitting out of the dark. But my horror was also mingled with a magical desire, for even in this dirtiest of mirrors I recognised something forgotten and now dimly felt again: here was the swamp-like world of the depths through which I had passed many years ago, and it now rose in my mind again with a phosphorescent glow. How strange was what this fantastic night offered me, suddenly revealing matters closed to me before, so that the darkest of my past, the most secret of my urges now lay open to me! Dim feelings revived from my forgotten boyhood years, when my timid glance was curiously attracted to such figures, yet felt afraid of them, a memory of the first time I followed one of them up a damp and creaking staircase to her bed—and suddenly, as if lightning had riven the night sky, I sharply saw every detail of that forgotten hour, the bad print of an oil painting over the bed, the good-luck charm she wore round her neck, I felt every fibre of that moment, the uncertain heat of it, the disgust, my first boyish pride. All that surged through my body at once. I was suddenly flooded with immeasurable clarity of vision, and—how can I say it, this infinite thing?—I suddenly understood all that bound me to these people with such burning pity, for the very reason that they were the last dregs of life, and my instinct, once aroused by my crime, felt for this hungry sauntering, so like my own on this fantastic night, felt for that criminal availability to any touch, any strange, chance-come desire. I was magnetically drawn to them, the wallet full of stolen money suddenly burned hot on my breast as at last I sensed beings over there, human beings, soft, breathing, speaking, wanting something from others, perhaps from me, only waiting as I was to offer myself up, burning in my fervent desire for human contact. And suddenly I understood what drives men to such creatures, I saw that it is seldom just the heat in the blood, a growing itch, but is usually simply the fear of loneliness, of the terrible strangeness that otherwise rises between us, as my inflamed emotions felt for the first time today. I remembered when I had last dimly felt something like this: it was in England, in Manchester, one of those steely cities that roar under a lightless sky with a noise like an underground railway, and yet at the same time are frozen with a loneliness that seeps through the pores and into the blood. I had been staying there with relatives for three weeks, but spent all my evenings wandering around bars and clubs, visiting the glittering music hall again and again just to feel some human warmth. And then, one evening, I had found such a woman, whose gutter English I could scarcely understand, but suddenly I was in a room, drinking in laughter from a strange mouth, there was a warm body there, something of this earth, close and soft. Suddenly the cold, black city melted away, the dark and raucous lonely space: a being you did not know, who just stood there waiting for all comers, could release you, thaw the frost; you could breathe freely again, feel life, all light and bright in the middle of the steely dungeon. How wonderful for those who are lonely, shut up in themselves, to know or guess that there is something to support them in their fear, something to cling to, though it may be dirty from much handling, stiff with age, eaten away by corrosion. And this, this of all things I had forgotten in that hour of ultimate loneliness from which, staggering, I rose that night. I had forgotten that somewhere, in one final corner, there are always these creatures waiting to accept any devotion, let any desolation rest in their breath, cool any heat for a small coin, which is never enough for the great gift they give with their eternal readiness, the gift of their human presence.

Beside me the orchestrion of the carousel started droning away again. This was the last ride, the last fanfare of the circling light going round in the darkness before Sunday passed into the workaday week. But no one was riding now, the horses went round empty in their crazy circle, the tired woman at the cash desk was raking together the day's takings and counting them, the errand boy was ready with a hook to bring the shutters rattling down over the booth after this last ride. Only I stood there alone, still leaning against the post, and looked out at the empty square where nothing but those figures moved, fluttering like bats, seeking something just as I was seeking, waiting as I was waiting, yet with an impassably strange space between us. Now, however, one of them must have noticed me, for she slowly made her way forwards, and I looked closely at her from under my lowered eyelids: a small, crippled, rickety creature without a hat, wearing a tasteless and showy cheap dress with worn dancing shoes peeping out from under it, the whole outfit probably bought bit by bit from a street stall or junk shop at third-hand, crumpled by the rain or some indecent adventure in the grass. She came over with an ingratiating look and stopped beside me, casting out a sharp glance like a fishing line and showing her bad teeth in an inviting smile. My breath stopped short. I could not move, could not look at her, and yet I could not tear myself away: as if I were under hypnosis, I felt that a human being was walking around me hopefully, that someone was wooing me, that with a word, with a gesture I could finally rid myself of my terrible loneliness, my painful sense of being an outcast. But I could not move, I was wooden as the post against which I was leaning, and in a kind of lascivious powerlessness I felt only—as the melody of the carousel wearily wound down—this close presence, the will to attract me, and I closed my eyes for a moment, to feel to the full this magnetic attraction of something human coming out of the darkness of the world and flowing over me.

The carousel stopped, the waltz tune was cut short with a last groaning sound. I opened my eyes just in time to see the figure beside me turn away. Obviously she felt it tedious to wait beside a man standing here like a block of wood. I was horrified. I suddenly felt very cold. Why had I let her go, the only human being who had approached me this fantastic night, who was receptive to me? Behind me the lights were going out; the shutters rolled down with a rattle and a clatter. It was over.

And suddenly—oh, how can I describe to myself that warm sense like spindrift suddenly spraying up?—suddenly—and it was as abrupt, as hot, as red as if a vein had burst in my breast—suddenly something broke out of me, a proud, haughty man fully armoured with cool social dignity, something like a silent prayer, a spasm, a cry: it was my childish yet overpowering wish for this dirty, rickety little whore to turn her head again so that I could speak to her. For I was not too proud to follow her—my pride was all crushed, trodden underfoot, swept away by very new feelings—no, I was too weak, too much at a loss. So I stood there, trembling and in turmoil, alone at the martyr's stake of darkness, waiting as I had never waited since my boyhood years, as I had waited only once before, standing by a window in the evening as a strange woman slowly began undressing, and I kept lingering and hesitating as she unwittingly stripped herself naked—I stood crying out to God with a voice I did not recognise as my own for a miracle, for this crippled thing, this last scum of humanity, to try me once more, to turn her eyes to me again.

And yes—she did turn. Once more, quite automatically, she looked back. But so strong must my convulsive start have been, so strong the leaping of intense feeling into my eyes, that she stopped and observed me. She half-turned again, looked at me through the darkness, smiled and nodded her head invitingly over to the shadowy side of the square. And at last I felt the terrible spell of rigidity in me give way. I could move again. I nodded my consent.

The invisible pact was made. Now she went ahead over the dimly lit square, turning from time to time to see if I was following. And I did follow: the leaden feeling had left my legs, I could move my feet again. I was magnetically impelled forwards, I did not consciously walk but flowed along behind her, so to speak, drawn by a mysterious power. In the dark of the alley between the booths of sideshows she slowed her pace. Now I was beside her.

She looked at me for a few seconds, scrutinising me distrustfully; something made her uncertain. Obviously my curiously timid lingering there, the contrast between the place and my elegance, seemed to her somehow suspicious. She looked round several times, hesitated. Then, pointing down the street that was black as a mine shaft: "Let's go there. It's dark behind the circus."

I could not answer. The dreadful vulgarity of this encounter numbed me. I would have liked to tear myself away somehow, bought myself off with a coin, an excuse, but my will had no more power over me. I felt as if I were on a toboggan run flinging myself round a bend, racing at high speed down a steep incline of snow, when the fear of death somehow mingles pleasantly with the intoxication of speed, and instead of braking you give yourself up to the sense of falling without your own volition, with delirious yet conscious weakness. I could not go back now, and perhaps I didn't want to. She pressed herself intimately against me, and I instinctively took her arm. It was a very thin arm, the arm not of a woman but of an underdeveloped, scrofulous child, and no sooner did I feel it through her lightweight coat than I was overcome, in the midst of my intense access of feeling, by gentle, overwhelming pity for this wretched, downtrodden scrap of life washed up against me by the night. And instinctively my fingers caressed the weak, feeble joints of her hand more respectfully and purely than I had ever touched a woman before.

We crossed a dimly lit road and entered a little grove where huge treetops held the sombre, evil-smelling darkness in their embrace. At that moment, and although you could hardly make out an outline any more, I noticed that she turned very carefully on my arm, and did the same thing again a few steps later. And strangely enough, while I was, as it were, numbed and rigid as I slipped into this indecent adventure, my senses were perfectly bright and alert. With clear vision that nothing escaped, that took conscious note of every movement, I realised that something was following quietly behind us on the borders of the path we had crossed, and I thought I heard a dragging step. And suddenly—as when a crackling, white flash of lightning leaps across a landscape—I guessed, I knew it all: I was to be lured into a trap, this whore's pimps were lurking behind us, and in the dark she was taking me to the appointed place where I was to be their victim. I saw it all, with the supernatural clarity that one is said to have only in the concentrated seconds between life and death, and I considered every possibility. There was still time to get away, the main road must be close, for I could hear the electric tram rattling along its rails, a shout or a whistle could summon aid. All the possibilities of flight and rescue leapt up in my mind, in sharply outlined images.

But how strange—this alarming realisation did not cool me but only further inflamed me. Today, awake in the clear light of an autumn day, I cannot explain the absurdity of my actions to myself: I knew, I knew at once with every fibre of my being that I was going into danger unnecessarily, but the anticipation of danger ran through my nerves like a fine madness. I knew there was something terrible and perhaps deadly ahead, I trembled with disgust at the idea of being forced into a criminal, mean and dirty incident somewhere here, but even death itself aroused a dark curiosity in me in my present state of life-induced intoxication, an intoxication I had never known or guessed at before, but now it was streaming over me, numbing me. Something—was it that I was ashamed to show fear, or was it weakness?—something drove me on. I felt intrigued to climb down to this last sewer of life, to squander my whole past, gamble it away. A reckless lust of the spirit mingled with the low vulgarity of this adventure. And although all my nerves scented danger, and I understood it clearly with my senses and my reason, I still went on into the grove arm-in-arm with this dirty little Prater tart who physically repelled rather than attracted me, and who I knew was bringing me this way just for her accomplices. Yet I could not go back. The gravitational pull of criminality, having taken hold of me that afternoon during my adventure on the racecourse, was dragging me further and further down. And now I felt only the daze, the eddying frenzy of my fall into new depths, perhaps into the last depths of all, into death.

After a few steps I stopped. Once again her glance flew uncertainly around. Then she looked expectantly at me.

"Well—what are you going to give me?"

Oh yes. I'd forgotten that. But the question did not sober me, far from it. I was so glad to give her something, to make her a present, to be able to waste my substance. I hastily reached into my pocket and tipped all the silver in it and a few crumpled banknotes into her outstretched hand. And now something so wonderful happened that even today my blood warms when I think of it: either this poor creature was surprised by the size of the sum—she must have been used to getting only small change for her indecent services—or there was something new and unusual to her in the way I gave it readily, quickly, almost with delight, for she stepped back, and through the dense and evil-smelling darkness I felt her gaze seeking me in great astonishment. And at last I felt what I had not found all evening: someone was interested in me, was seeking me, for the first time I was alive to someone else in the world. The fact that it should be this outcast, this creature who carried her poor abused body round in the darkness, offering it for sale, and who had thrust herself on me without even looking at the buyer, who now turned her eyes to mine, the fact that she was wondering about the human being in me only heightened my strange sense of intoxication, clear-sighted and dizzy as I was at one and the same time, both fully conscious and dissolving into a magical apathy. And already the stranger was pressing closer to me, but not in the businesslike way of a woman doing a duty that had been paid for. Instead, I thought I felt unconscious gratitude in it, a feminine desire for closeness. I gently took her thin, rickety, childish arm, felt her small, twisted body, and suddenly, looking beyond all that, I saw her whole life: the borrowed, smeared bedstead in a suburban yard where she slept from morning to noon among a crowd of other people's children; her pimp throttling her; belching drunks falling on her in the dark; the special hospital ward; the lecture hall where her abused body was put on show, sick and naked, as a teaching aid to cheerful young medical students; and the end somewhere in a poorhouse to which she would be carted off in a batch of women and left to die like an animal. Infinite pity for her, for all of them came over me, a warmth that was tenderness without sensuality. Again and again

I patted her small, thin arm. And then I bent down and kissed the astounded girl.

At that moment there was a rustle behind me. A twig cracked. I jumped back. And a coarse, vulgar male voice was laughing. "There we are. I thought so."

Even before I saw them I knew who they were. Not for one second, dazed and confused as I was, had I forgotten that I was surrounded, and indeed this was what my mysteriously lively curiosity had been waiting for. A figure now emerged from the bushes, and a second behind it: a couple of rough fellows boldly taking up their positions. The coarse laugh came again. "Turning a trick here, eh? A fine gentleman, of course! Well, we'll see to him now." I stood perfectly still, the blood beating in my temples. I felt no fear. I was simply waiting for what came next. Now I was in the very depths at last, in the final abyss of ignominy. Now the blow must come, the shattering end towards which I had half-intentionally been moving.

The girl had moved quickly away from me, but not to join them. She was in a way standing between us; it seemed that she did not entirely like the ambush prepared for me. The men, for their part, were vexed because I did not move. They looked at each other, obviously expecting some protest from me, a plea, some display of fear. "Oh, so he's not talking!" said one of them at last, threateningly. The other approached me and said in commanding tones, "You'll have to come down to the police station with us."

I still did not answer. One of the men put his hand on my shoulder and gave me a slight push. "Move," he said.

I began to move. I did not defend myself, for I did not want to: the extraordinary, degraded, dangerous nature of the situation left me dazed. But my brain remained perfectly clear: I knew that these fellows must fear the police more than I did, that I could buy myself off for a few crowns—but I wanted to relish the depths of horror to the full, I was enjoying the dreadful humiliation of the situation, in a kind of waking swoon. Without haste, entirely automatically, I went the way they had pushed me.

But the very fact that I moved towards the light so obediently and without a word seemed to confuse the men. They whispered softly, and then began to talk to each other again in deliberately raised voices. "Let him go," said one (a pockmarked little fellow), but the other replied, with apparent decision: "No, that won't do. If poor starving devils like us do such things they put us behind bars. But a fine gentleman like this—he really deserves punishment." I heard every word, and in their voices I detected their clumsily expressed request for me to begin negotiating with them; the criminal in me understood the criminal in them, understood that they wanted to torment me with fears, while I was tormenting them with my docility. It was a silent battle between us, and—oh, how rich in experience this night was!—and in the midst of deadly danger, here in this insalubrious grove on the Prater, in the company of a couple of ruffians and a whore, I felt the frenzied enchantment of gambling for the second time in twelve hours, but this time for the highest of stakes, for my whole comfortable existence, even my life. And with all the force of my quivering nerves, tensed as they were to breaking point, I abandoned myself to this great game, to the sparkling magic of chance.

"Hey, there goes the cop," said a voice behind me. "Our fine gentleman won't like this, he'll be behind bars a week or more." It was meant to sound like a grim threat, but I heard the man's hesitant uncertainty. I went placidly towards the dim light, where I did indeed see light glint on a police officer's spiked helmet. Twenty more paces and I would have reached him. Behind me, the men had fallen silent. I realised they were slowing down. Next moment, I knew, they must retreat like cowards into the dark, into their own world, embittered by the failure of their trick, perhaps to vent their anger on the poor woman. The game was over: again, for the second time today, I had won, I had cheated other strangers of their malicious designs. Pale lantern light was already flickering ahead, and when I turned I looked for the first time into the two ruffians' faces: bitterness and a craven shame looked out of their uncertain eyes. They still stood there, but downcast and disappointed, ready to slink back into the dark. For their power was gone: it was *me* they feared now.

At that moment I was suddenly overcome—and it was like fermentation within me, bursting the staves in the barrel of my breast to pour out hot feeling into my blood—I was suddenly overcome by an infinite, fraternal sympathy for these two men. What had they wanted from me, these poor hungry, ragged fellows, what had they wanted from me, a satiated parasite, but a few miserable crowns? They could have strangled me there in the dark, they could have robbed me, killed me, but they had not; they had only tried to frighten me in a clumsy, amateurish way for the sake of the loose silver in my pocket. How could I, who had become a thief on a whim, out of a sense of audacity, who had turned criminal for the pleasure of my nerves, how could I dare to torment these poor devils further? And my infinite sympathy was mingled with infinite shame at having toyed with their fear and impatience for my own amusement. I pulled myself together: now that I was safe and the light of the nearby street protected me, I must go along with them and banish the disappointment from those bitter, hungry eyes.

With a sudden movement I stepped up to one of them. "Why would you want to report me to the police?" I said, taking care to inject a touch of stress and fear into my voice. "What good will it do you? Perhaps I'll be locked up, perhaps not. But it won't do you any good. Why do you want to make my life a misery?"

They both stared at me in embarrassment. They must have expected anything: cries, threats to make them cringe like growling dogs, not this subservience. At last one of them said, not threateningly at all, but as it were apologetically: "Justice have got to be done! We're only doing our duty, right?"

This comment was obviously prepared for such cases, yet it rang false. Neither of the pair dared look at me. They were waiting. And I knew what they were waiting for. They were waiting for me to beg for mercy and offer them money.

I still remember everything about those seconds. I recollect every nerve that stirred in me, every thought that shot through my mind. And I know what I maliciously wanted at first: I wanted to make them wait, torment them a little longer, relish the pleasure of keeping them on tenterhooks. But soon I forced myself to beg, because I knew it was time for me to relieve these two of their anxiety. I began putting on a show of being terrified, I begged for mercy, asked them to keep all this quiet and not make me wretched. I saw these poor amateur blackmailers begin to feel awkward, and the silence between us was milder now.

And then at last, at last I said what they had been longing to hear all this time. "I'll… I'll give you… I'll give you a hundred crowns."

All three started and looked at each other. They had not expected so much, not now that all was really lost for them. At last one of them, the pockmarked man with the shifty eyes, pulled himself together. He started to speak twice, but couldn't get it out. Then he said—and I felt that he was ashamed as he spoke—"Two hundred crowns."

"Oh, shut it!" the girl suddenly intervened. "You be glad he gives you anything. He ain't done nothing, he didn't hardly touch me. This is too much."

She was shouting at them in genuinely embittered tones. And my heart sang. Someone was sorry for me, someone was speaking up for me, kindness was born of something low and mean, blackmail gave rise to some dim desire for justice. How good it felt, how it responded to the swelling tide of my feelings! No, I must not play with these people or torment them in their fear and shame any longer—enough, enough!

"Very well, two hundred crowns."

All three fell silent. I took out my wallet. Slowly, very openly I held it in my hand. With one move they could have snatched it from me and fled into the dark. But they looked shyly away. There was some kind of secret pact between them and me, not a conflict and a gamble any more but a condition of trust and justice, a human relationship. I took the two notes from the bundle of stolen money and handed them to one of the men.

"Thank you," he said automatically, and turned away. He himself obviously felt how ridiculous it was to thank me for money obtained by blackmail. He was ashamed, and his shame—for I could feel everything that night, I could read the meaning of every gesture—his shame distressed me. I did not want a human being to feel ashamed in front of me, one of his own kind, a thief like him, weak, cowardly, lacking in willpower. I felt pain for his humiliation, and wanted to lift it from him. So I refused his thanks.

"No, it is for me to thank you," I said, surprised at the amount of true feeling in my voice. "If you had reported me to the police I'd have been done for. I'd have had to shoot myself, and you'd have gained nothing by that. It's better this way. I will go right over there, and perhaps you will go the other way. Goodnight."

They stood silent for a moment longer. Then one man said: "Goodnight," and then the other, and last the whore, who had stayed in the dark all this time. The words sounded warm and heartfelt, like true good wishes. I sensed in their voices that somewhere deep in their dark natures they liked me, they would never forget this strange moment. It might perhaps return to their minds again in the penitentiary or the hospice; something of me lived on in them, I had given them something. And the pleasure of giving it filled me as no emotion had ever done before.

I walked alone through the night to the exit from the Prater. All inhibition had left me, I had been like a man missing, presumed dead, but now I felt my nature flowing out into the whole infinite world in a plenitude I had never known before. I sensed everything as if it lived for me alone, and as if in its own turn it linked me with that flow. The black trees stood around me, rustling, and I loved them. Stars shone down from above, and I breathed in their white salutation. I heard singing voices somewhere, and I felt they were singing for me. Now that I had torn away the carapace from my breast everything was suddenly mine, and the joy of lavish abandonment swept me on. Oh, how easy it is, I thought, to give pleasure and rejoice in that pleasure yourself: you have only to open yourself up and the living current will flow from one human being to another, falling from the heights to the depths, rising up again like spindrift from the depths into infinity.

At the exit of the Prater, beside a cab rank, I saw a street trader, tired and bowed over her paltry wares. She had baked goods for sale, covered with dust, and a few fruits; she had probably been sitting there since morning bending over the few coins she had earned, and weariness bent her back. Why not make her happy too, I thought, now that I am happy? I chose a small pastry and put a banknote down in front of her. She began busily looking for change, but I was already walking on and saw only her start of delight, saw the bent back suddenly straighten, while her open mouth, frozen in amazement, sent a thousand good wishes after me. Holding the pastry, I went up to a horse standing wearily in the shafts. It turned and gave me a friendly snort, and its dark eyes showed gratitude when I stroked its pink nostrils and gave it the sweet morsel. And as soon as I had done that I wanted more: to give more pleasure, to feel how a few silver coins, a few notes printed on coloured paper can conquer fear, kill want, kindle merriment. Why were there no beggars here? Why no children who would have liked to have the bunches of balloons on strings which a surly, white-haired cripple was taking home, disappointed by the poor business he had done all this long, hot day. I went up to him. "I'll take the balloons." "Ten hellers each," he said suspiciously, for what would this elegant gentleman of leisure want with his coloured balloons at midnight? "I'll take them all," I said, giving him a ten-crown note. He swayed on his feet, looked at me as if something had dazzled him, and then, trembling, gave me the string that held the whole bunch together. I felt the taut string tug at my finger; the balloons wanted to be gone, to be free, to fly through the air. Go then, fly where you like, be free! I let go of the strings, and up they suddenly rose like so many coloured moons. Laughing people came up from all sides, lovers emerged from the shadows, drivers cracked their whips and called to each other, pointing out the freed balloons drifting over the trees towards the houses and rooftops. The onlookers all glanced cheerfully at each other, enjoying my happy folly.

Why did I never know before how easy and how good it is to give pleasure? All of a sudden the banknotes were burning a hole in my wallet again, twitching in my fingers like the strings of the balloons just now. They wanted to fly away from me into the unknown too. And I took them, those I had stolen from Lajos and my own—for I felt no difference between them now and no guilt—and kept them ready to be given to any who wanted one. I approached a street-sweeper morosely sweeping the deserted Praterstrasse. He thought I wanted to ask him the way, and looked up with a surly expression; I smiled and held out a twenty-crown note. He started, uncomprehending, then finally took it and waited to see what I wanted in return. But I just smiled at him again, said: "Buy something you like," and went on. I kept looking around to see if anyone wanted something from me, and when no one came up I just handed the money out myself: I gave a note to a whore who accosted me, two notes to a lamplighter, I threw one into the open hatch of a basement bakery, and so I went on, leaving behind me a wake of amazement, thanks and pleasure, I walked on and on. Finally I crumpled notes up and scattered them around the empty street and on the steps of a church, liking the idea of the old ladies who would come to morning service, find all those banknotes and thank God, or of a poor student, a girl or a workman on their way out coming upon the money in amazement and delight, just as I had discovered myself in amazement and delight that night.

I couldn't say now where and how I scattered all those banknotes, and finally my silver too. There was some kind of delirium in me, an outpouring like lovemaking, and when the last pieces of paper had fluttered away I felt light, as if I could fly, and I knew a freedom I had never known before. The street, the sky, the buildings, all seemed to flow together and towards me, giving me an entirely new sense of possession and of belonging: never, even in the most warmly experienced moments of my life, had I felt so strongly that all these things were really present, that they were alive, that I was alive, and that their lives and mine were one and the same, that life is a great and mighty phenomenon and can never be hailed with too much delight. It is something that only love grasps, only devotion comprehends.

There was one last dark moment, and that came when, having walked happily home, I put the key in my door and the corridor leading to my rooms opened up black before me. I was suddenly overcome by fear that I would be returning to my old life if I entered the apartment of the man I had been until this moment, if I lay down in his bed and found myself once more connected with everything from which this night had so wonderfully released me. No, I must not be what I had been before, remote from the real world, I must not be the correct, unfeeling gentleman of yesterday and all the days before. I would rather plunge into any depths of crime and horror, but I must have the reality of life! I was tired, inexpressibly tired, yet I feared that sleep might close over me, and then its black silt would sweep away all the hot, glowing, living emotions that this night had aroused in me, and I might find that the whole experience had been as fleeting and without foundation as a fantastic dream.

But I woke cheerfully to a new morning next day, and none of that gratefully flowing emotion had run away into the sand. Four months have passed since then, and my old paralysis of feeling has not returned. I still bloom warmly as I face the day. The magical intoxication of my experience when the ground of my old world suddenly gave way under my feet, plunging me into the unknown, when I felt the delirium of speed mingled with the profundity of all life as I fell into my own abyss—yes, that flowing heat is gone, but since that hour I have been conscious of my own warm blood with every breath I take, and I daily feel new lust for life. I know I am a different man now, with different senses; different things arouse me, and I am more aware than before. I dare not say, of course, that I have become a better man; I know only that I am a happier man because I have found some kind of meaning in an existence that had been so cold, a meaning for which I can find no term but life itself. Since then I hold back from nothing, for I feel the norms and formalities of the society in which I live are meaningless, and I am not ashamed in front of others or myself. Words like honour, crime, vice, have suddenly acquired a cold, metallic note, I cannot speak them without horror. I live by letting myself draw on the power I so magically felt for the first time on that night. I do not ask where it will carry me: perhaps to some new abyss, into what others call vice, or perhaps to somewhere sublime. I don't know and I don't want to know. *For only he who lives his life as a mystery is truly alive.*

But never—and I am sure of this—have I loved life more fervently, and now I know that all who are indifferent to any of the shapes and forms it takes, commit a crime (the only crime there is!). Since I began to understand myself, I have understood much of many other things: someone's avid glance into a shop window can distress me, the playfulness of a dog can delight me. I suddenly care for everything; I am indifferent to nothing now. In the paper (which I used to consult only in search of entertainment and auction sales) I read of a hundred things that excite me every day; books that once bored me suddenly reveal their meaning to me. And the strangest thing of all is that I can suddenly talk to people outside the bounds of polite conversation. My manservant, who has been with me for seven years, interests me and I often talk to him; the caretaker whom I used to pass by, thinking no more of him than if he were a moving pillar, recently told me about his little daughter's death, and it affected me more than the tragedies of Shakespeare. And this change—although I continue to lead my life in circles of polite tedium so as not to give myself away—this change seems to be gradually becoming evident. I find that many people are suddenly on terms of warm good friendship with me; for the third time this week a strange dog ran up to me in the street. And friends tell me with a certain pleasure, as if speaking to one who has recovered from an illness, that I am quite rejuvenated.

Rejuvenated? I alone know that I am only just beginning to live. Well, it is a common delusion to think the past was nothing but error and preparation for the present, and I can well see that it is presumptuous of me to think that taking a cold pen in a warm, living hand and recording my feelings on dry paper means that I am really alive. But if it is a delusion, then it is the first ever to delight me, the first to warm my blood and open my senses to me. And if I write about the miracle of my awakening here, then I do it for myself alone, for I know the truth of this more profoundly than any words can say. I have spoken to no friend about it; my friends never knew how dead to the world I was, and they will never know how I live and flourish now. And should death strike me in the middle of this life of mine, and these lines should fall into another's hands, that idea does not alarm or distress me. For he who has never known the magic of such an hour will not understand, as I myself could not have understood half-a-year ago, that a few fleeting, apparently disconnected incidents on a single evening could so magically rekindle a life already extinguished. I feel no shame before such a man, for he will not understand me. But he who knows how those incidents are linked will not judge or feel pride. And I feel no shame before him, for he *will* understand me. Once a man has found himself there is nothing in this world that he can lose. And once he has understood the humanity in himself, he will understand all human beings.

LETTER FROM AN UNKNOWN WOMAN

WHEN R., *the famous novelist, returned to Vienna early in the morning, after a refreshing three-day excursion into the mountains, and bought a newspaper at the railway station, he was reminded as soon as his eye fell on the date that this was his birthday. His forty-first birthday, as he quickly reflected, an observation that neither pleased nor displeased him. He swiftly leafed through the crisp pages of the paper, and hailed a taxi to take him home to his apartment. His manservant told him that while he was away there had been two visitors as well as several telephone calls, and brought him the accumulated post on a tray. R. looked casually through it, opening a couple of envelopes because the names of their senders interested him; for the moment he set aside one letter, apparently of some length and addressed to him in writing that he did not recognize. Meanwhile the servant had brought him tea; he leant back in an armchair at his ease, skimmed the newspaper again, leafed through several other items of printed matter, then lit himself a cigar, and only now picked up the letter that he had put to one side.*

It consisted of about two dozen sheets, more of a manuscript than a letter and written hastily in an agitated, feminine hand that he did not know. He instinctively checked the envelope again in case he had missed an explanatory enclosure. But the envelope was empty, and like the letter itself bore no address or signature identifying the sender. Strange, he thought, and picked up the letter once more. It began, "To you, who never knew me," which was both a salutation and a challenge. He stopped for a moment in surprise: was this letter really addressed to him or to some imaginary person? Suddenly his curiosity was aroused. And he began to read:

My child died yesterday—for three days and three nights I wrestled with death for that tender little life, I sat for forty hours at his bedside while the influenza racked his poor, hot body with fever. I put cool compresses on his forehead, I held his restless little hands day and night. On the third evening I collapsed. My eyes would not stay open any longer; I was unaware of it when they closed. I slept, sitting on my hard chair, for three or four hours, and in that time death took him. Now the poor sweet boy lies there in his narrow child's bed, just as he died; only his eyes have been closed, his clever, dark eyes, and his hands are folded over his white shirt, while four candles burn at the four corners of his bed. I dare not look, I dare not stir from my chair, for when the candles flicker shadows flit over his face and his closed mouth, and then it seems as if his features were moving, so that I might think he was not dead after all, and will wake up and say something loving and childish to me in his clear voice. But I know that he is dead, I will arm myself against hope and further disappointment, I will not look at him again. I know it is true, I know my child died yesterday—so now all I have in the world is you, you who know nothing about me, you who are now amusing yourself without a care in the world, dallying with things and with people. I have only you, who never knew me, and whom I have always loved.

I have taken the fifth candle over to the table where I am writing to you now. For I cannot be alone with my dead child without weeping my heart out, and to whom am I to speak in this terrible hour if not to you, who were and are everything to me? Perhaps I shall not be able to speak to you entirely clearly, perhaps you will not understand me—my mind is dulled, my temples throb and hammer, my limbs hurt so much. I think I am feverish myself, perhaps I too have the influenza that is spreading fast in this part of town, and I would be glad of it, because then I could go with my child without having to do myself any violence. Sometimes everything turns dark before my eyes; perhaps I shall not even be able to finish writing this letter—but I am summoning up all my strength to speak to you once, just this one time, my beloved who never knew me.

I speak only to you; for the first time I will tell you everything, the whole story of my life, a life that has always been yours although you never knew it. But you shall know my secret only once I am dead, when you no longer have to answer me, when whatever is now sending hot and cold shudders through me really is the end. If I have to live on, I shall tear this letter up and go on preserving my silence as I have always preserved it. However, if you are holding it in your hands, you will know that in these pages a dead woman is telling you the story of her life, a life that was yours from her first to her last waking hour. Do not be afraid of my words; a dead woman wants nothing any more, neither love nor pity nor comfort. I want only one thing from you: I want you to believe everything that my pain tells you here, seeking refuge with you. Believe it all, that is the only thing I ask you: no one lies in the hour of an only child's death.

I will tell you the whole story of my life, and it is a life that truly began only on the day I met you. Before that, there was nothing but murky confusion into which my memory never dipped again, some kind of cellar full of dusty, cobwebbed, sombre objects and people. My heart knows nothing about them now. When you arrived I was thirteen years old, living in the apartment building where you live now, the same building in which you are holding my letter, my last living breath, in your hands. I lived in the same corridor, right opposite the door of your apartment. I am sure you will not remember us any more, an accountant's impoverished widow (my mother always wore mourning) and her thin teenage daughter; we had quietly become imbued, so to speak, with our life of needy respectability. Perhaps you never even heard our name, because we had no nameplate on the front door of our apartment, and no one came to visit us or asked after us. And it is all so long ago, fifteen or sixteen years; no, I am sure you don't remember anything about it, my beloved, but I—oh, I recollect every detail with passion. As if it were today, I remember the very day, no, the very hour when I first heard your voice and set eyes on you for the first time, and how could I not? It was only then that the world began for me. Allow me, beloved, to tell you the whole story from the beginning. I beg you, do not tire of listening to me for a quarter of an hour, when I have never tired of loving you all my life.

Before you moved into our building a family of ugly, mean-minded, quarrelsome people lived behind the door of your apartment. Poor as they were, what they hated most was the poverty next door, ours, because we wanted nothing to do with their down-at-heel, vulgar, uncouth manners. The man was a drunk and beat his wife; we were often woken in the night by the noise of chairs falling over and plates breaking; and once the wife, bruised and bleeding, her hair all tangled, ran out onto the stairs with the drunk shouting abuse after her until the neighbours came out of their own doors and threatened him with the police. My mother avoided any contact with that couple from the first, and forbade me to speak to their children, who seized every opportunity of avenging themselves on me. When they met me in the street they called me dirty names, and once threw such hard snowballs at me that I was left with blood running from my forehead. By some common instinct, the whole building hated that family, and when something suddenly happened to them—I think the husband was jailed for theft—and they had to move out, bag and baggage, we all breathed a sigh of relief. A few days later the "To Let" notice was up at the entrance of the building, and then it was taken down; the caretaker let it be known—and word quickly went around—that a single, quiet gentleman, a writer, had taken the apartment. That was when I first heard your name.

In a few days' time painters and decorators, wallpaper-hangers and cleaners came to remove all trace of the apartment's previous grubby owners; there was much knocking and hammering, scraping and scrubbing, but my mother was glad of it. At last, she said, there would be an end to the sloppy housekeeping in that apartment. I still had not come face to face with you by the time you moved in; all this work was supervised by your manservant, that small, serious, grey-haired gentleman's gentleman, who directed operations in his quiet, objective, superior way. He impressed us all very much, first because a gentleman's gentleman was something entirely new in our suburban apartment building, and then because he was so extremely civil to everyone, but without placing himself on a par with the other servants and engaging them in conversation as one of themselves. From the very first day he addressed my mother with the respect due to a lady, and he was always gravely friendly even to me, little brat that I was. When he mentioned your name he did so with a kind of special esteem—anyone could tell at once that he thought far more of you than a servant usually does of his master. And I liked him so much for that, good old Johann, although I envied him for always being with you to serve you.

I am telling you all this, beloved, all these small and rather ridiculous things, so that you will understand how you could have such power, from the first, over the shy, diffident child I was at the time. Even before you yourself came into my life, there was an aura around you redolent of riches, of something out of the ordinary, of mystery—all of us in that little suburban apartment building were waiting impatiently for you to move in (those who live narrow lives are always curious about any novelty on their doorsteps). And how strongly I, above all, felt that curiosity to see you when I came home from school one afternoon and saw the removals van standing outside the building. The men had already taken in most of the furniture, the heavy pieces, and now they were carrying up a few smaller items; I stayed standing by the doorway so that I could marvel at everything, because all your possessions were so interestingly different from anything I had ever seen before. There were Indian idols, Italian sculptures, large pictures in very bright colours, and then, finally, came the books, so many of them, and more beautiful than I would ever have thought possible. They were stacked up by the front door of the apartment, where the manservant took charge of them, carefully knocking the dust off every single volume with a stick and a feather duster. I prowled curiously around the ever-growing pile, and the manservant did not tell me to go away, but he didn't encourage me either, so I dared not touch one, although I would have loved to feel the soft leather of many of their bindings. I only glanced shyly and surreptitiously at the titles; there were French and English books among them, and many in languages that I didn't know. I think I could have stood there for hours looking at them all, but then my mother called me in.

After that, I couldn't stop thinking of you all evening, and still I didn't know you. I myself owned only a dozen cheap books with shabby board covers, but I loved them more than anything and read them again and again. And now I couldn't help wondering what the man who owned and had read all these wonderful books must be like, a man who knew so many languages, who was so rich and at the same time so learned. There was a kind of supernatural awe in my mind when I thought of all those books. I tried to picture you: you were an old man with glasses and a long white beard, rather like our geography teacher, only much kinder, better-looking and better-tempered—I don't know why I already felt sure you must be good-looking, when I still thought of you as an old man. All those years ago, that was the first night I ever dreamt of you, and still I didn't know you.

You moved in yourself the next day, but for all my spying I hadn't managed to catch a glimpse of you yet—which only heightened my curiosity. At last, on the third day, I did see you, and what a surprise it was to find you so different, so wholly unrelated to my childish image of someone resembling God the Father. I had dreamt of a kindly, bespectacled old man, and now here you were—exactly the same as you are today. You are proof against change, the years slide off you! You wore a casual fawn suit, and ran upstairs in your incomparably light, boyish way, always taking two steps at a time. You were carrying your hat, so I saw, with indescribable amazement, your bright, lively face and youthful head of hair; I was truly amazed to find how young, how handsome, how supple, slender and elegant you were. And isn't it strange? In that first second I clearly felt what I, like everyone else, am surprised to find is a unique trait in your character: somehow you are two men at once: one a hot-blooded young man who takes life easily, delighting in games and adventure, but at the same time, in your art, an implacably serious man, conscious of your duty, extremely well read and highly educated. I unconsciously sensed, again like everyone else, that you lead a double life, one side of it bright and open to the world, the other very dark, known to you alone—my thirteen-year-old self, magically attracted to you at first glance, was aware of that profound duality, the secret of your nature.

Do you understand now, beloved, what a miracle, what an enticing enigma you were bound to seem to me as a child? A man whom I revered because he wrote books, because he was famous in that other great world, and suddenly I found out that he was an elegant, boyishly cheerful young man of twenty-five! Need I tell you that from that day on nothing at home, nothing in my entire impoverished childhood world interested me except for you, that with all the doggedness, all the probing persistence of a thirteen-year-old I thought only of you and your life. I observed you, I observed your habits and the people who visited you, and my curiosity about you was increased rather than satisfied, because the duality of your nature was expressed in the wide variety of those visitors. Young people came, friends of yours with whom you laughed in high spirits, lively students, and then there were ladies who drove up in cars, once the director of the opera house, that great conductor whom I had only ever seen from a reverent distance on his rostrum, then again young girls still at commercial college who scurried shyly in through your door, and women visitors in particular, very, very many women. I thought nothing special of that, not even when, on my way to school one morning, I saw a heavily veiled lady leave your apartment—I was only thirteen, after all, and the passionate curiosity with which I spied on your life and lay in wait for you did not, in the child, identify itself as love.

But I still remember, my beloved, the day and the hour when I lost my heart to you entirely and for ever. I had been for a walk with a school friend, and we two girls were standing at the entrance to the building, talking, when a car drove up, stopped—and you jumped off the running-board with the impatient, agile gait that still fascinates me in you. An instinctive urge came over me to open the door for you, and so I crossed your path and we almost collided. You looked at me with a warm, soft, all-enveloping gaze that was like a caress, smiled at me tenderly—yes, I can put it no other way—and said in a low and almost intimate tone of voice: "Thank you very much, Fräulein."

That was all, beloved, but from that moment on, after sensing that soft, tender look, I was your slave. I learnt later, in fact quite soon, that you look in the same way at every woman you encounter, every shop girl who sells you something, every housemaid who opens the door to you, with an all-embracing expression that surrounds and yet at the same time undresses a woman, the look of the born seducer; and that glance of yours is not a deliberate expression of will and inclination, but you are entirely unconscious that your tenderness to women makes them feel warm and soft when it is turned on them. However, I did not guess that at the age of thirteen, still a child; it was as if I had been immersed in fire. I thought the tenderness was only for me, for me alone, and in that one second the woman latent in my adolescent self awoke, and she was in thrall to you for ever.

"Who was that?" asked my friend. I couldn't answer her at once. It was impossible for me to utter your name; in that one single second it had become sacred to me, it was my secret. "Oh, a gentleman who lives in this building," I stammered awkwardly at last. "Then why did you blush like that when he looked at you?" my friend mocked me, with all the malice of an inquisitive child. And because I felt her touching on my secret with derision, the blood rose to my cheeks more warmly than ever. My embarrassment made me snap at her. "You silly goose!" I said angrily; I could have throttled her. But she just laughed even louder, yet more scornfully, until I felt the tears shoot to my eyes with helpless rage. I left her standing there and ran upstairs.

I loved you from that second on. I know that women have often said those words to you, spoilt as you are. But believe me, no one ever loved you as slavishly, with such dog-like devotion, as the creature I was then and have always remained, for there is nothing on earth like the love of a child that passes unnoticed in the dark because she has no hope: her love is so submissive, so much a servant's love, passionate and lying in wait, in a way that the avid yet unconsciously demanding love of a grown woman can never be. Only lonely children can keep a passion entirely to themselves; others talk about their feelings in company, wear them away in intimacy with friends, they have heard and read a great deal about love, and know that it is a common fate. They play with it as if it were a toy, they show it off like boys smoking their first cigarette. But as for me, I had no one I could take into my confidence, I was not taught or warned by anyone, I was inexperienced and naive; I flung myself into my fate as if into an abyss. Everything growing and emerging in me knew of nothing but you, the dream of you was my familiar friend. My father had died long ago, my mother was a stranger to me in her eternal sad depression, her anxious pensioner's worries; more knowing adolescent schoolgirls repelled me because they played so lightly with what to me was the ultimate passion—so with all the concentrated attention of my impatiently emergent nature I brought to bear, on you, everything that would otherwise have been splintered and dispersed. To me, you were—how can I put it? Any one comparison is too slight—you were everything to me, all that mattered. Nothing existed except in so far as it related to you, you were the only point of reference in my life. You changed it entirely. Before, I had been an indifferent pupil at school, and my work was only average; now I was suddenly top of the class, I read a thousand books until late into the night because I knew that you loved books; to my mother's amazement I suddenly began practising the piano with stubborn persistence because I thought you also loved music. I cleaned and mended my clothes solely to look pleasing and neat in front of you, and I hated the fact that my old school pinafore (a house dress of my mother's cut down to size) had a square patch on the left side of it. I was afraid you might notice the patch and despise me, so I always kept my school bag pressed over it as I ran up the stairs, trembling with fear in case you saw it. How foolish of me: you never, or almost never, looked at me again.

And yet I really did nothing all day but wait for you and look out for you. There was a small brass peephole in our door, and looking through its circular centre I could see your door opposite. This peephole—no, don't smile, beloved, even today I am still not ashamed of those hours!—was my eye on the world. I sat in the cold front room, afraid of my mother's suspicions, on the watch for whole afternoons in those months and years, with a book in my hand, tense as a musical string resounding in response to your presence. I was always looking out for you, always in a state of tension, but you felt it as little as the tension of the spring in the watch that you carry in your pocket, patiently counting and measuring your hours in the dark, accompanying your movements with its inaudible heartbeat, while you let your quick glance fall on it only once in a million ticking seconds. I knew everything about you, knew all your habits, every one of your suits and ties, I knew your various acquaintances and could soon tell them apart, dividing them into those whom I liked and those whom I didn't; from my thirteenth to my sixteenth year I lived every hour for you. Oh, what follies I committed! I kissed the door handle that your hand had touched; I stole a cigarette end that you had dropped before coming into the building, and it was sacred to me because your lips had touched it. In the evenings I would run down to the street a hundred times on some pretext or other to see which of your rooms had a light in it, so that I could feel more aware of your invisible presence. And in the weeks when you went away—my heart always missed a beat in anguish when I saw your good manservant Johann carrying your yellow travelling bag downstairs—in those weeks my life was dead and pointless. I went about feeling morose, bored and cross, and I always had to take care that my mother did not notice the despair in my red-rimmed eyes.

Even as I tell you all these things, I know that they were grotesquely extravagant and childish follies. I ought to have been ashamed of them, but I was not, for my love for you was never purer and more passionate than in those childish excesses. I could tell you for hours, days, how I lived with you at that time, and you hardly even knew me by sight, because if I met you on the stairs and there was no avoiding it, I would run past you with my head bent for fear of your burning gaze—like someone plunging into water—just to escape being scorched by its fire. For hours, days I could tell you about those long-gone years of yours, unrolling the whole calendar of your life, but I do not mean to bore you or torment you. I will tell you only about the best experience of my childhood, and I ask you not to mock me because it is something so slight, for to me as a child it was infinite. It must have been on a Sunday. You had gone away, and your servant was dragging the heavy carpets that he had been beating back through the open front door of the apartment. It was hard work for the good man, and in a suddenly bold moment I went up to him and asked if I could help him. He was surprised, but let me do as I suggested, and so I saw—if only I could tell you with what reverent, indeed devout veneration!—I saw your apartment from the inside, your world, the desk where you used to sit, on which a few flowers stood in a blue crystal vase. Your cupboards, your pictures, your books. It was only a fleeting, stolen glimpse of your life, for the faithful Johann would certainly not have let me look closely, but with that one glimpse I took in the whole atmosphere, and now I had nourishment for never-ending dreams of you both waking and sleeping.

That brief moment was the happiest of my childhood. I wanted to tell you about it so that even though you do not know me you may get some inkling of how my life depended on you. I wanted to tell you about that, and about the terrible moment that was, unfortunately, so close to it. I had—as I have already told you—forgotten everything but you, I took no notice of my mother any more, or indeed of anyone else. I hardly noticed an elderly gentleman, a businessman from Innsbruck who was distantly related to my mother by marriage, coming to visit us often and staying for some time; indeed, I welcomed his visits, because then he sometimes took Mama to the theatre, and I could be on my own, thinking of you, looking out for you, which was my greatest and only bliss. One day my mother called me into her room with a certain ceremony, saying she had something serious to discuss with me. I went pale and suddenly heard my heart thudding; did she suspect something, had she guessed? My first thought was of you, the secret that linked me to the world. But my mother herself was ill at ease; she kissed me affectionately once, and then again (as she never usually did), drew me down on the sofa beside her and began to tell me, hesitantly and bashfully, that her relation, who was a widower, had made her a proposal of marriage, and mainly for my sake she had decided to accept him. The hot blood rose to my heart: I had only one thought in answer to what she said, the thought of you.

"But we'll be staying here, won't we?" I just managed to stammer.

"No, we're moving to Innsbruck. Ferdinand has a lovely villa there."

I heard no more. Everything went black before my eyes. Later, I knew that I had fallen down in a faint; I heard my mother, her voice lowered, quietly telling my prospective stepfather, who had been waiting outside the door, that I had suddenly stepped back with my hands flung out, and then I fell to the floor like a lump of lead. I cannot tell you what happened in the next few days, how I, a powerless child, tried to resist my mother's all-powerful will; as I write, my hand still trembles when I think of it. I could not give my real secret away, so my resistance seemed like mere obstinacy, malice and defiance. No one spoke to me, it was all done behind my back. They used the hours when I was at school to arrange our move; when I came back, something else had always been cleared away or sold. I saw our home coming apart, and my life with it, and one day when I came in for lunch, the removals men had been to pack everything and take it all away. Our packed suitcases stood in the empty rooms, with two camp beds for my mother and me; we were to sleep there one more night, the last, and then travel to Innsbruck the next day.

On that last day I felt, with sudden resolution, that I could not live without being near you. I knew of nothing but you that could save me. I shall never be able to say what I was thinking of, or whether I was capable of thinking clearly at all in those hours of despair, but suddenly—my mother was out—I stood up in my school clothes, just as I was, and walked across the corridor to your apartment. Or rather, I did not so much walk; it was more as if, with my stiff legs and trembling joints, I was magnetically attracted to your door. As I have said before, I had no clear idea what I wanted. Perhaps to fall at your feet and beg you to keep me as a maidservant, a slave, and I am afraid you will smile at this innocent devotion on the part of a fifteen-year-old, but—beloved, you would not smile if you knew how I stood out in that ice-cold corridor, rigid with fear yet impelled by an incomprehensible power, and how I forced my trembling arm away from my body so that it rose and—after a struggle in an eternity of terrible seconds—placed a finger on the bell-push by the door handle and pressed it. To this day I can hear its shrill ringing in my ears, and then the silence afterwards when my blood seemed to stop flowing, and I listened to find out if you were coming.

But you did not come. No one came. You were obviously out that afternoon, and Johann must have gone shopping, so with the dying sound of the bell echoing in my ears I groped my way back to our destroyed, emptied apartment and threw myself down on a plaid rug, as exhausted by the four steps I had taken as if I had been trudging through deep snow for hours. But underneath that exhaustion my determination to see you, to speak to you before they tore me away, was still burning as brightly as ever. There was, I swear it, nothing sensual in my mind; I was still ignorant, for the very reason that I thought of nothing but you. I only wanted to see you, see you once more, cling to you. I waited for you all night, beloved, all that long and terrible night. As soon as my mother had got into bed and fallen asleep I slipped into the front room, to listen for your footsteps when you came home. I waited all night, and it was icy January weather. I was tired, my limbs hurt, and there was no armchair left in the room for me to sit in, so I lay down flat on the cold floor, in the draught that came in under the door. I lay on the painfully cold floor in nothing but my thin dress all night, for I took no blanket with me; I did not want to be warm for fear of falling asleep and failing to hear your step. It hurt; I got cramp in my feet, my arms were shaking; I had to keep standing up, it was so cold in that dreadful darkness. But I waited and waited and waited for you, as if for my fate.

At last—it must have been two or three in the morning—I heard the front door of the building being unlocked down below, and then footsteps coming upstairs. The cold had left me as if dropping away, heat shot through me; I quietly opened the door to rush towards you and fall at your feet… oh, I don't know what I would have done, such a foolish child as I was then. The steps came closer and closer, I saw the flicker of candlelight. Shaking, I clung to the door handle. Was it you coming?

Yes. It was you, beloved—but you were not alone. I heard a soft, provocative laugh, the rustle of a silk dress, and your lowered voice—you were coming home with a woman…

How I managed to survive that night I do not know. Next morning, at eight o'clock, they dragged me off to Innsbruck; I no longer had the strength to resist.

My child died last night—and now I shall be alone again, if I must really go on living. They will come tomorrow, strange, hulking, black-clad men bringing a coffin, and they will put him in it, my poor boy, my only child. Perhaps friends will come as well, bringing flowers, but what do flowers on a coffin mean? They will comfort me, and say this and that—words, words, how can they help me? I know that I must be alone again when they have gone. I felt it then, in those two endless years in Innsbruck, the years from my sixteenth to my eighteenth birthday, when I lived like a prisoner or an outcast in my family. My stepfather, a very placid, taciturn man, was kind to me; my mother seemed ready to grant all my wishes, as if atoning for her unwitting injustice to me; young people tried to make friends with me, but I rejected all their advances with passionate defiance. I didn't want to live happy and content away from you, I entrenched myself in a dark world of self-torment and loneliness. I didn't wear the brightly coloured new clothes they bought me, I refused to go to concerts or the theatre, or on outings in cheerful company. I hardly went out at all: would you believe it, beloved, I didn't come to know more than ten streets of the little town in the two years I lived there? I was in mourning, and I wanted to mourn, I became intoxicated by every privation that I imposed on myself over and beyond the loss of you. And I did not want to be distracted from my passion to live only for you. I stayed at home alone for hours, days, doing nothing but thinking of you again and again, always reviving my hundred little memories of you, every time I met you, every time I waited for you, staging those little incidents in my mind as if in a theatre. And that is why, because I went over every second of the past countless times, I retain such a vivid memory of my whole childhood that I feel every minute of those past years with as much heat and ardour as if they were only yesterday.

My life at the time was lived entirely through you. I bought all your books; when your name was in the newspaper it was a red-letter day. Would you believe that I know every line of your books by heart, I have read them so often? If anyone were to wake me from sleep at night and quote a random line from them, I could still, thirteen years later, go on reciting the text from there, as if in a dream: every word of yours was my Gospel and prayer book. The whole world existed only in relation to you; I read about concerts and premieres in the Viennese newspapers with the sole aim of wondering which of them might interest you, and when evening came I was with you, even though I was so far away: now he is going into the auditorium, now he is sitting down. I dreamt of that a thousand times because I had once seen you at a concert.

But why describe this raving, tragic, hopeless devotion on the part of an abandoned child feeling angry with herself, why describe it to a man who never guessed at it or knew about it? Yet was I really still a child at that time? I reached the age of seventeen, eighteen—young men turned to look at me in the street, but that only embittered me. To love, or even merely play at love with anyone but you was so inexplicable to me, so unimaginably strange an idea, that merely feeling tempted to indulge in it would have seemed to me a crime. My passion for you was the same as ever, except that my body was changing, and now that my senses were awakened it was more glowing, physical, womanly. And what the child with her sombre, untaught will, the child who had pressed your doorbell, could not guess at was now my only thought: to give myself to you, devote myself to you.

The people around me thought me timid, called me shy (I had kept my secret strictly to myself). But I was developing an iron will. All that I thought and did tended in one direction: back to Vienna, back to you. And I imposed my will by force, senseless and extraordinary as it might seem to anyone else. My stepfather was a prosperous man, and regarded me as his own child. But I insisted, with grim obstinacy, that I wanted to earn my own living, and at last I managed to get a position with a relation as an assistant in a large ready-to-wear dress shop.

Need I tell you where I went first when I arrived back in Vienna—at last, at last!—one misty autumn evening? I left my case at the station, boarded a tram—how slowly it seemed to be going, I bitterly resented every stop—and hurried to the apartment building. There was light in your windows; my whole heart sang. Only now did the city, strange to me these days with its pointless roar of traffic, come to life, only now did I come to life again myself, knowing that I was near you, you, my only dream. I did not guess that in reality I was as far from your mind now, when only the thin, bright glass pane stood between you and my radiant gaze, as if valleys, mountains and rivers separated us. I merely looked up and up; there was light there, here was the building, and there were you, the whole world to me. I had dreamt of this hour for two years, and now I was granted it. I stood outside your windows all that long, mild, cloudy evening, until the light in them went out. Only then did I go home to the place where I was staying.

Every evening after that I stood outside your building in the same way. I worked in the shop until six; it was hard, strenuous work, but I liked it, because all the activity there made me feel my own restlessness less painfully. And as soon as the iron shutters rolled down behind me I hurried to my desired destination. My will was set on seeing you just once, meeting you just once, so that my eyes could see your face again, if only from a distance. And after about a week it finally happened: I met you at a moment when I didn't expect it. Just as I was looking up at your windows, you came across the street. Suddenly I was that thirteen-year-old child again, and felt the blood rise to my cheeks. Instinctively, against my innermost urge to feel your eyes on me, I lowered my head and hurried past you, quick as lightning. Afterwards I was ashamed of my timid flight, the reaction of a schoolgirl, for now I knew very clearly what I wanted: I wanted to meet you, I was seeking you out, I wanted you to recognize me after all those years of weary longing, wanted you to take some notice of me, wanted you to love me.

But it was a long time before you really noticed me, although I stood out in your street every evening, even in flurries of snow and the keen, cutting wind of Vienna. I often waited in vain for hours, and often, in the end, you left the building in the company of friends. Twice I saw you with women, and now that I was an adult I sensed what was new and different about my feeling for you from the sudden tug at my heartstrings, wrenching them right apart, when I saw a strange woman walking so confidently arm in arm with you. I was not surprised. After all, I knew about your succession of women visitors from my childhood days, but now it hurt me physically, and I was torn between hostility and desire in the face of your obvious intimacy with someone else. One day, childishly proud as I was and perhaps still am, I stayed away from your building, but what a terrible, empty evening of defiance and rebellion I spent! Next evening, once again, I was standing humbly outside your building waiting, waiting, just as I had spent my whole life standing outside your life, which was closed to me.

And at last one evening you did notice me. I had already seen you coming in the distance, and I steeled my will not to avoid you. As chance would have it, a cart waiting to be unloaded obstructed the street, and you had to pass close to me. Involuntarily your absent-minded gaze fell on me, and as soon as it met the attention of my own eyes—oh, what a shock the memory gave me!—it became that look you give women, the tender, all-enveloping, all-embracing gaze that also strips them, the look that, when I was a child, had made me into a loving woman for the first time. For one or two seconds that gaze held mine, which neither could nor wished to tear itself away—and then you had passed me. My heart was beating fast; instinctively I slowed my pace, and as I turned, out of a curiosity that I could not master, I saw that you too had stopped and were still looking at me. And the way you observed me, with such interest and curiosity, told me at once that you did not recognize me.

You did not recognize me, neither then nor ever, you never recognized me. How can I describe to you, beloved, the disappointment of that moment? That was the first time I suffered it, the disappointment of going unrecognized by you. I have lived with it all my life, I am dying with it, and still you do not recognize me. How can I make you understand my disappointment? During those two years in Innsbruck, when I thought of you every hour and did nothing but imagine our next meeting back in Vienna, I had dreamt of the wildest—or the most blissful—possibilities, depending on my mood at the time. I had dreamt, if I may so put it, of everything;

in dark moments I had pictured you rejecting me, despising me for being too uninteresting, too ugly, too importunate. In passionate visions I had gone through all forms of your disfavour, your coldness, your indifference—but in no moment of dark emotion, not even in full awareness of my inferiority, had I ventured to envisage this, the worst thing of all: the fact that you had never even noticed my existence. Today I understand it—ah, you have taught me to understand it!—I realize that, to a man, a girl's or a woman's face must have something extraordinarily changeable in it, because it is usually only a mirror reflecting now passion, now childishness, now weariness, and passes by as a reflection does; so that a man can easily forget a woman's face because age changes its light and shade, and different clothes give her a new setting. Those who are resigned to their fate really know that. However, still a girl at the time, I could not yet grasp your forgetfulness, because somehow my immoderate, constant concern with you had made me feel—although it was a delusion—that you, too, must often think of me, you would be waiting for me; how could I have gone on breathing in the certainty that I was nothing to you, no memory of me ever touched you, however lightly? And this moment, when your eyes showed me that nothing in you recognized me, no thin gossamer line of memory reached from your life to mine, was my first fall into the depths of reality, my first inkling of my destiny.

You did not recognize me at that time. And when, two days later, we met again, your eyes rested on me with a certain familiarity, you still did not recognize me as the girl who loved you and whom you had woken to life, but only as the pretty eighteen-year-old who had met you in the same place two days earlier. You looked at me in surprise, but in a friendly manner, with a slight smile playing round your mouth. Once again you passed me, once again immediately slowing your pace; I trembled, I rejoiced, I prayed that you would speak to me. I felt that, for the first time, you saw me as a living woman; I myself slowed down and did not avoid you. And suddenly I sensed you behind me; without turning round I knew that now, for the first time, I would hear your beloved voice speaking directly to me. Expectation paralysed me; I feared I would have to stop where I was because my heart was thudding so violently—and then you were beside me. You spoke to me in your easy, cheerful way, as if we had been on friendly terms for a long time—oh, you had no idea about me, you have never had any idea of my life!—so captivatingly free and easy was the way you spoke to me that I was even able to answer you. We walked all down the street side by side. Then you suggested that we might go and have something to eat together. I agreed. What would I ever have dared to deny you?

We ate together in a small restaurant—do you still know where it was? No, I am sure you don't distinguish it now from other such evenings, for who was I to you? One among hundreds, one adventure in an ever-continuing chain. And what was there for you to remember about me? I said little, because it made me so infinitely happy to have you near me, to hear you speaking to me. I did not want to waste a moment of it by asking questions or saying something foolish. I shall never forget my gratitude to you for that hour, or how entirely you responded to my passionate reverence, how tender, light and tactful you were, entirely without making importunate advances, entirely without any hasty, caressing gestures of affection, and from the first moment striking a note of such certain and friendly familiarity that you would have won my heart even if it had not been yours long ago, given with all my goodwill. Ah, you have no idea what a wonderful thing you did in not disappointing my five years of childish expectation!

It was getting late; we left the restaurant. At the door you asked me whether I was in a hurry or still had time to spare. How could I have failed to show that I was ready for you? I said that I could indeed spare some time. Then you asked, quickly surmounting a slight hesitation, whether I would like to go to your apartment and talk. "Oh, most happily," I said, and it came out of the fullness of my feelings so naturally that I noticed at once how you reacted, in either embarrassment or pleasure, to my quick tongue—but you were also visibly surprised. Today I understand why you were astonished; I know it is usual for women, even when they long to give themselves, to deny that readiness, pretending to be alarmed or indignant, so that first they have to be reassured by urgent pleading, lies, vows and promises. I know that perhaps only prostitutes, the professionals of love, or perhaps very naive adolescents, respond to such an invitation with such wholehearted, joyful consent as mine. But in me—and how could you guess that?—it was only my will put into words, the concentrated longing of a thousand days breaking out. In any case, you were struck; I began to interest you. I sensed that, as we were walking along, you glanced sideways at me with a kind of astonishment while we talked. Your feelings, your magically sure sense of all that is human, immediately scented something unusual here, a secret in this pretty, compliant girl. Your curiosity was awakened, and I noticed, from your circling, probing questions, that you wanted to discover the mystery. But I evaded you; it would be better to seem foolish than to let you know my secret.

We went up to your apartment. Forgive me, beloved, when I tell you that you cannot understand what that corridor, that staircase meant to me—what turmoil and confusion there was in my mind, what headlong, painful, almost mortal happiness. Even now I can hardly think of it without tears, and I have none of those left. But imagine that every object in the building was, so to speak, imbued with my passion, each was a symbol of my childhood, my longing: the gate where I had waited for you thousands of times, the stairs from which I always listened for your footsteps, and where I had seen you for the first time, the peephole through which I had stared my soul out, the doormat outside your door where I had once knelt, the click of the key at which I had always leapt up from where I was lying in wait. All my childhood, all my passion were here in those few metres of space; this was my whole life, and now it came over me like a storm, everything, everything was coming true, and I was with you, going into your, into our apartment building. Think of it—it sounds banal, but I can't put it any other way—as if going only as far as your door had been my reality all my life, my sombre everyday world, but beyond it a child's magic realm began, the realm of Aladdin, remember that I had stared a thousand times, with burning eyes, at the door through which I now stepped, almost reeling, and you will guess—but only guess, you can never entirely know, beloved!—what that tumultuous minute meant in my life.

I stayed with you all night. You did not realize that no man had ever touched me before, had ever felt or seen my body. But how could you guess that, beloved, when I offered no resistance, showed no bashful hesitancy, so that you could have no idea of my secret love for you? It would certainly have alarmed you, for you love only what is light and playful, weightless, you are afraid of intervening in someone else's life. You want to give of yourself to everyone, to the world, but you do not want sacrificial victims. If I tell you now, beloved, that I was a virgin when I gave myself to you, I beg you not to misunderstand me! I am not accusing you, you did not entice me, lie to me, seduce me—it was I who pressed myself on you, threw myself on your breast and into my own fate. I will never, never blame you for anything, I will only thank you for the richness of that night, sparkling with desire, hovering in bliss. When I opened my eyes in the dark and felt you at my side, I was surprised not to see the stars above me, I could feel heaven so close—no, I never regretted it, beloved, for the sake of that hour. I never regretted it. I remember that when you were asleep and I heard your breathing, felt your body, while I was so close to you, I shed tears of happiness in the dark.

In the morning I was in a hurry to leave early. I had to go to the shop, and I also wanted to be gone before your manservant arrived; I couldn't have him seeing me. When I was dressed and stood in front of you, you took me in your arms and gave me a long look; was some dark and distant memory stirring in you, or did I merely seem to you beautiful, happy as indeed I was? Then you kissed me on the mouth. I gently drew away, about to go. "Won't you take a few flowers with you?" you asked, and I said yes. You took four white roses out of the blue crystal vase on the desk (which I knew from that one stolen childhood glance) and gave them to me. I was still kissing them days later.

We had arranged to meet again another evening. I went, and again it was wonderful. You gave me a third night. Then you said you had to go away—oh, how I hated those journeys of yours even in my childhood!—and promised to get in touch with me as soon as you were back. I gave you a poste restante address. I didn't want to tell you my name. I kept my secret. And again you gave me a few roses when you said goodbye—goodbye.

Every day for two whole months I went to ask if any post had come… but no, why describe the hellish torment of waiting, why describe my despair to you? I am not blaming you, I love you as the man you are, hot-blooded and forgetful, ardent and inconstant, I love you just as you always were and as you still are. You had come back long ago, I could tell that by the light in your windows, and you did not write to me. I have not had a line from you to this day and these last hours of mine, not a line from you to whom I gave my life. I waited, I waited in despair. But you did not get in touch with me, you never wrote me a line… not a line…

My child died yesterday—he was also yours. He was your child, beloved, conceived on one of those three nights, I swear it, and no one tells lies in the shadow of death. He was our child, and I swear it to you, because no man touched me between those hours when I gave myself to you and the time when he made his way out of my body. I was sacred to myself because of your touch; how could I have shared myself with you, who had been everything to me, and other men who passed by touching my life only slightly? He was our child, beloved, the child of my conscious love and your careless, passing, almost unconscious affection, our child, our son, our only child. You will ask—perhaps alarmed, perhaps only surprised—you will ask, beloved, why I kept the child secret all these long years, and mention him only today, now that he lies here sleeping in the dark, sleeping for ever, ready to leave and never return, never again? But how could I have told you? You would never have believed me, a stranger who showed herself only too willing on those three nights, who gave herself to you without resistance, indeed with desire, you would never have believed the anonymous woman of your fleeting encounter if she said she was keeping faith with you, the faithless—you would never have considered the child your own without suspicion! Even if what I said had seemed probable to you, you would never have been able to dismiss the secret suspicion that I was trying to palm off some other man's child on you because you were prosperous. You would have suspected me, a shadow would have remained, a fugitive, tentative shadow of distrust between us. I didn't want that. And then I know you; I know you rather better than you know yourself. I know that it would have been difficult for you, who love the carefree, light-hearted, playful aspect of love, suddenly to be a father, suddenly responsible for someone else's life. You can breathe only at liberty; you would have felt bound to me in some way. You would have hated me for that—I know that you would have done so, against your own conscious will. Perhaps only for hours, perhaps only for fleeting minutes I would have been a burden to you, a hated burden—but in my pride I wanted you to think of me all your life without any anxiety. I preferred to take it all on myself rather than burden you, I wanted to be the only one among all your women of whom you always thought with love and gratitude. But the fact is that you never thought of me at all, you forgot me.

I am not blaming you, my beloved, no, I am not blaming you. Forgive me if a touch of bitterness flows into my pen now and then, forgive me—my child, our child lies dead in the flickering candle-light; I clenched my fists against God and called him a murderer, my senses are confused and dulled. Forgive my lament, forgive me! I know that deep in your heart you are good and helpful, you help everyone, even a total stranger who asks for help. But your kindness is so strange, it is open to all to take as much of it as they can hold, it is great, infinitely great, your kindness, but it is—forgive me—it is passive. It wants to be appealed to, to be taken. You help when you are called upon to help, when you are asked for help, you help out of shame, out of weakness, and not out of joy. You do not—let me say so openly—you do not like those who are in need and torment any better than their happier brothers. And it is hard to ask anything of people like you, even the kindest of them. Once, when I was still a child looking through the peephole in our door, I saw you give something to a beggar who had rung your bell. You gave him money readily before he asked you, even a good deal of it, but you gave it with a certain anxiety and in haste, wanting him to go away again quickly; it was as if you were afraid to look him in the face. I have never forgotten your uneasy, timid way of helping, fleeing from gratitude. And so I never turned to you. Certainly I know that you would have stood by me then, even without any certainty that the child was yours. You would have comforted me, you would have given me money, plenty of money, but never with anything but a secret impatience to push what was unwelcome away from you; yes, I believe you might even have asked me to do away with the child before its birth. And I feared that more than anything—because what would I not have done if you wanted it, how could I have denied you anything? However, that child meant everything to me, because it was yours, yourself again but no longer as a happy, carefree man whom I could not hold, yourself given to me for ever—so I thought—there in my body, a part of my own life. Now at last I had caught you, I could sense your life growing in my veins, I could give you food and drink, caress and kiss you when my heart burned for that. You see, beloved, that is why I was so blissfully happy when I knew that I was carrying a child of yours, that is why I never told you, because then you could not escape from me again.

To be sure, beloved, they were not such blissful months as I had anticipated in my mind, they were also months of horror and torment, of revulsion at the vileness of humanity. I did not have an easy time. I could not work in the shop during the final months, or my relative would have noticed and sent news home. I did not want to ask my mother for money—so I eked out an existence until the baby's birth by selling what little jewellery I had. A week before he was born, my last few crowns were stolen from a cupboard by a washerwoman, so I had to go to the maternity hospital where only very poor women, the outcasts and forgotten, drag themselves in their need. And the child—your child—was born there in the midst of misery. It was a deadly place: strange, everything was strange, we women lying there were strange to each other, lonely and hating one another out of misery, the same torment in that crowded ward full of chloroform and blood, screams and groans. I suffered the humiliation, the mental and physical shame that poverty has to bear from the company of prostitutes and the sick who made our common fate feel terrible, from the cynicism of young doctors who stripped back the sheets from defenceless women with an ironic smile and felt them with false medical expertise, from the greed of the nurses—in there, a woman's bashfulness was crucified with looks and scourged with words. The notice with your name in such a place is all that is left of you, for what lies in the bed is only a twitching piece of flesh felt by the curious, an object to be put on display and studied—the women who bear children at home to husbands waiting affectionately for the birth do not know what it means to give birth to a baby alone and defenceless, as if one were on the laboratory table! If I read the word "hell" in a book to this day, I suddenly and against my conscious will think of that crowded, steamy ward full of sighs, laughter, blood and screams, that slaughterhouse of shame where I suffered.

Forgive me, forgive me for telling you about it. I do so only this one time, never again, never. I have said nothing for eleven years, and I will soon be silent for all eternity; just once I must cry out and say what a high price I paid for my child, the child who was all my bliss and now lies there with no breath left in his body. I had forgotten those hours long ago in his smile and voice, in my happiness, but now he is dead the torment revives, and I had to scream out from my heart just this one time. But I do not accuse you—only God, only God, who made that torment pointless. I do not blame you, I swear it, and never did I rise against you in anger. Even in the hour when I was writhing in labour, when my body burned with shame under the inquisitive eyes of the students, even in the second when the pain tore my soul apart, I never accused you before God. I never regretted those nights or my love for you, I always blessed the day you met me. And if I had to go through the hell of those hours again and knew in advance what was waiting for me I would do it again, my beloved, I would do it again a thousand times over!

Our child died yesterday—you never knew him. Never, even in a fleeting encounter by chance, did your eyes fall on him in passing. I kept myself hidden away from you for a long time once I had my son; my longing for you had become less painful, indeed I think I loved you less passionately, or at least I did not suffer from my love so much now that I had been given the child. I did not want to divide myself between you and him, so I gave myself not to you, a happy man living without me, but to the son who needed me, whom I must nourish, whom I could kiss and embrace. I seemed to be saved from my restless desire for you, saved from my fate by that other self of yours who was really mine—only occasionally, very occasionally, did my feelings humbly send my thoughts out to where you lived. I did just one thing: on your birthday I always sent you a bunch of white roses, exactly the same as the roses you gave me after our first night of love. Have you ever wondered in these ten or eleven years who sent them? Did you perhaps remember the woman to whom you once gave such roses? I don't know, and I will never know your answer. Merely giving them to you out of the dark was enough for me, letting my memory of that moment flower again once a year.

You never knew our poor child—today I blame myself for keeping him from you, because you would have loved him. You never knew the poor boy, never saw him smile when he gently opened his eyelids and cast the clear, happy light of his clever, dark eyes—your eyes!—on me, on the whole world. Oh, he was so cheerful, such a dear; all the light-hearted nature of your being came out again in him in childish form, your quick, lively imagination was reborn. He could play with things for hours, entranced, just as you play with life, and then sit over his books, serious again, his eyebrows raised. He became more and more like you; the duality of gravity and playfulness that is so much your own was visibly beginning to develop in him, and the more like you he grew to be, the more I loved him. He studied hard at school, he could talk French like a little magpie, his exercise books were the neatest in the class, and he was so pretty too, so elegant in his black velvet suit or his white sailor jacket. Wherever he went he was the most elegant of all; when I took him to the Adriatic seaside resort of Grado, women stopped on the beach to stroke his long, fair hair; in Semmering, when he tobogganed downhill, everyone turned admiringly to look at him. He was so good-looking, so tender, so attractive; when he went to be a boarder at the Theresian Academy last year he wore his uniform and his little sword like an eighteenth-century pageboy—now he wears nothing but his nightshirt, poor boy, lying there with pale lips and folded hands.

You may perhaps be wondering how I could afford to bring the child up in such luxury, allowing him to live the cheerful, carefree life of the upper classes. Dearest, I speak to you out of the darkness; I am not ashamed, I will tell you, but do not alarm yourself, beloved—I sold myself. I was not exactly what they call a streetwalker, a common prostitute, but I sold myself. I had rich friends, rich lovers; first I went in search of them, then they sought me out, because I was—did you ever notice?—very beautiful. Everyone to whom I gave myself grew fond of me, they all thanked me and felt attached to me, they all loved me—except for you, except for you, my beloved!

Do you despise me now for telling you that I sold myself? No, I know you do not; you understand everything, and you will also understand that I did it only for you, for your other self, your child. Once, in that ward in the maternity hospital, I had touched the worst aspect of poverty, I knew that the poor of this world are always downtrodden, humiliated, victims, and I would not have your child, your bright, beautiful son growing up deep down in the scum of society, in the dark, mean streets, the polluted air of a room at the back of an apartment building. I did not want his tender mouth to know the language of the gutter, or his white body to wear the fusty, shabby garments of the poor—your child was to have everything, all the riches, all the ease on earth; he was to rise to be your equal, in your own sphere of life.

That, my beloved, was my only reason for selling myself. It was no sacrifice for me, since what people usually call honour and dishonour meant nothing to me; you did not love me, and you were the only one to whom my body truly belonged, so I felt indifferent to anything else that happened to it. The caresses of those men, even their most ardent passion did not touch me deeply at all, although I had to go very carefully with many of them, and my sympathy for their unrequited love often shook me when I remembered what my own fate had been. All of them were good to me, all of them indulged me, they all showed me respect. There was one in particular, an older man, a widower who was an imperial count, the same man who wore himself out going from door to door to get my fatherless child, your child, accepted into the Theresian Academy—he loved me as if I were his daughter. He asked me to marry him three or four times—I could be a countess today, mistress of an enchanting castle in the Tyrol, living a carefree life, because the child would have had a loving father who adored him, and I would have had a quiet, distinguished, kindly husband at my side—but I did not accept him, however often he urged me, and however much my refusals hurt him. Perhaps it was folly, for then I would be living somewhere safe and quiet now, and my beloved child with me, but—why should I not tell you?—I did not want to tie myself down, I wanted to be free for you at any time. In my inmost heart, the depths of my unconscious nature, my old childhood dream that one day you might yet summon me to you, if only for an hour, lived on. And for the possibility of that one hour I rejected all else, so that I would be free to answer your first call. What else had my whole life been since I grew past childhood but waiting, waiting to know your will?

And that hour really did come, but you do not know it. You have no inkling of it, beloved! Even then you did not recognize me—you never, never, never recognized me! I had met you a number of times, at the theatre, at concerts, in the Prater, in the street—every time my heart leapt up, but you looked past me; outwardly I was so different now, the shy child had become a woman, said to be beautiful, wearing expensive clothes, surrounded by admirers: how could you detect in me that shy girl in the dim light of your bedroom? Sometimes the man who was with me greeted you, you greeted him in return and looked at me, but your glance was that of a courteous stranger, appreciative but never recognizing me: strange, terribly strange. Once, I still remember, that failure to recognize me, although I was almost used to it, became a burning torment. I was sitting in a box at the Opera House with a lover and you were in the box next to ours. The lights dimmed during the overture, and I could no longer see your face, I only felt your breath as near to me as it had been that first night, and your hand, your fine and delicate hand lay on the velvet-upholstered partition between our boxes. And at last I was overcome by longing to bend down to that strange but beloved hand, the hand whose touch I had once felt holding me, and kiss it humbly. The music was rising tempestuously around me, my longing was more and more passionate, I had to exert all my self-control and force myself to sit there, so powerfully were my lips drawn to your beloved hand. After the first act I asked my lover to leave with me. I could not bear it any more, knowing that you were sitting beside me in the dark, so strange to me and yet so close.

But the hour did come, it came once more, one last time in my buried, secret life. It was almost exactly a year ago, on the day after your birthday. Strange: I had been thinking of you all those hours, because I always celebrated your birthday like a festival. I had gone out very early in the morning to buy the white roses that I asked the shop to send you, as I did every year, in memory of an hour that you had forgotten. In the afternoon I went out with my son, I took him to Demel's café and in the evening to the theatre; I wanted him, too, to feel from his early youth that this day, although he did not know its significance, was in some mystical fashion an occasion to be celebrated. Then next day I was out with my lover of the time, a rich young manufacturer from Brünn who adored and indulged me, and wanted to marry me like the rest of them—and whose proposals I had turned down apparently for no good reason, as with the rest of them, although he showered presents on me and the child, and was even endearing in his rather awkward, submissive way. We went together to a concert, where we met cheerful companions, had supper in a restaurant in the Ringstrasse, and there, amidst laughter and talking, I suggested going on to the Tabarin, a café with a dance floor. I normally disliked cafés of that kind, with their organized, alcoholic merriment, like all similar kinds of "fun", and usually objected to such suggestions, but this time—as if some unfathomable magical power in me suddenly and unconsciously caused me to suggest it in the midst of the others' cheerful excitement—I had a sudden, inexplicable wish to go, as if something special were waiting for me there. Since I was accustomed to getting my way, they all quickly stood up, we went to the Tabarin, drank champagne, and I fell suddenly into a fit of hectic, almost painful merriment, something unusual in me. I drank and drank, sang sentimental songs with the others, and almost felt an urge to dance or rejoice. But suddenly—I felt as if something either cold or blazing hot had been laid on my heart—I stopped short: you were sitting with some friends at the next table, looking admiringly at me, with an expression of desire, the expression that could always send my entire body into a state of turmoil. For the first time in ten years you were looking at me again with all the unconsciously passionate force of your being. I trembled, and the glass that I had raised almost fell from my hands. Fortunately my companions did not notice my confusion: it was lost in the noise of the laughter and music.

Your gaze was more and more ardent, immersing me entirely in fire. I did not know whether at last, at long last, you had recognized me, or you desired me again as someone else, a stranger. The blood shot into my cheeks, I answered my companions at our table distractedly. You must have noticed how confused your gaze made me. Then, unseen by the others, you signed to me with a movement of your head a request to go out of the café for a moment. You ostentatiously paid your bill, said goodbye to your friends and left, not without first indicating to me again that you would wait for me outside. I was trembling as if in frost, as if in a fever, I could not answer anyone, I could not control my own racing blood. As chance would have it, at that very moment a pair of black dancers launched into one of those newfangled modern dances with clattering heels and shrill cries; everyone was watching them, and I made use of that second. I stood up, told my lover that I would be back in a moment, and followed you.

You were standing outside the cloakroom, waiting for me; your expression brightened as I came out. Smiling, you hurried to meet me; I saw at once that you didn't recognize me, not as the child of the past or the young girl of a couple of years later. Once again you were approaching me as someone new to you, an unknown stranger.

"Would you have an hour to spare for me, too, sometime?" you asked in confidential tones—I sensed, from the assurance of your manner, that you took me for one of those women who can be bought for an evening.

"Yes," I said, the same tremulous yet of course compliant "Yes" that the girl had said to you in the twilit street over a decade ago.

"Then when can we meet?" you asked.

"Whenever you like," I replied—I had no shame in front of you. You looked at me in slight surprise, the same suspiciously curious surprise as you had shown all that time ago when my swift consent had startled you before.

"Could it be now?" you asked, a little hesitantly.

"Yes," I said. "Let's go."

I was going to the cloakroom to collect my coat. Then it occurred to me that my lover had the cloakroom ticket for both our coats. Going back to ask him for it would have been impossible without offering some elaborate reason, but on the other hand I was not going to give up the hour with you that I had longed for all these years. So I did not for a second hesitate; I just threw my shawl over my evening dress and went out into the damp, misty night without a thought for the coat, without a thought for the kindly, affectionate man who had been keeping me, although I was humiliating him in front of his friends, making him look like a fool whose lover runs away from him after years the first time a stranger whistles to her. Oh, I was entirely aware of the vile, shameful ingratitude of my conduct to an honest friend; I felt that I was being ridiculous, and mortally injuring a kind man for ever in my madness—but what was friendship to me, what was my whole life compared with my impatience to feel the touch of your lips again, to hear you speak softly close to me? I loved you so much, and now that it is all over and done with I can tell you so. And I believe that if you summoned me from my deathbed I would suddenly find the strength in myself to get up and go with you.

There was a car outside the entrance, and we drove to your apartment. I heard your voice again, I felt your tender presence close to me, and was as bemused, as childishly happy as before. As I climbed those stairs again after more than ten years—no, no, I cannot describe how I still felt everything doubly in those seconds, the past and the present, and in all of it only you mattered. Not much was different in your room, a few more pictures, more books, and here and there new pieces of furniture, but still it all looked familiar to me. And the vase of roses stood on the desk—my roses, sent to you the day before on your birthday, in memory of someone whom you did not remember, did not recognize even now that she was close to you, hand in hand and lips to lips. But all the same, it did me good to think that you looked after the flowers: it meant that a breath of my love and of myself did touch you.

You took me in your arms. Once again I spent a whole, wonderful night with you. But you did not even recognize my naked body. In bliss, I accepted your expert caresses and saw that your passion draws no distinction between someone you really love and a woman selling herself, that you give yourself up entirely to your desire, unthinkingly squandering the wealth of your nature. You were so gentle and affectionate with me, a woman picked up in the dance café, so warmly and sensitively respectful, yet at the same time enjoying possession of a woman so passionately; once more, dizzy with my old happiness, I felt your unique duality—a knowing, intellectual passion mingled with sensuality. It was what had already brought me under your spell when I was a child. I have never felt such concentration on the moment of the act of love in any other man, such an outburst and reflection of his deepest being—although then, of course, it was to be extinguished in endless, almost inhuman oblivion. But I also forgot myself; who was I, now, in the dark beside you? Was I the ardent child of the past, was I the mother of your child, was I a stranger? Oh, it was all so familiar, I had known it all before, and again it was all so intoxicatingly new on that passionate night. I prayed that it would never end.

But morning came, we got up late, you invited me to stay for breakfast with you. Together we drank the tea that an invisible servant had discreetly placed ready in the dining room, and we talked. Again, you spoke to me with the open, warm confidence of your nature, and again without any indiscreet questions or curiosity about myself. You did not ask my name or where I lived: once more I was just an adventure to you, an anonymous woman, an hour of heated passion dissolving without trace in the smoke of oblivion. You told me that you were about to go away for some time, you would be in North Africa for two or three months. I trembled in the midst of my happiness, for already words were hammering in my ears: all over, gone and forgotten! I wished I could fall at your feet and cry out, "Take me with you, recognize me at last, at long last, after so many years!" But I was so timid, so cowardly, so slavish and weak in front of you. I could only say, "What a pity!"

You looked at me with a smile. "Are you really sorry?"

Then a sudden wildness caught hold of me. I stood up and looked at you, a long, hard look. And then I said, "The man I loved was always going away too." I looked at you, I looked you right in the eye. Now, now he will recognize me, I thought urgently, trembling.

But you smiled at me and said consolingly, "People come back again."

"Yes," I said, "they come back, but then they have forgotten."

There must have been something odd, something passionate in the way I said that to you. For you rose to your feet as well and looked at me, affectionately and very surprised. You took me by the shoulders. "What's good is not forgotten; I will not forget you," you said, and as you did so you gazed intently at me as if to memorize my image. And as I felt your eyes on me, seeking, sensing, clinging to you with all my being, I thought that at last, at last the spell of blindness would be broken. He will recognize me now, I thought, he will recognize me now! My whole soul trembled in that thought.

But you did not recognize me. No, you did not know me again, and I had never been more of a stranger to you than at that moment, for otherwise—otherwise you could never have done what you did a few minutes later. You kissed me, kissed me passionately again. I had to tidy my hair, which was disarranged, and as I stood looking in the mirror, looking at what it reflected—I thought I would sink to the ground in shame and horror—I saw you discreetly tucking a couple of banknotes of a high denomination in my muff. How I managed not to cry out I do not know, how I managed not to strike you in the face at that moment—you were paying me, who had loved you from childhood, paying me, the mother of your child, for that night! I was a prostitute from the Tabarin to you, nothing more—you had paid me, you had actually paid me! It was not enough for you to forget me, I had to be humiliated as well.

I reached hastily for my things. I wanted to get away, quickly. It hurt too much. I picked up my hat, which was lying on the desk beside the vase of white roses, my roses. Then an irresistible idea came powerfully to my mind: I would make one more attempt to remind you. "Won't you give me one of your white roses?"

"Happily," you said, taking it out of the vase at once.

"But perhaps they were given to you by a woman—a woman who loves you?" I said.

"Perhaps," you said. "I don't know. They were sent to me, and I don't know who sent them; that's why I like them so much."

I looked at you. "Or perhaps they are from a woman you have forgotten."

You seemed surprised. I looked at you hard. Recognize me, my look screamed, recognize me at last! But your eyes returned a friendly, innocent smile. You kissed me once more. But you did not recognize me.

I went quickly to the door, for I could feel tears rising to my eyes, and I did not want you to see them. In the hall—I had run out in such a hurry—I almost collided with your manservant Johann. Diffident and quick to oblige, he moved aside, opened the front door to let me out, and then in that one second—do you hear?—in that one second as I looked at the old man, my eyes streaming with tears, a light suddenly came into his gaze. In that one second—do you hear?—in that one second the old man, who had not seen me since my childhood, knew who I was. I could have knelt to him and kissed his hands in gratitude for his recognition. As it was, I just quickly snatched the banknotes with which you had scourged me out of my muff and gave them to him. He trembled and looked at me in shock—I think he may have guessed more about me at that moment than you did in all your life. All, all the other men had indulged me, had been kind to me—only you, only you forgot me, only you, only you failed to recognize me!

My child is dead, our child—now I have no one left in the world to love but you. But who are you to me, who are you who never, never recognizes me, who passes me by as if I were no more than a stretch of water, stumbling upon me as if I were a stone, you who always goes away, forever leaving me to wait? Once I thought that, volatile as you are, I could keep you in the shape of the child. But he was your child too: overnight he cruelly went away from me on a journey, he has forgotten me and will never come back. I am alone again, more alone than ever, I have nothing, nothing of yours—no child now, not a word, not a line, you have no memory of me, and if someone were to mention my name in front of you, you would hear it as a stranger's. Why should I not wish to die since I am dead to you, why not move on as you moved on from me? No, beloved, I do not blame you, I will not hurl lamentations at you and your cheerful way of life. Do not fear that I shall pester you any more—forgive me, just this once I had to cry out what is in my heart, in this hour when my child lies there dead and abandoned. Just this once I had to speak to you—then I will go back into the darkness in silence again, as I have always been silent to you.

However, you will not hear my cries while I am still alive—only if I am dead will you receive this bequest from me, from one who loved you above all else and whom you never recognized, from one who always waited for you and whom you never summoned. Perhaps, perhaps you will summon me then, and I will fail to keep faith with you for the first time, because when I am dead I will not hear you. I leave you no picture and no sign, as you left me nothing; you will never recognize me, never. It was my fate in life, let it be my fate in death. I will not call for you in my last hour, I will leave and you will not know my name or my face. I die with an easy mind, since you will not feel it from afar. If my death were going to hurt you, I could not die.

I cannot write any more… my head feels so dulled… my limbs hurt, I am feverish. I think I shall have to lie down. Perhaps it will soon be over, perhaps fate has been kind to me for once, and I shall not have to see them take my child away… I cannot write any more. Goodbye, beloved, goodbye, and thank you… it was good as it was in spite of everything… I will thank you for that until my last breath. I am at ease: I have told you everything, and now you know—or no, you will only guess—how much I loved you, and you will not feel that love is any burden on you. You will not miss me—that consoles me. Nothing in your happy, delightful life will change—I am doing you no harm with my death, and that comforts me, my beloved.

But who… who will always send you white roses on your birthday now? The vase will be empty, the little breath of my life that blew around you once a year will die away as well! Beloved, listen, I beg you… it is the first and last thing I ask you… do it for me every year on your birthday, which is a day when people think of themselves—buy some roses and put them in that vase. Do it, beloved, in the same way as others have a Mass said once a year for someone now dead who was dear to them. I do not believe in God any more, however, and do not want a Mass—I believe only in you, I love only you, and I will live on only in you… oh, only for one day a year, very, very quietly, as I lived near you… I beg you, do that, beloved… it is the first thing that I have ever asked you to do, and the last… thank you… I love you, I love you… goodbye.

*

His shaking hands put the letter down. Then he thought for a long time. Some kind of confused memory emerged of a neighbour's child, of a young girl, of a woman in the dance café at night, but a vague and uncertain memory, like a stone seen shimmering and shapeless on the bed of a stream of flowing water. Shadows moved back and forth, but he could form no clear picture. He felt memories of emotion, yet did not really remember. It was as if he had dreamt of all these images, dreamt of them often and deeply, but they were only dreams.

Then his eye fell on the blue vase on the desk in front of him. It was empty, empty on his birthday for the first time in years. He shivered; he felt as if a door had suddenly and invisibly sprung open, and cold air from another world was streaming into his peaceful room. He sensed the presence of death, he sensed the presence of undying love: something broke open inside him, and he thought of the invisible woman, incorporeal and passionate, as one might think of distant music.

THE INVISIBLE COLLECTION

An episode from the time of German inflation

TWO STATIONS AFTER DRESDEN an elderly gentleman got into our compartment, passed the time of day civilly and then, looking up, expressly nodded to me as if I were an old acquaintance. At first I couldn't remember him; however, as soon as he mentioned his name, with a slight smile, I recollected him at once as one of the most highly regarded art dealers in Berlin. In peacetime I had often viewed and bought old books and autograph manuscripts from him. We talked of nothing much for a while, but suddenly and abruptly he said: "I must tell you where I've just come from—this is the story of about the strangest thing that I've ever encountered, old art dealer that I am, in the thirty-seven years I've been practising my profession." And the story as he told it follows.

You probably know for yourself what it's like in the art trade these days, since the value of money started evaporating like gas; all of a sudden people who have just made their fortunes have discovered a taste for Gothic Madonnas, and incunabula, old engravings and pictures. You can't conjure up enough such things to satisfy them—why, you have to be careful they don't clear out your house and home. They'd happily buy the cufflinks from your sleeves and the lamp from your desk. It's getting harder and harder to find new wares all the time—forgive me for suddenly describing as *wares* items that, to the likes of you and me, usually mean something to be revered—but these philistines have accustomed even me to regard a wonderful Venetian incunabulum only as if it were a coat costing such-and-such a sum in dollars, and a drawing by Guercino as the embodiment of a few hundred franc notes. There's no resisting the insistent urging of those who are suddenly mad to buy art. So I was right out of stock again overnight, and I felt like putting up the shutters, I was so ashamed of seeing our old business that my father took over from my grandfather with nothing for sale but wretched trash, stuff that in the past no street trader in the north would have bothered even to put on his cart.

In this awkward situation, the idea of consulting our old business records occurred to me, to look up former customers from whom I might be able to get a few items if they happened to have duplicates. A list of old customers is always something of a graveyard, especially in times like the present, and it did not really tell me much: most of those who had bought from us in the past had long ago had to get rid of their possessions in auction sales, or had died, and I could not hope for much from the few who remained. But then I suddenly came upon a bundle of letters from a man who was probably our oldest customer, and who had surfaced from my memory only because after 1914 and the outbreak of the World War, he had never turned to us with any orders or queries again. The correspondence—and I really am not exaggerating!—went back over almost sixty years; he had bought from my father and my grandfather, yet I could not remember him ever coming into our premises in the thirty-seven years of my personal involvement with the family business. Everything suggested that he must have been a strange, old-fashioned oddity, one of that lost generation of Germans shown in the paintings and graphic art of such artists as Menzel and Spitzweg, who survived here and there as rare phenomena in little provincial towns until just before our own times. His letters were pure calligraphy, neatly written, the items he was ordering underlined in red ink, with a ruler, and he always wrote out the sum of money involved in words as well as figures, so that there could be no mistake. That, as well as his exclusive use of blank flyleaves from books as writing paper and old, reused envelopes, indicated the petty mind and fanatical thrift of a hopeless provincial. These remarkable documents were signed not only with his name but with the elaborate title: Forestry and Economic Councillor, retd; Lieutenant, retd; Holder of the Iron Cross First Class. Being a veteran of the Franco-Prussian War, he must therefore, if still alive, be at least eighty. However, as a collector of old examples of graphic art this ridiculously thrifty oddity showed unusual acumen, wide knowledge and excellent taste. As I slowly put together his orders from us over almost sixty years, the first of them still paid for in silver groschen, I realized that in the days when you could still buy a stack of the finest German woodcuts for a taler, this little provincial must have been assembling a collection of engravings that would probably show to great advantage beside those so loudly praised by the *nouveaux riches*. For what he had bought from us alone in orders costing him a few marks and pfennigs represented astonishing value today, and in addition it could be expected that his purchases at auction sales had been acquired equally inexpensively.

Although we had had no further orders from him since 1914, I was too familiar with all that went on in the art trade to have missed noticing the auction or private sale of such a collection. In that case, our unusual customer must either be still alive, or the collection was in the hands of his heirs.

The case interested me, and on the next day, that's to say yesterday evening, I set off for one of the most provincial towns in Saxony; and as I strolled along the main street from the station it seemed to me impossible that here, in the middle of these undistinguished little houses with their tasteless contents, a man could live who owned some of the finest prints of Rembrandt's etchings, as well as engravings by Dürer and Mantegna in such a perfectly complete state. To my surprise, however, when I asked at the post office if a forestry or economic councillor of his name lived here, I discovered that the old gentleman really was still alive, and in the middle of the morning I set off on my way to him—with my heart, I confess, beating rather faster.

I had no difficulty in finding his apartment. It was on the second floor of one of those cheaply built provincial buildings that might have been hastily constructed by some builder on spec in the 1860s. A master tailor lived on the first floor, to the left on the second floor I saw the shiny nameplate of a civil servant in the post office, and on the right, at last, a porcelain panel bearing the name of the Forestry and Economic Councillor. When I tentatively rang the bell, a very old white-haired woman wearing a clean little black cap immediately answered it. I gave her my card and asked if I might speak to the Forestry Councillor. Surprised, and with a touch of suspicion, she looked first at me and then at the card; a visitor from the outside world seemed to be an unusual event in this little town at the back of beyond and this old-fashioned building. But she asked me in friendly tones to wait, took my card and went into the room beyond the front door; I heard her whispering quietly, and then, suddenly, a loud male voice. "Oh, Herr R. from Berlin, from the great antiques dealers there… bring him in, bring him in, I'll be very glad to meet him!" And the little old lady came tripping out to me again and asked me into the living room.

I took off my coat and followed her. In the middle of the modest little room an old but still-vigorous man stood erect. He had a bushy moustache and wore a frogged, semi-military casual jacket, and he was holding out both hands in heartfelt welcome. But this gesture, unmistakably one of happy and spontaneous greeting, contrasted with a curious rigidity in the way he held himself. He did not come a step closer to me, and I was obliged—feeling slightly alienated—to approach him myself in order to take his hand. As I was about to grasp it, however, the way he held both hands out horizontally, not moving them, told me that they were not searching for my own but expecting mine to find them. And the next moment I understood it all: this man was blind.

Even from my childhood I had always been uncomfortable facing someone blind; I was never able to fend off a certain shame and embarrassment in sensing that the blind person was entirely alive and knowing, at the same time, that he did not experience our meeting in the same way as I did. Now, yet again, I had to overcome my initial shock at seeing those dead eyes, staring fixedly into space under bushy white brows. However, the blind man himself did not leave me feeling awkward for long; as soon as my hand touched his he shook it powerfully, and repeated his welcome with strong and pleasingly heartfelt emotion. "A rare visitor," he said, smiling broadly at me, "really, it's a miracle, one of the great Berlin antiques dealers making his way to our little town... however, it behoves us to be careful when one of those gentlemen boards the train. Where I come from, we always say: keep your gates and your purses closed when the gypsies are in town... yes, yes, I can guess why you seek me out... business is going badly these days in our poor country; now that our unhappy land of Germany's come down in the world, there are no buyers left, so the great gentlemen of the art world think of their old customers and go in search of those little lambs. But I'm afraid you won't have much luck here, we poor old retired folk are glad if we can put a meal on the table. We can't match the crazy prices you ask these days... the likes of us are finished with all that for ever."

I told him at once that he had misunderstood me; I had not come to sell him anything, I just happened to be in this neighbourhood, and didn't want to miss my chance of calling on him, as a customer of our house over many years, and paying my respects to one of the greatest collectors in Germany. As soon as I said, "one of the greatest collectors in Germany", a remarkable change came over the old man's face. He was still standing upright and rigid in the middle of the room, but now there was an expression of sudden brightness and deep pride in his attitude. He turned towards the place where he thought his wife was, as if to say, "Did you hear that?" and his voice as he then turned to me was full of delight, with not a trace of the brusque, military tone in which he had spoken just now; instead it was soft, positively tender.

"That's really very, very good of you... and you will find you have not come here in vain. You shall see something that can't be seen every day, even in the grandeur of Berlin... a few pieces as fine as any in the Albertina in Vienna or in that damn city of Paris… yes, if a man collects for sixty years he comes upon all kinds of things that aren't to be found on every street corner. Luise, give me the key to the cupboard, please!"

But now something unexpected happened. The little old lady standing beside him, listening courteously and with smiling, quietly attentive friendliness to our conversation, suddenly raised both hands to me in an imploring gesture, at the same time shaking her head vigorously, a sign that at first I failed to understand.

Only then did she go over to her husband and lightly laid both hands on his shoulder. "Oh, Herwarth," she admonished him, "you haven't even asked the gentleman if he has time to spare to look at your collection. It's nearly lunchtime, and after lunch you must rest for an hour, you know the doctor expressly said so. Wouldn't it be better to show our visitor your things after lunch, and Annemarie will be here as well then, she understands it all much better than I do, she can help you!"

And once again, as soon as the words were out of her mouth, she repeated that urgently pleading gesture as if over her husband's head, leaving him unaware of it. Now I understood her. I could tell that she wanted me to decline an immediate viewing, and I quickly invented a lunch engagement. It would be a pleasure and an honour to be allowed to see his collection, I said, but it wouldn't be possible for me to do so before three in the afternoon. Then, however, I would happily come back here.

Cross as a child whose favourite toy has been taken away, the old man made a petulant gesture. "Oh, of course," he grumbled, "those Berlin gentlemen never have time for anything. But today you'll have to find the time, because it's not just three or five good pieces I have, there are twenty-seven portfolios, one for each master of the graphic arts, and all of them full. So come back at three, but mind you're punctual or we'll never get through the whole collection."

Once again he put out his hand into the air, in my direction. "I warn you, you may like it, or you may be jealous. And the more jealous you are the better I'll be pleased. That's collectors for you: we want it all for ourselves and nothing for anyone else!" And once again he shook my hand vigorously.

The little old lady accompanied me to the door. I had noticed a certain discomfort in her all this time, an expression of anxious embarrassment. But now, just before we reached the way out, she stammered in a low voice, "Could you… could you… could my daughter Annemarie join you before you come back to us? That would be better for… for various reasons… I expect you are lunching at the hotel?"

"Certainly, and I will be delighted to meet your daughter first. It will be a pleasure," I said.

And sure enough, an hour later when I had just finished my lunch in the little restaurant of the hotel on the market square, a lady not in her first youth, simply dressed, came in and looked enquiringly around. I went up to her, introduced myself and said I was ready to set out with her at once to see the collection. However, with a sudden blush and the same confused embarrassment that her mother had shown, she asked if she could have a few words with me first. I saw at once that this was difficult for her. Whenever she was bringing herself to say something, that restless blush rose in her face, and her hand fidgeted with her dress. At last she began, hesitantly, overcome by confusion again and again.

"My mother has sent me to see you… she told me all about it, and… and we have a request to make. You see, we would like to inform you, before you go back to see my father… of course Father will want to show you his collection, and the collection… the collection, well, it isn't entirely complete any more… there are several items missing… indeed, I'm afraid quite a number are missing…"

She had to catch her breath again, and then she suddenly looked at me and said, hastily: "I must speak to you perfectly frankly… you know what these times are like, I'm sure you'll understand. After the outbreak of war Father went blind. His vision had been disturbed quite often before, but then all the agitation robbed him of his eyesight entirely. You see, even though he was seventy-six at the time he wanted to go to France with the army, and when the army didn't advance at once, as it had in 1870, he was dreadfully upset, and his sight went downhill at terrifying speed. Otherwise he's still hale and hearty: until recently he could walk for hours and even go hunting, his favourite sport. But now he can't take long walks, and the only pleasure he has left is his collection. He looks at it every day… that's to say, he can't see it, he can't see anything now, but he gets all the portfolios out so that he can at least touch the items in them, one by one, always in the same order; he's known their order by heart for decades. Nothing else interests him these days, and I always have to read the accounts of all the auction sales in the newspaper to him. The higher the prices he hears about the happier he is, because… this is the worst of it, Father doesn't understand about prices nowadays… he doesn't know that we've lost everything, and his pension will keep us for only two days in the month… in addition, my sister's husband fell in the war, leaving her with four small children. But Father has no idea of the material difficulties we're in. At first we saved hard, even more than before, but that didn't help. Then we began selling things—we didn't touch his beloved collection, of course, we sold the little jewellery we had, but dear God, what did that amount to? After all, for sixty years Father had spent every pfennig he could spare on his prints alone. And one day there was nothing for us to sell, we didn't know what to do, and then… then Mother and I sold one of the prints. Father would never have allowed it, after all, he doesn't know how badly off we are, how hard it is to buy a little food on the black market, he doesn't even know that we lost the war, and Alsace and Lorraine are part of France now, we don't read those things to him when they appear in the paper, so that he won't get upset.

"It was a very valuable item that we sold, a Rembrandt etching. The dealer offered us many, many thousands of marks for it, and we hoped that would provide for us for years. But you know how money melts away these days… we had deposited most of it in the bank, but two months later it was all gone. So we had to sell another work, and then another, and the dealer was always so late sending the money that it was already devalued when it arrived. Then we tried auctions, but there too we were cheated, although the prices were in millions… by the time the millions reached us they were nothing but worthless paper. And so gradually the best of his collection left us, except for a few good items, just so that we could lead the most frugal of lives, and Father has no idea of it.

"That's why my mother was so alarmed when you came today—because if he opens the portfolios and shows them to you, it will all come out… you see, we put reprints or similar sheets of paper in the old mounts instead of the prints we had sold, so that he wouldn't notice when he touched them. If he can only touch them and enumerate them (he remembers their order of arrangement perfectly), he feels just the same joy as when he could see them in the past with his own eyes. There's no one else in this town whom Father would think worthy of seeing his treasures… and he loves every single print so fanatically that I think his heart would break if he guessed that they all passed out of his hands long ago. You are the first he has invited to see them in all these years, since the death of the former head of the engravings department in the Dresden gallery—he meant to show his portfolios to him. So I beg you…"

And suddenly the ageing woman raised her hands, and tears gleamed in her eyes.

"…We beg you… don't make him unhappy… don't make us all unhappy… don't destroy his last illusion, help us to make him believe that all the prints he will describe to you are still there… he wouldn't survive it if he only suspected. Maybe we have done him an injustice, but we couldn't help it. One must live, and human lives, the lives of four orphaned children as well as my sister, are surely worth more than sheets of printed paper. To this day, what we did hasn't taken any of his pleasure from him; he is happy to be able to leaf through his portfolios for three hours every afternoon, talking to every print as if it were a human being. And today… today would perhaps be the happiest day of his life; he's been waiting years for a chance to show a connoisseur his darlings. Please… I beg and pray you, please don't destroy his happiness!"

My account of her plea cannot express the deep distress with which she told me all this. My God—as a dealer I have seen many such people despicably robbed, infamously deceived by the inflation, people who were persuaded to part with their most precious family heirlooms for the price of a sandwich—but here Fate added a touch of its own, one that particularly moved me. Of course I promised her to keep the secret and do my best.

So we went back to the apartment together—on the way, still full of my bitter feelings, I heard about the trifling amounts that these poor women, who knew nothing of the subject, had been paid, but that only confirmed me in my decision to help them as well as I could. We went up the stairs, and as soon as we opened the door we heard the old man's cheerfully hearty voice from the living room. "Come in, come in!" With a blind man's keen hearing, he must have heard our footsteps as we climbed the stairs.

"Herwarth hasn't been able to sleep at all, he is so impatient to show you his treasures," said the little old lady, smiling. A single glance at her daughter had already set her mind at rest: I would not give them away. Piles of portfolios were arranged on the table, waiting for us, and as soon as the blind man felt my hand he took my arm, without further greeting, and pressed me down into an armchair.

"There, now let's begin at once—there's a great deal to see, and I know you gentlemen from Berlin never have much time. The first portfolio is devoted to that great master Dürer and, as you'll see for yourself, pretty well complete—each of my prints finer than the last. Well, you can judge for yourself, look at this one!" he said, opening the portfolio at the first sheet it contained. "There—the Great Horse!"

And now, with the tender caution one would employ in handling something fragile, his fingertips touching it very lightly to avoid wear and tear, he took out of the folio a mount framing a blank, yellowed sheet of paper, and held the worthless scrap out in front of him with enthusiasm. He looked at it for several minutes, without of course really seeing it, but in his outstretched hand he held the empty sheet up level with his eyes, his expression ecstatic, his whole face magically expressing the intent gesture of a man looking at a fine work. And as his dead pupils stared at it—was it a reflection from the paper, or a glow coming from within him?—a knowledgeable light came into his eyes, a brightness borrowed from what he thought he saw.

"There," he said proudly, "did you ever see a finer print? Every detail stands out so sharp and clear—I've looked at it beside the Dresden copy, which was flat and lifeless by comparison. And as for its provenance! There—" and he turned the sheet over and pointed to certain places on the back, which was also blank, so that I instinctively looked at it as if the marks he imagined were really there after all—"there you see the stamp of the Nagler collection, here the stamps of Remy and Esdaile; I dare say the illustrious collectors who owned this print before me never guessed that it would end up in this little room some day."

A cold shudder ran down my back as the old man, knowing nothing of what had happened, praised an entirely blank sheet of paper to the skies; and it was a strange sight to see him pointing his finger, knowing the right places to the millimetre, to where the invisible collectors' stamps that existed only in his imagination would have been. My throat constricted with the horror of it, and I didn't know what to say; but when, in my confusion, I looked at his wife and daughter I saw the old woman's hands raised pleadingly to me again, as she trembled with emotion. At this I got a grip on myself and began to play my part.

"Extraordinary!" I finally stammered. "A wonderful print." And at once his entire face glowed with pride. "But that's nothing to all I still have to show you," he said triumphantly. "You must see my copy of the Melancholia, or the Passion—there, this one is an illuminated copy, you won't see such quality in one of those again. Look at this—and again his fingers tenderly moved over an imaginary picture—"that freshness, that warm, grainy tone. All the fine dealers in Berlin, and the doctors who run the museums there, they'd be bowled over."

And so that headlong, eloquent recital of his triumphs went on for another good two hours. I can't say how eerie it was to join him in looking at a hundred, maybe two hundred blank sheets of paper or poor reproductions, but in the memory of this man, who was tragically unaware of their absence, the prints were so incredibly real that he could describe and praise every one of them unerringly, in precise detail, just as he remembered the order of them: the invisible collection that in reality must now be dispersed to all four corners of the earth was still genuinely present to the blind man, so touchingly deceived, and his passion for what he saw was so overwhelming that even I almost began to believe in it.

Only once was the somnambulistic certainty of his enthusiasm as he viewed the collection interrupted, alarmingly, by the danger of waking to reality; in speaking of his copy of Rembrandt's *Antiope* (the print of the etching was a proof and must indeed have been inestimably valuable), he had once again been praising the sharpness of the print, and as he did so his nervously clairvoyant fingers lovingly followed the line of it, but his ultra-sensitive nerves of touch failed to feel an indentation that he expected on the blank sheet. The suggestion of a shadow descended on his brow. His voice became confused. "But surely... surely this is the *Antiope*?" he murmured, with some awkwardness, whereupon I immediately summoned up all my powers, quickly took the mounted sheet from his hands, and enthusiastically described the etching, which I myself knew well, in every detail. The tension in the blind man's expression relaxed again. And the more I praised the merits of the collection, the more did a jovial warmth bloom in that gnarled old man's face, a simple depth of feeling.

"Here's someone who understands these things for once," he rejoiced, turning triumphantly to his family. "At last, at long last a man who can tell you what my prints are worth. You've always been so cross with me for putting all the money I had to spare into my collection, that's the truth of it: over sixty years no beer, no wine, no tobacco, no travelling, no visits to the theatre, no books—I was always saving and saving for these prints. But one day, when I'm gone, you'll see—you two will be rich, richer than anyone in this town, as rich as the richest in Dresden, then for a change you'll be glad of my folly. However, as long as I live not a single one of these prints leaves the house—they'll have to carry me out first and only then my collection."

And as he spoke, his hand passed lovingly over the portfolios that had been emptied of their contents long ago, as if they were living things—I found it terrible, yet at the same time touching, for in all the years of the war I had not seen so perfect and pure an expression of bliss on any German face. Beside him stood the women, looking mysteriously like the female figures in that etching by the German master, who, coming to visit the tomb of the Saviour, stand in front of the vault, broken open and empty, with an expression of fearful awe and at the same time joyous ecstasy. As the women disciples in that picture are radiant with their heavenly presentiment of the Saviour's closeness, these two ageing, worn, impoverished ladies were irradiated by the childish bliss of the old man's joy—half laughing, half in tears, it was a sight more moving than any I had ever seen. As for the old man himself, he could not hear enough of my praise, he kept stacking the portfolios up again and turning them, thirstily drinking in every word I said, and so for me it was a refreshing change when at last the deceitful portfolios were pushed aside and, protesting, he had to let the table be cleared for the coffee things. But what was my sense of guilty relief beside the swelling, tumultuous joy and high spirits of a man who seemed to be thirty years younger now! He told a hundred anecdotes of his purchases, his fishing trips in search of them, and rejecting any help tapped again and again on one of the sheets of paper, getting out another and then another print; he was exuberantly drunk as if on wine. When I finally said I must take my leave, he was positively startled, he seemed as upset as a self-willed child, and stamped his foot defiantly: this wouldn't do, I had hardly seen half his treasures. And the women had a difficult time making him understand, in his obstinate displeasure, that he really couldn't keep me there any longer or I would miss my train.

When, after desperate resistance, he finally saw the sense of that, and we were saying goodbye, his voice softened. He took both my hands, and his fingers caressed the joints of mine with all the expressiveness conveyed by the touch of a blind man, as if they wanted to know more of me and express more affection than could be put into words. "You have given me the greatest pleasure—at long, long last I have been able to look through my beloved prints again with a connoisseur. But you'll find that you haven't come to see me, old and blind as I am, in vain. I promise you here and now, before my wife as my witness, that I will add a clause to my will entrusting the auction of my collection to your old-established house. You shall have the honour of administering these unknown treasures"—and he placed his hand lovingly on the plundered portfolios—"until the day when they go out into the world and are dispersed. Just promise me to draw up a handsome catalogue: it will be my tombstone, and I couldn't ask for a better memorial."

I looked at his wife and daughter, who were holding each other close, and sometimes a tremor passed from one to the other, as if they were a single body trembling in united emotion. I myself felt a sense of solemnity in the touching way the old man, unaware of the truth, consigned the invisible and long-gone collection to my care as something precious. Greatly moved, I promised him what I could never perform; once again his dead pupils seemed to light up, and I felt his inner longing to feel me physically; I could tell by the tender, loving pressure of his fingers as they held mine in thanks and a vow.

The women went to the door with me. They dared not speak, for his keen hearing would have picked up every word, but their eyes beamed at me, warm with tears and full of gratitude! Feeling dazed, I made my way down the stairs. I was in fact ashamed of myself; like the angel in the fairy tale I had entered a poor family's house, I had restored a blind man's sight, if only for an hour, by helping him with what amounted to a white lie, when in truth I had gone to see him only as a mean-minded dealer hoping to get a few choice items out of someone by cunning. But what I took away with me was more: I had once again felt a sense of pure and lively enthusiasm in a dull, joyless time, a kind of spiritually irradiated ecstasy bent entirely on art, something that people these days seem to have forgotten entirely. And I felt—I can't put it any other way—I felt a sense of reverence, although I was still ashamed of myself, without really knowing why.

I was already out in the street when I heard an upstairs window open, and my name was called; the old man had not wanted to miss looking with his blind eyes in the direction where he thought I would be standing. He leant so far forwards that the two women had to support him, waved his handkerchief and called, "*Bon voyage!*" with the cheerful, fresh voice of a boy. It was an unforgettable moment: the white-haired old man's happy face up at the window, high above all the morose, driven, busy people in the street, gently elevated from what in truth is our dismal world on the white cloud of a well-meant delusion. And I found myself remembering the old saying—I think it was Goethe's—"Collectors are happy men."

TWENTY-FOUR HOURS IN THE LIFE OF A WOMAN

In the little guest house on the Riviera where I was staying at the time, ten years before the war, a heated discussion had broken out at our table and unexpectedly threatened to degenerate into frenzied argument, even rancour and recrimination. Most people have little imagination. If something doesn't affect them directly, does not drive a sharp wedge straight into their minds, it hardly excites them at all, but if an incident, however slight, takes place before their eyes, close enough for the senses to perceive it, it instantly rouses them to extremes of passion. They compensate for the infrequency of their sympathy, as it were, by exhibiting disproportionate and excessive vehemence.

Such was the case that day among our thoroughly bourgeois company at table, where on the whole we just made equable small talk and cracked mild little jokes, usually parting as soon as the meal was over: the German husband and wife to go on excursions and take snapshots, the portly Dane to set out on tedious fishing expeditions, the distinguished English lady to return to her books, the Italian married couple to indulge in escapades to Monte Carlo, and I to lounge in a garden chair or get some work done. This time, however, our irate discussion left us all still very much at odds, and if someone suddenly rose it was not, as usual, to take civil leave of the rest of us, but in a mood of heated irascibility that, as I have said, was assuming positively frenzied form.

The incident obsessing our little party, admittedly, was odd enough. From outside, the guest house where the seven of us were staying might have been an isolated villa—with a wonderful view of the rock-strewn beach from its windows—but in fact it was only the cheaper annexe of the Grand Palace Hotel to which it was directly linked by the garden, so that we in the guest house were in constant touch with the hotel guests. And that same hotel had been the scene of an outright scandal the day before, when a young Frenchman had arrived by the midday train, at twenty-past twelve (I can't avoid giving the time so precisely because it was of importance to the incident itself, and indeed to the subject of our agitated conversation), and took a room with a view of the sea, opening straight on to the beach, which in itself indicated that he was in reasonably easy circumstances. Not only his discreet elegance but, most of all, his extraordinary and very appealing good looks made an attractive impression. A silky blond moustache surrounded sensuously warm lips in a slender, girlish face; soft, wavy brown hair curled over his pale forehead; every glance of his melting eyes was a caress—indeed everything about him was soft, endearing, charming, but without any artifice or affectation. At a distance he might at first remind you slightly of those pink wax dummies to be seen adopting dandified poses in the window displays of large fashion stores, walking-stick in hand and representing the ideal of male beauty, but closer inspection dispelled any impression of foppishness, for—most unusually—his charm was natural and innate, and seemed an inseparable part of him. He greeted everyone individually in passing, in a manner as warm as it was modest, and it was a pleasure to see his unfailingly graceful demeanour unaffectedly brought into play on every occasion. When a lady was going to the cloakroom he made haste to fetch her coat, he had a friendly glance or joke for every child, he was both affable and discreet—in short, he seemed to be one of those happy souls who, secure in the knowledge that their bright faces and youthful attractions are pleasing to others, transmute that security anew into yet more charm. His presence worked wonders among the hotel guests, most of whom were elderly and sickly, and he irresistibly won everyone's liking with the victorious bearing of youth, that flush of ease and liveliness with which charm so delightfully endows some human beings. Only a couple of hours after his arrival he was playing tennis with the two daughters of the stout, thick-set manufacturer from Lyon—twelve-year-old Annette and thirteen-year-old Blanche—and their mother, the refined, delicate and reserved Madame Henriette, smiled slightly to see her inexperienced daughters unconsciously flirting with the young stranger. That evening he watched for an hour as we played chess, telling a few amusing anecdotes now and then in an unobtrusive style, strolled along the terrace again with Madame Henriette while her husband played dominoes with a business friend as usual; and late in the evening I saw him in suspiciously intimate conversation with the hotel secretary in the dim light of her office. Next morning he went fishing with my Danish chess partner, showing a remarkable knowledge of angling, and then held a long conversation about politics with the Lyon manufacturer in which he also proved himself an entertaining companion, for the stout Frenchman's hearty laughter could be heard above the sound of the breaking waves. After lunch he spent an hour alone with Madame Henriette in the garden again, drinking black coffee, played another game of tennis with her daughters and chatted in the lobby to the German couple. At six o'clock I met him at the railway station when I went to post a letter. He strode quickly towards me and said, as if apologetically, that he had been suddenly called away but would be back in two days' time. Sure enough, he was absent from the dining room that evening, but only in person, for he was the sole subject of conversation at every table, and all the guests praised his delightful, cheerful nature.

That night, I suppose at about eleven o'clock, I was sitting in my room finishing a book when I suddenly heard agitated shouts and cries from the garden coming in through my open window. Something was obviously going on over at the hotel. Feeling concerned rather than curious, I immediately hurried across—it was some fifty paces—and found the guests and staff milling around in great excitement. Madame Henriette, whose husband had been playing dominoes with his friend from Namur as usual, had not come back from her evening walk on the terrace by the beach, and it was feared that she had suffered an accident. The normally ponderous, slow-moving manufacturer kept charging down to the beach like a bull, and when he called: "Henriette! Henriette!" into the night, his voice breaking with fear, the sound conveyed something of the terror and the primeval nature of a gigantic animal wounded to death. The waiters and pageboys ran up and down the stairs in agitation, all the guests were woken and the police were called. The fat man, however, trampled and stumbled his way through all this, waistcoat unbuttoned, sobbing and shrieking as he pointlessly shouted the name "Henriette! Henriette!" into the darkness. By now the children were awake upstairs, and stood at the window in their night dresses, calling down for their mother. Their father hurried upstairs again to comfort them.

And then something so terrible happened that it almost defies retelling, for a violent strain on human nature, at moments of extremity, can often give such tragic expression to a man's bearing that no images or words can reproduce it with the same lightning force. Suddenly the big, heavy man came down the creaking stairs with a changed look on his face, very weary and yet grim. He had a letter in his hand. "Call them all back!" he told the hotel major-domo, in a barely audible voice. "Call everyone in again. There's no need. My wife has left me."

Mortally wounded as he was, the man showed composure, a tense, superhuman composure as he faced all the people standing around, looking at him curiously as they pressed close and then suddenly turned away again, each of them feeling alarmed, ashamed and confused. He had just enough strength left to make his way unsteadily past us, looking at no one, and switch off the light in the reading room. We heard the sound of his ponderous, massive body dropping heavily into an armchair, and then a wild, animal sobbing, the weeping of a man who has never wept before. That elemental pain had a kind of paralysing power over every one of us, even the least of those present. None of the waiters, none of the guests who had joined the throng out of curiosity, ventured either a smile or a word of condolence. Silently, one by one, as if put to shame by so shattering an emotional outburst, we crept back to our rooms, while that stricken specimen of mankind shook and sobbed alone with himself in the dark as the building slowly laid itself to rest, whispering, muttering, murmuring and sighing.

You will understand that such an event, striking like lightning before our very eyes and our perceptions, was likely to cause considerable turmoil in persons usually accustomed to an easygoing existence and carefree pastimes. But while this extraordinary incident was certainly the point of departure for the discussion that broke out so vehemently at our table, almost bringing us to blows, in essence the dispute was more fundamental, an angry conflict between two warring concepts of life. For it soon became known from the indiscretion of a chambermaid who had read the letter—in his helpless fury, the devastated husband had crumpled it up and dropped it on the floor somewhere—that Madame Henriette had not left alone but, by mutual agreement, with the young Frenchman (for whom most people's liking now swiftly began to evaporate). At first glance, of course, it might seem perfectly understandable for this minor Madame Bovary to exchange her stout, provincial husband for an elegant and handsome young fellow. But what aroused so much indignation in all present was the circumstance that neither the manufacturer nor his daughters, nor even Madame Henriette herself, had ever set eyes on this Lovelace before, and consequently their evening conversation for a couple of hours on the terrace, and the one-hour session in the garden over black coffee, seemed to have sufficed to make a woman about thirty-three years old and of blameless reputation abandon her husband and two children overnight, following a young dandy previously unknown to her without a second thought. This apparently evident fact was unanimously condemned at our table as perfidious deceit and a cunning manoeuvre on the part of the two lovers: of course Madame Henriette must have been conducting a clandestine affair with the young man long before, and he had come here, Pied Piper that he was, only to settle the final details of their flight, for—so our company deduced—it was out of the question for a decent woman who had known a man a mere couple of hours to run off just like that when he first whistled her up. It amused me to take a different view, and I energctically defended such an eventuality as possible, even probable in a woman who at heart had perhaps been ready to take some decisive action through all the years of a tedious, disappointing marriage. My unexpected opposition quickly made the discussion more general, and it became particularly agitated when both married couples, the Germans and the Italians alike, denied the existence of the *coup de foudre* with positively scornful indignation, condemning it as folly and tasteless romantic fantasy.

Well, it's of no importance here to go back in every detail over the stormy course of an argument conducted between soup and dessert: only professionals of the table d'hôte are witty, and points made in the heat of a chance dispute at table are usually banal, since the speakers resort to them clumsily and in haste. It is also difficult to explain how our discussion came to assume the form of insulting remarks so quickly; I think it grew so vehement in the first place because of the instinctive wish of both husbands to reassure themselves that their own wives were incapable of such shallow inconstancy. Unfortunately they could find no better way of expressing their feelings than to tell me that no one could speak as I did except a man who judged the feminine psyche by a bachelor's random conquests, which came only too cheap. This accusation rather annoyed me, and when the German lady added her mite by remarking instructively that there were real women on the one hand and 'natural-born tarts' on the other, and in her opinion Madame Henriette must have been one of the latter, I lost patience entirely and became aggressive myself. Such a denial of the obvious fact that at certain times in her life a woman is delivered up to mysterious powers beyond her own will and judgement, I said, merely concealed fear of our own instincts, of the demonic element in our nature, and many people seemed to take pleasure in feeling themselves stronger, purer and more moral than those who are 'easily led astray'. Personally, I added, I thought it more honourable for a woman to follow her instincts freely and passionately than to betray her husband in his own arms with her eyes closed, as so many did. Such, roughly, was the gist of my remarks, and the more the others attacked poor Madame Henriette in a conversation now rising to fever pitch, the more passionately I defended her (going far beyond what I actually felt in the case). My enthusiasm amounted to what in student circles might have been described as a challenge to the two married couples, and as a not very harmonious quartet they went for me with such indignant solidarity that the old Dane, who was sitting there with a jovial expression, much like the referee at a football match with stopwatch in hand, had to tap his knuckles on the table from time to time in admonishment. "Gentlemen, please!" But it never worked for long. One of the husbands had jumped up from the table three times already, red in the face, and could be calmed by his wife only with difficulty—in short, a dozen minutes more and our discussion would have ended in violence, had not Mrs C suddenly poured oil on the stormy waters of the conversation.

Mrs C, the white-haired, distinguished old English lady, presided over our table as unofficial arbiter. Sitting very upright in her place, turning to everyone with the same uniform friendliness, saying little and yet listening with the most gratifying interest, she was a pleasing sight from the purely physical viewpoint, and an air of wonderfully calm composure emanated from her aristocratically reserved nature. Up to a certain point she kept her distance from the rest of us, although she could also show special kindness with tactful delicacy: she spent most of her time in the garden reading books, and sometimes played the piano, but she was seldom to be seen in company or deep in conversation. You scarcely noticed her, yet she exerted a curious influence over us all, for no sooner did she now, for the first time, intervene in our discussion than we all felt, with embarrassment, that we had been too loud and intemperate.

Mrs C had made use of the awkward pause when the German gentleman jumped brusquely up and was then induced to sit quietly down again. Unexpectedly, she raised her clear, grey eyes, looked at me indecisively for a moment, and then, with almost objective clarity, took up the subject in her own way.

"So you think, if I understand you correctly, that Madame Henriette—that a woman can be cast unwittingly into a sudden adventure, can do things that she herself would have thought impossible an hour earlier, and for which she can hardly be held responsible?"

"I feel sure of it, ma'am."

"But then all moral judgements would be meaningless, and any kind of vicious excess could be justified. If you really think that a *crime passionnel*, as the French call it, is no crime at all, then what is the state judiciary for? It doesn't take a great deal of good will—and you yourself have a remarkable amount of that," she added, with a slight smile, "to see passion in every crime, and use that passion to excuse it."

The clear yet almost humorous tone of her words did me good, and instinctively adopting her objective stance I answered half in jest, half in earnest myself: "I'm sure that the state judiciary takes a more severe view of such things than I do; its duty is to protect morality and convention without regard for pity, so it is obliged to judge and make no excuses. But as a private person I don't see why I should voluntarily assume the role of public prosecutor. I'd prefer to appear for the defence. Personally, I'd rather understand others than condemn them."

Mrs C looked straight at me for a while with her clear grey eyes, and hesitated. I began to fear she had failed to understand what I said, and was preparing to repeat it in English. But with a curious gravity, as if conducting an examination, she continued with her questions.

"Don't you think it contemptible or shocking, though, for a woman to leave her husband and her children to follow some chance-met man, when she can't even know if he is worth her love? Can you really excuse such reckless, promiscuous conduct in a woman who is no longer in her first youth, and should have disciplined herself to preserve her self-respect, if only for the sake of her children?"

"I repeat, ma'am," I persisted, "that I decline to judge or condemn her in this case. To you, I can readily admit that I was exaggerating a little just now—poor Madame Henriette is certainly no heroine, not even an adventuress by nature, let alone a *grande amoureuse*. So far as I know her, she seems to me just an average, fallible woman. I do feel a little respect for her because she bravely followed the dictates of her own will, but even more pity, since tomorrow, if not today, she is sure to be deeply unhappy. She may have acted unwisely and certainly too hastily, but her conduct was not base or mean, and I still challenge anyone's right to despise the poor unfortunate woman."

"And what about you yourself; do you still feel exactly the same respect and esteem for her? Don't you see any difference between the woman you knew the day before yesterday as a respectable wife, and the woman who ran off with a perfect stranger a day later?"

"None at all. Not the slightest, not the least difference."

"*Is that so?*" She instinctively spoke those words in English; the whole conversation seemed to be occupying her mind to a remarkable degree. After a brief moment's thought, she raised her clear eyes to me again, with a question in them.

"And suppose you were to meet Madame Henriette tomorrow, let's say in Nice on the young man's arm, would you still greet her?"

"Of course."

"And speak to her?"

"Of course."

"If… if you were married, would you introduce such a woman to your wife as if nothing had happened?"

"Of course."

"*Would you really?*" she said, in English again, speaking in tones of incredulous astonishment.

"*Indeed I would,*" I answered, unconsciously falling into English too.

Mrs C was silent. She still seemed to be thinking hard, and suddenly, looking at me as if amazed at her own courage, she said: "I don't know if I would. Perhaps I might." And with the indefinable and peculiarly English ability to end a conversation firmly but without brusque discourtesy, she rose and offered me her hand in a friendly gesture. Her intervention had restored peace, and we were all privately grateful to her for ensuring that although we had been at daggers drawn a moment ago, we could speak to each other with tolerable civility again. The dangerously charged atmosphere was relieved by a few light remarks.

Although our discussion seemed to have been courteously resolved, its irate bitterness had none the less left a faint, lingering sense of estrangement between me and my opponents in argument. The German couple behaved with reserve, while over the next few days the two Italians enjoyed asking me ironically, at frequent intervals, whether I had heard anything of '*la cara signora Henrietta*'. Urbane as our manners might appear, something of the equable, friendly good fellowship of our table had been irrevocably destroyed.

The chilly sarcasm of my adversaries was made all the more obvious by the particular friendliness Mrs C had shown me since our discussion. Although she was usually very reserved, and hardly ever seemed to invite conversation with her table companions outside meal times, she now on several occasions found an opportunity to speak to me in the garden and—I might almost say—distinguish me by her attention, for her upper-class reserve made a private talk with her seem a special favour. To be honest, in fact, I must say she positively sought me out and took every opportunity of entering into conversation with me, in so marked a way that had she not been a white-haired elderly lady I might have entertained some strange, conceited ideas. But when we talked our conversation inevitably and without fail came back to the same point of departure, to Madame Henriette: it seemed to give her some mysterious pleasure to accuse the errant wife of weakness of character and irresponsibility. At the same time, however, she seemed to enjoy my steadfast defence of that refined and delicate woman, and my insistence that nothing could ever make me deny my sympathy for her. She constantly steered our conversation the same way, and in the end I hardly knew what to make of her strange, almost eccentric obsession with the subject.

This went on for a few days, maybe five or six, and she never said a word to suggest why this kind of conversation had assumed importance for her. But I could not help realising that it had when I happened to mention, during a walk, that my stay here would soon be over, and I thought of leaving the day after tomorrow. At this her usually serene face suddenly assumed a curiously intense expression, and something like the shadow of a cloud came into her clear grey eyes. "Oh, what a pity! There's still so much I'd have liked to discuss with you." And from then on a certain uneasy restlessness showed that while she spoke she was thinking of something else, something that occupied and distracted her mind a great deal. At last she herself seemed disturbed by this mental distraction, for in the middle of a silence that had suddenly fallen between us she unexpectedly offered me her hand.

"I see that I can't put what I really want to say to you clearly. I'd rather write it down." And walking faster than I was used to seeing her move, she went towards the house.

I did indeed find a letter in her energetic, frank handwriting in my room just before dinner that evening. I now greatly regret my carelessness with written documents in my youth, which means that I cannot reproduce her note word for word, and can give only the gist of her request: might she, she asked, tell me about an episode in her life? It lay so far back in the past, she wrote, that it was hardly a part of her present existence any more, and the fact that I was leaving the day after tomorrow made it easier for her to speak of something that had occupied and preyed on her mind for over twenty years. If I did not feel such a conversation was an importunity, she would like to ask me for an hour of my time.

The letter—I merely outline its contents here—fascinated me to an extraordinary degree: its English style alone lent it great clarity and resolution. Yet I did not find it easy to answer. I tore up three drafts before I replied:

I am honoured by your showing such confidence in me, and I promise you an honest response should you require one. Of course I cannot ask you to tell me more than your heart dictates. But whatever you tell, tell yourself and me the truth. Please believe me: I feel your confidence a special honour.

The note made its way to her room that evening, and I received the answer next morning:

You are quite right: half the truth is useless, only the whole truth is worth telling. I shall do my best to hide nothing from myself or from you. Please come to my room after dinner—at the age of sixty-seven, I need fear no misinterpretation, but I cannot speak freely in the garden, or with other people near by. Believe me, I did not find it easy to make my mind up to take this step.

During the day we met again at table and discussed indifferent matters in the conventional way. But when we encountered each other in the garden she avoided me in obvious confusion, and I felt it both painful and moving to see this white-haired old lady fleeing from me down an avenue lined with pine trees, as shy as a young girl.

At the appointed time that evening I knocked on her door, and it was immediately opened; the room was bathed in soft twilight, with only the little reading lamp on the table casting a circle of yellow light in the dusk. Mrs C came towards me without any self-consciousness, offered me an armchair and sat down opposite me. I sensed that she had prepared mentally for each of these movements, but then came a pause, obviously unplanned, a pause that grew longer and longer as she came to a difficult decision. I dared not inject any remark into this pause, for I sensed a strong will wrestling with great resistance here. Sometimes the faint notes of a waltz drifted up from the drawing room below, and I listened intently, as if to relieve the silence of some of its oppressive quality. She too seemed to feel the unnatural tension of the silence awkward, for she suddenly pulled herself together to take the plunge, and began.

"It's only the first few words that are so difficult. For the last two days I have been preparing to be perfectly clear and truthful; I hope I shall succeed. Perhaps you don't yet understand why I am telling all this to you, a stranger, but not a day, scarcely an hour goes by when I do not think of this particular incident, and you can believe me, an old woman now, when I say it is intolerable to spend one's whole life staring at a single point in it, a single day. Everything I am about to tell you, you see, happened within the space of just twenty-four hours in my sixty-seven years of life, and I have often asked myself, I have wondered to the point of madness, why a moment's foolish action on a single occasion should matter. But we cannot shake off what we so vaguely call conscience, and when I heard you speak so objectively of Madame Henriette's case I thought that perhaps there might be an end to my senseless dwelling on the past, my constant self-accusation, if I could bring myself to speak freely to someone, anyone, about that single day in my life. If I were not an Anglican but a Catholic, the confessional would long ago have offered me an opportunity of release by putting what I have kept silent into words—but that comfort is denied us, and so I make this strange attempt to absolve myself by speaking to you today. I know all this sounds very odd, but you agreed unhesitatingly to my suggestion, and I am grateful.

As I said, I would like to tell you about just one day in my life—all the rest of it seems to me insignificant and would be tedious listening for anyone else. There was nothing in the least out of the ordinary in the course of it until my forty-second year. My parents were rich landlords in Scotland, we owned large factories and leased out land, and in the usual way of the gentry in my country we spent most of the year on our estates but went to London for the season. I met my future husband at a party when I was eighteen. He was a second son of the well-known R family, and had served with the army in India for ten years. We soon married, and led the carefree life of our social circle: three months of the year in London, three months on our estates, and the rest of the time in hotels in Italy, Spain and France. Not the slightest shadow ever clouded our marriage, and we had two sons who are now grown up. When I was forty my husband suddenly died. He had returned from his years in the tropics with a liver complaint, and I lost him within the space of two terrible weeks. My elder son was already in the army, my younger son at university—so I was left entirely alone overnight, and used as I was to affectionate companionship, that loneliness was a torment to me. I felt I could not stay a day longer in the desolate house where every object reminded me of the tragic loss of my beloved husband, and so I decided that while my sons were still unmarried, I would spend much of the next few years travelling.

In essence, I regarded my life from that moment on as entirely pointless and useless. The man with whom I had shared every hour and every thought for twenty-three years was dead, my children did not need me, I was afraid of casting a cloud over their youth with my sadness and melancholy—but I wished and desired nothing any more for myself. I went first to Paris, where I visited shops and museums out of sheer boredom, but the city and everything else were strange to me, and I avoided company because I could not bear the polite sympathy in other people's eyes when they saw that I was in mourning. How those months of aimless, apathetic wandering passed I can hardly say now; all I know is that I had a constant wish to die, but not the strength to hasten the end I longed for so ardently.

In my second year of mourning, that is to say my forty-second year, I had come to Monte Carlo at the end of March in my unacknowledged flight from time that had become worthless and was more than I could deal with. To be honest, I came there out of tedium, out of the painful emptiness of the heart that wells up like nausea, and at least tries to nourish itself on small external stimulations. The less I felt in myself, the more strongly I was drawn to those places where the whirligig of life spins most rapidly. If you are experiencing nothing yourself, the passionate restlessness of others stimulates the nervous system like music or drama.

That was why I quite often went to the casino. I was intrigued to see the tide of delight or dismay ebbing and flowing in other people's faces, while my own heart lay at such a low ebb. In addition my husband, although never frivolous, had enjoyed visiting such places now and then, and with a certain unintentional piety I remained faithful to his old habits. And there in the casino began those twenty-four hours that were more thrilling than any game, and disturbed my life for years.

I had dined at midday with the Duchess of M, a relation of my family, and after supper I didn't feel tired enough to go to bed yet. So I went to the gaming hall, strolled among the tables without playing myself, and watched the mingled company in my own special way. I repeat, in my own special way, the way my dead husband had once taught me when, tired of watching, I complained of the tedium of looking at the same faces all the time: the wizened old women who sat for hours before venturing a single jetton, the cunning professionals, the *demi-mondaines* of the card table, all that dubious chance-met company which, as you'll know, is considerably less picturesque and romantic than it is always painted in silly novels, where you might think it the *fleur d'élégance* and aristocracy of Europe. Yet the casino of twenty years ago, when real money, visible and tangible, was staked and crackling banknotes, gold Napoleons and pert little five-franc pieces rained down, was far more attractive than it is today, with a solid set of folk on Cook's

Tours tediously frittering their characterless gaming chips away in the grand, fashionably renovated citadel of gambling. Even then, however, I found little to stimulate me in the similarity of so many indifferent faces, until one day my husband, whose private passion was for chiromancy—that's to say, divination by means of the hand—showed me an unusual method of observation which proved much more interesting, exciting and fascinating than standing casually around. In this method you never look at a face, only at the rectangle of the table, and on the table only at the hands of the players and the way they move. I don't know if you yourself ever happen to have looked at the green table, just that green square with the ball in the middle of it tumbling drunkenly from number to number, while fluttering scraps of paper, round silver and gold coins fall like seedcorn on the spaces of the board, to be raked briskly away by the croupier or shovelled over to the winner like harvest bounty. If you watch from that angle, only the hands change—all those pale, moving, waiting hands around the green table, all emerging from the ever-different caverns of the players' sleeves, each a beast of prey ready to leap, each varying in shape and colour, some bare, others laden with rings and clinking bracelets, some hairy like wild beasts, some damp and writhing like eels, but all of them tense, vibrating with a vast impatience. I could never help thinking of a racecourse where the excited horses are held back with difficulty on the starting line in case they gallop away too soon; they quiver and buck and rear in just the same way. You can tell everything from those hands, from the way they wait, they grab, they falter; you can see an avaricious character in a claw-like hand and a spendthrift in a relaxed one, a calculating man in a steady hand and a desperate man in a trembling wrist; hundreds of characters betray themselves instantly in their way of handling money, crumpling or nervously creasing notes, or letting it lie as the ball goes round, their hands now weary and exhausted. Human beings give themselves away in play—a cliché, I know, but I would say their own hands give them away even more clearly in gambling.

Almost all gamblers soon learn to control their faces—from the neck up, they wear the cold mask of impassivity; they force away the lines around their mouths and hide their agitation behind clenched teeth, they refuse to let their eyes show uneasiness, they smooth the twitching muscles of the face into an artificial indifference, obeying the dictates of polite conduct. But just because their whole attention is concentrated on controlling the face, the most visible part of the body, they forget their hands, they forget that some people are watching nothing but those hands, guessing from them what the lips curved in a smile, the intentionally indifferent glances wish to conceal. Meanwhile, however, their hands shamelessly reveal their innermost secrets. For a moment inevitably comes when all those carefully controlled, apparently relaxed fingers drop their elegant negligence. In the pregnant moment when the roulette ball drops into its shallow compartment and the winning number is called, in that second every one of those hundred or five hundred hands spontaneously makes a very personal, very individual movement of primitive instinct. And if an observer like me, particularly well-informed as I was because of my husband's hobby, is used to watching the hands perform in this arena, it is more exciting even than music or drama to see so many different temperaments suddenly erupt. I simply cannot tell you how many thousands of varieties of hands there are: wild beasts with hairy, crooked fingers raking in the money like spiders; nervous, trembling hands with pale nails that scarcely dare to touch it; hands noble and vulgar, hands brutal and shy, cunning hands, hands that seem to be stammering—but each of these pairs of hands is different, the expression of an individual life, with the exception of the four or five pairs of hands belonging to the croupiers. Those hands are entirely mechanical, and with their objective, businesslike, totally detached precision function like the clicking metal mechanism of a gas meter by comparison with the extreme liveliness of the gamblers' hands. But even those sober hands produce a surprising effect when contrasted with their racing, passionate fellows; you might say they were wearing a different uniform, like policemen in the middle of a surging, agitated riot. And then there is the personal incentive of getting to know the many different habits and passions of individual pairs of hands within a few days; by then I had always made acquaintances among them and divided them, as if they were human beings, into those I liked and those I did not. I found the greed and incivility of some so repulsive that I would always avert my gaze from them, as if from some impropriety. Every new pair of hands to appear on the table, however, was a fresh experience and a source of curiosity to me; I often quite forgot to look at the face which, surrounded by a collar high above them, was set impassively on top of an evening shirt or a glittering décolletage, a cold social mask.

When I entered the gaming hall that evening, passed two crowded tables, reached a third, and was taking out a few coins, I was surprised to hear a very strange sound directly opposite me in the wordless, tense pause that seems to echo with silence and always sets in as the ball, moving sluggishly, hesitates between two numbers. It was a cracking, clicking sound like the snapping of joints. I looked across the table in amazement. And then I saw—I was truly startled!—I saw two hands such as I had never seen before, left and right clutching each other like doggedly determined animals, bracing and extending together and against one another with such heightened tension that the fingers' joints cracked with a dry sound like a nut cracking open. They were hands of rare beauty, unusually long, unusually slender, yet taut and muscular—very white, the nails pale at their tips, gently curving and the colour of mother-of-pearl. I kept watching them all evening, indeed I kept marvelling at those extraordinary, those positively unique hands—but what surprised and alarmed me so much at first was the passion in them, their crazily impassioned expressiveness, the convulsive way they wrestled with and supported each other. I knew at once that I was seeing a human being overflowing with emotion, forcing his passion into his fingertips lest it tear him apart. And then—just as the ball, with a dry click, fell into place in the wheel and the croupier called out the number—at that very moment the two hands suddenly fell apart like a pair of animals struck by a single bullet. They dropped, both of them, truly dead and not just exhausted; they dropped with so graphic an expression of lethargy, disappointment, instant extinction, as if all was finally over, that I can find no words to describe it. For never before or since have I seen such speaking hands, hands in which every muscle was eloquent and passion broke almost tangibly from the pores of the skin. They lay on the green table for a moment like jellyfish cast up by the sea, flat and dead. Then one of them, the right hand, began laboriously raising itself again, beginning with the fingertips; it quivered, drew back, turned on itself, swayed, circled, and suddenly reached nervously for a jetton, rolling the token uncertainly like a little wheel between the tips of thumb and middle finger. And suddenly it arched, like a panther arching its back, and shot forwards, positively spitting the hundred-franc jetton out on the middle of the black space. At once, as if at a signal, the inactive, slumbering left hand was seized by excitement too; it rose, slunk, crawled over to its companion hand, which was trembling now as if exhausted by throwing down the jetton, and both hands lay there together trembling, the joints of their fingers working away soundlessly on the table, tapping slightly together like teeth chattering in a fever—no, I had never seen hands of such expressive eloquence, or such spasmodic agitation and tension. Everything else in this vaulted room, the hum from the other halls around it, the calls of the croupiers crying their wares like market traders, the movement of people and of the ball itself which now, dropped from above, was leaping like a thing possessed around the circular cage that was smooth as parquet flooring—all this diversity of whirling, swirling impressions flitting across the nerves suddenly seemed to me dead and dull compared to those two trembling, breathing, gasping, waiting, freezing hands, that extraordinary pair of hands which somehow held me spellbound.

But finally I could no longer refrain; I had to see the human being, the face to which those magical hands belonged, and fearfully—yes,

I do mean fearfully, for I was afraid of those hands!—my gaze slowly travelled up the gambler's sleeves and narrow shoulders. And once again I had a shock, for his face spoke the same fantastically extravagant language of extremes as the hands, shared the same terrible grimness of expression and delicate, almost feminine beauty. I had never seen such a face before, a face so transported and utterly beside itself, and I had plenty of opportunity to observe it at leisure as if it were a mask, an unseeing sculpture: those possessed eyes did not turn to right or left for so much as a second, their pupils were fixed and black beneath the widely opened lids, dead glass balls reflecting that other mahogany-coloured ball rolling and leaping about the roulette wheel in such foolish high spirits. Never, I repeat, had I seen so intense or so fascinating a face. It belonged to a young man of perhaps twenty-four, it was fine-drawn, delicate, rather long and very expressive. Like the hands, it did not seem entirely masculine, but resembled the face of a boy passionately absorbed in a game—although I noticed none of that until later, for now the face was entirely veiled by an expression of greed and of madness breaking out. The thin mouth, thirsting and open, partly revealed the teeth: you could see them ten paces away, grinding feverishly while the parted lips remained rigid. A light-blond lock of hair clung damply to his forehead, tumbling forwards like the hair of a man falling, and a tic fluttered constantly around his nostrils as if little waves were invisibly rippling beneath the skin. The bowed head was moving instinctively further and further forwards; you felt it was being swept away with the whirling of the little ball, and now, for the first time, I understood the convulsive pressure of the hands. Only by the intense strain of pressing them together did the body, falling from its central axis, contrive to keep its balance. I had never—I must repeat it yet again—I had never seen a face in which passion showed so openly, with such shamelessly naked animal feeling, and I stared at that face, as fascinated and spellbound by its obsession as was its own gaze by the leaping, twitching movement of the circling ball. From that moment on I noticed nothing else in the room, everything seemed to me dull, dim and blurred, dark by comparison with the flashing fire of that face, and disregarding everyone else present I spent perhaps an hour watching that one man and every movement he made: the bright light that sparkled in his eyes, the convulsive knot of his hands loosening as if blown apart by an explosion, the parting of the shaking fingers as the croupier pushed twenty gold coins towards their eager grasp. At that moment the face looked suddenly bright and very young, the lines in it smoothed out, the eyes began to gleam, the convulsively bowed body straightened lightly, easily—he suddenly sat there as relaxed as a horseman, borne up by the sense of triumph, fingers toying lovingly, idly with the round coins, clinking them together, making them dance and jingle playfully. Then he turned his head restlessly again, surveyed the green table as if with the flaring nostrils of a young hound seeking the right scent, and suddenly, with one quick movement, placed all the coins on one rectangular space. At once the watchfulness, the tension returned. Once more the little waves, rippling galvanically, spread out from his lips, once again his hands were clasped, the boyish face disappeared behind greedy expectation until the spasmodic tension exploded and fell apart in disappointment: the face that had just looked boyish turned faded, wan and old, light disappeared from the burnt-out eyes, and all this within the space of a second as the ball came to rest on the wrong number. He had lost; he stared at the ball for a few seconds almost like an idiot, as if he did not understand, but as the croupier began calling to whip up interest, his fingers took out a few coins again. But his certainty was gone; first he put the coins on one space, then, thinking better of it, on another, and when the ball had begun to roll his trembling hand, on a sudden impulse, quickly added two crumpled banknotes.

This alternation of up and down, loss and gain, continued without a break for about an hour, and during that hour I did not, even for a moment, take my fascinated gaze from that ever-changing face and all the passions ebbing and flowing over it. I kept my eyes fixed on those magical hands, their every muscle graphically reflecting the whole range of the man's feelings as they rose and fell like a fountain. I had never watched the face of an actor in the theatre as intently as I watched this one, seeing the constant, changing shades of emotion flitting over it like light and shade moving over a landscape. I had never immersed myself so wholeheartedly in a game as I did in the reflection of this stranger's excitement. If someone had been observing me at that moment he would surely have taken my steely gaze for a state of hypnosis, and indeed my benumbed perception was something like that—I simply could not look away from the play of those features, and everything else in the room, the lights, the laughter, the company and its glances, merely drifted vaguely around me, a yellow mist with that face in the middle of it, a flame among flames. I heard nothing, I felt nothing, I did not notice people coming forwards beside me, other hands suddenly reaching out like feelers, putting down money or picking it up; I did not see the ball or hear the croupier's voice, yet I saw it all as if I were dreaming, exaggerated as in a concave mirror by the excitement and extravagance of those moving hands. For I did not have to look at the roulette wheel to know whether the ball had come to rest on red or black, whether it was still rolling or beginning to falter. Every stage of the game, loss and gain, hope and disappointment, was fierily reflected in the nerves and movements of that passionate face.

But then came a terrible moment—something that I had been vaguely fearing all this time, something that had weighed like a gathering thunderstorm on my tense nerves, and now suddenly ripped through them. Yet again the ball had fallen back into the shallow depression with that dry little click, yet again came the tense moment when two hundred lips held their breath until the croupier's voice announced the winning number—this time it was zero—while he zealously raked in the clinking coins and crackling notes from all sides. At that moment those two convulsively clasped hands made a particularly terrifying movement, leaping up as if to catch something that wasn't there and then dropping to the table again exhausted, with no strength in them, only the force of gravity flooding back. Then, however, they suddenly came to life yet again, feverishly retreating from the table to the man's own body, clambering up his torso like wild cats, up and down, left and right, nervously trying all his pockets to see if some forgotten coin might not have slipped into one of them. But they always came back empty, and the pointless, useless search began again ever more frantically, while the roulette wheel went on circling and others continued playing, while coins clinked, chairs were shifted on the floor, and all the small sounds, put together a hundredfold, filled the room with a humming note. I trembled, shaking with horror; I felt it all as clearly as if my own fingers were rummaging desperately for a coin in the pockets and folds of my creased garments. And suddenly, with a single abrupt movement, the man rose to his feet opposite me, like a man standing up when he suddenly feels unwell and must rise if he is not to suffocate. His chair crashed to the floor behind him. Without even noticing, without paying any attention to his surprised and abashed neighbours as they avoided his swaying figure, he stumbled away from the table.

The sight petrified me. For I knew at once where the man was going: to his death. A man getting to his feet like that was not on his way back to an inn, a wine bar, a wife, a railway carriage, to any form of life at all, he was plunging straight into the abyss. Even the most hardened spectator in that hellish gaming hall could surely have seen that the man had nothing to fall back on, not at home or in a bank or with a family, but had been sitting here with the last of his money, staking his life, and was now staggering away somewhere else, anywhere, but undoubtedly out of that life. I had feared all along, I had sensed from the first moment, as if by magic, that more than loss or gain was staked on the game, yet now it struck me like a bolt of dark lightning to see the life suddenly go out of his eyes and death cast its pale shadow over his still living face. Instinctively—affected as I was by his own graphic gestures—I clutched at myself while the man tore himself away from his place and staggered out, for his own uncertain gait was now transferred to my own body just as his tension had entered my veins and nerves. Then I was positively wrenched away, I had to follow him; my feet moved without my own volition. It was entirely unconscious, I did not do it of my own accord, it was something happening to me when, taking no notice of anyone, feeling nothing myself, I went out into the corridor leading to the doors.

He was standing at the cloakroom counter, and the attendant had brought him his coat. But his arms would no longer obey him, so the helpful attendant laboriously eased them into the sleeves, as if he were paralysed. I saw him automatically put his hand in his waistcoat pocket to give the man a tip, but his fingers emerged empty. Then he suddenly seemed to remember everything, awkwardly stammered something to the cloakroom attendant, and as before moved forwards abruptly and then stumbled like a drunk down the casino steps, where the attendant stood briefly watching him go, with a smile that was at first contemptuous and then understanding.

His bearing shook me so much that I felt ashamed to have seen it. Involuntarily I turned aside, embarrassed to have watched a stranger's despair as if I were in a theatre—but then that vague fear suddenly took me out of myself once again. Quickly, I retrieved my coat, and thinking nothing very definite, purely mechanically and compulsively I hurried out into the dark after the stranger."

Mrs C interrupted her story for a moment. She had been sitting calmly opposite me, speaking almost without a break with her characteristic tranquil objectivity, as only someone who had prepared and carefully organised the events of her tale in advance could speak. Now, for the first time, she stopped, hesitated, and then suddenly broke off and turned directly to me.

"I promised you and myself," she began, rather unevenly, "to tell you all the facts with perfect honesty. Now I must ask you to believe in my honesty, and not assume that my conduct had any ulterior motives. I might not be ashamed of them today, but in this case such suspicions would be entirely unfounded. And I must emphasise that, when I hurried after that ruined gambler in the street, I had certainly not fallen in love with him—I did not think of him as a man at all, and indeed I was over forty myself at the time and had never looked at another man since my husband's death. All that part of my life was finally over; I tell you this explicitly, and I must, or you would not understand the full horror of what happened later. On the other hand, it's true that I would find it difficult to give a clear name to the feeling that drew me so compulsively after the unfortunate man; there was curiosity in it, but above all a dreadful fear, or rather a fear of something dreadful, something I had felt invisibly enveloping the young man like a miasma from the first moment. But such feelings can't be dissected and taken apart, if only because they come over one too compulsively, too fast, too spontaneously—very likely mine expressed nothing but the instinct to help with which one snatches back a child about to run into the road in front of a motor car. How else can we explain why non-swimmers will jump off a bridge to help a drowning man? They are simply impelled to do it as if by magic, some other will pushes them off the bridge before they have time to consider the pointless bravery of their conduct properly; and in just the same way, without thinking, without conscious reflection, I hurried after the unfortunate young man out of the gaming room, to the casino doors, out of the doors and on to the terrace.

And I am sure that neither you nor any other feeling human being with his eyes open could have withstood that fearful curiosity, for a more disturbing sight can hardly be imagined than the way the gambler, who must have been twenty-four at the most but moved as laboriously as an old man and was swaying like a drunk, dragged himself shakily and disjointedly down the steps to the terrace beside the road. Once there, his body dropped on to a bench, limp as a sack. Again I shuddered as I sensed, from that movement, that the man had reached the end of his tether. Only a dead man or one with nothing left to keep him alive drops like that. His head, fallen to one side, leant back over the bench, his arms hung limp and shapeless to the ground, and in the dim illumination of the faintly flickering street lights any passer-by would have thought he had been shot. And it was like that—I can't explain why the vision suddenly came into my mind, but all of a sudden it was there, real enough to touch, terrifying and terrible—it was like that, as a man who had been shot, that I saw him before me at that moment, and I knew for certain that he had a revolver in his pocket, and tomorrow he would be found lying lifeless and covered with blood on this or some other bench. For he had dropped like a stone falling into a deep chasm, never to stop until it reaches the bottom: I never saw such a physical expression of exhaustion and despair.

So now, consider my situation: I was standing twenty or thirty paces from the bench and the motionless, broken man on it, with no idea what to do, on the one hand wishing to help, on the other restrained by my innate and inbred reluctance to speak to a strange man in the street. The gaslights flickered dimly in the overcast sky, few figures hurried past, for it was nearly midnight and I was almost entirely alone in the park with this suicidal figure. Five or ten times I had already pulled myself together and approached him, but shame or perhaps that deeper premonitory instinct, the idea that falling men are likely to pull those who come to their aid down with them, made me withdraw—and in the midst of this indecision I was clearly aware of the pointless, ridiculous aspect of the situation. Nonetheless, I could neither speak nor turn away, I could not do anything but I could not leave him. And I hope you will believe me when I say that for perhaps an hour, an endless hour, I walked indecisively up and down that terrace, while time was divided up by thousands of little sounds from the breaking waves of the invisible sea—so shaken and transfixed was I by the idea of the annihilation of a human being.

Yet I could not summon up the courage to say a word or make a move, and I would have waited like that half the night, or perhaps in the end my wiser self-interest would have prevailed on me to go home, and indeed I think I had already made up my mind to leave that helpless bundle of misery lying there—when a superior force put an end to my indecision. It began to rain. All evening the wind had been piling up heavy spring clouds full of moisture above the sea, lungs and heart felt the pressure of the lowering sky, and now drops suddenly began to splash down. Soon a heavy rain was falling in wet torrents blown about by the wind. I instinctively sheltered under the projecting roof of a kiosk, but although I put up my umbrella gusts of wind kept blowing the rain on my dress. I felt the cold mist thrown up by the falling raindrops spray my face and hands.

But—and it was such a terrible sight that even now, two decades later, the memory still constricts my throat—but in the middle of this cloudburst the unfortunate man stayed perfectly still on his bench, never moving. Water was gurgling and dripping from all the eaves; you could hear the rumble of carriages from the city; people with their coat collars turned up hurried past to right and to left; all living creatures ducked in alarm, fled, ran, sought shelter; man and beast felt universal fear of the torrential element—but that black heap of humanity on the bench did not stir or move. I told you before that he had the magical gift of graphically expressing everything he felt in movement and gesture. But nothing, nothing on earth could convey despair, total self-surrender, death in the midst of life to such shattering effect as his immobility, the way he sat there in the falling rain, not moving, feeling nothing, too tired to rise and walk the few steps to the shelter of the projecting roof, utterly indifferent to his own existence. No sculptor, no poet, not Michelangelo or Dante has ever brought that sense of ultimate despair, of ultimate human misery so feelingly to my mind as the sight of that living figure letting the watery element drench him, too weary and uncaring to make a single move to protect himself.

That made me act; I couldn't help it. Pulling myself together, I ran the gauntlet of the lashing rain and shook the dripping bundle of humanity to make him get up from the bench. 'Come along!' I seized his arm. Something stared up at me, with difficulty. Something in him seemed to be slowly preparing to move, but he did not understand. 'Come along!' Once again, almost angry now, I tugged at his wet sleeve. Then he slowly stood up, devoid of will and swaying. 'What do you want?' he asked, and I could not reply, for I myself had no idea where to take him—just away from the cold downpour where he had been sitting so senselessly, suicidally, in the grip of deep despair. I did not let go of his arm but dragged the man on, since he had no will of his own, to the sales kiosk where the narrow, projecting roof at least partly sheltered him from the raging attack of the stormy rain as the wind tossed it wildly back and forth. That was all I wanted, I had nothing else in mind, just to get him somewhere dry, under a roof. As yet I had thought no further.

So we stood side by side on that narrow strip of dry ground, the wall of the kiosk behind us and above us only the roof, which was not large enough, for the insatiable rain insidiously came in under it as sudden gusts of wind flung wet, chilly showers over our clothes and into our faces. The situation became intolerable. I could hardly stand there any longer beside this dripping wet stranger. On the other hand, having dragged him over here I couldn't just leave him and walk away without a word. Something had to be done, and gradually I forced myself to think clearly. It would be best, I thought, to send him home in a cab and then go home myself; he would be able to look after himself tomorrow. So as he stood beside me gazing fixedly out at the turbulent night I asked, 'Where do you live?'

'I'm not staying anywhere… I only arrived from Nice this morning… we can't go to my place.'

I did not immediately understand this last remark. Only later did I realise that the man took me for… for a *demi-mondaine*, one of the many women who haunt the casino by night, hoping to extract a little money from lucky gamblers or drunks. After all, what else was he to think, for only now that I tell you about it do I feel all the improbability, indeed the fantastic nature of my situation—what else was he to think of me? The way I had pulled him off the bench and dragged him away as if it were perfectly natural was certainly not the conduct of a lady. But this idea did not occur to me at once. Only later, only too late did his terrible misapprehension dawn upon me, or I would never have said what I did next, in words that were bound to reinforce his impression. 'Then we'll just take a room in a hotel. You can't stay here. You must get under cover somewhere.'

Now I understood his painful misunderstanding, for he did not turn towards me but merely rejected the idea with a certain contempt in his voice: 'I don't need a room; I don't need anything now. Don't bother, you won't get anything out of me. You've picked the wrong man. I have no money.'

This too was said in a dreadful tone, with shattering indifference, and the way he stood there dripping wet and leaning against the wall, slack and exhausted to the bone, shook me so much that I had no time to waste on taking petty offence. I merely sensed, as I had from the first moment when I saw him stagger from the gaming hall, as I had felt all through this improbable hour, that here was a human being, a young, living, breathing human being on the very brink of death, and I must save him. I came closer.

'Never mind money, come along! You can't stay here. I'll get you under cover. Don't worry about anything, just come with me.'

He turned his head and I felt, while the rain drummed round us with a hollow sound and the eaves cast water down to splash at our feet, that for the first time he was trying to make out my face in the dark. His body seemed to be slowly shaking off its lethargy too.

'As you like,' he said, giving in. 'It's all one to me… after all, why not? Let's go.' I put up my umbrella, he moved to my side and took my arm. I felt this sudden intimacy uncomfortable; indeed, it horrified me. I was alarmed to the depths of my heart. But I did not feel bold enough to ask him to refrain, for if I rejected him now he would fall into the bottomless abyss, and everything I had tried to do so far would be in vain. We walked the few steps back to the casino, and only now did it strike me that I had no idea what to do with him. I had better take him to a hotel, I thought quickly, and give him money to spend the night there and go home in the morning. I was not thinking beyond that. And as the carriages were now rapidly drawing up outside the casino I hailed a cab and we got in. When the driver asked where to, I couldn't think what to say at first. But realising that the drenched, dripping man beside me would not be welcome in any of the best hotels—on the other hand, genuinely inexperienced as I was, with nothing else in mind—I just told the cabby, 'Some simple hotel, anywhere!'

The driver, indifferent, and wet with rain himself, drove his horses on. The stranger beside me said not a word, the wheels rattled, the rain splashed heavily against the windows, and I felt as if I were travelling with a corpse in that dark, lightless rectangular space, in a vehicle like a coffin. I tried to think of something to say to relieve the strange, silent horror of our presence there together, but I could think of nothing. After a few minutes the cab stopped. I got out first and paid the driver, who shut the door after us as if drunk with sleep. We were at the door of a small hotel that was unknown to me, with a glass porch above us providing a tiny area of shelter from the rain, which was still lashing the impenetrable night around us with ghastly monotony.

The stranger, giving way to his inertia, had instinctively leant against the wall, and water was dripping from his wet hat and crumpled garments. He stood there like a drunk who has been fished out of the river, still dazed, and a channel of water trickling down from him formed around the small patch of ground where he stood. But he made not the slightest effort to shake himself or take off the hat from which raindrops kept running over his forehead and face. He stood there entirely apathetically, and I cannot tell you how his broken demeanour moved me.

But something had to be done. I put my hand into my bag. 'Here are a hundred francs,' I said. 'Take a room and go back to Nice tomorrow.'

He looked up in astonishment.

'I was watching you in the gaming hall,' I continued urgently, noticing his hesitation. 'I know you've lost everything, and I fear you're well on the way to doing something stupid. There's no shame in accepting help—here, take it!'

But he pushed away my hand with an energy I wouldn't have expected in him. 'You are very good,' he said, 'but don't waste your money. There's no help for me now. Whether I sleep tonight or not makes not the slightest difference. It will all be over tomorrow anyway. There's no help for me.'

'No, you must take it,' I urged. 'You'll see things differently tomorrow. Go upstairs and sleep on it. Everything will look different in daylight.'

But when I tried to press the money on him again he pushed my hand away almost violently. 'Don't,' he repeated dully. 'There's no point in it. Better to do it out of doors than leave blood all over their room here. A hundred or even a thousand francs won't help me. I'd just go to the gaming hall again tomorrow with the last few francs, and I wouldn't stop until they were all gone. Why begin again? I've had enough.'

You have no idea how that dull tone of voice went to my heart, but think of it: a couple of inches from you stands a young, bright, living, breathing human being, and you know that if you don't do your utmost, then in a few hours time this thinking, speaking, breathing specimen of youth will be a corpse. And now I felt a desire like rage, like fury, to overcome his senseless resistance. I grasped his arm. 'That's enough stupid talk. You go up these steps now and take a room, and I'll come in the morning and take you to the station. You must get away from here, you must go home tomorrow, and I won't rest until I've seen you sitting in the train with a ticket. You can't throw your life away so young just because you've lost a couple of hundred francs, or a couple of thousand. That's cowardice, silly hysteria concocted from anger and bitterness. You'll see that I'm right tomorrow!'

'Tomorrow!' he repeated in a curiously gloomy, ironic tone. 'Tomorrow! If you knew where I'd be tomorrow! I wish I knew myself—I'm mildly curious to find out. No, go home, my dear, don't bother about me and don't waste your money.'

But I wasn't giving up now. It had become like a mania obsessing me. I took his hand by force and pressed the banknote into it. 'You will take this money and go in at once!' And so saying I stepped firmly up to the door and rang the bell. 'There, now I've rung, and the porter will be here in a minute. Go in and lie down. I'll be outside here at nine tomorrow to take you straight to the station. Don't worry about anything, I'll see to what's necessary to get you home. But now go to bed, have a good sleep, and don't think of anything else!'

At that moment the key turned inside the door and the porter opened it.

'Come on, then!' said my companion suddenly, in a harsh, firm embittered voice, and I felt his fingers span my wrist in an iron grip. I was alarmed… so greatly alarmed, so paralysed, struck as if by lightning, that all my composure vanished. I wanted to resist, tear myself away, but my will seemed numbed, and I… well, you will understand… I was ashamed to struggle with a stranger in front of the porter, who stood there waiting impatiently. And so, suddenly, I was inside the hotel. I wanted to speak, say something, but my throat would not obey me… and his hand lay heavy and commanding on my arm. I vaguely felt it draw me as if unawares up a flight of steps—a key clicked in a lock. And suddenly I was alone with this stranger in a strange room, in some hotel whose name I do not know to this day."

*

Mrs C stopped again, and suddenly rose to her feet. It seemed that her voice would not obey her any more. She went over to the window and looked out in silence for some minutes, or perhaps she was just resting her forehead on the cold pane; I did not have the courage to look closely, for I found it painful to see the old lady so agitated. So I sat quite still, asking no questions, making no sound, and waited until she came back, stepping firmly, and sat down opposite me.

"Well—now the most difficult part is told. And I hope you will believe me when I assure you yet again, when I swear by all that is sacred to me, by my honour and my children, that up to that moment no idea of any… any relationship with the stranger had entered my mind, that I really had been suddenly plunged into this situation against my own will, indeed entirely unawares, as if I had fallen through a trapdoor from the level path of my existence. I have promised to be honest with you and with myself, so I repeat again that I embarked on this tragic venture merely through a rather overwrought desire to help, not through any other, any personal feeling, quite without any wishes or forebodings.

You must spare me the tale of what happened in that room that night; I myself have forgotten not a moment of it, and I never will. I spent it wrestling with another human being for his life, and I repeat, it was a battle of life and death. I felt only too clearly, with every fibre of my being, that this stranger, already half-lost, was clutching at his last chance with all the avid passion of a man threatened by death. He clung to me like one who already feels the abyss yawning beneath him. For my part, I summoned everything in me to save him by all the means at my command. A human being may know such an hour perhaps only once in his life, and out of millions, again, perhaps only one will know it—but for that terrible chance I myself would never have guessed how ardently, desperately, with what boundless greed a man given up for lost will still suck at every red drop of life. Kept safe for twenty years from all the demonic forces of existence, I would never have understood how magnificently, how fantastically Nature can merge hot and cold, life and death, delight and despair together in a few brief moments. And that night was so full of conflict and of talk, of passion and anger and hatred, with tears of entreaty and intoxication, that it seemed to me to last a thousand years, and we two human beings who fell entwined into its chasm, one of us in frenzy, the other unsuspecting, emerged from that mortal tumult changed, completely transformed, senses and emotions transmuted.

But I don't want to talk about that. I cannot and will not describe it. However, I must just tell you of the extraordinary moment when I woke in the morning from a leaden sleep, from nocturnal depths such as I had never known before. It took me a long time to open my eyes, and the first thing I saw was a strange ceiling over me, and then, looking further an entirely strange, unknown, ugly room. I had no idea how I came to be there. At first I told myself I must still be dreaming, an unusually lucid, transparent dream into which I had passed from my dull, confused slumber—but the sparkling bright sunshine outside the windows was unmistakably genuine, the light of morning, and the sounds of the street echoed from below, the rattle of carriages, the ringing of tram bells, the noise of people—so now I knew that I was awake and not dreaming. I instinctively sat up to get my bearings, and then—as my glance moved sideways—then I saw, and I can never describe my alarm to you, I saw a stranger sleeping in the broad bed beside me… a strange, perfectly strange, half-naked, unknown man… oh, I know there's no real way to describe the awful realisation; it struck me with such terrible force that I sank back powerless. But not in a kindly faint, not falling unconscious, far from it: with lightning speed, everything became as clear to me as it was inexplicable, and all I wanted was to die of revulsion and shame at suddenly finding myself in an unfamiliar bed in a decidedly shady hotel, with a complete stranger beside me. I still remember how my heart missed a beat, how I held my breath as if that would extinguish my life and above all my consciousness, which grasped everything yet understood none of it.

I shall never know how long I lay like that, all my limbs icy cold: the dead must lie rigid in their coffins in much the same way. All I know is that I had closed my eyes and was praying to God, to some heavenly power, that this might not be true, might not be real. But my sharpened senses would not let me deceive myself, I could hear people talking in the next room, water running, footsteps shuffling along the corridor outside, and each of these signs mercilessly proved that my senses were terribly alert.

How long this dreadful condition lasted I cannot say: such moments are outside the measured time of ordinary life. But suddenly another fear came over me, swift and terrible: the stranger whose name I did not know might wake up and speak to me. And I knew at once there was only one thing to do: I must get dressed and make my escape before he woke. I must not let him set eyes on me again, I must not speak to him again. I must save myself before it was too late, go away, away, away, back to some kind of life of my own, to my hotel, I must leave this pernicious place, leave this country, never meet him again, never look him in the eye, have no witnesses, no accusers, no one who knew. The idea dispelled my faintness: very cautiously, with the furtive movements of a thief, I inched out of bed (for I was desperate to make no noise) and groped my way over to my clothes. I dressed very carefully, trembling all the time lest he might wake up, and then I had finished, I had done it. Only my hat lay at the foot of the bed on the far side of the room, and then, as I tiptoed over to pick it up—I couldn't help it, at that moment I had to cast another glance at the face of the stranger who had fallen into my life like a stone dropping off a window sill. I meant it to be just one glance, but it was curious—the strange young man who lay sleeping there really was a stranger to me. At first I did not recognise his face from yesterday. The impassioned, tense, desperately distressed features of the mortally agitated man might have been entirely extinguished—this man's face was not the same, but was an utterly childlike, utterly boyish face that positively radiated purity and cheerfulness. The lips, so grim yesterday as he clenched his teeth on them, were dreaming, had fallen softly apart, half-curving in a smile; the fair hair curled gently over the smooth forehead, the breath passed from his chest over his body at repose like the mild rippling of waves.

Perhaps you may remember that I told you earlier I had never before seen greed and passion expressed with such outrageous extravagance by any human being as by that stranger at the gaming table. And I tell you now that I had never, even in children whose baby slumbers sometimes cast an angelic aura of cheerfulness around them, seen such an expression of brightness, of truly blissful sleep. The uniquely graphic nature of that face showed all its feelings, at present the paradisaical easing of all internal heaviness, a sense of freedom and salvation. At this surprising sight all my own fear and horror fell from me like a heavy black cloak—I was no longer ashamed, no, I was almost glad. The terrible and incomprehensible thing that had happened suddenly made sense to me; I was happy, I was proud to think that but for my dedicated efforts the beautiful, delicate young man lying here carefree and quiet as a flower would have been found somewhere on a rocky slope, his body shattered and bloody, his face ruined, lifeless, with staring eyes. I had saved him; he was safe. And now I looked—I cannot put it any other way—I looked with maternal feeling at the man I had reborn into life more painfully than I bore my own children. In the middle of that shabby, threadbare room in a distasteful, grubby house of assignation, I was overcome by the kind of emotion—ridiculous as you may find it put into words—the kind of emotion one might have in church, a rapturous sense of wonder and sanctification. From the most dreadful moment of a whole life there now grew a second life, amazing and overwhelming, coming in sisterly fashion to meet me.

Had I made too much noise moving about? Had I involuntarily exclaimed out loud? I don't know, but suddenly the sleeping man opened his eyes. I flinched back in alarm. He looked round in surprise—just as I had done before earlier, and now he in his own turn seemed to be emerging with difficulty from great depths of confusion. His gaze wandered intently round the strange, unfamiliar room and then fell on me in amazement. But before he spoke, or could quite pull himself together, I had control of myself. I did not let him say a word, I allowed no questions, no confidences; nothing of yesterday or of last night was to be explained, discussed or mulled over again.

'I have to go now,' I told him quickly. 'You stay here and get dressed. I'll meet you at twelve at the entrance to the casino, and I'll take care of everything else.'

And before he could say a word in reply I fled, to be rid of the sight of the room, and without turning back left the hotel whose name I did not know, any more than I knew the name of the stranger with whom I had just spent the night."

Mrs C interrupted her narrative for a moment again, but all the strain and distress had gone from her voice: like a carriage that toils uphill with difficulty but then, having reached the top, rolls swiftly and smoothly down the other side, her account now proceeded more easily:

"Well—so I made haste to my hotel through the morning light of the streets. The drop in the temperature had driven all the hazy mists from the sky above, just as my own distress had been dispelled. For remember what I told you earlier: I had given up my own life entirely after my husband's death. My children did not need me, I didn't care for my own company, and there's no point in a life lived aimlessly. Now, for the first time, a task had suddenly come my way: I had saved a human being, I had exerted all my powers to snatch him back from destruction. There was only a little left to do—for my task must be completed to the end. So I entered my hotel, ignoring the porter's surprise when he saw me returning at nine in the morning—no shame and chagrin over last night's events oppressed me now, I felt my will to live suddenly revive, and an unexpectedly new sense of the point of my existence flowed warmly through my veins. Once in my room I quickly changed my clothes, putting my mourning aside without thinking (as I noticed only later) and choosing a lighter colour instead, went to the bank to withdraw money, and made haste to the station to find out train times. With a determination that surprised me I also made a few other arrangements. Now there was nothing left to do but ensure the departure from Monte Carlo and ultimate salvation of the man whom fate had cast in my way.

It is true that I needed strength to face him personally. Everything yesterday had taken place in the dark, in a vortex; we had been like two stones thrown out of a torrential stream suddenly striking together; we scarcely knew each other face to face, and I wasn't even sure whether the stranger would recognise me again. Yesterday had been chance, frenzy, a case of two confused people possessed; today I must be more open with him, since I must now confront him in the pitiless light of day with myself, my own face, as a living human being.

But it all turned out much easier than I expected. No sooner had I approached the casino at the appointed hour than a young man jumped up from a bench and made haste towards me. There was something so spontaneous, so childlike, unplanned and happy in his surprise and in each of his eloquent movements; he almost flew to me, the radiance of a joy that was both grateful and deferential in his eyes, which were lowered humbly as soon as they felt my confusion in his presence. Gratitude is so seldom found, and those who are most grateful cannot express it, are silent in their confusion, or ashamed, or sometimes seem ungracious just to conceal their feelings. But in this man, the expression of whose every feeling God, like a mysterious sculptor, had made sensual, beautiful, graphic, his gratitude glowed with radiant passion right through his body. He bent over my hand and remained like that for a moment, the narrow line of his boyish head reverently bowed, respectfully brushing kisses on my fingers; only then did he step back, ask how I was, and look at me most movingly. There was such courtesy in everything he said that within a few minutes the last of my anxiety had gone. As if reflecting the lightening of my own feelings, the landscape around was shining, the spell on it broken: the sea that had been disturbed and angry yesterday lay so calm and bright that every pebble beneath the gently breaking surf gleamed white, and the casino, that den of iniquity, looked up with Moorish brightness to the damask sky that was now swept clean. The kiosk with the projecting roof beneath which the pouring rain had forced us to shelter yesterday proved to be a flower stall; great bunches of flowers and foliage lay there in motley confusion, in white, red, other bright colours and green, and a young girl in a colourful blouse was offering them for sale.

I invited him to lunch with me in a small restaurant, and there the young stranger told me the story of his tragic venture. It confirmed my first presentiment when I had seen his trembling, nervously shaking hands on the green table. He came from an old aristocratic family in the Austrian part of Poland, was destined for a diplomatic career, had studied in Vienna and passed his first examination with great success a month ago. As a reward, and to celebrate the occasion, his uncle, a high-ranking general-staff officer, had taken him to the Prater in a cab, and they went to the races. His uncle was lucky with his bets and won three times running; then they ate supper in an elegant restaurant on the strength of the fat wad of banknotes that were the uncle's gains. Next day, again to mark his success in the examinations, the budding diplomat received a sum of money from his father which was as much as his usual monthly allowance. Two days earlier this would have seemed to him a large sum, but now, seeing how easily his uncle had won money, it struck him as trifling and left him indifferent. Directly after dinner, therefore, he went to the races again, laid wild, frenzied bets, and fortune—or rather misfortune—would have it that he left the Prater after the last race with three times the sum he had brought there. Now a mania for gambling infected him; sometimes he went to the races, sometimes to play in coffee houses and clubs, exhausting his time, his studies, his nerves, and above all his money. He was no longer able to think or to sleep peacefully, and he was quite unable to control himself; one night, coming home from a club where he had lost everything, he found a crumpled banknote forgotten in his waistcoat pocket as he was undressing. There was no holding him; he got dressed again and walked the streets until he found a few people playing dominoes in a coffee house, and sat with them until dawn. On one occasion his married sister came to his aid, paying his debts to moneylenders who were very ready to give credit to the heir of a great and noble name. For a while he was lucky at play again—but then matters went inexorably downhill, and the more he lost, the more urgently did unsecured obligations and fixed-term IOUs require him to find relief by winning. He had long ago pawned his watch and his clothes, and at last a terrible thing happened: he stole two large pearl earrings that she seldom wore from his old aunt's dressing table. He pawned one of the pearls for a large sum, which his gambling quadrupled that evening. But instead of redeeming the pearl he staked all his winnings and lost. At the time when he left Vienna the theft had not yet been discovered, so he pawned the second pearl and on a sudden impulse travelled by train to Monte Carlo to win the fortune he dreamt of at roulette. On arrival he had sold his suitcase, his clothes, his umbrella; he had nothing left but a revolver with four cartridges, and a small cross set with jewels given him by his godmother, Princess X. He did not want to part with the cross, but it too had been sold for fifty francs that afternoon, just to let him try to satisfy his urge by playing for life or death one last time that evening.

He told me all this with the captivating charm of his original and lively nature. And I listened shaken, gripped and much moved, but not for a moment did it occur to me to feel horror that the man at my table was in sober fact a thief. Yesterday, if someone had so much as suggested to me that I, a woman with a blameless past who expected the company she kept to be strictly and conventionally virtuous, would be sitting here on familiar terms with a perfectly strange young man, not much older than my son, who had stolen a pair of pearl earrings, I would have thought he had taken leave of his senses and such a thing was impossible. But I felt no horror at all as he told his tale, for he spoke so naturally and passionately that it seemed more like the account of a fever or illness than a crime. Moreover, the word 'impossible' had suddenly lost its meaning for a woman who had known such an unexpected, torrential experience as I had the night before. In those ten hours, I had come to know immeasurably more about reality than in my preceding forty respectable years of life.

Yet something else about his confession did alarm me, and that was the feverish glint in his eyes, which made all the nerves of his face twitch galvanically as he talked about his passion for gambling. Even speaking of it aroused him, and his face graphically and with terrible clarity illustrated that tension between pleasure and torment. His hands, those beautiful, nervous, slender-jointed hands, instinctively began to turn into preying, hunting, fleeing animal creatures again, just as they did at the gaming table. As he spoke I saw them suddenly trembling, beginning at the wrists, arching and clenching into fists, then opening up to intertwine their fingers once more. And when he confessed to the theft of the pearl earrings they suddenly performed a swift, leaping, quick, thieving movement—I involuntarily jumped. I could see his fingers pouncing on the jewels and swiftly stowing them away in the hollow of his clenched hand. And with nameless horror, I recognised that the very last drop of this man's blood was poisoned by his addiction.

That was the one thing that so shattered and horrified me about his tale, the pitiful enslavement of a young, light-hearted, naturally carefree man to a mad passion. I considered it my prime duty to persuade my unexpected protégé, in friendly fashion, that he must leave Monte Carlo, where the temptation was most dangerous, without delay, he must return to his family this very day, before anyone noticed that the pearl earrings were gone and his future was ruined for ever. I promised him money for his journey and to redeem the jewellery, though only on condition that he left today and swore to me, on his honour, never to touch a card or play any other game of chance again.

I shall never forget the passion of gratitude, humble at first, then gradually more ardent, with which that lost stranger listened to me, how he positively drank in my words as I promised him help, and then he suddenly reached both hands over the table to take mine in a gesture I can never forget, a gesture of what one might call adoration and sacred promise. There were tears in his bright but slightly confused eyes; his whole body was trembling nervously with happy excitement. I have tried to describe the uniquely expressive quality of his gestures to you several times already, but I cannot depict this one, for it conveyed ecstatic, supernal delight such as a human countenance seldom turns on us, comparable only to that white shade in which, waking from a dream, we think we see the countenance of an angel vanishing.

Why conceal it? I could not withstand that glance. Gratitude is delightful because it is so seldom found, tender feeling does one good, and such exuberance was delightfully new and heart-warming to me, sober, cool woman that I was. And with that crushed, distressed young man, the landscape itself had revived as if by magic after last night's rain. The sea, calm as a millpond, lay shining blue beneath the sky as we came out of the restaurant, and the only white to be seen was the white of seagulls swooping in that other, celestial blue. You know the Riviera landscape. It is always beautiful, but offers its rich colours to the eye in leisurely fashion, flat as a picture postcard, a lethargic sleeping beauty who admits all glances, imperturbable and almost oriental in her ever-opulent willingness. But sometimes, very occasionally, there are days when this beauty rises up, breaks out, cries out loud, you might say, with gaudy, fanatically sparkling colours, triumphantly flinging her flower-like brightness in your face, glowing, burning with sensuality. And the stormy chaos of the night before had turned to such a lively day, the road was washed white, the sky was turquoise, and everywhere bushes ignited like colourful torches among the lush, drenched green foliage. The mountains seemed suddenly lighter and closer in the cooler, sunny air, as if they were crowding towards the gleaming, polished little town out of curiosity. Stepping outside, you sensed at every glance the challenging, cheering aspect of Nature spontaneously drawing your heart to her. 'Let's hire a carriage and drive along the Corniche,' I said.

The young man nodded enthusiastically: he seemed to be really seeing and noticing the landscape for the first time since his arrival. All he had seen so far was the dank casino hall with its sultry, sweaty smell, its crowds of ugly visitors with their twisted features, and a rough, grey, clamorous sea outside. But now the sunny beach lay spread out before us like a huge fan, and the eye leapt with pleasure from one distant point to another. We drove along the beautiful road in a slow carriage (this was before the days of the motor car), past many villas and many fine views; a hundred times, seeing every house, every villa in the green shade of the pine trees, one felt a secret wish to live there, quiet and content, away from the world!

Was I ever happier in my life than in that hour? I don't know. Beside me in the carriage sat the young man who had been a prey to death and disaster yesterday and now, in amazement, stood in the spray of the sparkling white dome of the sun above; years seemed to have dropped away from him. He had become all boy, a handsome, sportive child with a playful yet respectful look in his eyes, and nothing about him delighted me more than his considerate attentiveness. If the carriage was going up a steep climb which the horses found arduous, he jumped nimbly down to push from behind. If I named a flower or pointed to one by the roadside, he hurried to pluck it. He picked up a little toad that was hopping with difficulty along the road, lured out by last night's rain, and carried it carefully over to the green grass, where it would not be crushed as the carriage went by; and from time to time, in great high spirits, he would say the most delightful and amusing things; I believe he found laughter of that kind a safety valve, and without it he would have had to sing or dance or fool around in some way, so happily inebriated was the expression of his sudden exuberance.

As we were driving slowly through a tiny village high up on the road, he suddenly raised his hat politely. I was surprised and asked who he was greeting, since he was a stranger among strangers here. He flushed slightly at my question and explained, almost apologetically, that we had just passed a church, and at home in Poland, as in all strict Catholic countries, it was usual from childhood on to raise your hat outside any church or other place of worship. I was deeply moved by this exquisite respect for religion, and remembering the cross he had mentioned, I asked if he was a devout believer. When he modestly confessed, with a touch of embarrassment, that he hoped to be granted God's grace, an idea suddenly came to me. 'Stop!' I told the driver, and quickly climbed out of the carriage. He followed me in surprise, asking, 'Where are we going?' I said only, 'Come with me.'

In his company I went back to the church, a small country church built of brick. The interior looked chalky, grey and empty; the door stood open, so that a yellow beam of light cut sharply through the dark, where blue shadows surrounded a small altar. Two candles, like veiled eyes, looked out of the warm, incense-scented twilight. We entered, he took off his hat, dipped his hand in the basin of holy water, crossed himself and genuflected. When he was standing again I took his arm. 'Go and find an altar or some image here that is holy to you,' I urged him, 'and swear the oath I will recite to you.' He looked at me in surprise, almost in alarm. But quickly understanding, he went over to a niche, made the sign of the cross and obediently knelt down. 'Say after me,' I said, trembling with excitement myself, 'say after me: I swear… '—'I swear,' he repeated, and I continued, 'that I will never play for money again, whatever the game may be, I swear that I will never again expose my life and my honour to the dangers of that passion.'

He repeated the words, trembling: they lingered loud and clear in the empty interior. Then it was quiet for a moment, so quiet that you could hear the faint rustling of the trees outside as the wind blew through their leaves. Suddenly he threw himself down like a penitent and, in tones of ecstasy such as I had never heard before, poured out a flood of rapid, confused words in Polish. I did not understand what he was saying, but it was obviously an ecstatic prayer, a prayer of gratitude and remorse, for in his stormy confession he kept bowing his head humbly down on the prayer desk, repeating the strange sounds ever more passionately, and uttering the same word more and more violently and with extraordinary ardour. I have never heard prayer like that before or since, in any church in the world. As he prayed his hands clung convulsively to the wooden prayer desk, his whole body shaken by an internal storm that sometimes caught him up and sometimes cast him down again. He saw and felt nothing else: his whole being seemed to exist in another world, in a purgatorial fire of transmutation, or rising to a holier sphere. At last he slowly stood up, made the sign of the cross, and turned with an effort. His knees were trembling, his countenance was pale as the face of a man exhausted. But when he saw me his eyes beamed, a pure, a truly devout smile lit up his ecstatic face; he came closer, bowed low in the Russian manner, took both my hands and touched them reverently with his lips. 'God has sent you to me. I was thanking him.' I did not know what to say, but I could have wished the organ to crash out suddenly above the low pews, for I felt that I had succeeded: I had saved this man for ever.

We emerged from the church into the radiant, flooding light of that May-like day; the world had never before seemed to me more beautiful. Then we drove slowly on in the carriage for another two hours, taking the panoramic road over the hills which offers a new view at every turn. But we spoke no more. After so much emotion, any other words would have seemed an anti-climax. And when by chance my eyes met his, I had to turn them away as if ashamed, so shaken was I by the sight of my own miracle.

We returned to Monte Carlo at about five in the afternoon. I had an appointment with relatives which I could not cancel at this late date. And in fact I secretly wished for a pause in which to recover from feelings that had been too violently aroused. For this was too much happiness. I felt that I must rest from my overheated, ecstatic condition. I had never known anything like it in my life before. So I asked my protégé to come into my hotel with me for a moment, and there in my room I gave him the money for his journey and to redeem the jewellery. We agreed that while I kept my appointment he would go and buy his ticket, and then we would meet at seven in the entrance hall of the station, half-an-hour before the departure of the train taking him home by way of Genoa. When I was about to give him the five banknotes his lips turned curiously pale. 'No… no money… I beg you, not money!' he uttered through his teeth, while his agitated fingers quivered nervously. 'No money… not money… I can't stand the sight of it!' he repeated, as if physically overcome by nausea or fear. But I soothed him, saying it was only a loan, and if he felt troubled by it then he could give me a receipt. 'Yes, yes… a receipt,' he murmured, looking away, cramming the crumpled notes into his pocket without looking at them, like something sticky that soiled his fingers, and he scribbled a couple of words on a piece of paper in swift, flying characters. When he looked up damp sweat was standing out on his brow; something within seemed to be choking him, and no sooner had he given me the note than an impulse seemed to pass through him and suddenly—I was so startled that I instinctively flinched back—suddenly he fell on his knees and kissed the hem of my dress. It was an indescribable gesture; its overwhelming violence made me tremble all over. A strange shuddering came over me; I was confused, and could only stammer, 'Thank you for showing your gratitude—but do please go now! We'll say goodbye at seven in the station hall.'

He looked at me with a gleam of emotion moistening his eye; for a moment I thought he was going to say something, for a moment it seemed as if he were coming towards me. But then he suddenly bowed deeply again, very deeply, and left the room."

*

Once again Mrs C interrupted her story. She had risen and gone to the window to look out, and she stood there motionless for a long time. Watching the silhouette of her back, I saw it shiver slightly, and she swayed. All at once she turned back to me with determination, and her hands, until now calm and at rest, suddenly made a violent, tearing movement as if to rip something apart. Then she looked at me with a hard, almost defiant glance, and abruptly began again.

"I promised to be completely honest with you, and now I see how necessary that promise was. For only now that, for the first time, I make myself describe the whole course of those hours exactly as they happened, seeking words for what was a very complicated, confused feeling, only now do I clearly understand much that I did not know at the time, or perhaps would not acknowledge. So I will be firm and will not spare myself, and I will tell you the truth too: then, at the moment when the young man left the room and I remained there alone, I felt—it was a dazed sensation, like swooning—I felt a hard blow strike my heart. Something had hurt me mortally, but I did not know, or refused to know, what, after all, it was in my protégé's touchingly respectful conduct that wounded me so painfully.

But now that I force myself to bring up all the past unsparingly, in proper order, as if it were strange to me, and your presence as a witness allows no pretence, no craven concealment of a feeling which shames me, I clearly see that what hurt so much at the time was disappointment... my disappointment that... that the young man had gone away so obediently... that he did not try to detain me, to stay with me. It was because he humbly and respectfully fell in with my first attempt to persuade him to leave, instead... instead of trying to take me in his arms. It was because he merely revered me as a saint who had appeared to him along his way and did not... did not feel for me as a woman.

That was the disappointment I felt, a disappointment I did not admit to myself either then or later, but a woman's feelings know everything without words, without conscious awareness. For—and now I will deceive myself no longer—for if he had embraced me then, if he had asked me then, I would have gone to the ends of the earth with him, I would have dishonoured my name and the name of my children—I would have eloped with him, caring nothing for what people would say or the dictates of my own reason, just as Madame Henriette ran off with the young Frenchman whom she hadn't even met the day before. I wouldn't have asked where we were going, or how long it would last, I wouldn't have turned to look back at my previous life—I would have sacrificed my money, my name, my fortune and my honour to him, I would have begged in the street for him, there is probably no base conduct in the world to which he could not have brought me. I would have thrown away all that we call modesty and reason if he had only spoken one word, taken one step towards me, if he had tried to touch me—so lost in him was I at that moment. But… as I told you… the young man, in his strangely dazed condition, did not spare another glance for me and the woman in me… and I knew how much, how fervently I longed for him only when I was alone again, when the passion that had just been lighting up his radiant, his positively seraphic face was cast darkly back on me and now lingered in the void of an abandoned breast. With difficulty, I pulled myself together. My appointment was a doubly unwelcome burden. I felt as if a heavy iron helmet were weighing down on my brow and I was swaying under its weight; my thoughts were as disjointed as my footsteps as I at last went over to the other hotel to see my relatives. I sat there in a daze, amidst lively chatter, and was startled whenever I happened to look up and see their unmoved faces, which seemed to me frozen like masks by comparison with that face of his, enlivened as if by the play of light and shade as clouds cross the sky. I found the cheerful company as dreadfully inert as if I were among the dead, and while I put sugar in my cup and joined absently in the conversation, that one face kept coming before my mind's eye, as if summoned up by the surging of the blood. It had become a fervent joy to me to watch that face, and—terrible thought!—in an hour or so I would have seen it for the last time. I must involuntarily have sighed or groaned gently, for my husband's cousin leant over to me: what was the matter, she asked, didn't I feel well? I looked so pale and sad. This unexpected question gave me a quick, easy excuse; I said I did indeed have a migraine, and perhaps she would allow me to slip away.

Thus restored to my own company, I hurried straight to my hotel. No sooner was I alone there than the sense of emptiness and abandonment came over me again, feverishly combined with a longing for the young man I was to leave today for ever. I paced up and down the room, opened shutters for no good reason, changed my dress and my ribbon, suddenly found myself in front of the looking glass again, wondering whether, thus adorned, I might not be able to attract him after all. And I abruptly understood myself: I would do anything not to lose him! Within the space of a violent moment, my wish turned to determination. I ran down to the porter and told him I was leaving today by the night train. Now I had to hurry: I rang for the maid to help me pack—time was pressing—and as we stowed dresses and small items into my suitcases I dreamt of the coming surprise: I would accompany him to the train, and then, at the very last moment, when he was giving me his hand in farewell, I would suddenly get into the carriage with my astonished companion, I would spend that night with him, and the next night—as long as he wanted me. A kind of enchanted, wild frenzy whirled through my blood, sometimes, to the maid's surprise, I unexpectedly laughed aloud as I flung clothes into the suitcases. My senses, I felt from time to time, were all in disorder. And when the man came to take the cases down I stared at him strangely at first: it was too difficult to think of ordinary matters while I was in the grip of such inner excitement.

Time was short; it must be nearly seven, leaving me at most twenty minutes before the train left—but of course, I consoled myself, my arrival would not be a farewell now, since I had decided to accompany him on his journey as long and as far as he would have me. The hotel manservant carried the cases on ahead while I made haste to the reception desk to settle my bill. The manager was already giving me change, I was about to go on my way, when a hand gently touched my shoulder. I gave a start. It was my cousin; concerned by my apparent illness, she had come to see how I was. Everything went dark before my eyes. I did not want her here; every second I was detained meant disastrous delay, yet courtesy obliged me at least to fall into conversation with her briefly. 'You must go to bed,' she was urging me. 'I'm sure you have a temperature.' And she could well have been right, for the blood was pounding at my temples, and sometimes I felt the blue haze of approaching faintness come over my eyes. But I fended off her suggestions and took pains to seem grateful, while every word burned me, and I would have liked to thrust her ill-timed concern roughly away. However, she stayed and stayed and stayed with her unwanted solicitude, offered me eau de Cologne, would not be dissuaded from dabbing the cool perfume on my temples herself. Meanwhile I was counting the minutes, thinking both of him and of how to find an excuse to escape the torment of her sympathy. And the more restless I became, the more alarming did my condition seem to her; finally she was trying, almost by force, to make me go to my room and lie down. Then—in the middle of her urging—I suddenly saw the clock in the hotel lobby: it was two minutes before seven-thirty, and the train left at seven thirty-five. Brusquely, abruptly, with the brutal indifference of a desperate woman I simply stuck my hand out to my cousin—'Goodbye, I must go!'—and without a moment's thought for her frozen glance, without looking round, I rushed past the surprised hotel staff and out of the door, into the street and down it to the station. From the agitated gesticulating of the hotel manservant standing waiting there with my luggage I saw, well before I got there, that time must be very short. Frantically I ran to the barrier, but there the conductor turned me back—I had forgotten to buy a ticket. And as I almost forcibly tried to persuade him to let me on the platform all the same, the train began to move.

I stared at it, trembling all over, hoping at least to catch a glimpse of him at the window of one of the carriages, a wave, a greeting. But in the middle of the hurrying throng I could not see his face. The carriages rolled past faster and faster, and after a minute nothing was left before my darkened eyes but black clouds of steam.

I must have stood there as if turned to stone, for God knows how long; the hotel servant had probably spoken to me in vain several times before he ventured to touch my arm. Only then did I start and come to myself. Should he take my luggage back to the hotel, he asked. It took me a few minutes to think; no, that was impossible, after this ridiculous, frantic departure I couldn't go back there, and I never wanted to again; so I told him, impatient to be alone, to take my cases to the left luggage office. Only then, in the middle of the constantly renewed crush of people flowing clamorously into the hall and then ebbing away again, did I try to think, to think clearly, to save myself from my desperate, painful, choking sense of fury, remorse and despair, for—why not admit it?—the idea that I had missed our last meeting through my own fault was like a knife turning pitilessly within me, burning and sharp. I could have screamed aloud: that red-hot blade, penetrating ever more mercilessly, hurt so much. Perhaps only those who are strangers to passion know such sudden outbursts of emotion in their few passionate moments, moments of emotion like an avalanche or a hurricane; whole years fall from one's own breast with the fury of powers left unused. Never before or after have I felt anything like the astonishment and raging impotence of that moment when, prepared to take the boldest of steps—prepared to throw away my whole carefully conserved, collected, controlled life all at once—I suddenly found myself facing a wall of senselessness against which my passion could only beat its head helplessly.

As for what I did then, how could it be anything but equally senseless? It was foolish, even stupid, and I am almost ashamed to tell you—but I have promised myself and you to keep nothing back. I… well, I went in search of him again. That is to say, I went in search of every moment I had spent with him. I felt irresistibly drawn to everywhere we had been together the day before, the bench in the casino grounds from which I had made him rise, the gaming hall where I had first seen him—yes, even that den of vice, just to relive the past once more, only once more. And tomorrow I would go along the Corniche in a carriage, retracing our path, so that every word and gesture would revive in my mind again—so senseless and childish was my state of confusion. But you must take into account the lightning speed with which these events overwhelmed me—I had felt little more than a single numbing blow, but now, woken too abruptly from that tumult of feeling, I wanted to go back over what I had so fleetingly experienced step by step, relishing it in retrospect by virtue of that magical self-deception we call memory. Well, some things we either do or do not understand. Perhaps you need a burning heart to comprehend them fully.

So I went first to the gaming hall to seek out the table where he had been sitting, and think of his hands among all the others there. I went in: I remembered that I had first seen him at the left-hand table in the second room. Every one of his movements was still clear before my mind's eye: I could have found his place sleepwalking, with my eyes closed and my hands outstretched. So I went in and crossed the hall. And then… as I looked at the crowd from the doorway… then something strange happened. There, in the very place where I dreamt of him, there sat—ah, the hallucinations of fever!—there sat the man himself. He looked exactly as I had seen him in my daydream just now—exactly as he had been yesterday, his eyes fixed on the ball, pale as a ghost—but he it unmistakably was.

I was so shocked that I felt as if I must cry out. But I controlled my alarm at this ridiculous vision and closed my eyes. 'You're mad—dreaming—feverish,' I told myself. 'It's impossible. You're hallucinating. He left half-an-hour ago.' Only then did I open my eyes again. But terrible to relate, he was still sitting there exactly as he had been sitting just now, in the flesh and unmistakable. I would have known those hands among millions… no, I wasn't dreaming, he was real. He had not left as he had promised he would, the madman was sitting there, he had taken the money I gave him for his journey and brought it here, to the green table, gambling it on his passion, oblivious of all else, while I was desperately eating my heart out for him.

I abruptly moved forwards: fury blurred my vision, a frenzied, red-eyed, raging desire to take the perjurer who had so shamefully abused my confidence, my feelings, my devotion by the throat. But I controlled myself. With a deliberately slow step (and how much strength that cost me!) I went up to the table to sit directly opposite him. A gentleman courteously made way for me. Two metres of green cloth stood between us, and as if looking down from a balcony at a play on stage I could watch his face, the same face that I had seen two hours ago radiant with gratitude, illuminated by the aura of divine grace, and now entirely absorbed in the infernal fires of his passion again. The hands, those same hands that I had seen clinging to the wood of the prayer desk as he swore a most sacred oath, were now clutching at the money again like the claws of lustful vampires. For he had been winning, he must have won a very great deal: in front of him shone a jumbled pile of jettons and louis d'ors and banknotes, a disordered medley in which his quivering, nervous fingers were stretching and bathing with delight. I saw them pick up separate notes, stroke and fold them, I saw them turn and caress coins, then suddenly and abruptly catch up a fistful and put them down on one of the spaces. And immediately that spasmodic tic around his nostrils began again, the call of the croupier tore his greedily blazing eyes away from the money to the spinning ball, he seemed to be flowing out of himself, as it were, while his elbows might have been nailed to the green table. His total addiction was revealed as even more dreadful, more terrible than the evening before, for every move he made murdered that other image within me, the image shining as if on a golden ground that I had credulously swallowed.

So we sat there two metres away from each other; I was staring at him, but he was unaware of me. He was not looking at me or anyone else, his glance merely moved to the money, flickering unsteadily with the ball as it rolled back to rest: all his senses were contained, chasing back and forth, in that one racing green circle. To this obsessive gambler the whole world, the whole human race had shrunk to a rectangular patch of cloth. And I knew that I could stand here for hours and hours, and he would not have the faintest idea of my presence.

But I could stand it no longer. Coming to a sudden decision, I walked round the table, stepped behind him and firmly grasped his shoulder with my hand. His gaze swung upwards, for a second he stared strangely at me, glassy-eyed, like a drunk being laboriously shaken awake, eyes still vague and drowsy, clouded by inner fumes. Then he seemed to recognise me, his mouth opened, quivering, he looked happily up at me and stammered quietly, in a confused tone of mysterious confidentiality, 'It's going well… I knew it would as soon as I came in and saw that he was here… ' I did not understand what he meant. All I saw was that this madman was intoxicated by the game and had forgotten everything else, his promise, his appointment at the station, me and the whole world besides. But even when he was in this obsessive mood I found his ecstasy so captivating that instinctively I went along with him and asked, taken aback, who was here?

'Over there, the one-armed old Russian general,' he whispered, pressing close to me so that no one else would overhear the magic secret. 'Over there, with the white sideboards and the servant behind him. He always wins, I was watching him yesterday, he must have a system, and I always pick the same number… He was winning yesterday too, but I made the mistake of playing on when he had left… that was my error… he must have won twenty thousand francs yesterday, he's winning every time now too, and I just keep following his lead. Now—'

He broke off in mid-sentence, for the hoarse-voiced croupier was calling his '*Faites votre jeu!*' and his glance was already moving away, looking greedily at the place where the white-whiskered Russian sat, nonchalant and grave, thoughtfully putting first one gold coin and then, hesitantly, another on the fourth space. Immediately the fevered hands before me dug into the pile of money and put down a handful of coins on the same place. And when, after a minute, the croupier cried '*Zéro!*' and his rake swept the whole table bare with a single movement, he stared at the money streaming away as if at some marvel. But do you think he turned to me? No he had forgotten all about me; I had dropped out of his life, I was lost and gone from it, his whole being was intent only on the Russian general who, with complete indifference, was hefting two more gold coins in his hand, not yet sure what number to put them on.

I cannot describe my bitterness and despair. But think of my feelings: to be no more than a fly brushed carelessly aside by a man to whom one has offered one's whole life. Once again that surge of fury came over me. I seized his arm with all my strength. He started.

'You will get up at once!' I whispered to him in a soft but commanding tone. 'Remember what you swore in church today, you miserable perjurer.'

He stared at me, perplexed and pale. His eyes suddenly took on the expression of a beaten dog, his lips quivered. All at once he seemed to be remembering the past, and a horror of himself appeared to come over him.

'Yes, yes… ' he stammered. 'Oh, my God, my God… yes, I'm coming, oh, forgive me… '

And his hand was already sweeping the money together, fast at first, gathering it all up with a vehement gesture, but then gradually slowing down, as if coming up against some opposing force. His eyes had fallen once more on the Russian general, who had just made his bet.

'Just a moment,' he said, quickly throwing five gold coins on the same square. 'Just this one more time… I promise you I'll come then—just this one more game… just… '

And again his voice fell silent. The ball had begun to roll and was carrying him away with it. Once again the addict had slipped away from me, from himself, flung round with the tiny ball circling in the smooth hollow of the wheel where it leapt and sprang. Once again the croupier called out the number, once again the rake carried his five coins away from him; he had lost. But he did not turn round. He had forgotten me, just like his oath in the church and the promise he had given me a minute ago. His greedy hand was moving spasmodically towards the dwindling pile of money again, and his intoxicated gaze moved only to the magnet of his will, the man opposite who brought good luck.

My patience was at an end. I shook him again, hard this time. 'Get up at once! Immediately! You said one more game… '

But then something unexpected happened. He suddenly swung round, but the face looking at me was no longer that of a humbled and confused man, it was the face of a man in a frenzy, all anger, with burning eyes and furiously trembling lips. 'Leave me alone!' he spat. 'Go away! You bring me bad luck. Whenever you're here I lose. You brought bad luck yesterday and you're bringing bad luck now. Go away!'

I momentarily froze, but now my own anger was whipped up beyond restraint by his folly.

'I am bringing you bad luck?' I snapped at him. 'You liar, you thief—you promised me… ' But I got no further, for the maniac leapt up from his seat and, indifferent to the turmoil around him, thrust me away. 'Leave me alone,' he cried, losing all control. 'I'm not under your control… here, take your money.' And he threw me a few hundred-franc notes. 'Now leave me alone!'

He had been shouting out loud like a madman, ignoring the hundred or so people around us. They were all staring, whispering, pointing, laughing—other curious onlookers even crowded in from the hall next door. I felt as if my clothes were being torn from my body, leaving me naked before all these prying eyes. '*Silence, madame, s'il vous plaît*,' said the croupier in commanding tones, tapping his rake on the table. He meant me, the wretched creature meant me. Humiliated, overcome by shame, I stood there before the hissing, whispering curious folk like a prostitute whose customer has just thrown money at her. Two hundred, three hundred shameless eyes were turned on my face, and then—then, as I turned my gaze evasively aside, overwhelmed by this filthy deluge of humiliation and shame, my own eyes met two others, piercing and astonished—it was my cousin looking at me appalled, her mouth open, one hand raised as if in horror.

That struck home; before she could stir or recover from her surprise I stormed out of the hall. I got as far as the bench outside, the same bench on which the gambling addict had collapsed yesterday. I dropped to the hard, pitiless wood, as powerless, exhausted and shattered as he had been.

All that is twenty-four years ago, yet when I remember the moment when I stood there before a thousand strangers, lashed by their scorn, the blood freezes in my veins. And once again I feel, in horror, how weak, poor and flabby a substance whatever we call by the names of soul, spirit or feeling must be after all, not to mention what we describe as pain, since all this, even to the utmost degree, is insufficient to destroy the suffering flesh of the tormented body entirely—for we do survive such hours and our blood continues to pulse, instead of dying and falling like a tree struck by lightning. Only for a sudden moment, for an instant, did this pain tear through my joints so hard that I dropped on the bench breathless and dazed, with a positively voluptuous premonition that I must die. But as I was saying, pain is cowardly, it gives way before the overpowering will to live which seems to cling more strongly to our flesh than all the mortal suffering of the spirit. Even to myself, I cannot explain my feelings after such a shattering blow, but I did rise to my feet, although I did not know what to do. Suddenly it occurred to me that my suitcases were already at the station, and I thought suddenly that I must get away, away from here, away from this accursed, this infernal building. Taking no notice of anyone, I made haste to the station and asked when the next train for Paris left. At ten o'clock, the porter told me, and I immediately retrieved my luggage. Ten o'clock—so exactly twenty-four hours had passed since that terrible meeting, twenty-four hours so full of changeable, contradictory feelings that my inner world was shattered for ever. At first, however, I felt nothing but that one word in the constantly hammering, pounding rhythm: away, away, away! The pulses behind my brow kept driving it into my temples like a wedge: away, away, away! Away from this town, away from myself, home to my own people, to my own old life! I travelled through the night to Paris, changed from one station to another and travelled direct to Boulogne, from Boulogne to Dover, from Dover to London, from London to my son's house—all in one headlong flight, without stopping to think or consider, forty-eight hours without sleep, without speaking to anyone, without eating, forty-eight hours during which the wheels of all the trains rattled out that one word: away, away, away! When at last I arrived unexpectedly at my son's country house, everyone was alarmed; there must have been something in my bearing and my eyes that gave me away. My son came to embrace and kiss me, but I shrank away: I could not bear the thought of his touching lips that I felt were disgraced. I avoided all questions, asked only for a bath, because I needed to wash not only the dirt of the journey from my body but all of the passion of that obsessed, unworthy man that seemed to cling to it. Then I dragged myself up to my room and slept a benumbed and stony sleep for twelve or fourteen hours, a sleep such as I have never slept before or since, and after it I know what it must be like to lie dead in a coffin. My family cared for me as for a sick woman, but their affection only hurt me, I was ashamed of their respect, and had to keep preventing myself from suddenly screaming out loud how I had betrayed, forgotten and abandoned them all for the sake of a foolish, crazy passion.

Then, aimless again, I went back to France and a little town where I knew no one, for I was pursued by the delusion that at the very first glance everyone could see my shame and my changed nature from the outside, I felt so betrayed, so soiled to the depths of my soul. Sometimes, when I woke in my bed in the morning,

I felt a dreadful fear of opening my eyes. Once again I would be overcome by the memory of that night when I suddenly woke beside a half-naked stranger, and then, as I had before, all I wanted was to die immediately.

But after all, time is strong, and age has the curious power of devaluing all our feelings. You feel death coming closer, its shadow falls black across your path, and things seem less brightly coloured, they do not go to the heart so much, they lose much of their dangerous violence. Gradually I recovered from the shock, and when, many years later, I met a young Pole who was an attaché of the Austrian Embassy at a party, and in answer to my enquiry about that family he told me that one of his cousin's sons had shot himself ten years before in Monte Carlo, I did not even tremble. It hardly hurt any more; perhaps—why deny one's egotism?—I was even glad of it, for now my last fear of ever meeting him again was gone. I had no witness against me left but my own memory. Since then I have become calmer. Growing old, after all, means that one no longer fears the past.

And now you will understand why I suddenly brought myself to tell you about my own experience. When you defended Madame Henriette and said, so passionately, that twenty-four hours could determine a woman's whole life, I felt that you meant me; I was grateful to you, since for the first time I felt myself, as it were, confirmed in my existence. And then I thought it would be good to unburden myself of it all for once, and perhaps then the spell on me would be broken, the eternal looking back; perhaps I can go to Monte Carlo tomorrow and enter the same hall where I met my fate without feeling hatred for him or myself. Then the stone will roll off my soul, laying its full weight over the past and preventing it from ever rising again. It has done me good to tell you all this. I feel easier in my mind now and almost light at heart… thank you for that."

*

With these words she had suddenly risen, and I felt that she had reached the end. Rather awkwardly, I sought for something to say. But she must have felt my emotion, and quickly waved it away.

"No, please, don't speak… I'd rather you didn't reply or say anything to me. Accept my thanks for listening, and I wish you a good journey."

She stood opposite me, holding out her hand in farewell. Instinctively I looked at her face, and the countenance of this old woman who stood before me with a kindly yet slightly ashamed expression seemed to me wonderfully touching. Whether it was the reflection of past passion or mere confusion that suddenly dyed her cheeks with red, the colour rising to her white hair, she stood there just like a girl, in a bridal confusion of memories and ashamed of her own confession. Involuntarily moved, I very much wanted to say something to express my respect for her, but my throat was too constricted. So I leant down and respectfully kissed the faded hand that trembled slightly like an autumn leaf.

DOWNFALL OF THE HEART

DESTINY DOES NOT ALWAYS need the powerful prelude of a sudden violent blow to shake a heart beyond recovery. The unbridled creativity of fate can generate disaster from some small, fleeting incident. In clumsy human language, we call that first slight touch the cause of the catastrophe, and feel surprise in comparing its insignificance with the force, often enormous, that it exerts, but just as the first symptoms of an illness may not show at all, the downfall of a human heart can begin before anything happens to make it visible. Fate has been at work within the victim's mind and his blood long before his soul suffers any outward effects. To know yourself is to defend yourself, but it is usually in vain.

The old man—Salomonsohn was his name, and at home in Germany he could boast of the honorary title of Privy Commercial Councillor—was lying awake in the Gardone hotel where he had taken his family for the Easter holiday. A violent physical pain constricted his chest so that he could hardly breathe. The old man was alarmed; he had troublesome gallstones and often suffered bilious attacks, but instead of following the advice of his doctors and visiting Karlsbad to take the waters there he had decided, for his family's sake, to go further south and stay at this resort on Lake Garda instead. Fearing a dangerous attack of his disorder, he anxiously palpated his broad body, and soon realised with relief, even though he was still in pain, that it was only an ordinary stomach upset, obviously as a result of the unfamiliar Italian food, or the mild food poisoning that was apt to afflict tourists. Feeling less alarmed, he let his shaking hand drop back, but the pressure on his chest continued and kept him from breathing easily. Groaning, the old man made the effort of getting out of bed to move about a little. Sure enough, when he was standing the pressure eased, and even more so when he was walking. But there was not much space to walk about in the dark room, and he was afraid of waking his wife in the other twin bed and causing her unnecessary concern. So he put on his dressing gown and a pair of felt slippers, and groped his way out into the corridor to walk up and down there for a little while and lessen the pain.

As he opened the door into the dark corridor, the sound of the clock in the church tower echoed through the open windows—four chimes, first weighty and then dying softly away over the lake. Four in the morning.

The long corridor lay in complete darkness. But from his clear memory of it in daytime, the old man knew that it was wide and straight, so he walked along it, breathing heavily, from end to end without needing a light, and then again and again, pleased to notice that the tightness in his chest was fading. Almost entirely freed from pain now by this beneficial exercise, he was preparing to return to his room when a sound startled him. He stopped. The sound was a whispering in the darkness somewhere near him, slight yet unmistakable. Woodwork creaked, there were soft voices and movements, a door was opened just a crack and a narrow beam of light cut through the formless darkness. What was it? Instinctively the old man shrank back into a corner, not out of curiosity but obeying a natural sense of awkwardness at being caught by other people engaged in the odd activity of pacing up and down like a sleepwalker. In that one second when the light shone into the corridor, however, he had involuntarily seen, or thought he had seen, a white-clad female figure slipping out of the room and disappearing down the passage. And sure enough, there was a slight click as one of the last doors in the corridor latched shut. Then all was dark and silent again.

The old man suddenly began to sway as if he had suffered a

blow to the heart. The only rooms at the far end of the corridor, where the door handle had given away a secret by clicking… the only rooms there were his own, the three-roomed suite that he had booked for his family. He had left his wife asleep and breathing peacefully only a few minutes before, so that female figure—no, he couldn't be mistaken—that figure returning from a venture into a stranger's room could have been no one but his daughter Erna, aged only just nineteen.

The old man was shivering all over with horror. His daughter Erna, his child, that happy, high-spirited child—no, this was impossible, he must be mistaken! But what could she have been doing in a stranger's room if not… Like an injured animal he thrust his own idea away, but the haunting picture of that stealthy figure still haunted his mind, he could not tear it out of his head or banish it. He had to be sure. Panting, he groped his way along the wall of the corridor to her door, which was next to his own bedroom. But he was appalled to see, at this one door in the corridor, a thin line of light showing under the door, and the keyhole was a small dot of treacherous brightness. She still had a light on in her room at four in the morning! And there was more evidence—with a slight crackle from the electric switch the white line of light vanished without trace into darkness. No, it was useless trying to pretend to himself. It was Erna, his daughter, slipping out of a stranger's bed and into her own by night.

The old man was trembling with horror and cold, while at the same time sweat broke out all over his body, flooding the pores of his skin. His first thought was to break in at the shameless girl's door and chastise her with his fists. But his feet were tottering beneath the weight of his broad body. He could hardly summon up the strength to drag himself into his own room and back to bed, where he fell on the pillows like a stricken animal, his senses dulled.

*

The old man lay motionless in bed. His eyes, wide open, stared at the darkness. He heard his wife breathing easily beside him, without a care in the world. His first thought was to shake her awake, tell her about his dreadful discovery, rage and rant to his heart's content. But how could he express it, how could he put this terrible thing into words? No, such words would never pass his lips. What was he to do, though? What *could* he do?

He tried to think, but his mind was in blind confusion, thoughts flying this way and that like bats in daylight. It was so monstrous—Erna, his tender, well-brought-up child with her melting eyes… How long ago was it, how long ago that he would still find her poring over her schoolbooks, her little pink finger carefully tracing the difficult characters on the page, how long since she used to go straight from school to the confectioner's in her little pale-blue dress, and then he felt her childish kiss with sugar still on her lips? Only yesterday, surely? But no, it was all years ago. Yet how childishly she had begged him yesterday—*really* yesterday—to buy her the blue and gold pullover that looked so pretty in the shop window. "Oh please, dear Papa, please!"—with her hands clasped, with that self-confident, happy smile that he could never resist. And now, now she was stealing away to a strange man's bed by night, not far from his own door, to roll about in it with him, naked and lustful.

My God, my God! thought the old man, instinctively groaning. The shame of it, the shame! My child, my tender, beloved child—an assignation with some man… Who is he? Who can he be? We arrived here in Gardone only three days ago, and she knew none of those spruced-up dandies before—thin-faced Conte Ubaldi, that Italian officer, the baron from Mecklenburg who's a gentleman jockey… they didn't meet on the dance floor until our second day. Has one of them already?… No, he can't have been the first, no… it must have begun earlier, at home, and I knew nothing about it, fool that I am. Poor fool! But what do I know about my wife and daughter anyway? I toil for them every day, I spend fourteen hours a day at my office just to earn money for them, more and more money so that they can have fine dresses and be rich… and when I come home tired in the evening, worn out, they've gone gadding off to the theatre, to balls, out with company, what do I know about them and what they get up to all day long? And now my child with her pure young body has assignations with men by night like a common streetwalker… oh, the shame of it!

The old man groaned again and again. Every new idea deepened his wound and tore it open, as if his brain lay visibly bleeding, with red maggots writhing in it.

But why do I put up with this, he wondered, why do I lie here tormenting myself while she, with her unchaste body, sleeps peacefully? Why didn't I go straight into her room so that she'd know *I* knew her shame? Why didn't I beat her black and blue? Because I'm weak… and a coward… I've always been weak with both of them, I've given way to them in everything, I was proud that I could make their lives easy, even if my own was ruined, I scraped the money together with my fingernails, *pfennig* by *pfennig*, I'd have torn the flesh from my hands to see them content! But as soon as I'd made them rich they were ashamed of me, I wasn't elegant enough for them any more, too uneducated… where would I have got an education? I was taken out of school aged twelve, I had to earn money, earn and earn, carry cases of samples about from village to village, run agencies in town after town before I could open my own business… and no sooner were they ladies and living in their own house than they didn't like my honourable old name any more. I had to buy the title of Councillor, so that my wife wouldn't be just Frau Salomonsohn, so that she could be Frau Commercial Councillor and put on airs. Put on airs! They laughed at me when I objected to all that putting on airs of distinction, when I objected to what they call high society, when I told them how my mother, God rest her soul, kept house quietly, modestly, just for my father and the rest of us… they called me old-fashioned. "Oh, you're so old-fashioned, Papa!" She was always mocking me… yes, old-fashioned, indeed I am… and now she lies in a strange bed with strange men, my child, my only child! Oh, the shame, the shame of it!

The old man was moaning and sighing in such torment that his wife, in the bed beside his, woke up. "What's the matter?" she drowsily asked. The old man did not move, and held his breath. And so he lay there motionless in the coffin of his torment until morning, with his thoughts eating away at him like worms.

The old man was first at the breakfast table. He sat down with a sigh, unable to face a morsel of food.

Alone again, he thought, always alone! When I go to the office in the morning they're still comfortably asleep, lazily taking their ease after all their dancing and theatre-going… when I come home in the evening they've already gone out to enjoy themselves in company, they don't need me with them. It's the money, the accursed money that's ruined them, made them strangers to me. Fool that I am, I earned it, scraped it together, I stole from myself, made myself poor and them bad with the money… for fifty pointless years I've been toiling, never giving myself a day off, and now I'm all alone…

He felt impatient. Why doesn't she come down, he wondered, I want to talk to her, I have to tell her… we must leave this place at once… why doesn't she come down? I suppose she's too tired, sleeping soundly with a clear conscience while I'm tearing my heart to pieces, old fool that I am… and her mother titivating herself for hours on end, has to take a bath, dress herself, have a manicure, get her hair arranged, she won't be down before eleven, and is it any wonder? How can a child turn out so badly? It's the money, the accursed money…

Light footsteps were approaching behind him. "Good morning, Papa, did you sleep well?" A soft cheek bent down to his side, a light kiss brushed his hammering forehead. Instinctively he drew back; repelled by the sweetly sultry Coty perfume she wore. And then…

"What's the matter, Papa… are you in a cross temper again? Oh, coffee, please, waiter, and ham and eggs… Did you sleep badly, or have you heard bad news?"

The old man restrained himself. He bowed his head—he did not have the courage to look up—and preserved his silence. He saw only her manicured hands on the table, her beloved hands, casually playing with each other like spoilt, slender little greyhounds on the white turf of the tablecloth. He trembled. Timidly, his eyes travelled up the delicate, girlish arms which she had often—but how long ago?—flung around him before she went to sleep. He saw the gentle curve of her breasts moving in time with her breathing under the new pullover. Naked, he thought grimly, stark naked, tossing and turning in bed with a strange man. A man who touched all that, felt it, lavished caresses on it, tasted and enjoyed her… my own flesh and blood, my child… that villainous stranger, oh…

Unconsciously, he had groaned again. "What's the matter with you, Papa?" She moved closer, coaxing him.

What's the matter with me? echoed a voice inside him. A whore for a daughter, and I can't summon up the courage to tell her so.

But he only muttered indistinctly, "Nothing, nothing!" and hastily picked up the newspaper, protecting himself from her questioning gaze behind a barricade of outspread sheets of newsprint. He felt increasingly unable to meet her eyes. His hands were shaking. I ought to tell her now, said his tormented mind, now while we're alone. But his voice failed him; he could not even find the strength to look up.

And suddenly, abruptly, he pushed back his chair and escaped, treading heavily, in the direction of the garden, for he felt a large tear rolling down his cheek against his will, and he didn't want her to see it.

*

The old man wandered around the garden on his short legs, staring at the lake for a long time. Almost blinded by the unshed tears he was holding back, he still could not help noticing the beauty of the landscape—the hills rose in undulating shades of soft green behind silver light, black-hatched with the thin spires of cypress trees, and beyond the hills were the sterner outlines of the mountains, severe, yet looking down on the beauty of the lake without arrogance, like grave men watching the light-hearted games of beloved children. How mild it all lay there outspread, with open, flowering, hospitable gestures. How it enticed a man to be kindly and happy, that timeless, blessed smile of God at the south he had created! Happy! The old man rocked his heavy head back and forth, confused.

One could be happy here, he thought. I would have liked to be happy myself, just once, feel how beautiful the world of the carefree is for myself, just once, after fifty years of writing and calculating and bargaining and haggling, I would have liked to enjoy a few bright days before they bury me… for sixty-five years, my God, death's hand is in my body now, money is no help and nor are the doctors. I wanted to breathe easily just a little first, have something for myself for once. But my late father always said: contentment is not for the likes of us, we carry our pedlar's packs on our backs to the grave… Yesterday I thought I myself might feel at ease for a change… yesterday I could have been called a happy man, glad of my beautiful, lovely child, glad to give her pleasure… and God has punished me already and taken that away from me. It's all over now for ever… I can't speak to my own child any more, I am ashamed to look her in the eye. I'll always be thinking of this at home, at the office, at night in my bed—where is she now, where has she been, what has she done? I'll never be able to come happily home again, to see her sitting there and then running to meet me, with my heart opening up at the sight of her, so young and lovely… When she kisses me I'll wonder who had her yesterday, who kissed those lips… I'll always live in fear when she's not with me, I'll always be ashamed when I meet her eyes—a man can't live like this, can't live like this…

The old man stumbled back and forth like a drunk, muttering. He kept staring out at the lake, and his tears ran down into his beard. He had to take off his pince-nez and stand there on the narrow path with his moist, short-sighted eyes revealed, looking so foolish that a gardener's boy who was passing stopped in surprise, laughed aloud and called out a few mocking words in Italian at the bewildered old man. That roused him from his turmoil of pain, and he put his pince-nez on and stole aside into the garden to sit on a bench somewhere and hide from the boy.

But as he approached a remote part of the garden, a laugh to his left startled him again… a laugh that he knew and that went to his heart. That laughter had been music to him for nineteen years, the light laughter of her high spirits… for that laughter he had travelled third-class by night to Poland and Hungary so that he could pour out money before them, rich soil from which that carefree merriment grew. He had lived only for that laughter, while inside his body his gall bladder fell sick… just so that that laughter could always ring out from her beloved mouth. And now the same laughter cut him to the heart like a red-hot saw.

Yet it drew him to it despite his reluctance. She was standing on the tennis court, twirling the racket in her bare hand, gracefully throwing it up and catching it again in play. At the same time as the racket flew up, her light-hearted laughter rose to the azure sky. The three gentlemen admiringly watched her, Conte Ubaldi in a loose tennis shirt, the officer in the trim uniform that showed off his muscles, the gentleman jockey in an immaculate pair of breeches, three sharply profiled, statuesque male figures around a plaything fluttering like a butterfly. The old man himself stared, captivated. Good God, how lovely she was in her pale, ankle-length dress, the sun dusting her blonde hair with liquid gold! And how happily her young limbs felt their own lightness as she leapt and ran, intoxicated and intoxicating as her joints responded to the free-and-easy rhythm of her movements. Now she flung the white tennis ball merrily up to the sky, then a second and a third after it, it was wonderful to see how the slender wand of her girlish body bent and stretched, leaping up now to catch the last ball. He had never seen her like that before, incandescent with high spirits, an elusive, wavering flame, the silvery trill of her laughter above the blazing of her body, like a virginal goddess escaped in panic from the southern garden with its clinging ivy and the gentle surface of the lake. At home she never stretched that slender, sinewy body in such a wild dance or played competitive games. No, he had never seen her like this within the sombre walls of the crowded city, had never heard her voice rise like lark-song set free from the earthly confines of her throat in merriment that was almost song, not indoors and not in the street. She had never been so beautiful. The old man stared and stared. He had forgotten everything, he just watched and watched that white, elusive flame. And he would have stood like that, endlessly absorbing her image with a passionate gaze, if she had not finally caught the last of the balls she was juggling with a breathless, fluttering leap, turning nimbly, and pressed them to her breast breathing fast, face flushed, but with a proud and laughing gaze. "*Brava, brava!*" cried the three gentlemen, who had been intently watching her clever juggling of the balls, applauding as if she had finished an operatic aria. Their guttural voices roused the old man from his enchantment, and he stared grimly at them.

So there they are, the villains, he thought, his heart thudding. There they are—but which of them is it? Which of those three has had her? Oh yes, how finely rigged out they are, shaved and perfumed, idle dandies… while men like me still sit in offices in their old age, in shabby trousers, wearing down the heels of their shoes visiting customers… and for all I know the fathers of these fine fellows may still be toiling away today, wearing their hands out so that their sons can travel the world, wasting time at their leisure, their faces browned and carefree, their impudent eyes bright. Easy for them to be cheerful, they only have to throw a silly, vain child a few sweet words and she'll fall into bed… But which of the three is it, which is it? One of them, I know, is seeing her naked through her dress and smacking his lips. I've had her, he's thinking, he's known her hot and naked, we'll do it again this evening, he thinks, winking at her—oh, the bastard, the dog, yes, if only I could whip him like a dog!

And now they had noticed him standing there. His daughter swung up her racket in a salutation, and smiled at him, the gentlemen wished him good day. He did not thank them, only stared at his daughter's smiling lips with brimming, bloodshot eyes. To think that you can laugh like that, he thought, you shameless creature… and one of those men may be laughing to himself, telling himself—there goes the stupid old Jew who lies snoring in bed all night… if only he knew, the old fool! Oh yes, I do know, you fine fellows laugh, you tread me underfoot like dirt… but my daughter, so pretty and willing, she'll tumble into bed with you… and as for her mother, she's a little stout now, but she goes about all dolled up with her face painted, and if you were to make eyes at her, who knows, she might yet venture to dance a step or so with you… You're right, you dogs, you're right when they run after you, those shameless women, women on heat… what's it to you that another man's heart is breaking so long as you can have your fun, fun with those shameless females… someone should take a revolver and shoot you down, you deserve to be horsewhipped… but yes, you're right, so long as no one does anything, so long as I swallow my rage like a dog returning to his vomit… you're right, if a father is so cowardly, so shockingly cowardly… if he doesn't go to the shameless girl, take hold of her, drag her away from you… if he just stands there saying nothing, bitter gall in his mouth, a coward, a coward, a coward…

The old man clutched the balustrade as helpless rage shook him. And suddenly he spat on the ground in front of his feet and staggered out of the garden.

*

The old man made his way unsteadily into the little town. Suddenly he stopped in front of a display window full of all kinds of things for tourists' needs—shirts and nets, blouses and angling equipment, ties, books, tins of biscuits, not in chance confusion but built up into artificial pyramids and colourfully arranged on shelves. However, his gaze went to just one object, lying disregarded amidst this elegant jumble—a gnarled walking stick, stout and solid with an iron tip, heavy in the hand; it would probably come down with a good thump. Strike him down, thought the old man, strike the dog down! The idea transported him into a confused, almost lustful turmoil of feeling which sent him into the shop, and he bought the stout stick quite cheaply. And no sooner was the weighty, heavy, menacing thing in his hand than he felt stronger. A weapon always makes the physically weak more sure of themselves. It was as if the handle of the stick tensed and tautened his muscles. "Strike him down… strike the dog down!" he muttered to himself, and unconsciously his heavy, stumbling gait turned to a firmer, more upright, faster rhythm. He walked, even ran up and down the path by the shores of the lake, breathing hard and sweating, but more from the passion spreading through him than because of his accelerated pace. For his hand was clutching the heavy handle of the stick more and more tightly.

Armed with this weapon, he entered the blue, cool shadows of the hotel lobby, his angry eyes searching for the invisible enemy. And sure enough, there in the corner they were sitting together on comfortable wicker chairs, drinking whisky and soda through straws, talking cheerfully in idle good fellowship—his wife, his daughter and the inevitable trio of gentlemen. Which of them is it, he wondered, which of them is it? And his fist clenched around the handle of the heavy stick. Whose skull do I smash in, whose, whose? But Erna, misunderstanding his restless, searching glances, was already jumping up and running to him. "So here you are, Papa! We've been looking for you everywhere. Guess what, Baron von Medwitz is going to take us for a drive in his Fiat, we're going to drive all along the lake to Desenzano!" And she affectionately led him to their table, as if he ought to thank the gentlemen for the invitation.

They had risen politely and were offering him their hands. The old man trembled. But the girl's warm presence, placating him, lay soft and intoxicating against his arm. His will was paralysed as he shook the three hands one by one, sat down in silence, took out a cigar and bit grimly into the soft end of it. Above him, the casual conversation went on, in French, with much high-spirited laughter from several voices.

The old man sat there, silent and hunched, biting the end of his cigar until his teeth were brown with tobacco juice. They're right, he thought, they're right, I deserve to be spat at… now I've shaken their hands! Shaken hands with all three, and I know that one of them's the villain. Here I am sitting quietly at the same table with him, and I don't strike him down, no, I don't strike him down, I shake hands with him civilly… they're right, quite right if they laugh at me… and see the way they talk, ignoring me as if I weren't here at all! I might already be underground… and they both know, Erna and my wife, that I don't understand a word of French. They both know that, both of them, but no one asked me whether I minded, if only for form's sake, just because I sit here so foolishly, feeling so ridiculous. I might be thin air to them, nothing but thin air, a nuisance, a hanger-on, something in the way of their fun… someone to be ashamed of, they tolerate me only because I make so much money. Money, money, always that wretched, filthy lucre, the money I've spent indulging them, money with God's curse on it. They don't say a word to me, my wife, my own child, they talk away to these idlers, their eyes are all for those smooth, smartly rigged-out dandies… see how they smile at those fine gentlemen, it tickles their fancy, as if they felt their hands on bare female flesh. And I put up with it all. I sit here listening to their laughter, I don't understand what they say, and yet I sit here instead of striking out with my fists, thrashing them with my stick, driving them apart before they begin coupling before my very eyes. I let it all pass… I sit here silent, stupid, a coward, coward, coward…

"Will you allow me?" asked the Italian officer, in laborious German, reaching for his lighter.

Startled out of his heated thoughts, the old man sat up very erect and stared grimly at the unsuspecting young officer. Anger was seething inside him. For a moment his hand clutched the handle of the stick convulsively. But then he let the corners of his mouth turn down again, stretching it into a senseless grin. "Oh, I'll allow you!" he sardonically repeated. "To be sure I'll allow you, ha ha, I'll allow you anything you want—ha ha!—anything I have is entirely at your disposal… you can do just as you like."

The bewildered officer stared at him. With his poor command of German, he had not quite understood, but that wry, grinning smile made him uneasy. The gentleman jockey from Germany sat up straight, startled, the two women went white as a sheet—for a split second the air among them all was breathless and motionless, as electric as the tiny pause between a flash of lightning and the thunder that follows.

But then the fierce distortion of his face relaxed, the stick slid out of his clutch. Like a beaten dog, the old man retreated into his own thoughts and coughed awkwardly, alarmed by his own boldness. Trying to smooth over the embarrassing tension, Erna returned to her light conversational tone, the German baron replied, obviously anxious to maintain the cheerful mood, and within a few minutes the interrupted tide of words was in full flow once more.

The old man sat among the others as they chattered, entirely withdrawn; and you might have thought he was asleep. His heavy stick, now that the clutch of his hands was relaxed, dangled useless between his legs. His head, propped on one hand, sank lower and lower. But no one paid him any more attention, the wave of chatter rolled over his silence, sometimes laughter sprayed up, sparkling, at a joking remark, but he was lying motionless below it all in endless darkness, drowned in shame and pain.

The three gentlemen rose to their feet, Erna followed readily, her mother more slowly; in obedience to someone's light-hearted suggestion they were going into the music room next door, and did not think it necessary to ask the old man drowsing away there to come with them. Only when he suddenly became aware of the emptiness around him did he wake, like a sleeping man roused by the cold when his blanket has slipped off the bed in the night, and cold air blows over his naked body. Instinctively his eyes went to the chairs they had left, but jazzy music was already coming from the room next door, syncopated and garish. He heard laughter and cries of encouragement. They were dancing next door. Yes, dancing, always dancing, they could do that all right! Always stirring up the blood, always rubbing avidly against each other, chafing until the dish was cooked and ready. Dancing in the evening, at night, in bright daylight, idlers, gentlemen of leisure with time on their hands, that was how they charmed the women.

Bitterly, he picked up his stout stick again and dragged himself after them. At the door he stopped. The German baron, the gentleman jockey, was sitting at the piano, half turned away from the keyboard so that he could watch the dancers at the same time as he rattled out an American hit song on the keys, a tune he obviously knew more or less by heart. Erna was dancing with the officer; the long-legged Conte Ubaldi was rhythmically pushing her strong, sturdy mother forward and back, not without some difficulty. But the old man had eyes for no one but Erna and her partner. How that slender greyhound of a man laid his hands, soft and flattering, on her delicate shoulders, as if she belonged to him entirely! How her body, swaying, following his lead, pressed close to his, as if promising herself, how they danced, intertwined, before his very eyes, with passion that they had difficulty in restraining! Yes, he was the man—for in those two bodies moving as one there burnt a sense of familiarity, something in common already in their blood. He was the one—it could only be he, he read it from her eyes, half-closed and yet brimming over, in that fleeting, hovering movement reflecting the memory of lustful moments already enjoyed—he was the man, he was the thief who came by night to seize and ardently penetrate what his child, his own child, now concealed in her thin, semi-transparent, flowing dress! Instinctively he stepped closer to tear her away from the man. But she didn't even notice him. With every movement of the rhythm, giving herself up to the guiding touch of the dancer, the seducer leading her, with her head thrown back and her moist mouth open, she swayed softly to the beat of the music, with no sense of space or time or of the man, the trembling, panting old man who was staring at her in a frenzied ecstasy of rage, his eyes bloodshot. She felt only herself, her own young limbs as she unresistingly followed the syncopation of the breathlessly swirling dance music. She felt only herself, and the fact that a male creature so close to her desired her, his strong arm surrounded her, and she must preserve her balance and not fall against him with greedy lips, hotly inhaling his breath as she abandoned herself to him. And all this was magically known to the old man in his own blood, his own shattered being—always, whenever the dance swept her away from him, he felt as if she were sinking for ever.

Suddenly, as if the string of an instrument had broken, the music stopped in the middle of a bar. The German baron jumped up. "*Assez joué pour vous*," he laughed. "*Maintenant je veux danser moi-même.*"—"You've had your fun. Now I want to dance myself!" They all cheerfully agreed, the group stopped dancing in couples and moved into an informal, fluttering dance all together.

The old man came back to his senses—how he wanted to do something now, say something! Not just stand about so foolishly, so pitifully superfluous! His wife was dancing by, gasping slightly from exertion but warm with contentment. Anger brought him to a sudden decision. He stepped into her path. "Come with me," he said brusquely. "I have to talk to you."

She looked at him in surprise. Little beads of sweat moistened his pale brow, his eyes were staring wildly around. What did he want? Why disturb her just now? An excuse was already forming on her lips, but there was something so convulsive, so dangerous in his demeanour that, suddenly remembering the grim outburst over the lighter just now, she reluctantly followed him.

"*Excusez, messieurs, un instant!*" she said, turning back apologetically to the gentlemen. So she'll apologise to *them*, thought the agitated old man grimly, she didn't apologise to me when she got up from the table. I'm no more than a dog to her, a doormat to be trodden on. But they're right, oh yes, they're right if I put up with it.

She was waiting, her eyebrows sternly raised; he stood before her, his lip quivering, like a schoolboy facing his teacher.

"Well?" she finally asked.

"I don't want… I don't want…" he stammered awkwardly. "I don't want you—you and Erna—I don't want you mixing with those people."

"With what people?" Deliberately pretending not to understand, she looked up indignantly, as if he had insulted her personally.

"With those men in there." Angrily, he jerked his chin in the direction of the music room. "I don't like it… I don't want you to…"

"And why not, may I ask?"

Always that inquisitorial tone, he thought bitterly, as if I were a servant. Still more agitated, he stammered, "I have my reasons… I don't like it. I don't want Erna talking to those men. I don't have to tell you everything."

"Then I'm sorry," she said, flaring up, "but I consider all three gentlemen extremely well-brought up, far more distinguished company than we keep at home."

"Distinguished company! Those idlers, those… those…" Rage was throttling him more intolerably than ever. And suddenly he stamped his foot. "I don't want it, I forbid it! Do you understand that?"

"No," she said coldly. "I don't understand any of what you say. I don't know why I should spoil the girl's pleasure…"

"Her pleasure… her pleasure!" He was staggering as if under a heavy blow, his face red, his forehead streaming with sweat. His hand groped in the air for his heavy stick, either to support himself or to hit out with it. But he had left it behind. That brought him back to his senses. He forced himself to keep calm as a wave of heat suddenly passed over his heart. He went closer to his wife, as if to take her hand. His voice was low now, almost pleading. "You… you don't understand. It's not for myself… I'm begging you only because… it's the first thing I've asked you for years, let's go away from here. Just away, to Florence, to Rome, anywhere you want, I don't mind. You can decide it all, just as you like. I only want to get away from here, please, away… away, today, this very day. I… I can't bear it any longer, I can't."

"Today?" Surprised, dismissively, she frowned. "Go away today? What a ridiculous idea! Just because you don't happen to like those gentlemen. Well, you don't have to mingle with them."

He was still standing there, hands raised pleadingly. "I can't bear it, I told you… I can't, I can't. Don't ask me any more, please… but believe me, I can't bear it, I can't. Do this for me, just for once, do something for me…"

In the music room someone had begun hammering at the piano again. She looked up, touched by his cry despite herself, but how very ridiculous he looked, that short fat man, his face red as if he had suffered a stroke, his eyes wild and swollen, his hands emerging from sleeves too short for him and trembling in the air. It was embarrassing to see him standing there in such a pitiful state. Her milder feelings froze.

"That's impossible," she informed him. "We've agreed to go out for that drive today, and as for leaving tomorrow when we've booked for three weeks… why, we'd make ourselves look ridiculous.

I can't see the faintest reason for leaving early. I am staying here, and so is Erna, we are not—"

"And I can go, you're saying? I'm only in the way here, spoiling your… pleasure."

With that sombre cry he cut her short in mid-sentence. His hunched, massive body had reared up, he had clenched his hands into fists, a vein was trembling alarmingly on his forehead in anger. He wanted to get something else out, a word or a blow. But he turned abruptly, stumbled to the stairs, moving faster and faster on his heavy legs, and hurried up them like a man pursued.

Gasping, the old man went hastily up the stairs; he wanted only to be in his room now, alone, try to control himself, take care not to do anything silly! He had already reached the first floor when—there it came, the pain, as if a burning claw were tearing open his guts from the inside. He suddenly stumbled back against the wall, white as a sheet. Oh, that raging, burning pain kneading away at him; he had to grit his teeth to keep himself from crying out loud. Groaning, his tormented body writhed.

He knew at once what was wrong—it was his gall bladder, one of those fearful attacks that had often plagued him recently, but had never before tortured him so cruelly. Next moment, in the middle of his pain, he remembered that the doctor had prescribed 'no agitation'. Through the pain he grimly mocked himself. Easily said, he thought, no agitation—my dear good Professor, can you tell me how to avoid agitation when… oh, oh…

The old man was whimpering as the invisible, red-hot claw worked away inside his poor body. With difficulty, he dragged himself to the door of the sitting room of the suite, pushed it open, and fell on the ottoman, stuffing the cushions into his mouth. As he lay there the pain immediately lessened slightly; the hot nails of that claw were no longer reaching so infernally deep into his sore guts.

I ought to make myself a compress, he remembered, I must take those drops, then it will soon be better.

But there was no one there to help him, no one. And he himself had no strength to drag himself into the next room, or even reach the bell.

There's no one here, he thought bitterly, I shall die like a dog sooner or later, because I know what it is that hurts, it's not my gall bladder, it's Death growing in me. I know it, I'm a defeated man, no professors, no drinking the waters at spas can help me… you don't recover from this sort of thing, not at sixty-five. I know what's piercing me and tearing me from the inside, it's Death, and the few years I have left will not be life, just dying, dying. But when did I ever really live? Live my own life, for myself? What kind of life have I had, scraping money together all the time, always for other people, and now, what help is it to me now? I've had a wife, I married her as a girl, I knew her body and she bore me a child. Year after year we lay together in the same bed… and now, where is she now? I don't recognise her face any more… she speaks so strangely to me, and never thinks of my life, of all I feel and think and suffer… she's been a stranger to me for years now… Where has my life gone, where did it go?… And I had a child, watched her grow up, I thought I'd begin to live again through her, a brighter, happier life than was granted to me, in her I wouldn't entirely die… and now she steals away by night to throw herself at men. There's only me, I shall die alone, all alone… I'm already dead to those two. My God, my God, I was never so much alone…

The claw sometimes closed grimly inside him and then let go again. But another pain was hammering deeper and deeper into his temples; his thoughts, harsh, sharp, were like mercilessly hot gravel in his forehead, he mustn't think just now, mustn't think! The old man had torn open his jacket and waistcoat—his bloated body quivered, plump and shapeless, under his billowing shirt. Cautiously he pressed his hand to the painful place. All that hurts there is me, he felt, it's only me, only this piece of hot skin… and only what's clawing around in it there still belongs to me, it is *my* illness, *my* death… I am all it is… I am not a Privy Commercial Councillor any more, with a wife and child and money and a house and a business… this is all I really am, what I feel with my fingers, my body and the heat inside it hurting me. Everything else is folly, makes no sense now… because what hurts in there hurts only me, what concerns me concerns me alone. They don't understand me any more, and I don't understand them… you are all alone with yourself in the end. I never felt it so much before… But now I know, now I lie here feeling Death under my skin, too late now in my sixty-fifth year, just before dying, now while they dance and go for walks or drift aimlessly about, those shameless women… now I know it, I lived only for them, not that they thank me for it, and never for myself, not for an hour. But what do I care for them now… what do I care for them… why think of them when they never think of me? Better die than accept their pity… what do I care for them now?…

Gradually receding, the pain ebbed away; the cruel hand did not grasp into the suffering man with such red-hot claws. But it left behind a dull, sombre feeling, barely perceptible as pain now, yet something alien pressing and pushing, tunnelling away inside him. The old man lay with his eyes closed, attending carefully to this soft pushing and pulling; he felt as if a strange, unknown power were hollowing something out in him, first with sharp tools, then with blunter ones. It was like something coming adrift, fibre by fibre, within his body. The tearing was not so fierce now, and did not hurt any more. But there was something quietly smouldering and rotting inside him, something beginning to die. All he had lived through, all he had loved, was lost in that slowly consuming flame, burning black before it fell apart, crumbling and charred, into the lukewarm mire of indifference. Something was happening, he knew it vaguely, something was happening while he lay like this, reflecting passionately on his life. Something was coming to an end. What was it? He listened and listened to what was going on inside him.

And slowly his heart began to fail him.

The old man lay in the twilight of the room with his eyes closed. He was still half awake, half already dreaming. And then, between sleeping and waking, it seemed to him in the confusion of his feelings as if, from somewhere or other, something moist and hot was seeping softly into him from a wound that did not hurt and that he was unaware of having suffered. It was like being drained of his own blood. It did not hurt, that invisible flow, it did not run very strongly. The drops fell only slowly, like warm tears trickling down, and each of them struck him in the middle of the heart. But his heart, his dark heart, made no sound and quietly soaked up that strange torrent. Soaked it up like a sponge, became heavier and heavier with it, his heart was already swelling with it, brimming over, it was spilling into the narrow frame of his chest. Gradually filling up, overflowing with its own weight, whatever it was began gently pulling to expand itself, pulling at taut muscles, pressing harder and harder and forcing his painful heart, gigantic by now, down after its own weight. And now (oh, how this hurt!) now the weight came loose from the fibres of flesh—very slowly, not like a stone or a falling fruit, no, like a sponge soaked with moisture it sank deeper and ever deeper into a warm void, down into something without being that was outside himself, into vast and endless night. All at once it was terribly still in the place where that warm, brimming heart had been a moment ago. What yawned empty there now was uncanny and cold. No sensation of thudding any more, no dripping now, all was very still and perfectly dead inside him. And his shuddering breast surrounded that silent and incomprehensible void like a hollow black coffin.

So strong was this dreamlike feeling, so deep his confusion, that when the old man began to wake he instinctively put his hand to the left side of his chest to see whether his heart was still here. But thank God, he felt a pulse, a hollow, rhythmical pulse beating below his groping fingers, and yet it might have been beating mutely in a vacuum, as if his heart was really gone. For strange to say, it suddenly seemed as if his body had left him of its own accord. No pain wrenched at it any more, no memory twitched painfully, all was silent in there, fixed and turned to stone. What's this, he wondered, when just now I felt such pain, such hot pressure, when every fibre was twitching? What has happened to me? He listened, as if to the sounds in a cavern, to find out whether what had been there before was still moving. But those rushing sounds, the dripping, the thudding, they were far away. He listened and listened, no echo came, none at all. Nothing hurt him any more, nothing was swelling up to torment him; it must be as empty and black in there as a hollow, burnt-out tree. And all at once he felt as if he had already died, or something in him had died, his blood was so sluggish and silent. His own body lay under him cold as a corpse, and he was afraid to feel it with his warm hand.

There in his room the old man, listening to what was happening to him, did not hear the sound of church clocks down by the lake striking the hours, each hour bringing deeper twilight. The night was already gathering around him, darkness fell on the things in the room as it flowed away into the night, at last even the pale sky visible in the rectangle of the window was immersed in total darkness. The old man never noticed, but only stared at the blackness in himself, listening to the void there as if to his own death.

Then, at last, there was exuberant laughter in the room next door. A switch was pressed, and light came through the crack of the doorway, for the door was only ajar. The old man roused himself with a start—his wife, his daughter! They would find him here on the day bed and ask questions. He hastily buttoned up his jacket and waistcoat; why should they know about the attack he had suffered, what business of theirs was it?

But the two women had not come in search of him. They were obviously in a hurry; the imperious gong was striking for the third time. They seemed to be dressing for dinner; listening, he could hear every movement through the half-open doorway. Now they were opening the shutters, now they were putting their rings down on the washstand with a light chink, now shoes were tapping on the floor, and from time to time they talked to each other. Every word, every syllable came to the old man's ears with cruel clarity. First they talked about the gentlemen, mocking them a little, about a chance incident on the drive, light, inconsequent remarks as they washed and moved around, dressing and titivating themselves. Then, suddenly, the conversation turned to him.

"Where's Papa?" Erna asked, sounding surprised that he had occurred to her so late.

"How should I know?" That was her mother's voice, instantly irritated by the mere mention of him. "Probably waiting for us down in the lobby, reading the stock prices in the Frankfurt newspaper for the hundredth time—they're all he's interested in. Do you think he's even looked at the lake? He doesn't like it here, he told me so at mid-day. He wanted us to leave today."

"Leave today? But why?" Erna's voice again.

"I really don't know. Who can tell what he has in mind? He doesn't like the other guests here, the company of those gentlemen doesn't suit him—probably he feels how little his company suits them. Really, the way he goes around here is disgraceful, with his clothes all crumpled, his collar open… you should suggest that he might look a little more *soigné*, at least in the evenings, he'll listen to you. And this morning… I thought I'd sink into the ground to hear him flare up at the lieutenant when he wanted to borrow Papa's lighter."

"Yes, Mama, what was that all about? I wanted to ask you, what was the matter with Papa? I've never seen him like that before… I was really shocked."

"Oh, he was just in a bad temper. I expect prices on the stock exchange have fallen. Or perhaps it was because we were speaking French. He can't bear other people to have a nice time. You didn't notice, but while we were dancing he was standing at the door of the music room like a murderer lurking behind a tree. Leave today! Leave on the spot! Just because that's what he suddenly feels like doing. Well, if he doesn't like it here, there's no need for him to grudge us our pleasure… but I'm not going to bother with his whims any more, whatever he says and does."

The conversation ended. Obviously they had finished dressing for dinner. Yes, the door was opened, they were leaving the room, he heard the click of the switch, and the light went out.

The old man sat perfectly still on the ottoman. He had heard every word. But strange to say, it no longer hurt, it did not hurt at all. The clockwork in his breast that had been hammering and tearing at him fiercely not so long ago had come to a standstill; it must be broken. He had felt no reaction to the sharp touch of their remarks. No anger, no hatred… nothing, nothing. Calmly, he buttoned up his clothes, cautiously made his way downstairs, and sat down at the dinner table with them as if they were strangers.

He did not speak to them that evening, and for their part they did not notice his silence, which was as concentrated as a clenched fist. After dinner he went back to his room, again without a word, lay down on the bed and put out the light. Only much later did his wife come up from the evening's cheerful entertainment, and thinking he was asleep she undressed in the dark. Soon he heard her heavy, easy breathing.

The old man, alone with himself, stared open-eyed at the endless void of the night. Beside him something lay in the dark, breathing deeply; he made an effort to remember that the body drawing in the same air in the same room was the woman whom he had known when she was young and ardent, who had borne him a child, a body bound to him through the deepest mystery of the blood; he kept forcing himself to think that the warm, soft body there—he had only to put out a hand to touch it—had once been a life that was part of his own. But strangely, the memory aroused no feelings in him any more. And he heard her regular breathing only like the murmuring of little waves coming through the open window as they broke softly on the pebbles near the shore. It was all far away and unreal, something strange was lying beside him only by chance—it was over, over for ever.

Once he found himself trembling very slightly, and stole to his daughter's door. So she was out of her room again tonight. He did feel a small, sharp pang in the heart he had thought dead. For a second, something twitched there like a nerve before it died away entirely. That was over now as well. Let her do as she likes, he thought, what is it to me?

And the old man lay back on his pillow again. Once more the darkness closed in on his aching head, and that cool, blue sensation seeped into his blood—a beneficial feeling. Soon light slumber cast its shadow over his exhausted senses.

When his wife woke up in the morning she saw her husband already in his coat and hat. "What are you doing?" she asked, still drowsy from sleep.

The old man did not turn around. He was calmly packing his night things in a small suitcase. "You know what I'm doing. I'm going home. I'm taking only the necessities; you can have the rest sent after me."

His wife took fright. What was all this? She had never heard his voice like that before, bringing each word out cold and hard. She swung both legs out of bed. "You're not going away, surely? Wait… we'll come with you, I've already told Erna that…"

He only waved this vigorously away. "No, no, don't let it disturb you." And without looking back he made his way to the door. He had to put the suitcase down on the floor for a moment in order to press down the door handle. And in that one fitful second a memory came back—a memory of thousands of times when he had put down his case of samples like that as he left the doors of strangers with a servile bow, ingratiating himself with an eye to further business. But he had no business here and now, so he omitted any greeting. Without a look or a word he picked up his suitcase again and closed the door firmly between himself and his old life.

Neither mother nor daughter understood what had happened. But the strikingly abrupt and determined nature of his departure made them both uneasy. They wrote to him back at home in south Germany at once, elaborately explaining that they assumed there had been some misunderstanding, writing almost affectionately, asking with concern how his journey had been, and whether he had arrived safely. Suddenly compliant, they expressed themselves ready and willing to break off their holiday at any time. There was no reply. They wrote again, more urgently, they sent telegrams, but there was still no reply. Only the sum of money that they had said they needed in one of the letters arrived—a postal remittance bearing the stamp of his firm, without a word or greeting of his own.

Such an inexplicable and oppressive state of affairs made them bring their own return home forward. Although they had sent a telegram in advance, there was no one to meet them at the station, and they found everything unprepared at home. In an absent-minded moment, so the servants told them, the master had left the telegram lying on the table and had gone out, without leaving any instructions. In the evening, when they were already sitting down to eat, they heard the sound of the front door at last. They jumped up and ran to meet him. He looked at them in surprise—obviously he had forgotten the telegram—patiently accepted his daughter's embrace, but without any particular expression of feeling, let them lead him to the dining room and tell him about their journey. However, he asked no questions, smoked his cigar in silence, sometimes answered briefly, sometimes did not notice what they said at all; it was as if he were asleep with his eyes open. Then he got up ponderously and went to his room.

And it was the same for the next few days. His anxious wife tried to get him to talk to her, but in vain; the more she pressed him, the more evasively he reacted. Some place inside him was barred to her, inaccessible, an entrance had been walled up. He still ate with them, sat with them for a while when callers came, but in silence, absorbed in his own thoughts. However, he took no part in their lives any more, and when guests happened to look into his eyes in the middle of a conversation, they had the unpleasant feeling that a dead man's dull and shallow gaze was looking past them.

Even those who hardly knew him soon noticed the increasing oddity of the old man's behaviour. Acquaintances began to nudge each other on the sly if they met him in the street—there went the old man, one of the richest men in the city, slinking along by the wall like a beggar, his hat dented and set at a crooked angle on his head, his coat dusted with cigar ash, reeling in a peculiar way at every step and usually muttering aloud under his breath. If people greeted him, he looked up in surprise; if they addressed him he stared at them vacantly, and forgot to shake hands. At first a number of acquaintances thought he must have gone deaf, and repeated what they had said in louder tones. He was not deaf, but it always took him time to wake himself, as it were, from his internal sleep, and then he would lapse back into a strange state of abstraction in the middle of the conversation. All of a sudden the light would go out of his eyes, he would break off the discussion hastily and stumble on, without noticing the surprise of the person who had spoken to him. He always seemed to have emerged from a dark dream, from a cloudy state of self-absorption; other people, it was obvious, no longer existed for him. He never asked how anyone was; even in his own home he did not notice his wife's gloomy desperation or his daughter's baffled questions. He read no newspapers, listened to no conversations; not a word, not a question penetrated his dull and overcast indifference for a moment. Even what was closest to him became strange. He sometimes went to his office to sign letters. But if his secretary came back an hour later to fetch them, duly signed, he found the old man just as he had left him, lost in reverie over the unread letters and with the same vacant look in his eyes. In the end he himself realised that he was only in the way at the office, and stayed away entirely.

But the strangest and most surprising thing about the old man, to the whole city, was the fact that although he had never been among the most devoutly observant members of its Jewish community he suddenly became pious. Indifferent to all else, often unpunctual at meals and meetings, he never failed to be at the synagogue at the appointed hour. He stood there in his black silk cap, his prayer shawl around his shoulders, always at the same place, where his father once used to stand, rocking his weary head back and forth as he chanted psalms. Here, in the dim light of the room where the words echoed around him, dark and strange, he was most alone with himself. A kind of peace descended on his confused mind here, responding to the darkness in his own breast. However, when prayers were read for the dead, and he saw the families, children and friends of the departed dutifully bowing down and calling on the mercy of God for those who had left this world, his eyes were sometimes clouded. He was the last of his line, and he knew it. No one would say a prayer for him. And so he devoutly murmured the words with the congregation, thinking of himself as one might think of the dead.

Once, late in the evening, he was coming back from wandering the city in a daze, and was halfway home when rain began to fall. As usual, the old man had forgotten his umbrella. There were cabs for hire quite cheaply, entrances to buildings and glazed porches offered shelter from the torrential rain that was soon pouring down, but the strange old man swayed and stumbled on through the wet weather. A puddle collected in the dent in his hat and seeped through, rivulets streamed down from his own dripping sleeves; he took no notice but trudged on, the only person out and about in the deserted street. And so, drenched and dripping, looking more like a tramp than the master of a handsome villa, he reached the entrance of his house just at the moment when a car with its headlights on stopped right beside him, flinging up more muddy water on the inattentive pedestrian. The door swung open, and his wife hastily got out of the brightly lit the interior, followed by some distinguished visitor or other holding an umbrella over her, and then a second man. He drew level with them just outside the door. His wife recognised him and was horrified to see him in such a state, dripping wet, his clothes crumpled, looking like a bundle of something pulled out of the water, and instinctively she turned her eyes away. The old man understood at once—she was ashamed of him in front of her guests. And without emotion or bitterness, he walked a little further as if he were a stranger, to spare her the embarrassment of an introduction, and turned humbly in at the servants' entrance.

From that day on the old man always used the servants' stairs in his own house. He was sure not to meet anyone here, he was in no one's way and no one was in his. He stayed away from meals—an old maidservant brought something to his room. If his wife or daughter tried to get in to speak to him, he would send them away again with a vague murmur that was none the less clearly a refusal to see them. In the end they left him alone, and gradually stopped asking how he was, nor did he enquire after anyone or anything. He sometimes heard music and laughter coming through the walls from the other rooms in the house, which were already strange to him, he heard vehicles pass by until late at night, but he was so indifferent to everything that he did not even look out of the window. What was it to do with him? Only the dog sometimes came up and lay down by his forgotten master's bed.

*

Nothing hurt in his dead heart now, but the black mole was tunnelling on inside his body, tearing a bloodstained path into quivering flesh. His attacks grew more frequent from week to week, and at last, in agony, he gave way to his doctor's urging to have himself thoroughly examined. The professor looked grave. Carefully preparing the way, he said he thought that at this point an operation was essential. But the old man did not take fright, he only smiled wearily. Thank God, now it was coming to an end. An end to dying, and now came the good part, death. He would not let the doctor say a word to his family, the day was decided, and he made ready. For the last time, he went to his firm (where no one expected to see him any more, and they all looked at him as if he were a stranger), sat down once more in the old black leather chair where he had sat for thirty years, a whole lifetime, for thousands and thousands of hours, told them to bring him a cheque book and made out a cheque. He took it to the rabbi of the synagogue, who was almost frightened by the size of the sum. It was for charitable works and for his grave, he said, and to avoid all thanks he hastily stumbled out, losing his hat, but he did not even bend to pick it up. And so, bareheaded, eyes dull in his wrinkled face, now yellow with sickness, he went on his way, followed by surprised glances, to his parents' grave in the cemetery. There a few idlers gazed at the old man, and were surprised to hear him talk out loud and at length to the mouldering tombstones as if they were human beings. Was he announcing his imminent arrival to them, or asking for their blessing? No one could hear the words, but his lips moved, murmuring, and his shaking head was bowed deeper and deeper in prayer. At the way out of the cemetery beggars, who knew him well by sight, crowded around him. He hastily took all the coins and notes out of his pockets, and had distributed them when a wrinkled old woman limped up, later than the rest, begging for something for herself. In confusion, he searched his pockets, but there was nothing left. However, he still had something strange and heavy on his finger—his gold wedding ring. Some kind of memory came to him—he quickly took it off and gave it to the startled old woman.

And so, impoverished, empty and alone, he went under the surgeon's knife.

When the old man came round from the anaesthetic, the doctors, seeing the dangerous state he was in, called his wife and daughter, now informed of the operation, into the room. With difficulty, his eyes looked out from lids surrounded by blue shadows. "Where am I?" He stared at the strange white room that he had never seen before.

Then, to show him her affection, his daughter leant over his poor sunken face. And suddenly a glimmer of recognition came into the blindly searching eyes. A light, a small one, was kindled in their pupils—that was her, his child, his beloved child, that was his beautiful and tender child Erna! Very, very slowly the bitterly compressed lips relaxed. A smile, a very small smile that had not come to his closed mouth for a long time, cautiously began to show. And shaken by that joy, expressed as it was with such difficulty, she bent closer to kiss her father's bloodless cheeks.

But there it was—the sweet perfume that aroused a memory, or was it his half-numbed brain remembering forgotten moments?—and suddenly a terrible change came over the features that had looked happy only just now. His colourless lips were grimly tightened again, rejecting her. His hand worked its way out from under the blanket, and he tried to raise it as if to push something repellent away, his whole sore body quivering in agitation. "Get away!… Get away!" he babbled. The words on his pale lips were almost inarticulate, yet clear enough. And so terribly did a look of aversion form on the face of the old man, who could not get away, that the doctor anxiously urged the women to stand aside. "He's delirious," he whispered. "You had better leave him alone now."

As soon as the two women had gone, the distorted features relaxed wearily again into final drowsiness. Breath was still escaping, although more and more stertorously, as he struggled for the heavy air of life. But soon his breast tired of the struggle to drink in that bitter nourishment of humanity. And when the doctor felt for the old man's heart, it had already ceased to hurt him.

INCIDENT ON LAKE GENEVA

ON THE BANKS OF LAKE GENEVA, close to the small Swiss resort of Villeneuve, a fisherman who had rowed his boat out into the lake one summer night in the year 1918 noticed a strange object in the middle of the water. When he came closer, he saw that it was a raft made of loosely assembled wooden planks which a naked man was clumsily trying to propel forward, using a piece of board as an oar. In astonishment, the fisherman steered his boat that way, helped the exhausted man into it, used some fishing nets as a makeshift covering for his nakedness, and then tried questioning the shivering figure huddling nervously into the corner of the boat. But he replied in a strange language, not a word of which was anything like the fisherman's, so the rescuer soon gave up any further attempts, pulled in his nets, and rowed back to the bank, plying his oars faster than before.

As the early light of dawn showed the outline of the bank, the naked man's face too began to clear. A childlike smile appeared through the tangled beard around his broad mouth, he raised one hand, pointing, and kept stammering out a single word over and over again: a question that was half a statement. It sounded like "*Rossiya*", and he repeated it more and more happily the closer the keel came to the bank of the lake. At last the boat crunched on the beach; the fisherman's womenfolk, who were waiting for him to land his dripping catch, scattered screeching, like Nausicaa's maids in the days of old, when they caught sight of the naked man covered by fishing nets, and only gradually, on hearing the strange news, did several men from the village appear. They were soon joined by that local worthy the courthouse usher, eagerly officious and very much on his dignity. He knew at once, from various instructions that he had received and a wealth of wartime experience, that this must be a deserter who had swum over the lake from the French bank, and he was preparing to interrogate him officially, but any such elaborate process was quickly deprived of any dignity or usefulness by the fact that the naked man (to whom some of the locals had now thrown a jacket and a pair of cotton drill trousers) responded to all questions with his questioning cry of "*Rossiya? Rossiya?*" sounding ever more anxious and doubtful. Slightly irked by his failure, the usher ordered the stranger to follow him by means of gestures that could not be misunderstood, and the wet, barefoot figure, his jacket and trousers flapping around him, was escorted to the courthouse, surrounded by the vociferous youths of the village who had now come along, and was taken into custody there. He did not protest, he said not a word, but his bright eyes had darkened with disappointment, and his shoulders were hunched as if expecting blows.

By now news of this human catch had reached the nearby hotel, and several ladies and gentlemen, glad of this intriguing episode to relieve the monotonous course of the day's events, came over to look at the wild man. One lady gave him some confectionery, which he eyed as suspiciously as a monkey might, and did not touch. A gentleman took a photograph. They all chattered and talked vivaciously as they swarmed around him, until at last the manager of the large hotel, who had lived abroad for a long time and knew several languages, spoke to the terrified man first in German, then in Italian and English, and finally in Russian. No sooner did he hear the first sound of his native tongue than the frightened man started violently, a broad smile split his good-natured face from ear to ear, and suddenly he was telling his whole story frankly and with self-assurance. It was very long and very confused, and the chance-come interpreter could not always understand every detail, but in essentials the man's history was as follows:

He had been fighting in Russia, and then one day he and a thousand others were packed into railway trucks and taken a very long way, they were transferred to ships and had travelled in those for even longer, through regions where it was so hot that, as he put it, the bones were baked soft inside your body. Finally they were landed again somewhere or other, packed into more railway trucks, and then they were suddenly told to storm a hill, but he knew no more about that, because a bullet had hit him in the leg as soon as the attack began. The audience, for whom the interpreter translated his questions and the man's answers, immediately realised that this fugitive was a member of one of those Russian divisions fighting in France who had been sent half-way round the world, from Siberia and Vladivostok to the French front, and as well as feeling a certain pity they were all moved at the same time by curiosity: what could have induced him to make this strange attempt at flight? With a smile that was half-good-natured, half-crafty, the Russian readily explained that as soon as he was better he had asked the orderlies where Russia was, and they had pointed to show him the way. He had roughly remembered the direction by noting the position of the sun and the stars, and so he had escaped in secret, walking by night and hiding in haystacks from patrols by day. He had eaten fruit and begged for bread for ten days, until at last he reached this lake. Now his account became less clear. Apparently he himself came from Lake Baikal, and seeing the undulating curves of the opposite bank ahead of him in the evening light, he had thought that Russia must lie over there. At any rate, he had stolen a couple of planks from a hut, and lying face downwards over them, had used a piece of old board as a paddle to make his way far out into the lake, where the fisherman found him. As soon as the hotel manager had translated the anxious question which concluded his confused explanation—could he get home tomorrow?—its naivety at first aroused loud laughter, but that soon turned to pity, and everyone found a few coins or banknotes to give the poor man, who was now looking around him with miserable uncertainty.

By this time a telephone call to Montreux had brought the arrival of a senior police officer to take down an account of the case, rather an arduous task. For not only was the amateur interpreter's command of Russian inadequate, it was soon obvious that the man was uneducated to a degree scarcely comprehensible to Westerners. All he knew about himself was his own first name of Boris, and he was able to give only the most confused accounts of his native village, for instance that the people there were serfs of Prince Metchersky (he used the word serfs although serfdom had been abolished long ago), and that he lived fifty versts from the great lake with his wife and three children. Now a discussion of what was to be done with him began, while he stood amidst the disputants dull-eyed and hunching his shoulders. Some thought he ought to be handed over to the Russian embassy in Berne, others feared that such a measure would get him sent back to France; the police officer explained all the difficulty of deciding whether he should be treated as a deserter or a foreigner without papers; the local courthouse usher rejected out of hand any suggestion that the stranger should be fed and accommodated in Villeneuve itself. A Frenchman protested that there was no need to make such a fuss about a miserable runaway; he had better either work or be sent back. Two women objected strongly to this remark, saying that his misfortune wasn't his own fault, and it was a crime to send people away from their homes to a foreign country. It began to look as if this chance incident would lead to political strife when suddenly an old Danish gentleman intervened, saying in firm tones that he would pay for the man's board and lodging for a week, and meanwhile the authorities could come to some agreement with the embassy. This unexpected solution satisfied both the officials and the private parties.

During the increasingly agitated discussion the fugitive's timid gaze had gradually lifted, and his eyes were now fixed on the lips of the hotel manager, the only person in all this turmoil who, he knew, could tell him his fate in terms that he was able to understand. He seemed to be vaguely aware of the turmoil caused by his presence, and as the noisy argument died down he spontaneously raised both hands in the silence, and reached them out to the manager with the pleading look of women at prayer before a holy picture. This moving gesture had an irresistible effect on all present. The manager went up to the man and reassured him warmly, saying that he had nothing to fear, he could stay here and come to no harm, he would have accommodation for the immediate future. The Russian tried to kiss his hand, but the other man withdrew it and quickly stepped back. Then he pointed out the house next door, a small village inn where the Russian would have bed and board, said a few more words of reassurance to him, and then, with another friendly wave, went up the beach to his hotel.

The motionless fugitive stared after him, and as the only person who understood his language dwindled in the distance, his face, which had brightened, grew gloomy again. His avid glances followed the figure of the manager as he went away, going up to the hotel above the bank of the lake, and he took no notice of the others present who were smiling at his strange demeanour. When a sympathetic bystander touched him and pointed to the inn, his heavy shoulders seemed to slump, and he went to the doorway with his head bowed. The bar was opened for him. He sat down at the table, where the barmaid brought him a glass of brandy by way of welcome, and stayed there without moving all afternoon, his eyes clouded. The village children kept looking in at the windows, laughing and shouting something at him—he never raised his head. Customers coming in looked at him curiously, but he sat where he was, back bowed, eyes staring at the table, shy and bashful. And when a crowd of guests came in to eat at midday and filled the room with their laughter, while hundreds of words he did not understand swirled around him and he himself, horribly aware of being a foreigner here, sat deaf and mute amidst the general liveliness, his hands trembled so badly that he could hardly raise the spoon from his soup. Suddenly a large tear ran down his cheek and dropped heavily on the table. He looked timidly around him. The others present had noticed the tear, and suddenly fell silent. And he felt ashamed; his large, shaggy head sank closer and closer to the black wood of the table.

He sat like that until evening. People came and went; he did not notice them, and they had stopped noticing him. He sat in the shadow of the stove like a shadow himself, his hands resting heavily on the table. He was forgotten, and no one saw him suddenly rise when twilight came and go up the path to the hotel, plodding lethargically like an animal. He stood for an hour at the door there, cap humbly in his hand, and then for another hour, not looking at anyone. At last this strange figure, standing still and black as a tree stump outside the sparkling lights of the hotel entrance as if he had put down roots there, attracted the attention of one of the pageboys, who fetched the manager. Once again his dark face lightened a little when he heard his own language.

"What do you want, Boris?" asked the manager kindly.

"Forgive me," stammered the fugitive, "I only wanted… I wanted to know if I can go home."

"Of course, Boris, to be sure you can go home," smiled the manager.

"Tomorrow?"

Now the other man looked grave too. The words had been spoken in so pleading a tone that the smile vanished from his face.

"No, Boris… not just yet. Not until the war is over."

"When is that? When will the war be over?"

"God only knows. We humans don't."

"But before that? Can't I go before that?"

"No, Boris."

"Is it so far to go?"

"Yes."

"Many more days' journey?"

"Many more days."

"I'll go all the same, sir. I'm strong. I don't tire easily."

"But you can't, Boris. There's a border between here and your home."

"A border?" He looked blank. The word was new to him. Then he said again, with his extraordinary obstinacy, "I'll swim over it."

The manager almost smiled. But he was painfully moved, and explained gently, "No, Boris, that's impossible. A border means there's a foreign country on the other side. People won't let you through."

"But I won't hurt them! I threw my rifle away. Why wouldn't they let me go back to my wife, if I ask them in Christ's name?"

The manager was feeling increasingly heavy at heart. Bitterness rose in him. "No," he said, "they won't let you through, Boris. People don't take any notice of the word of Christ any more."

"But what am I to do, sir? I can't stay here! The people that live here don't understand me, and I don't understand them."

"You'll soon learn, Boris."

"No, sir." The Russian bowed his head. "I can't learn things. I can only work in the fields, that's all I know how to do. What would I do here? I want to go home! Show me the way!"

"There isn't any way at the moment, Boris."

"But sir, they can't forbid me to go home to my wife and my children! I'm not a soldier any more."

"Oh yes, they can, Boris."

"What about the Tsar?" He asked the question very suddenly, trembling with expectation and awe.

"There's no Tsar any more, Boris. He's been deposed."

"No Tsar any more?" He stared dully at the other man, the last glimmer of light went out in his eyes, and then he said very wearily, "So I can't go home?"

"Not yet. You'll have to wait, Boris."

The face in the dark grew ever gloomier. "I've waited so long already! I can't wait any more. Show me the way to go! I want to try!"

"There's no way, Boris. They'd arrest you at the border. Stay here and we'll find you work."

"People here don't understand me, and I don't understand them," he obstinately repeated. "I can't live here! Help me, sir!"

"I can't, Boris."

"Help me, sir, for the sake of Christ! Help me, I can't bear it any more!"

"I can't, Boris. There's no way anyone can help anyone else these days."

They faced each other in silence. Boris was twisting his cap in his hands. "Then why did they take me away from home? They said I had to fight for Russia and the Tsar. But Russia is far away from here, and the Tsar… what do you say they did to the Tsar?"

"They deposed him."

"Deposed." He repeated the word without understanding it. "What am I to do, sir? I have to go home! My children are crying for me. I can't live here. Help me, sir, help me!"

"I just can't, Boris."

"Can no one help me?"

"Not at the moment."

The Russian bent his head even further, and then said abruptly, in hollow tones, "Thank you, sir," and turned away.

He went down the path very slowly. The hotel manager watched him for a long time, and was surprised when he did not go to the inn, but on down the steps to the lake. He sighed deeply and went back to his work in the hotel.

As chance would have it, it was the same fisherman who found the drowned man's naked body next morning. He had carefully placed the trousers, cap and jacket that he had been given on the bank, and went into the water just as he had come out of it. A statement was taken about the incident, and since no one knew the stranger's full name, a cheap wooden cross was put on the place where he was buried, one of those little crosses planted over the graves of unknown soldiers that now cover the continent of Europe from end to end.

MENDEL THE BIBLIOPHILE

BACK IN VIENNA AGAIN, on my way home from a visit to the outer districts of the city, I was unexpectedly caught in a heavy shower of rain that sent people running from its wet whiplash to take refuge in such shelter as the entrances of buildings, and I myself quickly looked round for a place where I could keep dry. Luckily Vienna has a coffee house on every street corner, so with my hat dripping and my shoulders drenched, I hurried into one that stood directly opposite. Inside, it proved to be a suburban café of the traditional kind, almost a stereotype of a Viennese café, with none of the newfangled features that imitate the inner-city music halls of Germany. It was in the old Viennese bourgeois style, full of ordinary people partaking more lavishly of the free newspapers than the pastries on sale. At this evening hour the air in the café, which would always be stuffy anyway, was thick with ornate blue smoke rings, yet the place looked clean, with velour sofas that were obviously new and a shiny aluminium till. In my haste I hadn't even taken the trouble to read its name outside, and indeed, what would have been the point? Now I was sitting in the warm, looking impatiently through window panes veiled by blue smoke, and wondering when it would suit the vexatious shower to move a few kilometres further on.

So there I sat, with nothing to do, and began to fall under the spell of the passive lethargy that invisibly emanates, with narcotic effect, from every true Viennese coffee house. In that empty, idle mood I looked individually at the customers, to whom the artificial light of the smoke-filled room lent an unhealthy touch of grey shadow round the eyes, and studied the young woman at the till mechanically setting out sugar and a spoon for every cup of coffee served by the waiter; drowsily and without really noticing them I read the posters on the walls, to which I was wholly indifferent, and found myself almost enjoying this kind of apathy. But suddenly, and in a curious way, I was brought out of my drowsy state as a vague impulse began to stir within me. It was like the beginning of a slight toothache, when you don't know yet if it is on the right or the left, if it is starting in the upper or the lower jaw; there was just a certain tension, a mental uneasiness. For all at once—I couldn't have said how—I was aware that I must have been here once before, years ago, and that a memory of some kind was connected with these walls, these chairs, these tables, this smoky room, apparently strange to me.

But the more I tried to pin down that memory, the more refractory and slippery it was as it eluded me—like a luminous jellyfish unconsciously glowing on the lowest level of my mind, yet not to be seized and scrutinized at close quarters. In vain I stared at every item of furnishing; certainly much of it was new to me, for instance the till with the clinking of its automatic calculations, and the brown wallpaper imitating Brazilian rosewood. All that must have been imported later. Nonetheless, I knew I had been here once before, twenty years or more ago, and something of my own old self, long since overgrown, lingered here invisibly, like a nail hidden in wood. I reached out into the room, straining all my senses, and at the same time I searched myself—yet damn it all, I couldn't place that lost memory, drowned in the recesses of my mind.

I was annoyed with myself, as you always are when a failure of some kind makes you aware of the inadequacy and imperfection of your intellectual powers. But I did not give up hope of retrieving the memory after all. I knew I just had to lay hands on some tiny hook, for my memory is an odd one, good and bad at the same time: on the one hand defiant and stubborn, on the other incredibly faithful. It often swallows up what is most important, both incidents and faces, what I read and what I experience, engulfing it entirely in darkness, and will not give anything back from that underworld merely at the call of my will, only under duress. However, I need just some small thing to jog my memory, a picture postcard, a few lines of handwriting on an envelope, a sheet of newsprint faded by smoke, and at once what is forgotten will rise again like a fish on the line from the darkly streaming surface, as large as life. Then I remember every detail about someone, his mouth and the gap between the teeth in it on the left that shows when he laughs, the brittle sound of that laughter, how it makes his moustache twitch, and how another and new face emerges from that laughter—I see all that at once in detail, and I remember over the years every word the man ever said to me. But to see and feel the past so graphically I need some stimulus provided by my senses, a tiny aid from the world of reality. So I closed my eyes to allow me to think harder, to visualize and seize that mysterious hook at the end of the fishing line. Nothing, however, still nothing! All lost and forgotten. And I felt so embittered by the stubborn apparatus of memory between my temples that I could have struck myself on the forehead with my fists, as you might shake a malfunctioning automatic device that is unjustly refusing to do as you ask. No, I couldn't sit calmly here any longer, I was so upset by the failure of my memory, and in my annoyance I stood up to get some air.

But here was a strange thing: I had hardly taken a couple of steps across the room before the first phosphorescent glimmers of light began to dawn in my mind, swirling and sparkling. To the right of the cash desk, I remembered, there would be a way into a windowless room illuminated only by artificial light. And sure enough, I was right. There it was, not with the wallpaper I had known before, but the proportions of that rectangular back room, its contours still indistinct in my memory, were exactly the same. This was the card room. I instinctively looked for individual details, my nerves already joyfully vibrating (soon, I felt, I would remember it all). Two billiard tables stood idle, like silent ponds of green mud; in the corners of the room there were card tables, with two men who looked like civil servants or professors playing chess at one of them. And in the corner, close to the iron stove, where you went to use the telephone, stood a small, square table. Suddenly the realization flashed right through my entire mind. I knew at once, instantly, with a single, warm impulse jogging my memory: my God, that was where Mendel used to sit, Jakob Mendel, Mendel the bibliophile, and after twenty years here I was again in the Café Gluck at the upper end of Alserstrasse, to which he habitually resorted. Jakob Mendel—how could I have forgotten him for such an incredibly long time? That strangest of characters, a legendary man, that esoteric wonder of the world, famous at the university and in a small, eminent circle—how could I have lost my memory of him, the magician who traded in books and sat here from morning to evening every day, a symbol of the knowledge, fame and honour of the Café Gluck?

I had only to turn my vision inwards for that one second, and already his unmistakable figure, in three dimensions, was conjured up by my creatively enlightened blood. I saw him at once as he had been, always sitting at that rectangular table, its dingy grey marble top heaped high at all times with books and other writings. I saw the way he persistently sat there, imperturbable, his eyes behind his glasses hypnotically fixed on a book, humming and muttering as he read, rocking his body and his inadequately polished, freckled bald patch back and forth, a habit acquired in the *cheder*, his Jewish primary school in eastern Europe. He pored over his catalogues and books here, at that table, never sitting anywhere else, singing and swaying quietly, a dark, rocking cradle. For just as a child falls into sleep and is lost to the world by that rhythmically hypnotic rocking movement, in the opinion of pious Jews the spirit passes more easily into the grace of contemplation if one's own idle body rocks and sways at the same time. And indeed, Jakob Mendel saw and heard none of what went on around him. Beside him, the billiards players talked in loud voices, making a great deal of noise; the markers scurried about, the telephone rang, people came to scour the floor and heat the stove—he noticed none of it. Once a hot coal had fallen out of the stove, and was already burning and smoking on the wooden floor two paces away from him; only then did the infernal smell alert another of the guests in the café to the danger, and he made haste to extinguish the smoke. Jakob Mendel himself, however, only a couple of inches away and already affected by the fumes, had noticed nothing. For he read as other people pray, as gamblers gamble, as drunks stare into space, their senses numbed; he read with such touching absorption that the reading of all other persons had always seemed to me profane by comparison. As a young man, I had seen the great mystery of total concentration for the first time in this little Galician book dealer, Jakob Mendel, a kind of concentration in which the artist resembles the scholar, the truly wise resembles the totally deranged. It is the tragic happiness and unhappiness of total obsession.

An older colleague of mine from the university had taken me to see him. At the time I was engaged on research into Mesmer, the Paracelsian doctor and practitioner of magnetism, still too little known today, but I was not having much luck. The standard works on Mesmer proved to be unobtainable, and the librarian to whom I, as a guileless newcomer to the place, applied for information, replied in a surly tone that literary references were my business, not his. That was the occasion when my colleague first mentioned the man's name to me. "I'll go and see Mendel with you," he promised. "He knows everything, he can get hold of anything. He'll find you the most obscure book from the most forgotten of German second-hand bookshops. The ablest man in Vienna, and an original into the bargain, a bibliophilic dinosaur, the last survivor of a dying race from the prehistoric world."

So the two of us went to the Café Gluck, and lo and behold there sat Mendel the bibliophile, bespectacled, sporting a beard that needed trimming, clad in black, and rocking back and forth as he read like a dark bush blown in the wind. We went up to him, and he didn't even notice. He just sat there reading, his torso swaying over the table like a mandarin, and hanging on a hook behind him was his decrepit black overcoat, its pockets stuffed with notes and journals.

My friend coughed loudly by way of announcing us. But Mendel, his thick glasses close to his book, still didn't notice us. Finally my friend knocked on the tabletop as loudly and energetically as you might knock at a door—and at last Mendel looked up, automatically pushed his clumsy steel-rimmed glasses up on his forehead, and from under his bushy, ashen grey brows two remarkable eyes gazed keenly at us. They were small, black, watchful eyes, as nimble and sharp as the darting tongue of a snake. My friend introduced me, and I explained my business, first—a trick expressly recommended by my friend—complaining with pretended anger of the librarian who, I said, wouldn't give me any information. Mendel leant back and spat carefully. Then he just laughed, and said with a strong eastern European accent, "Wouldn't, eh? Not him—couldn't is more like it! He's an ignoramus, a poor old grey-haired ass. I've known him, heaven help me, these twenty years, and in all that time he still hasn't learnt anything. He can pocket his salary, yes, that's all he and his like can do! Those learned doctors—they'd do better to carry bricks than sit over their books."

This forceful venting of his grievances broke the ice, and with a good-natured wave of his hand he invited me, for the first time, to sit at the square marble-topped table covered with notes, that altar of bibliophilic revelations as yet unknown to me. I quickly explained what I wanted: works contemporary with Mesmer himself on magnetism, as well as all later books and polemics for and against his theories. As soon as I had finished, Mendel closed his left eye for a second, just like a marksman before he fires his gun. It was truly for no more than a second that this moment of concentrated attention lasted, and then, as if reading from an invisible catalogue, he fluently enumerated two or three dozen books, each with its place and date of publication and an estimate of its price. I was astonished. Although prepared for it in advance, this was more than I had expected. But my bafflement seemed to please him, for on the keyboard of his memory he immediately played the most wonderful variations on my theme that any librarian could imagine. Did I also want to know about the somnambulists and the first experiments with hypnosis? And about Gassner's exorcisms, and Christian Science, and Madame Blavatsky? Once again names came tumbling out of him, titles and descriptions; only now did I realize what a unique marvel of memory I had found in Jakob Mendel, in truth an encyclopaedia, a universal catalogue on two legs. Absolutely dazed, I stared at this bibliographical phenomenon, washed up here in the shape of an unprepossessing, even slightly grubby little Galician second-hand book dealer who, after reciting some eighty names to me full pelt, apparently without taking much thought, but inwardly pleased to have played his trump card, polished his glasses on what might once have been a white handkerchief. To hide my astonishment a little, I hesitantly asked which of those books he could, if need be, get hold of for me.

"Well, we'll see what can be done," he growled. "You come back here tomorrow, by then old Mendel will have found you a little something, and what can't be found here will turn up elsewhere. A man who knows his way around will have luck."

I thanked him courteously, and in all this civility I stumbled into a great act of folly by suggesting that I could write down the titles of books I wanted on a piece of paper. At the same moment I felt a warning nudge in the ribs from my friend's elbow. But too late! Mendel had already cast me a glance—what a glance!—that was both triumphant and injured, a scornful and superior, a positively regal glance, the Shakespearian glance of Macbeth when Macduff suggests to that invincible hero that he yield without a fight. Then he laughed again, briefly, the big Adam's apple in his throat rolling back and forth in an odd way. Apparently he had bitten back a sharp rejoinder with some difficulty. And good Mendel the bibliophile would have been right to make every imaginable sharp remark, for only a stranger, an ignoramus (*amhorez* is the Yiddish word he used for it) could offer such an insult as to write down the title of a book for him, Jakob Mendel, as if he were a bookseller's apprentice or a servant in a library, as if that incomparable, diamantine bibliophilic brain would ever have needed such a crude aid to his memory. Only later did I realize how much my civil offer must have injured the feelings of such an esoteric genius, for this small, squat Galician Jew, entirely enveloped in his own beard and hunchbacked into the bargain, was a Titan of memory. Behind that chalky, grubby brow, which looked as if it were overgrown by grey moss, there stood in an invisible company, as if stamped in steel, every name and title that had ever been printed on the title page of a book. Whether a work had first been published yesterday or two hundred years ago, he knew at once its exact place of publication, its publisher and the price, both new and second-hand, and at the same time he unfailingly recollected the binding, illustrations and facsimile editions of every book. He saw every work, whether he had held it in his own hands or had only seen it once from a distance, in a window display or a library, with the same optical precision as the creative artist sees the still-invisible forms of his inner world and those of other people. If, say, a book was offered for six marks in the catalogue of a second-hand bookseller in Regensburg, he immediately remembered that another copy of the same book could have been bought for four crowns in an auction in Vienna two years ago, and he also knew who had bought it; indeed, Jakob Mendel never forgot a title or a number, he knew every plant, every micro-organism, every star in the eternally oscillating, constantly changing cosmos of the universe of books. He knew more in every field than the experts in that field, he was more knowledgeable about libraries than the librarians themselves, he knew the stocks of most firms by heart better than their owners, for all their lists and their card indexes, although he had nothing at his command but the magic of memory, nothing but his incomparable faculty of recollection, which could only be truly explained and analysed by citing a hundred separate examples. It was clear that his memory could have been trained and formed to show such demonic infallibility only by the eternal mystery of all perfection: by concentration. This remarkable man knew nothing about the world outside books, for to his mind all the phenomena of existence began to seem truly real to him only when they were cast as letters and assembled as print in a book, a process that, so to speak, had sterilized them. But he read even the books themselves not for their meaning, for their intellectual and narrative content: his sole passion was for their names, prices, forms of publication and original title pages. Unproductive and uncreative in that last point, nothing but a list of hundreds of thousands of titles and names, stamped on the soft cortex of a mammalian brain as if written in a catalogue of books, Jakob Mendel's specifically bibliophilic memory was still, in its unique perfection, no less a phenomenon than Napoleon's memory for faces, Mezzofanti's for languages, the memory of a chess champion like Lasker for opening gambits or of a composer like Busoni for music. In a public place in the context of a seminar, that brain would have instructed and amazed thousands, hundreds of thousands of students and scholars, with results fertile for the sciences, an incomparable gain for those public treasuries that we call libraries. But that higher world was for ever closed to this small, uneducated Galician dealer in books, who had mastered little more than what he was taught in his studies of the Talmud, and consequently his fantastic abilities could take effect only as the secret knowledge shown when he sat at that marble-topped table in the Café Gluck. But some day, when there is a great psychologist who, with patience and persistence equal to Buffon's in arranging and classifying the entire animal kingdom, can do the same for all varieties, species and original forms of the magical power that we call memory, describing them separately and presenting their variants (a work as yet absent from our intellectual world)—then he would be bound to think of Jakob Mendel, that genius of prices and titles, that nameless master of the science of antiquarian books.

By trade, to be sure, Jakob Mendel was known to the ignorant only as a little dealer in second-hand books. Every Sunday the same standard advertisement appeared in the *Neue Freie Presse* and the *Neues Wiener Taghlatt*: "Old books bought, best prices paid, apply to Mendel, Obere Alserstrasse", and then a telephone number which in fact was the number of the Café Gluck. He would search through stockrooms, and every week, with an old servant bearded like the Emperor Joseph, brought back new booty to his headquarters and conveyed it on from there, since he had no licence for a proper bookshop. So he remained a dealer in a small way, not a very lucrative occupation. Students sold him their textbooks, and his hands passed them on from one academic year to the next, while in addition he sought out and acquired any particular work that was wanted, asking a small extra charge. He was free with good advice. But money had no place within his world, for he had never been seen in anything but the same shabby coat, consuming milk and two rolls in the morning, the afternoon and the evening, and at mid-day eating some small dish that they fetched him from the restaurant. He didn't smoke, he didn't gamble, you might even say he didn't live, but the two lively eyes behind his glasses were constantly feeding words, titles and names to this strange being's brain. And the soft, fertile substance of that brain absorbed this wealth of words greedily, like a meadow soaking up thousands upon thousands of raindrops. Human beings did not interest him, and of all the human passions perhaps he knew only one, although that, for sure, is the most human of them all: vanity. If someone came to him for information, after laboriously searching for it elsewhere to no avail, and he could provide it at once, that alone made him feel satisfaction, pleasure; and so too perhaps did the fact that a few dozen people who respected and needed his knowledge lived in and outside Vienna. Every one of those massive conglomerations of millions of people, a place that we would call a metropolis, is sprinkled here and there with several small facets reflecting one and the same universe in miniature, invisible to most and valuable only to the expert, who is related to another expert by virtue of the same passion. And these bibliophiles all knew Jakob Mendel. Just as if you wanted advice on sheet music you turned to Eusebius Mandyczewski at the Viennese Music Association, a friendly presence sitting there in his grey cap among his files and his scores, and he would solve the most difficult problem with a smile as he first looked up at you; just as today everyone wanting to know about the Altwiener Theater and its culture would still turn infallibly to Karl Glossy, who knows all about the subject—so a few devout Viennese bibliophiles, when they had a tough nut to crack, made their pilgrimage to the Café Gluck and Jakob Mendel.

Watching Mendel during one of these conversations gave me, as a young man full of curiosity, a particular kind of pleasure. If you put an inferior book in front of him he would close it scornfully, muttering only, "Two crowns"; but faced with some rarity, or a unique specimen, he would lean respectfully back, place a sheet of paper under it, and you could see that he was suddenly ashamed of his grubby, inky fingers with their black-rimmed nails. Then he would begin leafing tenderly, cautiously and with immense reverence through the rare volume, page by page. No one could disturb him at a moment like that, as little as you can disturb a devout believer at prayer; and indeed that looking, touching, smelling and assessing, each of those single acts, had about it something of the succession of rituals in a religious ceremony. His hunched back shifted to and fro, meanwhile he muttered and growled, scratched his head, uttered curious vowel sounds, a long-drawn-out, almost awe-stricken, "Ah" or "Oh" of captivated admiration, or then again a swift and alarmed, "Oy!" or "Oy vey!" if a page turned out to be missing, or had been nibbled by a woodworm. Finally he would weigh up the thick tome respectfully in his hands, sniff at the large rectangle and absorb its smell with half-closed eyes, as delighted as a sentimental girl enjoying the scent of tuberose. During this rather elaborate procedure, the owner of the book of course had to possess his soul in patience. Having ended his examination, however, Mendel was very happy, indeed positively delighted to give any information, which infallibly came with wide-ranging anecdotes and dramatic accounts of the prices of similar copies. At these moments he seemed to become brighter, younger, livelier, and only one thing could embitter him beyond all measure: that was if a novice tried to offer him money for his opinion. Then he would draw back with an air of injury, for all the world like the distinguished curator of a gallery when an American tourist passing through the city tries to press a tip into his hand.

Holding a precious book meant to Mendel what an assignment with a woman might to another man. These moments were his platonic nights of love. Books had power over him; money never did. Great collectors, including the founder of a collection in Princeton University Library, tried in vain to recruit him as an adviser and buyer for their libraries—Jakob Mendel declined; no one could imagine him anywhere but in the Café Gluck. Thirty-three years ago, when his beard was still soft and black and he had ringlets over his forehead, he had come from the east to Vienna, a crook-backed lad, to study for the rabbinate, but he had soon abandoned Jehovah the harsh One God to give himself up to idolatry in the form of the brilliant, thousand-fold polytheism of books. That was when he had first found his way to the Café Gluck, and gradually it became his workplace, his headquarters, his post office, his world. Like an astronomer alone in his observatory, studying myriads of stars every night through the tiny round lens of the telescope, observing their mysterious courses, their wandering multitude as they are extinguished and then appear again, so Jakob Mendel looked through his glasses out from that rectangular table into the other universe of books, also eternally circling and being reborn in that world above our own.

Of course he was highly esteemed in the Café Gluck, the fame of which was linked, so far as we were concerned, with Mendel at his invisible teacher's lectern rather than with the nominal patronage of that great magician Christoph Willibald Gluck, the composer of *Alceste* and *Iphigénie*. Mendel was as much a part of the fixtures and fittings as the old cherrywood cash desk, the two badly mended cues and the copper coffee pot, and his table was protected like a shrine—for his many customers and seekers after information were always urged by the staff, in a friendly manner, to place an order of some kind, thus ensuring that most of the profits of his knowledge disappeared into the broad leather bag worn at his hip by Deubler the head waiter. In return, Mendel the bibliophile enjoyed many privileges. He was free to use the telephone, his letters were fetched and anything he ordered from the restaurant brought in, the good old lady who looked after the toilets brushed his coat and sewed on buttons, and every week she took a little bundle of washing to the laundry for him. Lunch could be brought over from the nearby restaurant for him alone, and every day Herr Standhartner, the owner of the café, came to his table in person and said good morning (although usually Jakob Mendel, deep in his books, failed to notice the greeting). He arrived promptly at seven-thirty in the morning, and he left the café only when the lights were switched off. He never spoke to the other customers, and when Herr Standhartner once asked him courteously if he didn't find reading better by electric light than in the pallid, fitful illumination from the old Auer gas lamps, he gazed in surprise at the electric light bulbs; in spite of the noise and hammering of an installation lasting several days, this change had entirely passed him by. Only through the twin circles of his glasses, only through those two sparkling lenses that sucked everything in, did the billions of tiny organisms formed by the letters filter into his brain; everything else streamed over him as meaningless noise. In fact he had spent over thirty years, the entire waking part of his life, here at his rectangular table reading, comparing and calculating, in a continual daydream interrupted only by sleep.

So I was overcome by a kind of horror when I saw that the marble-topped table where Jakob Mendel made his oracular utterances now stood in this room as empty as a gravestone. Only now that I was older did I understand how much dies with such a man, first because anything unique is more and more valuable in a world now becoming hopelessly uniform. And then because, out of a deep sense of premonition, the young, inexperienced man I once was had been very fond of Jakob Mendel. In him, I had come close for the first time to the great mystery of the way what is special and overwhelming in our existence is achieved only by an inner concentration of powers, a sublime monomania akin to madness. And I had seen that a pure life of the mind, total abstraction in a single idea, can still be found even today, an immersion no less than that of an Indian yogi or a medieval monk in his cell, and indeed can be found in a café illuminated by electric light and next to a telephone—as a young man, I had sensed it far more in that entirely anonymous little book dealer than in any of our contemporary writers. Yet I had been able to forget him—admittedly in the war years, and in an absorption in my own work not unlike his. Now, however, looking at that empty table, I felt a kind of shame, and at the same time a renewed curiosity.

For where had he gone, what had happened to him? I called the waiter over and asked. No, he was sorry, he didn't know a Herr Mendel, no gentleman of that name frequented the café. But perhaps the head waiter would know. The head waiter ponderously steered his pot belly towards me, hesitated, thought it over. No, he didn't know any Herr Mendel either. But maybe I meant Mandl, Herr Mandl from the haberdashery shop in Florianigasse? A bitter taste rose to my mouth, the taste of transience: what do we live for, if the wind carries away the last trace of us from beneath our feet? For thirty years, perhaps forty, a man had breathed, read, thought and talked in this room of a few square metres, and only three or four years had to pass before there arose up a new king over Egypt, which knew not Joseph. No one in the Café Gluck knew anything now about Jakob Mendel, Mendel the bibliophile! Almost angrily I asked the head waiter if I could speak to Herr Standhartner, or was there anyone else from the old staff left in the house? Oh, Herr Standhartner, oh, dear God, he had sold the café long ago, he had died, and the old head waiter was living on his little property in the town of Krems. No, there was no one from the old staff here now… or yes! Yes, there was—Frau Sporschil was still here, the toilet lady (known in vulgar parlance as the chocolate lady). But he was sure she wouldn't be able to remember individual customers now. I thought at once, you don't forget a man like Jakob Mendel, and I asked her to come and see me.

She came, Frau Sporschil with her untidy white hair, her dropsical feet taking the few steps from her area of responsibility in the background to the front of the café and still hastily rubbing her red hands on a cloth; obviously she had just been sweeping or cleaning the windows of her dismal domain. From her uncertain manner I noticed at once that she felt uneasy to be summoned so suddenly into the smarter part of the café, under the large electric lights—in Vienna ordinary people suspect detectives and the police everywhere, as soon as anyone wants to ask them questions. So she looked at me suspiciously at first, glancing at me from under her brows, a very cautious, surreptitious glance. What good could I want of her? But as soon as I asked about Jakob Mendel she stared at me with full, positively streaming eyes, and her shoulders began to shake.

"Oh, my God, poor Herr Mendel—to think of anyone remembering him now! Yes, poor Herr Mendel"—she was almost weeping, she was so moved in the way of old people when they are reminded of their youth, of some good, forgotten acquaintanceship. I asked if he was still alive.

"Oh, my God, poor Herr Mendel, it must be five or six years he's been dead, no, seven years. Such a kind, good man, and when I think how long I knew him, more than twenty-five years, he was already coming here when I joined the staff. And it was a shame, a real shame, the way they let him die." She was growing more and more agitated, and asked if I was a relation. Because no one had ever troubled about him, she said, no one had ever asked after him—didn't I know what had happened to him?

No, I assured her, I knew nothing, and please would she tell me all about it? The good woman looked shy and embarrassed, and kept wiping her damp hands again and again. I realized that as the toilet lady she felt awkward standing here in the middle of the café, with her untidy white hair and stained apron. In addition, she kept looking anxiously to left and right in case one of the waiters was listening.

So I suggested that we might go into the card room, to Mendel's old table, and she could tell me all about it there. Moved, she nodded to me, grateful for my understanding, and the old lady, already a little unsteady on her feet, went ahead while I followed her. The two waiters stared after us in surprise, sensing some connection, and some of the customers also seemed to be wondering about the unlikely couple we made.

Over at Mendel's table, she told me (another account, at a later date, filled in some of the details for me) about the downfall of Jakob Mendel, Mendel the bibliophile.

Well then, she said, he had gone on coming here even after the beginning of the war, day after day, arriving at seven-thirty in the morning, and he sat there just the same and studied all day, as usual; the fact was they'd all felt, and often said so, that he wasn't even aware there was a war going on. I'd remember, she said, that he never looked at a newspaper and never talked to anyone else, but even when the newsboys were making their murderous racket, announcing special editions, and all the others ran to buy, he never got to his feet or even listened. He didn't so much as notice that Franz the waiter was missing (Franz had fallen at Gorlice), and he didn't know that Herr Standhartner's son had been taken prisoner at Przemyśl, he never said a word when the bread got worse and worse, and they had to serve him fig coffee instead of his usual milk, nasty stuff it was. Just once he did seem surprised because so few students came in now, that was all. "My God, the poor man, nothing gave him pleasure or grief except those books of his."

But then, one day, the worst happened. At eleven in the morning, in broad daylight, a policeman had come in with an officer of the secret police, who had shown the rosette badge in his buttonhole and asked if a man called Jakob Mendel came in here. Then they went straight over to Mendel's table, and he thought, suspecting nothing, they wanted to sell him books or ask for information. But they told him to his face to go with them, and they took him away. It had brought shame on the café; everyone gathered round poor Herr Mendel as he stood there between the two police officers, his glasses pushed up on his forehead, looking back and forth from one to the other of them, not knowing what they really wanted.

Frau Sporschil, however, said that she had instantly told the uniformed policeman this must be a mistake. A man like Herr Mendel wouldn't hurt a fly, but then the secret police officer shouted at her not to interfere in official business. And then, she added, they had taken him away, and it was a long time before he came back, two years. To this day she didn't really know what they'd wanted from him back then. "But I give you my oath," said the old woman, much upset, "Herr Mendel can't have done anything wrong. They made a mistake, I'd swear to it. It was a crime against that poor, innocent man, a real crime!"

And good, kind-hearted Frau Sporschil was right. Our friend Jakob Mendel really had not done anything wrong, only something stupid (and as I said, not until later did I learn all the details)—he had committed a headlong, touching and even in those crazy times entirely improbable act of stupidity, to be explained only by his total self-absorption, the oddity of his unique nature.

This was what had happened. One day the military censorship office, where it was the duty of the officials to supervise all correspondence sent abroad, had intercepted a postcard written and signed by one Jakob Mendel, properly stamped with sufficient postage for a country outside Austria, but—incredible to relate—sent to an enemy nation. The postcard was addressed to Jean Labourdaire, Bookseller, Paris, Quai de Grenelle, and on it the sender, Jakob Mendel, complained that he had not received the last eight numbers of the monthly *Bulletin bibliographique de la France*, in spite of having paid a year's subscription in advance. The junior censorship official who found it, in civil life a high-school teacher by profession and a scholar of Romance languages and literature by private inclination, who now wore the blue uniform of the territorial reserves, was astonished to have such a document in his hands. He thought it must be a silly joke. Among the 2,000 letters that he scanned every week, searching them for dubious comments and turns of phrase that might indicate espionage, he had never come across anything so absurd as someone in Austria addressing a letter to France without another thought, simply posting a card to the enemy country as if the borders had not been fortified by barbed wire since 1914, and as if, on every new day created by God, France, Germany, Austria and Russia were not killing a few thousand of each other's male populations. So at first he put the postcard in his desk drawer as a curio, and did not mention the absurdity to anyone else.

However, a few weeks later another card from the same Jakob Mendel was sent to a bookseller called John Aldridge, at Holborn Square in London, asking if he could procure the latest numbers of *The Antiquarian* for him; and once again it was signed by the same strange individual, Jakob Mendel, who with touching naiveté gave his full address. Now the high-school teacher felt a little uncomfortable in the uniform coat that he was obliged to wear. Was there, after all, some mysteriously coded meaning behind this idiotic joke? Anyway, he stood up, clicked his heels and put the two cards on the major's desk. The major shrugged his shoulders: what an odd case! First he asked the police to find out whether this Jakob Mendel actually existed, and an hour later Jakob Mendel was under arrest and, still stunned with surprise, was brought before the major. The major placed the mysterious postcards in front of him and asked whether he admitted to sending them. Agitated by the major's stern tone, and particularly upset because the police had tracked him down just when he was reading an important catalogue, Mendel said, almost impatiently, that of course he had written those postcards. He supposed a man still had a right to claim value for money paid as an advance subscription. The major turned in his chair and leant over to the lieutenant at the next desk. The two of them exchanged meaningful glances: what an utter idiot! Then the major wondered whether he should just tell this simpleton off in no uncertain terms and send him packing, or whether he ought to take the case seriously. In such difficult circumstances, almost any office will decide that the first thing to do is to write a record of the incident. A record is always a good idea. If it does no great good, it will do no harm either, and one more meaningless sheet of paper among millions will be covered with words.

This time, however, it unfortunately did do harm to a poor, unsuspecting man, for something very fateful emerged in answer to the major's third question. First the man was asked his name: Jakob, originally Jainkeff Mendel. Profession: pedlar (for he had no bookseller's licence, only a certificate allowing him to trade from door to door). The third question was the catastrophe: his place of birth. Jakob Mendel named a small village in Petrikau. The major raised his eyebrows. Petrikau, wasn't that in the Russian part of Poland, near the border? Suspicious! Very suspicious! So he asked more sternly when Mendel had acquired Austrian citizenship. Mendel's glasses stared at him darkly and in surprise: he didn't understand the question. For heaven's sake, asked the major, did he have his papers, his documents, and if so where were they? The only document he had was his permit to trade from door to door. The major's eyebrows rose ever higher. Then would he kindly explain how he came to be an Austrian citizen? What had his father been, Austrian or Russian? Jakob Mendel calmly replied: Russian, of course. And he himself? Oh, to avoid having to serve in the army, he had smuggled himself over the Russian border thirty-three years ago, and he had been living in Vienna ever since. The major was getting increasingly impatient. When, he repeated, had he acquired Austrian citizenship? Why would he bother with that, asked Mendel, he'd never troubled about such things. So he was still a Russian citizen? And Mendel, who was finding all this pointless questioning tedious, replied with indifference, "Yes, I suppose so."

Shocked, the major sat back so brusquely that his chair creaked. To think of such a thing! In Vienna, the capital of Austria, right in the middle of the war at the end of 1915, after Tarnów and the great offensive, here was a Russian walking around with impunity, writing letters to France and England, and the police did nothing about it! And then those fools in the newspapers are surprised that Conrad von Hötzendorf didn't advance directly to Warsaw, and on the general staff they are amazed that all troop movements are reported to Russia by spies. The lieutenant too had risen to his feet and was standing at his desk: the conversation abruptly became an interrogation. Why hadn't he immediately reported to the authorities as a foreigner? Mendel, still unsuspecting, replied in his sing-song Jewish tones, "Why would I want to go and report all of a sudden?" The major saw this reversal of his question as a challenge and asked, menacingly, whether he hadn't read the announcements? No! And didn't he read the newspapers either? Again, no.

The two of them stared at Mendel, who was sweating slightly in his uncertainty, as if the moon had fallen to earth in their office. Then the telephone rang, typewriters tapped busily, orderlies ran back and forth and Jakob Mendel was consigned to the garrison cells, to be moved on to a concentration camp. When he was told to follow two soldiers he stared uncertainly. He didn't understand what they wanted from him, but really he had no great anxiety. What ill, after all, could the man with the gold braid on his collar and the rough voice have in store for him? In his elevated world of books there was no war, no misunderstanding, only eternal knowledge and the desire to know more about numbers and words, titles and names. So he good-naturedly went down the steps with the two soldiers. Only when all the books in his coat pockets were confiscated at the police station, and he had to hand over his briefcase, where he had put a hundred important notes and customers' addresses, did he begin to strike out angrily around him. They had to overcome him, but in the process unfortunately his glasses fell to the floor, and that magic spyglass of his that looked into the intellectual world broke into a thousand pieces. Two days later he was sent, in his thin summer coat, to a concentration camp for civilian Russian prisoners at Komorn.

As for Jakob Mendel's experience of mental horror in those two years in a concentration camp, living without books—his beloved books—without money, with indifferent, coarse and mostly illiterate companions in the midst of this gigantic human dunghill, as for all he suffered there, cut off from his sublime and unique world of books as an eagle with its wings clipped is separated from its ethereal element—there is no testimony to any of it. But the world, waking soberly from its folly, has gradually come to know that of all the cruelties and criminal encroachments of that war, none was more senseless, unnecessary and therefore more morally inexcusable than capturing and imprisoning behind barbed wire unsuspecting civilians long past the age for military service, who had become used to living in a foreign land as if it were their own, and in their belief in the laws of hospitality, which are sacred even to Tungus and Araucanian tribesmen, had neglected to flee in time. It was a crime committed equally unthinkingly in France, Germany and England, in every part of a Europe run mad. And perhaps Jakob Mendel, like hundreds of other innocents penned up in a camp, would have succumbed miserably to madness or dysentery, debility or a mental breakdown, had not a coincidence of a truly Austrian nature brought him back to his own world just in time.

After his disappearance, several letters from distinguished customers had been delivered to his address. Those customers included Count Schönberg, the former governor of Styria and a fanatical collector of heraldic works; the former dean of the theological faculty at the university, Siegenfeld, who was working on a commentary on St Augustine; and the eighty-year-old retired Admiral the Honourable von Pisek, who was still tinkering with his memoirs—all of them, his faithful customers, had repeatedly written to Jakob Mendel at the Café Gluck, and a few of these letters were forwarded to the missing man in the concentration camp. There they fell into the hands of a captain who happened to have his heart in the right place, and who was surprised to discover the names of the distinguished acquaintances of this little half-blind, dirty Jew, who had huddled in a corner like a mole, grey, eyeless and silent, ever since his glasses had been broken (he had no money to buy a new pair). There must, after all, be something special about a man with friends like that. So he allowed Mendel to answer the letters and ask his patrons to put in a good word for him, which they did. With the fervent solidarity of all collectors, His Excellency and the Dean powerfully cranked up their connections, and their united support brought Mendel the bibliophile back to Vienna in the year 1917, after more than two years of confinement, although on condition that he reported daily to the police. However, he could return to the free world, to his old, cramped little attic room, he could walk past the window displays of books again, and above all he could go back to the Café Gluck.

Good Frau Sporschil was able to give me a first-hand account of Mendel's return to the café from an infernal underworld. "One day—Jesus, Mary and Joseph, thinks I, I can't believe my eyes!—one day the door's pushed open, you know what it's like, just a little way, he always came in like that, and there he is stumbling into the café, poor Herr Mendel. He was wearing a much-mended military coat, and something on his head that might once have been a hat someone had thrown away. He didn't have a collar, and he looked like death, grey in the face, grey-haired and pitifully thin. But in he comes, like nothing had happened, he doesn't ask no questions, he doesn't say nothing, he goes to the table over there and takes off his coat, but not so quickly and easily as before, it takes him an effort. And no books with him now, like he always brought—he just sits down there and don't say nothing, he just stares ahead of him with empty, worn-out eyes. It was only little by little, when we'd brought him all the written stuff that had come from Germany for him, he went back to reading. But he was never the same again."

No, he was not the same, he was no longer that *miraculum mundi*, a magical catalogue of all the books in the world. Everyone who saw him at that time sadly told me the same. Something in his otherwise still eyes, eyes that read only as if in his sleep, seemed to be destroyed beyond redemption. Something in him was broken; the terrible red comet of blood must, in its headlong career, have smashed destructively into the remote, peaceful, halcyon star that was his world of books. His eyes, used for decades to the tender, soundless, insect-like letters making up print, must have seen terrible things in that barbed-wire pen into which human beings were herded, for his eyelids cast heavy shadows over his once-swift and ironically sparkling pupils; sleepy and red-rimmed, they shed twilight on his formerly lively eyes as they peered through his glasses, now repaired by being laboriously tied together with thin string. And even more terrible: in the fantastic and elaborate structure of his memory, some prop must have given way, bringing the rest of it down in confusion, for the human brain, that control centre made of the most delicate of substances, a precision instrument in the mechanics of our knowledge, is so finely adjusted that a blocked blood vessel, even a small one, a shattered nerve, an exhausted cell or the shift of a molecule is enough to silence the heavenly harmony of the most magnificently comprehensive mind. And in Mendel's memory, that unique keyboard of knowledge, the keys themselves jammed now that he was back. If someone came in search of information now and then, Mendel would look wearily at him, no longer fully understanding; he heard things wrongly, and forgot what was said to him. Mendel was not Mendel any more, just as the world was no longer the world. Total immersion in reading no longer rocked him back and forth, but he usually sat there perfectly still, his glasses turned only automatically on a book, and you could not tell whether he was reading or only daydreaming. Several times, Frau Sporschil told me, his head dropped heavily on the book and he fell asleep in broad daylight; or he sometimes stared for hours on end at the strange and smelly light of the acetylene lamp they had put on his desk at this time when coal was in short supply. No, Mendel was not the old Mendel, no longer a wonder of the world but a useless collection of beard and clothes, breathing wearily, pointlessly sitting in his once-oracular chair, he was no longer the glory of the Café Gluck but a disgrace, a dirty mark, ill-smelling, a revolting sight, an uncomfortable and unnecessary parasite.

That was how the new owner of the café saw him. This man, Florian Gurtner by name, came from Retz, had made a fortune from shady deals in flour and butter during the starvation year of 1919, and had talked the unsuspecting Herr Standhartner into selling him the Café Gluck for 80,000 crowns in paper money, which swiftly depreciated in value. He set about the place with his firm rustic hands, renovating the old-established café to smarten it up, buying new armchairs for bad money at the right time, installing a marble porch, and he was already negotiating to buy the bar next door and turn it into a dance hall. Naturally enough, the odd little Galician parasite who kept a table occupied all day, and in that time consumed nothing but two cups of coffee and five rolls, was very much in the way of his hastily undertaken project to smarten up the café. Standhartner had, to be sure, specially commended his old customer to the new owner, and had tried to explain what an important man Jakob Mendel was; indeed he had, so to speak, transferred him along with the café's fixtures and fittings as someone with a claim on his goodwill. But along with the new furniture and the shiny aluminium cash register, Florian Gurtner had introduced the approach of a man out to earn all he could, and he was only waiting for an excuse to banish this last, annoying remnant of suburban shabbiness from his now-elegant café.

And a good reason to do so quite soon arose, for Jakob Mendel was in a bad way. The last banknotes he had saved had been pulverized in the paper mill of inflation, and his customers had disappeared. These days he was so exhausted that he lacked the strength to start climbing steps and going from door to door selling books again. There were a hundred little signs of his poverty. He seldom had something for lunch brought in from the restaurant now, and he was behind with paying the small sums he owed for coffee and rolls, once as much as three weeks behind. At that point the head waiter wanted to turn him out into the street. But good Frau Sporschil, the toilet lady, was sorry for Mendel and said she would pay his debt.

Next month, however, a great misfortune happened. The new head waiter had already noticed, several times, that when he was settling up accounts the money for the baked goods never worked out quite right. More rolls proved to be missing than had been ordered and paid for. His suspicions, naturally, went straight to Mendel, for the decrepit old servant at the café had come to complain, several times, that Mendel had owed him money for six months, and he couldn't get it out of him. So the head waiter kept his eyes open, and two days later, hiding behind the fire screen, he succeeded in catching Jakob Mendel secretly getting up from his table, going into the other front room, quickly taking two rolls from a bread basket and devouring them greedily. When it came to paying for what he had had that day, he denied eating any rolls at all. So that explained the disappearance of the baked goods. The waiter reported the incident at once to Herr Gurtner who, glad of the excuse he had been seeking for so long, shouted at Mendel in front of everyone, accused him of theft and made a great show of magnanimity in not calling the police at once. But he told Mendel to get out of his café immediately and never come back. Jakob Mendel only trembled and said nothing; he got up from where he sat, tottering, and went away.

"Oh, it was a real shame," said Frau Sporschil, describing this departure. "I'll never forget it, the way he stood there, his glasses pushed up on his forehead, white as a sheet. He didn't even take the time to put on his coat, although it was January, and you know what a cold year it was. And in his fright he left his book lying on the table, I didn't notice that until later, and I was going to follow him with it. But he'd already stumbled to the door, and I didn't dare follow him out into the streets, because there was Herr Gurtner himself standing by the door shouting after him so loud that people stopped and crowded together. Yes, I call it a shame, I felt shamed to the heart myself! Such a thing could never have happened when old Herr Standhartner was here, fancy chasing a man away just for a few rolls, with old Herr Standhartner he could have eaten them for free all his life. But folk these days, they've got no hearts. Driving away a man who sat here day after day for over thirty years—a shame, it really was, and I wouldn't like to have to answer to the Lord God for it, not me."

The good woman was greatly agitated, and with the passionate volubility of old age she repeated again and again that it was a real shame, and nothing like it would have happened in Herr Standhartner's day. So finally I had to ask her what had become of our friend Mendel, and whether she had seen him again. At that she pulled herself together, and then went on in even more distress.

"Every day when I passed his table, every time, believe you me, I felt a pang. I always wondered where he might be now, poor Herr Mendel, and if I'd known where he lived I'd have gone there, brought him something hot to eat, because where would he get the money to heat his room and feed himself? And so far as I know he didn't have any family, not a soul in the world. But in the end, when I still never heard a thing, I thought to myself it must all be over, and I'd never see him again. And I was wondering whether I wouldn't get a Mass read for him, because he was a good man, Herr Mendel, and we'd known each other more than twenty-five years.

"But then one day early, half past seven in the morning in February, I'm just polishing up the brass rails at the windows, and suddenly—I mean suddenly, believe you me—the door opens and in comes Herr Mendel. You know the way he always came in, kind of crooked and confused-looking, but this time he was somehow different. I can see it at once, he's torn this way and that, his eyes all glazed, and my God, the way he looked, all beard and bones! I think right away, he don't remember nothing, here he is sleepwalking in broad daylight, he's forgot it all, all about the rolls and Herr Gurtner and how shamefully they threw him out, he don't know nothing about himself. Thank God for it, Herr Gurtner wasn't there yet, and the head waiter had just had his own coffee. So I put my oar in quickly, I tell him he'd better not stay here and get thrown out again by that nasty fellow" (and here she looked timidly around and quickly corrected herself) "I mean by Herr Gurtner. So I call out to him. 'Herr Mendel,' I say. He stares at me. And at that moment, oh my God, terrible it was, at that moment it must all have come back to him, because he gives a start at once and he begins to tremble, but not just his fingers, no, he's trembling all over, you can see it, shoulders and all, and he's stumbling back to the door, he's hurrying, and then he collapsed. We telephoned for the emergency service and they took him away, all feverish like he was. He died that evening. Pneumonia, a bad case, the doctor said, and he said he hadn't really known anything about it, not how he came back to us. It just kind of drove him on, it was like he was sleepwalking. My God, when a man has sat at a table like that every day for thirty-six years, the table is kind of his home."

We talked about him for some time longer; we were the last two to have known that strange man—I, to whom in my youth, despite the minute scope of his own existence, little more than that of a microbe, he had conveyed my first inklings of a perfectly enclosed life of the mind, and she, the poor worn-out toilet lady who had never read a book, and felt bound to this comrade of her poverty-stricken world only because she had brushed his coat and sewn on his buttons for twenty-five years. And yet we understood one another wonderfully well as we sat at his old table, now abandoned, in the company of the shades we had conjured up between us, for memory is always a bond, and every loving memory is a bond twice over. Suddenly, in the midst of her talk, she thought of something. "Jesus, how forgetful I am—I still have that book, the one he left lying on the table here. Where was I to go to take it back to him? And afterwards, when nobody came for it, afterwards I thought I could keep it a memento. There wasn't anything wrong in that, was there?"

She hastily produced it from her cubby hole at the back of the café. And I had difficulty in suppressing a small smile, for the spirit of comedy, always playful and sometimes ironic, likes to mingle maliciously in the most shattering of events. The book was the second volume of Hayn's *Bibliotheca Germanorum Erotica et Curiosa*, the well-known compendium of gallant literature known to every book collector. And this scabrous catalogue—*habent sua fata libelli*—had fallen as the dead magician's last legacy into those work-worn, red and cracked, ignorant hands that had probably never held any other book but her prayer book. As I say, I had difficulty in keeping my lips firmly closed to the smile involuntarily trying to make its way out, and my moment of hesitation confused the good woman. Was it valuable after all, or did I think she could keep it?

I shook her hand with heartfelt goodwill. "Keep it and welcome. Our old friend Mendel would be glad to think that at least one of the many thousands who had him to thank for a book still remembers him." And then I went, feeling ashamed in front of this good old woman, who had remained faithful to the dead man in her simple and yet very human way. For she, unschooled as she was, had at least kept a book so that she could remember him better, whereas I had forgotten Mendel the bibliophile years ago, and I was the one who ought to know that you create books solely to forge links with others even after your own death, thus defending yourself against the inexorable adversary of all life, transience and oblivion.

LEPORELLA

HER REAL NAME WAS Crescentia Anna Aloisia Finkenhuber, she was thirty-nine years old, she had been born out of wedlock and came from a small mountain village in the Ziller valley. Under the heading of 'Distinguishing Marks' in the booklet recording her employment as a servant, a single line scored across the space available signified that she had none, but if the authorities had been obliged to give a description of her character, the most fleeting glance would have required a remark there, reading: resembles a hard-driven, strong-boned, scrawny mountain horse. For there was something unmistakably horsy about the expression of her heavy, drooping lower lip, the oval of her sun-tanned face, which was both long and harshly outlined, her dull, lashless gaze, and in particular the thick, felted strands of hair that fell greasily over her brow. Even the way she moved suggested the obstinacy and stubborn, mule-like manner of a horse used to the Alpine passes, carrying the same wooden panniers dourly uphill and downhill along stony bridleways in summer and winter alike. Once released from the halter of her work, Crescenz would doze with her bony hands loosely clasped and her elbows splayed, much as animals stand in the stable, and her senses seemed to be withdrawn. Everything about her was hard, wooden, heavy. She thought laboriously and was slow to understand anything: new ideas penetrated her innermost mind only with difficulty, as if dripping through a close-meshed sieve. But once she had finally taken in some new notion, she clung to it tenaciously and jealously. She read neither newspapers nor the prayer-book, she found writing difficult, and the clumsy characters in her kitchen records were curiously like her own heavy but angular figure, which was visibly devoid of all tangible marks of femininity. Like her bones, her brow, her hips and hands, her voice was hard too, and in spite of its thick, throaty Tyrolean accent, always sounded rusty—which was hardly surprising, since Crescenz never said an unnecessary word to anyone. And no one had ever seen her laugh. Here too she was just like an animal, for the gift of laughter, that release of feeling so happily breaking out, has not been granted to God's brute creation, which is perhaps a more cruel deprivation than the lack of language.

Brought up at the expense of the parish because of her illegitimate birth, put out to domestic service at the age of twelve, and then later a scullery maid in a carters' tavern, she had finally left that establishment, where she was known for her tenacious, ox-like capacity for work, and had risen to be cook at an inn that was popular with tourists. Crescenz rose there at five in the morning every day, worked, swept, cleaned, lit fires, brushed, cleared up, cooked, kneaded dough, strained food, washed dishes and did the laundry until late at night. She never took any holiday, she never went out in the street except to go to church; the fire in the kitchen range was her sun, the thousands and thousands of wooden logs it burned over the years her forest.

Men left her alone, whether because a quarter-century of dour, dull toil had taken every sign of femininity from her, or because she had firmly and taciturnly rejected all advances. Her one pleasure was in money, which she doggedly collected with the hamster-like instincts of the rustic labouring class, so that in her old age she would not have to eat the bitter bread of charity in the parish poorhouse yet again.

It was only for the money, in fact, that this dull-witted creature first left her native Tyrol at the age of thirty-seven. A woman who was a professional agent for domestic staff had come there on holiday, saw her working like a madwoman from morning to night in the kitchen and public rooms of the inn, and lured her to Vienna with the promise of a position at double the wages. During the railway journey Crescenz hardly said a word to anyone, and in spite of the friendly offers of other passengers to put the heavy wicker basket containing all her worldly goods up in the net of the luggage rack, she held it on her knees, which were already aching, for deception and theft were the only notions that her clumsy peasant brain connected with the idea of the big city. In her new place in Vienna, she had to be accompanied to market for the first few days, because she feared all the vehicles as a cow fears a motor car. But as soon as she knew her way down the four streets leading to the marketplace she no longer needed anyone, but trotted off with her basket, never looking up, from the door of the building where her employers lived to the market stalls and home again to sweep the apartment, light fires and clear out her new kitchen range just as she had cleared the old one, noticing no change. She kept rustic hours, went to bed at nine and slept with her mouth open, like an animal, until the alarm clock went off in the morning. No one knew if she liked her job; perhaps she didn't know herself, for she approached no one, answered questions merely with a dull "Very well", or if she didn't agree, with a discontented shrug of her shoulders. She ignored her neighbours and the other maids in the building; the mocking looks of her more light-hearted companions in domestic service slipped off the leathery surface of her indifference like water. Just once, when a girl imitated her Tyrolean dialect and wouldn't stop teasing her for her taciturnity, she suddenly snatched a burning piece of wood out of the range and went for the horrified, screaming young woman with it. From that day on, everyone avoided her, and no one dared to mock someone capable of such fury again.

But every Sunday morning Crescenz went to church in her wide, pleated skirt and flat peasant hat. Only once, on her first day off in Vienna, did she try taking a walk. As she didn't want to ride on the tram, and had seen nothing but more and more stone walls in her cautious exploration of the many bewildering streets, she went only as far as the Danube Canal, where she stared at the flowing water as at something familiar, turned and went back the way she had come, always keeping close to the buildings and anxiously avoiding the carriageway. This first and only expedition must obviously have disappointed her, for after that she never left the house again, but preferred to sit at the window on Sundays either busy with her needlework or empty-handed. So the great metropolis brought no change into the routine treadmill of her days, except that at the end of every month she held four blue banknotes instead of the old two in her gnarled, tough, battered hands. She always checked these banknotes suspiciously for a long time. She unfolded the new notes ceremoniously, and finally smoothed them out flat, almost tenderly, before putting them with the others in the carved, yellow wooden box that she had brought from her home village. This clumsy, heavy little casket was her whole secret, the meaning of her life. By night she put its key under her pillow. No one ever found out where she kept it in the day.

Such was the nature of this strange human being (as we may call her, although humanity was apparent in her behaviour only in a very faint and muted way), but perhaps it took someone with exactly those blinkered senses to tolerate domestic service in the household of young Baron von F—which was an extremely strange one in itself. Most servants couldn't put up with the quarrelsome atmosphere for any longer than the legally binding time between their engagement and the day when they gave notice. The irate shouting, wound up to hysterical pitch, came from the lady of the house. The only daughter of an extremely rich manufacturer in Essen, and no longer in her first youth, she had been at a spa where she met the considerably younger Baron (whose nobility was suspect, while his financial situation was even more dubious), and had quickly married that handsome young ne'er-do-well, ready and able as he was to display aristocratic charm. But as soon as the honeymoon was over, the newly-wedded wife had to admit that her parents, who set great store by solid worth and ability, had been right to oppose the hasty marriage. For it quickly transpired that besides having many debts to which he had not admitted, her husband, whose attentions to her had soon worn off, showed a good deal more interest in continuing the habits of his bachelor days than in his marital duties. Although not exactly unkind by nature, since at heart he was as sunny as light-minded people usually are, but extremely lax and unscrupulous in his general outlook, that handsome would-be cavalier despised all calculations of interest and capital, considering them stingy, narrow-minded evidence of plebeian bigotry. He wanted an easy life; she wanted a well-ordered, respectable domestic existence of the bourgeois Rhineland kind, which got on his nerves. And when, in spite of her wealth, he had to haggle to lay hands on any large sum of money, and his wife, who had a turn for mathematics, even denied him his dearest wish, a racing stables of his own, he saw no more reason to involve himself any further in conjugal relations with the massive, thick-necked North German woman whose loud and domineering voice fell unpleasantly on his ears. So he put her on ice, as they say, and without any harsh gestures, but none the less unmistakably, he kept his disappointed wife at a distance. If she reproached him he would listen politely, with apparent compassion, but as soon as her sermon was over he would wave her passionate admonitions away like the smoke of his cigarette, and had no qualms about continuing to do exactly as he pleased. This smooth, almost formal amiability embittered the disappointed woman more than any opposition. And as she was completely powerless to do anything about his well-bred, never abusive and positively overpowering civility, her pent-up anger broke out violently in a different direction: she ranted and raged at the domestic staff, wildly venting on the innocent her indignation, which was fundamentally justified but in those quarters inappropriately expressed. Of course there were consequences: within two years she had been obliged to engage a new lady's maid no less than sixteen times, once after an actual physical scuffle—a considerable sum of money had to be paid in compensation to hush it up.

Only Crescenz stood unmoved, like a patient cab-horse in the rain, in the midst of this stormy tumult. She took no one's side, ignored all changes, didn't seem to notice the arrival of strangers with whom she shared the maids' bedroom and whose names, hair-colour, body-odour and behaviour were constantly different. For she herself talked to no one, didn't mind the slammed doors, the interrupted mealtimes, the helpless and hysterical outbursts. Indifferent to it all, she went busily from her kitchen to market, from market back to her kitchen, and what went on outside that enclosed circle did not concern her. Hard and emotionless as a flail, she dealt with day after day, and so two years in the big city passed her by without incident, never enlarging her inner world, except that the stack of blue banknotes in her little box rose an inch higher, and when she counted the notes one by one with a moistened finger at the end of the year, the magic figure of one thousand wasn't far off.

But Chance works with diamond drills, and that dangerously cunning entity Fate can often intervene from an unexpected quarter, shattering even the rockiest nature entirely. In Crescenz's case, the outward occasion was almost as ordinary as was she herself; after ten years, it pleased the state to hold a new census, and highly complicated forms were sent to all residential buildings to be filled in by their occupants, in detail. Distrusting the illegible handwriting and purely phonetic spelling of his domestic staff, the Baron decided to fill in the forms himself, and to this end he summoned Crescenz to his study. When he asked for her name, age and date of birth, it turned out that as a passionate huntsman and a friend of the owner of the local game preserves, he had often shot chamois in that very corner of the Alps from which Crescenz came. A guide from her native village had actually been his companion for two weeks. And when, extraordinarily, it turned out that this same guide was Crescenz's uncle, the chance discovery led on the Baron, who was in a cheerful mood, to further conversation, in the course of which another surprising fact came to light: on his visit to the area, he had eaten an excellent dish of roast venison at the very same inn where she was cook. None of this was of any importance, but the power of coincidence made it seem strange, and to Crescenz, for the first time meeting someone who knew her home here in Vienna, it appeared miraculous. She stood before him with a flushed, interested face, bobbed clumsily, felt flattered when he went on to crack some jokes, imitating the Tyrolean dialect and asking if she could yodel, and talked similar schoolboy nonsense. Finally, amused at himself, he slapped her hard behind with the palm of his hand in the friendly peasant way and dismissed her with a laugh. "Off you go then, my good Cenzi, and here's two crowns because you're from the Ziller valley."

In itself this was not a significant emotional event, to be sure. But that five minutes of conversation had an effect on the fish-like, underground currents of Crescenz's dull nature like that of a stone being dropped into a swamp: ripples form, lethargically and gradually at first, but moving sluggishly on until they slowly reach the edge of consciousness. For the first time in years, the obdurate and taciturn Crescenz had held a personal conversation with another human being, and it seemed to her a supernatural dispensation of Providence that this first person to have spoken to her in the midst of the stony maze of the city knew her own mountains, and had even once eaten roast venison that she herself had prepared. And then there was that casual slap on the behind, which in peasant language represents a kind of laconic courtship of a woman. Although Crescenz did not make so bold as to suppose that such an elegant and distinguished gentleman had actually been expressing any intentions of that sort towards herself, the physical familiarity somehow shook her slumbering senses awake.

So that chance impetus set off movement in the underground realm within her, shifting stratum after stratum, until at last, first clumsily and then ever more clearly, a new feeling developed in her, like that sudden moment when one day a dog unexpectedly recognises one of the many two-legged figures around him as his master. From that hour on the dog follows him, greets the man whom Fate has set in authority over him by wagging his tail or barking, becomes voluntarily subservient and follows his trail obediently step by step. In just the same way, something new had entered the small circle of Crescenz's life, hitherto bounded by the five familiar ideas of money, the market, the kitchen range, church and her bed. That new element needed space, and brusquely pushed everything else forcefully aside. And with that peasant greed that will never let something it has seized out of its hands again, she drew it deep into herself and the confused, instinctive world of her dull senses. Of course it was some time before any change became visible, and those first signs were very insignificant: for instance, the particularly fanatical care she devoted to cleaning the Baron's clothes and shoes, while she still left the Baroness's to the lady's maid. Or she was often to be seen in the corridor of the apartment, eagerly making haste to take his hat and stick as soon as she heard the sound of the key in the front door. She redoubled her attention to the cooking, and even laboriously made her way to the big market hall so that she could get a joint of venison to roast specially for him. She was taking more care with her outward appearance too.

It was one or two weeks before these first shoots of new emotion emerged from her inner world, and many weeks more before a second idea was added to the first and grew, uncertainly in the beginning, but then acquiring distinct form and colour. This new feeling was complementary to the first: initially indistinct, but gradually appearing clear and plain, it was a sense of emergent hatred for the Baron's wife, the woman who could live with him, sleep with him, talk to him, yet did not feel the same devoted veneration for him as she herself did. Whether because she had perhaps—these days instinctively noticing more—witnessed one of those shameful scenes in which the master she idolized was humiliated in the most objectionable way by his irate wife, or whether it was that the inhibited North German woman's arrogant reserve was doubly obvious in contrast to his jovial familiarity—for one reason or another, at any rate, she suddenly brought a certain mulishness to bear on the unsuspecting wife, a prickly hostility expressed in a thousand little barbed remarks and spiteful actions. For instance, the Baroness always had to ring at least twice before Crescenz responded to the summons, deliberately slowly and with obvious reluctance, and her hunched shoulders always expressed resistance in principle. She accepted orders and errands wordlessly and with a glum expression, so that the Baroness never knew if she had actually understood her, but if she asked again to be on the safe side she got only a gloomy nod or a derisive "Sure I hears yer!" by way of answer. Or just before a visit to the theatre, while the Baroness was nervously scurrying around, an important key would prove to be lost, only to be unexpectedly discovered in a corner half-an-hour later. She regularly chose to forget about messages and phone calls to the Baroness: when charged with the omission she would offer, without the slightest sign of regret, only a brusque, "I fergot 'un". She never looked the Baroness in the face, perhaps for fear that she would not be able to hide her hatred.

Meanwhile the domestic differences between husband and wife led to increasingly unedifying scenes; perhaps Crescenz's unconsciously provocative surliness also had something to do with the hot temper of the Baroness, who was becoming more overwrought every week. With her nerves unstable as a result of preserving her virginity too long, and embittered by her husband's indifference, the exasperated woman was losing control of herself. In vain did she try to soothe her agitation with bromide and veronal; the tension of her overstretched nerves showed all the more violently in arguments, she had fits of weeping and hysteria, and never received the slightest sympathy or even the appearance of kindly support from anyone at all. Finally, the doctor who had been called in recommended a two-month stay in a sanatorium, a proposal that was approved by her usually indifferent husband with such sudden concern for her health that his wife, suspicious again, at first balked at the idea. But in the end it was decided that she would take the trip, with her lady's maid to accompany her, while Crescenz was to stay behind in the spacious apartment to serve her master.

The news that her master was to be entrusted to her care alone affected Crescenz's dull senses like a sudden tonic. As if all her strength and zest for life had been shaken wildly up in a magic flask, a hidden sediment of passion now rose from the depths of her being and lent its colour to her whole conduct. The sluggish heaviness suddenly left her rigid, frozen limbs; it was as if since she had heard that electrifying news her joints were suddenly supple, and she adopted a quick, nimble gait. She ran back and forth between the rooms, up and down the stairs, when it was time to make preparations for the journey she packed all the cases, unasked, and carried them to the car herself. And then, when the Baron came back from the railway station late in the evening, and handed her his stick and coat as she eagerly came to his aid, saying with a sigh of relief, "She's on her way!" something strange happened. All at once a powerful stretching movement became visible around Crescenz's narrowed lips, although in the normal way, like all animals, she never laughed. Now her mouth twisted, became a wide horizontal line, and suddenly a grin appeared in the middle of her idiotically brightening face. It displayed such frank, animal lack of inhibition that the Baron, embarrassed and surprised by the sight, was ashamed of his inappropriate familiarity with the servant, and disappeared into his study without a word.

But that fleeting second of discomfort quickly passed over, and during the next few days the two of them, master and maid, were united in their sense of shared relief, enjoying the precious silence and independence that did them both good. The departure of the Baron's wife had lifted a lowering cloud, so to speak, from the atmosphere; the liberated husband, happily freed from the constant necessity to account for himself, came late home that very first evening, and the silent attentions of Crescenz were an agreeable contrast to his wife's only too voluble reception of him. Crescenz flung herself into her daily work again with passionate enthusiasm, rose particularly early, scoured everything until it shone, polished doorknobs and handles like a woman possessed, conjured up particularly delicious menus, and to his surprise the Baron noticed, when she first served him lunch, that the valuable china and cutlery kept in the silver cupboard except on special occasions had been taken out just for him. Not an observant man in general, he couldn't help noticing the attentive, almost affectionate care that this strange creature was taking, and kindly as he was at heart, he expressed his satisfaction freely. He praised her cooking, gave her a few friendly words, and when next morning, which happened to be his name-day, he found that she had made an elaborate cake with his initials and coat of arms on it in sugar icing, he smiled at her in high spirits. "You really are spoiling me, Cenzi! And what am I to do when—heaven forbid!—my wife comes home again?"

All the same, he kept a certain control over himself for a few days before casting off the last of his scruples. But then, feeling sure from various signs that she would keep silent, he began living the bachelor life again, making himself comfortable in his own apartment. On his fourth day as a grass widower he summoned Crescenz and told her, without further explanation, that he would like her to prepare a cold supper for two that evening and then go to bed; he would see to everything else himself. Crescenz received the order in silence. Not a glance, not the faintest look showed whether the real purport of what he said had penetrated her low forehead. But her master soon saw, with surprised amusement, how well she understood his real intentions, for when he came home from the theatre late that evening with a little music student who was studying opera, not only did he find the table beautifully laid and decorated with flowers, but the bed next to his own in the bedroom was invitingly if brazenly turned down, and his wife's silk dressing gown and slippers were laid out ready. The liberated husband instinctively smiled at the far-sighted thoughtfulness of that strange creature Crescenz. And with that he threw off the last of his inhibitions about letting the helpful soul into his confidence. He rang next morning for her to help the amorous intruder get dressed, and that finally sealed the silent agreement between them.

It was in those days, too, that Crescenz acquired her new name. The merry little music student, who was studying the part of Donna Elvira and in jest liked to elevate her lover to the role of Don Giovanni, had once said to him, laughing, "Now, do call for your Leporella!" The name amused him, just because it was so grotesque a parody when applied to the gaunt Tyrolean woman, and from now on he never called her anything but Leporella. Crescenz, who looked up in surprise the first time but was then enchanted by the pleasing vocal music of her new name, which she did not understand in the least, regarded it as a sign of distinction; whenever her high-spirited master called for her by that name her thin lips would part, exposing her brown, horse-like teeth, and like a dog wagging its tail, she submissively hurried to receive her lord and master's orders.

The name was intended as a joke, but the budding operatic diva had unintentionally hit the mark, throwing her a verbal dress that magically suited her. For like Don Giovanni's appreciative accomplice as depicted by Da Ponte, this bony old maid who had never known love took a curious pride and pleasure in her master's adventures. Was it just her satisfaction at seeing the bed of the wife she hated so much tumbled and desecrated every morning by now one, now another young body, or did a secret sense of conspiratorial pleasure make her own senses tingle? In any case, the stern, narrow-minded spinster showed a positively passionate readiness to be of service to her master in all his adventures. It was a long time since her own hard-worked body, now sexless after decades of labour, had felt any such urges, but she warmed herself comfortably, like a procuress, on the satisfaction of seeing a second young woman in the bedroom after a few days, and then a third; her share in the conspiracy and the exciting perfume of the erotic atmosphere worked like a stimulant on her dulled senses. Crescenz really did become Leporella, and was nimble, alert and ready to jump to attention; strange qualities appeared in her nature, as if forced into being by the flowing heat of her burning interest, all kinds of little tricks, touches of mischief, sharp remarks, a curiosity that made her eavesdrop and lurk in waiting. She was almost frolicking. She listened at doors, looked through keyholes, searched rooms and beds, flew upstairs and downstairs in excitement as soon as, like a huntswoman, she scented new prey; and gradually this alertness, this curious, interested sympathy reshaped the wooden shell of her old dull lethargy into some kind of living human being. To the general astonishment of the neighbours, Crescenz suddenly became sociable, she chatted to the maids in the building, cracked broad jokes with the postman, began chatting and gossiping with the women at the market stalls, and once in the evening, when the lights in the courtyard were out, the maidservants sleeping in the building in a room opposite hers heard a strange humming sound at the usually silent window: awkwardly, in a muted, rusty voice, Crescenz was singing one of those Alpine songs that herdswomen sing on the pastures at evening. The monotonous melody staggered out of her unpractised lips with difficulty, in a cracked tone, but it did come out, a strange and gripping sound. Crescenz was trying to sing again for the first time since her childhood, and there was something touching in those stumbling notes that rose with difficulty to the light out of the darkness of buried years.

The unconscious author of this change in the woman who was so devoted to him, the Baron, noticed it less than anyone, for who ever turns to look at his own shadow? He knows it is following faithfully and silently along behind his own footsteps, sometimes hurrying ahead like a wish of which he is not yet conscious, but he seldom tries to observe its shape imitating his, or to recognise himself in its distortion. The Baron noticed nothing about Crescenz except that she was always there at his service, perfectly silent, reliable and devoted to him to the point of self-abnegation. And he felt that her very silence, the distance she naturally preserved in all discreet situations, was specially beneficial; sometimes he casually gave her a few words of appreciation, as one might pat a dog, now and then he even joked with her, pinched her earlobe in kindly fashion, gave her a banknote or a theatre ticket—small things for him, taken from his waistcoat pocket without a moment's thought, but to her they were holy relics to be treasured in her little wooden box. Gradually he had become accustomed to thinking out loud in front of her, and even entrusting complex errands to her—and the greater the signs he gave of his confidence in her, the more gratefully and assiduously did she exert herself. An odd sniffing, searching, tracking instinct gradually appeared in her as she tried to spy out his wishes and even anticipate them; her whole life, all she did and all she wished for, seemed to pass from her own body into his; she saw everything with his eyes, listened hard to guess what he was feeling, and with almost depraved enthusiasm shared his enjoyment of all his pleasures and conquests. She beamed when a new young woman crossed the threshold, and looked downcast, as if her expectations were disappointed, if he came home at night without such amorous company—her once sluggish mind was now working as quickly and restlessly as only her hands used to, and a new, vigilant light shone in her eyes. A human being had awoken in the tired, worn-out work-horse—a human being who was reserved and sombre but cunning and dangerous, thinking and then acting on her thoughts, restless and intriguing.

Once when the Baron came home unexpectedly early, he stopped in the corridor in surprise: wasn't that giggling and laughter behind the usually silent kitchen door? And then Leporella appeared in the doorway, rubbing her hands on her apron, bold and awkward at the same time. "'Scuse us, sir," she said, eyes on the floor, "it's the pastry-cook's daughter's here, a pretty girl she be, she'd like to meet sir ever so!" The Baron looked up in surprise, not sure whether he should be angry at such outrageous familiarity or amused at her readiness to procure for him. Finally his male curiosity won the day. "Well, let her have a look at me!"

The girl, a fresh, blond sixteen-year-old, whom Leporella had gradually enticed with flattering talk, appeared, blushing, and with an embarrassed giggle as the maid firmly pushed her through the doorway, and twirled clumsily in front of the elegant gentleman, whom she had indeed often watched with half-childlike admiration from the pâtisserie opposite. The Baron thought her pretty, and invited her to take a cup of tea in his study. Uncertain whether she ought to accept, the girl turned to look for Crescenz, but she had already disappeared into the kitchen with conspicuous haste, so there was nothing the girl could do, having been lured into this adventure, but accept the dangerous invitation, flushed and excited with curiosity.

But nature cannot leap too far: though the pressure of a distorted, confused passion might have aroused a certain mental agility in her dull and angular nature, Crescenz's newly acquired and limited powers of thought were not enough to overcome the next obstacle. In that, they were still related to an animal's short-term instincts. Immured in her obsession to serve the master she loved with doglike devotion in every way, Crescenz entirely forgot his absent wife. Her awakening was all the more terrible: it was like thunder coming out of a clear sky when one morning the Baron came in with a letter in his hand, looking annoyed, and brusquely told her to set everything in the apartment to rights, because his wife was coming home from the sanatorium next day. Crescenz stood there pale-faced, her mouth open with the shock: the news had struck her like a knife. She just stared and stared, as if she didn't understand. And so immeasurably and alarmingly did this thunderclap distort her face that the Baron thought he should calm her a little with a light-hearted comment. "It looks to me as if you're not best pleased either, Cenzi, but there's nothing anyone can do about it."

Soon, however, something began to move in her rigid face again. It worked its way up from deep down in her, as if coming out of her guts, a mighty convulsion that gradually brought dark red colour to the cheeks that had been white just now. Very slowly, forced out with harsh thrusts like heartbeats, words emerged: her throat was trembling under the pressure of the effort. And at last they were there and came dully through her gritted teeth. "Could be—could be summat as 'un could do..."

It had come out harsh as the firing of a deadly shot. And so evil, so darkly determined did that distorted face look after she had vented her feelings with such violence that the Baron instinctively started, flinching back in surprise. But Crescenz had already turned away again, and was beginning to scour a copper bowl with such convulsive zeal that she looked as if she meant to break her fingers on it.

With the home-coming of the Baron's wife, stormy winds filled the apartment again, slamming doors, blowing angrily through the rooms, sweeping away the comfortable, warm atmosphere like a cold draught. Whether the deceived wife had found out, from informers among the neighbours or anonymous letters, about the despicable way in which her husband had abused the freedom of the household, or whether the nervous and obvious ill temper that he did not scruple to show on her return had upset her, no one could tell—but in any case, two months in the sanatorium seemed to have done her strained nerves no good, for weeping fits now alternated with occasional threats and hysterical scenes. Relations between the couple became more insufferable every day. For a few weeks the Baron manfully defied the storm of her reproaches with the civility he had always preserved before, and replied evasively and indirectly when she threatened him with divorce or letters to her parents. But this cool, loveless indifference of his in itself drove the friendless woman, surrounded as she was by secret hostility, further and further into her nervous agitation.

Crescenz had armoured herself entirely in her old silence. But that silence had turned aggressive and dangerous. On her mistress's arrival she defiantly stayed in the kitchen, and when she was finally summoned she avoided wishing the Baroness well on her return. Shoulders obdurately braced, she stood there like a block of wood and replied with such surliness to all questions that her impatient mistress soon turned away from her. With one glance, however, Crescenz darted all her pent-up hatred at the unsuspecting woman's back. Her greedy emotions felt wrongfully robbed by the Baroness's return; from the delights of the service she had so passionately relished, she was thrust back into the kitchen and the range, deprived of her intimate name of Leporella. For the

Baron carefully avoided showing any liking for Crescenz in front of his wife. Sometimes, however, when he was exhausted by the unendurable scenes, and feeling in need of comfort and wanted to vent his feelings, he would slip into the kitchen and sit down on one of the hard wooden chairs, just so that he could groan, "I can't stand this any longer!"

These moments, when the master she idolized sought refuge with her from his excessive tension, were the happiest of Leporella's life. She never ventured to reply or say a word of consolation; silent and lost in thought, she just sat there, and only looked up sometimes with a sympathetic, receptive and tormented glance at her god, thus humiliated. Her silent sympathy did him good. But once he had left the kitchen, an angry fold would return to her brow, and her heavy hands expressed her anger by battering defenceless pieces of meat or savagely scouring dishes and cutlery.

At last the ominous atmosphere in the apartment since the wife's return discharged itself stormily; during one of the couple's intemperate scenes the Baron finally lost patience, abruptly abandoned the meekly indifferent schoolboy attitude he had adopted, and slammed the door behind him. "I've had enough of this," he shouted so angrily that all the windows in the apartment shook. And still in a furious temper, red in the face, he went out to the kitchen, where Crescenz was quivering like a bent bow. "Pack my case at once and find my sporting gun. I'm going hunting for a week. Even the Devil couldn't endure this hell any more. There has to be an end to it."

Crescenz looked at him happily: like this, he was master in his own house again! And a hoarse laugh emerged from her throat. "Sir be right, there have to be an end to 'un." And twitching with eager zeal, racing from room to room, she hastily snatched everything he would need from cupboards and tables, every nerve of the heavily built creature straining with tension and avidity. She carried the case and the gun out to the car herself. But when he was seeking words to thank her for her eager help, his eyes looked away from her in alarm. For that spiteful smile, the one that always alarmed him, had returned to her narrowed lips. When he saw her seeming to lie in ambush like that, he was instinctively reminded of the low crouching movement of an animal gathering itself to spring. But then she retreated into herself again, and just whispered hoarsely, with almost insulting familiarity, "I hopes sir has a good journey, I'll do 'un all."

Three days later the Baron was called back from his hunting trip by an urgent telegram. His cousin was waiting for him at the railway station. At his very first glance the anxious man knew that something terrible must have happened, for his cousin looked nervous and was fidgeting. After a few words solicitously designed to prepare him, he discovered what it was: his wife had been found dead in her bed that morning, with the whole room full of gas. Unfortunately a careless mistake was out of the question, said his cousin, because now, in May, the gas stove had not been lit for a long time, and his wife's suicidal frame of mind was also obvious from the fact that the unhappy woman had taken some veronal the evening before. In addition there was the statement made by the cook Crescenz, who had been alone at home that evening, and had heard her unfortunate mistress going into the room just outside the bedroom in the night, presumably on purpose to switch on the gas supply, which had been carefully turned off. On hearing this, the police doctor who had also been called in agreed that an accident was out of the question, and recorded death by suicide.

The Baron began to tremble. When his cousin mentioned the statement that Crescenz had made he suddenly felt the blood in his hands turn cold. An unpleasant, a dreadful idea rose in his mind like nausea. But he forcibly suppressed this seething, agonising sensation, and meekly let his cousin take him home. The body had already been removed; family members were waiting in the drawing room with gloomy and hostile expressions. Their condolences were cold as a knife. With a certain accusatory emphasis, they said they thought they should mention that, unfortunately, it had been impossible to hush up the 'scandal', because the maid had rushed out on the stairs that morning screaming, "The mistress has killed herself!" And they had decided on a quiet funeral—yet again that sharp, chilly blade was turned against him—because, deplorably, all kinds of rumours had aroused the curiosity of society to an unwelcome degree. The downcast Baron listened in confusion, and once instinctively raised his eyes to the closed bedroom door, but then cravenly looked away again. He wanted to think something out to the end, an unwelcome idea that kept surfacing in his mind, but all this empty, malicious talk bewildered him. The black-clad relations stood around talking for another half-hour, and then one by one they took their leave. He was left alone in the empty, dimly lit room, trembling as if he had suffered a heavy blow, with an aching head and weariness in his joints.

Then there came a knock at the door. "Come in," he said, rousing himself with a start. And along came a hesitant step, a dragging, stealthy step that he knew well. Suddenly, horror overcame him; he felt as if his cervical vertebrae were firmly screwed in place, while at the same time the skin from his temples to his knees was rippling with icy shudders. He wanted to turn, but his muscles failed him. So he stood there in the middle of the room, trembling and making no sound, his hands dropping by his sides and rigid as stone, and he felt very clearly how cowardly this guilt-ridden attitude must look. But it was useless for him to exert all his strength: his muscles just would not obey him. The voice behind him said, "I just wants ter ask, sir, will sir eat at home or out?" The Baron shivered ever more violently, and now the icy cold made its way right into his breast. He tried three times before he finally managed to get out the words, "No, I don't want anything to eat." Then the footsteps dragged themselves away, and still he didn't have the courage to turn. And suddenly the rigidity left him: he was shaking all over with spasms, or nausea. He suddenly flung himself at the door and turned the key in it, so that those dreadful footsteps following him like a ghost couldn't get at him. Then he dropped into a chair to force down an idea that he didn't want to entertain, although it kept creeping back into his mind, as cold and slimy as a snail. And this obsessive idea, though he hated the thought of coming close to it, filled all his emotions: it was inescapable, slimy, horrible, and it stayed with him all that sleepless night and during the hours that followed, even when, black-clad and silent, he stood at the head of the coffin during the funeral.

On the day after the funeral the Baron left the city in a hurry. All the faces he saw were too unendurable now: in the midst of their sympathy they had—or was he only imagining it?—a curiously observant, a painfully inquisitorial look. And even inanimate objects spoke to him accusingly, with hostility: every piece of furniture in the apartment, but more particularly in the bedroom where the sweetish smell of gas still seemed to cling to everything, turned him away if he so much as automatically opened the doors. But the really unbearable nightmare of his sleeping and waking hours was the cold, unconcerned indifference of his former accomplice, who went about the empty apartment as if nothing at all had happened. Since that moment at the station when his cousin mentioned her name, he had trembled at the thought of any meeting with her. As soon as he heard her footsteps a nervous, hasty restlessness took hold of him; he couldn't look at that dragging, indifferent gait any more, couldn't bear her cold, silent composure. Revulsion overcame him when he even thought of her—her croaking voice, her greasy hair, her dull, animal, merciless absence of feeling, and part of his anger was anger against himself because he lacked the power to break the bond between them by force, like a piece of string, although it was almost throttling him. So he saw only one way out—flight. He packed his case in secret without a word to her, leaving only a hasty note behind to say that he had gone to visit friends in Carinthia.

The Baron stayed away all summer. Returning once during that time, when he was called back to Vienna on urgent business concerning his late wife's estate, he preferred to come quietly, stay in a hotel, and send no word to that bird of ill omen waiting for him at home. Crescenz never learned of his presence because she spoke to no one. With nothing to do, dark-faced, she sat in the kitchen all day, went to church twice instead of once a week as before, received instructions and money to settle bills from the Baron's lawyer, but she heard nothing from the Baron himself. He did not write and he sent her no messages. She sat there silently, waiting: her face became harder and thinner, her movements were wooden again, and so she spent many weeks, waiting and waiting in a mysterious state of rigidity.

In autumn, however, urgent business no longer allowed the Baron to extend his stay in the country, and he had to return to his apartment. At the doorway of the building he stopped, hesitating. Two months in the company of close friends had almost made him forget a good deal of it—but now that he was about to confront his nightmare again in physical form, the person who perhaps was his accomplice, he felt exactly the same nauseating spasm as before. It made him retch. With every step he took as he went more and more slowly up the stairs, that invisible hand crept up his throat and tightened its grip. In the end he had to make a mighty effort to summon up all his will-power and force his stiff fingers to turn the key in the lock.

Surprised, Crescenz came out of the kitchen as soon as she heard the click of the key turning. When she saw him, she stood there looking pale for a moment, and then, as if ducking out of sight, bent to pick up the travelling bag he had put down. But she said not a word of greeting, and he said nothing either. In silence she carried the bag to his room; he followed in silence too. He waited in silence, looking out of the window, until she had left the room. Then he hastily turned the key in the door.

That was their first meeting after several months.

Crescenz waited. And so did the Baron, to see if that dreadful spasm of horror at the sight of her would pass off. It did not. Even before hc saw her, the mere sound of her footsteps in the corridor outside his room sent the sense of discomfort fluttering up in him. He did not touch his breakfast, he was quick to leave the house every morning without a word to her, and he stayed out until late at night merely to avoid her presence. He delivered the two or three instructions that he had to give her with his face averted. It choked him to breathe the air of the same room as this spectral creature.

Meanwhile, Crescenz sat silently on her wooden stool all day. She was not cooking anything for herself. She couldn't stomach food, she avoided all human company, she just sat with timidity in her eyes, waiting for the first whistle from her master, like a beaten dog which knows that it has done something bad. Her dull mind did not understand exactly what had happened, only that her lord and master was avoiding her and didn't want her any more. That was all that reached her, and it made a powerful impression.

On the third day after the Baron's return the doorbell rang. A composed, grey-haired man with a clean-shaven face was standing there with a suitcase in his hand. Crescenz was about to send him away, but the intruder insisted that he was the new manservant here, his master had asked him to arrive at ten, and she was to announce him. Crescenz went white as a sheet; she stood there for a moment with her stiff fingers spread wide in mid-air. Then her hand fell like a bird that has been shot. "Thassa way," she abruptly told the surprised man, turned to the kitchen and slammed the door behind her.

The manservant stayed. From that day on her master no longer had to say a word to her; all messages were relayed by the calm, elderly servant. She did not know what was going on in the apartment; it all flowed over her like a cold wave flowing over a stone.

This oppressive state of affairs lasted for two weeks, draining Crescenz like an illness. Her face was thin and haggard, the hair was suddenly going grey at her temples. Her movements froze entirely. She spent almost all the time sitting on her wooden stool, like a block of wood herself, staring blankly at the empty window, and if she did work she worked furiously, like someone in a violent outbreak of rage.

After those two weeks the manservant went to his master's room, and from his tactful air of biding his time the Baron realised that there was something he particularly wanted to say. The man had already complained of the sullen manner of that 'Tyrolean clod', as he contemptuously called her, and had suggested dismissing her. But feeling in some way painfully embarrassed, the Baron had initially pretended to ignore his proposal. Although at the time the servant had bowed and left the room, this time he stuck doggedly to his opinion, and with a strange, almost awkward expression he finally stammered that he hoped sir would not think he was being ridiculous, but he couldn't… no, he couldn't put it any other way… he was *afraid* of her. That surly, withdrawn creature was unbearable, he didn't think the Baron knew what a dangerous person he had in his home.

The Baron instinctively started at this warning. What did the man mean, he asked, what was he trying to say? The manservant did soften his statement by saying that he couldn't point to anything certain, he just had a feeling that the woman was like a rabid animal… she could easily do someone harm. Yesterday he turned to give her an order, and he had unexpectedly seen a look in her eyes—well, there wasn't much you could say about a look, but it had been as if she was about to spring at his throat. And since then he had been afraid of her—even afraid to touch the food she cooked. "You wouldn't have any idea, sir," he concluded, "what a dangerous person that is. She don't speak, she don't say much, but I think she's capable of murder." Startled, the Baron cast the man a quick glance. Had he heard anything definite? Had someone passed any suspicion on to him? He felt his fingers begin to shake, and hastily put his cigar down so that the trembling of his hands would not show. But the elderly man's face was entirely unsuspecting—no, he couldn't know anything. The Baron hesitated. Then he suddenly pulled himself together, knowing what he himself wanted to do, and made up his mind. "Well, wait a little while, but if she's so unfriendly to you again then I'll just give her notice."

The manservant bowed, and the Baron sat back in relief. Every thought of that mysteriously dangerous creature darkened the day for him. It would be best to do it while he was away, he thought, at Christmas, perhaps—the mere idea of the liberation he hoped for did him good. Yes, that will be best, he told himself once more, at Christmas when I'm away.

But the very next day, as soon as he had gone to his study after dinner, there was a knock at the door. Unthinkingly looking up from his newspaper, he murmured, "Come in." And then he heard that dreaded, hard tread that was always in his dreams. He started up: like a death's head, pale and white as chalk, he saw the angular face quivering above the thin black figure. A little pity mingled with his horror when he saw how the anxious footsteps of the creature, crushed as she looked, humbly stopped short at the edge of the carpet. And to hide his bemused state, he tried to sound carefree. "Well, what is it then, Crescenz?" he asked. But it didn't come out warm and jovial, as he had intended; against his own will the question sounded hostile and unpleasant.

Crescenz did not move. She stared at the carpet. At last, as you might push a hard object away with your foot, she managed to get the words out. "That servant, sir, he come ter see 'un. He say sir be going to fire 'un."

The Baron, painfully embarrassed, rose to his feet. He had not expected it to come so soon. He began to say, stammering, that he was sure it hadn't been meant like that, she ought to try to get on with his other servant, adding whatever other unthinking remarks came to his lips.

But Crescenz stayed put, her gaze boring into the carpet, her shoulders hunched. Bitter and dogged, she kept her head bowed like an ox, letting all his kindly remarks pass her by, waiting for just one word that did not come. And when at last he fell silent, exhausted and rather repelled by the contemptible role he was obliged to adopt, trying to ingratiate himself with a servant, she remained obstinate and mute. Then at last she got out something else. "I only wants ter know if sir himself tells Anton ter fire 'un."

She somehow got it out—harshly, reluctantly, violently. And already on edge as he was, he felt it like a blow. Was that a threat? Was she challenging him? All at once all his cowardice was gone, and all his pity. The hatred and disgust that had been dammed up in him for weeks came together with his ardent wish to make an end of it at last. And suddenly changing his tone entirely, and adopting the cool objectivity that he had learned at work in the ministry, he confirmed, as if it were of no importance, that yes, that was indeed so, he had in fact given the manservant a free hand to organise the household just as he liked. He personally wished her well, and would try to persuade Anton to change his mind about dismissing her. But if she still insisted on maintaining hostilities with the manservant, well, he would just have to dispense with her services.

And summoning up all his will-power, determined not to be deterred by any sly hint or insinuating remark, he turned his glance as he spoke these last words on the woman he assumed to be threatening him and looked straight at her.

But the eyes that Crescenz now raised timidly from the floor were those of a wounded animal, seeing the pack just about to break out of the bushes ahead of her. "Th… thank 'ee, sir," she got out, very faintly. "I be goin'… I won't trouble sir no more…"

And slowly, without turning, she dragged herself out of the door with her bowed shoulders and stiff, wooden footsteps.

That evening, when the Baron came back from the opera and reached for the letters that had arrived on his desk, he saw something strange and rectangular there. As the light flared up, he made out a wooden casket with rustic carving. It was not locked: inside, neatly arranged, lay all the little things that he had ever given Crescenz: a few cards from his hunting expeditions, two theatre tickets, a silver ring, the entire heaped rectangle of her banknotes, and there was also a snapshot taken twenty years ago in the Tyrol in which her eyes, obviously taken unawares by the flashlight, stared out with the same stricken, beaten look as they had a few hours ago when she left his study.

At something of a loss, the Baron pushed the casket aside and went out to ask the manservant what these things of Crescenz's were doing on his desk. The servant immediately offered to bring his enemy in to account for herself. But Crescenz was not to be found in the kitchen or anywhere else in the apartment. And only the next day, when the police reported the suicidal fall of a woman about forty years old from the bridge over the Danube Canal, did the two men know the answer to the question of where Leporella had gone.

DID HE DO IT?

PERSONALLY I'M AS GOOD AS CERTAIN that he was the murderer. But I don't have the final, incontrovertible proof. "Betsy," my husband always tells me, "you're a clever woman, a quick observer, and you have a sharp eye, but you let your temperament lead you astray, and then you make up your mind too hastily." Well, my husband has known me for thirty-two years, and perhaps, indeed probably, he's right to warn me against forming a judgement in too much of a hurry. So as there is no conclusive evidence, I have to make myself suppress my suspicions, especially in front of other people. But whenever I meet him, whenever he comes over to me in that forthright, friendly way of his, my heart misses a beat. And a little voice inside me says: he and no one else was the murderer.

So I am going to try reconstructing the entire course of events again, just for my own satisfaction.

About six years ago my husband had come to the end of his term of service as a distinguished government official in the colonies, and we decided to retire to some quiet place in the English countryside, to spend the rest of our days, already approaching their evening, with such pleasures of life as flowers and books. Our choice was a small village in the country near Bath. A narrow, slowly flowing waterway, the Kennet and Avon Canal, winds its way from that ancient and venerable city, passing under many bridges, towards the valley of Limpley Stoke, which is always green. The canal was built with much skill and at great expense over a century ago, to carry coal from Cardiff to London, and has many wooden locks and lock-keepers' stations along its length. Horses moving at a ponderous trot on the narrow towpaths to right and left of the canal used to pull the broad, black barges along the wide waterway at a leisurely pace. It was planned and built on a generous scale, and was a good means of transport for an age when time still did not mean much. But then came the railway to bring the black freight to the capital city far more cheaply and easily. Canal traffic ground to a halt, the canal fell into decay and dilapidation, but the very fact that it is entirely deserted and serves no useful purpose makes it a romantic, enchanted place today. Waterweed grows so densely from the bottom of the sluggish, black water that the surface has a shimmer of dark green, like malachite; pale water lilies sway on the smooth surface of the canal, which reflects the flower-grown banks, the bridges and the clouds with photographic accuracy. There is barely a ripple moving on the drowsy waterway. Now and then, half sunk in the water and already overgrown with plants, a broken old boat by the bank recalls the canal's busy past, of which even the visitors who come to take the waters in Bath hardly know anything, and when we two elderly folk walked on the level towpath where the horses used to pull barges laboriously along by ropes in the old days, we would meet no one for hours on end except, perhaps, pairs of lovers meeting in secret to protect, by coming to this remote place, their youthful happiness from neighbours' gossip, before it was officially declared by their engagement or marriage.

We were delighted by the quiet, romantic waterway set among rolling hills. We bought a plot of land in the middle of nowhere, just where the slope from Bathampton falls gently to the waterside as a beautiful, lush meadow. At the top of the rise we built a little country cottage, with a pleasant garden path leading past fruit trees, vegetable beds and flower beds and on down to the canal, so that when we sat out of doors on our little garden terrace beside the water we could see the meadow, the house and the garden reflected in the canal. The house was more peaceful and comfortable than anywhere I had ever dreamt of living, and my only complaint was that it was rather lonely, since we had no neighbours.

"Oh, they'll soon come when they see what a pretty place we've found to live in," said my husband, cheering me.

And sure enough; our little peach trees and plum trees had hardly established themselves in the garden before, one day, signs of another building going up next to our house suddenly appeared. First came busy estate agents, then surveyors, and after them builders and carpenters. Within a dozen or so weeks a little cottage with a red-tiled roof was nestling beside ours. Finally a removal van full of furniture arrived. We heard constant banging and hammering in the formerly quiet air, but we had not yet set eyes on our new neighbours.

One morning there was a knock at our door. A pretty, slender woman with clever, friendly eyes, not much more than twenty-eight or twenty-nine, introduced herself as our neighbour and asked if we could lend her a saw; the workmen had forgotten to bring one. We fell into conversation. She told us that her husband worked in a bank in Bristol, but for a long time they had both wanted to live somewhere more remote, outside the city, and as they were walking along the canal one Sunday they had fallen in love with the look of our house. Of course it would mean a journey of an hour each way for her husband from home to work and back, but he would be sure to find pleasant travelling companions and would easily get used to it. We returned her call next day. She was still on her own in the house, and told us cheerfully that her husband wouldn't be joining her until all the work was finished. She really couldn't do with having him underfoot until then, she said, and after all, there was no hurry. I don't know why, but I didn't quite like the casual way she spoke of her husband's absence, almost as if she were pleased not to have him there. When we were sitting over our meal alone at home, I commented that she didn't appear to be very fond of him. My husband told me I shouldn't keep jumping to hasty conclusions; he had thought her a very agreeable young woman, intelligent and pleasant, and he hoped her husband would be the same.

And it wasn't long before we met him. As we were taking our usual evening walk one Saturday, when we had just left our house, we heard footsteps behind us, brisk and heavy, and when we turned we saw a large, cheerful-looking man catching up with us, offering us a large, red, freckled hand. He was our new neighbour, he said, he'd heard how kind we had been to his wife. Of course he ought not to be greeting us like this in his shirtsleeves, without paying a formal visit first. But his wife had told him so many nice things about us that he really couldn't wait a minute longer to thank us. So here he was, John Charleston Limpley by name, and wasn't it a famous thing—they'd already called the valley Limpley in his honour long before he himself could ever guess that he'd be looking for a house here some day? Yes, here he was, he said, and here he hoped to stay as long as the good Lord let him live. He liked this place better than anywhere else in the world, and he would promise us here and now, hand on his heart, to be a good neighbour.

He talked so fast and cheerfully, with such a flow of words, that you hardly had a chance to get a word in. So I at least had plenty of time to scrutinise him thoroughly. Limpley was a powerful figure of a man, at least six foot tall, with broad, square shoulders that would have graced a navvy, but he seemed to have a good-natured, childlike disposition, as giants so often do. His narrowed, slightly watery eyes twinkled confidently at you from between their reddish lids. As he talked and laughed, he kept showing his perfect white teeth. He didn't know quite what to do with his big, heavy hands, and had some difficulty in keeping them still. You felt that he would have liked to clap you on the shoulder in comradely fashion with those hands, and as if to work off some of his strength he at least cracked the joints of his fingers now and then.

Could he, he asked, join us on our walk, in his shirtsleeves just as he was? When we said yes, he walked along with us talking nineteen to the dozen. He was of Scottish descent on his mother's side, he told us, but he had grown up in Canada. Now and then he pointed to a fine tree or an attractive slope; how beautiful, he said, how incomparably beautiful that was! He talked, he laughed, he expressed enthusiasm for everything almost without stopping. An invigorating current of strength and cheerfulness emanated from this large, healthy, vital man, infectiously carrying us away with it. When we finally parted, my husband and I both felt pleased with the warmth of his personality. "It's a long time since I met such a hearty, full-blooded fellow," said my husband who, as I have already indicated, is usually rather cautious and withdrawn in assessing character.

But it wasn't long before our first pleasure in finding such an agreeable new neighbour began to diminish considerably. There could not be the least objection to Limpley as a human being. He was good-natured to a fault, he was interested in others, and so anxious to be obliging that you were always having to decline his helpful offers. In addition he was a thoroughly decent man, modest, open and by no means stupid. But after a while it became difficult to put up with his effusive, noisy way of being permanently happy. His watery eyes were always beaming with contentment about anything and everything. All that he owned, all that he encountered was delightful, wonderful; his wife was the best woman in the world, his roses the finest roses, his pipe the best pipe ever seen, and he smoked the best tobacco in it. He could spend a full quarter-of-an-hour trying to convince my husband that a pipe ought to be filled just so, in exactly the way he filled his own, and that while his tobacco was a penny cheaper than more expensive brands it was even better. Always bubbling over as he was with excessive enthusiasm about the most unimportant, natural and indifferent of things, he evidently had an urge to expound the reasons for falling into such banal raptures at length. The noisy engine running inside him was never switched off. Limpley couldn't work in his garden without singing at the top of his voice, couldn't talk without laughing uproariously and gesticulating, couldn't read the paper without jumping up when he came upon a news item that aroused his interest and running round to tell us about it. His huge, freckled hands were always assertive, like his big heart. It wasn't just that he patted every horse and every dog he met; my husband had to put up with many a comradely and uninhibited Canadian slap on the knee when they sat comfortably talking together. Because his own warm, full heart, which constantly overflowed with emotion, took an interest in everything, he assumed that it was only natural for everyone else to take a similar interest, and you had to resort to all kinds of little tricks to ward off his insistent kindness. He respected no one's hours of rest or even sleep, because bursting as he was with health and strength he simply could not imagine anyone else ever feeling tired or downcast. You found yourself secretly wishing he would take a daily dose of bromide to lower his magnificent but near-intolerable vitality to a more normal level. Several times, when Limpley had spent an hour sitting with us—or rather not sitting, but leaping up and down and striding around—I caught my husband instinctively opening the window, as if the presence of that dynamic and somehow barbaric man had overheated the room. While you were with him, looking into his bright, kindly eyes—and they were indeed always brimming over with kindness—you couldn't dislike him. It was only later that you felt you were worn out and wished him at the Devil. Before we knew Limpley, we old folk had never guessed that such admirable qualities as kindness, goodness of heart, frankness and warmth of feeling could drive us to distraction in their obtrusive superfluity.

I now also understood what I had found incomprehensible at first, that it by no means showed lack of affection on his wife's part when she accepted his absence with such cheerful equanimity. For she was the real victim of his extravagant good humour. Of course he loved her passionately, just as he passionately loved everything that was his. It was touching to see him treat her so tenderly and with such care; she had only to cough once and he was off in search of a coat for her, or poking the fire to fan the flames, and if she went on an expedition to Bath he overwhelmed her with good advice as if she had to survive a dangerous journey. I never heard an unkind word pass between the two of them; on the contrary, he loved to sing her praises to the point where it became quite embarrassing. Even in front of us, he couldn't refrain from caressing her and stroking her hair, and above all enumerating her many beauties and virtues. "Have you noticed what pretty little fingernails my Ellen has?" he would suddenly ask, and in spite of her bashful protest he made her show us her hands. Then I was expected to admire the way she arranged her hair, and of course we had to taste every batch of jam she made, since in his opinion it was infinitely better than anything the most famous jam manufacturers of England could produce. Ellen, a quiet, modest woman, always sat with her eyes cast down on these embarrassing occasions, looking uncomfortable. She seemed to have given up defending herself against her husband's boisterous behaviour. She let him talk and tell stories and laugh, putting in only an occasional weary, "Oh, really?" or, "Fancy that."

"She doesn't have an easy life," commented my husband one day when we were going home. "But one can't really hold it against him. He's a good soul at heart, and she may well be happy with him."

"I'm not so sure about the happiness," I said rather sharply. "If you ask me, all that ostentatious happiness is too much to take—fancy making such a show of his feelings! I'd go mad living with so much excessive emotion. Don't you see that he's making his wife very *un*happy with all that effervescence and positively murderous vitality?"

"Oh, you're always exaggerating," said my husband, and I suppose he was right, really. Limpley's wife was by no means unhappy, or rather she wasn't even that any more. By now she was probably incapable of any pronounced feeling of her own; she was simply numbed and exhausted by Limpley's vast exuberance. When he went to his office in the morning, and his last cheery 'Goodbye' died away at the garden gate, I noticed that the first thing she did was to sit down or lie down for a little while without doing anything, just to enjoy the quiet atmosphere all around her. And there would be something slightly weary in her movements all day. It wasn't easy to get into conversation with her, for she had almost forgotten how to speak for herself in their eight years of marriage. Once she told me how they had met. She had been living with her parents in the country, he had strolled by on an outing, and in his wild way he had swept her off her feet; they were engaged and then married before she really knew what he was like or even what his profession was. A quiet, pleasant woman, she never said a word, not a syllable to suggest that she wasn't happy, and yet as a woman myself I sensed where the real crux of that marriage lay. In the first year they had taken it for granted that they would have a baby, and it was the same in the second and third years of their marriage. Then after six or seven years they had given up hope, and now her days were too empty, while her evenings were too full of his boisterous high spirits. It would be a good idea, I thought to myself, if she were to adopt a child, or take to some kind of sporting activity, or find a job. All that sitting around was bound to lead to melancholy, and melancholy in turn to a kind of hatred for his provoking cheerfulness, which was certainly likely to exhaust any normal person. She ought to have someone, anyone with her, or the tension would be too strong.

As chance would have it, I had owed an old friend of my youth who lived in Bath a visit for weeks. We had a comfortable chat, and then she suddenly remembered that she wanted to show me something charming, and took me out into the yard. At first all I could see in the dim light of a shed was a group of small creatures of some kind tumbling about in the straw, crawling over each other and mock-fighting. They were four bulldog puppies of six or seven weeks old, stumbling about on their big paws, now and then trying to utter a little squeal of a bark. They were indeed charming as they staggered out of the basket where their mother lay, looking massive and suspicious. I picked one of them up by his profuse white coat. The puppy was brown and white, and with his pretty snub nose he did credit to his distinguished pedigree, as his mistress explained to me. I couldn't refrain from playing with him, teasing him and getting him excited so that he snapped clumsily at my fingers. My friend asked if I would like to take him home with me; she loved the puppies very much, she said, and she was ready to give them away if she could be sure they were going to good homes where they would be well cared for. I hesitated, because I knew that when my husband lost his beloved spaniel he had sworn never to let another dog into his heart again. But then it occurred to me that this charming little puppy might be just the thing for Mrs Limpley, and I promised my friend to let her know next day. That evening I put my idea to the Limpleys. Mrs Limpley was silent; she seldom expressed an opinion of her own. However, Limpley himself agreed with his usual enthusiasm. Yes, yes, he said, that was all that had been missing from their lives! A house wasn't really a home without a dog. Impetuous as he was, he tried persuading me to go to Bath with him that very night, rouse my friend and collect the puppy. But when I turned down this fanciful idea he had to wait, and not until the next day did the bulldog puppy arrive at their house in a little basket, yapping and scared by the unexpected journey.

The outcome was not quite what we had expected. I had meant to provide the quiet woman who spent her days alone in an empty house with a companion to share it. However, it was Limpley himself who turned the full force of his inexhaustible need to show affection on the dog. His delight in the comical little creature was boundless, and as always excessive and slightly ridiculous. Of course Ponto, as he called the puppy, I don't know why, was the best-looking, cleverest dog on earth, and Limpley discovered new virtues and talents in him every day, indeed every hour. He spent lavishly on the best equipment for his four-footed friend, on grooming tools, leashes, baskets, a muzzle, food bowls, toys, balls and bones. Limpley studied all the articles and advertisements in the newspapers offering information on the care and nutrition of dogs, and took out a subscription to a dog magazine with a view to acquiring expert knowledge. The large dog industry that makes its money exclusively from such enthusiastic dog-lovers found a new and assiduous customer in him. The least little thing was a reason for a visit to the vet. It would take volumes to describe all the foolish excesses arising in unbroken succession from this new passion of his. We often heard loud barking from the house next door, not from the dog but from his master as he lay flat on the floor, trying to engage his pet in dialogue that no one else could understand by imitating dog language. He paid more attention to the spoilt animal's care than to his own, earnestly following all the dietary advice of dog experts. Ponto ate better than Limpley and his wife, and once, when there was something in the newspaper about typhoid—in a completely different part of the country—the animal was given only bottled mineral water to drink. If a disrespectful flea ventured to come near the sacrosanct puppy and get him scratching or biting in an undignified manner, the agitated Limpley would take the wretched business of flea-hunting upon himself. You would see him in his shirtsleeves, bent over a bucket of water and disinfectant, getting to work with brush and comb until the last unwanted guest had been disposed of. No trouble was too much for him to take, nothing was beneath his dignity, and no prince of the realm could have been more affectionately and carefully looked after than Ponto the puppy. The only good thing to come of all this foolishness was that as a result of Limpley's emotional fixation on his new object of affection, his wife and we were spared a considerable amount of his exuberance; he would spend hours walking the dog and talking to him, although that did not seem to deter the thick-skinned little creature from snuffling around as he liked, and Mrs Limpley watched, smiling and without the slightest jealousy, as her husband carried out a daily ritual at the altar of his four-footed idol. All he withdrew from her in the way off affection was the irritating excess of it, for he still lavished tenderness on her in full measure. We could not help noticing that the new pet in the house had perhaps made their marriage happier than before.

Meanwhile Ponto was growing week by week. The thick puppy folds of his skin filled out with firm, muscular flesh, he grew into a strong animal with a broad chest, strong jaws, and muscular hindquarters that were kept well brushed. He was naturally good-tempered, but he became less pleasant company when he realised that his was the dominant position in the household, and thanks to that he began behaving with lordly arrogance. It had not taken the clever, observant animal long to work out that his master, or rather his slave, would forgive him any kind of naughtiness. First it was just disobedience, but he soon began behaving tyrannically, refusing on principle to do anything that might make him seem subservient. Worst of all, he would allow no one in the house any privacy. Nothing could be done without his presence and, in effect, his express permission. Whenever visitors called he would fling himself imperiously against the door, well knowing that the dutiful Limpley would make haste to open it for him, and then Ponto would jump up proudly into an armchair, not deigning to honour the visitors with so much as a glance. He was showing them that he was the real master of the house, and all honour and veneration were owed to him. Of course no other dog was allowed even to approach the garden fence, and certain people to whom he had taken a dislike, expressed by growling at them, were obliged to put down the post or the milk bottles outside the gate instead of bringing them right up to the house. The more Limpley lowered himself in his childish passion for the now autocratic animal, the worse Ponto treated him, and improbable as it may sound the dog even devised an entire system of ways to show that he might put up with petting and enthusiastic encomiums, but felt not in the least obliged to respond to these daily tributes with any kind of gratitude. As a matter of principle, he kept Limpley waiting every time his master called him, and in the end this unfortunate change in Ponto went so far that he would spend all day racing about as a normal, full-blooded dog who has not been trained in obedience will do, chasing chickens, jumping into the water, greedily devouring anything that came his way, and indulging in his favourite game of racing silently and with malice aforethought down the slope to the canal with the force of a small bomb, head-butting the baskets and tubs of washing standing there until they fell into the water, and then prancing around the washerwomen and girls who had brought them with howls of triumph, while they had to retrieve their laundry from the water item by item. But as soon as it was time for Limpley to come home from the office Ponto, that clever actor, abandoned his high-spirited pranks and assumed the unapproachable air of a sultan. Lounging lazily about, he waited without the slightest welcoming expression for the return of his master, who would fall on him with a hearty, "Hello there, Ponty!" even before he greeted his wife or took off his coat. Ponto did not so much as wag his tail in response. Sometimes he magnanimously rolled over on his back to have his soft, silky stomach scratched, but even at these gracious moments he took care not to show that he was enjoying it by snuffling or grunting with pleasure. His humble servant was to notice that Ponto was doing him a favour by accepting his attentions at all. And with a brief growl that was as much as to say, "That's enough!" he would suddenly turn and put an end to the game. Similarly, he always had to be implored to eat the chopped liver that Limpley fed him piece by piece. Sometimes he merely sniffed at it and despite all persuasions lay down, scorning it, just to show that he was not always to be induced to eat his dinner when his two-legged slave served it up. Invited to go out for a walk, he would begin by stretching lazily, yawning so widely that you could see down to the black spots in his throat. He always insisted on doing something to make it clear that personally he was not much in favour of a walk, and would get off the sofa only to oblige Limpley. All his spoiling made him badly behaved, and he thought up any number of tricks to make sure that his master always assumed the attitude of a beggar and petitioner with him. In fact Limpley's servile passion could well have been described as more like doglike devotion than the conduct of the insubordinate animal, who played the part of oriental pasha to histrionic perfection.

Neither my husband nor I could bear to watch the outrageous behaviour of the tyrannical dog any longer. Clever as he was, Ponto soon noticed our lack of respect for him, and took care to show us his disapproval in the most obvious way. There was no denying that he was a dog of character. After the day when our maid turned him out of the garden in short order when he had left his unmistakable visiting card in one of our rose beds, he never again slipped through the thick hedge that formed the boundary between our two properties, and despite Limpley's pleas and persuasions could not be induced to set foot inside our house. We were glad to dispense with his visits; more awkward was the fact that when we met Limpley in his company walking down the road or outside our house, and that good-natured, talkative man fell into friendly conversation, the tyrannical animal's provocative behaviour made it impossible for us to talk at any length. After two minutes Ponto would begin to howl angrily, or growl and butt Limpley's leg, clearly meaning, "Stop it! Don't talk to these unpleasant people!" And I am sorry to say that Limpley always caved in. First he would try to soothe the disobedient animal. "Just a minute, and then we'll go on." But there was no fobbing off the tyrant, and his unfortunate servant—rather ashamed and confused—would say goodbye to us. Then the haughty animal trotted off, hindquarters proudly raised, visibly triumphant after demonstrating his unlimited power. I am not a violent woman, but my hand always itched to give the spoilt creature a smart blow with a dog whip, just once.

By these means Ponto, a perfectly ordinary dog, had managed to cool our previously friendly relations with our neighbours to a considerable extent. It obviously annoyed Limpley that he could no longer drop in on us every five minutes as he used to; his wife, for her part, was upset because she could see how ridiculous her husband's servile devotion to the dog made him in everyone else's eyes. And so another year passed in little skirmishes of this kind, while the dog became, if possible, even bolder and more demanding, and above all more ingenious in humiliating Limpley, until one day there was a change that surprised all concerned equally. Some of us, indeed, were glad of it, but it was a tragedy for the one most affected.

I had been unable to avoid telling my husband that for the last two or three weeks Mrs Limpley had been curiously shy, avoiding a conversation of any length with me. As good neighbours we lent each other this or that household item from time to time, and these encounters always led to a comfortable chat. I really liked that quiet, modest woman very much. Recently, however, I had noticed that she seemed embarrassed to approach me, and would rather send round her housemaid when she wanted to ask a favour. If I spoke to her, she seemed obviously self-conscious and wouldn't let me look her in the eye. My husband, who had a special liking for her, persuaded me just to go over to her house and ask straight out if we had done something to offend her without knowing it. "One shouldn't let a little coolness of that kind come between neighbours. And maybe it's just the opposite of what you fear. Maybe—and I do think so—she wants to ask you a favour and can't summon up the courage."

I took his advice to heart. I went round to the Limpleys' house and found her sitting in a chair in the garden, so lost in reverie that she didn't even hear me coming. I put a hand on her shoulder and said, speaking frankly, "Mrs Limpley, I'm an old woman and you needn't be shy with me. Let me speak first. If you are annoyed with us about something, do tell me what the matter is."

The poor little woman was startled. How could I think such a thing, she asked? She had kept from visiting me only because… And here she blushed instead of going on, and began to sob, but her sobs were, if I may say so, happy and glad. Finally she told me all about it. After nine years of marriage she had long ago given up all hope of being a mother, and even when her suspicion that the unexpected might have happened had grown stronger in the last few weeks, she said she hadn't felt brave enough to believe in it. The day before yesterday, however, she had secretly gone to see the doctor, and now she was certain. But she hadn't yet brought herself to tell her husband. I knew what he was like, she said, she was almost afraid of his extreme joy. Might it be best—and she hadn't been able to summon up the courage to ask us—might we be kind enough to prepare him for the news?

I said we'd be happy to do so. My husband in particular liked the idea, and he set about it with great amusement. He left a note for Limpley asking him to come round to us as soon as he got home from the office. And of course the good man came racing round, anxious to oblige, without even stopping to take his coat off. He was obviously afraid that something was wrong in our house, but on the other hand delighted to let off steam by showing how friendly and willing to oblige us he was. He stood there, breathless. My husband asked him to sit down at the table. This unusual ceremony alarmed him, and he hardly knew what to do with his large, heavy, freckled hands.

"Limpley," my husband began, "I thought of you yesterday evening when I read a maxim in an old book saying that no one should wish for too much, we should wish for only a single thing. And I thought to myself—what would our good neighbour, for instance, wish for if an angel or a good fairy or some other kindly being were to ask him—Limpley, what do you really want in life? I will grant you just one wish."

Limpley looked baffled. He was enjoying the joke, but he did not take it seriously. He still had an uneasy feeling that there was something ominous behind this solemn opening.

"Come along, Limpley, think of me as your good fairy," said my husband reassuringly, seeing him so much at a loss. "Don't you have anything to wish for at all?"

Half-in-earnest, half-laughing, Limpley scratched his short red hair.

"Well, not really," he finally confessed. "I have everything I could want, my house, my wife, my good safe job, my..." I noticed that he was going to say 'my dog', but at the last moment he felt it was out of place. "Yes, I really have all I could wish for."

"So there's nothing for the angel or the fairy to grant you?"

Limpley was getting more cheerful by the minute. He was delighted to be offered the chance to tell us, straight out, how extremely happy he was. "No... not really."

"What a pity," said my husband. "What a pity you can't think of anything." And he fell silent.

Limpley was beginning to feel a little uncomfortable under my husband's searching gaze. He clearly thought he ought to apologise.

"Well, one can always do with a little more money, of course… maybe a promotion at work… but as I said, I'm content… I really don't know what else I could wish for."

"So the poor angel," said my husband, pretending to shake his head sadly, "has to leave his mission unaccomplished because Mr Limpley has nothing to wish for. Well, fortunately the kind angel didn't go straight away again, but had a word with Mrs Limpley first, and he seems to have had better luck with her."

Limpley was taken aback. The poor man looked almost simple-minded, sitting there with his watery eyes staring and his mouth half-open. But he pulled himself together and said with slight irritation, for he didn't see how anyone who belonged to him not be perfectly happy, "My wife? What can *she* have to wish for?"

"Well—perhaps something better than a dog to look after."

Now Limpley understood. He was thunderstruck. Instinctively he opened his eyes so wide in happy surprise that you could see the whites instead of the pupils. All at once he jumped up and ran out, forgetting his coat and without a word of apology to us, storming off to his wife's room like a man demented.

We both laughed. But we were not surprised; it was just what we would have expected of our famously impetuous neighbour.

Someone else, however, *was* surprised. Someone who was lounging on the sofa idly, eyes half-open and blinking, waiting for the homage that his master owed him, or that he thought his master owed him—the well-groomed and autocratic Ponto. But what on earth had happened? The man went rushing past him without a word of greeting or flattery, on into the bedroom, and he heard laughter and weeping and talk and sobs, going on and on, and no one bothered about him, Ponto, who by right and custom received the first loving greeting. An hour passed by. The maid brought him his bowl of food. Ponto scornfully left it untouched. He was used to being begged and urged to eat until he was hand-fed. He growled angrily at the maid. They'd soon find out he wasn't to be fobbed off with indifference like that! But in their excitement his humans never even noticed that he had turned down his dinner that evening. He was forgotten, and forgotten he remained. Limpley was talking on and on to his wife, never stopping, bombarding her with concern and advice, lavishing caresses on her. In the first flush of his delight he had no eyes for Ponto, and the arrogant animal was too proud to remind his master of his existence by intruding. He crouched in a corner and waited. This could only be a misunderstanding, a single if inexcusable oversight. But he waited in vain. Even next morning, when the countless admonitions Limpley kept giving his wife to take it easy and spare herself almost made him miss his bus, he raced out of the house and past Ponto without a word to the dog.

There's no doubt that Ponto was an intelligent animal, but this sudden change was more than he could understand. I happened to be standing at the window when Limpley got on the bus, and I saw how, as soon as he had disappeared inside it, Ponto very slowly—I might almost say thoughtfully—slunk out of the house and watched the vehicle as it drove away. He waited there without moving for half-an-hour, obviously hoping that his master would come back and make up for the attention he had forgotten to pay him the evening before. He did not rush about playing, but only went round and round the house all day slowly, as if deep in thought. Perhaps—who knows how and to what extent sequences of thought can form in an animal mind?—he was brooding on whether he himself had done something clumsy to earn the incomprehensible withdrawal of the favours he was used to. Towards evening, about half-an-hour before Limpley usually came home, he became visibly nervous and kept patrolling the fence with his ears back, keeping an eye open to spot the bus in good time. But of course he wasn't going to show how impatiently he had been waiting; as soon as the bus came into view at its usual hour he hurried back into the living room, lay down on the sofa as usual and waited.

Once again, however, he waited in vain. Once again Limpley hurried past him. And so it went on day after day. Now and then Limpley noticed him, gave him a fleeting, "Oh, there you are, Ponto," and patted him in passing. But it was only an indifferent, casual pat. There was no more flattering, servile attention, there were no more caresses, no games, no walks, nothing, nothing, nothing. Limpley, that fundamentally kindly man, can hardly be blamed for this painful indifference, for he now had no thought in his head but to look after his wife. When he came home from work he accompanied her wherever she went, taking her for walks of just the right length, supporting her with his arm in case she took a hasty or incautious step; he watched over her diet, and made the maid give him a precise report on every hour of her day. Late at night, when she had gone to bed, he came round to our house almost daily to ask me, as a woman of experience, for advice and reassurance; he was already buying equipment in the big department stores for the coming baby. And he did all this in a state of uninterrupted busy excitement. His own personal life came nowhere; sometimes he forgot to shave for two days on end, and sometimes he was late at the office because the constant stream of advice he gave his wife had made him miss the bus. So it was not malice or unfaithfulness if he neglected to take Ponto for walks or pay him attention; only the confusion of a passionate man with an almost monomaniac disposition concentrating all his senses, thoughts and feelings on a single object. But if human beings, in spite of their ability to think logically of the past and the future, are hardly capable of accepting a slight inflicted on them without bearing resentment, how can a dumb animal take it calmly? Ponto was more and more nervous and agitated as the weeks went by. His self-esteem could not tolerate being overlooked and downgraded in importance, when he was the real master of this house. It would have been sensible of him to adopt a pleading, flattering attitude to Limpley, who would then surely have been aware of his dereliction of duty. But Ponto was too proud to crawl to anyone. It was not he but his master who was to make the first approach. So the dog tried all kinds of ruses to draw attention to himself. In the third week he suddenly began limping, dragging his left hind leg as if he had gone lame. In normal circumstances, Limpley would have examined him at once in affectionate alarm, to see if he had a thorn in his paw. He would anxiously have phoned the vet, he would have got up three or four times in the night to see how the dog was doing. Now, however, neither he nor anyone else in the house took the slightest notice of Ponto's pathetically assumed limp, and the embittered dog had no alternative but to put up with it. A couple of weeks later he tried again, this time going on hunger strike. For two days he made the sacrifice of leaving his food untouched. But no one worried about his lack of appetite, whereas usually, if he failed to lick the last morsel out of his bowl in one of his tyrannical moods, the attentive Limpley would fetch him special dog biscuits or a slice of sausage. Finally animal hunger was too much for Ponto, and he secretly and guiltily ate all his food with little enjoyment. Another time he tried to attract attention by hiding for a day. He had prudently taken up quarters in the disused henhouse, where he would be able to listen with satisfaction to anxious cries of "Ponto! Ponto, where are you?" But no one called him, no one noticed his absence or felt worried. His masterful spirit caved in. He had been set aside, humiliated, forgotten, and he didn't even know why.

I think I was the first to notice the change that came over the dog in those weeks. He lost weight, and his bearing was different. Instead of strutting briskly with his hindquarters proudly raised in the old way, he slunk about as if he had been whipped, and his coat, once carefully brushed every day, lost its silky gloss. When you met him he bowed his head so that you couldn't see his eyes and hurried past. But although he had been miserably humiliated, his old pride was not yet entirely broken; he still felt ashamed to face the rest of us, and his only outlet for his fury was to attack those baskets of washing. Within a week he pushed no less than three of them into the canal to make it clear, through his violence, that he was still around and he demanded respect. But even that was no good, and the only effect was that the laundry maids threatened to beat him. All his cunning ruses were in vain—leaving his food, limping, pretending to go missing, assiduously looking for his master—and he racked his brain inside that square, heavy head—something mysterious that he didn't understand must have happened that day. After it, the house and everyone in it had changed, and the despairing Ponto realised that he was powerless in the face of whatever had happened or was still happening. There could be no doubt about it—someone, some strange and ill-disposed power was against him. He, Ponto, had an enemy. An enemy who was stronger than he was, and this enemy was invisible and out of his reach. So the enemy, that cunning, evil, cowardly adversary who had taken away all his authority in the household, couldn't be seized, torn to pieces, bitten until his bones cracked. No sniffing at doorways helped him, no alert watchfulness, no lying in wait with ears pricked, no brooding—his enemy, that thief, that devil, was and remained invisible. In those weeks Ponto kept pacing along the garden fence like a dog deranged, trying to find some trace of his diabolical, unseen enemy.

All that his alert senses did pick up was the fact that preparations of some kind were being made in the house; he didn't understand them, but they must be to do with his arch-enemy. Worst of all, there was suddenly an elderly lady staying there—Mrs Limpley's mother—who slept at night on the dining-room sofa where Ponto used to lounge at his ease if his comfortably upholstered basket didn't seem luxurious enough. And then again, all kinds of things kept being delivered to the house—what for?—bedclothes, packages, the doorbell was ringing all the time. Several times a black-clad man with glasses turned up smelling of something horrible, stinking of harsh, inhuman tinctures. The door to the mistress of the house's bedroom was always opening and closing, and there was constant whispering behind it, or sometimes the two ladies would sit together snipping and clicking their sewing things. What did it all mean, and why was he, Ponto, shut out and deprived of his rights? All his brooding finally brought a vacant, almost glazed look to the dog's eyes. What distinguishes an animal's mind from human understanding, after all, is that the animal lives exclusively in the past and the present, and is unable to imagine the future or speculate on what may happen. And here, the dumb animal felt in torments of despair, something was going on that meant him ill, and yet he couldn't defend himself or fight back.

It was six months in all before the proud, masterful, Ponto, exhausted by his futile struggle, humbly capitulated, and oddly enough I was the one to whom he surrendered. I had been sitting in the garden one fine summer evening while my husband played patience indoors, and suddenly I felt the light, hesitant touch of something warm on my knee. It was Ponto, his pride broken. He had not been in our garden for a year-and-a-half, but now, in his distress, he was seeking refuge with me. Perhaps, in those weeks when everyone else was neglecting him, I had spoken to him or patted him in passing, so that he thought of me in this last moment of despair, and I shall never forget the urgent, pleading expression in his eyes as he looked up at me. The glance of an animal in great need can be a more penetrating, I might even say a more speaking look than the glance of a human being, for we put most of our feelings and thoughts into the words with which we communicate, while an animal, incapable of speech, expresses feelings only with its eyes. I have never seen perplexity more touchingly and desperately expressed than I did in that indescribable look from Ponto as he pawed gently at the hem of my skirt, begging. Much moved, I realised that he was saying, "Please tell me what my master and the rest of them have against me. What horrible thing are they planning to do to me in that house? Help me, tell me what to do." I really had no idea what to do myself in view of that pleading look. Instinctively I patted him and murmured under my breath, "Poor Ponto, your time is over. You'll have to get used to it, just as we all have to get used to things we don't like." Ponto pricked up his ears when I spoke to him, and the folds of skin on his brow moved painfully, as if he were trying to guess what my words meant. Then he scraped his paw impatiently on the ground. It was an urgent, restless gesture, meaning something like, "I don't understand you! Explain! Help me!" But I knew there was nothing I could do for him. He must have sensed, deep down, that I had no comfort to offer. He stood up quietly and disappeared as soundlessly as he had come, without looking back.

Ponto was missing for a whole day and a whole night. If he had been human I would have been afraid he had committed suicide. He did not turn up until the evening of the next day, dirty, hungry, scruffy and with a couple of bites; in his helpless fury he must have attacked other dogs somewhere. But new humiliation awaited him. The maid wouldn't let him into the house, but instead put his bowl of food outside the door and then took no more notice of him. It so happened that special circumstances accounted for this cruel insult, because Mrs Limpley had gone into labour, and the house was full of people bustling about. Limpley stood around helplessly, red-faced and trembling with excitement; the midwife was hurrying back and forth, assisted by the doctor; Limpley's mother-in-law was sitting by the bed comforting her daughter; and the maid had her hands more than full. I had come round to the Limpleys' house myself and was waiting in the dining room in case I could be useful in any way. All things considered, Ponto's presence could only have been a nuisance. But how was his dull, doggy brain to understand that? The distressed animal realised only that for the first time he had been turned out of the house—*his* house—like a beggar, unwanted. He was being maliciously kept away from something important going on there behind closed doors. His fury was indescribable, and with his powerful teeth he cracked the bones that had been thrown to him as if they were his unseen enemy's neck. Then he snuffled around; his sharpened senses could tell that other strangers had gone into the house—again, *his* house—and on the drive he picked up the scent of the black-clad man he hated, the man with the glasses. But there were others in league with him as well, and what were they doing in there? The agitated animal listened with his ears pricked up. Pressing close to the wall, he heard voices both soft and loud, groaning, cries, then water splashing, hurried footsteps, things being moved about, the clink of glass and metal—something was going on in there, something he didn't understand. But instinctively he sensed that it was hostile to him. It was to blame for his humiliation, the loss of his rights—it was the invisible, infamous, cowardly, malicious enemy, and now it was really there, now it would be in visible form, now at last he could seize it by the scruff of its neck as it richly deserved. Muscles tense and quivering with excitement, the powerful animal crouched beside the front door so that he could rush in the moment it opened. He wasn't going to get away this time, the evil enemy, the usurper of his rights and privileges who had murdered his peace of mind!

Inside the house no one gave a thought to the dog. We were too busy and excited. I had to reassure and console Limpley—no mean task—when the doctor and the midwife banished him from the bedroom; for those two hours, considering his vast capacity for sympathy, he may well have suffered more than the woman in labour herself. At last came the good news, and after a while Limpley, his feelings vacillating between joy and fear, was cautiously let into the bedroom to see his child—a little girl, as the midwife had just announced—and the new mother. He stayed there for a long time, while his mother-in-law and I, who had been through childbirth ourselves, exchanged reminiscences in friendly conversation.

At last the door opened and Limpley appeared, followed by the doctor. The proud father was coming to show us the baby, and was carrying her lying on a changing pad, like a priest bearing a monstrance; his broad, kind, slightly simple face almost transfigured by radiant happiness. Tears kept running unstoppably down his cheeks, and he didn't know how to dry them, because his broad hands were holding the child like something inexpressibly precious and fragile. Meanwhile the doctor behind him, who was familiar with such scenes, was putting on his coat. "Well, my job here is done," he said, smiling, and he shook hands and went to the door, suspecting no harm.

But in the split second when the doctor opened the door, with no idea what was about to happen, something shot past his legs, something that had been crouching there with muscles at full stretch, and there was Ponto in the middle of the room, filling it with the sound of furious barking. He had seen at once that Limpley was holding some new object that he didn't know, holding it tenderly, something small and red and alive that mewed like a cat and smelled human—aha! There was the enemy, the cunning, hidden enemy he had been searching for all this time, the adversary who had robbed him of his power, the creature that had destroyed his peace! Bite it! Tear it to bits! And with bared teeth he leapt up at Limpley to snatch the baby from him. I think we all screamed at the same time, for the powerful animal's movement was so sudden and violent that Limpley, although he was a heavy, sturdily built man, swayed under the weight of the impact and staggered back against the wall. But at the last moment he instinctively held the changing pad up in the air with the baby on it, so that no harm could come to her, and I myself, moving fast, had taken her from Limpley before he fell. The dog immediately turned against me. Luckily the doctor, who had rushed back on hearing our cries, with great presence of mind picked up a heavy chair and flung it. It landed with a heavy impact on the furious animal, cracking bones, as Ponto stood there with his eyes bloodshot and foaming at the mouth. The dog howled with pain and retreated for a moment, only to attack again in his frenzied rage. However, that brief moment had been long enough for Limpley to recover from his fall and fling himself on the dog, in a fury that was horrifyingly like Ponto's own. A terrible battle began. Limpley, a broad, heavy, powerful man, had landed on Ponto with his full weight and was trying to strangle him with his strong hands. The two of them were now rolling about on the floor in a tangle of limbs as they fought. Ponto snapped, and Limpley went on trying to choke him, his knee braced on the animal's chest, while Ponto kept wriggling out of his grasp. We old women fled into the next room to protect the baby, while the doctor and the maid, joining the fray, now joined the attack on the furious dog. They struck Ponto with anything that came to hand—wood cracked, glass clinked—they went for him with hands and feet, hammering and kicking his body, until the mad barking turned to heavy, stertorous breathing. Finally the animal, now completely exhausted, his breath coming irregularly, had his front and back legs tied by the doctor, the maid and my husband, who had come running from our house when he heard the noise. They used Ponto's own leather leash and some cord, and stuffed a cloth snatched off the table into his mouth. Now entirely defenceless and half-conscious, he was dragged out of the room. Outside the door they got him into a sack, and only then did the doctor hurry back to help.

Limpley, meanwhile, swaying like a drunk, staggered into the other room to make sure his child was all right. The baby was uninjured, and stared up at him with her sleepy little eyes. Nor was his wife in any danger, although she had been woken from her deep, exhausted sleep by all the noise. With some difficulty, she managed to give her husband a wan, affectionate smile as he stroked her hands. Only now was he able to think of himself. He looked terrible, his face white, mad-eyed, his collar torn open and his clothes crumbled and dusty. We were alarmed to see that blood was dripping from his torn right sleeve to the floor. In his fury he had not even noticed that, as he tried to throttle the animal, it had bitten him deeply twice in desperate self-defence. He removed his coat and shirt, and the doctor made haste to bandage his arm. Meanwhile the maid fetched him a brandy, for exhausted by his agitation and the loss of blood he was close to fainting, and it was only with some difficulty that we got him lying down on a sofa. Since he had had little rest for the last two nights as he waited in suspense for the baby's birth, he fell into a deep sleep.

Meanwhile we considered what to do with Ponto. "Shoot him," said my husband, and he was about to go home to fetch his revolver. But the doctor said it was his own duty to take him to have his saliva tested without a moment's delay, in case he was rabid, because if so then special measures must be taken to treat Limpley's bites. He would get Ponto into his car at once, he said. We all went out to help the doctor. The animal was lying defenceless outside the door, bound and gagged—a sight I shall never forget—but he was rolling his bloodshot eyes as if they would pop out of his head. He ground his teeth and retched and swallowed, trying to spit out the gag, while his muscles stood out like cords. His entire contorted body was vibrating and twitching convulsively, and I must confess that although we knew he was well trussed up we all hesitated to touch him. I had never in my life seen anything like such concentrated malice and fury, or such hatred in the eyes of any living creature as in his bloodshot and bloodthirsty gaze. I instinctively wondered if my husband had not been right in suggesting that the dog should be shot at once. But the doctor insisted on taking him away, and so the trussed animal was dragged to his car and driven off, in spite of his helpless resistance.

With this inglorious departure, Ponto vanished from our sight for quite a long time. My husband found out that he had tested negative for rabies under observation for several days at the Pasteur Institute, and as there could be no question of a return to the scene of his crime Ponto had been given to a butcher in Bath who was looking for a strong, aggressive dog. We thought no more of him, and Limpley himself, after wearing his arm in a sling for only two or three days, entirely forgot him. Now that his wife had recovered from the strain of childbirth, his passion and care were concentrated entirely on his little daughter, and I need hardly say that he showed as much extreme and fanatical devotion as to Ponto in his time, and perhaps made even more of a fool of himself. The powerful, heavy man would kneel beside the baby's pram like one of the Magi before the crib in the Nativity scenes of the old Italian masters; every day, every hour, every minute he discovered some new beauty in the little rosy creature, who was indeed a charming child. His quiet, sensible wife smiled with far more understanding on this paternal adoration than on his old senseless idolising of his four-footed friend, and we too benefited, for the presence of perfect, unclouded happiness next door could not help but cast its friendly light on our own house.

We had all, as I said, completely forgotten Ponto when I was surprisingly reminded of him one evening. My husband and I had come back from London late, after going to a concert conducted by Bruno Walter, and I could not drop off to sleep, I don't know why. Was it the echo of the melodies of the Jupiter Symphony that I was unconsciously trying to replay in my head, or was it the mild, clear, moonlit summer night? I got up—it was about two in the morning—and looked out of the window. The moon was sailing in the sky high above, as if drifting before an invisible wind, through clouds that shone silver in its light, and every time it emerged pure and bright from those clouds it bathed the whole garden in snowy brightness. There was no sound; I felt that if a single leaf had stirred it would not have escaped me. So I started in alarm when, in the midst of this absolute silence, I suddenly noticed something moving stealthily along the hedge between our garden and the Limpleys', something black that stood out distinctly as it moved quietly but restlessly against the moonlit lawn. With instinctive interest, I looked more closely. It was not a living creature, it was nothing corporeal moving there, it was a shadow. Only a shadow, but a shadow that must be cast by some living thing cautiously stealing along under cover of the hedge, the shadow of a human being or an animal. Perhaps I am not expressing myself very well, but the furtive, sly silence of that stealthy shape had something alarming about it. My first thought—for we women worry about such things—was that this must be a burglar, even a murderous one, and my heart was in my mouth. But then the shadow reached the garden hedge on the upper terrace where the fence began, and now it was slinking along past the railing of the fence, curiously hunched. Now I could see the creature itself ahead of its shadow—it was a dog, and I recognised the dog at once. Ponto was back. Very slowly, very cautiously, obviously ready to run away at the first sound, Ponto was snuffling around the Limpleys' house. It was—and I don't know why this thought suddenly flashed through my mind—it was as if he wanted to give notice in advance of something, for his was not the free, loose-limbed movement of a dog picking up a scent; there was something about him suggesting that he had some forbidden or ill-intentioned plan in mind. He did not keep his nose close to the ground, sniffing, nor did he walk with his muscles relaxed, he made his way slowly along, keeping low and almost on his belly, to make himself more inconspicuous. He was inching forward as if stalking prey. I instinctively leant forward to get a better look at him. But I must have moved clumsily, touching the window frame and making some slight noise, for with a silent leap Ponto disappeared into the darkness. It seemed as if I had only dreamt it all. The garden lay there in the moonlight empty, white and brightly lit again, with nothing moving.

I don't know why, but I felt ashamed to tell my husband about this; it could have been just my senses playing a trick on me. But when I happened to meet the Limpleys' maid in the road next morning, I asked her casually if she had happened to see Ponto again recently. The girl was uneasy, and a little embarrassed, and only when I encouraged her did she admit that yes, she had in fact seen him around several times, and in strange circumstances. She couldn't really say why, but she was afraid of him. Four weeks ago, she told me, she had been taking the baby into town in her pram, and suddenly she had heard terrible barking. As the butcher's van rolled by with Ponto in it, he had howled at her or, as she thought, at the baby in the pram, and looked as if he were crouching to spring, but luckily the van had passed so quickly that he dared not jump out of it. However, she said, his furious barking had gone right through her. Of course she had not told Mr Limpley, she added;

the news would only have upset him unnecessarily, and anyway she thought the dog was in safe keeping in Bath. But only the other day, one afternoon when she went out to the old woodshed to fetch a few logs, there had been something moving in there at the back. She had been about to scream in fright, but then she saw it was Ponto hiding there, and he had immediately shot away through the hedge and into our garden. Since then she had suspected that he hid there quite often, and he must have been walking around the house by night, because the other day, after that heavy storm in the night, she had clearly seen paw prints in the wet sand showing that he had circled the whole house several times. Did I think he might want to come back, she asked me? Mr Limpley certainly wouldn't have him in the house again, and living with a butcher Ponto could hardly be hungry. If he were, anyway, he would have come to her in the kitchen first to beg for food. Somehow she didn't like the way he was slinking about the place, she added, and did I think she ought to tell Mr Limpley after all, or at least his wife? We thought it over, and agreed that if Ponto turned up again we would tell his new master the butcher, so that he could put an end to his visits. For the time being, at least, we wouldn't remind Limpley of the existence of the hated animal.

I think we made a mistake, for perhaps—who can say—that might have prevented what happened next day, on that terrible and never-to-be-forgotten Sunday. My husband and I had gone round to the Limpleys', and we were sitting in deckchairs on the small lower terrace of the garden, talking. From the lower terrace, the turf ran down quite a steep slope to the canal. The pram was on the flat lawn of the terrace beside us, and I hardly need say that the besotted father got up in the middle of the conversation every five minutes to enjoy the sight of the baby. After all, she was a pretty child, and on that golden sunlit afternoon it was really charming to see her looking up at the sky with her bright blue eyes and smiling—the hood of the pram was put back—as she tried to pick up the patterns made by the sunlight on her blanket with her delicate if still rather awkward hands. Her father rejoiced at this, as if such miraculous reasoning as hers had never been known, and we ourselves, to give him pleasure, acted as if we had never known anything like it. That sight of her, the last happy moment, is rooted in my mind for ever. Then Mrs Limpley called from the upper terrace, which was in the shade of the veranda, to tell us that tea was ready. Limpley spoke soothingly to the baby as if she could understand him, "There, there, we'll be back in a minute!" We left the pram with the baby in it on the lawn, shaded from the hot sunlight by a cool canopy of leaves above, and strolled slowly to the usual place in the shade where the Limpleys drank afternoon tea. It was about twenty yards from the lower to the upper terrace of their garden, and you could not see one terrace from the other because of the rose-covered pergola between them. We talked as we walked, and I need hardly say what we talked about. Limpley was wonderfully cheerful, but his cheerfulness did not seem at all out of place today, when the sky was such a silky blue, it was such a peaceful Sunday, and we were sitting in the shade in front of a house full of blessings. Today, his mood was like a reflection of that fine summer's day.

Suddenly we were alarmed. Shrill, horrified screams came from the canal, voices of children and women's cries of alarm. We rushed down the green slope with Limpley in the lead. His first thought was for the child. But to our horror the lower terrace, where the pram had been standing only a few minutes ago with the baby dozing peacefully in it in perfect safety, was empty, and the shouting from the canal was shriller and more agitated than ever. We hurried down to the water. On the opposite bank several women and children stood close together, gesticulating and staring at the canal. And there was the pram we had left safe and sound on the lower terrace, now floating upside down in the water. One man had already put out in a boat to save the child, another had dived in. But it was all too late. The baby's body was not brought up from the brackish water, which was covered with green waterweed, until quarter-of-an-hour later.

I cannot describe the despair of the wretched parents. Or rather, I will not even try to describe it, because I never again in my life want to think of those dreadful moments. A police superintendent, informed by telephone, turned up to find out how this terrible thing had happened. Was it negligence on the part of the parents, or an accident, or a crime? The floating pram had been fished out of the water by now, and put back on the lower terrace on the police officer's instructions, just where it had been before. Then the Chief Constable himself joined the superintendent, and personally tested the pram to see whether a light touch would set it rolling down the slope of its own accord. But the wheels would hardly move through the thick, long grass. So it was out of the question for a sudden gust of wind, perhaps, to have made it roll so suddenly over the terrace, which itself was level. The superintendent also tried again, pushing a little harder. The pram rolled about a foot forward and then stopped. But the terrace was at least seven yards wide, and the pram, as the tracks of its wheels showed, had been standing securely some way from the place where the land began to slope. Only when the superintendent took a run up to the pram and pushed it really hard did it move along the terrace and begin to roll down the slope. So something unexpected must have set the pram suddenly in motion. But who or what had done it?

It was a mystery. The police superintendent took his cap off his sweating brow and scratched his short hair ever more thoughtfully. He couldn't make it out. Had any object, he asked, even just a ball when someone was playing with it, ever been known to roll over the terrace and down to the canal of its own accord? "No, never!" everyone assured him. Had there been a child nearby, or in the garden, a high-spirited child who might have been playing with the pram? No, no one! Had there been anyone else in the vicinity? Again, no. The garden gate had been closed, and none of the people walking by the canal had seen anyone coming or going. The one person who could really be regarded as an eyewitness was the labourer who had jumped straight into the water to save the baby, but even he, still dripping wet and greatly distressed, could say only that he and his wife had been walking beside the canal, and nothing seemed wrong. Then the pram had suddenly come rolling down the slope from the garden, going faster and faster, and tipped upside down as soon as it reached the water. As he thought he had seen a child in the water, he had run down to the bank at once, stripping off his jacket, and tried to rescue it, but he had not been able to make his way through the dense tangles of waterweeds as fast as he had hoped. That was all he knew.

The police superintendent was more and more baffled. He had never known such a puzzling case, he said. He simply could not imagine how that pram could have started rolling. The only possibility seemed to be that the baby might suddenly have sat up, or thrown herself violently to one side, thus unbalancing the lightweight pram. But it was hard to believe that, and he for one couldn't imagine it. Was there anything else that occurred to any of us?

I automatically glanced at the Limpleys' housemaid. Our eyes met. We were both thinking the same thing at the same moment. We both knew that the dog hated the child. We knew that he had been seen several times recently slinking around the garden. We knew how he had often head-butted laundry baskets full of washing and sent them into the canal. We both—I saw it from the maid's pallor and her twitching lips—we both suspected that the sly and now vicious animal, finally seeing a chance to get his revenge, had come out of hiding as soon as we left the baby alone for a few minutes, and had then butted the pram containing his hated rival fiercely and fast, sending it rolling down to the canal, before making his own escape as soundlessly as usual. But we neither of us voiced our suspicions. I knew the mere idea that if he had shot the raving animal after Ponto's attack, he might have saved his child would drive Limpley mad. And then, in spite of the logic of our thinking, we lacked any solid evidence. Neither the maid nor I, and none of the others, had actually seen the dog slinking around or running away that afternoon. The woodshed where he liked to hide—I looked there at once—was empty, the dry trodden earth of its floor showed no trace at all, we had not heard a note of the furious barking in which Ponto had always triumphantly indulged when he pushed a basket of washing into the canal. So we could not really claim that he had done it. It was more of a cruelly tormenting assumption. Only a justified, a terribly well justified suspicion. But the final, clinching certainty was missing.

And yet I have never since shaken off that dreadful suspicion—on the contrary, it was even more strongly confirmed over the next few days, almost to the point of certainty. A week later—the poor baby had been buried by then, and the Limpleys had left the house because they could not bear the sight of that fateful canal—something happened that affected me deeply. I had been shopping in Bath for a few household items when I suddenly had a shock. Beside the butcher's van I saw Ponto, of whom I had subconsciously been thinking in all those terrible hours, walking along at his leisure, and at the same moment he saw me. He stopped at once, and so did I. And now something that still weighs on my mind happened; in all the weeks that had passed since his humiliation, I had never seen Ponto looking anything but upset and distressed, and he had avoided any encounter with me, crouching low and turning his eyes away. Now he held his head high and looked at me—I can't put it any other way—with self-confident indifference. Overnight he had become the proud, arrogant animal of the old days again. He stood in that provocative position for a minute. Then, swaggering and almost dancing across the road with pretended friendliness, he came over to me and stopped a foot or so away, as if to say, "Well, here I am! Now what have you got to say? Are you going to accuse me?"

I felt paralysed. I had no power to push him away, no power to bear that self-confident and, indeed, I might almost say self-satisfied look. I walked quickly on. God forbid I should accuse even an innocent animal, let alone a human being, of a crime he did not commit. But since that day I cannot get rid of the terrible thought: "He did it. He was the one who did it."

THE DEBT
PAID LATE

MY DEAR ELLEN,
I know you will be surprised to receive a letter from me after so long; it must be five or perhaps even six years since I last wrote to you. I believe that then it was a letter of congratulations on your youngest daughter's marriage. This time the occasion is not so festive, and perhaps my need to confide the details of a strange encounter to you, rather than anyone else, may strike you as odd. But I can't tell anyone else what happened to me a few days ago. You are the only person who would understand.

My pen involuntarily hesitates as I write these words, and I have to smile at myself a little. Didn't we exchange the very same "You are the only person who would understand" a thousand times when we were fifteen or sixteen years old—immature, excitable girls telling each other our childish secrets at school or on the way home? And didn't we solemnly swear, long ago in our salad days, to tell each other everything, in detail, concerning a certain person? All that is more than a quarter of a century ago; but a promise, once made, must be kept. And as you will see, I am faithfully keeping my word, if rather late in the day.

This was how it all happened. I have had a difficult and strenuous time of things this year. My husband was appointed medical director of the big hospital in R., so I had all the complications of moving house to deal with; meanwhile my son-in-law went to Brazil on business, taking my daughter with him, and they left their three children in our house. The children promptly contracted scarlet fever one after the other, and I had to nurse them… and that wasn't all, because then my mother-in-law died. Everything was happening at once. I thought at first that I had survived all these headlong events pretty well, but somehow they must have taken more out of me than I knew, because one day my husband said, after looking at me in silence for some time, "Margaret, I think that now the children, thank goodness, are better again you ought to do something about your own health. You look overtired, you've been well and truly overdoing things. Two or three weeks at a sanatorium in the country, and you'll be your old self again."

My husband was right. I was exhausted, more so than I admitted to myself. I became aware of it when I realized that in company—and since my husband took up his post here, there have been many functions to host and many calls to be paid—after an hour I couldn't concentrate properly on what people were saying, while I forgot the simplest things more and more often in the daily running of the household, and had to force myself to get up in the morning. With his observant and medically trained eye, my husband had diagnosed my physical and mental weariness correctly. All I really needed was two weeks to recover. Fourteen days without thinking about the meals, the laundry, paying calls, doing all the everyday business—fourteen days on my own to be myself, not a mother, grandmother, housekeeper and wife of the medical director of a hospital all the time. It so happened that my widowed sister was available to come and stay, so everything was prepared for my absence; and I had no further scruples in following my husband's advice and going away by myself for the first time in twenty-five years. Indeed, I was actually looking forward quite impatiently to being invigorated by my holiday. I rejected my husband's suggestion only in one point: his idea that I should spend it at a sanatorium, although he had thoughtfully found one whose owner had been a friend of his from their youth. But there would have been other people whom I knew there, and I would have had to go on being sociable and mixing in company. All I really wanted was to be on my own for fourteen days with books, walks, time to dream and sleep undisturbed, fourteen days without the telephone and the radio, fourteen days of silence at peace with myself, if I may put it like that. Unconsciously, I hadn't wanted anything so much for years as this time set aside for silence and rest.

And then I remembered that in the first years of my marriage, when my husband was practising as an assistant doctor in Bolzano, I had once spent three hours walking up to an isolated little village high in the mountains. In its tiny marketplace, opposite the church, stood one of those rural inns of the kind so often to be found in the Tyrol, its ground floor built of massive stones, the first floor under the wide, overhanging wooden roof opening on to a spacious veranda, and the whole place surrounded by vine leaves that in autumn, the season when I saw it, glowed around the whole house like a red fire gradually cooling. Small outbuildings and big barns huddled to the right and left of it, but the house itself stood on its own under soft autumnal clouds drifting across the sky, and looked down at the endless panorama of the mountains.

At the time I had felt almost spellbound outside that little inn, and I wanted to go in. I'm sure you know what it's like to see a house from the train or on a walk, and think all of a sudden: oh, why don't I live here? I could be happy in this place. I think such an idea occurs to everyone sometimes, and when you have looked at a house for a long time secretly wishing to live happily in it, everything about it is imprinted on your memory. For years I remembered the red and yellow flowers growing in window boxes, the wooden first-floor gallery, where laundry was fluttering like colourful banners the day I saw it, the painted shutters at the windows, yellow on a blue background with little heart-shapes cut out of the middle of them, and the roof ridge with a stork's nest on the gable. When my heart felt restless I sometimes thought of that house. How nice it would be to go there for a day, I would think, in the dreamy, half-unconscious way that you think of something impossible. And now wasn't this my best chance to make my old, and by this time almost forgotten, wish come true? Wasn't the prettily painted house on the mountainside, an inn without the tiresome amenities of our modern world, with no telephone or radio, the very thing for overtired nerves? I would have no visitors there, and there would be no formalities. As I called it to mind again, I thought I was breathing in the strong, aromatic mountain air, and hearing the far-off ringing of rustic cowbells. Even remembering it gave me fresh courage and made me feel better. It was one of those ideas that take us by surprise apparently for no reason at all, although in reality they express wishes that we have cherished for a long time, waiting in the unconscious mind. My husband, who didn't know how often I had dreamt of that little house, seen only once years ago, smiled a little at first but promised to make enquiries. The proprietors replied that all of their three guest rooms were vacant at the moment, and I could choose whichever I liked. All the better, I thought, no neighbours, no conversations; and I went on the night train. Next morning, a little country one-horse trap took me and my small suitcase up the mountain at a slow trot.

It was all as delightful as I could have hoped for. The room was bright and neat, with its simple, pale pine furniture, and from the veranda, which was all mine in the absence of any other guests, I had a view into the endless distance. A glance at the well-scoured kitchen, shining with cleanliness, showed me, experienced housewife that I am, that I would be very well looked after here. The landlady, a thin, friendly, grey-haired Tyrolean, assured me again that I need not fear being disturbed or pestered by visitors. True, the parish clerk, the local policeman and a few of the other neighbours came to the inn every evening to drink a glass or so, play cards and talk. But they were all quiet folk, and at eleven they went home again. On Sunday after church, and sometimes in the afternoon, the place was rather livelier, because the locals came to the inn from their farms or the mountains; but I would hear hardly any of that in my room.

The day was too bright and fine, however, for me to stay indoors for long. I unpacked the few things I had brought, asked for a piece of good brown country bread and a couple of slices of cold meat to take out with me, and went walking over the meadows, climbing higher and higher. The landscape lay before me, the valley with its fast-flowing river, the surrounding snow-crowned peaks, as free as I was myself. I felt the sun on every pore of my skin, and I walked and walked and walked for an hour, two hours, three hours until I reached the highest Alpine meadows. There I lay down to rest, stretched out on the soft, warm moss, and felt a wonderful sense of peace come over me, together with the buzzing of the bees, the light and rhythmic sound of the wind—it was exactly what I had been longing for. I closed my eyes pleasurably, fell to dreaming, and didn't even notice when at some point I dropped off to sleep. I was woken only by a chill in the air on my limbs. Evening was coming on, and I must have slept for five hours. Only now did I realize how tired I had been. But I had good, fresh air in my nerves and in my bloodstream. It took me only two hours to walk back to the little inn with a strong, firm, steady step.

The landlady was standing at the door. She had been slightly anxious, fearing I might have lost my way, and offered to prepare my supper at once. I had a hearty appetite and was hungrier than I could remember feeling for years, so I was very happy to follow her into the main room of the inn. It was not large—a dark, low-ceilinged room with wood-panelled walls, very comfortable with its red-and-blue check tablecloths, the chamois horns and crossed shotguns on the walls. And although the big blue-tiled stove was not heated this warm autumn day, there was a comfortable natural warmth inside the room. I liked the guests as well. At one of the four tables the local policeman, the customs officer and the parish clerk sat playing cards together, each with a glass of beer beside him. A few farmers with strong, sun-browned faces sat at their ease at another, propping their elbows on it. Like all Tyroleans, they said little, and merely puffed at their long-stemmed porcelain pipes. You could see that they had worked hard all day and were relaxing now, too tired to think, too tired to talk—honest, upright men; it did one good to look at their faces, as strongly outlined as woodcuts. A couple of carters occupied the third table, drinking strong grain schnapps in small sips, and they too were tired and silent. The fourth table was laid for me, and soon bore a portion of roast meat so huge that normally I wouldn't have managed to eat half of it; but I had a healthy, even ravenous appetite after walking in the fresh mountain air.

I had brought a book down, meaning to read, but it was pleasant sitting here in this quiet room, among friendly people whose proximity was neither oppressive nor a nuisance. Sometimes the door opened, a fair-haired child came to fetch a jug of beer for his parents, or a farmer dropped in and emptied a glass standing at the bar. A woman came for a quiet chat with the landlady, who sat behind the bar darning socks for her children or grandchildren. There was a wonderful quiet rhythm to all this coming and going, which offered something for my eyes to see and was no burden on my heart, and I felt very well in such a comfortable atmosphere.

I had been sitting dreamily like that for a while, thinking of nothing in particular, when—it will have been about nine o'clock—the door was opened again, but not this time in the slow, unhurried way of the locals. It was suddenly flung wide, and the man who came in stood for a moment on the threshold filling the doorway, as if not quite sure whether to come in. Only then did he let the door latch behind him, much more loudly than the other guests, look around the room and greet all present with a deep-voiced and resonant, "A very good evening to you one and all, gentlemen!" I was immediately struck by his rather ornate and artificial vocabulary. In a Tyrolean village inn, people do not usually greet the "gentlemen" with such ceremony, and in fact this rather ostentatious form of address seemed to meet with an unenthusiastic response from the other guests in the room. No one looked up, the landlady went on darning grey woollen socks, and one of the carters was the only person to grunt an indifferent "Evening" in return, but in a tone of voice suggesting, "And to the devil with you!" No one seemed surprised by the strange guest's manner, but he was not to be deterred by this unforthcoming reception. Slowly and gravely, he hung up his broad hat with its well-worn brim—not a rustic item of headgear—on one of the chamois horns, and then looked from table to table, not sure where to sit down. Not a word of welcome came from any of them. The three card-players immersed themselves with conspicuous concentration in their game, the farmers on their benches gave not the slightest sign of moving closer to make room, and I myself, made to feel rather uncomfortable by the stranger's manner and fearing that he might turn out to be talkative, was quick to open my book.

So the stranger had no choice but to go over to the bar with a noticeably heavy, awkward step. "A beer, if mine hostess pleases, as fresh and delicious as your lovely self," he ordered in quite a loud voice. Once again I was struck by his dramatically emotional tone. In a Tyrolean village inn, such an elaborately turned compliment seemed out of place, and there was nothing whatsoever about that kindly old grandmother the landlady to justify it. As was to be expected, such a form of address failed to impress her. Without replying, she picked up one of the sturdy stoneware tankards, rinsed it out with water, dried it with a cloth, filled it from the barrel and pushed it to the newcomer over the bar, in a manner that was not exactly discourteous but was entirely indifferent.

Since the round paraffin lamp hung from its chains above him, right in front of the bar, I had a chance to take a better look at this unusual guest. He was about sixty-five years old, was very stout, and with the experience I had gained as a doctor's wife I immediately saw the reason for the dragging, heavy gait that I had noticed as soon as he came into the room. A stroke must have affected one side of his body to some extent, for his mouth also turned down on that side, and the lid of his left eye visibly drooped lower than his right eyelid. His clothes were out of place for an Alpine village; instead of the countryman's rustic jacket and lederhosen, he wore baggy yellow trousers that might once have been white, with a coat that had obviously grown too tight for him over the years and was alarmingly shiny at the elbows; his tie, carelessly arranged, hung from his fleshy, fat neck like a piece of black string. There was something run-down about his appearance in general, and yet it was possible that this man had once cut an imposing figure. His brow, curved and high, with thick, untidy white hair above it, had something of a commanding look, but just below his bushy eyebrows the decline set in: his eyes swam under reddened lids; his slack, wrinkled cheeks merged with his soft, thick neck. I was instinctively reminded of the mask of a late Roman emperor that I had once seen in Italy, one of those who presided over the fall of Rome. At first I did not know what it was that made me observe him so attentively, but I realized at once that I must take care not to show my curiosity, for it was obvious that he was already impatient to strike up a conversation with someone. It was as if he were under some compulsion to talk. As soon as he had raised his glass in a slightly shaky hand and taken a sip, he exclaimed in a loud voice, "Ah, wonderful, wonderful!" and looked around him. No one responded. The card-players shuffled and dealt the pack, the others smoked their pipes; they all seemed to know the new arrival and yet, for some reason of which I was unaware, not to feel any curiosity about him.

Finally there was no restraining him any longer. Picking up his glass of beer, he carried it over to the table where the farmers were sitting. "Will you gentlemen make a little room for my old bones?" The farmers moved together slightly and took no further notice of him. For a while he said nothing, pushing the half-full glass alternately forwards and backwards. Once again, I saw that his fingers trembled. Finally he leant back and began talking, in quite a loud voice. It was not really obvious whom he was addressing, for the two rustics sitting next to him had clearly shown that they were disinclined to embark on any conversation. He was, in fact, addressing everyone at large. He spoke—I sensed that at once—in order to speak and to hear himself speaking.

"Well, what a business that was today!" he began. "Well-meant of the Count, well-meant, I grant you. Meets me while he's driving along the road and stops his car, yes, indeed, he stops it specially for me. He's taking his children down to Bolzano to go to the cinema, says he, how would I like to go with them? Well, he's a distinguished man, a cultured, educated man, the Count knows where respect is due, and you don't say no lightly to such a man, not if you know what's right. So I go along with them, in the back seat of course, with his lordship the Count—after all, it's an honour, a man like that, and I let him take me into that magic-lantern show they've opened in the high street with such a fuss, advertisements and lights fit for a church festival. Well, I think, why shouldn't I see what those gentlemen the British and Americans are churning out over there, selling the stuff to us for good money? It's said to be quite an art, this cinema acting. Shame on them, say I"—and here he spat copiously—"shame on them for the rubbish they show on that screen of theirs! It's a disgrace to art, a disgrace to a world that has a Shakespeare and a Goethe in it! First came all that coloured nonsense with comical animals—well, I'll say nothing about that, it may be fun for children, it does no one any harm. But then they make a film of *Romeo and Juliet*—now that ought to be forbidden, forbidden in the name of art! The lines sound as if someone was croaking them into a stovepipe, those sacred lines of Shakespeare's, and all so sugary and sentimental! I'd have got up and walked out if I hadn't been there with his lordship the Count, on his invitation. Making such rubbish out of pure refined gold! And to think that we live in times like these!"

He grasped his glass of beer, took a large draught and put it down with a loud bang. His voice was very loud now, he was almost shouting. "And that's what actors do these days—they spit out Shakespearian lines into machines for money, filthy lucre, dragging their art in the dirt! Give me any tart in the street—I have more respect for her than for those apes with their smooth faces metres wide on the posters, raking in millions for committing a crime against art! Mutilating the word, the living word, shouting Shakespeare's verse into a funnel instead of edifying the public, instead of educating young people. A moral institution, that's what Schiller called the theatre, but that doesn't hold good any more. Nothing holds good any more but money, filthy money, and the spectacle they make of themselves. And anyone who doesn't know how to do that will die. Better die, say I—in my eyes, those who sell themselves to that sink of iniquity, Hollywood, should go to the gallows. To the gallows with them, I say, to the gallows!"

He had been shouting at the top of his voice and thumping the table with his fist. One of the trio at the card-players' table growled, "Keep quiet, can't you? We can't tell what cards we're playing through your stupid gabbling!"

The old man gave a start, as if to reply. For a moment there was strength and vigour in his dull gaze, but then he merely made a contemptuous gesture, as much as to imply that it was beneath him to answer. The two farmers beside him puffed at their pipes, and he stared silently ahead with glazed eyes, saying nothing, his expression sombre. You could tell it was not the first time he had forced himself to hold his tongue.

I was deeply shaken, and felt a pang. Something stirred in me at the sight of this humiliated man, who I felt at once must have seen better days, and yet somehow had sunk so low, perhaps because of drink. I could hardly breathe for fear that he or the others might embark on a violent scene. From the first moment when he came in and I had heard his voice, something in him—I didn't know what—had made me uneasy. But nothing happened. He sat still, his head sinking lower, he stared ahead, and I felt as if he were muttering something quietly to himself. No one took any more notice of him.

Meanwhile, the landlady had got up from the bar to fetch something from the kitchen. I took that as a chance to follow her and ask who the man was. "Oh," she said, unruffled, "poor fellow, he lives in the poorhouse here, and I give him a beer every evening. He can't afford to pay for it himself. But we don't have an easy time with him. He used to be an actor once somewhere or other, and it hurts his feelings that people don't really believe he ever amounted to much and show him no respect. Sometimes they poke fun at him, asking him to put on a show for them. Then he stands up and spouts stuff that nobody understands for hours. Sometimes they give him some tobacco for his pains, or buy him another beer. Sometimes they just laugh at him, and then he loses his temper. You have to go carefully with him, but he wouldn't hurt a fly. Two or three beers if someone will pay for them, and then he's happy—yes, poor devil, there's no harm in old Peter."

"What—what is his name?" I asked, startled without knowing why.

"Peter Sturzentaler. His father was a woodcutter in the village here, so they took him in at the poorhouse."

Well, my dear, you can imagine what had startled me so much. For at once I understood what might seem unimaginable. This Peter Sturzentaler, this down-at-heel, drunk, sick old man from the poorhouse, could be none other than the idol of our young days, the master of our dreams; the man who as Peter Sturz the actor, the male lead in our city theatre, had been the quintessence of all that was elevated and sublime, whom as you will remember, both of us—young girls who were still half children—had admired so madly, loved to such distraction. And now I also knew why something in the first words he spoke on entering the inn had troubled me. I had not recognized him—how could I have recognized him behind this mask of debasement, in such a state of change and decay?—but there had been something in his voice that found its way to my long-buried memory. Do you remember when we first saw him? He had come from some provincial city when our municipal theatre in Innsbruck offered him an engagement, and it so happened that our parents said we could go to the performance introducing him to Innsbruck audiences because it was a classic play, Grillparzer's *Sappho*, and he was playing the part of Phaon, the handsome young man who creates turmoil in Sappho's heart. But remember how he captured ours when he came on stage, in Greek costume, a wreath in his thick, dark hair, a new Apollo! He had hardly spoken his first lines before we were both trembling with excitement and holding hands with each other. We had never seen a man like this in our dull, sedate city of Innsbruck, and the young provincial actor, whose stage make-up and the artifice of whose presentation could not be seen from the gallery, seemed to us a divine symbol of all that was noble and sublime. Our foolish little hearts beat fast in our young breasts; we were different girls when we left the theatre, enchanted, and as we were close friends and did not want to endanger our friendship, we swore to each other to love and venerate him together. That was the moment when our madness began. Nothing mattered to us except him. All that happened at school, at home, in town was mysteriously linked with him, everything else paled beside him; we gave up loving books, and the only music we wanted to hear was in his voice. I think we talked of nothing else for months on end. Every day began with him; we hurried downstairs to get to the newspaper before our parents, to know what new part he had been given, to read the reviews; and none of them was enthusiastic enough for us. If there was a critical remark about him we were in despair, we hated any other actor who won praise. Oh, we committed too many follies for me to be able to remember a thousandth part of them today. We knew when he went out, and where he was going, we knew whom he spoke to, and envied everyone who could stroll down the street with him. We knew the ties he wore, the stick he carried; we hid photographs of him not only at home but inside the covers of our school textbooks, so that we could take a secret look at him in the middle of lessons; we had invented our own secret language so that at school we could signal, from desk to desk, that he was in our thoughts. A finger raised to the forehead meant, "I'm thinking of him now." When we had to read poems aloud, we instinctively imitated his voice, and to this day I can hardly see many of the plays in which I first saw him without hearing the lines spoken in his voice. We waited for him at the stage door and followed him, we stood in the entrance of a building opposite the café that he patronized, and watched endlessly as he read the newspaper there. But our veneration for him was so great that in those two years we never dared to speak to him or try to get to know him personally. Other, more uninhibited girls who also admired him would beg for his autograph, and even dared to address him in the street. We never summoned up the courage for that. But once, when he had thrown away a cigarette end, we picked it up as if it were a holy relic and divided it in two, half for you and half for me. And this childish idolatry was transferred to everything that had any connection with him. His old housekeeper, whom we envied greatly because she could serve him and look after him, was an object of our veneration too. Once, when she was shopping in the market, we offered to carry her basket for her, and were glad of the kind words she gave us in return. Ah, what folly wouldn't we have committed for Peter Sturz, who neither knew nor guessed anything about it?

Today, now that we have become middle-aged and therefore sensible people, it may be easy for us to smile scornfully at our folly as the usual rapturous fantasy of a girlish adolescent crush. And yet I cannot conceal from myself that in our case it had already become dangerous. I think that our infatuation took such absurd, exaggerated shape only because, silly children that we were, we had sworn to love him together. That meant that each of us tried to outdo the other in her flights of fancy, and we egged each other on further every day, thinking of more and more new evidence to prove that we had not for a moment forgotten the idol of our dreams. We were not like other girls, who by now were swooning over smooth-cheeked boys and playing silly games; to us, all emotion and enthusiasm was bent on this one man. For those two passionate years, all our thoughts were of him alone. Sometimes I am surprised that after this early obsession we could still love our husbands and children later with a clear-minded, sound and healthy love, and we did not waste all our emotional strength in those senseless excesses. But in spite of everything, we need not be ashamed of that time. For, thanks to the object of our love, we also lived with a passion for his art, and in our folly there was still a mysterious urge towards higher, purer, better things; they acquired, purely by coincidence, personification in him.

All this already seemed so very far away, overgrown by another life and other feelings; and yet when the landlady told me his name, it gave me such a shock that it is a miracle she didn't notice it. It was so startling to meet the man whom we had seen only surrounded by the aura of our infatuation, had loved so wholeheartedly as the very emblem of youth and beauty, and to find that he was a beggar now, the recipient of anonymous charity, a butt of the mockery of simple-minded peasants and already too old and tired to feel ashamed of his decline—so startling that it was impossible for me to go back into the main room of the inn. I might not have been able to restrain my tears at the sight of him, or I might have given myself away to him by some other means. I had to regain my composure first. So I went up to my room to think, to recollect clearly what this man had meant to me in my youth. The human heart is strange: for years and years I had not given him a single thought, although he had once dominated all my thoughts and filled my whole soul. I could have died and never asked what had become of him; he could have died and I would not have known.

I did not light a lamp in my room, I sat in the dark, trying to remember both the beginning and the end of it all; and all at once I seemed to be back in that old, lost time. I felt as if my own body, which had borne children many years ago, was a slender, immature girl's body again, and I was the girl who used to sit on her bed with her heart beating fast, thinking of him before she went to sleep. Involuntarily, I felt my hands turn hot, and then something happened that alarmed me, something that I can hardly describe to you. A shudder suddenly ran through me, and at first I did not know why. Something shook me severely. A thought, a certain thought, a certain memory had come back to me; it was one that I had shut out of my mind for years and years. At the very second when the landlady told me his name, I felt something within me lying heavily on my mind, demanding expression, something that I didn't want to remember, something that, as that Professor Freud in Vienna says, I "had suppressed"—had suppressed at such a deep level that I really had forgotten it for years on end, one of those profound secrets that one defiantly keeps even from oneself. I also kept it from you at the time, even after swearing to tell you everything I knew about him. I had hidden it from myself for years. Now it had been roused and was close to the surface of my mind again; and only now that it is for our children, and soon our grandchildren, to commit their own follies, can I confess to you what happened between me and that man at the time.

And now I can tell you my most intimate secret openly. This stranger, this old, broken, down-at-heel actor who would now deliver lines of verse in front of the local rustics for a glass of beer, and was the object of their laughter and contempt—this man, Ellen, held my whole life in his hands for the space of a dangerous minute. If he had taken advantage of that moment—and it was in his power to do so—my children would never have been born, and I do not know where or what I would have been today. The friend who is writing you this letter today would probably have been an unhappy woman, and might have been as crushed and downtrodden by life as he was himself. Please don't think that I exaggerate. At the time, I myself did not understand the danger I was in, but today I see and understand clearly what I did not understand at the time. Only today do I know how deeply indebted I was to that stranger, a man I had forgotten.

I will tell you about it as well as I can. You will remember that at the time, just before your sixteenth birthday, your father was suddenly transferred from Innsbruck, and I can still see you in my mind's eye weeping stormily in my room, sobbing out the news that you would have to leave me—and leave *him*. I don't know which was harder for you. I am inclined to believe that it was the fact that you would lose sight of him, the idol of our youth, without whom life seemed to you not worth living. You made me swear to tell you everything about him, write you a letter every week, no, every day, write a whole diary—and for some time I faithfully did it. It was hard for me to lose you, too, because whom could I confide in now, to whom could I describe the emotional high flights and blissful folly of my exuberant feelings? However, I still had him, I could see him, he was mine and only mine now; and in the midst of my pain there was a little pleasure in that. But soon afterwards—as you may have heard—there was an incident that we knew only in vague outline. It was said that Sturz had made advances to the wife of the manager of the theatre—at least, so I was told later—and after a violent scene he had been forced to accept dismissal. He was allowed one final benefit performance. He was to tread the boards of our theatre once more, and then I too would have seen him for the last time.

Thinking back to it today, I don't believe that any other day in my life was unhappier than the one when it was announced that Peter Sturz would be on stage in Innsbruck for the last time. I felt ill. I had no one to share my desperation with, no one to confide in. At school the teachers noticed how distracted and disturbed I looked; at home I was so violent and frantic that my father, guessing nothing, lost his temper and forbade me, on pain of punishment, to go to the theatre. I pleaded with him—perhaps too hard and too passionately—and only made matters worse, because my mother too now spoke against me, saying all that theatre-going had been a strain on my nerves and I must stay at home. At that moment I hated my parents—yes, I was so confused and deranged that day that I hated them and couldn't bear the sight of them. I locked myself into my room. I wanted to die. One of those sudden fits of melancholy that can actually endanger young people now and then overcame me; I sat rigid in my chair, I did not shed any tears—I was too desperate for that. Sometimes all was cold as ice inside me, and then I would suddenly feel feverish and go from room to room. I flung the window up and stared down at the yard three storeys below, assessing how far I would fall if I jumped out. And again and again my eyes went to my watch: it was only three in the afternoon, and the performance began at seven. He was going to act in our theatre for the last time, and I wouldn't hear him; everyone else would cheer him to the echo, and I wouldn't be there. Suddenly I couldn't bear it any more. I ignored my parents' prohibition on my leaving the house. I went out without a word to anyone, downstairs and out into the street—I don't know where I thought I was going. I believe I had some confused notion of drowning myself or doing something else senseless. I just didn't want to live any more without him, and I did not know how to put an end to my life. And so I went up and down the streets, ignoring friends when they hailed me. I was indifferent to everything, no one else in the world existed for me, he was the only one. Suddenly, I don't know how it happened, I was standing outside the building where he lived. You and I had often waited in the entrance to the building opposite to see if he might come home, or we looked up at his windows, and perhaps that vague hope of meeting him by chance some time had unconsciously driven me here. But he did not appear. Dozens of unimportant people, the postman, a carpenter, a fat woman from the market, left the building or went into it, hundreds and hundreds of people who didn't matter to me hurried past in the street; but he never put in an appearance.

I don't remember how the next part happened, but suddenly I felt drawn there. I crossed the road, went up the stairs to the second floor without stopping to get my breath back, and then went to the door of his apartment; I just had to be close to him, nearer to him! I had to say something to him, although I didn't know what. I really was in a state of possession by a madness that I couldn't account for to myself, and perhaps I ran up the stairs so fast in order to outrun any kind of circumspect thought. I was already—still without stopping for breath—pressing the doorbell. I can hear its high, shrill note to this day, and then there was a long wait in total silence, broken suddenly by the sound of my awakening heart. At last I heard footsteps inside: the firm, heavy tread I knew from his appearances at the theatre. And at that moment sober reflection returned to me. I wanted to run away from the door again, but everything in me was frozen in alarm. My feet felt paralysed, and my little heart stood still.

He opened the door and looked at me in surprise. I don't know if he knew or recognized me at all. Out in the street there were always dozens of his immature admirers, boys and girls alike, flocking around him. But the two of us who loved him most had been too shy, we had always fled rather than meet his eyes. And this time, too, I stood before him with my head bent, and dared not look up. He waited to hear what I had to say to him—he obviously thought I was an errand girl from one of the shops in town bringing him a message. "Well, my child, what is it?" he finally encouraged me in his deep, sonorous voice.

I stammered, "I only wanted to… but I can't say it here…" And I stopped again.

He said in a kindly tone, "Well, come in, then, child. What's it about?"

I followed him into his room. It was a large, simple place, rather untidy; the pictures had already been taken down from the walls, cases were standing around half-packed. "There now, tell me… who sent you here?" he asked again.

And suddenly it came bursting out of me in a torrent of burning tears. "Please stay here… please, please don't go away… stay here with us."

He instinctively took a step back. His brows shot up, and his mouth tightened in a sharp line. He had realized that I was another of those importunate admirers who kept pestering him, and I was afraid he would say something angry. But there must have been something about me that made him take pity on my childish despair. He came up to me and gently patted my arm: "My dear child,"—he spoke like a teacher addressing a pupil—"it's not my own doing that I am leaving this place, and it can't be altered now. It is very nice of you to come and ask me to stay. Who do we actors perform for if not the young? It has always been a particular joy to me if young people applaud us. But the die is cast, and I can't do anything about that. Well, as I said,"—and he stepped back again—"it was very, very nice of you to come and tell me what you have, and I thank you. Be a good girl, and I hope you will all think of me kindly."

I realized that he had said goodbye, but that only increased my desperation. "No, stay here," I exclaimed, sobbing, "for God's sake, stay here… I… I can't live without you."

"My dear child," he said soothingly, but I clung to him, clung to him with both arms—I who had never before had the courage even to brush against his coat. "No, don't go away," I went on, still sobbing in despair, "don't leave me alone! Take me with you. I'll go anywhere you like with you… anywhere… do what you like to me… only don't leave me."

I don't know what other nonsensical stuff I poured out in my despair. I pressed close to him as if I could keep him there like that, with no idea at all of the dangerous situation my passionate outburst was inviting. You know how naive we still were at the time, and what a strange and unknown idea physical love was to us. But I was a young girl and—I can say so today—a strikingly pretty girl; men were already turning in the street to look at me, and he was a man, thirty-seven or thirty-eight years old at the time. He could have done anything he liked to me; I really would have followed him, and whatever he had tried I would have offered no resistance. It would have been easy for him to take advantage of my ignorance there in his apartment. At that moment my fate was in his hands. Who knows what would have become of me if he had improperly abused my childish persistence, if he had given way to his vanity, and perhaps his own desires and the strength of temptation? Only now do I understand what danger I was in. There was a moment at which, I now feel, he was not sure of himself, when he sensed my body pressed to his, and my quivering lips were very close. But he controlled himself and slowly pushed me away. "Just a moment," he said, breaking free of me almost by force, and he turned to the other door. "Frau Kilcher!"

I was horrified. Instinctively, I wanted to run away. Was he going to hold me up to ridicule in front of his old housekeeper? Make fun of me in front of her? Then she came in, and he turned to her. "What do you think, Frau Kilcher," he said to her, "this young lady has come to bring me warm farewell wishes in the name of her whole school. Isn't that touching?" He turned to me again. "Please tell your friends I am very grateful. I have always felt that the beauty of our profession is having youth, and thus the very best thing there is on earth, on our side. Only young people appreciate the finer points of the stage, I assure you, only they. You have given me great pleasure, my dear young lady, and"—here he clasped my hands—"I will never forget it."

My tears dried up. He had not shamed me, he had not humiliated me. But his concern for me went even further, because he turned to his housekeeper again: "Well, if we didn't have so much to do, I would very much have liked to talk to this charming young lady for a little while. However, you will escort her down to the door, Frau Kilcher, won't you? My very good wishes to you, my very good wishes."

Only later did I realize how thoughtful of him it was to spare and protect me by sending the housekeeper down to the door of the building with me. After all, I was well known in the little city of Innsbruck, and some ill-disposed person might have seen me, a young girl, stealing out of the famous actor's apartment all by myself, and could have spread gossip. Although he was a stranger to me, he understood better than I, still a child, what endangered me. He had protected me from my own ignorant youth—how clear that was to me now, more than twenty-five years later.

Isn't it strange, my dear friend, doesn't it put me to shame that I had forgotten all that for years and years, because I was so ashamed that I *wanted* to forget it? That I had never felt truly grateful to this man, never asked after him, when he had held my life, my fate in his hands that afternoon? And now the same man was sitting downstairs over his glass of beer, a wreck of a failure, a beggar, despised by everyone; no one knew who he was and who he had been except for me. I was the only one aware of it. Perhaps I was the only person on earth who still remembered his name, and I was indebted to him. Now I might be able to repay my debt. All at once I felt very calm. I was no longer upset, only a little ashamed of my injustice in forgetting, for so long, that this stranger had once been generous to me at a crucial moment in my life.

I went downstairs and back into the main room of the inn. I suppose that only some ten minutes in all had passed. Nothing had changed. The card game was still going on, the landlady was at the bar, doing her mending, the local rustics were sleepily puffing their pipes. He too was still sitting in his place, with his empty glass in front of him, staring ahead. Only now did I see how much sorrow there was in that wreck of a face, his eyes dull under their heavy lids, his mouth grim and bitter, distorted by the stroke. He sat there gloomily with his elbows on the table so that he could prop his bowed head in his hands, warding off his weariness. It was not the weariness of sleep; he was tired of life. No one spoke to him, no one troubled about him. He sat there like a great grey bird with tattered feathers, crouching in its cage, perhaps dreaming of its former freedom when it could still spread its wings and fly through the air.

The door opened again and three more of the locals came in, with heavy, dragging footsteps, ordered their beer and then looked around for somewhere to sit. "Move up, you," one of them ordered him rather brusquely. Poor Sturz looked up. I could see that the rough contempt with which they treated him hurt his feelings. But he was too tired and humiliated by now to defend himself or dispute the point. He moved aside in silence, pushing his empty beer glass along with him. The landlady brought full tankards for the newcomers. He looked at them, I noticed, with an avid, thirsty glance, but the landlady ignored his silent plea with composure. He had already had his charity for that evening, and if he didn't leave then that was his fault. I saw he no longer had the strength of mind to stand up for himself, and how much more humiliation awaited him in his old age!

At that moment the liberating idea occurred to me at last. I couldn't really help him, I knew that. I couldn't make a broken, worn-out man young again. But perhaps I could give him a little protection against the pain of such contempt, retrieve a little esteem for him in this village at the back of beyond for the few months he had left to live, already marked as he was by the finger of Death.

So I stood up and walked over, making something of a show of it, to the table where he was sitting squeezed between the locals, who looked up in surprise at my arrival, and addressed him. "Do I by any chance have the honour of speaking to Herr Sturz, leading man at the Court Theatre?"

He started in surprise. It was like an electric shock going right through him; even the heavy lid over his left eye opened. He stared at me. Someone had called him by his old name, known to no one here, by the name that all except for him had long ago forgotten, and I had even described him as leading man at the Court Theatre, which in fact he never had been. The surprise was too great for him to summon up the strength to get to his feet. Gradually, his gaze became uncertain; perhaps this was another joke thought up by someone in advance.

"Well, yes… that is… that was my name."

I offered him my hand. "Oh, this is a great pleasure for me… and a really great honour." I was intentionally raising my voice, because I must now tell outright lies to get him some respect in this company. "I must admit that I have never had the good fortune of admiring you on stage myself, but my husband has told me about you again and again. He often saw you at the theatre when he was a schoolboy. I think it was in Innsbruck…"

"Yes, Innsbruck. I was there for two years." His face suddenly began coming to life. He realized that I was not setting out to make fun of him.

"You have no idea, Herr Sturz, how much he has told me, how much I know about you! He will be so envious when I write tomorrow to tell him that I was lucky enough to meet you here in person. You can't imagine how much he still reveres you. No other actor, not even Kainz, could equal you, he has often told me, in the parts of Schiller's Marquis of Posa and Max Piccolomini, or as Grillparzer's Leander; and I believe that later he went to Leipzig just to see you on stage there. But he couldn't pluck up the courage to speak to you. However, he has kept all your photographs from those days, and I wish you could visit our house and see how carefully they are treasured. He would be delighted to hear more about you, and perhaps you can help me by telling me something more about yourself that I can pass on to him… I don't know whether I am disturbing you, or whether I might ask you to join me at my table."

The rustics beside him stared, and instinctively moved respectfully aside. I saw that they were feeling both uneasy and ashamed. They had always treated this old man as a beggar to be given a beer now and then and used as a laughing stock. But observing the respectful manner that I, a total stranger, adopted towards him, they were overcome for the first time by the unsettling suspicion that he was well known and even honoured out in the wider world. The deliberately humble tone that I assumed in requesting the favour of a conversation with him was beginning to take effect. "Off you go, then," the farmer next to him urged.

He stood up, still swaying, as you might stand up on waking from a dream. "By all means… happily," he stammered. I realized that he had difficulty in restraining his delight, and that as a former actor he was now wrestling with himself in an effort not to show the others present how surprised he was, and taking great pains, if awkwardly, to behave as if such requests, accompanied by such admiration, were everyday matters to be taken for granted. With the dignity acquired in the theatre, he strode slowly over to my table.

"A bottle of wine," I ordered, "the best you have in the house, in honour of Herr Sturz of the Court Theatre." Now the card-players also looked up from their game and began to whisper. Their old acquaintance Sturzentaler a famous man who used to act at the Court Theatre? There must be something about him if this strange woman from the big city showed him such respect. And it was in a different manner that the landlady now set a glass down in front of him.

Then he and I passed a wonderful hour. I told him everything I knew about him by pretending that I had heard it from my husband. He could hardly contain his amazement at finding that I could enumerate every one of the parts he had taken at Innsbruck, the name of the theatre critic there, and every word that critic had written about him. And then I quoted the incident when Moissi, the famous actor Moissi, after giving a guest performance, had declined to come out to the front of the stage to receive the applause alone, but had made Sturz join him, addressing him in fraternal fashion. Again and again, he expressed his astonishment as if in a dream. "You know about that, too!" He had thought his memory dead and buried long ago, and now here came a hand knocking on its coffin, taking it out, and conjuring up for him fame of a kind that he never really had. But the heart is always happy to lie to itself, and so he believed in that fame of his in the world at large, and suspected nothing. "You even know that… why, I had forgotten it myself," he kept stammering, and I noticed that he had difficulty in not showing his emotion; two or three times he took a large and rather grubby handkerchief out of his coat pocket and turned away as if to blow his nose, but really to wipe away the tears running down his wrinkled cheeks. I saw that, and my heart shook to see that I could make him happy, I could give this sick old man one more taste of happiness before his death.

So we sat together in a kind of rapture until eleven o'clock. At that point the police officer came deferentially up to the table to point out courteously that by law it was closing time. The old man was visibly startled; was this heaven-sent miracle coming to an end? He would obviously have liked to sit here for hours hearing about himself, dreaming of himself. But I was glad of the official warning, for I kept fearing that he must finally guess the truth of the matter. So I asked the other men, "I hope you gentlemen will be kind enough to see Herr Sturz of the Court Theatre safely home."

"With the greatest pleasure," they all said at the same time; one of them respectfully fetched him his shabby hat, another helped him up, and I knew that from now on they would not make fun of him, laugh at him or hurt the feelings of this poor old man who had once been such a joy to us, such a necessity in our youth.

As we said goodbye, however, the dignity he had maintained at some expense of effort deserted him, emotion overwhelmed him, and he could not preserve his composure. Large tears suddenly streamed from his tired old eyes, and his fingers trembled as he clasped my hand. "Ah, you good, kind, gracious lady," he said, "give your husband my regards, and tell him old Sturz is still alive. Maybe I can return to the theatre some day. Who knows, who knows, I may yet recover my health."

The two men supported him on his right and left, but he was walking almost upright; a new pride had straightened the broken man's back, and I heard a different note in his voice. I had been able to help him at the end of his life, as he had helped me at the beginning of mine. I had paid my debt.

Next morning I made my excuses to the landlady, saying that I could not stay any longer; the mountain air was too strong for me. I tried to leave her money to give the poor old man a second and third glass of beer whenever he wanted it, instead of that single tankard. But here I came up against her own native pride. No, she would do that herself anyway. They hadn't known in the village that Sturzentaler had been such a great man. It was an honour to the village as a whole, the mayor had already decided that he should be paid a monthly allowance, and she herself would vouch for it that they would all take good care of him. So I merely left a letter for him, a letter of effusive thanks for his kindness in devoting an evening to me. I knew he would read it a thousand times before his death, and show the letter to everyone; he would blissfully dream the false dream of his own fame again and again before his end.

My husband was greatly surprised to see me back from my holiday so soon, and even more surprised to find how happy and reinvigorated those two days away had left me. He described it as a miracle cure. But I see nothing miraculous about it. Nothing makes one as healthy as happiness, and there is no greater happiness than making someone else happy.

There—and now I have also paid my debt to you from the days when we were girls. Now you know all about Peter Sturz, our idol, and you know the last, long-kept secret of

Your old friend

Margaret.

DATE OF FIRST PUBLICATION IN GERMAN

Forgotten Dreams (*Vergessene Träume*, 1900)

In the Snow (*Im Schnee*, 1901)

The Miracles of Life (*Die Wunder des Lebens*, 1903)

The Star Above the Forest (*Der Stern über dem Walde*, 1904)

A Summer Novella (*Sommernovellette*, 1906)

The Governess (*Die Gouvernante*, 1907)

Twilight (*Geschichte eines Unterganges*, 1910)

A Story Told in Twilight (*Geschichte in der Dämmerung*, 1911)

Wondrak [unfinished] (*Wondrak*, 1990—published posthumously but written during the First Word War)

Compulsion (*Der Zwang*, 1920)

Moonbeam Alley (*Die Mondscheingasse*, 1922)

Amok (*Der Amokläufer*, 1922)

Fantastic Night (*Phantastische Nacht*, 1922)

Letter from an Unknown Woman (*Vierundzwanzig Stunden aus dem Leben einer Frau*, 1925)

The Invisible Collection (*Die unsichtbare Samlung*, 1925)

Twenty-four Hours in the Life of a Woman
(*Vierundzwanzig Stunden aus dem Leben einer Frau*, 1927)

Downfall of a Heart (*Untergang eines Herzens*, 1927)

Incident on Lake Geneva (*Episode vom Genfer See*, 1927)

Mendel the Bibliophile (*Buchmendel*, 1929)

Leporella (*Leporella*, 1929)

Did He Do it? (*War er es?*, 1987—written between 1934-40)

The Debt Paid Late (*Die spät bezahlte Schuld*,
1951—date of writing unknown, c.1940)

Pushkin Press

Pushkin Press was founded in 1997, and publishes novels, essays, memoirs, children's books—everything from timeless classics to the urgent and contemporary.

Our books represent exciting, high-quality writing from around the world: we publish some of the twentieth century's most widely acclaimed, brilliant authors such as Stefan Zweig, Marcel Aymé, Antal Szerb, Paul Morand and Yasushi Inoue, as well as compelling and award-winning contemporary writers, including Andrés Neuman, Edith Pearlman and Ryu Murakami.

Pushkin Press publishes the world's best stories, to be read and read again.

*

Héctor Abad	*Recipes for Sad Women*
Olivier Adam	*Cliffs*
Flavia Arzeni	*An Education in Happiness: The Lessons of Hesse and Tagore*
François Augiéras	*A Journey to Mount Athos*
	Journey of the Dead
	The Sorcerer's Apprentice
Marcel Aymé	*Beautiful Image*
	The Man Who Walked through Walls
Salim Bachi	*The New Adventures of Sinbad the Sailor*
	The Silence of Mohammed
Philippe Beaussant	*Rendezvous in Venice*
Andrei Bely	*Petersburg*
Olivier Berggruen	*The Writing of Art*
Eduardo Berti	*Agua*
Filippo Bologna	*How I Lost the War*
	The Parrots
Peter Buwalda	*Bonita Avenue*
Marella Caracciolo Chia	*The Light in Between*

Velibor Čolić	*The Uncannily Strange and Brief Life of Amedeo Modigliani*
Louis Couperus	*Ecstasy*
	Eline Vere
	Inevitable
	Psyche
	The Hidden Force
Régis Debray	*Against Venice*
Penelope S. Delta	*A Tale Without a Name*
Charles Dickens	*Memoirs of Joseph Grimaldi*
Isak Dinesen	*The Necklace and The Pearls*
Mikhail Elizarov	*The Librarian*
Alain Elkann	*Envy*
	The French Father
Nicolas Fargues	*I Was Behind You*
Medardo Fraile	*Things Look Different in the Light and Other Stories*
Carlos Gamerro	*An Open Secret*
Gaito Gazdanov	*The Spectre of Alexander Wolf*
Julien Gracq	*A Dark Stranger*
	Chateau d'Argol
Julian Green	*The Other Sleep*
Brothers Grimm	*The Juniper Tree and Other Tales*
Pietro Grossi	*Fists*
	The Break
	Enchantment
Eduardo Halfon	*The Polish Boxer*
Peter Handke	*A Sorrow Beyond Dreams*
Hermann Hesse	*Hymn to Old Age*
E.T.A. Hoffmann	*The Nutcracker and The Strange Child*
Hugo von Hofmannsthal	*Andreas*
Peter Fröberg Idling	*Song for an Approaching Storm*
Yasushi Inoue	*Bullfight*
	The Hunting Gun
Pasi Ilmari Jääskeläinen	*The Rabbit Back Literature Society*
Henry James	*Letters from the Palazzo Barbaro*
	Letters to Isabella Stewart Gardner
Peter Stephan Jungk	*The Inheritance*
Erling Kagge	*Philosophy for Polar Explorers*
Søren Kierkegaard	*Diary of a Seducer*
Petr Král	*In Search of the Essence of Place*
	Loving Venice
	Working Knowledge
Maxim Leo	*Red Love: The Story of an East German Family*
Alexander Lernet-Holenia	*I Was Jack Mortimer*
Simon Liberati	*Anthology of Apparitions*

Oliver Matuschek	*Three Lives: A Biography of Stefan Zweig*
Guy de Maupassant	*The Necklace and The Pearls*
Jean-Euphèle Milcé	*Alphabet of the Night*
Paul Morand	*Hecate and Her Dogs*
	Tender Shoots
	The Allure of Chanel
	Venices
Ryu Murakami	*Popular Hits of the Showa Era*
	From the Fatherland, with Love
	Coin Locker Babies
	69
Andrés Neuman	*Traveller of the Century*
	Tallking to Ourselves
Auður Ava Ólafsdóttir	*Butterflies in November*
Umberto Pasti	*The Age of Flowers*
Marc Pastor	*Barcelona Shadows*
Edith Pearlman	*Binocular Vision*
Edgar Allan Poe	*The Journal of Julius Rodman*
Alexander Pushkin	*The Queen of Spades*
Raymond Radiguet	*Count d'Orgel*
	The Devil in the Flesh
Antoine de Saint-Exupéry	*Letter to a Hostage*
George Sand	*Laura: A Journey into the Crystal*
Friedrich von Schiller	*The Man Who Sees Ghosts*
Arthur Schnitzler	*Casanova's Return to Venice*
	Dying
	Fräulein Else
Adolf Schröder	*The Game of Cards*
Laurent Seksik	*The Last Days*
William Shakespeare	*Sonnets*
Nihad Sirees	*The Silence and the Roar*
Jan Jacob Slauerhoff	*The Forbidden Kingdom*
Simona Sparaco	*About Time*
Adalbert Stifter	*The Bachelors*
	Rock Crystal
Italo Svevo	*A Life*
Antal Szerb	*Journey by Moonlight*
	Love in a Bottle
	Oliver VII
	The Pendragon Legend
	The Queen's Necklace
	The Third Tower
Nadezhda Teffi	*Subtly Worded*
Friedrich Torberg	*Young Gerber*
Mark Twain	*The Jumping Frog and Other Sketches*

ELLEN ULLMAN — *By Blood*
Close to the Machine
The Bug

LOUISE DE VILMORIN — *Madame de*

ERNST WEISS — *Franziska*
Jarmila

EDITH WHARTON — *Glimpses of the Moon*

FLORIAN ZELLER — *Artificial Snow*
Julien Parme
Lovers or Something Like It
The Fascination of Evil

STEFAN ZWEIG — *Amok and Other Stories*
Beware of Pity
Burning Secret
Casanova: A Study in Self-Portraiture
A Chess Story
The Collected Stories of Stefan Zweig
Confusion
Fear
The Governess and Other Stories
Journey into the Past
Letter from an Unknown Woman and Other Stories
Magellan
Marie Antoinette
Mary Stuart
Mental Healers: Mesmer, Eddy, Freud
Selected Stories
Shooting Stars: Ten Historical Miniatures
The Struggle with the Daemon: Hölderlin, Kleist, Nietzsche
Twilight and Moonbeam Alley
The World of Yesterday
Wondrak and Other Stories